THEY SHALL NOT PASS

A novel of Madrid and Manhattan

I0649293

FREDERICK MARK KRAMER

Sagging
Meniscus

Set in Bembo with LaTeX.

ISBN: 978-1-963846-26-3 (paperback)
ISBN: 978-1-963846-27-0 (ebook)
Library of Congress Control Number: 2025930103

Sagging Meniscus Press
Montclair, New Jersey
saggingmeniscus.com

To Silas Orion,
Garrett Isaiah,
& Maple Louise,
my grandchildren

Dramatis Personae

Esmeralda, lover of Jacobo
Jacobo, grandfather of Joseph, former lover of Esmeralda
Joseph Peter Fuchs, grandson of Jacobo
Conchita, stage name **Cassandra**, granddaughter of Esmeralda

Secondary Characters

Fanny, neighbor of Joseph
Harold, her boarder
Yolanda, Carol, friends of Conchita from high school
Laszlo, comrade of Jacobo's
Zoltan, Laszlo's brother and friend of Jacobo later Joseph
Ferdinand, Zoltan's friend
Delores, born dead child of Esmeralda and Jacobo
Santiago, Esmeralda's first husband
Tomas, Esmeralda's second husband
Estrella, Tomas' second wife
Miriam, Jacobo's wife
Gloria, Esmeralda's daughter
Eric Clayton, English comrade of Jacobo
Dora, friend of Esmeralda
Julio, her son
Paul David, high school friend of Joseph
Harvey, childhood friend of Joseph
Katherine, his wife
Hector, boyhood friend of Conchita
Martha, acting teacher of Conchita
Mr. Martinez, chess teacher of Conchita
Johnnie, friend of Jacobo
Danielle, friend of Esmeralda
Jacoba, daughter of Joseph and Conchita
Lilliana, friend, lover of Joseph

They Shall Not Pass

'SO YOU ARE THE LOVE of my grandfather?' A woman came up to me rather was wheeled up to me in a wheelchair by a pretty young woman, a nice lovely girl, I was looking at the young girl not noticing the old lady otherwise I might have noticed the resemblance between the two when the old woman says Jacobo, Jacobo you haven't changed a bit, only I wasn't Jacobo, he had been dead almost five years after having a heart attack on our way home from the museum, I held his hand in the ambulance when he died, and I finally got what I wanted a room of my own only getting what I wanted is not what I wanted, I much rather him be alive and sharing the room with me than me having it all to myself—the room is empty without him, who else would tell me to shut that crap off, Elvis, Little Richard, Fats Domino, that I would listen to while he would put on classical music. He disliked rock 'n' roll because it appealed to emotion not intellect. We had a Victrola and he would fall asleep listening to Bach and when I awoke in the middle of the night would shut the turntable off as the hissing disturbed my sleep. I knew one day this would be my room until I actually got it then didn't want to go into the room without him and slept on the convertible couch until my parents woke up my father to go to work and my mother to pour milk into his cereal and I went to sleep in their bed. 'So you are the love of my grandfather?' She must be feeling good living longer is the best revenge, I thought, explaining that I look just like pictures of my grandfather when he was my age but I am not him and he didn't tell me much about you, occasional musings. He didn't realize how young I was and I never understood him but he would tell me he

FREDERICK MARK KRAMER

thought about you only twice the first thing in the morning and the last thing at night and how he was sorry but he was too fearful of bringing a Hispanic woman into the family yet Esmeralda was the last name on his breath before he slipped into unconsciousness. And he always mentioned we never marry the one we love but the one we love stays with you forever, I think about her from time to time whenever I do a smile comes upon my face, her laughter, her beauty, he said, opened up a world to me that I never knew existed, one of passion, of excitement but it was all a lie later on I went back to the world I knew; later on he amended that and said he no longer thinks about her it's time to move on. Yet she was the last word he said before losing consciousness, I was always amazed that someone could have a love like that. When grandma died he didn't even go to her funeral thought it would be hypocritical since he hadn't lived with her since my mother turned eighteen. He upped and left said he couldn't take it anymore and eventually moved in with my mother and her new husband when I was born and after the first six months of sharing a bedroom with my parents my crib was moved into his room and we shared it until it became mine. I have no awareness of that but he told me that story enough times I think it is mine. The young woman pushing the wheelchair blushed and I guessed they were related. She introduced me to her grandmother and I had only guessed that later back in my room that had no paintings on the wall, and the only furniture being a bed, a dresser, my *avuelo's* Telefunken radio my Zenith record player and a bridge table and chair that I kept behind my dresser and would open up as my desk, and my grandfather's little red fountain pen that he had bought in Woolworth's that my mother said was so cheap it would never last. It was my lucky pen in college whenever I took an exam with it did well. As I sat in my reading chair wondering if I ever was going to have a life now that I had graduated college, I actually had graduated City College and had always told myself when I finish I will begin, I doubt therefore I exist. I ended up crying on my 23rd birthday this is living? I was still living at home incapable of moving out of my parents' home, didn't have a girlfriend, but did have a job that I hated. My friends who had gone away to college and didn't save the money I did had all moved away, it looked so easy to move out with all the money I saved but here I am trapped in the old neighborhood, I had gone to City College but how I got in is a mystery to me, and in college whole series

2

of comprehensive exams needed in order to graduate were dropped or ceased to be a requirement and I received a D- on my last paper on Piers Plowman, for not answering the question with the comment you're in an English class not history stick to the text, don't talk about the transformation because of the Peasants Revolt. He obviously didn't understand he who doesn't answer the question passes the test—Kafka. I think I ran into that professor banging a drum vigorously at a Be-in at Central Park, but I was stoned on acid so who knows? I never recalled being bored as a child I always had something to distract me from myself but now there was nothing and I had to find my own way, it was terrifying. How did I get this way? I quickly started gaining weight, became dull and cynical even if I had promised myself I would never let this happen to me, school was a blur I had done all I was supposed to do not great, not good, but passing especially with a little help from my friends. When one guy complained I was cheating off him all I thought what kind of loser was that, I realized this sitting in my reading chair, belt open, pants open, eyes closed, pretending to be reading Thucydides in my room and I started crying on my birthday, hoping my life would be different but doing nothing to make it different, I wanted my past to be different for me to be more outgoing, social, have friends, to be more serious, that's what I wanted to be more serious for people to listen to what I have to say even if have nothing to say, to start my life not go through the motions of living yet intuitively realized all is tied together and that I just couldn't go back and change one part of my life without changing the whole thing—and if I could what would that be? Yet nothing that has happened to me exists independently of me, it's all connected and if I am to change it would be up to me not someone entirely different? How did I get so smart? To change one thing is to cease to be who I am, and let's face it I said to myself I graduated college and am glad of that even if I never learned anything there, no teacher left me on the edge of my seat, but I have a job that gets me out of bed in the morning even if I can't stand the railroad, at least it's unionized so it pays a decent wage, and if I want to be myself have to accept the good with the bad and it's not too late to learn; that's why I had found this comfortable reading chair as a birthday gift to myself, and wanted to sit and read and hope that reading could change my life, and if I changed one moment the whole damn thing would change like bubbles in a bubble can my favorite toy when I was five and my *avuelo* had taken a picture of me with his Brownie Camera so it is indelibly marked in my conscious memory, so much so I actually think I can picture myself running after the bubbles, smiling as I blew the bubbles and chasing them floating away. That reminded me I wanted to check my grandfather's photos and see if Esmeralda was among them, but the shoebox that contained them had no names or dates on the black-and-white photos, my mother would yell at him to identify them but they were his memories and when he passed he would have no need of them even if I would have been thrilled to learn more about his life before me. None of the people in the pictures did I know excluding the family and Zoltan. Surprise, surprise there were none of my grandmother. Why should there be he cursed her name whenever it was mentioned, that bitch. Once he said to me do you want to go to school? What kind of question was that? He had to ask. He said not to tell your mother, met me on the corner this was to be our little secret and took me for an outing. I thought we might be going to Brighton Beach or one of those little cafeterias that dotted the Upper West Side where he would go and sit with his chums, instead he took me for a breakfast at the Automat allowed me to drink coffee, my mother never would have allowed that, she always said it would stunt your growth, and when it was too bitter taught me to use sugar and cream, said you want to learn how to drink coffee to sit in cafés. I thought he meant candy stores, who knew of cafés in the Bronx, where you sit around all day drinking coffee, kibitzing and reading the papers. He surprised me taking me to the Museum of Modern Art because he knew I liked art and took me to my first installation by the artist Jean Tinguely, his machine that would destroy itself—the big and small wheels plus tubes and valves, old drums, and a piano that forgot to destroy itself. The machine made noise and caught on fire before it could destroy itself, and its only purpose was to destroy itself, and it couldn't even do that, the fireman had to complete the task by throwing foam on it, they must have been laughing that they had to destroy what was supposed to destroy, only the piano kept playing *Homage to New York* and the artist explained the only permanence is change—the eternal flux. Man must change grandfather said wondering if being is a unity or multiplicity while running to catch the subway as all New Yorkers do assuming this will be the last train, and had a heart attack on the platform and when the ambulance came and I held his hand and I kept saying *avuelo* are you okay are you all right he kept nodding until he could nod no more, but I thought I heard him whisper a name I had not heard again until this morning.

'You silly old goose, did you really think it was him?' Did I expect him to come up to me after all these years, but the way he walked, the way he looked it was as if clouds parted and there he was my heart skipped a beat—I thought I would never see him again and there he was right in front of me his profile, his full length beard, locks of curly red hair and him not even looking at me I just had to speak, I couldn't let the phantom pass I had to know and spoke without thinking, going without caffeine is like sloughing through soup, he must think I am happy to survive while his grandfather died, the young think that way rather than my anger at the futility of it all—all this sound and fury signifying nothing besides what does it matter if he's dead it's him as a young man I loved and he died years ago however this is the first I've heard of it. What must Conchita think? My grandmother has lost it all? Oldness has gotten to her? I lost it a long time ago only now she sees me as this helpless old lady. What did I expect him to say? That what I heard was true you were pregnant but I can't be blamed I had to go back, you know I was married had a child, however had I known you were pregnant I would have returned or at least helped support you, the child would have been well looked after but your letters came back unopened—we had a little fling but I had a wife and child I couldn't stand but I couldn't leave even if I eventually couldn't take it anymore and when my daughter finished elementary school couldn't take it anymore, when my life was falling apart and I wrote but my letters came back. How could I have known if you didn't tell me? We were best friends, I told you everything never have I spoken to anyone as I spoke to you, the horrible part of our breakup is the friendship lost, the sex was great but the friendship was better we would talk, I could talk to you like I couldn't even talk to myself we were always one, from the first night when we stayed up all night talking I never ended my conversation with you. Even in silence you were always besides me. His daughter quit school after the eighth grade, Joseph said, what does a woman need schooling for? Jacobo said, in order to help look after her baby brother yet the baby couldn't save the marriage. And that's all she was trained for. You silly goose thinking you can relive the past, you loved him as a young man not the old one he became, you think you can relive the past? How could I be what I became if I changed the past?

I had to live the life I led in order to have the life I wanted I just can't go tinker with one part of the past other parts would change as well not stay the same, I am grateful for the time we had it helped me become the person I wanted allowing me a gateway into life and that I wouldn't want to change, that I couldn't change and wouldn't change the past if it means changing the future. I was just existing appalled at my privilege and was finally able to do something and my fight for freedom became my crazy existence—freedom from a dictatorship but also freedom from an intolerable situation at home. But it would have been fun to see him one more time, he did look just like I remembered you. Your hatred must be honored did you actually stay with Miriam all those years like a poor schmuck dying unfulfilled—how many times did you tell me when you got back you were divorcing. And you were the hottest man I was ever with. But I also have to accept all that has led me to this life, including my heart attack that has left me weak, if you have a clot and it goes to your brain you have a stroke, if it goes to your heart you have a heart attack; half my body is paralyzed but my mind is crystal clear even if it would be better if I could walk, Jacobo your dying young spared you the pain of old age, to be able to change the past I would have to change the future but I can't do that all is connected, you left and I was able to survive it was all chance until I said no this is not the life I want to lead and that act did change the past or at least let me put it in perspective and managed to make my way to this country. It was good to be out of the dictatorship of Spain. I am what I am how I lived is who I am I wouldn't want to be anyone else, but my heart died a little when I saw you in front of me and I can never deny you are the most important person in my life, even more than my father—all my men were a variation of him and I had a difficult time understanding men, men are simply little boys, you were actually a *mensch*—the war years were the years of my intense living our moments were precious we could have died at any moment, you could have been blown up and I didn't want to die a virgin—you deflowered me gently and I could have gone to a 'Celestina' to sew me up but I was proud of my freedom not bound by the rules of the church—the new Soviet women, what a crock of shit they turned out to be treating women as chattel just like in the West, not giving them the freedom they promised, and nobody can take those eighteen months away from me those eighteen months in the trenches allowed me to grasp the life I wanted to lead and very few people can say that. Yes Conchita that boy was the grandson of the man I once loved. He seemed so handsome and sure of himself I thought it had to be him not one of those who only want to get into your pants or worse marry you because they are going off to war and want something to come back to. I took up with Jacobo then I thought with Jacobo I will live the rest of my life he is my future. I wonder did you get his phone number will he call; he was shy in a way Jacobo was not but he knew immediately what I was talking about so Jacobo talked about me. Does he have an education? Jacobo hated formal schooling but was one of the most educated men I knew.

Imagine grandma actually thought she saw an old boyfriend, she must be really losing it—who knew she had that type of life, she's always so prim and proper I hated going to her as a child, she always insisted I wear a dress that I couldn't roll around on the floor and she always pulled my finger out of my mouth, once even putting vinegar on my finger so I wouldn't suck saying sucking is for babies, but I was a baby and she never respected me as a person. Hard to imagine she was pretty once, my grandmother, I can't imagine her being pretty she always reminds me of the old world—I even changed my name to have no connection to that world, I don't even speak Spanish even if she wanted me to learn it my mother only spoke English to me at home. All I remember about her when little was how I hated going and my mother bribing me with a black and white cookie as a treat if I went with my mother to visit her mother, there was a local bakery near her that made the freshest black and white I still remember feeling cheated when I had one up in the Bronx packaged and stale. Now that I am her only living relative, grandpa is too old and lives too far away, I feel it as my obligation to take care of her, she did take care of me, and imagine being stuck inside the house all day and even if she could get down the stairs she'd be trapped on her block with this wheelchair, but she can't do long walks only short walks with her cane that she calls a walking stick with its mother of pearl handle on top and she says less old this way at least I can go to the grocery store before I get too tired, but soon she won't even be able to do that and will be trapped in the apartment all day. Bad enough now she can't even go on the fire escape because the super insisted upon putting gates on the window lest the colored break in. More and more Negros are moving into the building and there've been a number of burglaries and they'll break in, he said, sure we locked the roof door but hooligans climb down the fire escape; next I'm going to put barbed wire along the roof so they can't climb in from another rooftop but they will find a way, they always do, and so he installed fire safety window along the fire escape and now we can't even open the window and escape if there is a fire. She probably couldn't climb out the window anyway her balance is precarious. I've seen beautiful pictures of her as a young woman but there is a disconnect between that woman and my grandmother. Now she needs makeup, how ugly I've become we age so quickly, she says. That is the result of a hard life, I think, my mother always complained she had one purpose in life to ruin her life, I don't know if she accomplished it but my mother did accomplish it. She would embarrass me at every opportunity, I could never bring friends over to the apartment if I could help it. The one time she surprised my mother was when I started dating and my grandfather found out and said I could only date Catholic boys, which meant Spanish and my grandmother laughed in his face and said go with whomever you like a date is not marriage, don't be trapped in old-fashioned thinking but make sure you do not get pregnant by the first jerk who comes along and gave me rubbers to carry just in case because boys see a thrill in trapping women. How she had enough guts to walk into a pharmacy and buy them is beyond me. She doesn't want me burdened with a child before I have a chance to live, like my mother was with me. Of course my mother didn't listen to her and refused the condoms thinking she could take care of herself. Nine months later I was born and my mother had to drop out of high school to stay home with me. Welfare was generous back in the day and allowed a mother to raise a child and she was able to move up to an apartment in the Bronx with the help of welfare. All the girls did it in those days get pregnant by the Spanish Catholic boys who then abandoned them. Her history made interesting conversation around the dinner table during the holidays the only time I saw grandma. We would always go to her she rarely came up to us. My grandma always told me to move out when I became of age but my mother never heard of a girl living alone unless she became pregnant or married. It's just not done in our culture she would say and I would wonder what culture she was talking about, everywhere girls I knew lived with their parents until they married or became pregnant and moved into a place of their own. Grandma believes you have to keep recreating yourself but everything I do is to find jobs now that I am a working actress. I think I can inhabit a character but grandma thinks you only learn how a character acts by doing the character not by thinking about the character: you only learn what a character is by being that character you can't approach it from the outside. And even with all my difficulties with grandma she was the one who encouraged me, who took me in, who insisted I get a good high school education, even insisted I go to this boring out of town college. It had a good acting program. Who wanted to go away to school nobody ever heard of? I am the only one of my friends from the Bronx who actually went to college, excluding those Jewish girls who went to City College but I went away to school nobody else did that, and what I loved about that was getting away from my neighborhood even if it was a brave new world, but I didn't speak too much to my classmates who always studied. And some of the professors actually wrote the books we studied. I thought I was totally unprepared for this type of education and realized how little Walton high school had prepared me for serious learning and luckily I spent an extra year in a private high school when I moved in with grandma after my mother died.

When did history exist? When did it become so personal? I always figured grandpa joined the Spanish Civil War for personal reasons and overlaid grandiose ideas on it, he left because he couldn't stand grandma and my mother—at least that was the tale told at home but then why did he come back especially after he met that woman, Esmeralda? A conundrum: the historical versus the personal, and old and decrepit as she is now she certainly has a charm within her and I can see she was beautiful once or I could see it by looking at Cassandra her granddaughter, they say you get to look like your parents if you get to look like your parents then they have to look like you when they were young, I wonder does she still put on makeup? She didn't seem to dress like an old lady and I can see her getting pissed if some guy called her 'old lady' or worse 'young lady', she's the kind of woman you have to respect exudes dignity must have led an interesting life unlike my grandfather but then again he was only a shopkeeper who lived with us after he left his wife. I knew him all my life but never remember him talking about her. It is strange back then all my friends had a relative or a boarder in their house, nobody had their own room, now all kids seem to have a room of their own or share one with a brother or sister. I also thought it common for single people to live at home and saw nothing strange about a grownup living with his mother if he was single, who else was going to cook, clean and sew for him. And Fanny our next door neighbor rented out a room to an ex-serviceman Harold, after her son had died in the war and her husband a fruit dealer also died, to help defray expenses but the landlord wanted to kick her out because it was her husband's name on the lease and I remember thinking her husband's name is the same as hers, but the Law didn't see it that way. Luckily the *Post,* not the *New York Times* kicked up such a fuss, a veteran's mother that he chickened out backed down and the case didn't go to court where she might have lost—the law follows the golden rule, *avuelo* said, he who has the gold rules. It took a few more years before the courts decided even if a wife's name is not on the lease she has the legal right to occupy the apartment as long as she can pay the rent. Why I refused to study law that my mother kept insisting I do. All my friends not interested in science became lawyers, accountants or schoolteachers. I did study law for one semester but wasn't interested in the laws of the past, I was of the new generation not interested in the old hackneyed fee simple laws or inheritance when only men could inherit, own property or vote, I was of the new generation that was going to remake the world, and I knew I wouldn't be able to sit in an office all day I would have to be outside with low-life working with people—the professor who had taught that course on pre-law said law is not for you. How did he know? I loved listening to him talk about organic solidarity of law and the jus-tifications for law not about the mechanical reproductions that you have to obey but how law is transmitted through the values of the community. City College then was known as 'Jew City' and rumor had it over 90% of the students were Jewish and even when the student newspaper disputed the claim and not even half the students identified themselves as Jewish it didn't matter the story persisted. If I wasn't going to be a lawyer my father suggested I become a teacher, you always have a job as a teacher, summer's off so you could then be on the street, and a good pension. Pension I wasn't thinking about retirement but wondering if I was going to have a life and was afraid I wouldn't. *Avuelo* finally told me in a dream, his apparition, to go for it, don't settle, you're young yet there's enough time to settle for the crap society places on you. My parents liked the idea of me being a school teacher having a guaranteed income and that was enough to kill it for me. Grandfather said that night that I have a limited relationship with reality, but he didn't say what that was it would be interesting to ask him and why he came back. And in my junior year found this job on the railroad and saw no reason to leave it just yet it allowed me time to pursue my dreams even if I didn't know what they were. But I am good at following women and saw this woman on the street and followed her into Tompkins Square Park and made believe I had a relationship with her and then the old lady speaks to me. Grandfather always would say only your deeds count not what goes on inside your head, but I can only have fantasies inside my head never act upon them and even if this method failed all the time I kept up with it. I could chat with men freely but women were these strange unearthly creatures that I was afraid of, too bad I never had a sister then maybe I can see them as human beings, that's what a professor once said in class, he also said you can only become good by being bad, who knew what was going to come out of his mouth, he enjoyed shocking, you have to experience the bad in order to know the good, is you must have a passion in life that grips you in the essence, and lust and envy have to be part of your life in order to know decency. After listening to him I never wanted to be a lawyer or schoolteacher but when I took him again a couple of years later he didn't remember me nor how his ideas influenced me and he said he says things off the top of his head with no concern how it might affect others, like make love in the afternoon so you can get up early and study, he was a true academic talked but not lived ideas, his was a mediocre mind, at least I heard get up early and study previously by 6pm on Sunday night I would feel guilty for having done no studying. But hope and desire are different and he never recreated that first class. How the family sanitizes you, imagine Jacobo this avuncular man as a grandfather not the scruffy young man of my imagination, he probably only mentioned me in passing and not to his wife who wouldn't have understood passion—he knew who he was but never let on and when he talked about me it wasn't to his wife or daughter but only to his grandson who probably had no idea what he was talking about, who didn't know the difference between love and marriage, that you can't marry the one you love it's too intense that you must separate in order to breathe to learn who you are and that you can't have a life without the other but with the other you cannot live. Only memory allows that to happen that you when you separate appearance from reality, the outside from the inside, and no matter how you do it but because you want to be different than those around you and live free that at the same time makes you the loneliest individual because living inside yourself and worse knowing you are doing this so you won't be submerged in the other, even as you tell yourself a thousand times this is a mistake but on the thousandth and one you realize there is no old man with a beard, some judge, god, whatever, guaranteeing that you are doing the right thing, making the correct decision and that all you are is adrift in making decisions from your own gut, and only adding reasons afterwards, layered belief with thought thinking it's correct, but how can there be correct thought if there is no absolute unchanging authority by which to base them. Christians have it too easy with their absolute morality, why make living so easy, why not have no perfect answer and not be stuck in invalid old ways, there is no perfect thought only thought that is good if it's bold and love and freedom belong together and if you don't understand freedom there is no way you can grasp love. No doubt I could have done what was expected of me but I got nauseous around the family, knew I had to escape, and had one great adventure that seems to have lasted my entire life—fought the good fight, the noble war as if war can ever be noble, I saw enough suffering, gore and death to realize war could never be ennobling but in that destructive atmosphere was able to find the love of my life even if I never saw him again in the city even as I did look in the other's eyes always hoping to see him again, I would look for him in the strangest places but from what Joseph says he rarely left home unless to go to work and hardly came into the city, never hung with the artsy crowd or even went to the theater or concerts, and I always wondered how you could talk to a man who never engaged with art. I would laugh at him reading every chance he got, he thought books made you smart but only practical experience counted and yet he was crucial to who I would become because he had that intuitive knowledge I had to work so hard to get, I was too shy and modest only later did I begin to understand. Then I was willing to sacrifice myself for the cause only he wouldn't let me and stayed with me at all times so I wouldn't do anything foolish. Strange man. My body remembers him even after he has died and am talking to him as if he were alive. I should find out where he's buried. Why? He's now in a dreamless sleep. When we are dead we are not anywhere and only live inside the people we touch. I always admired his courage no matter what the situation and when I was stuck and could see no way out he was always taking care of me and would find practical solutions to everyday problems, he wasn't waiting for some Messiah to come that I had been indoctrinated into believing the difference between the Jews and the rest of us Christians we had the Messiah already Jews denied his existence; he didn't believe in a hidden reality behind everything only the here and now, because you can think the form of God doesn't mean a God exists. When I asked him if he would fight for his own people and I said to him after this I will go with him to Palestine he was flabbergasted, and only afterwards here in America did I realize he was not even circumcised. But now everyone in the States is circumcised so never again can the Nazis so easily identify Jews, doctors came up with this public health reason after the Second War after the war to end all wars failed so as not to allow Jews to be identified by simply pulling down their pants. Only Hispanic men in this country are not circumcised most are from the island not from Latin America or Spain and are barely educated so enthralled to the Catholic Church and have no idea they are supposed to be circumcised. And they follow their women around like puppy dogs. You rarely see an old Hispanic male they can't live without a woman. How many only wanted to get into my pants so I would cook, clean and sew for them as if I had nothing better to do than be a mother to them, it was better to have affairs when my ovaries started to squirm but was able to control myself and only needed them at certain times at others I was able to keep my desires under control, Jacobo taught me how to control myself, to learn self-discipline to live free not give into your passions all the time. That's all behind me now, now my difficulty is getting out of this damn wheelchair and wonder if I can continue without always looking back. All this is difficult to explain to Conchita I still somehow forget to call her by her stage name because she has a superficial view of acting and I talk so slowly now even if my thoughts rage inside my head but words stutter inside my mouth. At least she is no longer enamored with stardom and is learning her craft and has consented to take day jobs rather than going on the road so that she can be home for me. The road must be a lonely place but not as lonely as a foxhole, I still can't believe I actually did that to escape my parents' abode, I felt I had to fight for freedom, for Spain, for the democracy, as if the communists ever gave freedom to anyone, if we had won we would have become a Stalinist dictatorship. Jacobo wasn't caught up in the rhetoric he only wanted to escape a bad marriage. He could have gone to Palestine they needed fighters no he said they needed farmers who could roll up their sleeves and till the land and he wasn't a farmer but a city boy who had no connection to Eastern European Jews but was a Marrano.

'Conchita, Conchita, come inside you must have lunch you can't eat peaches and cream all the time', I can still hear my mother's voice ringing inside my head, she would always embarrass me never let me be, I can't remember a time when she wasn't concerned what the neighbors would think of her, I wasn't her concern but what others would think of her—at least grandma allowed me to wear blue-jeans, what a battle I had with my mother when I wanted to wear a pair of pants, young ladies don't wear pants they wear skirts, and I was not longer little so could wear what I wanted even when I was small she said I cried and made quite a fuss and didn't want to wear dresses to school but I had to otherwise they wouldn't let me in school. She could have let me go in dungarees maybe then I would have been shamed by all the girls for wearing pants but I doubt it I wasn't afraid of the public eye and would have gone my own way, I was never content to go with the crowd I was happy being with myself and I can only now imagine how angry I must have been because as a teenager she wouldn't let me wear jeans—there was no girls jeans back then and you had to fit them to boy's sizes, I remember specifically going up to Bobkoff's on Fordham Road because that's where all the boys bought them, I can remember the day quite well, a breezy fall day leaves everywhere and I walked the half mile usually I took a bus everywhere but today I wanted to save the fifteen cents so walked and the streets were jammed packed with people and barricades everywhere and I didn't know what was going on but it was difficult to cross the Grand Concourse until I saw a sign candidate Kennedy was coming to the Bronx and the whole Bronx was coming out to greet him but I wasn't interested and finally was able to cross the Concourse and walk down Fordham towards Kingsbridge, where Fordham and Kingsbridge Road met and the further I walked away from the Concourse the less crowded the streets became as everybody was walking up to the Concourse and Fordham Road to see John F. Kennedy, and when I walked into Bobkoff's the place was empty and I walked up to a salesman and said I would like a pair of dungarees for myself, young ladies don't wear dungarees they are what farmers used for shoveling manure but when I insisted he must have thought I was joking but when he saw the determined look said okay examined me and gave me a few pair to try on near my size in a boy's size, I learned a lesson that day you don't have to be a creature of your times I could create my own life, and he came up to me with three different sizes and thought one should fit and since there was nobody in the store was allowed to go into the changing room and try them on and since the first one fit, I peeled the labels off and walked out of the store wearing my bright new blue jeans. Too bad Bobkoff's didn't change with the times, soon The Gap came along and sold women's as well as men's jeans and they went out of business. I carried my dress in a bag and by the time I got back to the Grand Concourse I had missed our future president but had a nice pair of blue jeans that caused quite a stir with my mother, she said I couldn't wear them to school, girls were not allowed to wear pants according to their dress code, and we still had to wear white blouses on assembly days. I learned how to put up with this ridiculousness but boys thought me a tomboy when I wore jeans, even if I detested sports and didn't even know how a baseball game was scored. What I learned was that I hated shopping and as I aged would buy two of the same things so they would last and I wouldn't have to shop for a while. Ladies didn't wear pants at my all girls high school, it was as if we were being trained to serve tea and that was silly where most of the girls couldn't read and we all had difficulty with deportment, I envied Negro girls who were so free and always got into trouble and never listened to the teachers, who said we can't control 'them' and would ignore them. I was too afraid to do that and couldn't even pretend to be like them only their freedom didn't last long, Yolanda became pregnant her sophomore year and had to drop out—we were told nobody is allowed to continue high school pregnant—I too condemned her but if I could find out where she lived now would write her a letter apologizing for dissing her that way, but after she left that school rarely saw her again yet we always sat side by side in the gym while the girls played volleyball; she had mortgaged her potential in order to be a mother, of course the boy-father was nowhere to be found. I told myself that's not right. My mother said nothing how could she, she did the same thing. We both sat on the floor of the gym waiting for spring when we could walk outside and not be trapped inside, but spring never came for her by the middle of sophomore year she was history. The whole school was built like a fort, there were never comfortable chairs, the desks were immovable the library had hard wooden stools, nothing in the school was upholstered lest we become comfortable and not want to leave, even in the teachers' room didn't have comfortable sitting—there was no freedom, you needed a pass for everything, the hall, the bathroom, and if you actually went to class had to listen to teachers drone. Did they ever once look down upon their charges? Even in the theater looking away from the spotlight you can see if the audience is getting it and you can listen to their reaction; you have to listen and adjust accordingly make changes after a few performances if something isn't working while teachers never deviated from their designed spiel. Maybe if I hadn't been 'so cool' or realized they had a drama program could have gotten more out of high school, but I never wanted to stay after school, in fact the block the school was located on emptied of students in ten minutes, nobody wanted to be near that shit hole, we congregated blocks away and Yolanda and I would even walk home together. I should phone her, I don't dare, but of course I can't we have gone separate ways what could I say to her after all these years—maybe the next time I'm in a play I can let her know, she did call me after my mother was killed and came to the funeral with her little boy. She felt funny being in a Catholic church and I knew why they still preached marriage was sacred and sex was only for procreation and only God could break it and she was living in sin. She had never considered abortion, which was illegal, but I told her I knew where she could get one, but she stopped speaking to me after that—that was a sin against God, or as grandma said to me these superstitious people who think there is a next world live in a world of lies, this is the only true world, and I think that was the first time I ever heard someone say that, while the priest said mama was with God now. Grandma told me if I ever got pregnant I would have an abortion, that I must have a life and not be trapped even before I started to live. She was a feminist even before the word came into existence. Being a mother at your age is unacceptable and the Church's pronouncement that sex outside marriage is evil sounded as bad in Spanish as it did in Latin and in Spanish or Latin I had no idea what they were saying as grandma took me to a doctor for the pill. But their idea was that the little woman had to be protected from the big bad wolf. No wonder Yolanda rebelled. Older I would have yelled at the priest there is no God if there was how could he allow such evil to exist, even if would have answered allowing evil means there is a moral stance but then I could have replied if there is a God how could he allow such evil and only want worship, but I only thought such things after living with grandma for a while, even if I did foolish things I certainly wasn't a rebel like Yolanda; why I liked Yolanda so she wasn't a fraidy cat, when she left we lost contact and when I started college had other close friends, I had never planned on college but grandma insisted, I never gave much thought to my future figuring it would be just like my past but she said this is your last chance that it not be like your past, I didn't get that—I could get a job, buy a red mustang, get married, have four children, live in a house in the suburbs then buy a station wagon to drive the kids. But grandma didn't even want me to finish high school in the Bronx, she detested that place, as she told me she wouldn't come up there and live with me but that I would have to move downtown with her. She wanted me to transfer to a school closer to her home but all my friends were up in the Bronx so for a half a year commuted until grandma realized what a bad education I was getting and insisted I leave—back then nobody was interested in Hispanics going to college and she spoke to the principal who said my grades weren't good enough for City College and she explained to him America is a big place and there are more colleges than just City, he said not everybody is college material, but she would have none of it, and she knew someone who knew someone and imagine I had to spend my senior year all over again but this time in a private school, that I balked at, didn't want to be with rich kids learning how to serve tea, but had the time of my life at Calhoun, besides actually learning stuff I smoked pot all the time. It was so scary there at first, not only didn't they have walls but the desks weren't bolted to the ground and you could hear everyone from every class but soon you learned to drown them out. Then the counselor at The Calhoun School said colleges outside New York are interested in geographical diversity and the University of Pittsburgh has a good acting program, by then I was in the drama program, and grandma said this would be your last chance to change your life. I had no idea what she was talking about. Then she said if I go for one year then I can transfer back into the city, grandma said I was smart, she was the first person who ever said that to me, and even if I don't have good grades the last year you made decent grades and some school will accept you, not all schools care only if you have a high grade point average. She was so wrong I had to study so hard to keep up I was so unprepared for Calhoun and college was even more difficult because of my poor study habits, now from what I know in acting you must practice good habits in order to cultivate them—habit is the key to education along with good learning skills and creativity, all my mother cared about was good penmanship and respect for elders, her. I was so unprepared I never thought I would make it beyond the first semester, and I got below a C average but they didn't just kick me out let me have another semester to see if I could bring up my grades, which I did. They had this guerrilla theater acting program but they only let you continue the final two years if you did well on their exams, but by then I came around to believing at least I would have two years under my belt and would finish up in the city at the Open Theatre, where I had spent my summers honing my craft, grandma also knew someone who knew someone who said that was a good program. The audition was a breeze, I wasn't even nervous, I waited patiently until I was called then read my scene that I had been rehearsing for the last two years at Pitt, and besides acting there was physical training classes, diet, as well as dancing and singing—right away I knew this was a demanding program. Teachers were surprised I couldn't dance; don't all Hispanics know how to dance? I explained my family is from Spain not Puerto Rico, we have an intellectual history not a musical culture, and Grandma had made sure I read *Celestina* and had given me the play as a graduation present. And I had used that in my audition and what surprised me was that acting teachers who should be the smartest people in the world were so dumb and had never heard of the character let alone the play. They have so much time between auditions, call backs, scenes, why aren't they reading? I spend my time reading what I think the character might be reading, and sometimes of course it is a stretch because some characters are so poorly drawn that they can't read but if they could what would they? Yet I rarely see actors open a book. Once when I was dating a TV actor everyone thought how well-mannered and stable he was not believing when I said he's playing a well-mannered stable person but in reality he's a neurotic, insecure man. I wonder what happened to him? When he became violent the only way I could escape his clutches was call the police and he became afraid I was going to cause a scene and became the well-respected mild-mannered man he had played on the sitcom and I vowed never to put myself in that situation again, I learned from grandma you have to lead an independent life and not depend upon a man, and I have skills now waiting tables, hairdresser, even substitute teacher in order to pay my way, she more than my mother taught me art is a stimulant the energizer bunny of life.

Whoever expected to see him again, he claims to have looked us up in the phone book but probably followed us home and called and asked if he could come over, but he does look so much like Jacobo that I couldn't refuse even struggling to get the words out—it's so difficult to speak now, not to think but to talk, and I did invite him for tea. Conchita will be glad I know he came for her not to see me and she's in a fallow period now, working a day job to make ends meet and coming home to spend nights with me. What would I do without her? and yet I keep pushing her to go out more, to have a life, to look for work maybe even get married, as if marriage was ever so good to me. All I have is memory. I had to escape my home once again when travel was permitted not to live in a country where you couldn't express yourself, where you couldn't think, where everyone in public thought the same, where art and literature was in the service of the church, where the young didn't rebel only wanted to be good Christians as if the church had done any good in the world except keep people entwined in it, but still I think of marriage—those ideas once in your head are impossible to remove. So here comes this nice guy dressed as a preppie: tan pants, plaid shirt, penny loafers with no spots coat or tie, but wearing colorful socks, no less, luckily I didn't burst out laughing—imagine Jacobo dressed like that! but his flaming red hair and blue eyes reminds me of my old love and he laughs saying he only remembers his grandfather with white hair, because red turns quicker to gray and we had walked some from the park but we didn't invite him up for tea. When he came he was surprised that there were rugs on the floor not wall-to-wall carpet or linoleum on the floors like up in the Bronx, and that there was original art on the walls not paint by numbers paints, that Conchita explained to me when she too was surprised at original works of art, who would spend money on that when you could get cheaper posters or paint by the numbers art, or what she had Christian decoration motifs. He too was surprised by a library, hard-covered books and not an encyclopedia in sight. His mother had a set bought via green stamps, Conchita explained that in some of her friends' houses the only book was the Encyclopedia Britannica. He wanted to know about his grandfather, what is there to say we loved and parted when we were defeated but he was always besides me in conversation, I couldn't tell him that. He was so cute told us over tea that he had never had tea from a tea ball with fresh leaves only Lipton tea from bags, he may have lacked social graces but had a sharp mind and said you have to accept all that you have done in the past to become the person you are today and that you can't leave anything out to be the person you are today, and I could attest to that if I could have altered one thing would have had a much better life if only I went with him to America instead of moving back with my parents, who were wealthy enough to buy me out of trouble with the new authorities and would have lived a different life, maybe not happy who's happy but at least not living at home again, but he said you didn't alter your actions and that's what made you who you are today and there's not one specific moment in a life but life is a series of moments not one episode and we are responsible for who we become. Only the young think that. But his grandfather would have been proud of who he has become now if he only would stop living with his parents. I love listening to people tell the world how to change the world and still live at home with their parents; his mother still makes his bed, cooks for him and apparently also sews for him, why should a man leave that. American men are such little boys, not that Spanish men are much better, and colored boys go everywhere with their mother. Do men ever grow up? We sat in the living room drinking tea poured from the tea pot into nice cups and saucers and he was surprised that I had milk with tea he never saw that before but he never dated an Englishman. To an Englishman tea without milk is like cheese without bread to a Frenchman. He didn't know that either. Conchita sat on the other side of the table to be near the kitchen but I had to sit up close to see and hear and his gruff voice reminded me of Jacobo and if I closed my eyes I swear I could hear Jacobo speaking even if I can't remember what we ever spoke about no matter how hard I try and recall I can never recall a specific conversation but I know we never ran out of things to talk about, never tired of talking, we would spend the night making love and talking not sleeping and never have I been more alive than in his company—he had this firm belief that he could change his life and in changing his future life would change his past as well, he was no idealist and in his asking to change he was hoping not to be afraid alone at night and when he changed the future he would change how he remembered the past, and when he changed the past he would no longer be one who is afraid and become one who has courage; he said too long when Jews faced some pogrom and were about to go to their death they would sing a blessing to the Messiah, he wanted to sing the *Internationale*. Then I heard that Jews did just that during the Second World War before being executed by the Germans they sang the *Internationale*. What else can you do but piss off your enemies and not go gently into the night—nothing matters at the end you might as well show you're not afraid and military music unites us with a swelling of frenzied feeling that binds us together, unfortunately our bodies betray us at the end and we become afraid—like now when I have to go pee and I can't even go to the bathroom by myself, luckily I now carry around an extra set of underwear and a dress in reserve—you can only accept your life, as Joseph says if you accept your past, what Jacobo wanted to do but never was able to do, Joseph makes good points even if all he is doing is staring at Conchita but was too intimidated to have a conversation with her.

Got to get up enough guts to call Cassie, got to get up enough guts, and get Esmeralda and she does actually invite me over for tea, couldn't believe her grandmother answered, but if she would have called me my mother would have answered so I shouldn't be so surprised, and I had gone into the drug store with a fistful of nickels, dimes, quarters ready to be on the phone for hours to talk to her and ask her to see me again, screamed at the person who banged on the door, showed him my change until he finally realized I was going to be awhile—he probably thought I was a teenager talking to a girl and couldn't do it in front of my parents, he was close our phone line doesn't reach into the bathroom so you have no privacy in our apartment, but before stumbling into my spiel she invited me up to her house for tea, and I listened to my mother when she said you had to bring something. What? I went to best bakery I knew Lichtman's on West 86th and Amsterdam, the one with the green sign that I had walked past numerous times with my grandfather and the aroma was so delightful, and brought a Sachertorte, that started a big debate as my college friend suggested I go to a bakery in Forrest Hills that made the best, but a Sachertorte has to be made fresh with real chocolate not vanilla it's as if you had a vanilla egg cream, the essence is gone. I met this guy there who said they also make the best black and white's and that he escaped from East Germany, why would anyone want to leave that workers' paradise, I wondered. The baker says in his thick German accent this has to be served with whipped cream and Esmeralda says I know. I shaved my scruffy beard but didn't get a haircut but this time wore one of my grandfather's ties that I had saved even when my father said nobody wears wide ties anymore, but that his fountain pen and chess set were all I had left of his possessions and carried his inexpensive Shaeffer fountain pen in my shirt pocket instead of my usual expensive ones, that's how my mother knew I was dressing up, and was impressed when I saw wall-to-wall bookcases filled with hard-covered books, rugs on the floor, paintings on the wall, I had never seen an apartment like that, some friends who moved out had studio apartments with books on the floor or held together by bookcases held up with wine bottles, but most lived with roommates and said they wouldn't start getting good furniture until they married. They had a Bang and Olufsen sound system not a record player with a radio attached playing Esmeralda's favorite Franz Schubert's *String Quintet in C*, I mentioned *The Art of the Fugue* trying to impress them from music my grandfather played but she said he was a boring and banal composer. Esmeralda was just sitting there listening, her head propped up by her elbow, I never saw anyone listening so intently usually it was background to her it was foreground. So much for grandfather who also said only Germans really can listen to classical music. Only after the LP finished did she struggle out of her chair to greet me, she said classical music is to die for, literally, Stalin, that despot, was listening to Mozart's *Concerto #23* when he had a stroke and the record kept humming but nobody dared go in and check on him, but that wasn't what impressed me what impressed me is the way she discussed ideas after I handed her the Sachertorte and said it had to be served with whipped cream and she said she knew. This was my first true exposure to music and ideas and it was profound, a dialogue not a conversation, she actually mentioned books I hoped to read and said that Stalin was despot who destroyed a good idea, that the Jews infected Russians with their beliefs in toleration and rationalism. In my college culture some teachers talked communism but didn't live by them or have a creative bone in their body. These types of conversations never happened at home where my father's head was stuck in the *Daily News* and I watched television as we ate together. When grandfather was alive he wouldn't eat with us and waited until we were finished to eat my mother's cooking but he too had his head stuck in a newspaper only it was *The Daily Worker.* Who had discussions with tea and cake? I wondered if they were 'intellectual' I had met some in college but I thought that was for show, you could tell them apart, they wore berets, horn-rimmed glasses, took deep breathes between words and smoked, and I immediately gravitated to them as opposed to the crew cut, penny loafer white sock look, and Esmeralda and Cassie actually listened to what I had to say but quickly realized they had thought much more about what I thought than I did in my little quips, and they took ideas seriously. I found the dialogue intimidating and exhilarating at the same time, this was no ordinary conversation and while it was going on couldn't believe I was actually participating in an intellectual discussion about moral responsibility for our lives regardless of the consequences, that you must develop good habits to be able to appreciate beauty and then you can ascend to good by the mind. We must take responsibility for our lives but each time I tried thinking like that I became cynical and cracked a joke but these women were taking thoughts seriously. Esmeralda talked about Dulcinea and I wondered who she was and only later found out she was a character in *Don Quixote* who had a deeper understanding of men than men have of women, where men can't understand that women don't always have to be with a man and fuck. That was the first time I ever heard an older women curse, they were usually so polite and condescending in conversation but not Esmeralda, she spoke her mind, even as it took her a little while to say it with her stutter, but what a mind. I wanted to hear more about my grandfather but she said that was between them and she told me little but all of a sudden I spoke up of how *avuelo* and me went to the art exhibit and afterwards ran for the subway, as true New Yorkers, and he had a heart attack and I held his hand and he kept telling me he was okay as if he wasn't believing he had a heart attack and how he died mouthing Esmeralda in the ambulance with me holding his hand and when the ambulance attendant told me he was dead I realized I was holding a cold hand. I called my parents at the neighbor's apartment because we didn't have a phone yet, and they had to come down and identify the body, I was too young and the police officer came on the phone and explained it to my father and he knew immediately it was him because he could tell by the shoes he was wearing, as if all the time he was hoping it was a mistake. None of us could believe my grandfather was no more. My mother said the steps must have been too much for his heart, the doctor said he must take it easy and then my mother made me dinner, and the beef as usual stuck to my teeth, but tonight unlike other nights I didn't watch television nor did my father read the news, we sat in silence. Esmeralda then said there would be plenty of time to talk about Jacobo and automatically a smile came across my face, we would meet again, it also widened when she said I want to see more of me, just like in my dreams. And the next morning bright and early I pictured myself knocking on the door or a used bookshop on Bookseller's row, Fourth Ave, or Park Ave South, and saying let me in, let me in I have to get a book, but waited until they opened and bought my first hard-covered book that wasn't a textbook to find out who Dulcinea was went to Washington Square Park and listening to the bongo drums awakened my mind.

Here I am, dead. What do they want from me, I'm dead and buried in the cold ground, why do they keep bringing up my name? In actuality I led a shameful life didn't do what I wanted to do but what I thought I had to do—time put a severe burden on me, I saw so much killing and pain I couldn't take it anymore and ran home: enlisted for the noblest of causes to free Spain, to fight for freedom not what Miriam thought to escape her, but believed freedom was important and when one of my colored workers quit to go and fight over there at first I thought he was crazy, what about the battles that had to be fought for here but then saw the logic of his decision—over there, here, it doesn't matter freedom is freedom and loved how the Europeans were now fighting for freedom, Germans in Munich, Hungarians in Budapest, failed attempts at freedom right after the Great War but fighting for freedom from capitalistic exploiters and I wanted to be part of that struggle not just a shopkeeper, and with the help of the party made my way to Spain. A rough crossing on a tanker *Thersites*, I threw up most of the time, which should have been an omen only I'm not superstitious we live in secular times—there is literally a vanishing moment when religious time is no longer and scientific time takes over, now I no longer live and the sequence of moments changes to a repetition of moments but then off I went and saw sufferings a human being should not see. Because I am unaware of what is going on doesn't mean they are not not going on, there is no evidence after death of anything and yet here I am. When you sleep or under the influence of anesthesia and have pain but don't remember it does it go on? And awake absence of thought does not prove anything? There is no soul without a body and I didn't believe in soul only body but upon coming back my body was okay but my soul was defective, there may not be a world soul but there certainly is an individual soul—no matter what you call it. I think about the nightmares, the days I couldn't get out of bed in the morning filled with emptiness as I look in the faces of my dead comrades, oh how I had lost my being, my sense of feeling for other human beings, of how I could no longer be friends with anyone back in the States and one day couldn't get out of bed and had to move in with my daughter because I couldn't find the will to move, and only because my grandson loved me unconditionally was I able to be with him, and only when he came up to me and hugged me and asked me to take him places, when he started developing a self apart from his body. He was like a puppy dog all over me unlike those who forced me to shoot a traitor, or watch as men died in battle wondering if these feeling could ever go away, and only with schnapps did they recede never leave even if each day I wondered if I could ever lead a normal life again but the pain was too great and I couldn't and was glad it finally came sooner rather than later. I was surprised when I came home thought far away from the war it would go away but it only came back stronger, I couldn't understand it and I still jumped when a car backfired and I had pain but nobody could see it, doctors said I was physically fine but they were not in my skin, if by chance I was able to get out of bed, I would walk across the Concourse into Manhattan sunning myself drinking liquor out of a brown paper bag and if you are not in harmony with your soul you can only lead a discomforting life, body and soul are married and you need both if a person is to be whole otherwise time is out of joint, we must be in agreement with our selves before we can love our fellow woman. The one thing I learned from war is you can't love your fellow human being because you can't love yourself—those that can can find companionship others of us did the cruelest things without seeing the other as a human being a face-to-face encounter, imagine I had to shoot someone and see his face his face still haunts my dreams. I did the this without regard of the other because I didn't know what the self was and the sad part is you only learn after you do cruelty, you cannot live alone you have to live with others but not in a literary salon the kind I despised in my youth where you can talk the love of solitude and independence, free-thinking.

Too bad you can't live as a pure mind and communicate only with your thoughts but we live in a world and the body takes its revenge on us for our acts. And after my stroke no more caffeine or schnapps how was I supposed to live. Smoking was easy to give up my little grandson didn't want me to kiss him anymore because of my bad breath and I gave that up because I wanted to hug and kiss my only grandchild and I wanted him to sit in my lap. These doctors spoke so intently, so rationally, I always promised them I would give up drinking but never could, how was I to get through the night or the day, twenty years later and I still couldn't forget, the pain would always come back, his face would always be in my dream regardless of what or who I dreamt about, two balls rolling down the street it was his face chasing them, a friend waiting for me to go to the bar it was his face, the man I shot, and no matter how many times I tell myself I did not do it alone there were others in the firing squad it makes no difference I did it. My dreams are always associations from the war, when awake I lead a normal humdrum existence the same as everybody else, but asleep I am in my own private world, no longer back home but an exile; only my body was back home otherwise I was still in Spain even as I knew there was no other life than this. Nothing I could ever do could make up for the harm I did to other human beings when I disregarded the other as a human being. I never thought about that when I engaged in the noble fight for freedom but what I did was not noble at all, I killed, and saw people being killed and that wasn't noble and what was worse was watching how they suffered, I thought I would be immune to their pain because they were the enemy but they were also human beings even if I disagreed with them—the best and worst of times, away from Miriam and with people I was proud to call my brothers, people I admired and loved talking about a free Spain with and what we were going to do once we got back into the world—black and white together commanded by Oliver Law, a Negro general, who laughed the first time the Spanish saw him sitting in a court yard and tried to rub the dirt off his face, but the retaliation we gave because what they did to us made killing too easy, saying the other started it, war showed beneath our veneer a beast is waiting to be let out and once let out of the bottle couldn't put it back in again. Yet I still believed in the workers' movement until Hungary, when Soviet tanks invaded Hungary when Zoltan escaped to America as Soviet tanks crushed the Hungarian uprising of 1956, at first Laszlo, Zoltan's brother, my comrade, had welcomed the communists but he was in the first wave to be arrested only to be freed after the sun of the world died, up until then I thought communists would create a democratic socialist state. Zoltan called the Gulag the Kolyma, not even the God that failed saw the beast in man what class guilt was able to do to another and like Pandora's box we unleashed evils into the world.

I don't know if there is an unseen order to the universe or it all happens simply by chance but I acted as if I were in love and that attracted others to me, just like grandfather said it would, when you are in love you are happy and other people automatically surround you, and Esmeralda and Cassandra and I had a wonderful time; I loved how Esmeralda said in her stuttering voice because of her medication, which I quickly got used to, that she didn't have to wait for Khrushchev's revelation to turn against the communists, she saw it from the moment of the Hitler-Stalin pact and the collapse of the Left in the face of fascism—that is living with history, all dates to me, some points I heard in lectures at the yap, yap shop but living reality to her as she absorbed them and lived them and realized the seriousness of them. My grandfather always talked the interests of the working class even if his son-in-law, my father was the most reactionary worker there ever was, the only one in the family who voted Republican, republicans who stand for greed, lies and racism, and worse believed in their lies. He and my grandfather would argue about the future of the proletariat and after *avuelo* died my father continued the arguments with me, that's how we talked, we argued, and I replaced *avuelo* but I still have no doubt they both loved me. *Avuelo* told me after Spain he came back to be with the family that he couldn't violate the blood purity, I had no idea what he was talking about then now I realize how much the old ways grab onto you and won't let go, my mother thought he had a girlfriend in Spain because he was gone so long but he never mentioned it to her when I mentioned it to him he didn't want to talk about it, and I believed him believed anything he said. Yet he couldn't stand being with the family and spent as much of his time away from it as he could, except with me when we would go on walks throughout the city together when I was able to walk long distances—served me well in high school when I would wander the city instead of going to school. He hadn't left the party after Khrushchev's '56 speech and he may not even have believed it, only when Zoltan showed up, the brother of his old buddy from the

Spanish Civil War and he could no longer deny it. Zoltan was the one who gave me *Darkness at Noon* and while my buddies were afraid of being a phony I was reading serious history, and I made sure Miss Pellman my history teacher saw me carrying it but she didn't even know what it was. I should have carried Salinger instead or what some real cool boys were carrying *Tropic of Cancer*. Grandfather and I traversed the city together on weekends, walked or took the subway downtown, out of the Bronx, he even showed me Booksellers Row on Park Avenue South, Germantown in the East 80s, the Upper West Side, north of 96th Street where we'd go into the cafeterias and south where we would go to a café, he would schmooze with his friends, but what I really loved was when he would take me to Little Spain and he would splurge and we'd eat lunch in El Quixote that was on the ground floor of the Chelsea hotel and would speak Spanish to the waiters and customers. When we took the subway I insisted we go in the first car so I can look at the tracks and the twists and turn of the line, he thought I might be a motorman but my mother said head of the Transit Authority. He was the one who taught me to read a book, not the newspaper on a bus or train and I only realized later that reading had made school much easier when I got into the special high school because I read a lot or Zoltan had taken me to the art museum and allowed me to sit and paint all by myself. Esmeralda smiled said Jews read all the time and she liked it even if Cassandra didn't, she was groomed for college but never finished, the acting bug bit her too hard. She did say one of these days she's hopes to finish but hope needs content, only in action do we do things. She tells me after spending two unhappy years in Pittsburgh she couldn't stand it anymore she abandoned her student life put on a form-fitting sweater that she tucked into her jeans and a beret, smoking Chesterfields which she quickly abandoned as a vile habit when her grandmother yelled at her it ages you too quickly and if you want to be an actress and remember women actresses in America are only ingénues. And since nobody ever checks resumes in acting she put down she was a college graduate of the University of Pittsburgh, and in fallow times the 'college degree' did her well in her temporary assignments but she now says she has become a reader and viewer and realizes only in art is there truth, while Esmeralda thought the struggle for justice is truth, while I think it is the scientific method that distinguished belief from knowledge. If there is truth Cassandra says she finds it while waiting to audition and from that individual case I assumed all actors read, that's what actors do, read while waiting or between scenes. Boy was I surprised when I met other actors how little they actually knew when I confused them with the part they were playing. Not Cassandra. We began to share books, imagine I was having a real conversation with an older woman no less, something I had hoped would happen but something I never did anything about until now when I got up my guts and called them. Still no one is truly free if you live with your parents, grandparents don't count because she was the freest woman I ever met. And I had never heard women talk so intelligently about the world or on so many issues as Esmeralda and Cassandra—after Esmeralda's spiel about the failure of the Left to stand up to fascism, which of course was never mentioned in class or practically anywhere because when the Hitler-Stalin pact collapsed everyone talked about the how the communists fought the Germans not the two years they were their allies carving up Mitropa (Eastern Europe) between them, no one uses that term anymore instead say Eastern Europe as if it was always was East not part of Europe, she said, and showed me authors in her bookcase, Hermann Broch, Robert Musil, Joseph Roth who I never heard of alongside Kafka, Thomas Mann, everyone had heard of Thomas Mann even if I didn't know a soul who read him and Heinrich Mann, I didn't know Thomas had a brother Heinrich. I made a mental note of the authors for my search down on Booksellers row wondering if my grandfather would have appreciated that.

She was a philosemite—first time I ever heard that word and that strange young man reminded her of an old boyfriend, how little we know about the people we love, she has had a whole life that I know practically nothing about, and he is the grandson of my grandmother's lover, imagine that, but all I saw in him was a confused kid, a newfound college graduate who doesn't know his ass from a hole in the ground and was shocked to realize the world doesn't exist the way it does in books. An excitable type with limited experiences who wants to tell the world how to live while him mother still folds his laundry, claims never to have drunk wine before always considered it a bums' drink or what you do on religious holidays, he lives with fake solitude, an 'existential hero' who doesn't realize the bread must be shared, conversation and human companionship are crucial, but he does have a car so we can go places, a '61 Corvair, his father was surprised at how cheap he got it, it was so inexpensive for a car a few years old, but it's a stick shift and I can't drive that and grandma doesn't dare anymore, but he's promised to take us for a drive, it will be fun to get out of the city. He never knew a woman could drive a car let alone a stick shift until grandma said she would in her younger days, grandma can drive a stick shift because occasionally she drove an ambulance and they only have sticks—he must have seen women drive there are enough of us driving now, but he still thinks of a car as a man thing. Women drive all over Pittsburgh they have to there's no public transportation, a bus comes once a half hour, the only ones who walk are the Negroes living at the bottom of the hill, and they don't need to they're close enough to work, all others are trapped if they don't have a car. She wanted me to learn up in the Bronx but I had no interest back then, but I learned in drivers' education, even got credit for it and loved going back up to the Bronx and cruising around the block. We girls could then honk at boys. But I can't wait to smell spring again, here you can't smell a thing too much carbon monoxide in the air, car exhales, bus fumes, pollution from construction, but nobody cares because we call that progress. They almost built a highway through the Lower East Side and the Village like they did up in the Bronx—the Lower Manhattan Expressway, they even had a name for it like they do in the Bronx, the Cross Bronx Expressway, no creativity in names, they were going to destroy neighborhood after neighborhood in the lower part of the city to build a highway from the Holland tunnel to the Williamsburg Bridge, not caring about the smog, a new term we've learned from California, destroying Chinatown, Little Italy the Lower East Side and parts of Greenwich Village with their highway and access roads, inadequately called urban renewal, only the tremendous opposition by the Village people stopped it, grandma fought it, I thought she was crazy, but we still have our apartment where the East Village turns into the Lower East Side. Mostly I was in school and grandma would write me letters from the White Horse Tavern about the fight and how she got high on the night of the final victory, one of her few victories, only one old man wanted it built and he couldn't even drive and was chauffeured around everywhere, and she wrote that progress isn't all that it's cracked up to be. She complained that they were tearing down Pennsylvania Station but nobody is complaining except a few academics, that didn't catch the support of the people but luckily the expressway did and they were able to galvanize enough politicians, who at first were to chicken shit or really believed it was progress, to force the government to be for the people not big business interests. When grandma first came to the city she told me how dazzled she was by the big skyscrapers, loved looking at the Flatiron building the Chrysler, with the gargoyles lit up on the roof, the Empire State building thought it the most beautiful buildings in the world, she would ride the double-decker bus up Fifth Avenue just to look at those buildings, sometimes walking into the lobbies of these art-deco buildings—no buildings in Madrid or Barcelona were over five or six stories and here even apartment buildings have elevators. She thought that was the future, now she is no longer so sure bigger is better. Joseph had never been to any of these buildings and she promised to take him, said the lobbies were beautiful even if the Empire State building is a bit touristy. And he didn't know where the Chrysler or Flatiron building were. A true New Yorker grandma said. He never even had been to Penn Station, his mother never took him out of the Bronx she had been too frightened of the city and when he could go with his friends at first all they went to was South Ferry then to Central Park, later on in college he ventured to Washington Square Park by himself, ashamed to ask people where the park was as if he would know automatically but didn't want to be considered a hick from Jersey, and walked and walked until he came upon it. I was pretty much the same you never left your neighborhood. I agreed to be his chaperone, he wanted to see beatniks and was surprised to see they weren't how they were characterized on television. What me work? He saw people disgusted with the American acquisitive life style and were pulling away with no particular ax to grind. Grandma didn't like them too much she saw them as pure negativity who remained neutral in the fight for justice and weren't involved in the anti-parkway movement, civil rights movement, anti-war movement, they all talked about their complexes as if the problems of the world were psychological not social and that individuals had to fight to change the system, she thought of psychoanalysis as another blame-the-mother approach to childrearing. She thought the ideals of capitalism itself had to be questioned. What are needed are new ideas, but the standard of living is so high in America, the economy doing so well now after the war, that few people seem willing to challenge the existing way of life. She once told me she was so surprised when she first came to America that every house has its own bathroom and kitchen. What more could people want than indoor plumbing.

Go lead a decent life after all I've been through, I can control my happiness but not my unhappiness, I thought once I left Spain, once I got as far away as I could from European soil, once I secured passage on the *Ajax* Spain would all become a distant memory, okay maybe not at first but in time, I was sitting below deck just made the twenty-minute horn, I was first on the waiting list and to my surprise was able to flee— the ticket agent said bring your valise, which mainly had books in it, I had so few possessions, rented a deck chair on the sun deck and made believe I was truly first class, of course my parents might have paid but I no longer wanted anything to do with them, and started reading Dos Passos' *Manhattan Transfer* and remember how well it felt to be reading Dos Passos and know in a few weeks I would be in his Manhattan, later Orwell's reminiscences about the war, only I had never met Orwell, and the friends I fought with never met him either and wondered if he made it all up. I did hear Paul Robeson sing, however, Jacobo and I held hands the whole time his deep rich voice sang *Old Man River,* afterwards we talked as we usually did all night long about the party, the future after the war was won and analyzed it to pieces but never grasped the uncertainty that defined our actions, thinking what we believed had to be the truth and that we were all in it together, only later would I say those were the most profound days of my life, but the years right after were the worst years coming home in total defeat, but even when recalling peeing in my pants because I couldn't hold it any longer and afterwards only a deep drag of a cigarette could calm me down, and plenty of vodka and this was the best, otherwise all my life was one of lies, and dreams from those times have never gone away, as I keep telling myself I should have done more, or done this or that, done it differently a mode of excuses why I didn't board the boat with him—a noble cause leads to a noble lie and lies aren't good and I couldn't confront myself back in purgatory, it had to be purgatory because I knew I was getting out of Spain not going to end my life there even as I felt my life was over. In hell you don't even realize that you did wrong but I had to confront myself even as I told myself I don't want redemption, I did it and am responsible for my cowardice; evil cannot be erased and this place is pure evil and no matter how much I tried to camouflage it saying it was alright I knew I couldn't stay there as if it was all a bad dream. On first sitting on E-deck I tried to read but my mind wandered all over the place and I said okay it might be too soon to forget this place I need some time to absorb it all—maybe if the ship is torpedoed it would be for the best, I wouldn't have to continue but the ship wasn't torpedoed and we passed the Statue of Liberty after two weeks of smooth sailing and I finally was able to sit on the sun deck and stare at the foam and the waves, read words I didn't understand but I had my dictionary, and wrote notes in my little diary thinking I am getting further and further away from Europe the country I had fought for only a few years before—now I have to admit I am an American even if not native born, this country sinks its teeth into you, this country is so energetic and never asks who your parents are where you've been before, I never felt that being with the 'internationalists' they always considered me an inferior and that they were condescending to fight for the poor Spaniards who have no home or whose country is being overrun never seeing us as equals in our own right. Luckily I am good at languages and could hear them speak we used the same words but they had different meanings—they talked historical progress we talked about freedom to decide—the difference being Jacobo enriched my life most just grandstanded they were full of doubt I was sure this was the only world that made sense, yet it was only an aberration in time, a short moment in history that I was privileged to be part of as opposed to the greatest evil the Great War, the war of miscalculation that broke all the rules of civilized living that forced man into history and forced me to finally get out of Europe, the first war awakened and liberated the powers of freedom they could not be held back by the forces of reactionism, the greatest fraud perpetrated on Europeans was saying we had to go to war over some archduke being assassinated somewhere and that the men would be home by Christmas. I thought it cutesy when Joseph now wants to do a grand tour, from what I wanted to escape from, from what his grandfather left in defeat. Workers have it so good here laundromats every few blocks so you don't have to wash by hand, pumps for gasoline so you no longer had to pump by hand, they even bottle-fed babies, how disgusting not to breastfeed. I understood, I understood but still couldn't understand all the rape that was committed and just like the Russians I wanted revenge on the Germans even if you couldn't catch the individual soldier all Germans were guilty especially because the Germans supplied Franco.

Sure the child was mine, the birth happened after I got home and the Germans were preparing for another war but it was born dead and that little homunculus inside me that gave meaning to my actions. How do I know it didn't die and they just took her from me, I never could stand the smell of the dead and didn't see her after she was taken from me? Before Jacobo I thought women do their duty give birth and motherhood, our destiny was set in stone and nothing touched us even when the panic came we were alright as long as our children were alright, we never had a life of our own. When I landed here I didn't have the right pedigree and couldn't be a nurse instead became an unregistered nurse, husbands still expected blood on the sheet, the stain of purity, and I sewed young girls up. Young women still had to appear as virgins before their man. I was also a graphologist for a time analyzing handwriting for character a person wasn't even aware of until they no longer needed that. You got up each morning drank instant coffee, read the *New York Times*, put on the portable Bakelite radio and then did it again the next day only I quickly became bored with that routine but I quickly perfected my English because I didn't only stay with Spaniards, mostly uneducated people from the island, and hung around with the bohemians, independent women, they had a keen sense of seeing the injustice and trying to do something about it, they were no longer going to be a plaything of history, and a large number of them worked or actually went to college because the men were away and colleges wanted to keep enrollments up and allowed women in, only of course to want to end it after the war ended, but you couldn't put Pandora back in the jar so easily. In the full light of reason now however I can see that again I was the plaything of history and when the war ended those high-paying jobs dried up as well.

Now my companion goes out all the time and I tell myself I am not jealous, I'm ok with it, I tell myself she has the right to choose, the right to freedom, but what if she's lying in a ditch somewhere, she tells me that's a line men use to control women and she refuses to be controlled by a man or words used as tricks to control women. I am my grand-mother's daughter, she says. No longer are women content to be clerks, administrative assistants, teachers, social workers, or volunteer to be a do-cent at the museum but are now challenging male assumptions—all of a sudden there was a feminist position and I was caught up in it: while I believed in it still didn't want it to happen to me. I never realized we would change or at least she is the one who changed, but why should I be so surprised after all I am no longer the same thirteen-year-old boy, I just didn't realize it could happen to me. No longer would women marry and put a ring in their nose, women decided they could live without a man or if they stayed together it would be without marriage, look at how many doorbells in the city have more than one name on it, at least in the hipper parts of the city, up in the Bronx it was the same ole, same ole. When Cassie came home real late from a date, she hugged me and said I was the one who she lived with and that I didn't have to wait up for her, and that I didn't have to stay up and wait for her return that she always comes home to me at the end, and I was about to speak but she had rehearsed her lines and said I told you when we moved in together that you cannot curtail my life in the theater and the theater exists past midnight. We are so worked up after a performance that it takes us awhile to calm down and we go out carousing together, and I am an actress and all that interferes with acting I ignore. No you didn't you said you wouldn't move in with me unless I lived alone for at least a year not live with my parents but know what it's like living as an adult. And then I had a visual revelation and with all the money I saved living at home found an apartment on the Upper West Side from a guy who was finishing law school and his grandfather had moved to Miami and I shared an apartment with him. Never live with lawyers they make you sign all sorts of documents for subletting, for the furniture I was using, for pissing in the middle of the night, but at least it counted as moving out of my parents' place and taking the subway only to 96th was a blessing after my late night dinners at Esmeralda and Cassandra and didn't have to go home to my stop on the D train 167th street. And I found it weird that by sunset the streets were dark hardly a soul on the streets, and never women alone like in the Village, except for Broadway; the side streets, West End Avenue, Riverside Drive, and Columbus and Amsterdam were deserted and stores closed by sundown and soon would be putting iron gates in front of their windows. There is a pervasive atmosphere in the world that a woman should be home by midnight, the Cinderella affect but I can't wait to stay home waiting for a man to put a slipper on me to see if it fits. I agreed felt the corrosive masculine spirit that subordinates women to the home but I was not coercing her but she claims you can feel the testosterone in the air, the press makes fun of feminists, businesses won't allow women to work except in helping roles, stewardess can't work when they reach 30, all we are allowed to be are schoolteachers and social workers all other professions are closed to us, including acting—how few substantial roles are there for women over thirty. Sociology becomes psychology and the thought is a woman can't be free without a man. I wanted to move in with her and agree all that oppresses her is oppressive but I don't think I oppress her, and I did agree because I wanted to live with her that she could continue to work, it wouldn't have dawned on me to stop her and destroy her spirit and if she would have asked me to leave I would be so sad so we agreed but we didn't sign a contract as she suggested, I had enough of lawyers to be and had no intention of denying her freedom, but why couldn't she phone. I know what she's talking about after my grandfather died I didn't want to live alone in our room but eventually I had to come to terms with it, why can't she. I wanted to be with her despite our differences, or maybe because of them—why should it always be an older man marries a younger woman and I thought this is cool living with an older woman. She continues I don't mean to hurt you but I cannot change my life, you're awake before dawn but that's not the life of theater people we are up to all hours of the night unless there's an early call and since I don't do television and love being with others in the theater and even when not working are night-birds. As usual I caved, was quiet, seething within but quiet on the outside because she was correct I agreed with that but didn't accept it even as I kept telling myself to accept it I am a rational person and if I can see it in front of me can control it and understand it even as these atavistic images arose inside my mind and soon there would be no way that I could control them. I tried fighting it with words but words then flew out of my mouth that I didn't even realize I thought. When I spoke I realized the futility of rational thought all I was was misogynistic and thoughtful arguments were useless and my hand banged into the table so hard it even scared me. Feminism isn't about intellectual arguments it was a deep rooted primordial feeling, men used these or similar arguments to deprive women of equal opportunity, and she was partly raised by a strong grandmother and knew how to fight for her freedom; Esmeralda had been a communist because of their promise of freedom for women but she quickly saw how that faded in the Soviet Union, Hungary, Poland, Czechoslovakia and the other Soviet bloc countries, communism didn't set women free only imprisoned everybody—women were still responsible for holding the family together, do the cooking, household chores, laundry all while holding a full time job. Just like in the West even if women worked they made dinner and gave the kiddies a bath at night, that was considered their job. A crack did develop in feminism saying what Cassandra was talking about was only for the privileged few, uneducated workers still have no freedom. Men use anything to criticize women who rebel but at times women were their own worst enemy saying I am not oppressed being a housewife, I would beg my mother to get a job not for the money but to get her out of the house and off my back. As she spoke to me she lit a cigarette should have been a cigarillo, the cigar of women but they still didn't have enough guts to smoke them in public and she quickly put it out not because I hate the vile stench of cigarette smoke in the apartment but because Esmeralda has warned her of the hazards of smoking, a heart attack. After a few symbolic puffs she crushed it. There would be no make-up sex tonight, that aroma was too putrid for me. What never changes, she concludes is anti-feminism it is what it is only the words change or different methods but women have to struggle to lead independent lives and control their bodies and not be trapped with little ones before they are ready to handle it. I have seen too many of my girlfriends become mothers before they were adults and never had a chance to live, but now they tell me they will live when the children are grown, but by then it may be too late. Children have to be cared for and men won't let us have an abortion because then we wouldn't be trapped inside the house, at least now the attitude is changing towards abortion even if the law isn't. No longer is it an evil doctor who does abortions instead of being on the golf course while you're having your heart attack.

Did I ever have a thing with Trotsky? What kind of question is that from a little boy, what do they teach boys in school? I told him as a child I saw Trotsky walking on Southern Boulevard and my mother pointed him out to me, he was famous even then, but what does a boy studying for his bar mitzvah know about such things. He just laughed when I asked him about his periods at school, thinks women's body parts are jokes and he must learn this stuff on the street. Certainly my daughter wouldn't teach him that even if I wouldn't put it past his grandfather. I tell him not to play with the boys downstairs—Irish hooligans parents always having a beer in their hand, the twins whatever their names are, identical twins that he can tell apart and every time he stops by here he says hello to me and runs downstairs to play with them—I hope he doesn't start to smoke like them, I've seen them smoking on the street corner and they now even do it in front of their mother. Those boys will end up no good, I almost don't want him visiting because he spends so much time with them, but then when would I see him, I can't go over to my daughter's house with my husband there, I am already dreading the bar mitzvah next year when he will certainly be present. Atheist that he is he won't miss this family event. I can't stand the man; I spit on the ground he walks on. And me having an affair with Trotsky that's his grandfather talking to him, I was a child. Maybe Frida Kahlo is the kiss-and-tell type, who knows, she says she did but Trotsky is dead and can't deny it, and I only know all about this when my husband drags me down to Rockefeller Center not to see the tree but 'Crossroads' the mural of Diego Rivera that was later destroyed because it showed workers in a heroic light and had Lenin in it. Everyone made such a big deal over a mural that's when Jacobo told me Diego Rivera's wife was Frieda Kahlo—right before he left for Spain, and I said good riddance, then I had to become a bookkeeper, ride the local train everyday all the way into the city, spend a fortune on babysitters, my mother was already dead and I needed someone to take care of Molly and people are up in arms over a mural, getting excited about a mural while I was struggling to keep food on the table and pay the rent. Jacobo left and how was I to survive with a baby to support and soon another one on the way. Boys are always little boys and my husband goes off to fight for freedom in Spain not caring about his family here in the city. He demanded the right to be part of history, history, shimistry, what about his family. Who ever heard of such nonsense, I never understood him even after the butcher introduced us, we could never talk, he wanted to teach me everything only I didn't want to learn what he taught and he then began hanging out with his rabble workers who it wasn't enough they had a job they wanted more. His language is not the language of Jews then he goes and tells his grandson that grandma wouldn't kiss and tell as if I would ever have an affair with a man like that. What was he going to do pick me up? As if I would go out with a stranger. Now at least I no longer get angry at him, what do I have in common with him—he bore me Molly then left me, and only because I made a little money and with help of Jewish charities were we able to get by and then he comes back after fighting for the Spaniards, and for the sake of the children I take him back, barely recognized him at first, if it wasn't for the children I would have nothing to do with him but children need a father even if we never shared a bed again. Finally we bought one of those expensive Saks convertible couches at the Hub on Third Avenue because I could no longer stand being in the same room as him. I wanted to go to Hearns Department store but no he shops only at the best with my money, at least I got to show Molly Santa Claus there, she wanted to sit on his lap but for that you had to pay and I wasn't going to pay for that. I was nice to him when he returned fed him, clothed him, kept a kosher home a lot he cared and I would have tried harder if he didn't go traipsing off to his cronies in the city. And he drags me off to see a picture of Lenin in the corner as if this was an earth-shaking event and had no interest in the tree that was already lit up. Man at the *Crossroads,* as if men are not always at the crossroads because he never allows things to be always wants to change them but every time he goes against God's will havoc ensues. But man never learns and each time it gets worse and all it does is age women when we have to be totally responsible for the family. Our whole life is the family a lot he cared about his family. Before I was deceiving myself that he would come to his senses but age is real entirely independent of thinking and now I know he will never change, and when Molly moved up to the Concourse I knew I had to move to be closer to her. When he passes he made it clear he doesn't want me at his funeral but of course I will go to support my children, who cares what he wants. When he left he never wrote, up and gone for years without a word, I was trapped to that man. Why did my parents' consent to that marriage weren't they supposed to look out for me? Nowadays it's different children make their own choices, I wasn't even eighteen when they consented to this marriage, now I see children in the street wheeling babies thinking they are so mature, just wait soon it will dawn upon them their life is over before it ever began. What does a sixteen-year-old know. But now with radio, television, movies they know much more than I knew and make worse decisions than I made. Little Joey listens to Elvis the Pelvis, Joey had to tell me his name and I wondered who can understand such lyrics. Eventually I told my grandson that decent women don't have affairs especially when they are married and that you should marry in life not be alone all your life but you have time yet, because his grandfather had told him not to marry. What kind of man tells a twelve-year-old boy that? I didn't even realize he was interested in girls, but they start so young these days, all this freedom is not so good for them. Now all he does is run outside and play ball as soon as he gets home from school, forget homework, as soon as he drops off his books he's gone, Molly has to drag him to Hebrew school for bar mitzvah lessons, he won't go on his own and now that he learned the word no stopped music lessons, wants to pick up the guitar, with his throaty voice and he can't even carry a tune. It cost my daughter a fortune for violin lessons and now he just gives it up. He only wants to be a ballplayer, even wants to waste money on an expensive Willie Mays baseball glove and when I went to Davega Stores again at the Hub on Third Avenue and East 149th street, a salesman says nobody has Negro gloves, what does a white boy want with a colored glove, but that's all he wants for Chanukah. I can't even follow a baseball game but his uncle did take him a few times to Yankee Stadium, his grandfather would never do that he takes him to restaurants where old men sit and smoke all the time. He even was caught playing hooky from school when the truant officer caught him standing online for bleacher seats for a Giant opener, he complains if he had a few more cents he could have gone to grand stand and nobody would have questioned him there, and he was punished by having to stay late after school, and my daughter was called to school and they made a deal, she promised not to tell his father if he wouldn't do it again, only she did saying they called him at work, and he was mad at her for betraying him and shaming him in front of his grandfather because he saw how his grandfather suffered and didn't want to hurt him; but from now on a letter goes home to my daughter every day, which she has to sign saying he was at school and not misbehaving. He's so bored in school if they give him extra work it might be good for him forcing him to learn.

I packed my only suitcase I had to get out of the home I couldn't stand this place and refused to put up with it anymore—the question is why did I come back, she wanted to live next to her mother she couldn't be anywhere but near her mother so we moved close to her mother and she would visit her mother every day and consult with her mother about everything as if she never grew up and anything we did she first had to run it by her mother, so I put my two shirts underwear, socks not even an extra pair of pants but my toiletries, and at least I had a good pair of sturdy shoes learned that because a friend was a postal worker on his feet all day and insisted I get good shoes even if expensive they will pay off in the long run, and even if my clothes didn't last good leather shoes did even as I quickly realized if I was killed someone would take my shoes, hopefully somebody on the Republic's side, I didn't want to die on the Loyalists side and give a fascist the privilege of good-looking comfortable shoes. All I was able to come home with were those shoes but nothing else in that suitcase that I packed and walked out the door because I was finally convinced I was doing something right, everything else was torn to shreds even before I got to Spain, these shoes were meant for traipsing through the woods of the mountain trails and down goat-infested dusty roads over the Pyrenees, good workmanship trumps lousy conditions and I was able to climb in these shoes only I kept getting exhausted walking uphill, I'm a New Yorker the city is flat, the only hills I know are the stairs on the subway, man was not made to climb like a goat, but I kept telling myself finally my life is worth something finally I am fighting the good fight, justice, not simply my everyday needs but something beyond myself, not realizing my life would be split in two, divided, not be the same person I was when I came back even if I never expected to be back in the world again. My suitcase was quickly stolen when we finally reached Madrid, but it didn't matter because I had chosen what I wanted to do and it felt good to do what I wanted to do and said I was going to do and finally make a decision instead of doing what was expected of me, a job, married with a child I had no idea what I was getting into my life over so quickly before I even had a chance to make a choice, I was too young to marry I had never read a book, been to an art gallery seen a concert the only knowledge I had was from reading the newspapers—imagine that forced to work after 8th grade even if I wanted to work and not go to school, it should have been my father who insisted I continue, but we needed the money and he was afraid of education because it would detract from Jewish lore, so my only knowledge was what was described in the popular press, not even the *New York Times* because it was too big and nobody I knew read the *Times* only the *Daily News*, *The Post*, the *Journal American*, or the *Herald Tribune* and that meant you married and settled down after spending a few years on wild oats even if I never had wild oats to spend. I didn't want marriage only adventure. I acted intuitively not knowledgeably like the

English communists at Oxbridge insisting upon taking their exams first so they could blow England and fight the good fight. I took no exams. But on the boat there were no newspapers only books. The English were a remarkable bunch of men they fit well into our brigades, they had good discipline and were a significant outfit compared to us American boys— they always seemed to operate in the most efficient manner thinking things through, planning, acting with a complete absence of doubt yet they were deeply religious. It was my first time away from home on Thanksgiving ever, and the first time I spent mostly around non-Jews, ever, of course I knew goyim but only superficially here for the first time I got to know them as human beings, as people, to actually talk to them face to face about our dreams, not as caricatures of people who disliked Jews, and how even away from home they celebrated Christmas together and even invited us to participate with them. It was this Protestant spirit of can-do that really impressed me, how they changed religious thought into can-do thought tested through evidence. I really got to like these heathens before I was always surrounded by my own kind, and in a foxhole there are no Christians and Jews only doughboys and we became close even if we were from totally different worlds and it was the English who helped replace my stolen supplies and in particular when I saw my first dead man, he removed his pants and I hadn't even spoken to him, I thought he didn't even know I existed but said he won't be needing these and I knew in those words that if he were alive he would have fought like the devil to save him but once he was dead made sure his pants were put to good use. 'Honor who has it? he who died on Wednesday', Falstaff. We discussed our noble ideas of trying to make Spain a more just place, to treat people as ends not means, he was the one who suggested I write Molly but I didn't want strangers in the building reading my thoughts, besides I couldn't explain to her why I left carrying my suitcase down five flights of stairs doing what I wanted to do not what I had to do or what was expected of me, I wasn't as articulate as the English communists who claimed the right to exams first because they were off to fight a just war. And even if he was killed almost immediately after I got to know him his companions insisted I keep his Shakespeare plays because we were good friends. How I got to read Billy Bard and learn English history about how power works not only class conflict. And even if he was upper class and all he was a good chap and if he stayed home would have been bored with that type of life and even if was killed at least he died for what he believed in thought was best for all men, he told me that enough times that he believed in this fray even in freezing cold weather when nothing we could do would warm us up, and he always said no matter how miserable I am now if I had stayed in England I would be more miserable. But how miserable could he be being born to the manor.

I have this splitting headache and lie down and the next thing I know I wake up in the hospital thinking he was the most melancholic man I ever knew and Conchita is telling me I had a heart attack but I am okay now, and I'm wondering what she's talking about and I see myself attached to all these tubes, only I am not there I am looking down at myself wondering who that poor schlemiel is before coming to the realization it is me and quickly realize I didn't make history but history didn't destroy me, and Conchita goes on talking how Dora found me lying on the bed, white as a ghost, and immediately called the new 911 and an ambulance came and then she called me and you are in Downtown Beekman and the doctors say you are going to be alright and I am trying to absorb her words but she keeps on talking, she talks from the minute she opens her eyes in the morning until she goes to sleep at night one never has a moment's peace with her, and I am trying to understand her words through tears, and as I absorb one set of words she goes onto another one and I am wondering why I'm in the hospital, and the same time wondering if I can change the future I can change the past—you change the past and your future changes, who said that to me? and then I recall Jacobo, he said that to me the first night we met, I was dealt this blow a hard life of wealth until I realized we can develop our own spirit not be trapped by our parents and the culture we were born into, we all get dealt a dirty hand and it's only in learning to think for ourselves that we can begin to change, and Conchita goes on talking that I was going to be okay just have to take it easy but that the ambulance driver said he had seen this before it is not too severe, not to severe to who? and lying here above myself, I finally realize that running away doesn't solve my problem, ah if only I knew what I know now then, I want to say but the self down below is nodding to my granddaughter. I really felt I knew what I was doing and the next day wondered what I was doing, such are the vagaries of life—he was so beautiful to look at but the next day I wondered is this what I want he will hurt you a married man, that went against everything I stood for, the sacredness of marriage but he awakened feelings I had never known I had and power I never realized before. I tried to hold Conchita's hand but it was tied to an IV, and she reached down and held mine, it felt warm to the touch, I tried to close my eyes I couldn't believe this was happening to me, heart attacks happen to other people, old people not fiftyish people. I would like to forget this but can't this seems more profound than my years in war when I helped people, people didn't help me. I'm sorry I never kept up the journal I wonder how accurate my memory is and think maybe now I will if I ever get out of this place, but I want to forget this place as quickly as I can and when they ask me for a donation, I know hospitals do that for recovering patients thinking they will be grateful, I will not acknowledge their existence. What I would do for a cigarette right now. Shouldn't a doctor come around he probably will say no alcohol but if I am to leave this place must be able to live my life. Now is not the time to think of anything but getting well, Conchita says. I would like to die in my own home not a hospital room, Conchita says I am not going to die but you did give me a scare. I want to live free not as a patient even if that means doing what the doctor says is wrong, I hear myself thinking as I feel myself starting to cry, why am I crying Conchita wants to know you are alright we got you to the hospital on time and the ambulance driver told me if a heart attack doesn't kill you instantly you have a good chance of survival, I hear myself thinking while watching myself down below, that my desire to remake myself is stronger than the desire to sit home alone and brood about my fate and try and imagine myself home again lying on the couch not trapped in a hospital bed attached to tubes. They even have something on my nose attached to an oxygen tank so it is difficult to talk, which is okay because I have nothing to say my memories are too strong to put into words, I try and recall but only visual images come to my mind with feelings attached to the images and each time I try and put words to the image the image fades away. I didn't make history but history didn't destroy me and I was on the right side of history but I hate to think of that but on a personal level he was the only man I truly loved and am no longer fanatically committed to revolution. Why I understand Conchita's obsession with acting I was like that once, crazy, the only thing that mattered was the fight, and now all that matters to her is her acting, good for her. It took me a while to realize that because she had a chance at an education but she refused to take advantage of it as she said school was too slow for her and she finally said to me stop nagging me about school when I insisted she go to night school, you won't be the oldest in the class now housewives are going back because they feel old at thirty-five, imagine that's when you first begin to break free, if you don't do it by then when the hell are you going to do it. Maybe at fifty you start to live, that is if you have your health. Ha, ha. History never stops but we do. I found myself pregnant when Jacobo left but I didn't want him to come back to me out of a sense of responsibility only if he loved me, and I wanted my baby to be the pact between us, anything part of him was part of me, and who would have thought pregnant with another's child satisfied some men and it didn't stop them one bit from courting me, and since I couldn't work had to live with my parents or in the confines of a man, but I knew I could never live in a man's explanation that men and women see the world differently and couldn't allow myself to get caught up in their world, even if we live in the same house we see the world differently, men only see the superficial aspects of the world not the underlying phenomena and their thoughts are without stability because they are prone to follow feelings only and have no insight only interested in the here and now not the long-term effects of thought. Is there a world beyond sensation and the real world may not be the one of history? I may have been on the wrong side of history even if we were right. Try and sleep, grandma, that's all I hear my granddaughter saying. Slowly I feel myself sinking down into my body. Did I have to live with such certainty and not as if were subject to discussion, even as Jacobo told me you have thought about these things more than me all I have are bon mots, clichés, not real thought, and I love your brain. He didn't do too bad with my body either. Conchita wonders why I am smiling; thinking about Jacobo always brings a smile to my face, and embraces me she's glad to see me smiling, and I can hear her saying not to drink too much wine, since she came to live with me I no longer drink a bottle a night, she shares some with me; at first she thought of wine as Hombre, what winos drink having no idea of the aroma of the bouquet and the beauty of the color, I look down almost before losing consciousness and see I am attached to a catheter. How will I ever get out of this place? I know I can't walk and up those flights of stairs something to look forward to if I can begin to look forward, will I ever be able to get out of this bed. I want to say I want to walk but words can't come out of my mouth, too bad my daughter is no longer here she can be shocked at my thoughts but not my granddaughter, Jacobo once said my phrases are all connected and that puts a whole different light on all my actions, I'm still glad I did them but it's not going to be easy now is the last thought I think I have before falling asleep, besides I tell myself in my last last thought before falling asleep you don't change your life you are still the same individual there has to be more than a mere correction between thought and action if you are to change, it just can't be feeling it at a particular moment otherwise I can believe at any particular moment but now I can't think about this anymore my brain is becoming fuzzy and I'm sinking down into my body, I'm trapped in my body, only with tremendous effort can I find out who I am. I'm afraid to fall asleep if I fall asleep I will never wake up.

After my grandfather died what surprised me was the absence of feeling, I didn't know how I felt, was it pleasure he was gone, pain I would never have another, I don't know but I did feel glad at least I loved once. The first conscious memory I have is my grandfather taking me to the American Museum of Natural History and seeing the dinosaurs or was it the Thanksgiving Day parade and Hopalong Cassidy riding his white horse Topper at the end the parade, or maybe we did both on the same day, I know we did both but I don't recall if it was on the same day, but I do remember us getting lost and I helped find 81st street not 181st street. We simply took the train back down; the trains ran frequently in the old days, I do remember not wanting to go to the Catskills for the summer, I rather stay in the city with my friends but wasn't allowed to stay only with my grandfather. It was the worst summer I ever had walking in nature, swimming in a swimming hole, learning to fish, catching tadpoles and frogs, ugh, no ball playing, the only fun I had was when my grandfather took the two-hour bus ride up to the Catskills and we walked into town together, otherwise a total bore and he would never walk on trails or paths, said he already had done enough of that in Spain, the first time I ever heard him mention Spain. There he didn't mention Esmeralda, I'm sure I would have remembered it. We had a nice lunch in town and he surprised me giving me a couple of decks of baseball cards. I didn't even know he knew about them but he bought some in the local candy store in the Bronx, Ellenville was too far in the boonies to have baseball cards, but they did have a Cohen's bread shop and we brought raisin pumpernickel home to my folks, even if they only ate store-bought white bread with margarine. He even brought along his good clothes for when we ate dinner in the dining hall he would dress for dinner in his suit spiffy shined shoes and wide ties, luckily I didn't have to bring my white shirts but could wear blue jeans and a tee shirt. My mother had wanted me to keep the white shirts clean for assembly which we had once a week in public school and I had to wear a white shirt and tie. All the while I was thinking he was going to take me home with him, like he did when he took me home from camp early, and I was preparing myself to look out the bus window for two hours but then be back in the city with my friends but he left without me, explaining that the city is hot and muggy and it's a cool up here and you would enjoy it more. Ha. They never asked what I wanted. Neither did Cassandra she no longer wanted to live with us so she left not caring if I wanted her too or not, or Jacoba wanted her mother or not, or Esmeralda wanted her granddaughter or not. It's what she wanted that counted. I shouldn't have been in a rush to get back home when we finally went home right before school started my mother enrolled me in Jewish school to prepare for my bar mitzvah, I was only eight couldn't she wait until I was twelve, and boy did I have to suffer going to Hebrew school once a week interfering with my ball playing let alone their teaching Judaism as catechism not lived thought, their attempts at teaching us Hebrew for prayers only not as a discussion of the Bible—God as a moral act, the creation of the covenant, that I might have enjoyed I loved discussion and debate but they didn't know how to teach only allowed us to sit and suffer as a badge of our tribe. At least he took me to see my first Shakespeare play when it played up in a park near us. *Avuelo* when he once faced anti-Semitism said to the guy I beg your pardon I served in the war, got shot at to protect freedom and I have to come home to this bullshit, good sir why did I serve to fight for freedom only to come home and be discriminated against in the city, and the real estate manager apologized said it wasn't his fault that was what the owner wouldn't rent to a Jew. He played by the rules didn't shop there sounded indignant but of course never fought in the Second World War, my father did, he had had enough of killing. His service in the Spanish Civil War kept him out of the Second World War because it was assumed he was a Communist. He wrote a letter to the *New York Times* condemning the anti-Semitism that they never printed but the *Post* did and the laundromat wasn't affected by a letter to the editor. It would take another generation of fighting, mostly Civil Rights workers to end discrimination in public spaces but by then grandfather would be dead. And whenever I walked past that laundromat would spit on the window. He might not have thought too much about anti-Semitism he had met it before but this time it was close to home. This must have been the first time I met with anti-Semitism because everybody else around me was Jewish, except the supers in the buildings, and why later I wanted to move out and be with different people. On Jewish holidays teachers would ask the few not Jewish kids not to bother to come in. My universe was small called the East Bronx that can no longer be found on maps because the Bronx has expanded and what was East now became South and neighborhoods where boys played stickball, off the point, acey-deucy and girls jumped rope played potsy (hopscotch) and gossiped and where old folks would sit out on beach chairs on hot summer nights were destroyed by malignant neglect, fires, the Cross Bronx Expressway and drugs. Luckily my grandfather didn't have to move to Co-op City like my mother and neighbors did unless they moved to Miami first. My mother was angry at her father for always looking for trouble that's not the only laundromat in the city you can get another one, why are you always looking for trouble. That's also what she would say to me when I got into a fight in school or disobeyed the teacher, always taking their side never mine. He could laugh at his daughter and her prejudice of the eternal suffering of Jews, I didn't have it so easy she was my mother, but he said we are not ghetto people but modern people and we don't have to put up with that anymore, we must give up the old ways and shouldn't encourage prejudice, and he even marched with Negroes in Civil Rights movements, which she thought him crazy what have the colored ever done for us. I inherited my grandfather's double-entry bookkeeping, not one set of books for the IRS and a real set for the accountants, but a more sophisticated way of looking at the world—every action will invoke other actions and you see things in longer terms rather than just the moment: my first act of freedom was the divine visualization that I had to move out of an all-Jewish neighborhood to get Cassandra, I was free but lonely, the second was to move in with her and was not free but no longer lonely and now the third for her to move out on me I am not free but lonely. I realized that there is a physical life of the body and a different one for your thought, and that's what grandfather taught me—if only I could live that way.

I tricked myself into believing what I was doing was correct and thought what I was doing was perfectly alright, rational, as I with my own free will went on to destroy my life. After telling myself a million times after what happened to me I will never I will never give up my freedom I go and do it of my own free will, I can give love not my life and then I go give life not love. None of this would have happened, I know, if my mother hadn't gone and gotten herself killed when I was sixteen and I had to move in with my grandmother, she taught me freedom something I could never have known with my mother who was only concerned with what the neighbors thought. I couldn't stand her be around her and her man friends always smoking and drinking should have walked out but where could I go. One girl actually moved out and her mother had her hospitalized, I didn't want that, the other alternative was to go to jail, another option I didn't want, that was more for boys smoking pot, and I really didn't know grandma that well back then, my mother always criticized her so, there was nothing to do but continue go on as I went on until it was my turn to have a baby then welfare would have helped me move out, once I actually started to walk out and she yelled if you leave I will call the police and I am still your mother, but I no longer believed her threats and was tired of listening to her laments of perpetual unhappiness and her taking that unhappiness out on me as if I asked to be born and I finally learned to ignore her and her threats and we lived two separate lives in one apartment and no longer cared what she thought about me and couldn't wait until I finished school and moved out on my own. In gym class that's all Carol and I planned, we planned to be roommates and move as soon as we finished Walton high school. She was the one whose mother had her hospitalized because she was hearing voices, or so the psychiatrist and her mother said, she never said that to me. No longer did I believe my mother, the first time was when I was little and she said if I didn't take this terrible-tasting medicine I would end up in the hospital, and I took it and ended up in the hospital anyway, I should have known then. I spent three nights on the ward and she kept assuring me I would be home soon, but it was the first time I was away from her for three nights and four days and would cry myself to sleep, I hated that dreadful place Lincoln Hospital on 149th Street in the

Bronx, and only felt better when I figured outs how to get home from this place, which bus to take, walk up to the Grand Concourse and grab the number 1 bus all the way to Fordham then walk the rest of the way, as if a bus driver would let me on without money and in a hospital robe, but I felt better knowing how to get home. When I really had to leave my home grandma welcomed me with open arms and always had food in the refrigerator, I should have gone there in the first place and she wouldn't have been able to call my mother, we didn't have a telephone yet. I still don't understand my rush to get home to hear my mother call me an ungrateful bitch? But she was still my mother and I had to be with her until I could escape her when I finished school and I wasn't going to get into trouble and not finish, I wanted out. Once in college when grandma called me in the dormitory I let the house matron call out my name a few times so people would know I got a phone call, I never got calls, only grandma on Sunday night to wonder how my week went, but the first time she called our upstairs neighbor I knew something was up she sounded sad and blue and said I should come right down to the hospital my mother and it doesn't look good. That was the first time I went back to Lincoln hospital they took her there because they had a trauma center I took a taxi, the first time in my life and when I walked into the emergency room grandma hugged me and I knew it was too late. I felt no pain in her death only a sliver of serves you right for going to bars at all hours of the night, I pushed back her hair, and knew I would have to put makeup on her she never wanted to be seen without war paint even as she tried to teach me but I would have none of it. Grandma handled all of the funeral arrangements and was surprised at how many people came to her services, I didn't know she knew that many people or that they cared about her, she certainly didn't care about them but when I looked around it was mainly grandma's friends and a few of mine, even Yolanda came, how she knew I don't know but everyone in the neighborhood knew. Yet none of her previous man friends came, which was good since I always bad-mouthed them. Grandma also wrote to my school principal and I was excused from class and the school was ready to help me in any way I could, the counselor even called me out of class when I went back and said in the doorway don't hesitate to knock on my door if you want to talk. The teachers must have felt sorry for me because I did no work the rest of the term but still passed everything. Grandma said I might as well stay there until the term was over and all I had to do was show up. It was truly mind-blowing what happened to my mother and how quickly my life collapsed and I could no longer live by myself welfare wouldn't allow it and I easily leave the old neighborhood that Joseph had such a difficult time leaving, and move in with my grandma and she let me continue at my old high school but only for the term but every day before going home to grandma would walk past my old building and look up at my apartment and cry.

God is absent, man must renew what originally was given because after Auschwitz all bets are off, the old ways don't work anymore we cannot go silently to our graves but must ask why this was permitted to happen and if we were the cause of it to happen. We brought self-consciousness into the world changing primitive man and changing the equilibrium between man, nature and the natural world of animals, Rome had power, Greece philosophy, Phoenicia wealth while we had the covenant, but that is not enough we have to be strong, be a community, a nation that is ready to fight for its freedom otherwise we don't deserve it. Could I have said this? Such guts for a thirteen-year-old, all I remember however is being nervous in front of the congregation, scared of speaking in front of strangers, standing on the podium, even if in my dreams I could speak easily, but I hadn't realized there would be strangers there not just family and friends but the local congregation as well. *Avuelo* came up to me and calmed me down, he hated being inside a place of worship thought Judaism was responsible of its own demise, but he did come up to me seeing how nervous I was and told me to recite your prayers and give my speech just as I had practiced it then sit down look over the heads of your audience they will think you are looking at them, and you perform well under pressure, even if that was not the case, I usually struck out if the game was on the line and while I was saying my prayers to become a man was thinking I've got to get out of this place where there are only the same people and promised myself the first chance I get I am gone— too bad I didn't know about boarding school I would have been a perfect candidate, and should have gone out of state to college but the guidance counselor said City was the place for me, and even if I was accepted into another place my parents wouldn't have let me go since City College was free in those days and we didn't have much money. It was only when Cassandra gave me the ultimatum that I was able to break free and move to the Upper West Side, and then was afraid of walking past 96th Street, except walking the one block north to my apartment on 97th street, for the longest time and would only walk down Broadway at night, stopping in Parnassus a used bookstore on the east side of West 88th street and becoming friendly with the owner, and began to learn the way to be free is to move away from your parents abode and have to do your own laundry, cleaning and cooking, but I couldn't bite the bullet totally and still brought my laundry home. After my bar mitzvah we had a small party in our next door neighbor's apartment, it goes without saying *Avuelo* didn't come, grandma was there, but the next day he and Zoltan took me out on one of their walks with them, the best gift of all. I thought my speech would shock but nobody listens to a thirteen-year-old and they all said what a lovely little speech, but Zoltan said you read it with such passion you must believe in it the same way the old rabbis believed in interpreting the Bible they were arguing with God and that means they loved and there is a God, so maybe divine providence is at work and that the world does have a purpose and we are responsible for our own lives. That was my first moment of freedom at least inside my head if not in my body, a weird kind of freedom where I still couldn't grab life by the balls but at least wasn't trapped in the old neighborhood: no longer did I want to accept things as they are I wanted out to experience adventure to live, I was going to run at full speed only I ran in the wrong direction and it took time for me to realize that, at last the '60s occurred which gave me hope and fellow travelers and a new way of looking the world. The old left always talked about the economic base and how the base was related to the superstructure but had no idea how the superstructure could change the way we thought. We saw the old lefties as on the wrong side of history, talking about the uneven development of history, guys who were supposed to be on our side against the Vietnam war, for Black Power, and the onset of feminism were usually opposed to the new ideas, and they hated us because they said we were 'bourgeoisie' me bourgeois a true worker yet I had truck only with the educated ones not the workers, even as I adopted workers' garb of blue jeans, work shirt and boots, my long hair put me at odds with workers. Then of course I switched jobs. I even bought glasses to make believe I was the serious person I wasn't and started carrying around my grandfather's pocket watch and fountain pen, making sure people in the hood knew I was different from them.

Some had even thought me a beatnik and asked my mother if I bathed, because of my long hair, others a communist because I read Marx in college not realizing the good books were never on the curriculum. We never discussed important stuff in college just what past men thought not how to live a passionate life, professors always talked ideas but not how to live them. Here's where Esmeralda and Cassandra blew my mind, and it was only chance that I ran into them, if it had been another day or time we wouldn't have met in Tompkins Square Park and I would have been bereft of intellectual sustenance. Other girls I would see all the time and maybe one time would have enough strength to approach them but this was a one shot deal, even if Esmeralda saw my grandfather in me and Cassandra my aspiring intelligence as opposed to the macho men she had been dating, when I said Beethoven begins by composing as Mozart then like himself and finally like God, that either Zoltan or my *Avuelo* talked about on the day they took me out after my bar mitzvah to my first coffee house *La Fortuna* where I had my first cup of coffee a latte macchiato. Did I understand what I was talking about, back then I was sure I knew but now I am not so sure, it sounded good, profound but was it true. What I liked about my bar mitzvah was I was finished with Hebrew school more than the gifts, which was only money and my mother kept her hand out making sure I gave her every check or cash so I didn't lose it and it went into the college fund. But the thoughts I was having were different than the words I was saying, I memorized my portion of the Torah, called the Haftarah and didn't have the slightest idea what I read since it was all for-eign to me and I couldn't debate with the author what he meant and that I would have liked, when *Avuelo* or Zoltan talked it was profound and I enjoyed hearing the arguments for and against the tree of life, that man couldn't live in a garden, and if we ate a forbidden fruit did it have to be an apple, could it have been a fig? and men sentenced to a lifetime of banishment for a crime an ancestor committed, is that just? are we now all Marranos or is mankind forced to be free? But I wasn't taught living Hebrew so I could listen to what others had thought only how to read the language not understand the language so I had no idea the words I was mentioning and Hebrew was as dead to me as Latin was, only later in college I wanted to learn Latin, because Greek wasn't taught, and I thought it would be of interest to read Virgil in the original. Never did of course, like a lot of what I planned to do it got dropped by the wayside.

If only I had the strength to act on my feelings and didn't just think about them maybe life would be more than waiting to have a life. I still will not get good furniture until I move in with Cassandra, before everything is on hold, I'm still an outsider of life, still afraid of life, view it crossways, tired, but at least I don't nap anymore in the middle of the day unless it's for sexual relaxation and I love feeling that sticky stuff in my underwear, or when we do it in the afternoon, a real treat, she also insists we keep the light on or the shades open, who ever heard of such a thing, who would ever think of such a thing. When I finally got my driver's license, not that I needed one I didn't own a car but a man ain't a man unless he can drive, moved into my own apartment, and had sex with someone not myself, did I finally begin to realize maybe I am starting to live and then wondered is this living. Now I could actually drive down to the Village from up in the Bronx, did it a few times and realized the impossibility of finding parking and worse you couldn't read while driving and pretty soon gave up my father's car let him have it he needs it for work, I would sit and read on the subway. A true New Yorker Esmeralda said. I thought it would be easy going the opposite way of traffic only there is no op-posite way of traffic in the city there is always something that delays you. At least on the subway you could read sitting in the station waiting for the train to come or when it came and stalled between stations. Usually however I get so angry sitting and waiting that I can't read and think back to my childhood years but refuse to see them as golden years and if I ever see them as the best years of my life I had no life, for as *avuelo* said only as an adult can you taste freedom and what you do with it is your responsibility, he insisted I learn so that I could think, and when I was through with school at ten said wait a few more years then you can leave right now you're too young. I think about that sitting in the subway, or walking in the Village or going to my old buddies' weddings where they marry some nebbish from the neighborhood because that was the only way both could break free of their parents. All I had to do was pay more for a room on the Upper West Side than my parents did for an apartment up in the Bronx. Now I had some freedom but the only freedom I really had was inside my head, a pointless freedom but mine just the same.

I called in my professional voice without a hint of accent so his mother wouldn't get upset, begrudge him, or question him endlessly about a woman who called him at home and told her to have him call me back I am a friend of his, only he told me afterwards it did no good his mother didn't write down the number nor could barely remember the message and had no idea I had called, so when he called and came up to our apartment he had no idea that I had called and grandma wanted to see him again: he described our first get together as a transformation into a world he only hoped existed from one where he lived in shadows, and was blinded by our sunlight but quickly wanted to get back home because he was afraid of getting what he wanted, this freedom, these ideas, the aroma of healthy people (he had loved my wearing jeans, being braless, and the way I kept my legs open and not afraid, he said), he had never heard people speak so knowledgeably about issues before, were so charming, and had a sense of humor, and this climbing so high bamboozled him at first and it took him awhile to become accustomed to his new surroundings and sometimes even to this day he falls back on old ways but forces himself to face the truth that even if it is a mistake it is better to live this way than not to live as he was existing before. Luckily for him his mother didn't write down the number would he have been able to deal with a woman calling a man, most men couldn't and hated Sadie Hawkins Day, where girls were permitted to call boys and ask them out. Such a little effort on my part gave him such a thrill, even if I must admit I was a little nervous wondering if he would remember us, and I invited him here and when he came here actually invited me to a movie with him. The last movie I saw was *Last Tango in Paris* which everyone said was controversial but all I remember was that it cost $4.00, an outrageous price and that I had to go alone because my girlfriend wouldn't go with me because she got a date at the last moment and a date automatically overrode plans with friends. I felt uncomfortable going to a movie by myself but I didn't want to be denied the pleasure of seeing what everybody was talking about, I feel at home in the theater don't mind going alone otherwise I would hardly see anything but going to a move by myself on date-night made me feel uncomfortable—everyone in the world has a date but me. He asked if I wanted to see a midnight double bill at the New Yorker, who goes to the movies at midnight? and he surprised me by knowing who Beckett was having seen a student production at City College. It was from Beckett I learned to project character from her point of view not the director's and his film was on a double bill with a Jodorowsky film I never heard of a crazy cowboy film, because *El Topo* wasn't weird enough. He didn't know about Beckett's film or even who Buster Keaton was and he had a more complete education than I had. But he said we never discussed contemporary stuff in class only in the lunchroom of the south campus cafeteria, where we would have interesting conversations and one of the actors was in Godot otherwise he would never have seen the play. This was his friend from the old neighborhood who was going to Columbia and said to him I know you're busy with exams now but you have to promise to see *The Flies* after exams are over, here's where characters go at it instead of the superficial language of the classroom, really superficial topics that goes on in the yap yap shop, Orestes discovers he's free and responsible for what he does and seeing that helped him to understand what freedom is and afterwards read Aeschylus but it was nothing like seeing it performed, good theater surprises you and it blew his mind as the characters came alive and forced him to see the world differently. And when I went for an audition of *Happy Days* got it even if I barely understood the words spoken because of our constant conversations on Beckett and I understood more than I realized and became the downtown interpreter of Beckett and his meaninglessness of life. I consented to be his date, I made it easy said I would pay my own way but he would have none of it and I wanted to walk uptown but he thought no you don't walk that far uptown—downtown, uptown whenever you went into different neighborhoods you took the subway, I laughed down here we walk everywhere in the city only when I go up to the Bronx do I take the train. He then mentioned he was worried he wouldn't understand it, who would? that ever since he went to the Tinguely installation at the Museum of Modern Art of a machine that destroyed itself and had no lasting value he had given up on art, that was when his grandfather died and I could understand that, even if I had never been to MoMA, which surprised him and said we could go, as he tried to explain his philosophy of life, that moment was all and it affected his entire life because it was an decisive moment in his life, and he thinks he grew up in that moment when he had to wrestle with himself in coming to terms with his grandfather dying in his arms, one moment he is living the next he is not. And if I don't think about anything that moment keeps coming back into my head—that is a real moment with me that forces me into myself and I always think of art now asking what does it signify, as if art has to signify something, to him it does otherwise it's not a work of art.

I realize he experiences the true immediacy of the work while grandma likes to think about it. All this we discussed afterwards at *La Fortuna*, an opera coffee house he introduced me to, having the nerve to ask if I minded walking ten, fifteen blocks when I was the one who insisted we walk uptown, but he said the side streets are not so safe and we have to walk down Broadway and up 72nd St. to Columbus, but before we came to 72nd street we passed a homosexual bar and they started catcalling and he said I must get about a dozen a day but I said no they were meant for him, and he goes hey, hey, hey these guys show class and he tells me our discussion resembled the south cafeteria at City College where he would discuss ideas but they closed early and we all went home to our neighborhoods, here at least a café is open late, not just a bar. What I liked about this café is they didn't have folk music that was starting to dominate the Village scene and you had to listen to the performers instead of talking, and now the Village cafés were filled with kids from the sticks coming down to act cool and rowdy. Grandma said there was a European tradition of coffee houses where you could read the papers, talk, smoke, get your mail and generally spend the day there were different tables for communists, socialists, anarchists, but there was open seating, not true here each person or group had their own table. But what I did see were tables for playing chess but I wouldn't play because men don't like to be beaten by a woman. What you bring to a movie, or a play or a work of art, I said, is your own history, your own expectations, what you expect to see, and if you read about it accept previous interpretations, but a good work of art is to force you out of the old ways of seeing and nothing is truer than a good work of art that forces you to see the world differently. I am not my grandmother's granddaughter for nothing. And she never learned that in school she learned it on her own and we went out many nights to galleries, poetry readings, plays, and musical events, usually in the Village she never liked going north of 14th street thought that as alien part of town. She never waited for a man to take her, she said if you do that you stay home alone and taught me not to be dependent upon a man and not to be afraid to do things on my own. She would wear her ersatz wedding ring to keep off unwanted attractions, since single women alone must be in need of a man was the ongoing mantra, but she went to an event for the event not to pick up a man. For the first time in a long while I enjoyed the present being with Joseph and actually enjoyed the experience not so much concerned what he would think of me saw it for what it was a date to a weird movie and a short film beforehand and then a pleasant after hour's coffee but I didn't see any future in it, he was a nice boy but in the grand scheme of things too young for me even if he did go out of his way to try and please me.

Was I disappointed when I finally came home, the only nice part was passing the Statue of Liberty on our way up the Hudson River to our pier on the West Side, when passing the Statue of Liberty, I knew I was home, the crossing was uneventful I was stuck in a lower cabin most of the trip and only went on deck to see the Statue and I finally told myself now I am home, big deal, and we finally docked the inspector said why do you want to come here? Not welcome back but why do you want to come here, I told him I am home. Show me your papers, he asks, and I think I'm back in Spain again, I never had to show papers in the city this is home all of a sudden, the city I couldn't wait to leave and all I kept thinking about on the ship was how I would walk up to the Bronx, to feel the city under my feet once more, pavement, not rural roads, even if I have to walk through some unruly neighborhoods but I wasn't too worried my body now had a tough guy look to it after eighteen months at the front, not counting times away from the battle with Esmeralda, or in the hospital—and I couldn't wait to look up at the skyscrapers again even if I was going back to my shitty life in the Bronx that I had wanted to escape from and at least I know now that running away doesn't change a thing you're still the same person only in a different part of the world, and soon no matter how slow I walked I would soon be home and as I walked down the gangplank realized the city was the only true home I had even as I felt scared walking down the gangplank, wondering how Miriam would greet me—maybe she found somebody else? Nobody was here to greet me, how could they nobody knew I was coming home, La Pasionaria's speech still in my head, they shall not pass but they did and we had to go home, I tried to describe to myself the taste of defeat but was unable to, glad to be off the boat, scared to be going home not understanding how such a good cause could end in such an ignoble defeat. The attempted freedom of the Spanish people ended so miserably with the legitimate government being overthrown by the Falangists, we were fighting for truth, freedom, justice and these were such powerful ideas they shouldn't have been defeated but the Western powers didn't help, refused to give aid, arms, tanks, planes, only Hitler and Mussolini did and arms were more powerful than ideas; it seemed noble what we were attempting to end the suffering of the Spanish people and all we did was right to stand up to the injustice even in defeat, even if we didn't know we would be defeated because we were outgunned and who thought Hitler and Mussolini would interfere in violation of the Versailles treaty but the European powers were so afraid of another Great War they not only didn't help but did all they could not to let arms be smuggled in, a far cry when Spain ruled the world—libertarian socialism was correct but we didn't carry them out successfully we truly expected the rest of the world to join in but they didn't come though. I had plenty of time to think about this on the ship and now on my walk up to the East Bronx, we lived in the East Bronx then before we moved to the Grand Concourse when I became successful with my laundromats; crossing Tenth Avenue I started my walk through Hell's Kitchen, where I should be afraid but it's now broad daylight and you didn't have to fear the other guy, and if young punks wanted to start trouble let them and even if I had the best possible motive to fight them would have lost but at least I wouldn't have had to go home empty-handed—what did I expect a victory parade down Southern Boulevard like Franklin Roosevelt had in his campaign, my that was the biggest parade I had ever seen when his motorcade rode down Southern Boulevard, imagine a presidential candidate coming to the Bronx. But I didn't come home for a parade, but I left to leave my dull dreary life and I couldn't stand it this married-life anymore, my screaming daughter, my boring job and this was the only way out and at the same time do a good deed, so even if my motives weren't pure I was helping my fellow human beings. Walking up Tenth, I felt that I must have convinced myself of this as I boarded *Thersites* to Madrid, and the growl on my face may have convinced the young hooligans to keep away from me, and I still had my knife which I knew how to use and if felt good in my side pocket, and it felt so good to be walking again after being stuck in that hole for two weeks, and now at least I ain't walking up hills, how many times did I stumble walking the Pyrenees to get into Spain and wondered what did I get myself into. The first battle cured me of any romantic fantasies. In the first battle Eric dies, my newfound friend from England who had insisted he be allowed to take his exams first so he could go and fight and confessed to me he had never lived next to a Jew before and I had to tell him I knew no one from the Church of England, that renegade outfit all I knew were Jews, Catholics and a few Protestants but they were usually the bosses. We had to sneak into Spain via France the blockade was so strong the Western powers were letting nothing into the legitimate government, and only as I crossed 138th Street bridge and walked into the Bronx had I realized even before we got there the West was doing all it could to not allow us to win. Now reality hit me I was actually on my way home to Miriam and Molly, all that I wanted to escape from and all that I tried to do to defend had ended with me back in this place, back where I started and all that I had done failed even as I did everything possible to succeed, not only had I not managed to succeed but managed to deceive myself and now I was heading back to a banal reality that I tried so hard to escape from, I didn't have to come home only there was nowhere else to go. Now the Bronx felt polluted, of course, I was walking alongside Bruckner Boulevard, where I had my first store, and the smell from the busses and the cars makes this street unbearable, the noise from the cars even interferes with my thought and I can't get my imagination to work so I turn to walk towards Westchester Ave. not walking up to Southern Boulevard via Bruckner but under the El that only comes once in a while not every second and allows my thoughts to work, I can start with an idea and play with that but with all the noise from the traffic I couldn't get any ideas, but the tenement houses have their own noise coming through them down Jackson Avenue, but soon I will be on Westchester Avenue where the El hardly comes and there will be fewer cars but with the elevated train you can barely see the sky, the sky was blue however nowhere as blue as in Spain I have never seen a truer blue than in Spain. It is such a quick subway ride from Simpson Street to Jackson but a much longer walk than I thought but still pleasant, too bad I couldn't see the sky overhead, I wonder will I be able to see stars from the city that so amazed me on a moonless night outside Madrid. Will I ever forget Madrid? When it was dark and there was no moon you couldn't see ten steps in front of you and if you let your guard down you might become dead and you always had to be alert listening for animals, tree branches, grunts, you could pee in your pants if you heard a tree or a bush tweak but you had to keep your head about you. How many false alarms did we encounter with inanimate objects? But we learned to clear our minds of all thoughts and concentrate on the job at hand to figure out what was real object and if real to trust it or not and our head became a bridge to our senses, our immediate sense was of no use we had to think as well not just shoot or we'd accidentally kill one of our own, which happened too many times.

We all had to make difficult choices none of them good but they had to be made just the same, and we all managed to make the worst and a fissure opened up within me from the time in war to the time of defeat but the Party never cared about individuals: why I learned to hate the Party, only the Party had a monopoly on truth, as if anyone could have a monopoly on truth—they were not concerned with the good of the people but the good of the party it was always all for them not for the individual—a top-down directorate which we called top-headed as if they could see above and beyond us, better than us, the long range or as Jacobo said unaware that human people exist we are mere charnel to them. I don't care now that he is dead it doesn't change a thing I loved him as a young man, I saw him walk on the gangplank looking straight ahead I was against the wall and could only look straight ahead and he wouldn't turn around to see me and a fence is behind him where creatures walk and carry things and all I can see are shadows on the wall, but how do these guys who make directives, really most only follow orders but somewhere someone makes a directive, later we found out it was Stalin, the sun of the shining world, who didn't let history touch him because he knew the single truth and so wasn't caught up in the vicissitudes of life, the same way that it gives them the privilege of knowing what the long-term interests of the Party are; it would only make the dilemmas worse if they understood people and were concerned with individuals instead of the masses, so all life was for the Communist Party and we individuals have to think of nothing else. There was no other way or so I thought then even if now I think both the Party and the individual could have a better outcome instead I had to go home, the one place I had tried to escape from my parents to a life of boredom as a man sentenced to rolling a stone up the hill daily and watching it fall down again and having to roll it up again the next day, only there was no smile on my face, I went home to nothing, a failure, to have to see the smile on my mother's face and not even a bouquet of flowers greeted me, a total failure, broke, no future and pregnant. I needed shelter and if I had come home somewhat victorious could have told my parents, my younger sister that what we did was right, correct, for the good of the people, but our defeat meant it was wrong and I was back in my bedroom from which I thought I had escaped all I had was the ring on my finger that Jacobo gave me when we parted, but I was so downtrodden that I let them impose upon me their will, at first they wanted to marry me off so as not to disgrace the family and men were such silly creatures they said they would marry me even if the child wasn't there's finally the local druggist who worshipped me from afar was approached and I wouldn't be subject to his whims; I had seen enough in my short life to realize if married I wouldn't be subject to the whims of the family but to a man who worshipped me, that is until I married him and he thought he was the boss. Once a woman is married her freedom is curtailed. I couldn't accept that even as it gave me a legitimate existence—in my new home I simply stared at the baby inside me and lied in bed, and Santiago thought that I would be okay once the baby was born. My father did think I would run away from him once when I realized what I had done after the baby was born, and he promised to do what was best for me but he thought the baby should have a father of record that's the way it's done in a Spanish family, afterwards we would see. And the father's word was Law in the new government even if my mother made the decisions and all she cared was for me not to shame the family and came up with the idea to save face and that the baby was born prematurely and the family would be free of the weight of things and I was deflowered legitimately and such nonsense was believed as long as I wore Jacobo's ring. I refused to go all the way and wear a white dress but did go to the Priest but not to repent for my anti-royalist ways or the baby inside me, I did make the sign of the cross, genuflect, and he thought I was one of them and I told him all I had wanted is a little freedom and was asked to do no penance just a few Hail Mary's and I went back to my ground floor room and starred out the window, not even looking at the people passing by only at the spot the sun made on the floor, and couldn't even go walking by myself because respectable women didn't walk unescorted and both my father and mother had no time to simply walk like Jacobo and I did and my little sister was off to school learning to be a good obedient housewife and all I could do was sit on my chair starring at the spot the motes made in the air or at the baby inside me wondering if it would be boy, it just had to be a boy like Jacobo and I would call him Junior. Sometimes I would stare at the moon when it was full and overhead would wait for this sadness to leave me that my father said would pass only I knew it wouldn't pass that we had been defeated and had given up on the only world that was free, and immediately afterwards Stalin became Hitler's buddy and events would not go good for him. Sure they didn't care about the masses and could make decrees and we would have to go along with it because the Comintern is never wrong even as they made decisions based on desperation or something in the stars, but it lacked all substance and here I was this newly married pregnant woman even if Santiago thought of me as a little girl not a grown woman and wanted to care for me for eternity as if he could make up for all the loneliness in his life with me. He like the Comintern couldn't tell fantasy from reality. His mind is like the new American Swiss cheese imported here with its tastelessness and holes in it as compared to Emmental imported from Switzerland that has a sharp taste and no holes. Having lost the war and lost Jacobo I had nothing to hold onto and being back home in my parents' house was difficult after having tasted freedom I convinced myself I could be free in marriage and what was causing me anguish is that I lost the view of the sun outside my window or the light of the moon that I could stare at for hours in my old room. Now I was in bed all the time my head ached so because I couldn't lie down all the time so I was forced to sit up and only when Santiago came calling did I go back to bed—I couldn't be with such a boy for long after having met a man and it was unhealthy for me to stay inside all the time and so my mother would come and visit me and insisted I see the Priest even if to her he was a charlatan but she didn't have enough guts to say that, never, and I know she never believed in anything he said, but believed in obedience to God and the priest represents God.

The lies they told who could believe what lies historians wrote about the Spanish Civil War, I wondered if contemporary writers could write the truth about anything, they had no idea, no feel for what was going on, the struggle the closeness of the people involved all they talked about were the socio-political order not the activities of the people, how we finally got out of ourselves and were concerned about other people, it was the doing that was important, it's as if old fart after old fart who wasn't there and had no understanding of what it was like to be there and assumes an actuality that wasn't but that they can recognize, that is their bias, they bring to the writing of history, and didn't recognize the experiences of people there or if they did recognized them as not important in their large scale analysis of historical progress, as if there can be progress without understanding the moment that is lived—the difference of what was thought to what was perceived. Nobody remembered the balance of power after the Great War was whacked out of joint, Wilson's peace destroyed the Central Powers disrupting the original balance, allowing Italy to grow, Austria to shrink, Germany to have to pay and only France and England allowed to divide and conquer and only if they acted in unionism could the peace be maintained, but they so feared another conflagration action paralyzed them, the League of Nations was a dud could only act if England and France acted and they refused to act until it was too late and Europe was once again driven into a war only the Germans wanted; old Europe wanted peace not freedom, and wanted the peace of Metternich more than another war and again the balance of power was called into play, only like the first time it did not work. Because it had worked for a hundred years didn't mean it was going to work for another hundred as a result they tried to keep the Spanish Civil War a localized phenomenon within the borders of Spain so created an embargo on arms and food stuffs allowed to be supplied to the government only Germany and Italy didn't honor it shipping goods, arms, tanks, planes, resupplying Franco, and England and France didn't want to get involved and interfere in a local civil war, as they called it, not realizing these were the first shots fired in the Second World War. The Spaniards tried to warn them but the great powers weren't interested, didn't care about liberty only peace, that's the way grandma explained history to me and I explained it to Joseph, who grandma said had the face of Jacobo in him, that's why she confused the two, I think, neither of us learning anything about the Spanish Civil War in school, and me explaining that when I signed for my National Defense Student Loan, had to sign a waiver that I wasn't a member of the Abraham Lincoln Brigade which classmates hadn't even heard of, but which I knew all about even if they had disbanded way before I was born. I only went to their parades down 34th street after I moved in with grandma before they were ancient history to me. But Joseph didn't have student loans so knew nothing of it, all his parents had to pay for were textbooks, and they complained about that, why can't they give you books like they do in high school. And his grandfather never really talked about the war to him, nor about my grandma either. And when he asked his mother she replied we don't talk about such nonsense when he left the family—one day he had a neighbor pick me up from school and only comes back years later loudly knocks on the door, my mother, your grandmother, didn't even recognize him he changed so much, so thin, his red hair now grey, how did he know we didn't move he never wrote? He left his business in good hands his friend stole everything and he had to start over and instead of a garage bought a laundromat, and your grandmother had to go on relief, and then had to work in order to pay the bills his friend saddled the family with and we had so little money mama had to take a boarder in, she needed help in paying the bills now that there were two of us to feed, your uncle was born while he was gone and had never seen his father, but when he went into our room that night and he was frightened of this strange man, I stood up and hugged him knew immediately who he was and immediately loved him, while my brother could do no such thing, I had to miss school to take care of my little brother when a sitter couldn't be found. When she was in the eighth grade he moved out again and she had to finally drop out of school to take care of her little brother, understandable why Joseph doesn't know his family history and I had to put it together for him. All Joseph knew was his grandmother worked as a bookkeeper not even realizing she probably was working under the table so she could still get welfare. He laughed at that because his mother was always yelling about those welfare cheats, meaning colored. What do they want? she always asked. My grandmother, however, would talk incessantly about her finest hour when she stood for something and was proud of what she did, and Joseph was always interested in what she had to say, especially about his grandfather, as that was the only way he could learn some of his history. Joseph said his grandfather explained things to him but rarely talked about his experiences in the Spanish Civil War and never about Esmeralda, he assumed that those were too painful to talk about, at least that's what his father said to him, his son-in-law got along better with him than his daughter and it was he who insisted that the grandfather move in with them when he was at the end of his rope mentally and needed help and his wife would have nothing to do with him. They still hadn't divorced, divorce wasn't easy in those days and they both saw no reason to undergo the expense they simply lived apart and his uncle stayed with his mother until he couldn't stand her anymore and fled to California. None of this came out all at once but in the many conversations the three of us had over dinner when Joseph was all but a member of the family. The three of us would eat dinner together every night, even if I came home late from a performance they would wait for me and we'd eat at eleven at night, our family ritual and I began to look forward to it, and found him pleasant to talk to, not some dumb jerk from the Bronx. I had had enough of them; when I first moved down here would keep in contact with them, and when I told one I was going to go to private school he even said what's a matter public schools aren't good enough for you, that's when I began to realize I lead a double life from them and slowly started breaking away, but sometimes out of loneliness would go out with them, and then ohmygod, what nonsense, the movies they saw, how they couldn't keep quiet in the movie theater, how all they wanted to do was feel me up, at least the girls that didn't get pregnant or marry a local boy moved away the boys never left their neighborhood, I vowed never to date a Bronx boy again then along comes Joseph almost a decade younger than me and I thought no problem I'm not going to be attracted to a younger man and I thought it would be impossible to feel a sexual arousal for him and when I kissed him thought of it as sisterly and even if I wanted him was afraid of ruining our nice threesome, luckily grandma was the one who saw my attraction and said don't be afraid of desire, and now with the pill I could satisfy my lusts without fear of an unwanted child. I thought I don't have to fall for him only taste his young blood, but didn't think this through and did fall for him, my lust got the better of me, I gave into my desires but I worried he might change after sleeping with me, as men are wont to do after sleeping with a woman thinking they own the woman but no one is going to own me, my acting is too important for me to be owned by anybody. I held out, I was older more experienced, it would be me the one who decides and I did enjoy his willingness to be educated not simply go out on date night to a movie and a bar afterwards. He was happy seeing off-beat plays and insisted I continue my acting during my fallow periods, do stage readings to keep in shape even if the pay was dismal or non-existent. The only place both grandma and I refused to go was up to Lincoln Center that complex had displaced too many Latino families in the name of progress, or poor people removal as it was called in the barrios, racist in the colored community, displacement for the better good of the city in sociologese, Joseph had even thought it was slum clearance not a working neighborhood that was destroyed.

The perfect is the enemy of the good, we went to the Brooklyn Academy of Music, who knew there was such a place in Brooklyn, I hardly went to the outskirts of the city, and only passed through Brooklyn driving to Coney Island or walking the Brooklyn Bridge but then only to the promenade and back, luckily they had a bus to take us into the heart of Brooklyn we wouldn't have done it by subway. Only the dead know Brooklyn it was that far off our radar and we got our shots, passports, I made my last will and testament, but since Esmeralda and Cassie didn't want to see opera at Lincoln Center because of poor people displacement we travelled out to Brooklyn only the opera was fair I was used to spectacle at Lincoln Center and enjoyed it but here it was nice, all I could say about it, they even had candles five candles burning during the performance and that was the first time I had ever seen candles used other than a religious service and mainly I went to Lincoln Center so I could brag how sophisticated I was but did get caught up in the performance and begin to like opera. The first time I ever heard an opera was after the assassination of President Kennedy and everything was cancelled except the Metropolitan Opera on Radio and I had enough public mourning actually tuned it in as a diversion but it soon became central. Zoltan had called to tell me they killed your president, I had no idea what he was talking about but pretty soon found out and the public mourning was too much, now I am accustomed to it after the murder of King and the younger Kennedy, but back then we didn't have a television yet so I listened on radio and they WQXR actually broadcast the opera in the midst of the coverage. How I learned about opera. My head ached, my stomach felt fat but it was warm under the covers listening on the Telefunken radio that my grandfather bought because he couldn't stand the Philco and insisted we get a good one, wood instead of plastic, but after we got the television the radio was assigned to my bedroom and I listened to it. My mother hated a German radio and hated that my grandfather bought a German product and threw it out after he died. And Cassandra called with the same message about Dr. Martin Luther King, why these guys were mine is beyond me. His funeral wasn't on television but the riots were and kids rioting would be watching the riots on television rather than turning down the street to see them in person, as friends in the country who had an actual fireplace would be watching the yuletide log on WPIX channel 11 rather than the actual burning in their own fireplace. My headache went away, my stomach felt better but the cold on my feet because I wasn't wearing slippers gave me the sniffles and I said I would never answer the phone again without shoes on, the extension cord was not long enough to reach into the bedroom, and Walter Cronkite took off his glasses and said he was dead. Nobody talked that it was because of Negroes who were just then beginning to be called black and how they wanted to be treated as equals, no longer interested in second class citizenship. Only on Saturday when we had tickets to the performance of the opera, Dr. King was not as important as President Kennedy, everything continued as normal except people said oh well, that's too bad, no commentator wondered if they would have to believe their own rhetoric now of violence. The show must go on, people had paid for tickets and BAM didn't want to refund the money and it was a good break from the drama of the week when all talk was about the assassination and riots, Cassandra even got hit by stones, small rocks, walking home in the East Village when a group of black girls thought she was a haughty white woman, blood on her temple but nothing serious. This wasn't like President Kennedy who chafed at the notion he shouldn't go to Dallas it was too dangerous and that a president of the United States couldn't go into an American city, I thought of that as President Johnson had to sneak into New York to view the remains of Cardinal Spellman, as reported in the *Times* but couldn't announce it because he couldn't go anywhere in America without there being massive demonstrations, why he only spoke on military bases where armed guards could keep us protesters out. A mere five years later the president of the United States was trapped inside his home and couldn't go to any city for fear of massive demonstrations, which of course were kept blocks from him and it was always reported he never saw them. That's when I began to realize the press lies. Esmeralda laughs she's had more experience with the jackal press and said no European could ever believe the press after all the lies they told about the Spanish Civil War and even before the Great War. The first causality of war is the truth she said and then she said she blamed the German workers for the war, whoever heard of that, because before the war all the socialist workers signed agreements not to go to war, that it was a capitalist trick to deprive workers of their rights, and they wouldn't fight fellow workers, only when war was announced they all became nationalists. At the death of President Kennedy all the local churches and temples had memorial services, after King and Bobby's death it was normalized and maybe a special prayer was said in the weekly service but nothing special was planned, I no longer attended services, the last religious rite I went to was the burial of my grandfather when my mother rented a rabbi, I objected, he hated rabbis who he said never did a day's work in their life, but she said he couldn't be buried without one. He gave a fine speech for someone he didn't know, how he loved his family and supported them but hadn't touched on the essence of his life that he was my grandfather and I was the only one in the family he loved. So after the assassination of Doctor Martin Luther King the three of us got our shots, passports—Brooklyn is far away Lord, and took the subway to Brooklyn, it was closer than the Bronx, and it had neighborhoods just like the Bronx both Cassie and I said, and went to see *Tristan and Isolde* in a miniaturized version of the spectacle at the Met it was quirky but not profound more interested in the libretto and the acting than the music, you didn't even have to dress up at BAM, of course I was there in my Sunday best wearing one of my grandfather's ties—dress codes were lightening and nobody wore ties anymore to opera and there were no tuxedos to be seen on men and no women wore gowns, I always loved seeing a well-dressed woman. Cassandra put on a new pair of jeans. Too bad I hadn't saved his double-breasted suits but I thought nobody would ever wear them again. My father had said to keep the ties because you never know old styles do come back in but even he didn't think people would want to wear these bulky suits. I had shown Esmeralda a photo of him dressed in a zoot suit and we both saw the immediate traces of each other in our faces and was glad to give it to her as she kept telling me more about his life unlike my mother who told me so little about him, but my grandfather used to say she was born old and didn't have a chance to have a life. Esmeralda sat with her legs wide apart and smelled young.

Which comes first time or ideas? My memory is playing tricks on me I remember only parts, but I only come alive when I think of my past, and only when I force myself to go deeper inside myself do I truly recall what I superficially remember but I can never put myself to sleep with those memories, the actual lived memories that I want to remember but they are more complex than I remember them or the limited parts that my memory recalls of them, sometimes I can only catch a glimpse of them—he is not the same man as he once was, he is not even with us anymore, and I wonder did he ever think of me, to write a letter to me, of course I couldn't have received it left that place and after my parents died that place left our family possession and sometimes feel sorry for myself that we couldn't have been together longer my one true husband, whose ring I wear but who never married me; would our lives have been better together than apart, maybe I should have tricked him into marrying me except now I think like Conchita that marriage is slavery, the sign of the times—I don't even know how we didn't know that, but now we live in different times and women can have their own lives but what good was I without him? and when I recall him when I awake in the middle of the night or for no reason in the middle of the day I know I recall a connection that is not truly accurate, I keep telling myself and we never did have a chance to bloom together caught up as we were in the war, my life is the unreality of the life left behind and the arbitrary determination of my ideas that are not set in stone only this habit of thinking about him is set in stone and even if I am sick of it can't let go, habit is stronger than my feelings and even as I realize he is no more, or different it doesn't alter a thing—go figure, we had possibilities after the war that never were but we never expected to lose and that defeat totally destroyed all possibility, all chances we had to live together, afterwards there was no time and I went home to my parents to have the baby who two weeks before she was due decided she didn't want to be of this world, and I couldn't stand living by the old rules and as quickly as they could they arranged a man for me to marry, and I married him to go me from one prison house to another, and all along I knew I wouldn't impose myself on him, wouldn't look for him, wouldn't write him, wanted nothing from him except him wanting me, and when I came to New York wouldn't look him up in the phone book, which I later found out I couldn't do because according to Joseph they didn't have a phone, so I could not knock on his door, instead could make my own living in New York working for the police department and clients until they stopped believing, and doing 'Celestina' on the side a profession never goes out of date. When I couldn't find leeches to bleed people I knew I would have to go to my other skills, people in this country didn't believe in that type of medicine but they do believe in abortion or being a supposed virgin for their husband and

I could sew young girls up. Thank goodness for the Catholic church and their craziness kept me in money. All that was nonsense but I did what I had to do in order to survive but even here who knows how accurate my memory is and I do recall mistakes not because it isn't real but because I can only recall a small portion of what actually occurred, only remember the parts I want to remember and unless a cold chill emanates from my head then I am forced to remember what I don't want to remember, my life is not as pure as I make it out, that I deceived two husbands who did love me but try not to recall that next to my memory of my original memories: he said he never had time for things like the theater or coffee houses and when I add my thoughts to his want to show him what he missed in life but his thoughts added to my thoughts show the type of life I would have loved; I know I am the product of my actions, intentions don't count but these words pale before I think about Jacobo and afterwards the words are only figures of speech not the thirty years I lived after I met him—he is the world behind my words and my life makes much more sense in that tender world than this one. His was the right idea to die right before we reach old age and not have to put up with the humiliations, your body fails you and the sweet smell of pleasure fades, only the pleasure of our time together remains solid in my memory. This heart sports group is like wearing old lady shoes depressing and a necessary evil, my body is now ugly but my complexion still radiates light, according to Joseph because he loves it when I recall the past to him, he says I come alive when I talk about the past but I don't want to live in the past and then I recall the nice moments not the sadness, I refuse to cultivate sadness rather search my memory for pleasure even if at times a deeper memory intrudes and I know it couldn't have been the way I remember it and even if he had no idea how much he meant to me I refuse to believe he had no idea and when Delores was born considered him the lost child between us—he had to come back to me on his own he had my address but he couldn't leave his family once he came back to New York. The sunlight is starting to appear through the shade, Conchita is asleep and the night is difficult to get through, I dreamt of him wearing a blue chemise walking away and that started me thinking and I know being around his grandson allows me to dream about his grandfather. I always hoped I would see him at one of the concerts or plays I went to even if he told me he never went, but once my English improved I could start going to more modern theater and I always hoped he would be there, at least my love of the theater rubbed off on Conchita my taking her to classical ballet, Shakespeare, opera as a child whetted her appetite or at least got her away from the neighborhood and her silly friends, I despised her friends they were so dumb never opened a book, could only giggle when I tried to talk to them, thought men should take care of them never trying to learn ideas on their own, and the school was just terrible, this isn't the south where segregation is written into law it's more insidious there at least you know where you stand, but up here in the city there is an 'iron curtain' that constantly shifts and Latinos, Negros, the poor are stopped at the curtain, put in segregated schools or arrested forced to plea to something lest they spend decades in jail, most Latinos boys have been stopped at some point in their lives, the girls become mothers before they finish high school, I couldn't wait to get her out of that neighborhood, she would have been pregnant or a user she was such a susceptible kid without a brain in her head, at least Joseph read, he told me so himself he would go to the library and take books out and his friends would wonder is that required, but he read for ideas not requirements, at least he read, there were no books in my daughter's house, not even an encyclopedia, and once there she didn't even have a pencil. It was good to get her out of that neighborhood. I gotta get out of bed it's time to start making dinner.

I don't understand, really don't, did everything correct, played by the rules did everything right was an okay student, went to college like a good Jewish boy, found a unionized job so have plenty of money but still help with the rent, everything I was supposed to have done and how do I end up like this, so unhappy, drunk, lonely, scared, still living at home, I can't seem to break the chord. I have this nice reading chair from which I put a table next to and can drink my wine, or watch television, now I have a little TV in my room so I never have to go into the living room and watch what my parents watch, even if we watch the same thing, or I can fall asleep in it, and now when I get up to go to bed don't even care if I brush my teeth. True Cassandra has given me an ultimatum but can I act upon it. My father is ready to take over this room as soon as I'm gone. I get up in the morning for my new job and sit at a desk all morning long before I go out to make my orders. It sounded anti-Semitic or a joke when I first heard it sell good Jewish wine not the overly sweet kind used for religious rituals, and only on the weekends do I do things for me, go down to the Village in my tie dye jeans that my mother says make me look like a kid and people in the building wonder if I bathe. And in the Village actually found an old man's basketball court on West 3rd street that grownups play on, I can no longer play with kids all they do is argue and I can get a good game even as I bounce off ex-football players but at least playing with them my headaches go away and am not considered a kid who doesn't want to grow up, but they're mostly ex-jocks not interested in conversation only talking sports, and it is at Cassandra's and Esmeralda's that I have real conversation and can really enjoy myself. I even took this new job because of Cassandra, even if she had no idea of it, because I didn't want her to see me as this dumb worker rather as an intellectual with a job in an office wearing a suit a tie and not jeans and being assigned a dark and dingy desk with a window that faces a wall. Why I go to Esmeralda, even if there is no future with Cassandra she has made that clear to me even before the ultimatum, is the intellectual stimulation. When I am there we talk, have a dialogue, conversation, and am happy even if whatever I think is wrong, both know so much more than me, all I can do is give intuitive answers but both are very patient with me and don't let me get away with phoniness or simply what I believe is correct without thinking about it, now I have to subject my beliefs to examination and what comes out of me that seemed right before now has to be reexamined and this is a real education. We saw *Who's Afraid of Virginia Woolf?* and it shocked me what kind of family is that but Esmeralda said seething beneath the surface is hatreds of those who marry the wrong person, and we were all surprised when she came down the stairs wearing trousers, when Cassandra told me she had an abortion I was shocked, upset to no end, killing an innocent baby, which I had been taught or automatically believed not her not wanting to care for a child by a man she didn't love even if he was ready to play house with her. She even said the guy had offered to marry me because that is the honorable thing to do, and I was willing to propose to her in my fantasy because then I would finally have her and she would have to be grateful for me being her protector and giving someone else's child my last name. But she replied even before I could let the fantasy take shape in my head, the wifey thing, the kiddies, the house with the white picket fence, taking care of a little baby, was not for her, she would rather die than be in a situation like that and so would I, how could I live being the king of my castle!? as opposed to living at home with my parents, I quickly said, but Esmeralda, who had lived it, knew full well it couldn't be lived unless you wanted to, what sounds good on the outside may be a horror for those who live it, à la Virginia Woolf. Here I was this provincial a boy from the Bronx speaking to this sophisticated woman, even if I had graduated college I really hadn't left the old neighborhood, like some of the girls who did marry and call home every day and speak to their mother, I knew nothing about the ways of the world, didn't know anything about art, literature, romance, only what I saw in the movies or television, was even afraid at first to go to the movie of Virginia Woolf for fear I wouldn't understand it, yet had the nerve to think of myself as this sophisticated man who now was carrying a satchel to work. Cassandra asked why I got that and I told her I wasn't easily influenced but had seen Buster Keaton carrying one in *Film* and I found an old-fashioned briefcase in a thrift shop and now I carry around my journal in it and write—mostly the weather of the day and my feelings, nothing profound and not the deep thoughts I had hoped to write in it, but I found out I was shallow not deep and self-censorship was difficult to overcome and wouldn't even write about Cassandra's abortion lest the journal fall into the hands of the FBI and she get in trouble. I thought she did it with a coat hanger and Esmeralda laughed and said that's propaganda put out to scare little girls, abortion is a simple and safe procedure. Why am I so against it? Even thinking about it I realized it wasn't killing you can only kill if something is alive and a fetus isn't a person but thinking about it didn't change the way I feel that it is wrong not to give a fetus a chance to be alive and my vaunted reason didn't help; right then and there I believed in actual rights of living people not abstract ideas that could be applied everywhere. My first awakening. My thinking was out in left field somewhere while they thought thinking it all through even as their words didn't convince me it forced me to begin to think through a fundamental belief, and how else could I begin to think about something I was so sure I knew the answer to if not taking the first step and in watching Cassandra do what I thought was unthinkable, if I am to become this sophisticated person I want to become I have to reevaluate all my beliefs—I could just imagine being with my neighborhood or college friends and telling them my girlfriend had an abortion, boy would they look at me differently— better than with my horn-rimmed glasses, turtle neck and sports coat, my hair no longer slick with pomade and with Albee sticking out of my jacket pocket, as new truths emerge from my mouth even as I still felt a pit in my stomach and the words were a philosopher's stone distilling truth from falsehood but even if it was all alchemy all that matters is that I would be thought of differently to myself. What if everybody acted this way? soon the whole planet would be depopulated, Esmeralda smiled, understood where I was coming from, and slowly in her stuttering voice, which is getting stronger since she started going to a speech therapist and what doctors had thought was a permanent condition was improving, and she had the patience with the grandson of her old love, and her mind was still sharp even if her body wasn't, that mankind no longer lives in a small village but big cities and even before the towns were only small villages not cities and what one did there these effects would affect the others, but once you come to cities you are no longer in a town and these actions are not going to affect others and that in cities one has the right to make personal decisions without fear of the community hindering you and if they influence you it is only in minor ways. She obviously didn't live in the Bronx, the hood, where everybody knows your business and I couldn't do a thing as a child without my mother or grandmother finding out.

It matters the whole edifice is built on superstition the covenant never occurred, imagine there is no discussion of this, Jews automatically assumed it happened, or like my grandson at his bar mitzvah said even if it didn't historically happen (how could it have historically happened God came down from the mountain once and never again?) it happened that is the basis of Judaism—superstition, pure superstition, I was so proud of him not like these Eastern European superstitions have seeped into general thought, it reminds me of the time Joey and my daughter were watching *The Dybbuk* on television I just had to shut it off even if they were sitting on the edge of their chairs, how could she allow him to watch this superstitious nonsense, we're Sephardic Jews and we lived in a sophisticated Muslim culture until the Christians kicked us out and we went to Constantinople, Istanbul is just a mispronunciation of the Latin Constantinople and Spanish Jews settled in Pera on the other side of the Golden Horn an estuary of the Bosporus, as the Roman Jews settled on the other side of the Danube, Buda, at least the Spanish Jews dealt with the civilized Muslims, Eastern European Jews had to deal with the superstitious Christians. We of a fine intellectual descent not superstition. I get angry just thinking about it, all Jews did was accept this fact without thought, constrained, by habit, custom, listened to whatever elders said to them, this consent is an answer to superstitious belief not the basis of it. True I was like this also but I worked my way out of it but as Zoltan said it was easy for me I didn't have to live it all the time as he did or European Jews did by being the other. I couldn't wait until she came to my bedside and knew I was starting to feel better when I was able to masturbate to her image and the cold, flu whatever had no more thoughts and my head wasn't spinning anymore. I tried to walk, to stand up, but my head was spinning so fast I couldn't grab onto anything and fell down, even lying down my head was still spinning yet my mind stayed lucid I knew I was spinning and I thought water would help and since my head wasn't spinning a moment ago when I went to the outhouse to do my business said to myself I better get back to bed and lay down for an hour or so it's not even daylight and see if I can fall asleep and it will get better in the morning, and I went back to my cot and when I lay down my head was still spinning and I wondered why, I hadn't drunk the night before or hadn't drunk any more than I usually do and I don't drink much because I don't like waking up cold and shivering, no matter how good it feels going down but usually I go for a walk before I sleep to calm me down, even if I can't get a good night's sleep in a room full of twenty, thirty men on cots, one of them is always playing with himself and not quietly, except the ex-Catholics who still think it's a mortal sin even as they hate the priests but still won't do it because only priests can forgive you, luckily rabbis can't forgive all they do is open doors to the temple, I never saw as lazy a bunch of bums as them, at least the Protestants believe only God can forgive, others snore, I wonder what we Jews believe in but at least we can masturbate without guilt, only I couldn't because my head was spinning so even when I turned over and tried to lie on my back and thought maybe I slept too long so got up and put on my clothes, slowly, because my head still spun but I thought okay once I get up and wash my face I'll be okay, I wasn't cold, didn't have the chills or even a headache, I just couldn't get my balance and needed to hold onto the cot as I stood up thinking that a moment ago I was okay and now I can't get up without holding onto the cot, this can't be happening to me I said aloud to nobody in particular and waited to see if anyone would awaken and then see if I would answer myself, I always answer myself but this time I was silent, then said I should keep quiet lest I wake the men and went outside to pump a little water to wash my face have a drink of water then I will be okay as if I could have a miraculous recovery; how I could I think of that with my head still spinning is beyond me that all I needed was some water and I would be okay and even with my head spinning I didn't fall and didn't need to hold onto anything all I needed to do was walk outside and so I walked outside and the brisk air on my face did me good and I said to myself maybe the fresh air will stop my head from spinning because fresh air is better than moldy air and the sun was beginning to rise, I could see the rosy light even if I couldn't see the sun and this was the first time in my life I actually saw a sunrise and so the light with no sun surprised me, I actually had seen an occasional sunrise but didn't pay attention to it in the city when I went to bed with it not awoke with it, all around me now I could hear the hissing, buzzing, clicking, and birds tweeting and everywhere the noise was deafening as I made my way to the pump, cupped my hands and washed my face from the spigot but my head continued spinning and pretty soon all I could hear was the spinning inside my head not the noise outside and all of a sudden I could no longer stand up—the question then remained could I get up again and make it to the infirmary since nobody was around and I didn't want to be found lying face down in the mud, I didn't feel as if I had enough strength to yell for help and all I could do was try not to lose consciousness and die of suffocation if I couldn't lift my head: what a way to begin my first day in combat, and thought how Molly would be saddened by my death but would soon forget me, and I forced myself to rise, once you're down you always wonder if you can get up again, and walked to the infirmary all the while my head was still spinning but I was still able to think, usually when ill with a fever can't think at all but it seemed obvious to me I could still think and I didn't have a headache or a cold and shivers and since I don't have any of these symptoms should be able to walk and I knew this was the only place that never closed so it seemed logical to go there, maybe I could get some hot coffee that would make me feel better, so made my way there looking for a piece of wood that would help me balance but there was none around so I wobbly walked and the walk seemed like an eternity over a little peasant hill, a nothing after my jaunt over the Pyrenees, but it took forever to climb this little rise and I tried not to fall because the ground was wet but at times couldn't help myself, I couldn't keep my balance and all I hoped was that my intuition was leading me correctly because I couldn't see over the ridge but I could still think even with my head spinning and said this has to be the correct way but even if I go off in the wrong direction I'll eventually run into a sentry and he'll get me to the infirmary, but I realized I have a good sense of direction, then doubt slipped in only I didn't listen to that voice, in the city I can't get lost but out here in nature everything looks the same, and I no longer heard the hissing, buzzing and clicking but felt the sun on my back and the wet clothes on my ass and made my way to Esmeralda.

I have been having this weird dream, this weird dream I have been having now for nights and it's always the same dream in different variations but the same dream I am sure of that, that I am with someone lying on a beach or in front of a fireplace or lying in bed and all of a sudden I look up and see a nuclear explosion, I see the big mushroom cloud forming and I awaken in a cold sweat, and finally I went to the library, first I had to get a library card a pain because I didn't have two forms of identification on me, so instead read in the library these dream interpretation books and even asked my actress friend Meredith who's in therapy, all actors are in therapy, and she made believe the dream was hers and her analyst gave her the same answer the books gave me, that I am about to undergo a profound change in my life—why do you have to go to therapy for that if you can find the answer in books? Finally, I am a member of the 'We Look it up Club' that I had no interest in in the fourth grade when they first took us to the public library on Melrose Avenue on a class trip. This is a good sign, I now am feeling energetic again getting out of the passive tense, which allows me to control things not just let them happen, grandma said that now at least I don't have to marry to be respectable but I have no intention of tying myself down to a man. Having regular sex is allowing me to feel better again as good as I can feel—it was charming, me having to ask him and he wanting to wait to marriage and I had to explain that I am not the marrying type, he was a bit shy and I wondered if it was his first time, and at least it gets me to feel better again and maybe something good can come out of all this, and certainly I am careful now not saying if it's god's will I get pregnant so be it, grandma did insist upon birth control, and I was one of the first women in college to even use the pill, most were afraid to even ask about it, asking about it meant you were thinking of sex, and good girls didn't or expected boys to look out for them, but boys think a condom is like having sex with socks on, and I certainly don't want to have another abortion. Long-term goals can't be side-tracked by short-term desires, and now I realize sex is important to me I feel so much better with it, enjoy it, but it is not in my long-term interest to become pregnant to be a mommy, and I have to insist boys take some responsibility because the pill is not 100% effective and to become pregnant would suck to be stuck home and nobody will hire a pregnant actor and that would be the end of my acting career and my independence even if Joseph says he doesn't mind little kiddies, I could stand them a little when they are cute but I couldn't wait until they left the home no I can't be with a little one and all that goes with it, nor a husband I'm not through looking yet. I could never do it alone, look at my mother, but even if I do better than her each time a man came by I became jealous and was so scared I would lose my mother, the woman I couldn't stand. Yes, it's fun doing things with Joseph nor am I afraid I have gone too far with him and he will act like Carlos, the father of the child I aborted, who thought he owned me and didn't want me to have an abortion and even asked his priest to speak to me, the nerve of him, and every time he calls I speak to him in a flat voice and explained to Joseph that he was the father of the child I aborted and that he wanted to marry me but I wasn't ready for that just because an accident happened and I have no interest in giving up my freedom and moving in with him. He still calls now and then when he's lonely to talk but at least now no longer in the middle of the night. Grandma was supportive saying I should not give in to something I do not want and she supports my desire to act, which is only her life style that she gets to view not feel. If everybody did this the country would be in trouble but I'm not everybody only me and I know what I want or at least what I don't want, which is not to live free and independent, why I can't believe Joseph is still living with his parents, what kind of freedom is that? and how knowing this I have lived accordingly, but Joseph like all men thinks I will change for him and maybe I will change later on but right now this is the way I want to live and it renders all other questions superfluous even if it is not what everyone says I should want, but I'm me and won't live the way other people think I should live; my first response is to wonder how I feel not what other people think is correct and if I can reverse the order first comes the thought even if it is not the wisdom of the ages it comes first then the deed comes even as grandma says I want everything and nothing and she is correct, I want to be active not passive, and I am lucky to have her as she even approves of my relationship with Joseph—why shouldn't she approve of the grandson of her old lover, even if Joseph is really someone I like to do things and he is a pleasant young man who I feel I might be able to help in time—we can each do what is best for the other but if we do it for ourselves we would mess it up. Together we do better even if individually each of us does worse. And I have to admit he is handsome and since I've come to live with my grandmother not ashamed to have feelings for a man younger than me. Back in the Bronx I would never have gone out with a younger man nor called one either, the unwritten rules were so strict you just didn't even think of doing such things, the rules were so codified in your head you didn't even dare go out with a man who wasn't the same religion as you. Men must be of the same religion, older, taller, and you never could violate these norms they were so drummed into you like God, and if you violate these commandments western civilization would come tumbling down, only grandma would say live don't be so concerned with what others thought of you, they don't think about you that often and she said when she first landed in America the first thing she gained was her anonymity. I was surprised, however, when in my senior year of high school, my second, I wanted to go up to Times Square and watch the ball come down she said do it after you graduate college this is not appropriate behavior for a girl who hasn't graduated high school. Now who in their right mind wants to stand in freezing cold temperature to watch a ball drop down, but back then I was surprised at her behavior after telling me to live free and all that here she is restricting me. Now I can laugh but that was the only time I can remember her restricting me except when she wouldn't allow me to graduate saying I just didn't know enough and made me repeat my senior year, in college she made sure I had the pill even called up the school nurse who said don't worry we will make sure she has pills even if she forgets to order them, we take care of our women. That was the school for me, grandma said, even if I didn't want to leave the city, she said go you should do the best you can for yourself, live for yourself not what your friends think, but by then I had broken with most high school girls and had made a new set of friends and most if not all of them were going to school away from home, only one girl did go to Barnard and another boy to Columbia but they also didn't live at home but in a dormitory and that was routine behavior and I went along with the crowd and went out of town. Now for the first time I understand what she was talking about, she's cooler than I thought back then when I thought she didn't have a clue how young girls think or as Joseph says she's made tremendous progress since then.

The day I went back to my barber at the Sherry-Netherland Hotel I finally felt myself feeling better or at least back to normal, my hair had been getting long and when I played with it tied it into knots I finally decided okay, enough grabbed the N train to 5th Avenue and Central Park South and went to see Aldo again, he welcomed me with open arms wondered where I had been. Few women go for a haircut in a barber shop but I had discovered this place years ago, cheaper than a hair salon, quicker, and he cuts my hair in layers, I like being with men better than gossiping with women, now maybe I won't be afraid to look at myself in the mirror. I hate looking at old photographs of myself, except, of course, the one and only one taken with Jacobo, him standing with his beret and no ambiguity in his face as we smile into the camera together on the day he leaves Spain not like the dead man walking he seemed when he first entered with his high fever, and when I finally came to the States the first thing I wanted to do was look him up, went into the phone book to find out where he lived but couldn't find him, and thought of immediately going up to the Bronx and walking all around until I found him. What was I going to say do you remember me, or I am here, to his wife? And realized a girl can't chase a man, what a thought, I was born too early now with modern feminism wouldn't hesitate for a moment, I'm sorry we never had a painting of us, one artist/soldier wanted to paint us once but I couldn't spare the time nor did I want to be stared at all the time—modeling takes time photographs are quick. Conchita thinks I should label them but who will care after I am gone they are of no use to anyone but me, and I can barely remember most of the characters photographed, except of course for Jacobo, and that was all I had to hold onto as my father would scream at me you fool thinking you can create your own government and not have to bow to a higher authority, meaning God, which we thought had died in the trenches of the Great War. But he keeps sneaking back in, now the Soviets try and kill him but there are more religious people in their country now than even before the revolution. When people have no faith in the government they come to believe in a God that can save them even if that God has failed. Sitting down in the chair as Aldo rubbed his hands through my hair, he says still thick fine do you want the usual, and I say yes, yes, let my life come back to normal, at least I am able to walk now without a stick and was able to climb the subway stairs and cross the street to get here. Conchita wanted to come or if she couldn't Joseph would but I wanted to go alone, I enjoy pampering myself and want to see if I still do. A painting would have become of the permanent record photographs are transitory because it is a quick moment of time that doesn't add or subtract from the actual image—I actually thought of making a copy of this photograph and sending it to him for his 70th birthday, imagine the look on his face receiving a photograph from an old lover but he was dead already only I didn't know it, he was always young in my heart. Aldo starts unraveling my hair to begin to cut, first he sprays water on my hair then unravels strand after strand just as if he were cutting a Negro's hair, only they don't come here, some unwritten rule they only go to barber shops that specialize in their hair, I wonder what would happen if a black person would come in, of course they now could have to cut it with the Civil Rights Act but would they. As he puts a wet towel over my eyes I think, I didn't send it because I didn't want to hurt his wife that I didn't know he no longer lived with and she was also dead, but it would have surprised his daughter and grandson that he had a different life than they imagined, only Joseph told me he never talked about his experiences in the war, and I'm glad that I didn't hurt his family with my remembrances of things past, these remembrances are for me alone but I did think it there's no denying that just as I thought of going up to the Bronx to surprise him, and depending upon my mood would either knock on his door, or hide behind a tree and observe him, not realizing he lived in the back of an apartment building until Joseph told me, all along I assumed the front and he would look out the window and spot me and at first not believe it was me but eventually have to come down and check—who could believe in these big apartment buildings that have no view of the street, in the old world of course houses were walled off from the street but here in the new world everything is so open there are no courtyards. Oh my face feels smooth the warm water is doing its wonders and now I wonder did I love him so much that each time I think about him my memory stays on the outskirts not catching the moment of sheer inflection when my feelings changed from patient to lover. Aldo is starting to unravel my hair; his hands feel good on top of my head, I know I loved him without being able to explain the reasons why, he couldn't have been more exciting than I thought he was he was Jewish after all how wild can those people be but it was he who made me who I am today, a human being, who always is in the company of the melancholy, not only was he my lover but he is also my best friend, the only one I could talk to who understood all my words, but if I think a little harder realize this is impossible since he hadn't yet learned enough Spanish or me English but we had the passion of lovers who see the world the same way and that takes time, which we didn't have that much of but the pleasure of being in each other's company and sharing that began immediately. When he walked into the infirmary, shaking, shivering, and he couldn't stand up his head spinning all around trying to hold onto something and that something was me and never letting go until the day we were defeated, we were a couple of soulmates, seventeen, eighteen months together before Delores Ibárruri, 'La Pasionaria', the old battle axe communist, says: 'Mothers, women when we are a free country once again speak to your children tell them about the International Brigades how these men reached our shores as fighters for freedom these men are fighters for freedom we shall not forget you.' Luckily now my face is wet with that memory as these men boarded the ship and Aldo cannot see tears rolling down my eyes whenever I think of that last moment, those eighteen months were my years of living all the rest have been of existing, my granddaughter thinks because I can name those years it becomes unmasked but she reads too much Freud as if unmasking can free you of your thoughts and feelings, they go don't go away so easily, to realize something doesn't change anything, it's why I like being around Joseph his mannerisms remind me of his grandfather even if Conchita thinks it silly of me to confuse the two, she's of the opinion when it's over it's over, but she has only had lovers never a love. When he didn't want to give us his phone number both of us thought he was married only later did we find out he didn't want his mother asking him about girls calling, she would never leave him a moment's peace, never let up, and it's easier telling her nothing because she is going to ask is she

Jewish as if that is the only thing that matters. He could have told her I am in spirit. Aldo seems to be finishing up he asked me something and now I see his words forming, he must have taken the towel off my face but I didn't hear his words I was into my thoughts, now they are slowly forming in front of me, is this short enough and I say yes not even truly looking in the mirror as he holds up the mirror to my back and I agree he's done his excellent job as usual. Thinking about the pleasant moments with Jacobo allows me to think about myself as well, my desires, too bad I couldn't live an ascetic life my body had needs and this silly recapitulation of the past allows me to stay whole even with the other men in my life, only how do I know what I could have been if I had loved other men as passionately as I loved him or they loved me. I did try and make an effort but they were so boring, dull, insipid, nice, but once the sexual attraction wore off they had nothing, the physicalness of Jacobo never wore off and even if it did we still had each other but now it's only in thinking about him and when I think about him as Aldo wipes the hair off me and does a nice job vacuuming the hair that somehow always gets down my back, and he lets me comb my hair the way I like with the part of the right, and he says soon we will have to start dying the gray streaks but I mention they are mine I will not hide them, it is thinking about him with the thoughts that are in my head that gives me my identity not my gray hairs, an image of myself which I alone have access to that is the essence of me and when I try and communicate this it loses its matter-of-factness, my parents never understood and I couldn't talk like this to my husbands so it is better to continue living inside my fully cut haircut than having a living conversation with a live person where I would have to explain myself over and over—one thing that I immediately noticed when I first came to this city that people never listen to one another, as I say goodbye to Aldo and shakes my hand, men here don't kiss and tells me to come back and not be such a stranger, I have gotten accustomed to the lack of conversation with so much noise, the busses, the trains, the El, the construction, and now the television always on there is no place you can go where there is no noise, only when I wake up in the middle of the night can I actually hear the clock ticking otherwise it is drowned out by the sounds of the day. I wish I had enough strength to walk home I use to love walking home after my martini, first stopping in the hotel bar for one even if a few men would never stop pestering me with their chatter until I would tell them the Playboy Club is around the corner but never could drive them away until I found this nice Café Nicholson on 58th street near the 59th street bridge and could sit for hours over a glass of tea, gay men know how to leave a woman alone, then enjoy the long walk home, never walking here because I wanted to get it over with and would take the subway up but would enjoy the solitary walk home, now I have to take the subway once more and the noise of the train station doesn't allow me to think of Jacobo but I tell myself to go look for the photograph when I get home, and maybe I should have a painting made of the photograph but who knew that would be the last time we would see each other but the picture does remind me that I lived in Spain but not how I felt leaving Spain with an American GI.

When I started reading Beckett and talking with Joseph about her did I begin to understand her emptiness always having to think never able to live on her own never allowed to live on her own; initially I thought this was her age an old lady afraid after a heart attack, then I thought from the part of the world she grew up in where women couldn't do anything on their own and if they were without a man they were old maids—she told me enough times she escaped Spain to the new world to get away from their frightful culture of the Church and the spiritual condition of death which was everywhere in all their symbols and sacred places, that their time was always the past and in the United States of A. she could leave all that behind this is the land of the future, she explained to me with the loss in the war a woman couldn't step out of the house without a man and she had to be with other women, cousins, but never seen with a man without a chaperone because women had one purpose in life to be a mother, two purposes really to avoid shaming the family, bringing disgrace upon the family was even worse than not being a mother and so she married her erstwhile suitor even as she despised him by convincing herself that she would eventually come to love him when all she was doing was attempting to get away from her parents and thinking once in her own home she would have more freedom—why can't women ever live free why must they be at the beck and call of a culture, at least feminism is now giving us more choices, and when we are allowed to earn money have some more freedom, and the man she married knew she was pregnant she was too far along not to let him know but the pharmacist thought it would be okay he was happy to have a younger woman as his wife and realized people would look at him with new respect, he was a boy according to grandma, a grown up man with the brains of a little boy, a silly grown up man with silly ideas of a boy, who thought women were these fragile creatures needing protection from the big bad wolf and now that she was his wife and soon to be mother he had saved her, in marrying her he had fulfilled his Christian duty even if she no longer believed and told him she was an atheist, he just couldn't imagine that, I thought she married so the child could have a father not that she could escape her parents, how little I know of my own grandmother. Joseph said he thought my mother was born from the loins of his grandfather not the loins of my father her second husband, an American GI after her first husband enlisted in the Blue Division the sop volunteers that Franco created to fight the Bolsheviks and not have to confront England and was killed in the siege of Leningrad. When she married Tomas she was able to come to the States with my mother, quite a conniver. She could no longer stay in that patriarchal culture and at the first opportunity escaped with him to America it would have been impossible to get a divorce in Spain but here you can live apart and nobody knows anything, she stayed with my grandfather for a long time but parted pretty quickly and at least was able to get out of Spain and she did work with the American Jewish Committee to ferret Jews out of Spain to America, and the same Jewish lobby made her transition to the States easier, from them she knew which hands to bribe, whose ego to flatter, who to call on in the bureaucracy to get things done. Grandma was able to help she said where other Spaniards thought Jews were the devil with lying eyes, pale look, uptight grins that recall a hyena, all this surprised Joseph who of course knew about anti-Semitism, but never heard it spoken so brutally in real time and he had never truly encountered it living in the city, or if he encountered prejudice didn't even realize it was anti-Semitism thought that was something of bygone days, of course not everybody in Spain felt that but then most remained silent, that 'inner emigration' thing Germans claimed they had when the Nazis were in power and what Americans do now during the Vietnam war, remain silent even if they disagree with the war, some even afraid to sign petitions against the war lest their bosses find out. How many men have I met on the street who couldn't sign the petition but told me they agree with me? And black men are hopeless all they want to do is get me to wrap my legs around them, thinking that's all a woman wants are black men in bed. How Jews were still thought of as the devil was a surprise to Joseph, after all he said, there hasn't been a Jew in Spain since they were kicked out over 400 years ago, not that the church hadn't kept alive that bogeyman, and the church is not one to repent for fear of not seeming infallible but grandma didn't have that prejudice and could work with them and talk to them if they knew Ladino, but most knew only Yiddish or German or some other foreign language but she helped them just the same and some greeted her when she came to the States without Tomas because he still had to fight the Nazis. Theoretically Tomas is not my grandfather but he is the only grandfather I know, he was this lovely man who never liked to see me cry and would never let me go to bed crying if he was around, and he saw me as his grandchild and he was the one who finally told me the truth when I turned eighteen that I was not his granddaughter by birth but that I was his granddaughter, he wanted me to know the truth. My mother was already dead and I was angry at her and grandma for not telling me the truth and when I went away to college he told me this was my last chance to redeem myself, I didn't know what he was talking about but I was glad to get away from the lies of the family. Joseph couldn't understand this type of family all his family hated each other but stayed together he could not imagine them leaving or even divorcing, he never heard of anything like this and said Jews don't do that, as if he could talk for the whole Jewish race and they aren't even a race but a religion, he had even laughed when I told him back in the Bronx some girls said Jews have tails like the devil, the snout of a vampire, the filthy kike, it's your blood they want, they're unclean circumcised, but he never grasped the true hatred that was sometimes said about them, he only heard the other side of the coin from his non-Jewish friends that Jews were smart. When I mentioned this to him it rendered him speechless, the practical stuff said behind closed doors, his education hadn't prepared him for this he thought this was dark ages stuff not stuff of the modern world, school is like light comedy not tragedy which he has to learn on his own, as he said he only began to be educated once he finished school and he can no longer see light comedies of school where teachers talked a good game but didn't act upon thought. Once he started going to the theater he opened up to a new way of thinking that mediocre teachers rarely talked about. And the few plays he saw in college were not very good you need good actors to bring out the dynamics of a play otherwise it is dull and insipid, if you see a Beckett, Brecht, or a Sartre you see it is not entertainment where you go to relax, he was surprised by these dramas not grandma who even if she didn't go to theater in Spain had grown up with serious thoughts that she acquired by meeting his grandfather and why he was such a blessing to her and other men don't measure up to him. Still it is very difficult for her to live but she has a strong will and has been going to physical therapy and she seems never to have missed my grandfather or other men in her life and she keeps wondering when I will marry, as if it's been so good to her, but she has never been defined by the men she was with underneath it all was always her and overcame her upbringing where Jews were thought of as dogs. The important thing modern feminism has given women is that we can live without a man we don't need one to define us, even if the culture of television and movies, magazines and newspapers only gives us easily digestible works even novels sometimes end up as pulp and I realized I would never find myself living through somebody else and grandma did encourage me that way but she also thought I should marry and settle down. But even deeper she was for me in childhood she was the one who took me to plays, the zoo, concerts, made sure I saw something of the wider world not simply trapped in the neighborhood, how many of my friends had never even been to Manhattan? she even took me to the South Ferry and I remember asking are we moving yet when we were in the middle of the bay. She showed me another world existed and while it was true I resisted her at first about going to private school that was because the only private schools I knew were Catholic not independent schools where you smoke pot out on the street even if at first I thought they were ritzy and I didn't like being with stuck-up kids who drank tea—never did I learn such bad habits as I did in private school, we all smoked but these kids did it in front of their parents. At least she let me finish the year up in the Bronx but said I didn't know enough to go to college, who wanted to go to college, and she insisted I take my senior year over again and learn something, and all I learned was how to have sex with a condom, all the girls wanted to do was lose it before college but she didn't care and the only condition she imposed upon me was that I finish in a good high school even if it was somewhere I didn't belong and felt out of place so that I would be free of the hood and so I was forced to go to a progressive high school that insisted I go to college away from the city. How can she hold such contradictory thoughts in her head?

The first time I ever heard of the Palestinians was when I applied for a job with a wine merchant after college, I did my due diligence and read up all about Israel and its foreign policy, how it came to be, and how they were now trying to sell wine and I had an interview with the manager who said most who come here usually stay unless they move to *Yerushalaim* I had no idea what that was, Esmeralda told me afterwards it was Jerusalem in Hebrew: the only reason this position is open because the person before me decided to move with his family to Israel, and for that they understand and forgive him even if it means more work for us it is good for the Jewish state when Jews move to Israel—at that I kept quiet and nodded because I hadn't the slightest intention of ever wanting to go to Israel unless it was on the way to Paris and the Latin quarter where I thought life would be grand, and had even taught myself how to drink coffee so I could sit in *Deux Magots* all day long but realized I shouldn't say this and agreed with him when he said President Truman was a great president for immediately recognizing Israel's right to exist, that Israel was founded because of the Holocaust that they had fought wars of self-defense and they had made the desert bloom, but Esmeralda said afterwards that's not the issue the issue really is what happens to the native people the Jews displaced and they are the Palestinians. Who? that was the first I ever heard of them and she explained that they were promised the right of return by their Arab neighbors and that's what the wars were about. It is when they are allowed to return and Israelis figure out how to live with them that peace will come to the region. I had never heard of them before and they would only come on the world stage after the 1972 Olympics when they killed their hostages and were themselves killed but they existed in the 1967 war which doubled the size of the Israeli state and some argued we should give the newly conquered land back to the Palestinians and live in peace, not as occupiers of East Jerusalem which meant apartheid, and I wondered what nation would do that but Esmeralda said Jews are held in higher standards than other people, the moral law of Judaism is justice. Usually all I heard from the goyim was they killed Jesus. Israel will be a just state or it won't be able to exist, she said. It took me years to convince liquor store owners to stock Israeli drek (wine) and usually I would get an occasional order to keep me in shekels and only after Israel was threatened with annihilation by the United Arab Republic of Egypt, Syria and Jordon did liquor store owners consent to stock more of its wine because they liked the way Israel had stood up to the bad guys. All of a sudden it was hip to be Jewish, that's when they invaded and occupied East Jerusalem, the West Bank, Gaza and the Golan Heights in one fell swoop and the joke was you want to visit the pyramids visit Israel. Now I had a platform to sell my wine and made a killing in the wine market and said nothing that would make me seem like a self-hating Jew even as I hoped Israel would give the land to the Palestinians and live in peace especially since Israel had destroyed the Egyptian air force so were no longer threatened and the war was essentially over but the occupation increased Israeli territory dramatically and made them an imperialist power. That I could do nothing about unless I moved to Israel and became a peacenik but I had my own worries with Vietnam, I didn't want to serve in the United States war of aggression so I certainly wasn't going to move to Israel and be eligible for their draft, it was easier to ignore it and continue making money with all my new orders. Finally my potential was paying off now I was making more money than I had on the railroad, when I first took this job the pay was less but my boss explained I had the potential to make a lot more, and I liked the challenge. What I didn't know and only found out later the only reason they hired me I found out from my boss when we were out drinking and he mentioned under his breath that nobody in the firm really wanted me but they hired me because I was the only Jewish candidate because they wanted a nice Jewish boy to hawk their product even if I had no salesmen skills nor any idea of Jewish culture and no idea of wines but was a recent college graduate, they liked the idea of a college graduate and could write because I had been on the student newspaper for two years—what a way to get a job, a mindless job but I could wear a suit and tie and was considered white-collar worker not like my union job, and I wrote copy writing what others had written and changing only a few words and the Golan Heights became a veritable wine growing area like California not only did it secure Israel from attack by Syria but it became profitable and to avoid controversy we insisted wine growers not put on the labels where the wine was actually made and all of a sudden Israeli wine expanded and I was caught up in the boom as Israeli wine went into liquor stores and restaurants overcoming an earlier prejudice.

For a few years she loved me then she no longer loved me. I never heard of a woman leaving a man. Imagine that! I was a good husband, provider, never interfered with her running of the household, loved her daughter as if she were my own, felt bad we couldn't have children but never said a word considered Gloria mine and she loved me always visited, at least Esmeralda didn't deny me that pleasure and her daughter Conchita—when she told me I had to leave I thought eventually she would come to her senses even if she said she wanted nothing more to do with me. I still think she truly loved me when I brought her here and I really became a 'big shot' on my block bringing home a foreign bride and I would even have allowed her to go back to Spain for a whole month at a time, but she wouldn't set foot in that country as long as Franco ruled but I wanted her to keep in contact with her parents and also so Gloria would learn Spanish, which my mother couldn't believe she couldn't speak and my mother would only speak Spanish to her but she would answer in English, she understood her but answered back in English, true my parents never really loved Esmeralda thought she was a snooty European from Spain not from the island and she would correct their Spanish as if Spain was the king's English—and she never liked rice and beans. What I missed most was the rice and beans, neither at home or in the service did they give me that. My wife refused to cook it as well, why I had to spend so much time at my mother's place but I did it with Gloria even if she didn't love rice and beans as much as me. I took Gloria everywhere in the city, to the Empire State building, Statue of Liberty, South Ferry, Radio City Music Hall, the tree at Rockefeller Center even Pennsylvania Station before they knocked it down, even as she got older was embarrassed by my Puerto Rican accent—the army couldn't get rid of that for me even if it got me out of Puerto Rico and taught me how to repair radios and so always had a job, even taught myself television repair, even if I never owned a shop always have a job, and we were the first on our block to own a television and all the kids would come over to our house to look at the 12-inch screen. She was the one who insisted we live in an integrated neighborhood hating living with all Puerto Ricans up in Spanish Harlem where they only spoke Spanish, she considered herself European not Hispanic, so we moved downtown but my parents stayed uptown and finally moved to the Bronx when I was able to get them here. They came by plane the first time anybody in the village had ever been on a plane. My father because he worked as a handyman learned some English my mother never because she rarely left the house of the South Bronx and could get by with her little English. Esmeralda who lived in Madrid had never been to a bull fight, why do you live in Spain if you don't go to see a bull fight. It was our first date, she was horrified of all that machismo and that the bull had been castrated, I hadn't known that, and had the saddest eyes you ever saw—she looked away at the killing and didn't care that the bull had fought honorably only saw it as part of the dominant culture that had come back after the Falangists had destroyed the legitimate government of Spain but she was decent to me and realized I was treating her in good faith and thinking she would be someone I would like and I believed her when she said she had seen too much death to want to see it voluntarily again and I was glad she told me it created a bond between us, and I was sensitive to her needs after I saw her looking away and didn't suggest it again and the next time we went to the Prado even as my friends in the barracks laughed at me going to a museum, they had never been to an art museum in their lives and the only paintings in their home were their drawings from kindergarten, some even admitted no paintings on the wall except religious icons, like in our house on the island, all we had was a picture of the Crucifixion and some magazine cut-outs on the walls, at first I felt uncomfortable, what pleasure can you have looking at paintings on the wall when you can be out in the sunlight, but I had to admit it was a delight to see those old fogies dressed in the most ridiculous costumes as Esmeralda explained not all pleasure has to be physical, you can have enjoyment in the delight of looking at something soothing—but I think she also liked to practice her English with me, and she was the one who put her hand through mine and I was most grateful. Spanish women have the reputation of being standoffish and here she was in a crowd letting me define her not letting the crowd define her but felt strong enough to walk with me holding my hand and she even went out without a chaperone because she thought it silly for a grown woman not to be allowed to walk by herself, and even if she wouldn't have dared go out at night by herself in the daytime she refused those unwritten restrictions—she felt those uncodified, unwritten traditions of roots which would keep alive a dead civilization and she wanted no part of that past. She would always live her own life and that's what I liked about her until she turned on me and that leads to enormous loneliness and I should stop drinking at night because I know it's going to kill me but the nights are terrible and I can't sit home alone even with the TV on. It was a mistake to buy a home in this godforsaken part of the Bronx, a two-fare zone, the difference in the neighborhood was immediate here they roll up the streets at 8 o'clock and hardly anyone is out, back in Spanish Harlem the streets were always full and now not only do I own a home but have to own a car as well but I do love getting into the city early finding a place to park it beats having to take a bus to the train station and then the train downtown but I can no longer drink coffee out of the thermos unless I'm willing to pee by the side of the car that I refuse to do because it reminds me too much of bums who urinate in the street, but now I also keep another pair of clothes in the shop for accidents. My mother said I should never have married a European woman should have stuck to my own kind they would never leave you Puerto Rican women don't have these new-fangled ideas. She didn't even go to church, the only trouble is after Esmeralda I can't stand those fat whiny women who know nothing.

I can never find pleasure in the moment always thinking ahead or behind never can enjoy myself instead always worrying about the future and if only I could act upon my desires instead of always being frightened, I enjoy being with Esmeralda and Conchita why can't I call why must I wait for her to call me, and I want to be with Cassandra alone not Esmeralda, so what? is it irrational to want pleasure to have her want to put her tush on my face and fart, she thought that disgusting but did say when I licked her ass that it was wonderful, and I now masturbate to her image not a random woman I see on the subway or passing me on the street but because I hope for it doesn't mean it's going to occur—stop being such a nervous nelly and make the phone call. Should I call again or should I simply enjoy the chance encounter we had but if it was cool I wouldn't deny myself this moment of pleasure, but what if she rejects me—ecstasy can never be repeated and even if I die now this has to be one of the highlights of my life and wouldn't it be nice to end upon such a high note, and just to be on the safe side while taking the subway home made sure not to stand to close to the edge of the platform—not that I would jump but in case I got bumped but then my last thought could have been at the pleasure spent not the anxiety of the future that my father said was full of promise now that I had a college degree but

I only felt scared, which is happening right now as I stand outside their apartment hoping they will come out and I can 'accidentally' bump into them only I won't do it in front of their apartment but would follow for a bit and maybe on the street, If I would do it at all—too bad there's no outdoor market here like the La Marqueta in Spanish Harlem everyone goes there, and I'd be sure to spot them, I knew about that place since I was a kid when my mother made me go with her to visit an elderly cousin who still lived in Harlem even as white people kept moving out but he had lived in the building since the '30s and felt too old to move and felt so comfortable in the neighborhood that he didn't even like to take the railroad up to Westchester to visit his son and daughter-in-law nor the grandchildren and so my mother adopted him and was the only one to visit since his wife died so unexpectedly, and we would make our weekly visit together and as a treat would go to La Marqueta and get a Chinese apple, called that because Chinese men were the only ones who sold pomegranate apple and fresh halvah not the prepackaged ones sold in candy stores, and as I got older could play in the street games with the local boys, stickball, acey-ducey, off the point, street games boys played in neighborhoods that didn't have parks and we also played in my neighborhood, and even if she didn't like me to play with Spanish boys I never felt lonely or scared we enjoyed the games, and if we got into a fight I could hold my own, I don't know when I became afraid to fight but as a kid was a terror if need be. And I would walk down there on my own when I was bored with high school and the friends I cut with was surprised I knew my way in Spanish Harlem, but I was surprised some of them knew their way around Central Park and even Washington Square Park in the Village and when I discovered them lost interest in Spanish Harlem. Also then I could hop over the turnstile and didn't need a token. My mother claimed I learned that from the Spanish boys I played with in Harlem but the truth was I showed it to them. Once when I was 8 got it in my head to walk down and see him and walked all the way, a true New Yorker I knew my way around the city even if I had never walked it before and since we didn't have a phone my cousin had to take me home up in the Bronx and I had to show him the way but not before we stopped in La Marqueta and got some fresh vegetables not the stuff you found in supermarkets, my grandfather insisted upon that. Now waiting in front of their apartment building a little to the side so they can't spot me if they actually come out I think of my previous misdeeds, I thought I would be punished for that but my grandfather defended me and I was told not to do that again, he was also the one who defended me for my low marks in conduct at school, saying not that I was bored but I didn't like bending to authority figures so wouldn't be submissive later in life, and then my mother had to walk my cousin to the subway not the El because he couldn't walk up all those stairs, I laughed how can you not be able to walk up three flight of stairs, we do it every day to our apartment, wait until you get old my grandfather said. At his funeral when I couldn't look at his body my grandfather said good he's not the same as before and my mother said he died of a broken heart because he was being kicked out of his small apartment building to make way for a brand new housing project—urban renewal to clear up the slums. Outside Conchita's apartment building waiting, wondering if I could repeat that experience coming unannounced to my cousin's place do I have enough guts to ring the bell, I felt the urine move inside my penis luckily it didn't go all the way out and actually did it before I could think about it and someone looked through the peep hole surprised to see me and invited me in. I didn't know who I was or who she was it was done so fast I didn't have time to think about it but then thought trying to justify my acts, I was in the neighborhood and justification is reason enough and as I rang I wondered was this where I was last time when she said not to be a stranger and Esmeralda said she wanted to see me again and what I wanted was to be part of their lives never before had I had such a nice experience of being treated like an adult, certainly not at home where I was always treated like a baby, and when she recognized me and opened up the door, I never saw so many locks on a door, a top lock, a bottom lock a police lock, the neighborhood was changing. Cassandra wasn't there but Esmeralda showed me in I don't know what she thought but she offered me some tapas said it had pork inside, I thought I would burn in hell but loved it, here was the first pork I had eaten, and I wondered if I had the correct apartment but she spoke like Esmeralda, only without the makeup, and told me Cassandra has a day job, I thought she was a working actress and she was but working actresses don't necessarily get paid, the first time I had heard you work without getting paid for the beauty of the work and when she spoke Spanish I understood some of it because I had taken it in Junior high school, high school and college and could conjugate verbs even if I never had a Spanish conversation. I added two and two and immediately got five, as Esmeralda switched from English to Spanish because the medication confused her and when I asked her to speak English she translated her Spanish back into Spanish.

The first time I realized I wasn't Christian was when I saw your grandfather in the hut, even then dizzy and barely able to stand up he impressed me by the way he moved and wanted him to notice me even if he was too weak to notice anybody and he sat down expecting to throw up only he didn't just sat still and when I came over tried to stand up but fell down still dizzy, I placed a cold compress on his head, undressed him and placed him on a cot, he thanked me, one of the few who ever did that to a nurse, we nurses appreciated when that was done it was done so rarely most think that's our job and why do you have to thank someone for being so gentle with you, even if the next morning he said he didn't remember it, but enjoyed it when I came over and held his hand and thanked me again for being so gentle with him and he told me had no memory of last night and I told him it was two nights ago he had lost one day of his life asleep, he said he didn't have that much time to waste but his body dictated the course of action, and when awake was able to hold down a little broth, I asked if he was hungry and he said now that you mention it I am hungry and I brought him some broth and he said he was glad it wasn't chicken soup he hated chicken soup that his mother would make for him when he was ill. He wanted a little schnapps but I said he has to be a little stronger for that and have something in his stomach, he wanted to get up and fight, couldn't stand lying in a cot all day said he was okay but I didn't want to let him out of my sight and in the afternoon was able to feed him some meat which he said he had never eaten before it tasted different maybe my taste buds are messed up but even chewing on the back of his teeth he said no this is different I have a good sense of taste and I said who hasn't eaten pork before and he spit it out. Interesting Joseph says because he would make me a succulent roast pork with fresh onions, garlic, mushrooms and real vegetables not the canned my mother used, even if my grandmother, mother and father would never touch the stuff. My mother's idea of cooking was heating frozen dinners or frying the taste out of everything and then bringing in cold margarine straight from the refrigerator to the table to be enjoyed with store-bought white bread—her food had no taste. The first time I realized food had taste was he bought a Russian pumpernickel bread and real soft butter to go along with it, the time we were in the country. Your grandfather spat it out thought he would choke, I felt terrible forgot that I had learned Jews didn't eat pork they had strange dietary restrictions, but he laughed as he spat it out and wanted more, insisted upon more, that they pound this religious thing into him since he was little that you get to believe it, he said, and you have to fight it with all your strength otherwise you succumb to it and he actually ate another piece commenting on how good it is, he was the first person I knew who questioned aloud the falsity of religious belief instead of just going along with what the system had but not taking it seriously, after all we were fighting with the godless communists but he said he had to join the party because that was the only way to get to Spain, he didn't believe in them anymore than he believed in God, he had no heroes, I always believed people who were polite were decent and I admired the way he struggled with ideas and prejudices and would fight them when he could. He had thought coming to Spain was the right thing to do and for no other reason did he come, and right away we got into a discussion about ends and means and he liked people who treated others as human beings not as a mean to something else yet he couldn't stand his family where you only treat people as ends but of course treat them as means, and even weak as he was his eyes gave off a certain glow that he was happy doing what he was doing even as he had no idea what's wrong with him all of a sudden he got so dizzy he could barely stand, that had never happened to him before, one moment you are well the next ill without a transition of feeling bad. I thought he might be malnourished that's why I gave him some food in the first place but it came right up even schnapps didn't slow it down but I cleaned him up and he was able to lie down once again said he was feeling better after vomiting but we stuck to broth not food the next go around. He lay on the cot and I still had my regular duties but continued to stop by his bedside and hold his hand and see how he was doing, covered him when he kicked his blanket off, washed his face with a cold compress to keep his fever down, we had no other medications, oh we did but not many and we had to ration them for more serious illnesses or gunshots. The allies not only didn't allow arms in they forbade medicines also, even he said if I have to see a doctor this is serious but it wasn't serious and the fever broke and he was able to hold down food, and looked forward to pieces of pork and by the time he was well we were already laughing together and I had told him I said a novena for him and he laughed and said god doesn't help a godless Jew, and he wondered was I going to live my life devoted to God if a miracle occurred and he would be saved but I said I didn't love him that much to give up my life and he held my hand firmly, fleshy love proved I was human and could prove I loved more than Jesus. He loved my logic and also that I wasn't afraid of sex. *Fakakta* logic, Joseph said and I had to translate for Conchita who I thought would have heard that word, I thought everyone at least in New York knew that word, silly, but Conchita never heard of Yiddish didn't want to learn Yiddish or Ladino only Spanish. Conchita asked if she minded if she smoked, I said I didn't mind even if she could see by the expression on my face I did, as I shook my head no and said yes, but finally asked her not to it's not good to breathe in that polluted air, and I continued on my memory that passion in the Christian world is a cardinal sin but your grandfather thought it the most wonderful aspect of being alive, the best part of life as long as it's taken in moderation, and we both laughed. He didn't understand anything about Christianity and that I found refreshing, someone going to a Christian country fighting for a Christian country hadn't a clue to the Passion of Christ, and here I had to explain that concept to Joseph again I thought everybody in America realized the Passion of Christ that Christianity occurs between the Last Supper and His death on the Cross at Mount Calvary—salvation history, you can't know God only love him. He really didn't understand what I was saying but nodded in agreement this time his head and words going in the same direction but the food was exploding in his mouth saying this was the best meal he ever had, not only does it have taste and now realize you have to chew it slowly to get every morsel of flavor out of the meat, not that he was a sloppy eater and if he ate slowly he wouldn't embarrass himself like his grandfather did. His grandfather liked to eat while reading papers, the first time I ever saw somebody eating a meal and reading a paper. He said at home he would eat watching the news and reading a paper not having a discussion at least not since his grandfather died, but he rarely at with the family and he couldn't remember him sitting around the table except at holidays or when guests came over, which was rarely. I had thought we would eat with Zoltan but he usually left before I came home from school in the afternoon. And after his grandfather died there was no one left to talk to, only Zoltan, who he found out afterwards his grandfather had asked him to look after Joey when he was gone, but they wouldn't meet in his apartment. The fruit of the forbidden tree was the most venial sin Jacobo said, he offered me a cigarette I was embarrassed good girls didn't smoke in public but he said bad girls can do anything and we laughed, I realized god remained outside thought and for Christianity that becomes sin, not all at once even if my family saw me as a heretic but slowly in conversation with your grandfather, and what pleasure did I have in those conversations especially when he said humans are not angels and only perfect beings can perfectly solve problems we can only solve problems that there is an answer to and call the others mysterious: what is wrong with man wanting to be like a God, the sin of pride, that's silly, all religion is silly people trying to stop you from what you want to do and they say you are not supposed to do.

Never have I thought so much about my grandfather as I do when meeting with this couple it's as if he's with me and I can hear him saying goodbye to me over again, it wasn't a speech he never lectured me always conversed with me, even as a baby I don't recall him talking baby talk with me, he always had a conversation with me, ever since the first time he held me in his arms and I stopped crying, so he told me and walking me back and forth in our small apartment said even when I am dead I will be near you even if you only see part of me even if I could never tell you all that goes on in my mind for you are yet too young—not yet old enough to know how he despises grandma, I only found that out later when he refused to go to her funeral, I hadn't even realized they were once a couple and now separated until an older friend told me that they simply hadn't divorced, somehow I thought grandma and grandpas live apart, now his telling me don't be in a rush to marry makes more sense, and now after he's gone and I'm of age I can truly begin to look inside him, after all he gave me enough hints, did he tell me about Esmeralda on his deathbed or did he just mention her name? and now even if he has no sense of corporeal presence his ideas are part of me and even as I lead my own life and to me the gates of paradise opened when I came into the city when I left my neighborhood and took the subway into Manhattan and now especially with Esmeralda and Cassandra and the livid memory of my grandfather even if he now is nothing he is like asleep, in sleep you are no more but upon awakening you grasp the idea of living—too bad there is no immortal soul that is indivisible that can survive the body when the body disintegrates and becomes pure, only humans are never pure we are a mixture of the good the evil the non-existent soul and the ever present body there is no scission, religious people may see human nature as corrupt and priests make us feel guilty, at least in Judaism it isn't the rabbi he's only the doorkeeper they have no forgiving powers, for us it's our mothers as we fight not to hear their voice inside us. So when I finally leave this earth I will not be in the hands of the almighty because God is no longer a real presence, still it is fun when trying to fall asleep to wonder which level of hell I would be in, not the first that's reserved for all those born before Christ, nor the seventh or eighth the seventh's reserved for schoolteachers the eighth for regicides, why should Dante have assigned Brutus to hell he was a democrat who killed a tyrant and should be honored? and Lucifer, maybe the fifth for the unbelievers or those who challenge Christ, but I don't challenge Christ don't even think about him in temple when I would read the Greek playwrights not Dante. What if he did appear to the ancients and never again then he certainly the Hidden One since the burning bush was never consumed, never went out. Grandfather insisted I read Nietzsche when I become old enough. I tried at sixteen but couldn't understand him yet impressed teachers by carrying Zarathustra to class and by the time I graduated understood even less. What I recalled was that he was thirty and by that time I would be an old married man, settled, with real furniture, laughing about my misspent youth. Who knew there would be life after college? But I can hear him saying your soul will perish with your body—you will never truly know what I think but I have given you enough kisses that you can keep my memory alive within you even if I am not able to pass on my thoughts even if you are the only one who truly knows them even if you were too young to understand what I am saying. That can't be true because he never told me about his war experiences and how he fought for the freedom of others when it had nothing to do with his own self, or later when he participated in Civil Rights demonstrations to the dismay of my mother and father, what do the colored have to do with us? Strangers needed his help and he answered the call yet he never spoke about this to me. He had no true love for my grandma but didn't have the courage of his convictions to divorce her, he did say, at least I think he said, love more than anything else transforms us, Eros and agape and they don't last forever. I still have no idea what he was talking about and again wonder if he was truly all there my mother always would pooh-pooh his thoughts but he was her father and when he didn't have the will to get out of bed my mother did take him in even as she moved closer to grandma so she could see her every day. Once I went home to look for Nietzsche a little miracle found him, was surprised my mother hadn't given it away, when something works do actually think it's a miracle, she did throw out most my childhood possessions now that I no longer lived there, she said she needed the space and my comic books, paperback books, and 45 records were all dumped in the trash. She threw them in the big mound of trash in front of our building and the only saving grace that came from this is she received a summons from the Sanitation department for illegally dumping garbage on the street—the arc of justice may run slow but it runs. Years ago Zoltan had retrieved my grandfather's library so at least that was spared and he said whenever I want it I can have it. So far I hadn't wanted it but now think I should go up to his place and get them before his roommate throws them out. I wonder if he left a diary it would be fun to read what he had to say to know I am not alone in loneliness that he faced the same problems as me a life out of joint. But he did tell me he burned his journals and all that is left is his few hardback books unless Zoltan's roommate has destroyed them as well and all traces of his existence will vanish from the earth. He probably thought he had years left and his death caught him by surprise and he didn't have to face old age, as Zoltan said, even if I had thought sixty was old, he was never sick a day in his life, he died with a full head of white hair so I never saw portraits of him with red hair, besides the only photographs I have are in black and white so I couldn't see red anyway, photographs are a snatched moment freed from time and space and I didn't need to filter it through consciousness as I do with painting, literature and the theater. He never had a portrait done of himself and Zoltan said he wouldn't sit for one but was sorry that he didn't paint one for me from memory or his desk mask, he said he could never paint from a photograph he needed the light and shadows on a face and photographs obliterate those. I've been to his apartment where he had drawn self-portraits all over the wall and in back of the portraits he painted copies of his modernist paintings, and it's fun to see how his face changed from a dashing young man to an old geezer, but he was no Rembrandt where you could see in the eyes of his self-portraits god do with me what you will but I am going to paint. Can I have a life or must I be at the mercy of my passions but I can't deny these feelings they make me who I am but if only I could have a strong desire to do something, maybe I could if I could be with Cassandra all the time then I could begin to live.

If I could go back if I could do it all over again would I do it the same way, would I say or do something different, make a stronger statement, act stronger, the shiver that still runs down my spine as I think of what I didn't do but I should have done, letting him aboard the *Polyphemus* without a firm time to meet again just sure we would meet, having no doubt we would meet again, not knowing how we would meet again, I think back then really meaning now, my body is failing me but I still have to work, no pension, and not even eligible for social security being an abortionist and like Spanish farmers being kicked off their land I will be at the mercy of welfare. The Fascists did nothing to protect tenants only the owners and didn't guide the change so one could live with it and slowly adjust, improvements are okay but social dislocation on a large scale was unendurable, and I have no pension plan, and can't sell my business only now that abortion has become legal, if not acceptable I should be able to get back to work and I have to actually think of old age, but since I am not a nurse practitioner will still be working off the books. Thank goodness my granddaughter moved back in with me otherwise I would be out on the street, Joseph says it's a good thing I had the heart attack it has given me a new lease on life, but I wouldn't go that far: would I have to move back in with Tomas, he would have enjoyed that hidden his sadistic intent but would have been smiling all the same me dependent upon him once again, living under his roof once again, or if not his roof because even in my scariest fantasies couldn't live where he lives but if he supports me he will think I owe him something, better dead than lose the liberty that I worked so hard to get, he of course would love to have me under his control again, it took me a long time to extract myself from living with him to want to easily go back to it. Joseph claims I am entitled to part of his social security because we had been married at least ten years but don't even know his social security number, Joseph says the government will find it for you, but I want nothing to do with him, if relief doesn't force me I see no reason to contact him again. Joseph says he doesn't even have to know and you are legally eligible—he is a smart boy knows how to research the law. Now Dominican girls don't need to be seen as virgins and Puerto Ricans still want babies even if I can do legal abortions. Young Hispanic women never seem to want to reflect on their condition, seem to be dropping out of school in record numbers and think having a baby is the answer to all their problems, I have to remake my business because now few girls feel the need to be sewn up and my business seems to involve more co-eds than poor girls, not so much rich families but young women who don't want to be trapped home all day with a baby at least not before they've had a chance to live a little, passion is natural for them but babies are not, at least they can pay. Now I have co-eds and an occasional high school student for abortions but the business of sewing girls up has declined girls are proud of not being virgins. Women still don't like to go to clinics too afraid their parents will find out so I can treat them until clinics become more organized, only difficulty is women still see abortion as wrong and are forced to act accordingly and keep it secret, somehow girls still think the FBI is going to tell their parents; however mature women are fighting the government and the state legislature actually did something for once and abortion is now legal in New York, which means girls from Jersey and Connecticut will be coming here for the day, like young boys do to buy liquor. I hide my laughter when young women come disguised with a wig or when mothers who are against abortion bring their daughter instead of being strapped with an unwanted child, but that is rare most parents have no idea what their kid does. But it's these women deans at college that protect their charges and it's not only so their colleges don't get a bad reputation, but because they are educated and realize twenty year-olds don't make good mothers. I survive on Barnard, NYU, Marymount, never the City universities and before the change in law, Vassar. I wonder if they will come into the city now. Joseph asked if a man has ever brought his daughter, never. Mothers still want to control their daughters and fathers are more for freedom, of course, they never think their daughter is doing it, or their wives either, mothers know. At least boys when they graduate college are allowed to go off and live alone, girls never or at least those from the boroughs until married they have to live with their parents, my favorite story of this one Italian girl from Brooklyn, Italian, the father wouldn't let her do it under his roof, so she did it in the car, aborted, was engaged to be married, found an apartment that her fiancé was living in already but she couldn't move in until after she married, and she saw nothing wrong with that. Hopefully I can keep my restructured business, and it is a business not a profession and cater to these college students, I've put out feelers to other deans, at least Conchita is not judgmental as Gloria was when she found out what her mother did to keep her in fine garments and to pay the rent. At least now I can talk about sex before you had to speak in hushed tones, nor of women seeking pleasure that was drowned out by talks of responsibility or what would God say or do you want to end up in hell. At least educated girls now can separate the two even if they believe premarital sex wrong and would become silent when they heard the carillon of bells calling them to mass, which they would go to after the procedure—this is the rupture between women and angels and it was very difficult for those who still saw the Bible as the word of God not a fairy tale—imagine thinking you are guilty from the moment you are born. At least young women are not making themselves attractive to men by playing meek and helpless and need a man to open a door for them instead demanding they have a right to sit on juries just like men and bingo the legislature agreed doubling the size of the jury pool. Now our august city council wants to ban homosexuals from holding hands in public because it is disgusting, exactly what they said in the South about white women and black men, it's not normal but at least women are standing up to this nonsense saying it isn't first impressions that count but reflective impressions, freedom is difficult has to be fought for, or as Jacobo once remarked we didn't lose because democratic socialism of voluntary associations and workers control of the workplace were bad ideas we lost because Franco had stronger artillery even had reconnaissance aircraft while we were fighting blind because the allies refused to resupply us with military or medical supplies, kept up the phony Non-Intervention Pact they were for neutrality while the Fascists supplied arms and equipment to Franco, and when I talk about this here in America it's like I am from another planet nobody knows what I am talking about or how little Americans know of history: time speeds up as you age and my memories are nodes in time episodes that don't have a linear order.

All of a sudden I come up against this wall I'm in a new play almost the leading role and I feel bored realizing I shouldn't be doing this, and this is what I want to do nothing pleases me more than acting or at least the thought of acting but being with actors all day long is very difficult, so charming on stage so boring off, but even if I can find another thing to do what would it be, I'm always somewhere else never in the moment, except on stage, and when I leave the performance late at night refuse to go along with them drinking rather walk home all by myself to calm myself down yet the city is becoming so crime-ridden that I can only walk on main streets and even then grandma says I should take a taxi, I feel as if I came out of chemo so exhausted and nothing to show for it; and I can't keep myself from using that image even as I realize how bad it is: I don't have cancer and people undergoing chemo have no choice I have chosen to do this. Chosen as if I could walk away, I walked into it and now it's too late to walk out of it, what else could I do? I could become a secretary or temporary worker, and here I am getting what I want an almost leading role in an off-Broadway production and I could say it's not Broadway then I would say it's not Hollywood, and I don't want Hollywood nor do I really want Broadway, I am getting what I truly want this is the moment I truly want and I can't stand it and am now wondering is this what I want—is this what I really want? usually I can't go with the flow make no plans whatever happens happens, a free spirit, a free bird—my thoughts never give me a moments peace; my mother would always say stop thinking but not grandma who had passion in her life, even if she was more in love with being in love than love itself—why can't I be old and look back at an exciting life like her, now everything appears black—metaphysically not in reality, in reality I'm doing fine, a new boyfriend, grandma on the mend, a starring or almost starring role yet I can see myself wearing a black veil—work will set you free ha, I always thought if I got what I wanted but now I have what I wanted so what. I never advanced in any of my day jobs so I would have time to audition and be ready to leave when the moment came and now it has come and I am frightened. Is what I say what I really want. What's going to happen when it's over; an actor is only as good as his current role your past doesn't count and the future is going to be the same ole, same ole, hoping for a role, immersing myself in it, really loving it just to say goodbye to it. My life is going fine right now and all I can see is disaster upon the horizon, why can't a woman go out with a younger man, men do it all the time, and the age difference is not so great grandma says, but she's the feminist not me all I believe in is equal pay for equal work, but I love his sense of humor, his curiosity, the way he holds his head to the side when he listens, how his eyes light up when I tell him my plans he is totally involved with me, his chin and mouth quiver with the excitement when he speaks and how my heart races when he stops by and feels sad when he goes home, but what I want is not to be bored, I have it all and am bored out of my mind—each new project excites at first but pretty soon I am bored and want to be somewhere else can't even enjoy being where I am, only on stage can I feel committed to a character and now worrying about what I'm going to do next otherwise I constantly want to withdraw from what I'm doing now and do something else, just pack up and leave—my one great fear is to forget my lines in the middle of a performance and simply say that's it, goodbye, and walk off the stage and walk out of the theater without looking back—how dramatic would that be? Leave them all hanging like that that I want nothing more to do with them—that would be taking the first step towards a new life that grandma says would be the same as the old one, you can't change your life by wishing, hoping, running away, and she of all people knows that—the crucial thing is to change yourself not your environment, trying to start your life over again somewhere else is running away is a false start because you think you can be someone else but we carry the same baggage with us where ever we go yet when I changed my name I did change my life. But the inside didn't change I'm still the same person inside that I was before the name change but I feel better with my new name, but it's our way of thinking that counts so that what we do in life corresponds to what we believe in, and I thought I was too old to change and then I met Joseph and he has gotten me to change and I no longer believe in changing the world only in changing myself—grandma laughs she's seen the Soviet experiment change into red bureaucracy and even laughed at Solzhenitsyn's *Letter to the Soviet Leaders* thinking he had to write to Brezhnev the moment he was expelled from the Soviet Union and thinking he was going to convince them to change their ways by his words and they were going to listen, she's too cynical for that but Joseph marveled at the words and still believes, says Solzhenitsyn stayed human under extreme conditions of the Gulag. Imagine a novelist having such a world stage. We watched the media circus on television loved the part where he condemned western materialism, it was irreal. But grandma can live with herself, Joseph still hasn't lived yet, at least he's out of his parents apartment now and found a job with a future but I'm in the middle of this joy ride and nothing satisfies me, I keep looking for new things and when I find them I am so dissatisfied I want the old things back or want to start all over again with a headlong flight to somewhere, ironically never Pittsburgh, I had enough of that place even as I realize I can't leave grandma she still needs someone to care for her like she cared for me even if I have a valise packed in the corner of my closet ready to burst out of there, and every six months wash all my clothes in it and keep my passport in my dresser drawer, that I learned from grandma in case you have to escape it is better to be ready because in flight you might not be able to choose the correct time. It was mostly the young Jews who survived the Holocaust they could flee in an instant their parents always said they would wait until the perfect moment until there were no moments left, the correct moment never came for them or if it came it was too late and they couldn't flee because it was always the wrong moment until it was too late it was never the correct moment until there were no moments left, according to Grandma. Is that what is going to happen to me? Or is it like my chemo analogy not the correct one to use because we are free here in the West and we are responsible for our own hell. Grandma would insist I leave and for that reason couldn't leave, who would care for her. She is getting stronger and that is something I thought would never happen when I saw her lying flat on her back in St. Vincent's with all sorts of tubes inside her and when you're flat on your back you don't know if you'll ever be able to get up again but the exercise is making her stronger—her doctor said the heart is a muscle use it or lose it. But if I don't leave now will I be able to choose another moment from which to go.

For 5,000 years men fooled women telling them they weren't smart enough to work or that they had to stay at home in the kitchen and not think, and they bought it, now in one generation that is all being overturned, we saw photos of Shirley MacLaine in China with liberated women, and I would always beg my mother to get a job not because I needed more spending loot but because I wanted her out of my hair, eat your breakfast, come up for lunch, she would even call grandma to put a red kerchief out of her window when it was time for me to come home—I didn't want or need lunch or even want to come home all I wanted to do was play ball and hang on the streets and I'm still pissed that they didn't allow me to go away to college but made me attend City, where you lived at home and she even complained that they had to spend $100 dollars a year for books, can't they give them to you for free like high school. And get rid of them you don't need a bookcase. At least Esmeralda insisted Cassandra go away to school you can only become an adult living away from me and gain your independence. In our local temple where there were all these sophisticated men who spoke three or four languages Hebrew, Ladino, Romanian and some Spanish or French no one in my family encouraged me to go, especially not my grandfather who wanted nothing to do with organized religion saw it as the opium of the masses created by man to hide their fear of death and in a more sophisticated culture God becomes more abstract and immortal god becomes perfect because humans are not so; I ragged the whole thing and my friend Harvey and I would laugh at these old geezers especially when they tried to tell us something or give us a piece of advice and wanted nothing to do with them, but now realize maybe I could have learned something from them. The rabbi was a bad example turned me off to Judaism but the congregants were very smart people and when they would see me carrying books home from City often discuss the works with me surprising me in that I thought I was the only one in the neighborhood who had heard of these men. You mean I wasn't the first generation to become absorbed in utopian fantasy. This morning as I was heading to work a stranger comes up to me and asks am I Jewish, what do I have in common with the Jews? but they needed a few more men to make up a minyan—a quorum the ten men required for a Jewish service so that a Jew is never alone with God—I am because you are, and I thought why not help them and out of basic decency went inside the temple so they could get started, never expecting to be touched by the service, for me true religiosity is having a cup of coffee and a bagel with the sports section of the *Times*. What about women Cassandra wanted to know, they don't count they don't understand the sophisticated prayers, I said. That was soon to change Esmeralda said proving she understood more about Judaism than I did. Cassandra laughed but Esmeralda said I did the right thing even if Jews don't count women they will someday it's simply all their lives they have been taught not to count women but what's going on in the world now will force them to reexamine their ways, and here I laughed saying they've been doing this for thousands of years they're not going to change now. Why Christians no longer hold mass in Latin, times change, religions change to meet the times or they fall by the wayside. I explained that the part of the Bible read was where to save Sodom God said he would if they could find ten righteous people and she wanted to know why ten was so holy, ten commandments, ten men needed for prayers to begin, ten plagues, no it's not all ten it's the 8th day for boys that is crucial, the wound of perfection! Christianity only says you need love to change your life but Jews don't believe personal wishes only impersonal forces it's only in relationship to God that the world moves. She thinks Jewish thinkers, Marx, Freud, Einstein, have been some of the most influential thinkers in the world always challenging the existing order of things the status quo but I think back to my synagogue days and those educated people accepting the rabbis *mishegoss* but she disagreed thinking being part of a community was something holy, special, even if she ran away from Spain to escape that. I remember never liking the rabbi and whenever a prayer was transliterated into English would be challenging those thoughts—I had a fine internal dialogue going on inside my head so much so I thought language developed for internal communication first because whenever I tried to express those thoughts they came out muddled, insipid and grownups would laugh at my formulations, that is except my Grandfather and later Zoltan. They both conversed with me and took me seriously while my parents and grandma always treated me as a four-year-old, they couldn't get it into their head that little boys grow up. Once when I made a joke to my mother my father said how can you joke at a time like this when your grandma is dying. No one bothered to tell me they kept insisting she was getting better in the hospital, how was I supposed to know they never confided in me anything, children were to be seen not heard and I learned from those experiences not to tell them anything, so they never knew I didn't want to go to City College and live at home or that I even knew her father's lover, who my mother would call a home wrecker even as her father came home to fulfill his responsibilities and raise her: the fun in that thought is imagining me introducing her to Esmeralda just to see the look on her face. After grandma's funeral where my grandfather was conspicuously absent the few relatives and friends came over to our house and my mother prepared food for them, closing the kitchen door, heating up frozen foods taking them out of their pouches, containers, aluminum foil, and serving them as if she had made them fresh. No one knew except me. That was the moment I became fully conscious of death and the lies we tell about it and no longer believed in religion and had not gone into temple since saying *Kaddish*, the mourner's prayer for *avuelo*, until this morning. From that moment on I started planning my escape from the Bronx, even if it got delayed by a few years because of college, and I had constantly refused to date Jewish girls from the neighborhood, and back then some of the girls were getting married right after high school—can you believe it? now at least they wait until college graduation. I wanted to do away with my circumcision, Esmeralda finally informed me you couldn't and Cassandra told me the best sex she ever had was with a circumcised boy in college, and that satisfied me no end. I never thought of sex as sin nor did it change anything in my relationship to Cassandra only it showed me I wouldn't be forever condemned to live with my parents even if my grandfather once mentioned sooner or later you end up where you began I rather it be later than sooner, and I could see myself at 83 having another Bar Mitzvah but not before and here I was walking into temple of my own free will listening to the Torah's call for justice—reading the Torah is a categorical imperative, the moral person is the decent person.

Jacobo, Jacobo you've been dead all these years, I even went to the March on Washington with the Abraham Lincoln brigade secretly hoping to see you only you were dead by then. Does it matter, does it make a difference? you are still in my mind you're always part of my internal conversation maybe I still desire to have sex with you only angels have no bodies, inside my head there is always the two of us, you were the first person ever really loved, to listen to my thoughts, to have conversations with, and not simply mouth clichés but to actually think what I want and not be afraid to say it to myself with utmost sophistication and complexity, and my talking to myself has actually been greater especially with you by my side than a real live people next to me—it's only with you that I learned to express myself my dear husband, with others it's only words with you I learned to express thoughts that sometimes make sense but my inner dialogue with you goes to the core—you were always at my side even if we haven't been together in a million years, it's silly this desire over so many years but with you I know no time, besides why should what happens now be more important than what happened then, just because I can remember the now and the then is a blur and you are physically no longer—when I first came to this country all I hoped to do was run into you but I wouldn't go looking for you, yes I can admit that now to my face that I didn't come to New York because the streets were paved with gold but for the fleeting chance I might run into you even if I denied it I saw it clearly right away just didn't want to admit it but I came to this country just as Puerto Ricans started coming and I saw how they were treated with this paternalistic welfare system that continued to deprive them of dignity—how decent men and women were forced into beggary and lying, with drink and no jobs and so were forced to go on relief—the state was trying to help but only make it worse and the children of these immigrants saw relief as a right and refused to stand up on their own two feet and I hid my Hispanic heritage because Americans couldn't tell the difference of a Spaniard with a European culture from a PR with a farming culture, and the PR's continued their old ways of plenty of children and the man had to be absent from the home in order to get welfare. And even if this is now all past you are not past you are my future, oh Jacobo why did you have to die without me seeing you, maybe if I saw you I could have gotten over you, but I doubt it my dear husband, I would have been disappointed that's for sure no one can live up to the image I made of you inside my head but it would have been fun seeing you one last time, especially if I could have seen you and you not have seen me. I should ask Joseph where you are buried and make a pilgrimage and put stones on your grave as you did to fallen comrades even if they weren't Jewish, I had never seen that before, it was the first time I saw men buried without a cross, which surprised me at first but later on got used to it, volunteers wanted nothing to do with Christ and didn't even believe in an afterlife, imagine that nobody in the war thought about the next life or that if you behave honorably in this the next would be honky-dory or you would get what's coming to you in the next, that fear was not part of them and you scoffed at such superstitious nonsense, when I mentioned Purgatory you laughed at Christian hieroglyphics the idea of purging the soul in between heaven and hell, for you hell was the Bronx, where you went back to live, and Joseph says you died so quickly you probably didn't even realize it's happening and Joseph says he puts stones on your grave just to let others know he's visited—you never believed in this idea of divine justice thought that was a crock of shit why should man be born guilty we are guilty only with our acts, I never heard such thoughts before and you opened up a new way of thinking for me and really conversing with me taking me seriously not laughing at me and because of you I am never able to shut my mind off, with you there was a constant laughter, banter, sex we never worried about having something to say to each other we could also be silent with one another holding hands while walking. All of a sudden I began to learn things that I never thought about before and we talked and talked what we usually refuse to even tell ourselves let alone friends, and it was our friendship that sustained you more than the desire for your body even if I now realize they are linked—we walked around the camp avoiding others and others knew to let love blossom and wouldn't bother us and we didn't need anybody else's company but would walk round and round the same little land that we reclaimed, sometimes we could walk a little further but never too far from the base camp because that was always dangerous and you always claimed that the highest good is what we were doing now fighting for a free Spain and there is no need for a God to tell us that or for us to be rewarded in the afterlife, you hated all astral beliefs, only the moment of history always disappoints and if we had won the next generation probably would have taken up arms against us, there can never be a utopian order only fanatics believe that, all we can do is live the way we live nothing noble or great in living it's just like fire rising and rocks falling only we know about it because we can think about it and give it some purpose, and I remember on our honeymoon how you loved looking at the arches formed by marble pieces of two different colors in Madrid, something I never paid any attention to because I had seen it all my life or walking on Mejia Lequerica with the sun shining down upon our heads and the ground uneven between our feet how you forced me to begin to think in a different language and take deep breathes between thoughts and examine what we say more clearly and you saying you always take me along with you but now I see life more puzzling than you presented but you gave me the basic tools that language is more than mere words piled upon words and helped me grasp some mysteries of existence and when I had to go back to my parents after the defeat because there was nowhere else to go, young women in the defeated republic could no longer travel alone, and I was exhausted emotionally and physically not to mention pregnant with your child that you never knew existed and that was too much for me and the child was born dead.

That could have been the moment I stopped believing not your words since the priest said the baby could not go into heaven because he wasn't baptized and I thought what kind of shit was this my baby must sit in limbo because of me going with a Jew. I laughed your laugh thinking what you said what we still carry the original sin? Should the sin of our parents be passed unto us? Children must defy their parents otherwise you become like them only if they break free of their influence do they have a chance in life otherwise they become them and live the same way as them.

While out walking by myself, what I love about this city is the same thing grandma loves about this city, the ability to walk by yourself and be alone in front of a million people, forget the mountains, forget the parks, walking city streets is the most fun there is, here no one thinks you're indecent, and you can even go into bars alone now: no longer can they put up signs against no unescorted ladies after 8pm, as if all unattached women are prostitutes, why not no single men they are all pansies, and now that I can go into bars unescorted refuse to go into bars, instead head for the waterfront, I love the busy city streets, the crowds, the noise, and while Joseph loves the parks I still don't feel comfortable walking there alone, that's when I realized he has an influence on me, when I started walking everywhere again instead of the subway or bus, of course, the crime on the subways doesn't hurt, I don't even realize where I am walking just out walking and brooding thinking about my part, I can tell when I'm on my game and the role encompasses me and all I do is think about it, inch work, and the best way is walking then I feel I'm truly an actor, all I remember is making sure I didn't keep making right turns then you'd get right back where you started but now I have no idea how I got to the waterfront, lucky I wasn't hit by a car but my inner radar kept me safe, and even if it's deserted it still is the middle of the day and safe and now as I walk I try and recapture the route that took me here but have no idea, did I walk down 8th street, Christopher street, no I wouldn't do that too crowded with tourists and homosexuals, I like the more quiet streets, maybe 9th via Bleecker street, I always liked Bleecker full of small shops but I don't recall looking in on any windows, yes, yes, I did look into the sandal shop thinking maybe I should get a pair made instead of store-bought ones, I walk enough in sandals maybe I deserve a good pair and wondered if I should spend the money at Leo's the gyp then laughed that was an old toy store that we nicknamed up in the Bronx, a Jewish store owner who always sold merchandise higher than everybody else, still I admire myself I can't get lost in the Village, even with its crooked streets, when I first came here couldn't figure anything out and now I know my way like a native. What I dislike about the waterfront is the piers are rotting so you have to stay along the shore and then you can feel the cars up above their noise, exhaust, from the highway above and the drone of the exhaust never allows you to complete a thought, it's a loud enough noise to penetrate your conscious whereas walking down the side streets and avoiding red lights means you don't have to stop and you can follow a thought and play with it. Men actors now tell me they enjoy that when jogging of how they can follow a thought to completion when they get into the zone as they call it, and insist I try it, instead of tai-chi but I am too much of a lady and besides they look so exhausted after a run that it's hard to believe they had a thought and I can't see how it is pleasurable; it's like Joseph's mother saying you'll get a heart attack walking all the way to the Village from Co-op City where she moved after her husband died with practically her whole building, in the northeastern section of the Bronx in a dull high-rise apartment complex, but which he says, is actually a beautiful apartment with a terrace, a nice view and a lot of sunlight, even if it's in the middle of nowhere but apparently the subway is going to be run there, yea sure, but it's a nice idea for people to buy their apartment, imagine that, and when they leave they sell the apartment back for what they paid plus interest, and meanwhile they have a nice place to live or as Esmeralda calls it white people housing away from blacks and Hispanic because blacks and Hispanics don't have the money for the down payment and don't understand owning an apartment instead of renting, it's not as if it's a house which you buy. However he enjoys walking all over the city especially in the parks along the East River but now has to stop when a group of black teenagers saw his walking over the Third Avenue Bridge and decided to swoop down on him only he had enough presence of mind to run faster but then decided not to go on long walks through Harlem, he even carried an anti-gravity knife until grandma persuaded him it was better not to carry it lest the police arrest him not the muggers for carrying a concealed weapon, now he takes the subway from Gun Hill Road down into the city, it's terrible what this city is coming to now that we have to watch out for the other guy. Each day the dailies lead off with a murder or an attempted or successful rape. Here in the West Village it is safer than the East Village where squatters are moving into some buildings and heroin is the drug of choice. Still grandma doesn't want to move our rent is affordable. But the Village is no longer as safe as it was when I first moved here a decade ago. I'm afraid for the next generation they will give in easy to temptation, when I was growing up my mother said never take a cigarette from a stranger it might be marihuana and one joint and you'll be hooked for life. Idiot. It's cigarettes that hook you for life look at the trouble grandma is having not being allowed to smoke by her doctor, but he said pot is good for you. It certainly was to Joseph. The first person I saw actually smoking dope was up at Calhoun not our local high school, when she pulled out this rolled-up cigarette with a pungent odor right in front of the school, this quiet unassuming girl was a pothead and offered me a joint but I was too frightened, in fact she became one of the first in this new wave of feminists she actually went to law school and according to the alumni bulletin is lawyering now. A nice Jewish girl couldn't get into Harvard, Columbia or Yale but instead of going to Brooklyn Law School went to Chicago instead, a real smart brain and she would let me cheat off her and once I saw her on the subway but didn't want to go up to her thinking she wouldn't remember me or think me a junky wanting a fix because it was late at night and while she was dressed nice I was in jeans coming from a rehearsal. She was so well-dressed I was surprised to find her on the subway only the taxis were on strike so she was forced to ride the subway, she probably wouldn't have dissed me but I just didn't have enough strength to try and we ignored each other. Still she was so well-dressed and I made sure I could never become as successful as her by quitting school to act, to make sure that could never happen to me, even as my counselor said don't do something you later on will regret and that was the exact reason I did it, even if I couldn't admit it to myself back then that I didn't want my future self to fall into the trap, didn't want to become a conservative know-it-all middle-aged frau, never believing I would get old or have different values always thinking I would be forever young not to become like my mother, ah if I could do it over again. How the mother never let's go. The past has shaped my future, but Joseph thinks I should finish up at Hunter they have a good night program but that would be the road to perdition and I won't allow him to influence me that way, he has to accept me as I am, he has to accept me not his image of me. I will never be a good frau. Joseph still has conventional ideas even if he thinks it's okay for a woman to work, he still thinks women should make dinner, sew and do the laundry—why I never learned to type or sew, my mother did try and teach me but I refused to learn and it cost a fortune in the dry cleaners to pay for routine sewing but it's worth it, I only learned to cook when grandma couldn't anymore and it's too expensive to eat out all the time. At Walton they had courses in home economics but was surprised at Calhoun they didn't have that shit, they insisted we use our minds that was the culture shock teachers expected us to go to college, imagine that, even helped and not especially to City College they wanted us to go away from home and warned us against marrying too young life will grab you by the balls quick enough she said don't go rushing into it, why I never truly worry about the future but am only concerned with the now.

I must admit when I first saw these boys with long hair, hair down to their waist, effeminate boys a sense of nausea overcame me—is it a woman or a man? and I had to walk to the gutter and a little vomit trickled out, however one of the boys/girls came over to me and asked if I was okay— not really he was the one who caused me to swoon, the closest I ever came to a swoon like that was when I first saw Jacobo and after we parted said I would never let myself be hurt like that again, never going all the way in again, feeling his absence and letting his absence teach me two things: one that I had love at one time and two, not to let myself get carried away like that again, that a love like that took away all my reason, but he held my hand and it was nice feeling the warmth of his hand on my ice cold hand even if he was the cause of my distress and tried to control my emotions, what I feel should not be what I think even as I knew it was and maybe by concentrated effort I could regain control of my emotions and at least he helped me walk away from the street so people wouldn't think it was me who made the putrid stink, but I couldn't walk too far as I am still a little weak and also felt comfortable on his arm, told him I was okay but what I wanted was a stiff shot but still can't drink, doctor's orders, even as Conchita says now it's okay for a woman to go into a bar unescorted, I still follow the old rules, I feel liberated now that I wear pants so I don't have to push my luck and instead he helps me to the Market Diner for a cup of tea without a madeleine but with a Danish just to get some food in me. He doesn't want to join me, a pity. I'm sure a little food will make me feel better upset of myself that a boy with long hair could shock me so: what's it to me if a boy wears his hair down to his waist that I should get so upset, when I was a nurse in war could see men's insides hanging outside and I didn't blanche but gently tried to help them die, but emotions are from the gut and go from the gut to the brain not the other way around and I couldn't help what I do it came on me so suddenly I've seen long hair on boys before and recently saw Elvis Presley on television and remarked what short hair he has, and it couldn't have been because this is the first time I've seen it up close, I live in the Village after all and these kids from the boroughs come down every Saturday night, and he was so nice helping an old lady instead of the usual young laughing at old people; it's almost as if he sought me out to listen he was so friendly and he enjoyed being with an older person instead of stiffing them maybe he realizes he'll actually be old someday most never do think the twenties will last forever as Conchita says do things now because when you become old you'll do nothing: walk out in the middle of the term so that you can't go back by making sure to get straight F's by not officially withdrawing, not simply withdrawing but running away instead of saying family emergency but she wanted to guarantee she would never go back. I couldn't convince her she would have a future and in that future she would be smarter and regret her decision, if I could have done that she would already be on the road to recovery realizing she would have a future but she wanted to burn all her bridges behind her: an actress or nothing, she didn't want to be a sellout; didn't want to have anything fall back on. The tea feels good, and I can only enjoy it while dunking my Danish, that too I learned from Jacobo. And she saw how actors between jobs sometimes would get comfortable in their current position and didn't want to give herself the chance to become bourgeois she rather hangs on the edge of hunger but that hunger became a trap of low-level-paying jobs with all of the vanity and envy—she still sees the surface as it were depth, but who am I to complain she wants to live a life of freedom no matter how difficult it is and I have to respect her for this, I could never see her going out with a mafia bozo like Gloria, what the hell was she thinking, and that's it she wasn't thinking just getting caught up in the glamour of a man taking her to expensive nightclubs, I'm catching my breath beginning to feel better tea works wonders for my system now that I can't have a stiff shot, and what is good about acting is you can do it all your life of your own free will no one forces you to act and you can continue to hone your craft, life-long learning not bored for doing the same ole, same ole, only the rejections can be so painful that it may be difficult for her to keep it up. Hopefully her crazy act will give her courage not despair, and she's now going with a younger man and for that I am proud of her, it's not every day a woman can skirt convention and Joseph is a wonderful fellow even if he thinks living is the best revenge and I must be happy because I survived his grandfather but it's not a victory only the young think that really all you see is the senselessness of life, an ephemeral world of folly. I hope they marry. Why? Did my marriages go so well? I feel strong enough now one more sip of tea, too bad I can't order another cup but then I wouldn't make it home it one piece. At least she didn't marry after high school imagine she could have a son now almost ready for college and she could be a grandmother at thirty-five that I see so many young girls now old disheveled women of thirty-five and they won't even have affairs to try and keep themselves young. At least her ideas are important to her and Joseph also insists she continue to act, of course, she would probably leave him if he insisted otherwise and he even told me he doesn't want a stay-at-home mom like his mother, her only purpose in life was to ruin his childhood, he likes old people and even thinks it will be fun to be old and dispense advice, but he will have his comeuppance nobody listens to old people and you even become unsure of the knowledge you gained through time and experience but you know it's not wisdom—the only wisdom I have is finally learning cheap is less that it's better to buy one good fan rather than three cheap ones the good one lasts longer than the three cheap ones and thus is more practical, next time I see one of those boys with long hair I'll give him the black power salute, I rather be with the young I get no pleasure from the aged only their health history.

Can you believe it? Joseph actually had a nose job. He was ashamed of being Jewish. Grandma, however, says he wanted to be more American— Rhinoplasty as she calls it, to fit into the culture, to be more American, I never would have believed it to be more American than the pope but he claims it broke him out of his shyness allowed him not to feel scared all the time to be a social misfit all the time and he could be the dude he wanted to be, of course he never became 'the dude' but feels at least he isn't ugly. The first time he actually saw what he looked like in a three-way mirror in Gimbals up on 86th street while he was shopping for his first suit, he never saw himself in profile before that and could see why people laughed at his hooked nose and decided to do something about it and for one day of pain and two days in the hospital over Easter break missing only a couple of classes with bandages on his face, because that was the first appointment he could get, didn't even want to wait until summer when classes were out wanted it done immediately before he changed his mind and he made sure not to watch television while recovering only the people in the ward always had a television on couldn't live without it so he insisted that he could, and only stayed in his bed reading Nietzsche no matter how uncomfortable he was, he said, what held him together and pushed him forward was all the girls he was going to meet, but to his surprise afterwards people still thought he had a hooked nose, nobody really looks at people and those who didn't know about the operation assumed he was the same. He didn't meet more women he was still the same shy person that didn't change but afterwards he says he became a reader and achieved a greater balance in his life even if his shyness didn't automatically disappear as he thought it would, and he also began lifting weights to give himself a physique and he thinks girls would like that. Too bad he didn't have a sister so as not to see women as these strange creatures who only fall for physical attributes never the struggles of what girls want and boys always give girls exactly what they don't want and leaving us trapped in a world that we thought we wanted never occurring to us, unless you have a grandma like I do; we have no interest in that type of life or that even if we wanted it there is no way we could be happy in it. Boys with sisters have a more realistic interpretation of women. How many of my old school chums fell for that hook, line and sinker; it's true I'm now with Joseph but my name is on the doorbell as well I live with him but I will not marry him even if grandma approves of him I cannot give myself to him body and soul, I am myself. Don't get me wrong I said to him if I didn't have him I told him there would be a great absence in my life as there was before I knew him and I am grateful that I now have him and nobody will take you from me but at the same time I have to be myself and pursue my dreams and the thought of little ones frighten me. He can't even bring me up to the Bronx to meet his mother because she is shocked we are living together in sin. People still believe that. All along I learned how to make a living so I wouldn't have to be dependent upon a man and am even learning computers now because typing may become a thing of the past but I never would have done what he did just to fit in—how many directors told me to straighten my hair or dye it blonde, okay I did that for a part but I wasn't going to do no breast augmentation to fulfill men's fantasies. I drew the line at big boobs, okay to escape ethnic identity changed my name because I thought I wasn't getting roles because of it and I was better than the other girls, and for a role dyed my hair, but nothing permanent, no thank you for pain in order to be good looking. I don't have the enmity of the past that he has for me the past is over and done with he carries it with him like a hunchback wherever he goes, the past, his grandfather, weighs like a ton on his shoulders. I've enjoyed aging and living in the moment Spanish history is ancient history to me who cares about the civil war I don't want to suffer because of what others had done—their pain is not my pain, if his mother doesn't want to see me that's her loss not the intended joy she could have in sharing meals with us and meeting grandma and me. She will remember her pain but I will not remember her absence except for maybe a bad feeling in my mouth but she will have loneliness stuck in her craw. At least Joseph had the memory of the intended joy he thought he would get as well as the pain of the operation and walking around the street in bandages, even if he refused to go out until the bandages were finally removed by the doctor a few days after he came home, and then he said he waited until the swelling went down, even if had to miss some class, he didn't care his attendance record was already shattered by the operation and he kept up his assignments at home. Not only did he do this to impress some unknown woman if he only had a woman while this was going on I could understand it better but he said he didn't want to postpone it until it was too late but I think he did it too early, if he had waited a few more years wouldn't have needed to do it, but that's not how he thought he said it had to be done exactly at this moment before he turned twenty-one or insurance wouldn't cover it and he thought this was the most important thing he had ever done, more important than good grades, can you imagine that—if I had been as good a student as him school could have been bearable, and even if he had to spend another semester in school it would have been worth it, but his reading did him well instead he got totally better grades from all his reading. and he was surprised afterwards when one of his professor's met him in the hall and said he should go to grad. school and would be willing to write a powerful letter of recommendation. He thought all letters of recommendation were good letters. He learned there is a difference between good and powerful. It was a big-named professor and he thinks with it he could have gotten into Yale but he had the draft to consider and besides he wasn't interested in graduate school. Probably a good move if New Haven is like Pittsburgh the school may be okay but the town is dudsville, life and culture non-existent. There he made the correct decision better to live as a day laborer in New York than a king in dudsville. But his nose would not have affected the way I felt for him but he said it affected the way he approached me, yea by stalking. If only he had more confidence in his innate abilities and didn't see us women as these strange creatures.

It was unnatural what my father said, it went against the laws of nature and it wasn't that she wasn't Jewish he didn't care about that, my mother did, not that she was older than me, he didn't care about that, my mother did, not that her grandmother was my grandfather's lover, he didn't care about that, my mother did, all he ever said to me is that I could be anything I want except what he was and that I couldn't get drafted into the army, the army doesn't make a man of you, he insisted I go to college, no if ands or buts, and he wouldn't have minded that she was a modern woman, he always wondered why my mother didn't work, and he was extremely nice to Cassandra when we met on the street and this old geyser came up to me and Cassandra was surprised I knew him and he invited her up to the house, but Cassandra doesn't like to go back to the Bronx. I think he was proud of me but now the more I think about it I think he was proud of himself for insisting I get an education before he died and avoid the army, he knew he was doing his duty fulfilling his responsibility to me and after he did that the quality of life just ended for him. Smoking three packs a day for thirty years finally did him in, not the first one, but by the second he was too old and weak to have open heart surgery, he would have died with the anesthesia and they couldn't keep him alive via drugs so he had a fatal heart attack and left my mother a widow at the ripe old age of 64, I couldn't imagine living without him even if he never interfered in my life he was always there for me and he and my grandfather stood up for me when my mother would be called into school for my free-spirited behavior that my grandfather knew as boredom. Interestingly he was called once, but that was a lie, my mother told him and expected him to punish me for some misdeed, only I was too angry to let it bother me, she had promised the teacher that she wouldn't tell my father and grandfather and in her passive-aggressive style immediately tells them and they make up the lie that he was called at work, as if they would ever bother a man at work with school problems. They always speak to the mother. When I went back to the Bronx I ran into an old friend and we chat at promising to keep in touch, exchange phone numbers, and she didn't even realize I no longer lived at home. She had heard about my father's death through the grapevine and sent a card of condolence, and actually came and visited my mother during *shivah*, the mourning after the burial not before which surprised Cassandra and she commented that you bury very quickly but Esmeralda said it's good to bury quickly and then mourn. All is vanity, the mirrors were covered lest we look at ourselves at a time like this, and the neighbors made a meal for the few people who were at the gravesite, cousins I hadn't seen since my bar mitzvah friends of my father that I hadn't even known he had, but no woman throwing herself on his grave saying I can't go on without you, that would have been something. As far as I knew my mother was the only woman he was with but as Esmeralda said all you need is one. Cassandra actually made her way up the Bronx, Esmeralda feigned illness, like my father had done the last few years of his life whenever they were invited anywhere he was always sick on that day, and she was treated politely but coldly by my mother still there are certain rituals you perform for the dead and she came almost as if this was an anthropology expedition—so the Jews do this, mirrors are covered, there's rip in the lapel showing a sign of mourning, sit on boxes and wear slippers. My mother made a fine distinction between nature and human nature and the gap between them and she wonders why I went to college if all I do is go out with goyim, what's going to happen when her youth fades her beauty dissipates and her ugliness is to the bone, is this what they taught you in college? but since it is only human nature I can think about I always wondered why I had to do what everyone expected me to do, isn't real education leaving the stupor of the usual mores and defining yourself against society's expectations besides couldn't imagine Cassandra as an old woman. I had had this talk once with my father where he insisted I go to college and not become an uneducated slob like him and then he said I could do whatever I want as long as I had an education to fall back on. When I wanted to quit school in the fifth grade because I hated it so much he said I would be derelict in my duty if I let you leave, you'll be miserable for the rest of your life if I let you quit so instead transferred all my thoughts to dreams of blowing up the school and would plant the explosives at different points in the school to make sure not a brick was left standing nor the teachers, we knew nothing about progressive education that Cassandra found at least the repeat year of her last year of high school that she said was the best year of her schooling, to be left back seemed to be the biggest fear but big deal she graduated a little later there's no rush. If my mother had been cool and a little more sophisticated she would have hugged and kissed her welcomed her into the home and I would have dropped her in an instant, who wants a woman your mother approves of. Even if it is her physical beauty that actually attracted me to her it's her gentleness, kindness, wit, humor and intelligence that keeps me tied to her I am not only smitten by physical appearance it's her whole healthy way of life that captures me, I still remember the way she sat with her legs spread open the first time we met and I could smell a healthy woman. I haven't the slightest idea what she's wearing I realize that when I look around the living room for her and say she's wearing a brightly colored scarf but she isn't in fact she's actually wearing a dress and a hat, and I can't recall her ever doing that, she dressed up for paying respects to the dead. Luckily she smiles when she sees me and her smile could have launched a thousand ships and I can stop talking to Bonnie my seventh grade girlfriend who actually said do what you want with me, back then, and I was so shy that I lightly kissed her on the cheek and she said that's all later on as teenagers sitting on the stoop talking making a racket at 2AM some bozo has the audacity to yell at us to shut up and we get the bright idea of making him suffer by ordering pizza and Chinese food on the phone giving his name and apartment number. I loved walking with Cassie and the status it gave me in front of my family, even if they saw it differently, and I don't mind that she is more experienced than me I love being on bottom anyway. My mother could have pulled a fast one and say a *Kaddish,* the mourner's prayer for the dead, the rabbis seemed to be making a big business out of this when a child marries a non-Jew, she's dead to the family but she isn't the type and now we have to say the real one. When Bonnie's father wouldn't let her drive the family car she stole the keys, my father had left them in plain sight and when I passed my driver's test told me to be careful and let me drive only I wasn't allowed to drink and drive, if I drank I had to take the subway or bus home. I was not allowed to drive with alcohol under my breath we would pick up the car the next day. It was difficult for him to keep a relationship up with his child during the sixties when we were challenging everything he stood for but we spoke every Sunday night and I occasionally would go up to dinner in the Bronx so he wouldn't consider me dead and he never cared that I was living with a non-Jewish older woman but said I should be careful and not marry her family as well. When I was afraid I was going to be drafted during Vietnam and said I would flee the country he took me seriously and said you don't say that aloud you just do it, but it was Esmeralda who was the practical one, and said she knew a doctor the doctor was a psychiatrist and when I went to the draft board on Gerard Ave. came in with a note from Dr. Hartogs that I was addicted to marihuana and the army didn't want a drug fiend who isn't moral enough to kill women and children. It was better than being a consciousness objector then I would need a rabbi to write something and I hadn't been in temple since before the flood. And my father approved of this even if he thought the communists evil he didn't want me to go even as I yelled at him it makes no sense what you say. Esmeralda said wait until you have a child of your own then you'll understand or wait until you get older then you'll understand as Cassandra said, but I never wanted to think like him, I expected to age, obviously, but thought I would always think the same, he said to me do you still want to be a shortstop for the Giants? I never understood but always enjoyed spring because me and my friends would work out as if we were going to spring training even if we were always in shape playing Little League in the spring and summer and two hand touch football and half-court basketball in the fall and winter. No wonder I could never play a musical instrument sport got in the way, literally after school I had to go to Hebrew school to prepare for my bar mitzvah and only when I couldn't take it anymore and refused to go and my grandfather taught me the prayers at home was I free at last, free at last to play ball with my friends but still refused to take music lessons, if I had as much ambition to play the violin as I did to play center field I could be a virtuoso by now instead I became a prisoner of childhood. In the meantime when I moved out he had taken over my bedroom so he no longer had to sleep with my mother in their double bed that was too small for one person let alone two, he was happy having a room of his own. Now that I had my room back minus all my childhood toys that my mother had tossed, she was finally called to Co-op City and since most of the building was moving there and there was nothing holding her to this neighborhood anymore she moved in. I did all the moving and the paperwork. I dreaded it but found it quit easy once you simply sit down and start to fill out forms it's not as difficult as it appears to be. As Cassandra says I am a whiz at paperwork. What a talent?

Is what she doing correct? I have to think about this nudity, Joseph objected to it, asked if she had to appear naked on stage, is it proper, won't you get arrested? She was. The music is too loud I don't have to think about that, it's difficult to tell the boys from the girls anymore, but so what if they want to express themselves that way but now the theater has gone berserk with this nudity—back in the day priests wouldn't even allow us to perform *Berenice* because of her unconsummated passions that would be a bad example for the young, if a play wasn't morally uplifting, socially beneficial it couldn't be acted, they had one objection only, truly, nudity wasn't even thought of—next he's going to say I only want verse in a play when tell him about Racine and says he never heard of Racine or read him. A fine education he received. But can I compare this to Racine, is this gratuitous nudity simply women without clothes showing off the female body or is it passion exercising itself, still it's not the male who is nude only young nubile female bodies, that I can understand nobody wants to see my body but it would be more profound to show aged women up there not only young girls and what about older men, the ones with face lifts, male enhancements, wrinkles, gray hair or balding instead of always emphasizing the cult of young beauty as if people never grow old, as if we are eternally young, okay I can buy all that but this dirty language that I am having a difficult time getting my head around, while all Joseph objects to is the nakedness not nudity in general but nakedness in particular, Conchita's, and phrases it in the usual doublespeak of Marxists, priests and politicians is it good for society, are they taking theater away from individual concerns and emotions and how they get mixed up in our head with objective conditions, as if there are any objective conditions without a connection to emotions and feelings—an insolvable difficulty but the dirty language is not allowing me to use my time in the theater as a space for reflection, we humans are part of the animal kingdom but we can also tell tales because we have language and are able to comment upon our condition, that's why we have theater, I never liked theater that lied to people and made life Pollyanna and saying this is the way life is, only drama that gets me out of myself and I get pleasure in realizing my difficulties are not that much, now I get it, I think, nudity shakes things up, it's compelling forcing us to see things in a new way not simply being entertainment where we sit and say how nice and walk away without thinking a moment about it—nudity explodes that situation and speculates on the human experience. She claims never to become as excited as she was having an orgasm on stage, while the male actor only felt anxiety each time he had to perform. If the theater is going to have some moment of truth, and that's all you can ask of a work of art, Joseph wanted to walk out I refused if an artist has the guts to put something up on stage I will watch it, never walk out on a work of art it's not there to be entertaining, to move you, or be morally uplifting but to engage you. Does she really need to be naked to do that? Joseph wanted to know and now that I think about it, yes, otherwise you are denying her right to free expression of ideas—a woman's cunt is really provocative too bad they couldn't show the male penis as well. Sexuality and dirty language take theater into new grounds from intellectualization of our emotions into the raw and how they are mixed in with our thoughts and only by being conscious of the world can we have an accurate reflection of the world—no stone age theater has ever been uncovered even if stone age drawings have, only in theater can we break free of the humdrum monstrosity of the everyday, we all have dark sides we show nobody and it's good that the theater explores them. Calculated nudity has dramatic effect. Conchita didn't see it that way she was ashamed at first, but slowly she got into the role, Joseph still has a difficult time wrapping his head around his girlfriend appearing on stage nude, naked as he says, he claimed he was afraid she would get in trouble what men always use to control women, she says all they can do is arrest me but he claims that's not so pleasant and the charge for public exposure can be severe and compares it to his former roommate who got arrested in a public bathroom for an indecent act and now because he pleaded guilty to a felony is not allowed to practice law. But it was this loud music, even Dylan has gone electric, I heard of Dylan but didn't know anything about him until Joseph, told me about the controversy at the Newport Folk Festival, but he doesn't appeal to me with his high pitched voice baby squeaking, but this certainly isn't the theater I am use to. That's okay I should stay with it. But now it's dangerous to walk the streets at night and Joseph and I waited for Cassandra afterwards in a bar, and I can't remember the last time I was out in a bar must have been over a decade ago before my heart attack when I would walk over to the White Horse Tavern, but now in any bar women can walk in alone but I have Joseph on my arm and we were silent walking here as if we both were gathering up our thoughts and she will meet us afterwards because she is hyper after her performance, why the theater goes past midnight actors are all worked up after the performance while all the spectators want to do is go home actors head for a bar. Too bad New York doesn't have all night coffee houses where you could sit and read the papers and talk all night long like the famous Deux Magots or Café Flore of France, or Megalomania Café in Berlin or the Hawelka in Vienna, if I ever travel to Europe again all I am going to do is sit in cafés who cares about sights I just want to sit with people, Joseph and Conchita don't know what I'm talking about they think I mean a restaurant, don't understand café culture where you read, talk, play chess, receive your mail and of course they were all heated while many apartments didn't have central heat unlike America, even when I first landed here noticed immediately apartments are hot in the winter, nobody wears sweaters in their apartment they are so overheated and you have to sometimes open the windows wide in the middle of winter it's so hot inside. When I went to theater with the one I loved the stage was a little platform above the ground and actors played their parts without scenery or costumes and music had a simple beat, but it was real theater, the actors had deep meanings with what they were saying, you were carried away into a different world by the seriousness of the performers both to themselves and to the audience. I loved that theater with no loud music, simple or no costumes, and an empty stage engaged in its strangeness not blaring music to tell me how to think. Joseph hated the strobe lights even as I realized it enhanced the performance, Conchita when she came in said she really liked the lights it enhanced nudity and forced everyone to look at her and the physical sensations she was going through, it didn't take away from her body only gave it dramatic effect and she thinks this theater will force legislators to enact new laws related to our new morality. Hard to believe people still think this way. Only way you change morality is to do it not wait for legislators to make it legal, law is always behind the times. Joseph claims you can't simply destroy the past for something new that the past has good elements in it, even if I can't name one except keeping women subjugated to patriarchal laws, and even when he fought for equal rights he still wanted women to make a home, be submissive. Can the theater the harbinger of the new? So few people actually go it's as if you're speaking to the converted but only in dramatic performances can old ways be challenged the past destroyed, especially here in New York where the old is constantly being destroyed to make way for the new and the new term that's history has entered the lexicon and the past is a forgotten country or if they conjure up the past it's anachronistically as if it's the present with only the clothes s being the past, as I said that I heard Joseph and Conchita laughing boy am I getting old defending modern theater of nudity but not loud noise. Who cares about the words, it's the emotions, feelings, backside of thought that now counts and the words only display those. They think me too old to have feelings, thoughts, that I am waiting for the grave, when I refused to wear old lady shoes that were so unstylish and clunky and flat out ugly—the ugly becomes laughable and I refused and they find it odd an older women wearing sneakers. I don't have to dress young I think older women are sexy if they feel sexy and I'm comfortable with my gray hair, wrinkles and not perfect body but I can't be with people my own age all the time why I insist upon coming to the theater even if Joseph thinks only old people go to the theater, they are older than him but still quit young and usually they go to be entertained not as theater being the most valuable of human activities. He claims college students never go; he hardly went therefore all college students don't go, is how Conchita put it, but he is correct when movies are so much cheaper now and you don't have to dress for movies maybe nudity and loud music will draw them in—when I first came it was mostly European emigre intellectual couples that I saw at performances but they are now getting old who will replace them. Today I rarely see a Hispanic couple or a black couple only middle-class people dressed up, who's the theater going to attract next. Will the Caribbean or Koreans support theater? At least Joseph and I can enjoy the unease together but I'm not sure if I enjoy the theater or the conversation we have afterwards more but I don't think you can have one without the other.

What about sex? Can I have a life with only pleasures of the self even if doing it a few times a day is fun but will I ever be able to have

IT again. I remember the joy of actually having it so many times that I lost count, hard to imagine me having sex so many times that I lost count, especially after waiting so long of a time to lose my virginity—the first time wasn't the best time that was only to get it over with, some girl I can't even recall her name on some couch somewhere—not that it was much better with Cassandra the first time, I was so uncomfortable I was so quiet, mostly embarrassed, Esmeralda was in the next room and even Cassandra told me she sleeps like a log and besides she's a grown up woman and it's okay with her, I still felt intimidated even as she said realizing our passions are natural and sex is not a sin even if I wasn't taught to save myself for marriage the way girls were, I was taught only to date Jewish girls and Jewish girls didn't go in for premarital sex. From our little chatting she led me into the bedroom after Esmeralda went to sleep, the transition was so sudden, a nice little conversation led into something else and I totally forgot what we were talking about a moment before as I undressed and watched her undress, she neatly folded her clothes and hung them up, mine were strewn all over the floor, only my socks were in my shoes so I could always find them, and I quickly realized you shouldn't be talking about your parents while you are making love and at the same time amazed she could actually talk about this—the window was open so I was cold watching and waiting for her to get into bed, while she spoke about her crazy mother and how she almost ruined her childhood but her act of getting herself killed allowed her to live and I wondered what she was gabbing about how do you let yourself be killed but I was more concerned with keeping it up, I practiced a lot when I was alone but it usually came very quickly, and she wanted to fondle, I quickly found out the best part was the foreplay and the after play the act itself was liberating but the love talk and holding were to me more important. She talked about the wandering Jew who was super-sexual, smelly, crafty, intelligent and I wondered who she was talking about and she didn't talk about my athletic abilities but of course she didn't know them I had given up sports by the time I went to college but I liked being thought of as this super sensual stud from the hood, and you could only talk about that with educated people who knew some history and knew how these terms were used, those who only saw the present had no inborn sexuality or imagination and weren't cultured the way Cassandra is. As Cassandra put it Puerto Rican girls, who are confused with Hispanic, are dropping out of school like flies that's why Esmeralda insisted on getting me away from the local high school, Walton in the Bronx and into a progressive school in Manhattan even if I didn't want to go and I shamefully took my mother's side that what was good enough for her was good enough for me and I didn't want to go with rich snobs and I didn't care to learn the social graces, which fork to use, keep your elbows close to the side, chew in small bites—and I too was shocked she had to pay for an education, I knew of parochial schools but there tuition was reasonable this all seemed unreasonable, paying for what the state offers for free, then we stopped chatting and she climbed on top of me, wasn't I to do it to her but I loved the way she strode on top of me and wrapped her legs around my sides and squeezed and even before I knew it came, and we talked and played some more and I was able to do it again when she straddled me, then the nicest part we cuddled in the bed under covers so I was no longer cold, and I could put my undershirt back on, she said she wanted to dress me in more colorful undergarments and I didn't even know what she was talking about having been raised my mother who only brought me milky white wife beaters and underpants. Who knew there were colors, for tee shirts yes but not underwear. I thought I looked cool in my gray tee shirt. Passion had overcome reason and we were into a different type of relationship when she simply grabbed my hand and led me into the bedroom; we had talked and held hands before, but this time it went further I thought to the time she wouldn't give me a blow job meaning we weren't going to have sex together and held back from then on, but she wasn't against blow jobs just thought the first date was too soon. She led the way having more experience and as usual my imagination went full throttle but it was my bodily needs that pushed my imagination and I had to fight my body to slow down rapidity in motion and be gentle. This was all I was asking for and it was a miracle even if I no longer believed and thought this was more of the devil than the good lord even as I was surprisingly quite not wanting to wake Esmeralda, and was prepared to leave and take the train back to my place on the Upper West Side in the middle of the night even if I planned to first stop into a dinner for a cup of coffee and making sure people saw me in case of legal difficulties. Where did I get that fear from? But Cassandra said there was no need we are adults. We are? She is. I'm still the kid. And I still never introduced any woman to my mother and to have to undergo her interrogation. And the second time we did it I was afraid sex would ruin our friendship but it enhanced it and made it more pleasant even if all I wanted was sex all the time and Esmeralda to go to sleep so we could get on with it. And I even said that she had the right to go with others I will not be controlling but of course didn't believe it. That was after she told me about her previous relationship and how the boy thought because he slept with her he had rights over her and when he became too demanding had to break it off. I didn't want that. And Esmeralda was also too much a part of my life she got me to thinking about my past and grandfather again so Cassandra was my future and Esmeralda my past no longer simply the past is ancient history and I should only be concerned about my future. You can look backward but also forward, that human time is concerned with face-to-face communication not some abstract entity called time, so much so that I actually called Zoltan who I had slowly lost contact with after the death of my grandfather and he was glad to hear from me and invited me to the New Museum that was featuring one of his paintings, a museum challenging boredom of traditional art. Time is time Esmeralda said, a second is a second, she said, but time is not only an objective condition, and when I think back to the dislocation of going back to my parents and the forced marriage to escape them and then my husband's death and how I projected myself as a widow but really glad to be free of him but this memory is not painful and if I don't think about it can barely recall it but I can remember everyday living with your grandfather, that I feel is with me still all these years later, I can't change that past but can live it with pleasure. That's what we talked about the first breakfast when I came out of Cassandra's room as opposed to waking up alone in my apartment and going and going out for a breakfast special at Bickford's on the corner of 96th street, or at home with my mother yelling at me how come I didn't call and tell her when I would be home you know I don't like to be home alone. A double-sided paradox I could talk to Cassandra and Esmeralda of everything and my mother nothing. If I told her about Cassandra she would be planning the wedding while wondering if she was Jewish. I wonder what she would have said about Esmeralda being grandfather's lover, she didn't care so much about the Laws of Moses only what the neighbors would think and only that I dressed nicely and now that I bathed and had short hair and not look like a hippie, so she wouldn't be embarrassed.

The biggest thrill still is when the houselights go down and the stage lights come up even if I am so nervous beforehand that I am in the bathroom right up until the performance and the penultimate night cannot even get a good night's sleep—I learned in a mime class if your audience is bored it's your fault and it's up to you to wake them up from their indifference you can't say they are not sophisticated enough it's you who has to create the rupture from the everyday when the magic of the curtain rises—it is inaccessible for them to expect anything other than a break from the everyday and unless they are too depressed it is up to me to awaken them and I am thrilled to be a part of this, or as grandma likes to say you're much happier being an actor than a waiter even if rarely wait on tables instead work in offices with the most boring men who like to hit on me even a wedding ring doesn't stop them. Joseph has been pretty insistent that I don't start climbing the corporate ladder afraid I will lose touch with acting, you are smart, he says, you will soon be making too much money and then you won't want to go on auditions because it will interfere with your work life or you won't take a job because it pays so little, too many talented actors have left the profession this way. But it would also keep me under his control because then he makes money and I don't and I'm not accustomed to not paying my way. I will support us means I am his vassal. He has no idea how physically exhausting such low skilled work actually is albeit clerical, administrative or sales besides getting automated out of existence, so I guess I will have to continue to become bourgeois but not too bourgeois and I spend most of my time juggling between auditions and work and asking people to cover for me and if I can't get someone don't come in that day. But he claims all artists need support and women have supported men artists forever so why can't he do it for me, he claims I have the one thing that is crucial to be an artist in the city, a rent-controlled apartment, that is grandma's. Grandma I understand, she has wisdom, and she too wants me to continue along my given path you have talent it would be a sin, and it's the only time I ever heard her use that word, a sin if you didn't continue to develop it. She still goes to all my performances even if I know she would rather stay home at night, but every opening night she is there and many another night as well, she is trying not to get into complacency and is always on the go, I should have her energy when I reach her age, the heart attack was not enough to fell her even if she now admits she's getting old, her exercise has gotten her stronger and she no longer needs her walking stick but she carries it for comfort even if doesn't get her a seat on the subway, because some women work now men don't feel the need to be chivalrous however a woman with a stick should receive special treatment. Men don't have to stand for me, take off their cap for me but it wouldn't hurt to give grandma a seat on the train. My name is getting known now, and I have an agent, and if a play works especially here in the Village it's good for a long run and when the house lights dim there is no feeling as magical as the anticipation but still it is difficult to put those thoughts into words, especially for people who have never had it, which was most of the men I dated, it's so hard to believe but I feel so comfortable around Joseph even with the difference in our ages, and he comes most of the time sometimes it's a little too much still he's not suffocating and when he isn't there after the performance I am disappointed, time with him is well spent. How I go through time, time on stage zooms by the same time waiting for a performance to begin drags and I look at my watch every fifteen minutes but why should it drag so it is the same before or during a performance only I feel it differently. Time is how you feel not simply moments strung together on a clock, and I recall my first meal with Joseph and how grandma and I thought it would be a short little chat who expected it to last twelve hours, of course the wine didn't hurt, and I appreciated her having a case of wine in the house, and here I am so lucky again because I am bored stiff with conventional drama and refused to work in the provinces and then found this profound play, I feel sorry for those actors stuck there unable to feel the moments of serendipity but realize that might be their lot in life if I want to continue to act and I want to continue to act not rise in the world to a position of non-importance but with plenty of money. Not now but you never know, that is the mantra actors have to live by: no longer do I even listen to plays on the radio with their beautiful-sounding voices now I want the whole gamut, the acting, the scenery, the interplay, not just the words—it is actors who portray inner life that fascinates me it's time out of joint, it's in those rare moments when you can truly believe and the whole thing becomes brutal that's when a performance takes off, the sincerity of the performance that is no longer visible to the naked eye you're so caught up in the play in those moments that you forget you are in the theater or even the nudity of the actors, the mere externals that most actors are so good at mimicking but when the inner person behind the shell comes to the surface—unlike men who seem to fall for fashion models and think what they're getting is the inner beauty when all they are getting is the shell. Unfortunately, grandma says, women fall for that too when they become engaged to powerful men thinking their outer shell is actually them and quickly become bored with them, or as my mime teacher quickly pointed out if you lose the audience it's your fault and you must banish everything from your mind except the moment you are in—on stage there is no past or future you are in the moment, the character resonates the moment no false images there is only one now, besides why should the future be connected with the past, past passions are not forgotten even if the pain is in the memory but they are nonexistent until they become now. Lucky for me more and more modern theater is getting away from traditional narrative starting sometimes at the end of a complicated story and we act out the events leading up to it; I love it the way producers now hire musical consultants to compose original music instead of canned music even if it's easier for the canned you don't even need them in the same theater they can be played from across the street and piped in, a small live group playing live music adds so much more to a performance, as what's going on in the country at large. *The Pentagon Papers* now are showing the lies of the government that our government lied to us that they knew all along the military couldn't win in Southeast Asia but so what they continued to send young men to their deaths so politicians wouldn't be accused of losing Vietnam, no wonder Nixon tried to cover it up you'd never guess he's the enemy of the people and television, movies, the press rarely get into it only theater attempts to keep truth alive and that's why I was arrested for being nude, obscenity, it shocked too many decent law-abiding people who believe what nobody can believe, grandma laughed said Europeans know governments lie they were lied to them about the Great War but the First World War didn't really affect us, Joseph says, and the second is seen as a noble cause to stop tyranny, but that's why our production survives and it is downtown theater that is challenging the whole conception of truth. The District Attorney wanted to fine us 250 dollars and fifteen days on the island, Rikers, for showing intimate parts of my body but the judge said it was protected under the first amendment, I wonder if it would have been a woman judge if she would have done that.

The young really don't know what it's like to be old, at least the old were young once so we have some idea of the young the young have no idea of the superfluousness of it all—one craving after another and when one of them is fulfilled another comes to take its place: Conchita thinks all I do is live in my past memories but even if some of them were good others were bad and it would be illogical just to remember the good and when I remember the past it's not the war but Jacobo, who was the bright and shiny moment in my past he was my best friend from the first moment we had our intense conversation—I may have suffered plenty because of him but not when I was with him and I remember thinking that after he boarded that boat, I went home and cried but not a cry of abandonment because I just knew we would be together again even if I couldn't cry on his shoulder, but if I were truly Spanish would wear black forever, imagine walking down the street with a black veil, but when I thought about that laughed even if the thought itself gave me a moment's pleasure to think of myself doing that, just think what people would say—oh how she must have suffered and so young, and I would be considered a holy woman, wouldn't even have to go to a nunnery but on further reflection realized that's not me that is the past it's over I cannot change the past, I will feel regret yes but I will not live my whole life in the past and only as I thought this, realized this, and I knew that would make a difference, it would take time but I would not be trapped in the past, I still would be saddened that is true but the thought helped change the memory of it, I would not let it overwhelm me: he remained the one true love of my life even if I continued on my way with other men and no thought could overcome that and even when young I knew in a few years I would not forget him, nor did I want to forget how I felt when with him it was too pleasurable even as I finally had to accept the fact he forgot me like I have forgotten my two husbands after him, I never think about them and I guess he never thought about me, even if I find that difficult to believe. Still I do not forget him as I realize he forgot me. One of the biggest errors of my life is thinking I could act rationally when it is irrational to believe you can behave rationally and Marxists never took that into consideration when they planned their future utopias. Why should an event that has passed affect me so doesn't make logical sense yet it is true and there is absolutely nothing I can do about it yet there is no satisfaction in looking backward nor regret—a fitting distinction for a misspent life which is all mine and I would have no other way, and there still is a joy in the past and future even if not in the present and it's done without anger just longing, and I am always amazed at myself becoming the being I am despite all my errors yet errors are part of the process and even if I found men who were like pussycats I really thought so little of them that I left them but I couldn't with Jacobo who was so gentle I still find it difficult to believe he carried a gun—he was not only my lover but also my best friend and he may not have been the world's greatest lover but he was the world's greatest friend—I should have gone looking for him up in the Bronx, I could have hid behind a light fixture, and just watched him exit the building that might have given me enough of a thrill only I know myself too well I would have wanted more and made myself available to him to see where it would go but he was married and I didn't want to cause pain to his people, I remembered the pain when he left and I didn't want to inflict that on others, to be the cause of this pain on his wife and children and no matter how in my madness wanted it wouldn't allow myself to do it. For him to run away with me and leave his wife for me would be a fantasy for him and when the fantasy blew over he would be trapped with me and that I would not want, it would have been easier to have an affair with him because then he would have a place to go home to when it was over and I would not be the one who broke up his family, even if at first I thought they too deserve it after all the pain I suffered but after a moment's hesitation into that type of thought realized I couldn't do that it might be fun to contemplate but not a nice action, and I always think about my actions even if they are not sins they are moral, language is not for God but for man to get beyond his primitive feelings, and maybe my language was so weak at first that I gave into feelings but as I slowly began to see how powerful my feelings are but they are more powerful if thought is based upon them and after Santiago died trying to impress me, that poor man nothing he could do could impress me and his dying on the wrong side no less thinking I would be proud of him fighting against the Judeo-Bolshevik Freemason experience as he called it in his last letter to me not realizing the British had bribed Franco with gold to keep him out of the war—he only enlisted to impress me he had no notion of the Republican cause and afterwards Jacobo came to me in a dream caressed my feet and talking to me in a gentle way how soft my feet were not boney or wrinkled and he told me that what I did was not a sin but a mistake and I shouldn't do it again and when I tried to console myself in his arms his body faded away but before he parted he said stop trying to hurt yourself by hurting others and when I awoke knew from then on I would behave decently not causing shame or inflicting pain upon others, which rebounded back on me. When Santiago died it would have been normal to wear black but that thought didn't even enter my head what should have occurred to me was now I was free of him but that didn't even occur to me I simply didn't think about him anymore. Poor Santiago this must be the first time I've thought about him since his death, and I'm surprised I even remembered his name, no, no, that's not true his baby sister constantly brought up his name she alone was the one who constantly thought about him—I wonder if she is still alive, if she is his memory is still alive, we lost all contact when I came to the states with Tomas, she actually thought I should wear black forever and be true to his memory. Jacobo convinced me to get on with my life and actually gave me permission to marry Tomas saying the death of Santiago means he is no longer alive there is no afterlife no resurrected soul only a grave where a body lies with no more feelings, sensations or thoughts, he never thought of it as an entrance to another world, and that I have an obligation to myself to live my life not become a prisoner of someone beyond the grave but to forge a future, not to forget the past but not to live in it either and that my present sadness and my past love are part of my future desires. Did he also say I should act in a moral way? That I don't recall.

An autodidact was thought of unkindly in educated circles, that there were large gaps in their education and only a thorough-going college education could make you well-rounded but that never really made sense to me because I remember my grandfather reading all the time or Zoltan explaining art to me while my father would be listening to the radio and later watching television or saying you could get an education by just reading the *New York Times*, which I found difficult to believe, while my mother read her romance magazines; all the while my grandfather and Zoltan were some of the most educated people I knew. Both always read hardcover books and my mother was always angry with her father for keeping so many books around the house that he finally brought them to his laundries where he set up a lending library but nobody wanted the books he had placed on the shelves there, you didn't even need a library card just a promise you would read them and pass them on, few women would take them and some women would even ask for romance novels or easier works but he said only plays or novels tell truth history is bunk just victors talking but only novels or plays can get you into the 'lived time' of people living those moments and you could use these novels or plays to get you to examine your own life and reflect upon your life, which is what most of his customers' didn't want to do. They would look at him strangely as if saying you can't change your life from a book and *avuelo* would answer back maybe not but it can help you grasp ideas, events, the past is the gateway to the future but it sounded a deaf ear on my mother who couldn't forgive her father for abandoning them even as she took him in when he could no longer live alone; however since I came of age, 5 or 6, when I could walk or ride the subways with him he never let living with her hinder us, and one thing the Bronx has is good subway lines going to both the East and West side of Manhattan, and we took the subways into the city on weekends, or afternoons after I came home for lunch from morning prison only it was called elementary school, until I became strong enough to walk all the way into the city with him. I said no to Hebrew school, an inaudible yes to public school but didn't say no to my grandfather and it was only with him that I was able to feel free, except, of course, also playing with my friends in the street, and later on when Zoltan joined us after he left Hungary after 56. He insisted I take up an instrument but I was stubborn and didn't want to waste my time practicing when it would interfere with my being a ballplayer, but did go once a week to Vinny Roberts studio where he would take me and the teacher kept saying I had to practice more, quickly he realized I hated the institutional character of the school and found me a private teacher who lived and died by the violin but it was too serious for me, he didn't approve of my fifteen tortuous minutes of practice and insisted upon hours but those hours were devoted to baseball and street games. He also gave me musical theory that made no sense to me I couldn't see how that would help me play, nothing could help me play and my lessons lasted less than a year when my family decided enough 'war' and left me alone. Maybe with some encouragement would have stuck to it but my parents thought all my effort should be spent on school not frivolous activities. At least they didn't let me quit school and become a menial worker and all along insisted I go to a technical high school so I could learn a trade and always be able to find a job. Only my grandfather insisted that I go to college. He employed enough high school dropouts and had to give them instructions and sometimes actually had to read to them as they repaired the machines and I laugh now as Esmeralda says he was all thumbs, because he was the handiest man I knew when he was around machines—he could look at them and make them work or at least immediately knew what was wrong with them. When I wanted to go to Samuel Gompers or Aviation high school to be like him he discouraged me and insisted I take the test to the special high schools because I was smart enough and Zoltan suggested Music and Art high school because he saw how much I liked art when he took me to art shows and museums said it's not good for an artist to play catch up it's better to learn while young, and I quickly agreed because they had girls, it wasn't an all-boys school like my junior high school or the technical high schools were, and *avuelo* thought I could get a good education there and go to college even if I dreamt I would be an all-star on the baseball team because artists and musicians can't play ball, but that didn't last long, but it was horrible going there on the subway, back then the subways had no air conditioning only ceiling fans, and wicker seats but at least I left the neighborhood. However I did learn to read the books *avuelo* gave me on the subway to school. I was the only one in class who knew who Trotsky was how he was the greatest general ever to come out of the Bronx and how he was assassinated on August 20th 1940. The surprise of high school was Mrs. Booker an English teacher taking us to Sheridan Square an off-Broadway show, before then I had never been to the theater only had gone with my grandfather and Zoltan to an occasional half-assed play in a union hall, and we were going to go at night and I doubted if my father would let me stay out so late at night but he said for school that would be okay, and my father waited for me in the automat then surreptitiously walked me home from the theater so none of my friends realized it was my father when I came home so late at night. He waited in the automat over a long cup of coffee but it was with my grandfather that I talked the next day about *The Serpent* about how we are neither not guilty, nor guilty, there is no innocence and that virtue doesn't admit degrees and to lead a happy life you must live by your beliefs, I'm sure he appreciated being lectured to by a fifteen-year-old. But he and Zoltan insisted upon going with me and the next Saturday we went and Zoltan liked it because the words were pretty static, not Talmudic, so he could understand them, his English not being that good yet, and the acting was slow and deliberate non-naturalistic and an attack on the fourth wall where the actors are on stage and we are supposed to imagine they are different than us, and afterwards we met one of the actors on the subway and we had a fine chat about the play but all I remember was being surprised he too lived in the Bronx, I thought all actors lived in Greenwich Village, but he said the Village has now become too expensive, he complained that he probably won't be able to stay in this company that he needs money to support his family and may have to go to Hollywood or television. A pity grandfather said how we abandon our dreams because of our need for security and we need a steady job to support our family.

The mole keeps sneaking up on me but these are dead ideas history is the path of old ideas I keep telling myself, I have to break free of them and go deeper underground and lately it has become difficult being with people my own age all they talk about are grandchildren and health issues and I see myself burrowing deeper into ground so as not to be around such people but it is boring here all by myself and I have to force myself to get out at night otherwise I will become like them or maybe I should move into one of those retirement communities down in Florida, but I know that's all talk I can't move down there even if the weather is appealing, the boredom with them will be so overwhelming, and besides I say this every year in the dead of winter but once spring comes and I can see the leaves on the trees forget what I said in the winter—I love seeing the first blossom of trees in early March, an occasional leaf on a tree a sky that turns bright blue not gray, no snow on the ground that never gets shoveled away now it's a fight I have with myself daily whether to go outside or not. Only when I finally go stir crazy do I force myself outside, unless it's to go shopping, which I now do a few times a day out of boredom, but I have to be careful now not only because of the sleet and black ice but because of the other guy, the streets around here are no longer safe for old people, young hooligans think it only fun not only to steal a purse but bash a head in and whenever you need a cop they are not around—who would ever think I would be supporter of law and order, somehow these punks think they're beating up on their mother, of course not their own mother, she is a saint, even if they probably deserve it for raising a hooligan, so junkies take it out on old people, easy marks, yet these tough punks bitch and moan when they get caught. 7th street is losing its allure, at one time I knew everybody on the block all my neighbors, now the city is moving in 'welfare addicts' who are destroying the street and this once nice safe neighborhood is becoming a war zone, it's not 'benign neglect' it's conscious destruction of parts of the city bringing strangers into our midst and forcing law-abiding citizens to move out to the country, what we in New York euphemistically call the suburbs yet it was 'benign neglect' that laid the intellectual foundations for the moratorium on federal housing programs and without these subsidies the city defaulted on its bonds and became bankrupt. Even Joseph's mother left the Bronx with practically her whole apartment complex and moved into Co-op City, what do you think is going to happen to that neighborhood when middle-class families abandon it? It's these real estate developers ruining the city they want to empty the block and put in Corbusier modernist ugly Soviet-style apartment houses, and are taking advantage of East Village liberalism to use unreliables to burn apartments down, just like they're doing up in the Bronx now. We defeated Robert Moses when he wanted to put the Cross Manhattan Lower Expressway through the neighborhood, what did he care that people live here only now we have slum clearance i.e. poor people removal in order to appease landlords. Does the city even realize that the smaller questions are truly the hardest questions and where people live determines the quality of lives or are they so blind to this fact and don't care what junkies do and are so desperate to move them anywhere they can find—with the destruction of neighborhoods the city is becoming a cesspool. Joseph wants to show me how it's happening in the Bronx as landlords burn down buildings all around the East Bronx for the insurance money and in Forest Hills they want to destroy a functioning middle-class neighborhood in order to save it by building another housing project right in the middle of a community, at least after Jane Jacobs led a revolt citizens are not passively accepting a government fiat and are fighting city hall, but here we are sitting ducks the city always comes here to put people nobody else will take, even small shops grocery stores, shoemakers, dry cleaning, watch repair shops are being forced out by chain stores or theft and burglaries, worse even used old bookstores on 4th avenue can't survive anymore, Joseph even no longer buys hardcover books they are so expensive yet he has money for theater, liquor or the movies but only buys paperbacks so he can read on the subway. Who would have believed this could happen if it were only 'benign neglect' but it's with the conscious effort of elected officials to destroy itself, and yet I must not give in to my malaise must join some organization to fight this destruction: Conchita brought me this color television set and I have to get rid of it, it's now much easier to stay home watching television than going out to meetings, and sometimes I find myself underlining television shows on Sunday night that I want to watch during the week. When I caught myself doing that I crumbled the newspaper in disgust and realized I have to fight my moral lassitude, unlike Joseph who loves being home at night, and make sure I get out of the house at least one night a week even if I have to take a cab I refuse to be trapped indoors all the time. We now have gates on the windows too many junkies have been climbing through windows in the neighborhood and when one neighbor was robbed in this building we all banded together formed a tenant's organization and bought window bars, we even have a police lock on the door, Joseph insisted and the front door is now locked you can only get in if you are buzzed in but I still feel uncomfortable not allowing black people in it reeks of racism but Joseph says wait until you get mugged. I can hardly wait. I can't keep burrowing deeper and deeper especially when Conchita goes out and I am home alone with Joseph and his television-watching, he can lie on the couch all night watching his basketball then fall asleep I'm too active for that. I could go to the senior center and talk health issues and the ungratefulness of children while playing bingo but it's only old ladies there, men are more solitary, I much rather do my exercises at the Y. Joseph warns me to be careful but as my doctor said the heart is a muscle strengthen it and even if I'm not a young kid anymore and I spent my time at the Y walking on the treadmill, lifting weights, and on the rowing machine, I'm not ready for old age I do have some choices. Physically I've strengthened my heart but mentally the fear of death never goes away, thoughts of mortality have taken up permanent residence inside me. What Joseph dislikes about this neighborhood is there are so few basketball courts anymore, the junkies take them over and the parks aren't safe so he no longer goes out and dribbles, he claims when he would feel down, or have a headache he could always go out on a basketball court and get into a zone and his headache would go away but now only high school kids play basketball and he can't stand the constant arguing, luckily he has started jogging on weekend mornings as exercise. Exercise slows the aging process down and helps me with my balance and breaks the natural order of aging. I love watching those young nubile women who dance and Conchita now uses it to slow down the wear and tear on her body so she can continue to act, and always feels exhausted yet gratified after coming home from a dance class, she claims to get the same high Joseph did when he played basketball and is so glad now that women are exercising because she's really into it but before felt self-conscious about doing it and people thinking she was still acting like a kid not a grown woman. Better than Joseph going out for a green pepper steak at his local Cuban Chinese restaurant at midnight because he was bored and couldn't sleep, like junkies who say I can quit anytime but never can, or women staying at home hoping to meet Prince Charming who will change their lives. I rather be me than these young of today who can't lead a solitary life and must only be with people, that reason is the fruit of passion the highpoint of our existence but it must be balanced by a life of movement. The further I get from my origins the closer I come to them and maybe one day will even grasp them.

How is this different? Grandma always said that I don't have to follow traditional roles yet it's scary how she won't believe that I am doing this of my own free will, she has given up certain thoughts as she ages, she's now becoming an old woman all she is missing is cats, I worry about her being out alone but she claims she doesn't want to be a homebody, trapped, forced to stay indoors all the time, and no matter what weather goes out, walks, even if the neighborhood is no longer safe, garbage strewn all over the street sanitation never comes by here to pick it up, rats bigger than cats, the streetlights no longer work, crack houses in the abandoned buildings, marihuana dealers put out of business because of the demand for crack-cocaine, she still refuses to take taxis something we modern women have now added to our budget, even now asking the driver to wait until we're inside the lobby. Joseph even jokes that he can get a job as 'muscle' because so many women have asked him to walk with them to the subway station, to the car, or home when they work late at night, they feel much more protected with a man's arm to lean on, sometimes even complain that he's not listening to them when all he's really doing is surveying the block to make sure he sees if anybody is hiding in the shadows. We all know now how dangerous it is to walk down a deserted street or get into an empty subway car, all except grandma who calls America a third-world country forcing single women indoors when the sun goes down. We recently drove up to Montreal and what surprise it was seeing women riding their bicycles around at 2am without a fear there the streets are safe. I was transported into a different world, the city was a European city, grandma said, small streets, curved, only thing that ruined it according to grandma is they want to create high-rise housing, which looks so pretty but is detrimental to street life, it's only when people see each other have a face-to-face interaction that a city thrives. How quickly you forget that I use to walk out at all hours of the night, and Joseph continually says in college he always knew he could go to the L-shaped (two entrances) Bickford's on the Concourse, near Fordham Road, at two in the morning and could always find some of his buddies hanging around over a cup of coffee and a cheesecake, all the boys would meet there after their dates and talk the night away. It's only the girls who had to be home by a special time, usually midnight but when I went to the progressive school it was girls who were allowed to stay out later than boys, now that's changed and we don't go out at all. But it was fun in college to see these small town girls finally allowed some freedom and didn't come back to the dorm until after 2 and drunk, even if they had to sneak in, no longer were they going to allow them to be confined to the dormitory room and this was with or without a boyfriend. The future is not what we expect it to be who would have thought after liberation women would still be confined to their homes, or when I first wore a mini-skirt boys would act like animals and stare all the time as if they've never seen knees before, so I wore a dress a little above my knees but then I had guts, now I won't even go braless because I don't feel like dealing with their catcalls and won't let Joseph jokingly run his fingers through my underwear on the street lest men get the wrong idea—this neighborhood is changing and if they see Joseph playfully touching me they think they can do it as well; now I'm beginning to understand what grandma is saying that the old cultured immigrants are dying out or moving out and the new residents don't know how to cope with the new values, and many Hispanic men live here without women and the catastrophe of being displaced from peasant to city life is too much for them, women when they come stick with families but men here are all alone, no job, no self-respect, their way of life destroyed and farming skills useless in the city, and they become so bored that at first all they can do is drink but now the new epidemic drugs destroys any semblance of life they had; it gives them something to do and you can blot out more of life with crack-cocaine quicker than with Hombre, a cheap red wine. No longer are they winos but crackheads but crack is illegal so you need money so they have to be ready to rob, steal, mug constantly be on the lookout for more money, and the police are useless and wherever law breaks down man becomes wolf to man, jail is no longer considered a disgrace but a badge of honor among the young and you can always meet a homebody there more people in the neighborhood in Rikers than at the local high school—this is true 'benign neglect' schools no longer care if their charges roam the streets, in fact they don't want them because they cause so much trouble and the schools are so overcrowded let the community deal with them but we can't. Two boys in the building dropped out of high school this week and grandma had to console their mothers she couldn't stop them they said drugs are everywhere and they knew they would get hooked unless they left and now are studying for the high school equivalency, Joseph is helping them unfortunately they have to wait until 18 to take the test, one is a serious student he says only the math might trip them up but he hopes that by working with them can get their reading skills sharper then will be able to understand the math questions. I'll never forget when a mother complained that the judge wouldn't lock her boy up, I was playing a woman whose son uses and the director suggested I go to criminal court to get some understanding what's going on and I sat and listened at the arraignment and couldn't believe my ears at how many Hispanics there were, and some of the mothers couldn't even speak English and kept begging the court for help, the junkies were all fiends and the women, oh my god, man crazy, going to do time for their man, carrying drugs for them, guns for them, doing it all of their own free will, and not even realizing that it's the man who ratted them out, he has to name someone to plea bargain with but women only know their boyfriend and would never implicate him. These courts can't solve society problems I wanted to standup and yell, you can't use the courts for justice all they're concerned with is the law, but I listened and couldn't believe my ears really wanted to shut off my ears at the helplessness of these mothers, and it was always mothers never fathers—no one time a father did come and the boy got a slap on the wrist the judge must have been thinking a father knows how to treat a boy, I found out later it was the son of a writer who knew how prejudiced the court was to women and flew in from California to stand by his son knowing the court would treat his son better with a man than with a woman, and I saw all the destruction of families they simply couldn't adjust to life in the big city after being forced or coming to the city for better opportunities. Grandma wants them to go to my plays but the few kids in the building who we know want nothing to do with art, laugh when she suggests it and never open a book let alone go to a play saying they have no time for 'white people's culture' refusing to see ideas as belonging to all people and have no interest in anything but their physical needs, even Joseph is having difficulty with one of the boys because he keeps saying I want a job not seeing that an education can lead to a better job. I've even offered to give them comps but they laugh at me seeing me as a sellout but the older one thought maybe I was coming on to him, such an imagination and he's not even 18. As if I would want to have sex with a dumb-witted teenage boy but he probably sees me with Joseph and thinks nothing of an older woman going with a younger man and it might as well be him except he's a stupid teenager with a man's body but a boy's brain, interesting how he assumes I'm an old biddy but have the sexual appetite of a monkey. Or maybe he thinks I want one last fling before I go into the retirement home. Grandma was flummoxed when she overheard the boys talking because I don't speak Spanish they assumed grandma doesn't, and the three of us laughed that I would be interested in such a 'dumb fuck' or that he could even think such a thing, I made no sexual contact with him not even flirting he's Joseph's project not mine—it's terrible what men think of women if you give them a little smile: next he'll expect to have an affair with me but go gently in the night when his true love comes along, a young girl his age, and I'm supposed to realize I'm making a fool of myself expecting a younger man to be interested in permanently having a relationship with me. If we only had some more women playwrights that could imagine stories from a woman's point of view instead of a man's fantasy all the time? And boys believe this nonsense never allowing women to think for themselves and see us as a product of their fantasies instead of having a life of our own. I don't know if grandma was angry or sad but I certainly am angry at the way boys think of women, Joseph thinks his mother would probably have thought the same way and when he came in from his late night carousing in high school expected his mother to make him a snack, which she did and he never thought anything about it until Grandma confronted him and said you expected your mother to get up out of bed at 4 in the morning? Yes. If you have no one showing you how to think outside the box, you see things only the way your culture presents them to you and the conventional newspapers, television, movies only support those beliefs as opposed to showing us another way. As Joseph says that's what college life is for intellectual discussions about solitary reflection between thought and silence. He had a better educational experience than me.

Why did she have to come home? She should have been out shopping and nobody else was home it was the middle of the day when women are supposed to be shopping. I didn't mean to hurt her, I don't even recall hitting her she just scared me when she burst in like that it was all instinctive she startled me and I didn't know what to do and she just got in the way. I shouldn't even be charged with this I have no memory of hitting her, should I be held responsible if I can't remember it? Shouldn't I be held responsible for what I can remember? I didn't use a gun sure I had one on me but I didn't use it didn't even take it out of my fanny pack, she thought I am this little boy that Joseph tutored in the building, but he would get angry with me when I read silently while moving my lips because I couldn't make out the words, she would give candy to me on the staircase or give me pennies to buy candy, a sweet old lady, but I've grown up since and once she didn't even recognize me on the street I had become so tall, so how come she recognizes me now? When I saw her in the lobby of my grandmother's building what was I to do steal from my grandmother, her window was all open it was broad daylight all I had to do was walk down the fire escape how hard is that, didn't even have to climb down from the roof or scuttle under the wire that all roofs now have so you can't get from one to the other, it was all so easy who expected her to walk in—it's her fault couldn't she realize she was being robbed. Now my lawyer tells me that since a person was involved it's not breaking and entering but robbery and I shoved her, hit her, not hard just so I could get out, and the only way out of this is if I plea to the Rockefeller program as a junkie I will do less time, I'm not an addict, I can stop anytime I want, all I do it is for kicks to get my rocks off and not have to feel anything and there was nothing left to pawn and my mother locked me out of the house because I took the television, so I went to grandma's what else could I do live on the street? Sell my body on 42nd street, I'm not a fag. I saw her window was open from the street it was an easy walk down two flights, if I didn't do it someone else would have and I needed another fix and didn't have any more money so what could I do? I'm not like those junkies who will do anything for a nickel bag but once I get my shot the world is cool again, nodding out gets rid of all the pain. I tried explaining that to the lawyer but he never listens all I wanted him to do was tell the judge I didn't want to hurt anybody that finally I got something that makes me feel good and the world's against me. I have to steal in order to get money what do they want me to do kill somebody? I'll tell the judge what do I need this damn lawyer for all he wants me to do is cop a plea so he gets credit for saving me but I'm no junkie I ain't going to admit what I'm not. He thinks because I occasionally shoot up, the guy won't listen they never do, and he couldn't get the charges reduced to disorderly conduct or carrying works that's what a good lawyer does, they didn't find me with any of the stuff why can't he get them to file lesser charges, maybe I should ask for a new lawyer—it's so fuckin noisy here I can hardly think and the only help I need is for someone to get me out of here, if I can only be a delinquent not a junkie and they didn't even have a warrant to search me all charges should be thrown out, they just can't come into grandma's place and say they saw bits of jewelry. My lawyer said that might have worked if it was the first offense but now that I have a rap sheet they aren't going to buy that. Because of my record I now have to plead guilty, he says, admit I'm a junkie, which I'm not, in order to get into this drug bullshit program where all you do is talk drugs, a seminar in crime my lawyer calls it where the older teach the younger so you have something to do when you get out, otherwise I could be spending real time in jail, and it's so boring there. I asked grandma to get me a real fuckin lawyer not one of these court-appointed ones but she said it was too late for that, and then my mother telling the judge to lock him up, what kind of mother is that, she's my mother she's supposed to love me says I'm out of control and then grandma says she's ashamed of me. It was me or her, and I only knocked her down didn't hit her she only hurt herself falling, is that my fault, not by me hitting her and when she yelled Julio it scared me but I didn't even hear her come in and I was safe in grandma's place until the pigs come and she lets them in and they slam me against the wall, handcuff me search me arrest me find some works but no drugs and they take me to the station and I gotta get fingerprinted and they keep me for night court. I was sure she wouldn't turn me in everyone said she's a good ole sort who didn't like the police, next time I'm not going to let anyone be a witness. I didn't hurt the old lady why is she's doing this to me. How could my mother abandon me at a time like this telling the judge lock me up for my own good he's going to get killed using drugs. Some mother, she's supposed to look after her son not send them upriver. If I ever get out of here I'm going to resort to a life of crime fuckem all. And how Esmeralda treat me like that she always gave me candy when I visited grandma, and I liked her place so much that I would go downstairs and visit with her when grandma started watching her soap operas, and she always encouraged me to read and the guy who lives with them is even teaching me to read even when I told him I don't need to read I want to be a basketball player and he said that's one in a million, I didn't care I knew I was good enough and I've never shot up in my legs, he would always say go study and make something of yourself, what did he know I'm good enough to be in the pros. She would always give me books and I never told them I stopped going to school, who can go to school where they treat you like shit, teachers never liked Spanish students always forced us to speak English never understood us and that's where I learned about drugs.

This is silly. My making such good money on such a useless product as if we are sitting around a symposium discussing Eros, how I enjoyed that in college where we would sit around and talk all day and night with coffee or booze depending upon where we were and would solve the problems of the world—it wasn't the irrational we feared but how we can bring knowledge and understanding to the unconscious. Now all I do is go from one liquor store to another and encourage them to try our wines and since there is a boom in wine consumption, everybody is now drinking wine no longer just hobos and their Hombre, Thunderbird on skid row, now college grads have gotten more sophisticated we've found a nice niche of good wines at reasonable prices, you can't price wine too low people are still self-conscious about buying cheap wine, but no longer do they have to drink $100 bottles to be considered sophisticated, nor worry about which wine with meat or fish—that's for the bourgeoisie, our customers are the newly educated who also can't stand instant coffee—we sell life style not just wine, our ads always have people with a house full of books, paintings on the wall, rugs on the floor, not paperback books, or photographs or even carpets on the floor, and always drinking out of a crystal wine goblet, we insist wine tastes better coming from crystal than a juice glass—and we're correct sales are booming, the sale of wine glasses has increased along with the consumption of wines, and I have this ability, not unique but good enough to ride this trend, I have a likeable personality and liquor store owners want to buy from me that I am making too much money for a man of my age, I can actually afford to buy a Mustang, cash only, just like a drug dealer as Esmeralda says, but the thought of driving in the city is a nightmare to me, besides the only solitary time I have now is on my subway rides and walks to the different liquor stores, and I'm no longer a voracious reader because this job eats time from me and even if the work doesn't satisfy me the money does. And I do enjoy the weekly pay check instead of the bi-weekly or monthly ones that some of my friends get, I'm never short of cash and am actually saving some: my father would be proud of me, he always said it wouldn't be this easy, but what did he know living during the Depression, we're in a booming economy and the government won't allow a crash to happen again, downturns yes but no major free fall. A laissez-faire but no more unstable economy, at least we fixed that and now we work for money without guilt only for my own selfish interests but is that what I want? At least it's something to get me out of bed in the morning but there is no moral duty associated with this job, at least Cassie enlightens people with her art, all I think about is quitting yet can't quite pull the trigger because I have no idea what I would do. What do I want to do? Wish I knew. Friends suggested I go for my Masters, the Jewish solution more education but in what? I could go for Ebonics, black English I would do well in that I'm from the Bronx, but enough school. Then everyday would be like Sunday and Sundays are impossible to get through, but the Left has become so preachy wanting to overturn the government, Zoltan and I spoke last Sunday, finally a pleasant Sunday we met at P.S. 1 in Long Island City, a museum that is in a former public school, that was so unique art that explored the building itself rotting floors, peeling paint and walked through the spaces, and I'm still surprised at him taking notes in front of peeling walls and rotting floors and occasionally even stopping to draw part of an installation that intrigues him, who carries a sketchbook around in a backpack. He was really animated saying the communists were winning everywhere and you Americans don't understand the viciousness of them, they've won in Vietnam, and Cambodia and I'm afraid if the Soviets advance into Europe the United States won't honor its treaties and let them win. Only in Spain were the Spanish able to defeat the communists and they didn't even realize how lucky they were with all their deaths and suffering it would have been much worse if the Reds had won. We will not see the demise of the Soviet Union in my lifetime and nobody in America truly realizes what's going on. I was happy to see us defeated in Vietnam, but he kept going on, all the while still sketching that first Eastern Europe was given to the Soviets at Yalta, he talked as if Yalta were a living document, the next day I had to go to a public library and spend hours searching through history books to find out what Yalta was, now they had Vietnam and Cambodia he said, they're winning in Latin America, Africa and the Middle East and your country is hardly aware of their long range goals. I couldn't see Israel going communist but he said there are more countries in the Middle East than Israel but I couldn't see Muslims going communist either. I thought he was exaggerating besides when he first came here had never even heard of Trotsky so what kind of history could he know. He didn't even know Eastern Europe was really Central Europe and never realized they were part of Western Europe not the Soviet bloc. Besides now such abstract thought bored me. But I did learn from him not to be a revolutionary that you don't want governments overturned too many people die, suffer, and nothing much happens, he was the one who told me you don't want a revolution it's too painful and he should know having participated in the attempted overthrow of the communists in his native Hungary. I still can never forget how he came to visit my grandfather because he was the younger brother of Lazlo and his brother had given him his address in New York and Zoltan memorized his name and address and explained to us that his brother had died somewhere off in Siberia when the Russians took over the country, and he was one of those waiting for them with open arms that is until they deported him, and in his limited English explained how he had been a Freedom Fighter for the four days Hungary had some freedom in '56 and how he had helped tear down the statue of Stalin in Stalin Square and had placed a flower in the boot that hadn't cracked but when the Soviets invaded with all the countries of the Warsaw pact he had to flee and his aunt said look you're going to be on some list you have to escape to Israel, and before the border was closed completely managed to get to Austria actually planning on going to Israel but then decided Israel was a farming country and he wasn't a farmer and thought about New York and his brother's friend from the Spanish Civil War. What had surprised me was that he came in the morning and when I came home from school in the afternoon he was still there. I had met some other of *avuelo's* friends but usually they were gone when I came back from school. He lived with us for months and in his broken English introduced me to the horrors of Socialism and the all-powerful state, and he told me about his brother being a communist in Spain but I was more interested in his love affair with a Dutch woman and how he never found out what happened to her after he went back to Budapest, but that his brother was active in the anti-fascistic movement and the revolution at home until he was denounced as a traitor and he was sent to forced labor in Siberia to a language he couldn't speak and he was almost forty years of age and could probably not survive those harsh cold winters and he was never to be heard from again, at least that was as much as I could pick up from his broken English and from my *avuelo's* retelling the story. He soon joined us on our walks. I gathered he was fortunate that we had just gotten a telephone and grandfather's name was in the phone book otherwise he would not have been able to find us, we no longer lived in the East Bronx. He was the first to tell me in capitalism man is wolf to man but in communism it is the reverse. Of course I didn't understand then, he thought me older or wiser than my years but he was the one with some of the first money he earned to buy me a real fielder's mitt not like the baby one my grandmother got me. This one, however, was endorsed by Mickey Mantle my arch enemy not by Willie Mays, they still were not making gloves endorsed by Negroes even as they had transformed the game, and I had found out Willie was wearing Jackie Robinson's number only in reverse. When we walked I got the impression he was religious saying things like pride is the original sin and we must stand up to it by going back to work, he was the first man I met who actually wore a bow tie, and since we had to wear a white shirt and tie to assembly once a week I asked him to teach me how to tie one, I refused to wear clip-ons, and even if some of the boys could already tie a Windsor knot I was cool wearing a bow tie. I wonder if I still have them or did my mother discard them when she moved to Co-op City? I can always buy another but who wears ties anymore. I learned to hate communism from Zoltan but still felt glad the U.S. was defeated in Vietnam but I never saw the Soviet Union as the paragon of virtue my leftist friends did. One guy even said *Pravda* is the truth, the true newspaper of record not the *New York Times*. I was still surprised anyone read newspapers they seemed so devoid of truth. I read books. *Avuelo's* influence. Still no longer could you change your life by a book you were reading, nobody does that anymore and I now get up every morning wondering why I should go out and do it but I was good at doing what I was doing so there was no chance of me getting fired and unemployment then maybe I could stand in the unemployment line and read books, go to foreign films in glorious black and white but if I was to leave I would have to do it on my own but the money is too good and I can renounce my passion for freedom by looking at my savings account and how it grows, it keeps me boxed in, and I have weekly deposited money in my savings automatically from my checking account.

It brought back memories, I remember it as if it were yesterday I never received phone calls and in the middle of the night no less, I had just been studying studying is not exactly the correct word I was learning how to pronounce artists this was the first time I had heard them pronounced correctly, it was Plato not Play-Doh, Antigone not Anti-gone Titian not Titan, and when I received the phone call didn't know what to do, I just couldn't leave the show must go on and I had a leading role, luckily I was a trained actress and could compartmentalize finished my performance and rushed over to the emergency room, Joseph had said she was okay and he would stay with her but still I knew I had to be there and by the time the performance was over and I was at the hospital she was being seen by a doctor, most of the time at Downtown Beekman she was waiting in the emergency room, which is a good thing if you come to think of it but not while you are waiting wondering if you will live, she only had bruises and contusions on her body, arms, and face, nothing life-threatening except maybe her pride but not a reoccurring heart attack and no long-term physical damage as far as the doctors could see. When the police came to interview her she said she couldn't remember what happened and didn't know who did it to her but I immediately knew she was protecting someone but it didn't do Julio any good everyone in the building knew it was him, and when the police arrived Julio was arrested simply because he had climbed up the fire escape and someone saw him. Now Grandma would have to testify against the grandson of her neighbor. I would have pulled the switch myself I was so angry at Julio, he could have gotten the electric chair as far as I was concerned beating up an old lady who gave him candy and pennies to buy candy, how many people were that nice to him and when Joseph explained to grandma that we had to get him off the street before he really hurts someone and that he's already been thrown out of his mother's house for stealing and it would be for his own good, but grandma said prison is never for your own good, and not good for society either you only come out worse for the treatment you go through not a better person, but I didn't care after what he put my grandma through and the biggest indignity was having her having to submit to an interrogation by the police officer and he asked embarrassing questions, of course, grandma wasn't embarrassed when he asked did he molest her, did he touch you, but she said no only she became scared when he hit her but more humiliation than pain that this little punk hits me, and the shock that he would actually do that to me and how quickly his anger turned to violence and what's going to become of a boy who can't control his temper. She was more worried about him than herself. Joseph had come by knocked a few times and heard moaning he used his key and saw her bleeding on the floor, he almost had a heart attack and when he saw blood immediately called an ambulance, the new emergency number 911 and within minutes an ambulance came, grandma didn't want to go to the hospital but Joseph and the ambulance workers insisted, afterwards she said she was more embarrassed that people were making a fuss over her until Joseph claimed we're taxpayers and have a right to city services and she laughed, a police car came with the ambulance and the officer immediately knew it was a robbery and told Joseph to get gates and a police lock, which he did the next day, and by the next night there were a police lock with a steel rod, and window guards on the windows, by the fire-escape we had one that could be open from the inside in case of fire and we weren't trapped and could die of smoke inhalation, on the other windows locked by a combination lock with the number taped on the back because we knew we couldn't remember lists of numbers; we never wanted this because it looks like a jail, but now nobody could come in even if we thought that if we were robbed once it probably wouldn't happen again, but a police officer disillusioned us of that type of thinking. The little shit was walked out of the building in handcuffs good let him be shamed even if grandma thought nothing would embarrass him if he hits a friend of his grandma's and a Spanish lady to boot even if grandma does feel superior to people of the Island, it wasn't because they were not true Spanish it was because of their lack of education, he was a crude boy who thought it was cool to get girls pregnant then leave them. Joseph said that when he gets out of jail in a few years he'll have to come back here and we'll have to be on the lookout, who knew about the Rockefeller program and he was back on the street in six months—but by then we tenants came together at a building meeting and formed a tenant patrol, chipped in twenty-five dollars then dues of ten dollars a month and we had the landlord install a second door and buzzer system so you couldn't just walk into the building unannounced and took turns sitting downstairs monitoring who came in at night—no more unannounced guests, and the fence on the roof was reinforced with barbed wire, another building on the block hired a guard who actually protected a woman from being mugged but was himself arrested for carrying an illegal Saturday night special. A new group called the Guardian Angels formed wearing distinctive red berets and offered to patrol our block but grandma called them Falangists, blue shirts, not as famous as the Nazi brown-shirts they wore blue instead of brown but like the Nazi and Italian fascists they were set to take over the city as the police abandoned block by block of the city and we now had to look out for the other guy, and I had to start taking taxis home late at night, which put a crimp in my budget but I soon learned to share rides with fellow actors. Joseph felt like Sir Galahad having to walk so many people to their car or the subway station late at night, he liked being considered muscle. Luckily he never was approached he was no muscle but women felt secure walking on the arm of a man.

My understandings have limits, once I believed masturbation causes blindness until Jacobo cured me of that thought, a nineteenth century superstition, he said, pleasuring yourself can't be bad, who know why that little snot nose hurt me, someone who was nice to him or as Joseph says if you are nice to people they will see it as weakness and take advantage of you, it makes no sense did he think I wouldn't know who he was but that's just it, he didn't think, it is deeper he knew what he was doing and wanted to do it, using drugs as an excuse to hurt people, thinking couldn't have stopped him from doing it, I looked like an easy mark like diving into a clear pool of water from a bridge it looks so beautiful even if you'll drown at the end of it and no amount of thought can stop you. Did you ever see Hockney's *Pool Party* it's so inviting you want to jump in even if you know it's a painting? Julio's thoughts were directed at hurting himself and took the open window connected to his grandma's fire escape and even if he knew it was my place and a friend of his grandmother he only thought easy pickings didn't even concern himself if I was home or not. Did he really think he could get away with it, that he wouldn't get caught did it ever enter into his mind? And some revolutionary leftists are saying these junkies are the new proletariat fighting 'the Man' it's only because I dislike the police more than him that I won't testify against him, but I wouldn't mind if he came by to apologize, see me as a person not simply an old lady he can steal from. He must have been hurt terribly as a child; Conchita and Joseph can't seem to grasp this fundamental fact those who hurt others have been hurt themselves, too bad the young can't lap up wisdom from the aged and think of me as a grandma not a human being, not that society has failed him when it didn't give him an opportunity to learn to think—a dropout in the sixth grade has no chance in America of today, and he must have mentally quit even earlier he can't even read a comic according to Joseph without moving his lips, can't write his name only print it, and thinks he's cool, except he's into herd culture can only do what his friends do and a whole generation of kids like him are becoming junkies, disposable people—how is this possible? Can he have any dignity forget about economic productivity maybe he could have a better life if he learned a trade learned to make something of himself learned to do something for himself maybe that could help him become a *mensch*—instead of being a puppet, someone is pulling strings and he moves to them. The absence of a father means he doesn't know what a man is, all he sees are superficial men who have no connection to family life and he doesn't realize real men stay put and put up with the indignities of life for the children to raise children and in so doing repress their pleasure to reason and the outside is connected to the inside and that is the only way we become whole, we find our other half, not our lover but ourselves. He never had a chance to know the security of childhood which later on you must leave but at least you have a base from which to begin with. What did he have? I don't want to see him spending the rest of his life in jail that would be a waste but he's not going to outgrow his childhood dependence upon drugs by acting tough—it's probably better for him if he can dive into a pool of water from a bridge, the temptation would be too great and he's probably not even connected to his thoughts to realize he should be depressed for his years of misery ahead of him, instead his only bent will be how to beat the system. Joseph and Conchita are adamant that he not be allowed on the streets and think this Rockefeller drug program a sham and would rather he go to Phoenix House or Odyssey House a private program where they have militarism, as if the military ever made a man of somebody not a zombie and they claim they help only those who finish the program, but few actually do finish most cop out when the obedience gets too tough, heck the army doesn't even want these kids how many of them wanted to join the army to get out of going to jail but the army said no thanks we don't want a junkie in a foxhole. Now even the army almost admits it has a problem with junkies and ex-soldiers are quick to say they got hooked in the army but the truth is they were users before. Now Dora has moved up to her daughter's place she's so embarrassed what her grandson did, and we have this tenant association now that has brought strangers together, we should thank junkies for that, but the whole building knows it was her grandson and she doesn't want to show her face in the building. He only knocked me down, hit me, she thought he raped me, so the police, but he probably can't get it up most rapists can't all they have is the power, and fear, and I was frightened when I saw a blur in my bedroom riffling through my underwear, I always thought I could lecture a mugger but it happened so quickly I didn't know what was happening. Conchita threw it all out and bought me new underwear she wouldn't allow me to wear anything he got his paws on, Joseph was embarrassed when they went to Lord and Taylor's for woman's underwear but he insisted she get nice, i.e. expensive, underwear she deserved it, he said, Conchita told me, after what I had been through I deserve nice undergarments. But I feel uncomfortable wearing such expensive undies. He now literally is making so much money that it didn't seem expensive to him and I feel uncomfortable wearing such soft undergarments, but Conchita says Joseph says I will get used to it. Here he sounds just like his grandfather who said in Spain for the first time he was learning to live with joy before all he did was go through the motions. It's from childhood on we learn how to live and what the family doesn't teach it's up to the schools to teach but that type of learning gets you only so far then you have to go off on your own and learn about reason, love, avoidance of pain what pleases you all that we get as we learn to distinguish—Joseph wonders if he went to a nice dark gloomy church he could reform, but how much did I hate hearing those preachers preach but he says that's because I learned to think and knew enough to realize preachers use thou shalt not while I made ethical choices—sure deceiving men with my beauty so I could get out of my parents' house and finally to America, he thinks I had a rational discussion with myself—impossible you only think of the pleasure in what other people see in you; only later do you learn what is right or wrong in itself. As a little girl artists wanted to paint my picture in a flower bed of tulips and roses, I'm sure that's exactly what my parents thought, and when I ran away and fought with the legitimate government, the Popular Front, how many letters did they send begging me to come back nobody knows yet we've told them you are visiting your aunt in Barcelona, and my mother must have worn out the prayer stool kneeling so much begging me to come to my senses—one of my nicest fantasies was bringing Jacobo home and for them to realize I was finally free of them.

I can't believe what grandma said in front of Joseph no less, she must be going through her second childhood, senility is similar to childhood only you don't grow out of it, children eventually learn to reason she seems to have lost hers. Does she feel no shame? It's worse than calling a man, I get that today's young girls can now phone a boy back in the day we girls had to sit by the phone waiting for boys to call, and I can understand with feminism girls not wanting to be passive but for her to say what she said in front of Joseph—to me it's bad enough but Joseph isn't even a member of the family, even if she considers him one—it must be because J. is driving her insane looking so much like his grandfather and he didn't even know about grandma, he kept that from his family, at least grandma told my mother and my mother mentioned it to me but old people in love never interested me, what could they know about love, love is for the young, or at least that's what I thought when I was young. I thought grandma and Tomas as a happy couple I had no idea she couldn't stand him and finally threw him out, I thought he cheated on her but he didn't cheat on her she just didn't want to live with him anymore and asked him to leave, no reason given. I never knew that. He was long gone by the time I came to live with her after my mother was killed but not the hooligan she was going out with in a gangland killing. What was she doing going out with a punk like that? But she was easily charmed and he probably carried a wad of bills in his pocket and willing to spend it on her, now we no longer carry large amount of cash on us for fear of robberies, but back then that was the sign of a tough guy—a twenty on top as grandma would say and all singles underneath. Now Joseph has credit cards up the wazoo and even insisted I get one since the new law doesn't allow discrimination against women, so widowed, divorced and single women can now own them, of course I have nowhere near the amount of credit Joseph does, but as he says they are good for emergencies—he wants enough credit so that if he gets fired he can live for at least a year before declaring bankruptcy. He knows the lay of the land I would never think of doing that. But back to grandma saying passion is everything Joseph grasped it immediately but it took me a bit to understand what she was getting at, she talked of unconscious conscious motives—what does a woman her age have a right to talk about lovers, passion, sex, she should be over that by now but J. quickly understood she wanted one more chance at life that she had been celibate for too many years and now she's having these weird dreams where she takes a lover. I've never been so embarrassed. She can't recall them but she wakes up and has to go the bathroom and her nipples are aching and burning with desire down below and she had thought she had long since passed that stage of madness, after all she can't have babies anymore why does she crave sex, have hot flashes, rage and vaginal dryness, shouldn't she be over that by now. For the pleasure Joseph said, imagine that a woman her age wanting sex just because she found love in the past does that mean she can find it in the future. She's a grandmother for god's sake. And she always complained to me that old men are so set in their ways but we women have to dye our hair, put on a false face, make a conscious effort to be gay around them. Gray hair in men is distinguished, in a woman the sign of old age, and now thinks this newfound libido of hers is not new but was just hidden and now that she sees us as a couple she is getting interested in men again, her doctor prescribed estrogen, isn't that unnatural? The aim of a woman is not to be a prisoner at home after dark—her imagination is coming alive once more and loves going out to the theater where before she thought the theater nonsense just a place for entertainment not a discussion of serious ideas and what she likes is what Joseph liked in college afterwards discussing ideas. At her age! She even now goes to the library to get the play and read it after seeing it—a sign she says her brain is coming alive and when it lives it also lives for Eros. It's been dormant too long, she says, and now it includes sexual images. Imagine that! A life of the mind opens up doors you don't expect Joseph says, I think it's shameful, but she thinks living so long is, and she needs all the aids she can get, she thinks the mind has become the instrument of her rebirth, her reawakening, her passions, since she began going to plays again she started thinking again and thinking is awareness of our bodies and her body is telling her something. I always laughed at her thinking like that but I'm not laughing now this is serious what is she going to do pick up men, Joseph is cool about grandma but admits he would be mortified if his mother married another man, ask Hamlet—he doesn't even believe they had sex more than once for him and can't imagine his mother having sex. He swears he was virgin born! I asked him to ask his mother, he thought I was crazy but that's just how I feel with grandma. It's a pity she no longer has women friends her own age to talk to about this and she has to talk to us, I always thought by the time I got to her age I would be over this; at least I wouldn't talk about it in front of my children, even if I never want children. Grandma always appreciated it that we don't talk slowly to her as if cooing to a child or infantilizing old people, even doctors do that to her especially after her heart attack and she left one doctor when all he talked to her was in baby talk about what he thought not respecting her rights until she found one who said to her your life is not over and you have to exercise and walk everyday not become stuck in the house and the more you do physical activity the more you will be able to do and high-fived her telling her she would live at least twenty more years, and now she's overloaded her mental thoughts into overlapping strands of memory and recalls the great love of her life and wants to reconnect with it, but you can't step into the same river twice life is continually flowing but she sees a unity of her life because of her memory of it and remembers when she was in love and wants that once more in her life. No she said I want sex, my body is aching for sex. But what she's doing is not right how can a woman of her age think of sex, all that is supposed to be behind you once you reach menopause but here she is thinking of having an affair, as of yet she has nobody in mind but thinks going out with a married man would be the safest, no strings attached. How can she think like that? Joseph ever the practical one wonders if we should knock before we come in, but how is she going to find a man they don't fall off trees like ripe fruit. Imagine her dating again, who would want to go through that! What I do enjoy about J. is not having to go out having someone to be at home with sex is an added bonus. Is it impossible for grandma to start again, learn again, is this like riding a bicycle you never forget? She claims her dreams convey to her the dissatisfaction of her life and her desire for gratification but it must come from somewhere else, I thought the joy of old age is the freedom from this madness.

When did it happen? How? Is there a precise moment when I realized I was unhappy or that childhood was over or was it the moment grand-father died, my protector and confidant and now I am thinking about him once again standing in front of my mother's casket trying to think of some words to say to her—they let me in early before the ceremony so I could say my final goodbyes, my father had said them enough times to her that he was leaving and going to live in a nursing home, of course he never did one of his empty threats in a life full of empty threats, yet he stayed with my mother and made sure I was raised, he couldn't have gone anyway how could my parents have separated they were my parents I just couldn't imagine them living apart, besides he wouldn't have liked that place there is no solitariness, you live in dorm-like rooms and lead a regimented life, you don't start life over there you end it. As soon as I moved out he moved into my room, finally a room of his own and lived silently only coming out to eat. I never understood what he did there since he no longer read newspapers, and never read books, and to him all music was noise; not only rock 'n' roll but he never even liked Bach, the late Beethoven string quartets or Schubert's *String Quintet in C major* that I now listen to religiously every evening trying to pick up the melody and variations and then back to the melody, and he only listened to the radio for the horse-racing results, not that he was a gambler but near the end he did get in the habit of betting on sure things and not losing too much as Off Track Betting became available in the city and he would be with his few cronies discussing horse racing, he was bored he didn't know how to live in retirement. He would sit in my room in the dark and in silence my mother would complain only coming out to eat, but still it was my home, I always felt if I blew it I could go back there and live, now I am an orphan there's no home to go home to. Now here I am in a funeral home on Eastchester Road that I took two buses because I wanted to walk in the old neighborhood first before I went and buried my mother and it is easier to get to Eastchester Road by buses than trains and I took #1 bus down the Grand Concourse to the Bx. 12 east to Eastchester Road walking a few blocks and here I am in front of my mother, only it's her body not her all made up with rouge and I'm trying to think of some farewell words but all I remember is when my friends said they saw me smoking a cigarette and she lit into me and wouldn't believe me that I wasn't smoking and they only wanted to get me into trouble, it was only when *avuelo* came home and said the boy doesn't lie that she relented. Shouldn't I be thinking nicer thoughts, I say to myself, I must have been happy at one time even if no such words came out of my lips—can I speak symbolically isn't that what thought is symbolic language, but am I the same person she raised, would she be the one person who could recognize me now as I was then. One of our neighbors offered us a puppy after her dog gave birth and I was so excited, must have been 5 or so but then was sad when the puppy died in childbirth, only to hear afterwards from Harvey that my puppy hadn't died they just said that because my parents didn't want a dog. I must have promised to take care of him but my words fell on deaf ears. Now her body is looking up at me but it's not her it's only a shell of herself she's not in the room with me—remember the good points I tell myself as anger overcomes me, she's dead feel for her and it becomes a thought I am thinking but not feeling, a thought being thought but not felt is not a thought just a mirage. Why? She loved me, there's no question about that. She loved me so much that she didn't allow me to live or maybe she loved me so much that she probably never loved me but couldn't say that to herself—she never let me grow. She never listened to my desires, feelings, experiences always seeing me as a little baby and never took my wishes into account like when I couldn't sleep in the bedroom the night grandfather died—that I can feel and I could no longer stand to be around her, and she never grasped that, oh I visited every Sunday but it was an obligation not a visit. After grandfather died in my arms in the ambulance I was making plans to move out even if it took me forever to carry them out. I still recall my friend Paul David, two first names, who moved out at 17 because he couldn't stand his parents and got a small room in Far Rockaway and registered in Far Rockaway high school all before he was 18. How he had the guts do it is beyond me but he did and I would go and visit him every chance I got until we both finished high school and lost touch. My mother constantly complained about the tracks I left on my underwear but later my first girlfriend loved seeing the shit stains on my underwear as she did the wash, it turned her on. How does a thought manifest itself: how does a molecule go from a feeling to a word and then back into a feeling once again if the word doesn't quite capture the feeling because now I am so confused about my feelings I'm not sure what I think? I know I loved my mother but at the same time she said a mother is a son's best friend, give me a break, she was always my mother never my friend, I expect more from a friend—she was my conscience that forced me to examine my behavior, forced me to come to grips with my actions, her voice is always inside me I doubt if I will ever be able to shut it off, she was the one who wouldn't allow me to do crazy things because I feared what if my mother found out like stealing from Alexander's on Fordham Road when all my friends considered that the thing to do and we called it our supply house, but I never could or would tell her anything that was going on in my life that stopped after grandma had gone into the hospital. Grandma gave me sweets I never had to perform for her and only at her funeral did I grasp the full family connection she was married to *avuelo* but grandfather wasn't at the funeral. Home in our small bedroom I waited awake in the dark until he came in and asked if he was married to her why he didn't go to her funeral? He said it would be hypocritical, I didn't know what that word meant but I knew what he meant, and I wanted nothing to do with her and may her soul burn in hell even if there is no hell. I must have learned of hell from Paul David and other Catholic school friends because they believed in an afterlife, I now recall these memories without feelings but I do remember being shocked when grandfather said this. Why can't I have a breakthrough moment where my feelings actually correspond to my thoughts, a spontaneous moment where I can act, feel, desire, all at the same time not always wondering what other people will think of me when they are probably not even thinking of me at all? How does one act the grieving son? Should I wear black, a tear in my coat? Cassandra said they would come to the service but I said they don't need to Esmeralda said we are doing it for you the dead don't need mourners only the living do. I search after the fact for reasons but I'm glad I won't be alone at the gravesite. Will it be like the time at grandfather's gravesite when after we all shoveled dirt over the coffin they all left and I stood there until my mother came up to me and said come on he doesn't need you anymore but I didn't want to leave him alone.

He asked me to go to the opera with him, usually I say no I can't stand opera no nothing about it seems like screaming on stage and I can never understand the story, something I think I would snore through, only the rich went to opera, it's weird, besides governor Rockhead destroyed a vibrant Hispanic community, San Juan Hill, to build a playground for the rich up at Lincoln Center and in the back of the Center was a wall to keep the people out, as if they would even think of going there, and wanted to raze some buildings so he could see his creation from his home across the park at 810-12 Fifth Avenue. But lately that neighborhood has been getting better, it's no longer desolate at night where culturists would flee from as soon as the performance was over, now restaurants were opening up along Broadway, the side streets all the way up to Columbus Avenue thanks to the homosexual population who had two incomes and could afford to go into those restaurants. Now Joseph says even straight people are moving into the neighborhood, the Upper West Side has been rediscovered. Slums have to go to make way for progress Joseph says but I call it poor people removal and at first it was a clean well-lit graveyard but now it was starting to liven up, in the daytime it was safe to walk there but at night I was always told to be careful. Besides who goes uptown? Joseph called, at first I called him Joey he told me how he hated that name, if I am to call him anything it's *The Lone Ranger* his favorite radio program that he would listen to with his grandfather, and was surprised when they finally got a television it was on there as well but nowhere as grand as in his imagination. So I immediately called him Joseph but figured he must have had a difficult time in school because a kid is always called by the diminutive. I really had no interest but then thought what am I going to do stay home and watch soaps, *The Price is Right*, *Strike it Rich* why not have a different experience and he was excited, I remember that, and told me to eat before because we wouldn't have much time but all I knew about Ricard Wagner was that he was an anti-Semite and he was long and boring. How could he a Jew like him, didn't he preclude Hitler? And when I had seen the newsreels of the extermination camps and what they had done to the Jews I almost vomited in the theater, I was still in Spain but it made it more clear to me I had to get out of Europe and to America and they filmed the horror and showed it to the world and was so glad to be out of Europe when more of that footage was shown. How could they do that to human beings? This was mass execution unknown to the world, even the Falangists killed only a few men and woman in comparison and buried them in unmarked graves compared to the systematic slaughter of a whole race of people. He had been told as a child we don't go see Wagner so of course he had to go. As he explained it Wagner died before Hitler was born so he could not have been a Nazi, even if his anti-Semitism had led the way it was not the killing of whole group of people Wagner just didn't like the Jews in art, as I explained to him Solzhenitsyn said Jews infected the Russians with their communism not that the Jews couldn't live a decent life in Russia, forced to live beyond the pale in settlements outside big cities, couldn't make a living, couldn't own land, couldn't farm so became peddlers and cobblers and decided that maybe communism with its promise of equality was a better way to live, silly them blaming the promise of communism for a better way of life. Same with Wagner he was an artist who in his personal life was anti-Semitic but his music was revolutionary. Joseph was able to get free tickets because the wife of his boss refused to go with him and he wouldn't go without his wife who was anti-German to the core. I liked his spunk and besides Conchita was out acting so why stay home alone but then wondered what to wear, men have it easy they can wear a business suit we women have to dress for fashion even if one of the goals of the new feminism is to free us from the iron grip of fashion that it hasn't reached me yet and I wore a nice dress even if we can now wear pants I still feel uncomfortable in them, it's not easy rejecting early training and thought, but when I saw Elizabeth Taylor wear them in *Who's Afraid of Virginia Woolf* coming down the stairs that was a powerful emotional statement and made the play real for me but even if Conchita can now wear them they seem inappropriate for a woman my age. But you can't wear to the opera what you wear around the house and I spent the entire afternoon choosing my wardrobe, when I should have gone to the library to read the libretto. It's always nicer to know what you're listening to. It was Jacobo who would read Shakespeare even if he never actually saw his plays and the lesson rubbed off on Joseph as he did go to the music library and listen to the opera before we went. Conchita didn't even understand what he was talking about reading a performance before you see it, you're going to see it why read it? She wished us well having never wanting to go to another opera after seeing the one in Brooklyn. He told me I had to get over my prejudice about going uptown and I agreed it would be fun to go out for a night on the town and I insisted we go to *The Ginger Man* afterwards to talk about it, I had even heard of that bar. Joseph wanted to pick me up but I said no it's okay I can take the subway but he did insist on taking me home. We met under a Marc Chagall mural one of those boring murals of life in old Russia as a phantasmagoria the charming life of a shtetl, ten in a room, with chickens, no heat ah the wonderful times before the communists came and ruined it all, I hated the nostalgia kick. As Joseph said I have strong opinions. I never saw so many well-dressed men and women, women wearing gowns, men tuxedos, one man even had a cape and top hat another with a walking stick, and bourgeoisie women in full armor with their heels and jewelry Joseph came in his new blue jeans and he was carrying his expensive Parker pen that he would only use for special occasions, that he considered dressed up. I thought there might be some anti-Semitism but there was none only a dwarf named Alberich who was evil but he was no eviler than Iago or Richard III. And I had to explain the Christian references to him, he knew none of that association of love and death yet we both loved the harmonies, sexual imagery, the music even if he didn't get the Christian apologetics, and there wasn't even that much of them only the typical man's view that woman is the devil that I've heard a thousand times before and you have to preach chastity to them otherwise they will swallow you whole. But you don't go to an opera for the story only the music and even if there was no chorus or famous arias that you could whistle to and the story line is silly a woman who only wants to seduce men and drive them away from their true goal and the only answer is renunciation—the devil is a woman and she must suffer because she laughed at Christ on the Cross leaves a lot to be desired but the music was out of this world. Why can't a woman have a life of her own, a true love not be a reborn as a man's fantasy giving up on her own life and renouncing sex. That's what's wrong with the story. Thank goodness I didn't have to truly know the libretto to love the opera. It did go on forever starting at six and ending at a quarter to midnight and he was too tired to go for a drink afterwards, but insisted upon taking me downtown because it was such a late hour and he didn't mind he could do his work as a zombie, but it took me a few days to get back on schedule I had gotten home so late, even as Conchita said what kind of world is this where the grandmother comes home later than the granddaughter. I thought I would dream about it and maybe I did but it was so remote I could only dream about Jacobo and only afterwards realized Joseph certainly looks like him and it's his image that is stuck in my head not the dwarf.

I know I should be doing something, doing more, something different writing my play, going to a poetry class, doing more exercise, but telling myself I should be doing more is not enough I have to do it; all I did was go down to 100 Centre Street find the courtroom and as I walked into part A, B, Q, who knows, but with courtroom personals help found the correct court room as we waited our turn, I know I wasn't the defendant, Cassandra told me this is an adventure but I felt my chest constrict, heavy breathing, pointless I know, I wasn't the defendant, but I was scared I was the designated worrier but it wasn't about me but all I thought was I can't wait for this to be over and I'm out on the street walking home and this would all be over but once out on the street the same fear overcame me even as I kept telling myself it's all over I'm walking arm in arm with Cassie and she says let's go for Chinese, but all I wanted to do was walk, how can she be so calm, she's laughing she could have almost been in jail, now there's an emptiness in me I expected a fierce legal battle, a courtroom clash over freedom of speech, I had my speech planned debating the issues that never came up. Charged with public lewd and indecent behavior, nudity, resisting arrest, violating community standards and god knows what else, out of shame and probably the promptings of the ACLU the prosecution quietly dropped the case and I felt so relieved even if her lawyer was itching for a legal fight, I think he was about to retire and he could go down in a blaze of glory defending freedom and make a name for himself, but since it was agreed no sexual coitus occurred only simulated and maybe because New York is being overrun by crime they decided not prosecute theater people? Who knows? She took me to this great Chinese restaurant near the court house and I had my first sweet-and-sour pork, I had never eaten pork before, except sausage, bacon or ham, I had no prejudice against pork certainty not religious it just never was made its way into my mother's repertoire so I never ordered it in restaurants. I didn't know what it tastes like. It was delicious. A whole new food was added to my diet. And now we would go there at least once a week or we did something I had never heard of anyone from the Bronx doing, we ordered in. Never back in my parents' house had we done that, and none of my friends' parents did either, of course we would eat out once in a while as a treat but never ever order outside food in, mothers cooked. I had enough money now to order out and it was easier than cooking, so there went my plans to buy real furniture. My landlord had given me his old crap even asked me to sign a contract for this shit, and I agreed knowing full well I would soon get my own stuff and he could have all this back—at first I was insulted what you don't take my word for it, but then Esmeralda said a contract is a good idea so you can give it back to him whenever and he can't complain it's in your favor, besides you don't want to live in an unfurnished room then you'll go out and buy junk just to furnish it now you can take your time. That never occurred to me, also what never occurred to me was to get quality furniture not the cheapest but she explained that the cheapest cost more in the long run and is not as pleasant, you want to get the best you can afford. Easy for her to say she's an old lady I'm use to crap uncomfortable furniture, cheap appliances, ill-fitting clothes functional stuff not exquisite stuff and she went with me and helped me find a good bed and said you just buy it, and it was easy with her; alone I hemmed and hawed, tore my hair out, aggravated, thought, debated back and forth and said when I am married will get good stuff and never did anything but have an uncomfortable desk chair and wobbly desk full of papers so I could never work, when I cleaned it up I would write my masterpiece. But I did get a queen-sized bed because Cassandra liked to sleep in my arms as she said she loves to sleep in my arms like she did with her boyfriend in college, only that was a single bed. How the hell could two people sleep in a single bed? I'm still in awe that she actually moved away from home and went to college not staying at home like most of my friends. It has taken me forever to do that. I wondered how do I know if I am unaware of its existence; I had thought as soon as I moved out I would begin my life, start writing my masterpiece even if I had no idea what I wanted to write and would stare at the blue-lined paper day in and day out, even bought an electric typewriter a good one the salesman said this isn't for an occasional letter or a term paper you are a writer and will have to use it constantly as it sat there silently upon my desk. I loved hearing the sound of typing only it never came. But what I could do was lie on my unmade bed and pleasure myself over and over. My desk was so cluttered that I actually took the bridge table from my mother's place and would set it up and move the typewriter there when I was in the mood to write, usually the typewriter stayed put. My plan was to write after dinner only I was too bloated and then took my constitutional to Bickford's but then I was too tired to write, so I came home took a nap, then ate, and then would write only I was too groggy then, my other thought was to get up at 2am and write for an hour or two then go back to bed, only I hated getting out of bed in the middle of the night just to stare at a blank sheet of paper, and the thought of opening the bridge table, moving the typewriter and starting especially in the cold morning hours was too much, it was easier to go out and get a green pepper steak at my local Cuban Chinese restaurant. I just couldn't write: when I am ready I will do it, I kept telling myself. Zoltan told me to begin every day all over again is the hardest and that you have to start by doing baby steps and he mentioned Prometheus and I thought of the sculpture at the ice-skating ring of Rockefeller Center, and I had never truly seen it until he mentioned it and I had to go see it again a god bringing fire to man to start civilization, the heroic age disintegrating to the age of iron—but not only did he steal fire from the gods so that they could be together, they were also able to live together in a city and create tragedy because tragedy can only develop in a city, and we developed a new way of thinking, for that Zeus punished him by having a vulture devour his liver, but we never talked about the consequences of his action, do you think he's smiling? Esmeralda also told me the story of Diego Rivera and the socialist mural he painted that Rockefeller destroyed because of the working-class consciousness he portrayed. Yes, Governor Rockhead the great connoisseur of modern art who chided people when they didn't know anything about art but whose family destroyed one of the great murals in the 20th century. Lucky nobody told Rockefeller that Marx considered himself a modern-day Prometheus bringing the torch of truth to the masses. Interesting story but if nobody knows it what good is it? People view sculpture as perceptual not moral. Still I had a good look at a local icon I never really noticed before or saw it only as a decoration never realizing the importance of it and said want to do something like that, make demands upon myself stop being lazy with myself and living in 'bad faith' which all sounded fine and dandy but I still went home to my cluttered desk and bridge table slid between the wall and desk but didn't even think of taking it out tonight. This is not the kind of life I wanted, this is not what I expected after I finished college when I resolutely said now I would begin learning, the only intellectual activities I have are going with Cassandra to court and Esmeralda who's almost as old as my mother to the opera. Yet I never did anything with my mother, she had to nag me incessantly for me to even take her to see some relatives because she's now afraid to ride the bus alone and didn't know how to get anywhere from Co-op City. One night I actually typed up a whole page, single space no less, no paragraphs just straight thoughts and said if I could only keep this up but for the next two weeks refused to even look at my typewriter, that's when Zoltan suggested I start first with a journal, which Esmeralda saying the same thing only called it a diary, but I didn't do anything interesting to write down what I did, what I did do is get up in the morning, dress for work, go to work, come back home eat dinner go for a walk or sit at my bridge table saying I should write this down— how earthshattering, it was so earthshattering I couldn't even remember it. Saw Jonas Mekas films of everyday life *Walden* and said god almighty this is three hours of boredom nothing is going on, there's no tumult, a home movie if it was at least of me would be interesting, however he's doing something what am I doing I don't even have a comfortable reading chair but Esmeralda said you're too young to read all the time you should be doing things. Will Cassandra be pissed if I do things without her?

Theater starts with wonder, I can't remember who said that or the first play I ever saw it must have been in grade school, we would have to sit and watch plays of the older students and when it became my turn I didn't want to perform in front of my classmates, I was ashamed. I'm lucky the school didn't ruin plays for me—I recall in the fifth grade we did something about the planets and I was supposed to play Pluto but not only didn't I tell my mother I was in it but snuck out of the classroom and refused to be in the play even when the assistant principal found me hiding in the bathroom and brought me back to the classroom; thank goodness my teacher said we don't need her and we'll do it without you and someone else did my part and the girl was congratulated for stepping in on such short notice and I was angry they weren't congratulating me and at the same time glad that I wasn't on stage in front of all my friends even if I wanted the admiration. And it's still true that I am so nervous before I step out on stage even if I do love the applause—certain memories of childhood haunt you and you still blush twenty years later other memories are simply distant and I can barely recall them like seeing a breath of fresh air coming out of my mouth, my occasionally going to grandma's and being bored stiff there or the museums she took me to where she explained everything to me and I would be saying yes, yes, why am I here when I rather be with my friends, but she reminded me how much I liked the Central Park Zoo because the animals came up so close to you as opposed to the Bronx Zoo where the cages are so much further back. Yet I went with my girlfriends to the Bronx Zoo really to look for boys when I was a little older, but she's wrong it was Café Nicholson's near the zoo but closer to the 59th street bridge where we walked down a long hallway to the dining room with silk pillows, that had the best dessert an apple calvados soufflé filled with ice cream, that I loved even if I wasn't a rich kid holding onto a teddy bear, not the animals at the zoo, even later after the Bronx Zoo we'd go to Jahns up on Kingsbridge Road eating their famous Kitchen Sink, what they called their big ice cream bowl filled with all their flavors that one person couldn't eat alone and all of us would dip into was more fun than being with grandma. I had to fight with my mother for some money for that, or when we bought a pizza pie, what do you need a pie for here's 25 cents get a slice and a soda, she had no idea of sharing. At least grandma understood that and allowed me to cut school that is until she started paying tuition and said not at these prices so what we girls did was hang out in Riverside Park smoking. But Calhoun did put on better performances than public schools or high school and they weren't only educational where school teachers in my local schools only thought in conformist ways preparing us for a boring life at Calhoun teachers thought your inner life was important and their plays attempted to teach mastery of the soul—these were serious dramatic teachers not just teaching to have weak pleasures and avoid pain, they wanted to make sure we had fun and said when life grabs you by the balls as it surely will all life does, make sure you simply don't give up and fight the good fight, of course I had no idea what she was talking about even if already was thrown for a loop by my mother's death. Martha thought your mind and body had to be correctly trained, grandma defended her and not only did she listen to me but I actually invited her to my play, something I never did with my mother, and she would mention how she came of age during the Depression, ancient history to me, and how she found this job and felt lucky she didn't have to be in a service job but still it was only temporary but it lasted a lifetime because she liked being with students. Can you believe they pay me for this! and I get to teach you how to act, something I wished I had a chance to do but couldn't because I had to earn a living for my family. This was unlike teachers in public school who seemed destined to waste their lives and I needn't feel sorry for them—grandma had told me I didn't have to listen to teachers who led mediocre lives while my mother swore by them. Then Martha, we always called teachers by their first name in this progressive school, asks me to come to tryouts for a meaningful play— the school produced *Celestina* I never knew Spain produced such a play I immediately grasped the subtext love of honor, the challenge to honor; and because I was repeating my senior year Martha thought I was mature enough to play the lead role and it did give me perks, once when rehearsing my classmates broke into applause at how well I did my speech, I was the one who bought beer to parties because I was over eighteen and could buy it legally, taught the younger girls how to smoke, but they taught me pot, but more important the actors sprouted real words not made-up junk. Convincing dialogue. Martha had said that we didn't live in these tragic times anymore Christianity talks about a promised land to come and Marxism of a better future, problems are fixable, no more do the unjust suffer while grandma didn't like this fuzzy logic and said there still is failure of the living. This was my first realistic play where actors were actually commenting upon life and characters could show themselves from their own point of view, and I even told grandma about the performance and I couldn't believe how much fun it was to act, the applause was secondary the good acting primary and from good acting other things can come. Martha was the one who insisted I apply to the University of Pittsburgh she said it had an excellent acting program and she wrote a letter of recommendation for me. What I liked about acting was the sense of freedom and rebellion, you could play the part any way you wanted where the actors could pull the strings on the character's moral development, which dominates the performance and allows reason to have fun and it was that reason, that fun, that awakened me to the world of theater and surprise the world of ideas. I surprised myself by becoming interested in something and all of a sudden, not all of a sudden but the whole second senior year, found for the first time school was a joy. At my old high school, they forced us to take gym all we did was talk about graduating getting a job meeting a boy and moving away from home. Not one of us ever mentioned college now here I was accepted to college and I would have been stuck up there had not fate intervened with my mother getting herself shot in a gangland killing when there was a power grab in the Bonanno crime family and a mafia punk tried to kill one of Bonanno's small-time hoods shot him five times and he survives, my mother was shot once in the head and killed only because she was in the car with him when he shot, a Mafia free-for-all where the young Turks wanted to take power from the old geezers and grandma had to take me in. That happened over Christmas, she let me finish the school year up in the Bronx and the school was willing to let me graduate but grandma said I wasn't ready to graduate yet and she registered me into this independent school where I thought all I was going to learn is how to serve tea and which fork to use at dinner. I was totally lost in that environment imagine they didn't learn how to serve tea they took learning seriously, they carried books around with them, they read them, before I never had any need for books, I didn't know what to make of it but I liked the boys and slowly I stopped going up to the Bronx and started finding out who I was and concerned with seeing who I was and trying to please my newfound friends and both joy and sadness became part of me and for the first time actually thought about making something of myself and what was so weird actually being able to say it aloud. But I couldn't say that up in the Bronx and slowly stopped going, stopped answering phone calls from old girlfriends and found new friends who were no longer always bored with everything.

Do you ever know the exact moment your life changes? I thought it did when my grandfather died, but now that I am in love I think the precise moment is when we moved in together and I hugged her three times just to see the smile on her face and her the glow on mine, why is my grandfather's face coming up is it because I am now in love or is it because my mother died alone in the hospital and I've never felt so alone in my life? By the time the hospital called and I arrived she was already dead and her face had that blank stare on it and seemed to be saying leave me alone, I want nothing to do with you anymore, and I never want to look at another dead body again. The nurse said call your funeral home there is nothing more you can do for her here. She had to repeat it I didn't comprehend what she said at first and after she said the second time I called the funeral home and it was all taken out of my hands all I had to do was mourn. I expected an outpouring of emotion, grief, tearing my hair out but that was hogwash I stood in silence, mourned in silence realized how useless my imagination was always wanting to begin living and so far not doing anything and I wanted to be a little boy again and start all over again a do-over, not my fear that would I end up like her, not a tear coming to my eye and when I left the hospital went to the first diner I saw and had a big breakfast, wondering if my grandfather would stop by open up his newspaper and read in front of me, that's what I remember about him when we ate together, as I tried to visualize my life at home—my job on Saturday night, when I was allowed to go out at night by myself, was to get the *Times* before that he only read the dailies and the Jewish press, but now he could stick his head around the Sunday *Times* forever. Trying to find out who I was, at the same time wondering who I was, but I couldn't grab hold of the image until all of a sudden there it was in front of me, if only I could stop being a disguise to myself, and it would take him a week to finish it, if only life would seize me by the throat, passion, love, lust, he must have stopped reading books after he started the Sunday *Times*, because he no longer had a book by his bed and I would sometimes have to ask him to shut the light in the middle of the night when it woke me up, usually it didn't I am a sound sleeper, how pathetic I felt, it was from him that I learned to take ideas seriously, and yet look at me, as I now stood in front of my mother, only it's not my mother, but an empty shell of a woman who was my mother, and I wonder, wonder why I can't get a coherent thought in my head and say I can't wait until I am out of here into the diner across the street, only it isn't across the street that one is closed I have to walk a few blocks until I come to a subway station and by a subway station there's always a Three or Four Brothers Greek diner and it is there I sit at a booth not the counter without the *Times* that I wanted to read to distract me but most newspaper kiosks in the Bronx don't sell the *Times* or the *Village Voice*, you have to know where to go and I don't know this neighborhood, so I am stuck with the *Post*, I quickly read Pete Hamill's column then am forced to read the rest of the *Post* to get my money's worth—terrible paper I only like their movie clock and the column of Pete Hamill and so it is not distracting enough for me. After this I vowed to carry a paperback book with me so I wouldn't get stuck again. Inwardly now I feel that I am looking at the world in a different way I am an orphan, at least Cassandra has her grandmother, who do I have? I knew I could declare my love but women now hang scalps on their belt but still I feel connected to her in ways I never felt before unlike an old girlfriend when we parted all I missed was the sex not her, I enjoy being by Cassie's side and just listening to her speak and the certitude of my thoughts are only relevant unless I discuss it with her, share it with her, nothing really happens unless I can discuss it with her, the act is meaningless unless shared with her and her grandmother. Does all this depend upon my bio-chemical system am I nothing but my moods—better living through chemistry, can I figure out when my whole way of life changed, when did she stop being a friend and became a lover? Not when she first led me into the bedroom in her grandma's place I was that before even if I didn't admit that to myself, that was the physical culmination of feelings I had, this is a much deeper change in mood not a superficial pining. My mother thought it was unnatural that I went out with an older woman, she was over thirty, it just wasn't done, a man should be older was what she thought or at least within a few months of each other's ages, also taller, but that was my prejudice not hers, until I saw that Truffaut movie where Antoine Doinel only dated taller women, and that she wasn't Jewish, she would have excused everything except that. That's why it was easier not to say much, we never had much to say to each other. Did Cassandra take me to that? Was that the first French movie I ever saw? Couldn't be I had seen some in college, I think, recalling how difficult it was at first trying to remember what I just read and forgetting to look at the acting, I wondered why I enjoyed it. But I remember being too cool to go to movies in college. The college world was lost on me; I saw it as extended high school even I learned to read books on the subway instead of comic books, I was in college now I shouldn't be reading comic books I said to myself. I remember there was even discount tickets to *The Deputy* but nobody wanted to go with me and I was afraid to go alone to Broadway, I would feel too embarrassed. But once I started reading some of the masterpieces did want more only too much of the reading assignments were ordinary stuff that got in the way of my more profound readings. My first play was *The Play's the Thing* after some professor, who? said avoid theater it gives the illusion of profundity but really it's false illusion but if I was going to live in New York I should take advantage of theater otherwise why not move to some warm climate; Zoltan and I took each other, it was experimental theater and I was afraid I wouldn't like it, we saw it down in Greenwich Village, which my mother associated with beatniks and dirty girls but it was only a subway ride and a brave new world away, someday I knew I had to leave the Bronx even if I kept coming home at night and I studied my map of New York City that my grandfather had so that I didn't have to ask directions when I got off the train at West 4th Street easily found the Theatre de Lys on Christopher Street, but was surprised how much Zoltan knew of avant-garde works outside of painting, he wanted to see the play because it was written by a Hungarian Ferenc Molnar, but didn't like it said it was entertaining but not serious; seeing it live blew my mind why couldn't it be serious and comic at the same time, and I wondered why they never took us to a live performance it is so different than reading a play. A play is meant to be acted. Zoltan then told me about theater in the Weimar Republic—Germany WW1? I wasn't sure, but he talked about the clash of values, the collapse of one era and the start of another, and that they had predicted the Gulag, Holocaust and the A bomb. Here I didn't have to worry about translated the words I knew exactly what they meant even if I didn't understand every word. Why did it take me so long to figure that out? But should I be caught up in the opinion of the foolish or listen to the wise. You can't learn until you are ready Esmeralda told me and you can't be ready until you have a smattering of education, she told me, so should I be grateful for those college years I wondered? In my senior year I had no desire to go to law school or graduate school like some of my classmates, one friend even got accepted to Yale in the MFA program in theater and I wondered why go why not just write, but it seems like we need a degree for everything now, even was surprised when a couple of ex-soldier boys, army veterans coming back to school on the GI bill said don't rush it it's not so good to be out there but I couldn't wait to begin learning: learning meant leaving, freedom and independence but there I was still at home with no freedom or independence until I chanced into meeting Cassandra and Esmeralda. I wasn't looking for wisdom only adventure until by chance happened upon it.

How can they not believe? What gives them the right to think my ways of using the past are wrong but theirs are right? After all my ways go from before psychology, history, they can buy this myth that all I want to do is sleep with my father and kill my mother or that the working class will inherent the earth but not that the stars influence our lives, I read my sign today that today is the first day of my new life, and newspapers carry more of astrology than they do of psychology or class-conflict, and my horoscope said that today is the first day of my new life, so I know I had to do something to make this day memorable and so I did, I don't even recall if I thought about it before, in fact I know I didn't and I don't even think my subconscious worked on it because I don't think I have a subconscious—I read my horoscope and acted knew I had to do something to change my life, that's what it said, like the time Conchita became Cassandra without thinking about it. I had gone for another audition at school but I didn't think too much would come of it I had gone before gotten callbacks but it never really came to anything I never got the part but this time the director asks what impressed me in reading the play and I replied how Ajax kept his hatred going he wanted nothing to do with Odysseus even when he meets him in Hades and the shade of Ajax still turns his back on him, and he knew I had done my homework, Ajax still lives on the old code of honor, he said he would commit suicide and does, while Odysseus lives in the modern world and didn't share in the old values he just deceived, placated and was ruthless. When Cassandra spoke her first lines walking on the purple carpet knowing she was doomed in grief and terror the director was impressed and I got the part right on the spot, he said I changed wasn't the same timid actress I had been in previous years. What he didn't know was I had lost my shyness someone had ticked my clock, I lost my virginity, Conchita became Cassandra without any hesitation and on my resume whited-out my old name and typed in my new name. Grandma thought it was because I didn't want to be identified as Puerto Rican, Americans had a difficult time distinguishing

Spanish culture and thought all Spanish people came from Puerto Rico back then, and that has helped me. How can they not believe the starts influence our lives there are magnetic fields, cosmic rays are bombarding the earth all the time why shouldn't they have an influence upon the way we think, and there's plenty of evidence of flying saucers, even pilots have seen them but the government covers it all up. They believe because *The New York Times* doesn't cover it it's not real, and Joseph thinks because I no longer believe in the Church that I believe in this, but I don't believe in God nor the church, religion has become irrelevant for me, especially when they started having a Spanish mass thinking that would draw me into the church it further turned me away, the Pope also said the Jews didn't kill Christ that must have come as a surprise to Father Morales. I don't speak Spanish anyway, but desire answers no matter where they come from and when I'm with my actor friends we all believe even if took us awhile to admit it to each other. Actors are a superstitious lot. Politicians can only think of war as the answer to any question, Joseph laughs thinks I am part of the *Ancien Regime* not part of the modern world and Enlightenment, yes the Enlightenment of imperialism, world wars, the Holocaust, all in the name of freedom of thought, that the world never again would permit torture ha, ha how can grandma not believe in the occult after all she's been though, after all the good guys lost, defeated badly, she lost the love of her life, and is an exile from her own country. I thought surely she would go back at least for a visit now that Franco has died, but she says the forces of the republic still haven't recovered the arc of history grinds slowly, here she means the working class, that is my father who couldn't wait to escape the factory and become his own boss. These false truths of science are only temporary, these modern thinkers only guessing, science can't even cure the modern cold which they even say doesn't come from the cold air but from germs, give me a break, these scientists never get beyond the superficial causation not into pleasure and pain, joy and sadness, which makes the world go around, they're missing the point looking for small mechanical answers to huge questions, and the stars and all the relationship of the stars to the planets is needed to get at the truth, the essence of a thing, the order of a connection, the relationship between our birth and where our planet was at the time of our birth. Everybody knows their sign. Recently I was at a Happening in Central Park where Hare Krishnas were playing their tambourines and they seemed happier than the morbid hippies. I brought some incense home and grandma said it had a putrid smell, pot has a better aroma and I really don't like the smell of pot, but this is safer I said, she laughed. How does she know about marihuana anyway? I asked her what is the sound of one hand clapping, but she said don't devise koans that sound clever but are empty of thought. You can't give in to their nonsense, she said. Right the Western mind is so correct that it has to destroy different cultures; we've had our day it's just so stupid meeting primitive cultures and destroying their way of life thinking our way of life is so superior there are other wisdoms than those found in the West, these great thinkers of the West here I include Joseph who says he's Jewish but doesn't believe in a Supreme Being and is more interested in social justice than theology, he laughs since he doesn't believe anymore he's so busy in making a living, but who still thinks science is the only way; I gave up on religion in my dope-smoking hippie days in college. I suggested we stop eating meat the flesh of a live animal both laughed, anything out of their scientific materialism they see as primitive thought and can't understand how anyone can believe that nonsense. But I believe we can take little steps to control our lives not fight them but go with them, besides what harm does it do? If we find life in outer space won't that be significant that we are not unique creatures, and what about all the signs, cave drawings, crop rotations, Machu Picchu, Stonehenge, Easter Island doesn't that show we were visited by ancient aliens and if we were visited once we will probably be visited again, all religions allow the gods to procreate with women rarely a goddess with a man, pure sexism—one drama teacher once asked how many people read their horoscopes daily and the whole class raised their hand, that has to mean something such insightful people believing, astrology at least provides answers: it tells us what to do and doesn't leave us in the cold empty vastness of space, and at least with astrology you don't have to buy into this myth of historical progress things are getting better all the time. Yea toys are getting bigger, better, now I can type on a screen not a piece of paper on this behemoth of a computer, but does it make my life easier, better, in fact Joseph told me not to do it they would consider me a typist forever but I did it and am now more important to the bank since secretaries are afraid of the computer, so much so they are letting me take a computer course so I can learn to code, but most of us are lost in the modern world; astrology offers relief the way the church used to before they lost their way blessing both the killer and the killed not wanting to become involved in dirty sordid politics and maybe spacemen can visit us again and show us the way. Can a belief be wrong if it's accepted by a majority of the people even if is contrary to the principles of science? Grandma and Joseph condemn it only because the answers are easier than science.

When I came home I was no longer the dutiful daughter, no longer this servile young girl known for her beauty not her brains, no longer did boys follow me around, write letters to my friends asking to be introduced to me, and when I didn't respond wrote to the school principal saying that I stayed out into all hours of the night with boys and was a bad girl, luckily the principal didn't believe a word of it and had the boy expelled. Our family was wealthier we drove a Hispano a luxury car, the Mercedes of Spain, at least my father did he never let a girl drive, he said a young lad like that should know his place, a country boy easily corrupted by city life he should stay in the country where he belongs, god only knows whatever happened to him. I was part and parcel of a new makeup city kids who were so much more sophisticated than our country bumpkins and I began realizing that I was becoming a new person, even frightened by my budding sexuality, but knowing I couldn't stop the new person I was being and I knew I couldn't do anything about it, besides I liked the new person I was becoming, it was like my name I couldn't change that nor could I change the person I was becoming but it was me and it wasn't me I was undergoing a metamorphosis, that's what love does to you even if it fails you can't go back to the old ways, and I would be sitting up in my room staring at the ceiling or looking out the bay window seeing nothing while my parents and sister thought I was ashamed of what I had done, imagine that, they knew me so little they think I was ashamed of standing up for freedom and fought the irrational demagogy of the fascists and their desire to return to feudalism not believing I had seen the future and there was no going backwards, but I was wrong the future came but not how I thought it would come, the family wasn't destroyed, the church didn't collapse, the state didn't wither away, the old ways continued and we went on living as if before only I wasn't the same anymore, the world may not have collapsed but I certainly changed, and when my mother and father found out I was pregnant they immediately arranged a match for me, even if I was never alone with him before marriage and my aunt would go everywhere with us as a chaperone and we could never have a real conversation, still realizing how banal he was I jumped at the opportunity to escape from my parents thinking in my own home at least I would have freedom, he didn't mind I was carrying someone else's child he wanted to play house with me and said he would love it as his own, but if he knew it was a Jew who got me pregnant I wonder what he would have thought, since he thought abortion was akin to murder he couldn't have wanted that, but the Jew was the devil incarnate he could never have raised a Jewish child, he hated Judeo-Bolshevism so. But it was a Jew who infected me with ideas of freedom, initially I joined just out of noblesse oblige sympathy for the peasants, but Jacobo was the one who taught me how to read and how to learn to think, even if he was wrong thinking a socialist economy could meet the needs of the masses. Who knew it would ever be so horrible? The reprisals started, the terror was beginning I was safe at first but who knew how long that would last. It's true the Church, the aristocrats, the government out of power were all united for one purpose to stop the spread of Judeo-Bolshevism, that is the secret history of the '30s: after the Great War, what I was trained to call the First World War, when revolutions broke out in Berlin, Vienna, Budapest, Munich, people expected it to succeed all over Europe but it came to fruition only in the Soviet Union where it swept away in the most backward of all countries the old existing monarchy—no developed country fell for the Soviet machinations, Spain was as backward as the Soviet Union mainly agricultural, no electricity, a corrupt priesthood, so we thought it only natural to be their allies, the only difference is that we had a strong right-wing repressive regime that did get the trains to run on time, build roads, started electrification, and it went well until the Wall Street crash that had worldwide effects on international finance—financiers wanted debts repaid and that led the way to the economic collapse, the rise of workers soviets, the election of left-wing politicians and the final collapse when land reform failed, exports fell, unemployment trebled as countrysiders made their way to the cities looking for work, scaring city folk—all these men coming to the city without women could only mean trouble—young men living without women will be up to no good—communists couldn't organize the men and they became armed thugs of the Franco state, and the leftist government wasn't a true communist government they wanted to reform capitalism not destroy it and never stood up for the abolishment of private property, all they begged for was relief from our allies but only Hitler airlifted supplies to Franco and because of his superior airpower we never had a chance; we couldn't raise the consciousness of the workers let alone the masses they still believed in superstitious nonsense, the church, the family, and they were against the new and we failed to capture the hearts and minds of the peasants—we fought but I was back in my room in less than two years and I had to continue all alone without Jacobo or my friends and was forced to act the passive young girl, which I wasn't, otherwise I would have had no future at all, and after the baby was stillborn I had this sudden fear I would never see Jacobo again, and no longer cared at all what happen to me I was so depressed, but I had engaged in some serious reading and now more than simply a gut feeling I wanted intellectual thought and when I stayed in my room or walked outside with a chaperone the only people I could engage with were educated Catholics who were allowed to read unholy works so as to be able to criticize them better but I wasn't interested in the critical parts just the *Economic and Philosophical Manuscripts* that were in the custody of the Soviet Union and were finally translated into Spanish and I began to see Marx was not a communist, and that there had been two strains in Marxism, and in my conversations with Jacobo he was the first man I was ever friends with who was also a lover and admired my brain, who believed man is part of nature and by transforming nature in social production develops from labor, but there are chances, accidents, it's not one long road to development like the communists contend, they had such a simplistic view of history, the narcissism of history, I still bounce all my ideas off him and he's really the other half of my mind, the two hemispheres in my brain, and I became a different person because of him, I should forget already he's dead and we lost, but even if he's dead and we lost that's not in my mind and still recall those days with joy and warmth.

Who would believe I have all this leisure time nobody checks attendance, nobody checks up on me, I have no time clock to punch, and I've developed a good rapport with liquor stores and they buy my wines that seem to be selling like hot cakes so I don't have to work 9–5 and I don't even feel guilty that I have it so easy, besides liquor stores don't open until 11AM and usually it's later in the day that the boss comes in, the managers could be selling socks for all they cared, and most liquor stores make money off booze not wine, but owners usually like wine and they're happy to be around someone who likes wine as well and some even want me to feature my wine at wine tastings, they'll supply the cheese, it's better to get people into the shop with a wine opening than selling lotto. At least at a wine opening customers buy. And of course I have to taste my product so by the middle of the evening am a little tipsy, a nice glow and in the afternoon tastings would always take a nap much better than my college nap but Esmeralda said I should learn to use my free time not fritter it away—how many people have such free time and make money like you, at first I thought get a second job work at a desk in a hotel or dishwasher at a restaurant, but she said you don't need more money don't do what you hate use your time productively but productively meant more work, in college I would count the seconds until class was over no professor had me on the edge of my seat excited wondering what would come next, a person who believed in the passion of ideas, in fact not only didn't they entertain me they rarely moved from behind the lectern or raised their voice and all I thought about was getting free of this place and having a job and now that I had one was as bored as I was in college and only have another fifty years to go before retiring. Esmeralda said you're no longer a student now it's time to start learning and you can now become something you never dreamed of, use what you learned from your grandfather, you don't have to see the world as a zero-sum game and that he who makes the most money in the end wins, nor do you have to follow the path of least resistance you can strike out on your own not follow what everyone does such a benchmark is a misunderstanding of other ways of life, easy for her to say she was old I still had to live, I thought I might be able to learn to use my leisure time productively but all I did after her speech is not go back to take a nap and began walking in earnest, only going back to the office to fill out the paperwork, but since I hated going into the office in a basement of a brownstone would leave it to the last moment and then would have to spend a whole day filling out all my order forms, and I learned to make decisions on the basis of my free time, unfortunately there were not many places you could walk in the afternoon, no longer could you just walk and avoid red lights never stopping because now you could only stay on main streets the city is so dangerous even in the afternoon so I joined the Y and jogged around the track and people thought I was in shape because I could run a few miles or lift some weights, at least until my back gave out from lifting too heavy of a weight, that scared me and I started doing stretching exercise which I hated but had to to relieve the pain. That's when I got into tai-chi, no longer was I 'the kid', immortal. Exercise became boring but the foreign film culture had moved from the Upper East Side down to the Village and that was great more fun than libraries where I would fall asleep because they were so over heated, and I really wasn't a bar person in the afternoon, and you don't go into a bar to drink wine so few people did that the wine had turned to vinegar and left a bad taste in my mouth. I found myself in a state of transition, wanting excitement, pleasure, but nothing I did gave me excitement or pleasure only boredom and now all I was doing was trying to avoid boredom but could not enjoy myself when not working and had done my job so fast and easily I didn't have to work that much. Such difficulties we should all have Cassandra said. Nothing grand, no great philosophical insight all I did was make a mental calculation to try and use my time more productively, I had enough money to continue especially if I didn't feel guilty not working, and I began to realize I had two distinct ways of doing things: one, just do it gut feeling, and two, think about doing it before I do it, but it was the first way that was bringing me in a fortune and I would never ever have called up Cassandra if I had thought about it—the fear of rejection would have been too great, yet even as I called said I can't do without thinking that can only lead to disaster and I tried to balance my divided self: one hand doing something the other half thinking about doing something except I was now beginning to realize that I couldn't do that and I had to leap into the unknown my choice was passion or boredom as success dogged me and I saw how easily I could rise up in the hierarchy I was getting so good at what I was doing but is the rise to the top what I want. I admired Cassandra for getting what she wanted, true she had a day job, but she made sure it didn't interfere with her acting even as she juggled appointments she always went to auditions and always took what was offered her, she rather act than wait for the perfect part, I am not me I am the character, she would always say. After I dodged the draft thanks to my addiction to marihuana, I thought all my problems would be solved; but now the draft was finished, the lottery in and not only was I not called but didn't even need it got a high number so wasn't called and was now free of the damn thing, but it didn't change the rest of my life, yes it did, I had seen some friends come back from 'Nam all messed up, into drugs, alcohol trying to blot memory and they refused to talk about it because they were afraid that would make them feel weak, I couldn't spend much time with Harvey my former friend, who gave up his student deferment because he didn't think it fair a poor person should go in his place, who was now into a world of his own and for him time had stopped when he went into the service, he still calls me Joey not the Joseph I started calling myself when I saw it on my college diploma. I have no idea where my diploma is, I know my mother kept it but I can't remember if I ever took it to my place, all I remember was being disappointed it wasn't in Latin, I thought that would be cool in a dead language that nobody could read: it could have said this idiot graduated we should all give back our diplomas, but nobody would know and it would look so sophisticated in a dead language. What good is it? That's why I always wanted to learn it it had no practical implications and now I have the time but not the inclination to do it but make a mental note when I retire to learn Latin. And it didn't stop me from putting on my resume that I could read Latin that seemed to turn people on as I were truly educated and employers were impressed with my false rigor, imagine if anyone asked me to translate it. *Caveat Emptor!*

I keep saying that I am the same person even if I don't believe it. I have a right and left hand side of the brain and they refuse to communicate with one another, it all started when my mother died and I had to move in with Grandma, I was numb didn't know what I was doing but never felt so lonely as when I left my friends and at first was commuting up there every day, supposedly for school but only to hang with my friends, smoke in the bathroom, cut classes and dream how we were going to get a job after graduation and live together, and then grandma comes up to my school sees my homeroom with drawings on the wall and the loud noise in the classroom frightens her and she wants to immediately get me out of this place. I refuse. It's the only place I feel at home. Instead of transferring me she lets me finish the semester, the school allows me to graduate after what I've been through even as I barely go to class and my grandma even comes to graduation but at graduation she has a surprise for me she asks how I can live having so little knowledge and it's true I don't even know the name of the mayor and she says that next year you will go to the Calhoun School, a private school on the Upper West Side, where she has a connection and I was shocked you had to pay tuition, why pay for school when it is free but she said you get what you pay for, and since it was only one year agreed even if I already had my high school diploma, I could have spent four years repeating high school I knew so little but I refused and only with her constant nagging did I spend one more year in high school and it worked my grades became better, I tried acting, and even got into a good college, something that had never entered my mind before, I had had enough school. I still wouldn't give up my old friends, but they wouldn't/couldn't come down to see me they were afraid of the Village with its dirty people and loose morals, and never left the neighborhood unless to go to work. I had two different set of thoughts depending upon who I was with, sensations when I was up in the Bronx with my bad-ass friends, drugs when I was with my newfound friends in the city and when I was with one wanted to be with the other I was never happy where I was and thought it had to be me but now I can see it was two different sets of people my body and mind were on opposite ends of the spectrum and it didn't occur to me that it was out there not me. In Walton we read *My Antonia* which is supposed to be a good book but it certainly didn't convey that to me and I continued to read my *Archies*, at Calhoun I read *Marks of Identity* by Goytisolo where for the first time I realized what history was and those Spanish men were not like the Spanish boys I knew in the Bronx. Back then we were told by parents, priests, schoolteachers, stick to your own kind, don't go out with boys from another racial group, don't be uppity and for the first time read about Spaniards as human beings, thinkers, not simply victims and it was from an drama teacher that I heard about the book and found it in grandma's bookcase in English, and it had this intriguing cover and I read it mostly to have something to read on the subway as opposed to my comics or keeping my hands in my pocket and humming songs to myself, however my English teacher did say it is a good place to read instead of dream—who would not believe he was a partisan after that and I began to understand about grandma after that, only I would have worn black forever but she isn't that type of woman, but I thought it would be cool to wear black for the rest of my life. That second senior year, my super senior year, at Calhoun transformed me not only did I learn to read but I learned to act, from a dumpy girl who just threw her wrinkled clothes on to a sophisticated one who learned how to color coordinate even as

I wore jeans they were now ironed, from one who wore makeup all the time to one that went braless but most of all I found the stage. Not only did we do *La Celestina* we did *The Visit* and I loved playing Claire the woman who comes back and seeks vengeance on her old lovers, imagine doing that in high school I expected parents would have objected but to my surprise no parent objected we even had a cast party in one of their houses and grandma was so proud one of the parents even tried to get Dürrenmatt to come to the school but he became ill and decided not to make the transatlantic flight. My mother would have been aghast she thought theater should only be entertaining not make you think, it's always too early to do things then it's too late, as grandma said, and I could see my mother not understanding why it wasn't a musical that we performed. How quickly I forgot her she wasn't a good mother always concerned what other people would say about her never concerned with me, dating hooligans, big shots, what kind of woman goes with such riff-raff one who wants to be showered with material possessions and didn't care how she was doing it only how she looked and she really thought people were jealous of her because of all the baubles the gangster bought, he even thought he could win me over bringing me jewelry—the jerk didn't even realize I was too young to wear jewelry, but he rarely spoke to me instead honked his horn and my mother came running. Still I am sad at her death but not like Joseph who tears up when talking about his mother's demise—but it was that event that changed my life got me out of the neighborhood showed me another world and that my mother's world wasn't the only world—moving in with grandma showed me a brave new world, but I keep wondering what I would be like if I stayed up in the Bronx: fat with two kids and an ex-husband by now, marrying the first jerk who came along, afterwards when I went back to the old neighborhood I would look on the doorbells of my old friend's buildings but most of them were gone I could recognize no names, I ran into Hector a boy I knew since kindergarten and he confirmed only the boys remained still living at home and he asked where I had been he hadn't seen me in a while, I told him I live in the Village now, which village, he wanted to know. There was hardly anyone left a few years after high school, so maybe I too would have left and not gotten pregnant and trapped, but as I later found out the girls left to marry and wanted to move to Queens and home owning but it was lily white and our kind were not welcomed there so moved to Yonkers or Long Island and home owning; as Joseph pointed out no one of my friends like no one of his friends moved down into the city only out of the city. This dividing up of me continues to this day the two different sets of experiences that occupy it the body and the mind and I speak differently now my Spanish accent accented when I went uptown to my girlfriends downtown with deep breathes and pauses between words, I didn't even realize that until Joseph pointed it out as if I'm two different people residing in one body and I'm not at home totally in either world.

I'm always in a state of agitation, imperceptible before the heart attack but perceptible afterwards, when I see a work of art and wonder what it means and wonder how contemplative it is or is it supposed to make you feel better, Conchita and Joseph mix up the two and think I am depressed when it is really this work of art that is depressing or in more modern terms, meaningless—what does it mean? As if art should have a moral meaning, to prepare us to be better robots instead of discriminating thinkers, reconnecting us to nature instead of disconnecting us like speech does from the animal kingdom, I like art that forces you to think, that knocks your socks off as Joseph once said even if he seems to be going to more entertainment now, entertain me from my rough day, but I do like art that forces me to reconsider my thoughts—Jacobo never did he wanted art to add to the social revolution and wanted it to have social meaning, arouse the masses, as if art could do that, and initially I saw art from his point of view but as I've aged see art in a different light, I want more love the non-rational stuff not calculation where everything fits into place—interestingly I love looking at paintings of nature but despise being in nature with the heat, bugs, uneven ground on which to walk, but do enjoy looking at the Hudson River School portrait of the beauty of nature and the struggle of men and women in nature, Joseph claims the Hudson River painters taught him to appreciate nature as if nature is benevolent with pastoral scenes and gently flowing rivers and sweet smelling flowers, not mud, bugs, stench and the rotting of dead bodies, but when you look only for contemplation you look for meaning in pleasure a rational account of what is going on: at first I did feel uncomfortable seeing Conchita on stage naked asking what purpose does it serve? Is it only gratuitous titillating men's fantasies, but when I was sitting in the Café Nicholson up on 58th street after my haircut with their parrot screaming I'm a parrot, and had a cup of tea and their delicious chocolate soufflé chatting with some of the queer folks there, many a time I am the only woman in the café, and one of those queer types said talking about it is important, get to the real you, and with his help got to see it in a different light, like pain and pleasure moving my body in different directions and what drives my body doesn't necessarily drive my mind and I want to force reason to be the dominant chord, I'm not hard-wired and I struggle with new ideas and am now happy I have people to discuss these different ideas with, even if they see me as this adult not an equal—now a young man is changing me who I thought was set in my ways and it's forcing me out of the house instead of always staying home, even if I was never a homebody more and more I was becoming one unfortunately men and women my age have little to offer me, most no longer even read books let alone go out after it gets dark and he has encouraged Conchita to read again, after she dropped out of college she said she would never read a book again, but Joseph takes me to performances of hers and has encouraged her to read about the plays and really get into the character—they are alive and that has added a depth to my existence I thought was gone, no longer do I go through the motions I enjoy the moments—really lived time not passing time, my imagination is being turned loose, who would have thought it at my age, at first I felt funny going out with him what would the neighbors think? But of course they don't think about me and even if they do what difference does it make they would only see him as my son-in-law but Conchita says it's like I have my old lover back but I do not see sex I have been celibate too long, washed up, wasted, now I live intimately again but celibate then all of a sudden felt this screaming upon me and I have to be careful lest I see myself calling Tomas, he's easy, willing, but I don't want to go back to those old ways and of course won't do it with Joseph that would be hurting Conchita and she would see it correctly as my wanting to hurt her sleeping with her boyfriend—soon pretty soon they will have a baby, she has a bun in the oven and she's going to be a mother at thirty-six, pretty old, how did she get so old, she was born yesterday and when we celebrated her birthday I miscalculated and thought she was only thirty-four and she said no and I should know it's been nineteen years since we've been living together and that she had such a difficult time at first always going back to her friends in the old neighborhood but she had no other family to go to after her mother passed, Tomas had moved out of the city by then and we both knew she was too young to live alone, even if she was dreaming welfare would allow her to keep the apartment but she was too young and Tomas and I agreed to the 'noble lie' that we couldn't afford two places—he's a decent man too bad he has nothing upstairs, and when we first moved here he couldn't understand anything I was talking about from the color of red, which he only saw as fire engine red as compared to my pinkish hue, to apricots that I said they were tasteless and he said apricots are apricots, he never liked my mind, but he did help out even if he is still angry at me for deserting him. I wonder if he ever got a divorce. In my more cynical moments I think he's trying to 'guilt trip' me with his niceness but he is a nice man and I have self-control except for one slip up, which I vowed never to do again and fall into the old trap once again he thought we were a couple once again, but when those hormones are raging it's easy going with a man you know, no I won't make that mistake again and it's easier now that those desires don't hit me as strongly or as long—I recall how I couldn't wait to get my hands on Jacobo, balling him, now I'm more mature—god I'm really becoming an old lady and I remember hating those old biddies who would even complain about a woman and man holding hands in public, recently some of them complained when a black man and white woman walked through the streets arm in arm, and this is the new world even here and men and women can't be affectionate in public all affection should be behind closed doors as if the totality of life is good behavior. When I finally asked Tomas to leave I gave him the television and I kept the stereo, I knew he would never need that, but he always lay on the couch watching television so let him have it, I would have no use for it as I bought myself an Alfred Kubin ink-and-watercolor drawing, a nice little treat to myself, for having spent so many years with him and later sold it to buy a drawing by Basquiat. Was there a moment I fell out of love with him, of course not, there was never a moment I was in love with him, only upon reflection did I convince myself I was in love with him but now realized he was my get-out-of-jail card, getting me out of Spain but I couldn't abandon him he was so nice, who would do his laundry, but not make his favorite rice and beans every day, as opposed to my first husband who died for the Blue Shirts, the Franco-created misfit army to appease Hitler who wanted him to control Gibraltar so that he could get to the Middle East, but Franco knew he couldn't defeat Britain and sent these jerks to fight Judeo-Bolshevism instead to appease Hitler, and him thinking that would impress me, he was so unsophisticated he didn't even realize I fought against the army, the church and the family. He thought the Falange were the workers not that they were anti-worker, it's so sad to see how easily he was manipulated but there's no proletarian class consciousness except for the intellectuals whose ideas are so abstract that they are never fully grasped. Why I am so excited again when I see a good work of art the juices start flowing again imagine for me to be able to begin again, to pull myself up when I should have one foot in the grave after a heart attack, now I can have a chance again to live able to get up after being flat on my back crying inwardly, wondering if I would ever leave the hospital alive, to walking straight and my body slowly coming back and to be using my mind once again, the mind is a terrible thing to waste.

A girl talks to me and right away I imagine running away with her and starting a new life. Shame on me for believing this at my age don't I ever grow up—you think I'm white with white people's problems at least I'm not Negro but still at my age how many pretty women talk to me and then I immediately think she will be a cure for my loneliness, but now I realize nobody can be a cure to my loneliness it's inside me, but with her at least, for one brief moment, I was able to come out of my shell to see the world as an oyster not as a peanut, but now I am back again in my loneliness with the television set on every night and me lying on the couch with a beer, too lazy to even go out at nights and play softball with my friends, they've started this over-55 softball league and I was invited to play, and one guy I know loves it so much that he had a hip replacement in January so he could play ball in the summer and did the exercise so religiously that he actually is now able to run again, but I have no desire to be outside. I saved up enough money to buy this place, to have a place of my own, worked two jobs would have worked three but needed to sleep yet coming home alone was painful, I left the light on and the radio on so it wouldn't feel so frightening not that I was scared only lonely, never hanging out at the bar or went for a drink with the boys always hurried to my second job as a repairman, I'm in demand I am good with my hands and could work in television repair shops after hours and fixing things was better than driving a cab, too many livery drivers get killed my mother said, junkies, okay robbing them but why do they have to go kill them, I'm a mamma's boy couldn't go against her. I couldn't even do it behind her back what if she found out so I found this safe job instead repair man fixing things, first in my apartment, then in a little workroom in the basement, and finally a shop hired me and I made extra money that I squirreled away for this place. I would have made more as a livery driver but how do you know if one of your customers is a hooligan, but I wouldn't have picked up blacks even if they were well-dressed nobody does, but a spic could do it to me as well, there's no brotherly love, honor among thieves, especially DR's, they would have thought I dissed them and shot me their ego is so small, it's almost as if I am ashamed of my heritage these guys give Hispanics such a bad name but now retirement has taken its toll on me and I never leave the house, now all I do is occasional repair work in the Village otherwise I would never see anyone and am preparing to spend the rest of my years alone, since I doubt anyone will ever talk to me again like Esmeralda. The furthest I go out now is for a little walk to the sports field and watch the little ones play soccer, even girls play now, I'm not big on softball soccer was the game of choice on the island, at first I was uncomfortable seeing girls play soccer but soon realized they have as much right to have fun as boys and nothing gave me as much pleasure as running, jumping and chasing the ball before I joined the army, I should have finished school instead of enlisting to get off the island, Esmeralda told me it wasn't too late I could take night classes but I was too proud. She even said she would do my homework but I wouldn't learn if I didn't do the homework. Besides then I would have to be on the street with Gloria and I didn't want men to see me babysitting, a man who took care of children, that was women's work. Now if Conchita has a child they couldn't keep me away from it. How times have changed, but she has told me she doesn't want children— she's going with this Jew younger than her, I've got nothing against Jews they make good husbands everybody knows that, but if he would give my granddaughter a little one I would love him to death. I have to be careful with her, she's been with men before but it never lasts, she's too much like her grandmother, who I still am angry at and won't call, I'll be there for her but she has to call me I won't call her, I don't need her I'm doing alright for myself have my own little place and can watch television all I want go for little walks out of the noisy city, and if I get too lonely go down to the diner near the train station with the boys, one former co-worker is there and he's always invited me and I go once in a while to be with the boys, they even invited me to play softball with them but I have no interest. I had these job friends but when you leave a job you rarely see them again, no I rather be alone then hang with them even if I once borrowed a glove and ran after the ball but it's too boring of a game standing around most of the time waiting for the ball to be hit and then wondering if I could catch it. Most of these guys played ball growing up so were naturals while I played soccer but who could run around like that now. These new big gloves are great you can never miss a ball but I much rather kick one, love to watch the kids at the school bus heading the ball like we would do back on the island. Now I'm becoming afraid, and for the first time can admit that to myself I can no longer justify myself to myself, no longer do I do anything when I was with Esmeralda she would drag me to things that I didn't want to go to she wanted a man to lean on and I went because I didn't want to be home alone with Gloria: Esmeralda the educative. I always felt uncomfortable wearing a tie. But I was proud of her knowledge was the one who told her to go and become a schoolteacher she knew English well enough and Gloria was in public school so she could take her education courses. But she would rather have her teeth pulled without novocaine than be a school teacher. She still thought of them as nuns and never took the teacher's side when Gloria was misbehaving it was always something wrong with the teacher and wouldn't force Gloria to do her homework. I was the one who went to her school on open school week she wouldn't set foot inside that place. Maybe I should have gone back to school I could have helped her with her math, but now it's too late, it's always been too late for me because I didn't want to do anything and wanted to be out playing football, American soccer, and my father did me no service when he allowed me to quit school at fourteen but I did the same when Gloria got pregnant but then they wouldn't allow her back in school.

The first words spoken after sex are in grief and terror and my director was surprised at their power, and I finally got the part of Cassandra and now here I am going back to my high school, not the one up in the Bronx I would never go there but the one that gave me my start in life to address young kids about being an actress, all I can say is have a heart of steel to prepare you for the rejections. I never even knew a place like this existed when I was up in the Bronx and here instead of cutting class and going to Coney Island, we'd go to Riverside Park up on this rock outcrop and smoke pot regardless of the weather just to sit and dream, and when the wind was slight and the sun glistening off the Hudson you could smell the azaleas and dream you were an adventurer in a foreign country. Should I tell the kids that? Here I am again only this time the Broadway train took forever, I always thought it was a good subway line and back in the day was, now it's rated the worst in the city, Joseph laughs how I use the old names, they changed in '67 or '8 he says we now call them by numbers or letters. Ok the #1 line is the worst in the city. However I never took the A train to Harlem but went further up to the Cloisters and listened to Gregorian Chants at the Cloisters, during college breaks, or in the summer recess: it was so peaceful and quiet and it's here that I memorized my lines until a boy would stop by, boys always thought a girl alone was in search of a man, and then I would leave and walk a little further north to the park overlooking the Hudson River, but this time I could sit on a bench not a rock outcrop and watch the sunset and it still bounced off the river and you didn't need sunglasses and continue to memorize lines or if I got bored wonder who I was and what's going to happen to me. I need to know what I was searching for in order to be relevant to these kids of today. How could I know now what I didn't know then and make it relevant to these kids who today have it so easy, no drugs, no sex, the fear of AIDS rampant, Hepatitis C all over the place that they are celibate because of this primordial fear. I don't have an answer except maybe steel your heart and I never found one up in the Northern reaches of Manhattan all I was able to do was spend a quiet day away from everybody. I think I knew the answer as soon as I popped the question it's not as if I was learning anything in college most of it was gobbledygook, maybe if I tried harder but I was always afraid to try and find out I couldn't do it no matter how hard I tried, should I tell the kids that? And I did enjoy the boys hitting on me thinking I was a college student not a little high school girl, it was so easy I always carried Tolstoy in my bag, only college students read Tolstoy or Dostoyevsky on summer breaks some drama teacher said, you could always tell a co-ed in the summer they're reading a good thick Russian novel. Then I would leave the garden and walk the Fort Tyron park stopping off at the, Silver Tree, Lime Lean I can't recall the name of the restaurant and have a nice cup of tea, you could blot out the whole world up there and try and figure out who I was. Grandma said I had many possibilities but I couldn't see any, true she told me that while making sure I had birth control pills, she wasn't messing around wouldn't allow me to grow up like my mother whose life was over before it began by becoming pregnant with me and at first I thought these pills immoral if God wishes you to be pregnant should you stop it, but later on saw this as an excuse for so many women not to have a life, but back then it meant you were thinking about sex not letting it happen spontaneously, I was surprised when Grandma talked to me about this but she said she didn't want to make the same mistake twice saying I should make something of my life not hide behind a child afraid to live. Should I tell the kids this? Now women's lives can be free and you can have a child when you are ready even if the thought of a child hadn't really occurred to me, back in the Bronx yes all of us girls always talked about it, but once I went to high school in the city college became our number one requirement and then losing it but not becoming pregnant as Ruth did only she was able to get an abortion, nobody we knew back then could do that except her mother insisted and her father was a stock broker who knew doctors, and even if we thought of it as murder she said it's only murder if the fetus becomes a person but she was Jewish. Yet I was ready to give it all up for a child, to be able to grow up with a child to be its friend, like my mother was to me but grandma said you can't be a friend to a child they need a mother. And at the same time realized or must have realized that having a kid would be the end of me, oh I wouldn't have perished but I wouldn't have been me, and this is without anyone to have the child with; it wasn't as if I was pinned and I knew if I had a child the father would be a college boy not a high school dropout, but those boys were honorable back then and would have insisted upon marrying me making a legitimate woman of me and I could never become the person I wanted to be even if I had no idea who I wanted to be except what I wasn't back then. Should I explain that to the kids? That the image of boys as love'em and leave'em, footloose and fancy free is a joke all they want is a little woman to take care of them and make believe they are men and using my freedom to become an adjunct in their lives. They do things while we sit home and clean the apartment. The devil could use scripture for his purpose, and slowly I began to realize if I wanted something I had to do it it wouldn't come if I only hoped, hope is for slaves. And I was fighting not to be like my mother, believe me what was driving me back then was not to end up like my mother, that probably spurred me on more than my fear of an illegitimate child; at least now we no longer use that word single parent is now becoming more appropriate rather than illegitimate since so many white girls are now having babies out of wedlock or with their boyfriend but they refuse to marry and lose their freedom. And all of a sudden I got so much better as an actor that's what the director said he didn't realize I just got laid and turned on by getting laid, and still made sure I was on the pill not just popping them in my mouth just before sex—I must have been the last girl in the dorm to do that, except for the religious few who were still saving themselves for marriage. How about if I mention that to these seniors? I wonder is it the senior class or only acting students and that include 9th graders? I should have found out who my audience is but was thrilled when the school called me thought it would be a nice feather in my cap and agreed before I had a chance to ask questions or think it through. But losing my virginity was not the eye-opening experience I thought it would be it was done and best it be done quickly, that's all I thought, and the desire was gone but not the awareness of desire but finally I couldn't stand the small town life of Pittsburgh and us only performing the classics and wanted to do guerrilla theatre and you could only do that back in the city, even if it disappointed grandma. In the city I joined the Bread and Puppet Theater, we did surprise public performances against the war in Vietnam, for Civil Rights, in favor of Feminism, it was called agitprop I didn't even know what that meant. A friend said I had to go to San Francisco, the mecca of public performances but that was only for rich kids, or you could hitch across country but I found that too daunting but Joseph actually did that and said it was horrible you usually didn't get rides and to his humiliation had to call his parents and asked them to send him some money to come home; after that he got his first credit card so he would never have to ask his parents again, I didn't have enough money to make the trip nor knew anyone from there where I could stay and it never even dawned on me to apply for a credit card, women back then couldn't get them unless in their husband's name. My most fun in guerrilla theatre was when threw down dollar bills off the balcony of the New York Stock Exchange protesting the war and boy did the newspapers eat that up, I even had my picture on the front page of the *Daily News*. I should tell the kids that story. And now, will I ever find out who I am after such a start, all I do is code in RPG2 and juggle my schedule to go on auditions, I haven't accomplished anything except Joseph in his immutable charm asked do you want to get married? At least he didn't get down on his knees, I would have died laughing but he did ask grandma for my hand, but what difference does it make we live together and I wouldn't feel any different towards him if we were married, even if he is much younger than me we get along well, and grandma doesn't mind if we aren't hitched she likes the bohemian life and is not embarrassed that he lives with us but we each still have our freedom and I would have to give it all up if I married him and I cannot give it all up. Should I tell the class that?

We Shall Beat our Ploughshares into Swords, whatever the fuck that means but I think it means no more swords, or my mother hates me, whatcha mean? those little fuckers saying that or that I have no love for anyone, she actually thinks I should believe that or the priests you must believe in God, the truth is I have no idea what either is talking about when they say you have no love for anyone but yourself, you hurt people: all I need is a job when I get out and I will be alright none of their lecturing shit. What has my mother done to them? I love my mother love her even as the social worker was pointing out I was slamming my fist into the palm of my hand, but I meant I was blaming her for thinking that she would hate me, I love my mother and the priest who wanted to meet me once I went back to the city to help me I can tell that look he wanted up my ass. I don't turn for no fuckin priest but at least he writes letters home for me. Upstate is no joke nobody visits me up here and I can't write no letters by myself, and nobody phones me it's too expensive. How do these guys know anything? All I need is a job and they tell me this cracker shit. We sit around in a circle and they expect us to talk and every time we say something they jump on us, I know better than to show weakness—you never show weakness especially not in front of brothers, guards trained as pimps buying into the white man's game only worse making believe they are on our side, unlike the social worker and priest who you know is up to no good because they're here to help us. I hate them more than social workers and priests at least they're upfront; upfront in bullshit like school teachers but I'm learning my bunkmates are teaching me how to play the game so I get out a little early, spill a little shit and they lap it up, they write it down as if they actually found the real me, as if they could know the real me instead of what I show them and tell them that's me but I'm playing them to get out of here early, that's what my bunkmates taught me, but I have to be careful and not let the real me come out in actions: how many times do I want to stand up and hit those motherfuckers, curse them out, let the real me come out. At first I was glad to be here kept me out of prison but I didn't expect to be moved up river, that's prison shit, but the guys at Rikers told me you spend less time in prison if you cop to the Rockefeller, probably get out in less than a year and it's really easy not like prison, now I'm sorry I listened to them prison time is easier even if it's longer you don't have to take these silly classes there you do your job, mind your own business then it's over, here I have to go to religious instruction, group therapy, educational classroom, they never leave you alone and they change schedules all the time I never know if I'm going to catechism where I'm supposed to write letters to my mother and grandmother, therapy where I have no love because my mother supposedly hates me, or school where I sit and draw pictures and look up at big thick books that I can't read, in prison at least you do the same thing every day. The school is so shitty they keep trying to teach me to read, what do I need to read for I need a job. If I could sit behind a desk every day I can have my secretary write letters, I don't have to be able to write, that's all I want let them give me a job so I can go to work every day come home to mom she makes dinner then I watch TV. Only I wouldn't watch TV every night some nights I'd hang out on street corners with my friends the social worker says, how the shit does she know? is she me? the Spic must have told her but still it's nobody's business but mine and I never tell anybody my business but I overhear them all they want to do is carry guns, soon they say a new law is going to be passed and they will be allowed to carry guns, and shit then they'll act tough. They spoke as if I wasn't there they don't think I can understand Spanish. I never thought of myself as Hispanic only here you have to choose sides and the whites won't let me be white and I don't want to be with the colored. Too few brothers here, more guard then bros. Never really spoke Spanish before only grandma spoke it to me but I can understand some words. I didn't force her to move, I didn't want to hurt her, the judge wouldn't even let her hug me, kiss me after he sentenced me said he wasn't the sentimental type but she was crying anyway but she probably didn't want to hug me and my mother thinks she will be dead by the time I get out. Shut up don't think that way. I can con my way out of anything and in a few months can be out of this place, I know how to be a good nigger, those dumb fucks fight all the time I don't get into fights play by the rules do my time and never come back: as the guard says do the crime pay the time. Even if I smell a joint, no problem, won't do drugs, even if all the talk here is about drugs, how can that one hour of bullshit compare with eight hours of talking drugs, and the only time we get excited is when drugs are mentioned. Nobody cares about nothing except scoring. We all like the little white social worker because she wears a dress ain't got to wear no uniform. And the priest wears colored underwear I never saw that before everybody else wears milky white but he showed it to me once when we were alone, says you want to see my war wound, shows me a scar but really I know he wants to show his underpants, and says he can get me some when I get out. He says he learned that from Hispanic men who dressed sharply on the outside and also wore jewelry, but the social worker wears no jewelry lest she be an easy mark, not even earrings or a necklace only her wedding ring. She came here from the city wants to live good life she says away from the noise and the pollution, and wants to live the simple life, she says. Only the simple life doesn't pay much and this life she gets city pay, which is more than country pay. My mother has already told me I will have to sleep on the couch when I come home, grandma has my old bed, she didn't have to I already figured that out. And that bitch Esmeralda talked against me in court angry that I broke holes in her wall, but I was looking for the safe she didn't have much jewelry about and no free cash so I figured she must have it all in the safe and when I couldn't find a safe thought okay maybe it's in her drawers but there was nothing there and her stereo was too big to carry so I grabbed the few trinkets I could grab and a clock radio and climbed upstairs, is this worth two year in prison? Nothing feels better than smoking a joint and now shooting up and nodding out that's the best feeling I've ever had in life and no white man is going to take that from me it feels too good and makes up for all the crap I gotta put up with, I like feeling pleasure only problem is coming down and then I have to have scratch for another high, that's why I went into Esmeralda's house I thought she would have a lot of money, she used to give me nickels not pennies on the staircase nobody else did that to me, she once even gave me a five-dollar bill when she went to her purse I thought she was going to give me a dollar, nobody ever even gave me that but she gave me a five-dollar bill, then I knew she was rich. But later she tells my grandma and I get in trouble because I already spent it with my friends and my grandma is mad at me for spending all that money on my friends she wanted me to save it. Shit she didn't even have any loose change around, you can get a lot of money just stealing loose change, people leave loose change not bills around, only my mother knew how much change she had in her purse. Her daughter said I'm ignorant and she thinks she got it made living with a white boy, she don't know me I never did anything to her and I didn't mean to hurt her mother I don't hit women she just scared me coming in like that I was looking for some stuff I could hock on the street when she burst in I didn't put a hand on her only shoved her and she faked the rest, thinks she's helping me out by me getting treatment but I've never learned so much about drugs as I've had up here. That's all we talk about have nothing else in common I sometimes even talk to the colored boys but usually the white boys colored boys are too wild and they beat me but not the white boys there are too many of them, and I don't like to be around them I'm not colored, but there aren't enough brothers to protect me, but still we stick together and smoke together, the guards smuggle in cigarettes to us—there goes my commissary pay.

I take my happiness wherever I can find it that's the lesson I learned from my grandfather when we went out walking or when he took me to Coney Island when I was ten, or even the cafeterias or movies, it was with him I learned to explore the city, especially by walking the city— he was a confirmed walker, we would even get off a subway a stop or two before our location and walk to it; he never took me to see the sights, that was my mother's job she took me to the South Ferry, Empire State Building, Statue of Liberty, but it was my grandfather who took me to Pennsylvania Station to see it before it was destroyed for progress, to see it before the bulldozer wrecked it and I still remember him saying that but have no memory of Penn Station even when I see its beauty in old photographs—Esmeralda said it was lovely the most European of all train stations, Cassandra says she saw it but was too cool to appreciate it and saw it only as a train station you went to when you went upstate. Nobody laments the passing of olde New York—I first realized it was going, going gone when Howie and some students were protesting the destruction of trees on campus and chaining themselves to the trees and

I'm saying what the fuck? But they passed out signs that said preservation is important and I'm thinking don't these tree huggers realize we have to make way for progress, nature exists to be destroyed by mankind for the new, and the students protesting were relics of an older age and I never missed the trees, and the construction of the new building was only a cumbersome obstacle to walk around—what I do remember is some students wanted to see the progress of the new building but the authorities said it was too dangerous so some students snuck in and one of them fell and was hurt, nothing serious, because It didn't happen to me, but Howie did break some bones and lo and behold the following week some dean arranged for tours of the construction site, which nobody was interested in—what I learned is that authorities never learn that if you ban somebody from something the desire becomes stronger. My desire was not stronger than my fear. I wondered how to live? And Howie was bored stiff in the hospital so his mother brought him his books and he studied all the time, I wished I had that discipline imagine being able to study for hours at a time, and when it was my turn did learn from him, I envied him, broken bones and all, and wondered if he became smarter after his stay in the hospital and did he see it as a turning point, did he become conscious of his self and use that moment for reflection, and would I ever be able to have a moment like that albeit without the broken bones. I stayed clear of tree lovers all I dreamed of dreams of having a passion but I had no passion that I could never conjure up always lived in time that passed slowly hoping for a time that could pass more quickly when I finished school and could engage in something, can you just know how to live or does it depend upon context? Time flew by when I was out with my friends playing ball or when I was with my grandfather but never in school where I counted seconds and couldn't wait until I finished one grade but the next was no better—freedom came one day when I realized I no longer had to worry about exams or performing in front of the class and that from now on my life was my own even if after that initial joy nothing much happened—a river has to flow between its banks but at least I didn't have to suffer in school, that has to be some accomplishment even if I was a top student I never learned anything but how to parrot and was never really there and time really did stand still. Now all I had to worry about was the draft, and watching good ole white boys from Gadsden Alabama clash with blacks from Newark or DC, they really hated each other according to my friend, or not getting killed in 'Nam, all that school for naught, but it wasn't serious at first, the Berlin crisis was over and President Kennedy only played tough sending another ten thousand advisors to Vietnam but after he was assassinated the war began in earnest when two destroyers claimed to have been attacked off the Gulf of Tonkin even as they suffered no damage and could never prove it, this fake attack led to Congress giving President Johnson authority to send me to Vietnam, but luckily I was already addicted to marihuana; I knew it was a possibility draftees were always the cannon fodder thrown in the first line to keep the professional soldiers safe and not wanting them to get killed too quickly and saving them for the important battles, veterans had explained that to me and the difference between them and me is they had experience in the world and were in no rush to graduate while I couldn't wait to become free. Freedom became solitude and whenever I became scared or too lonely thought of going back for my graduate degree until I calmed myself saying I rather be alone and here than back in graduate school, even if I no longer knew anyone. Surely living must be known not debated and truth is not amenable to discussion? Couldn't I just know how to live not have to make incremental progress? Soon I had a new circle of friends and even if it was false starts I remember chasing after a girl with big boots who I could say hi to and once had said some nice things to me even if I didn't like her because I wanted someone to talk to not chat with even if I couldn't think of anything to say but she was too far ahead of me and I couldn't catch up and two weeks later ran into Cassie and Esmeralda and my life changed, that is the turning point of my life when I became free, an adult, had a relationship, had friends, childhood left behind. For the first time I fought my fear, gave into my desire, wanted to be with them and actually did become part of their crowd and started living the way I always wanted to live as opposed to thinking about living the life I wanted to live but the life I was living had no relationship to the life I wanted except I knew it wasn't the life I wanted and refused either to go back to school or go to Israel to find myself. My mother thought law school was for me because I talked a lot but that was another no brainer instead I learned to take deep breaths before I spoke and said nothing. I could talk on anything but truly had nothing to say. I found this wine-selling job and people said I was a born salesman but nobody is a born salesman simply the wine became better, no longer the 'hammer wine' Manischewitz concord grape, and I was able to ride the wave and became free-floating in this culture and was able to move out of the Bronx, which Esmeralda said is the longest journey the one leaving your parents' home and finding out where you want to live. I like to think grandfather would have approved even if he came back to a world he didn't want that maybe his grandson could do better than him. Of course the economic depression of the thirties had something to do with it, and I lived in a booming economy and I thought yes we are not totally free but at least I am able to have some money in my pocket and that I didn't live when the extreme form of capitalism fascism was on the horizon and you didn't know if you would be alive the next day, I don't want to get too antsy this life won't last forever and as grandfather said take happiness where you can find it, it won't last forever.

First belief then questioning, as a child I always had to be with my mother or friends could never be alone by myself but slowly came to realize I live by myself not in the culture and I never could stand the people I was supposed to love, why I ran off first chance I got to fight in the civil war yet I laughed when Joseph said the gates of paradise opened up to him when he took the subway into Manhattan, then realized that's exactly how I felt when escaping the entrails of my family yet I still needed to be with people could not be alone with myself until I met Jacobo; the war was the turning point of my life, I was never so involved in life—the secret history of war is it gets the endorphins and adrenaline going a sense of exultation and you only want to be with your friends: he came along just at the right moment when I no longer could be with my family nor did I want to be alone with myself, and he had that wonderful smile, sharp blue eyes, red locks, chin covered in a beard, long still neck, and powerful body that I associated with my freedom—and even if now hate war those feelings still remain, he would lead me to the Promised Land, only nobody can lead you out of yourself you must do that yourself, and by the time I turned thirty saw the world completely different that there is no planned goal, no ending, that we have to make our way by ourselves, other people can't lead us and we follow along like sheep, we have to develop our own sense of what we want: freedom, even as we step into many blind alleys but people kept saying how can such a pretty woman believe in this? and along the way I made mistakes as I begin to realize life. There is a difference between then and now and I enjoy now because I can be alone with myself and don't always need a man by my side only in Spain you needed a husband to legitimize your life even going out at night unmarried women didn't do that and even if your husband never went with you if you had one sitting at home you became legitimate in the eyes of the bourgeoisie, and not a loose woman; but when I turned thirty realized that I didn't need to walk with a man on my arm, unlike now where women actually do need a man to walk the streets with at night because of junkies who see nothing wrong with pistol-whipping old ladies for their purse and having to show them they take no shit from a woman and they're the boss and can't let them dis me, a new word I recently learned when some hooligan was quoted as saying it after he had shot an old woman who disrespected him by trying to lecture him into leading a good life. Yet it was in realizing that I had to live in the world and developing my own likes and dislikes learning what is important and what is flimflam, a dialogue with myself knowing I have to live in the world and at the same time finding my way in the world especially as I began to realize the world wasn't going to change because I wanted it to, nor did I need the Church hammering it down upon my neck: if bad we will not go to heaven. What kind of belief is it where the only pleasure is seeing the wicked suffer in hell—the priests came back with a vengeance when let out of jail, when the revolution failed, and they had a ready-made explanation God's will not that Franco had more military supplies, guns, ammunition, tanks, planes, if we had that God's will would be on the other side. Then when I neared sixty had a heart attack, somehow I always thought I would be exempt from the ravages of old age and would age gracefully before I simply faded away but no the attack forced me out of myself and made me realize I wanted to exist and to continue to exist I had to take care of myself and I couldn't be fixated upon Jacobo, and what difference did it make that he was already dead, he had a good forty-year run inside my head what more does a girl need? And even when he wasn't around his ideas were crucial in my life, what made me want to smile was his friendship he was the first man who saw me as a person not just a beauty, boys would always talk about my beauty not my mind, write letters to my teeth not to me, the oppression of a beautiful woman, but it is his friendship that I keep closest to my heart, and of course that I could shock my parents bringing home a Wandering Jew, who knows which made me love him more but it's certainly true at first

I had many opportunities to marry but as I aged those opportunities fell by the wayside yet my path became one of those less taken, and now realize what I loved about him is that he was the exact opposite of my father, I see that in Joseph, his impulsive characteristics rather than his thinking characteristics who quits a job with such a good pension to impress Conchita that he is more than a workman. One day he couldn't go in anymore up and left said he couldn't give them thirty-five years of his life just for a pension and even if I will regret it when I am fifty-five, he took the lowest age of retirement, can't waste my life for a future that would kill me now, and that's why he went into work every day afraid if he stayed home one day he would make a habit of it. And he was correct. Took an iffy job but with more potential to make money like Jacobo bored with his life decided upon some adventure and enlisted, had to join the communist party because they were the only ones sending people to Spain as much as he disdained them for their dogmatic thinking and lack of humor, they were always so ponderous and could only enjoy life after the revolution. And now that I am over sixty the decisions of youth don't look as noble and great as I thought they were when I made them, I see things differently we should accept our circumstances but make the most of them and nobody has a monopoly on the truth and nobody has a freer culture than those here in the States. The young look at what's bad about the States, Vietnam, Civil Rights, a corrupt government, the CIA assassinating foreign leaders, the FBI investigating legitimate student groups, both out of control but not about the pill, intellectual freedom, and the space to start over again. If there is one place to be where no one cares about your family history, your pedigree it's here in U.S. of A. My life has been this fight between myself and my circumstances and even when I changed my circumstances, to the Gates of Paradise as Joseph so aptly put it, when I came to New York, New York is different than other cities in America just as the Village is different from the other boroughs of New York, but it didn't mean as much as I thought I still had to struggle to be free, I had broken away from my surrounding but was only more depressed in this strange land but I did feel at home here especially when I finally found enough nerve to walk the streets by myself and could get out of the house everyday just by walking not having to wait for someone to go with me and I loved hearing the sounds of the street exploring the neighborhood finding the piers on the Hudson River and the benches along the East River where I could sit and dream and watch the ships go by. Even when Conchita tells me she feels old I tell her wait you'll know when you're old and not to be afraid of differences of ages, that is only a cultural constraint if you love him be with him, if he makes you happy stay with him, don't let the age difference get in your way, this is only a cultural prohibition for a woman not to live with a younger man, not a moral one; besides ten years is only that much when you are young. What if he finds someone younger? always what if? What does what if mean? Now not now, do don't. Since time immemorial parents and priests have been asking that question trying to force people to do what they don't want to do. It may not work out there are no guarantees but if you don't think about it, try it, see where it leads, you'll never know where it goes. Does what if exist? And if you don't do it while young it gets harder old. But I am old she says, and I laughed, just wait I said, the first sign of old age is not your first gray hairs it's when you start thinking like your parents. That scared her. Joseph thinks it's when men let their hair grow long to cover their bald spot and Conchita has said she will dye her hair when gray becomes noticeable, while now I do love my gray. You can't change your life by changing your clothes or looks or even location even if it is a beginning there is more work that needs to be done, you have to find out who you are, what you like and be able to stand the silence and not give in to the force of temptation or the manipulation this culture or any culture imposes upon you, poor Jacobo finally found a vocation, made some money had a nice apartment, nice clothes, the only thing he didn't have was a house in the country, but was unhappy; he lived in dark times that ate up all his energy but he never achieved freedom, always unhappy, in a loveless marriage that he ended but never divorced from so he had an excuse not to live, poured his love into his grandson who now is becoming afraid like him. History is dead to him. He could live a lie for a long time but not be with me, but once you begin to see the truth it's difficult to go back to the old ways, the truth is different than lies and you wake up with truth not lies—I had no idea how I got to the ICU all I remember are shortness of breath and a sudden pain in my chest, but Conchita told me how I got there and she even brought me a blanket because I was freezing there and I said to myself if I ever get out of this will try only to live in truth that I had been living a lie all these years, that I couldn't wait to run into Jacobo always thinking I spotted him walking city streets, and I had my greetings prepared and when I woke up from the heart attack realized my thoughts were all for naught and now want to live for myself not merely words but in actions we must act in order to live free otherwise its existence not life.

Does he have this mommy thing? Why is he going with an older woman, did he really love his mother that much that he wants to replicate it that he wants to marry a woman like her? Is he confusing me with his mother? I am nothing like her, don't even have the same character traits that she had, granted he says I only saw her near the end of her life when life had beaten her down not in her prime when she made sure he had no fun, always worried what the neighbors would think, and wanted me to be a good little boy, the only thing I could never be. I don't even have her hazel eyes, my hair is dark, my smile is nothing like hers but she was his first love and maybe he sees in me a substitute and I've become her by his convoluted logic, even as he says I am in no way like his mother and that's why he likes me I am intelligent, clever, smart, independent not this whining woman who never did anything, he loves it that I act, claims I should only do that and he will support me but I don't want to be dependent upon anyone, why I continue at the bank until my big break comes. As it is off-off-Broadway roles simply don't pay enough to live. Grandma thinks men always feel totally abandoned when the last parent dies that's when their childhood is finally over when you are no longer special and can no longer be treated like a prince—all of a sudden he is alone and that scares the boogie-woogie out of him, for the first time in his life he is truly a stranger in the universe, he has no brothers or sisters and now it is not like his play-acting but is a real loneliness especially when he breaks up his mother's apartment, imagine walking into her place and finding her dead at the breakfast table stiff as a board her hand on her head and he has to call the police and they take her away and now he has to go back up there weekly to unload all her furniture, he's pretty decent, I think, selling it to people in the building at very low prices so some neighbors have a wooden dining room set, a brand new, less than a year-old color television, new bed, relaxing chair that she couldn't use because it was too deep and she couldn't get up without help, here grandma is preparing in the gym she now lifts weights so that even as her heart gets stronger her body will too and she won't be trapped in those deep chairs, but he must feel the dread of loneliness even if he denies it, and when he comes back he brings a bottle of wine with him having found a cheap liquor store up in the Bronx near the subway station that is having a sale on California wines and he always brings home some nice Swiss Colony burgundy. The kosher wines are too expensive for him, he laughs, and he's not a wine snob, he says, and California wines are as good as French, and we now drink wine with our meal all the time, sometimes we laugh when we want a glass of wine but will not drink before 6pm to show we have some control and are not winos. What's going on with him he now has to stop and think and recall what he has just done and I sometimes have to tell him what he just said before he can remember, while talking to me he's thinking about how he found his mother and thought she was asleep at the kitchen table then called 911 to rush her to the emergency room and he was preparing himself for that again, as he did with his father in the hospital when he would be looking at his watch every fifteen minutes wondering when he could get the hell out of there it was so depressing and feeling good when he succeeded in not looking for a whole fifteen minutes, but he didn't have to this time the technician said she was dead. Immediately he thought the police would think he killed her but they were kind and gentle and had dealt with cases like this before and said call the funeral home they take care of everything. He can now talk about it but cannot recapture the feeling the sense of shock when he walked into her apartment, and of course he's reimagining not only his father's death but his grandfather's as well. As he says he's now an orphan. He identified the body searched the house for insurance papers made sure to get a few death certificates for the bank, the co-op, the insurance company and wasn't too concerned about the high cost of a funeral because he knew she left money for her to be buried and made sure she had a nice coffin not the pine box his grandfather and father were buried in but something that she deserved even if she would have been appalled at how much money he spent on the coffin and her funeral dress. He didn't have the casket open for us to say our final goodbyes and it's really difficult for me to get used to how quick she was buried but he liked it that way, said it is our custom, her friends came and said goodbye he wanted to have her cremated but the rabbi said Jews don't do that and he had to deal with the funeral parlor, but this time didn't sit in the back of the black hearse like he did with his grandfather when they drove him to the cemetery but rented a car so he could be alone only he wasn't alone, of course, grandma and I were with him. He was surprised at how many people showed up but she had all these friends from the old apartment who had moved like her to Co-op City and wanted to pay their final respects. He wasn't going to tell her brother on the west coast why should he have to come in but grandma said you can't keep it from him and when he called found out he moved into a nursing home and his daughter told him she would call her father right away, but he didn't make the trip to New York for the funeral he was too old. That was the last he would see of his family, he said. When my mother passed all my girlfriends came up with me to the funeral home, one even came to my home with a cake, their first act as an adult, but we cremated her and had her ashes spilled over the Bronx, not even realizing it was illegal. Grandma greeted them and treated them as if they were grownups. Now Joseph feels out of body and just going through the motions, I felt the same way, exactly how I felt but I couldn't put words to it back then, engaging in magical thinking that my mother was an angel overlooking her burial, maybe that's why he loves me we have similar experiences but grandma says love defies reason and we can only make up reasons afterwards but attraction is the real reason, unlike the dream I had last night where we were in an enclosed barge together out in the middle of the sea and wave after wave shook us until I said there's a big one and it came over the barge and the barge was totally immersed and we were underwater for a long time until it finally passed and I said let's leave this place or I said that when scared and I awoke, and immediately understood the sexual imagery of the wave, and I can't remember having so many orgasms, that the sex is so good with him and now I see myself in something I never thought would happen to me, I thought I was this new type of feminist woman who could do without a man, now he's not simply a man I once slept with but a human being I don't want to be without, previously I had difficulty when I slept with men in their thinking they owned me, but if he owns me he doesn't show it he so supportive in my activities and insists I continue to act even when I think it's too much with this high-pressured job, he claims it would change who I am and grandma did say these men are rare; especially the men at the bank who want a down-and-dirty affair from me or for me to mother them, who only see women as potential mothers not of their children but of them—is that all men do search for their eternal mother. I feel myself split in half, half wants to be with him and share our future but the other side fears the consequences of our relationship, maybe he's into you now but years from now maybe you won't be this pretty woman and some young girl will tickle his fancy—but then if I have him for twenty years wouldn't that be better than not having him at all even if he does leave me for a younger woman. But will I recall this when he leaves me but grandma thinks he's a keeper. And it is true most of the men I've dated treat me with such condescension and he treats me as an equal. My act of wondering if we should marry worries me even as my passion for him remains but my explanations are concerned with this mommy thing even if we do make a perfect couple.

No longer am I the child of my parents as Esmeralda said, if it was her voyage to America that shaped her, the death of them shaped me, I no longer have any friends from the Bronx, I can't even recall the last time I saw Harvey or any of my neighborhood friends and after walking the streets of my old neighborhood after my mother died I haven't been up there since. Co-op City was not my home but the Concourse was and I walked all around asked a couple doormen on the Concourse if so-and-so still lived there and was told their parents did, but I didn't go up, wondered if I would run into anybody I knew but the neighborhood is mostly black and Hispanic now and the young kids were new to me. Interestingly I didn't feel scared, could have gotten myself killed as Cassie said, you think just because it is your old neighborhood these young hooligans care and she recites tales of how many old boys go back to the old neighborhood and get mugged or worse shot. But for boys the old neighborhood is home. Yes, she says like you men and your tools, I, of course, can't even hammer in a nail without banging my fingers. It was because of her and Esmeralda I took some of the unlabeled, unnamed, black-and-white photographs from my mother's old place but since she didn't date or name them had no idea who they were and even if I enjoyed the photograph had no idea who they were so didn't keep them. They said you don't throw out old photographs. Why not, these people are no longer alive and I have no idea if they have relatives I could send them to, I have no false sentimentality. The few old ones of my mother and father, which I did not even recognize at first, especially as they looked happy, I kept. Of my grandfather I kept every last one. But of strangers saw no reason, especially since they weren't labeled. I did keep my father's watch that my mother wore but when I had to spend more money than it was worth to repair simply kept it in my desk drawer, next to my grandfather's pocket watch, which also didn't work. I was into the new computer watches that you bought in Chinatown for ten dollars so if you got mugged you could laugh as they took your watch, not be frightened like those who had a Rolex. The only possession I carried around with me was the marble green Parker fountain pen that I used it the correct way without cartridges filling it with black ink, which made sure my fingers were always black with ink, and Cassandra complained there was ink stains all over the kitchen if I didn't dry my hands properly. Now my body isn't even the same as before, before I dabbled in sports now I exercised regularly and jogging reshaped my body, and I lost my freshman twenty that had taken me a few years to accumulate and was surprised when I started jogging the pain in my bottom teeth, the shortness of breath and the exhaustion I felt from a little jog, how quickly you lose your childhood pizzazz, but even if I ran slower and couldn't pick up my feet in a run by the end of the year could actually jog a mile and went up from there. Lucky we live down by the East River and we have one of the few tracks in the city and I started getting up before breakfast to jog along the river, it's not even a river it has salt water nor is the Hudson still a river it is so polluted, and bringing home fresh raisin pumpernickel bread or a chocolate swirl as a treat from Moishe's Kosher bakery for breakfast with Esmeralda and sometimes Cassie if she didn't get home late from the theater. In this way I was able to think through one whole thought while jogging and that's how I slowly began to realize I'm not the same person I was before my mother died. When I first started jogging a police car would follow me and occasionally stop me wondering where I was running to, and I had to start carrying identification, which was difficult because jogging shorts had no pockets, but finally started carrying a passport-pocket holder around my neck but by then there were enough joggers out that the police left us alone, joggers helped take back the parks from junkies because we were out at all hours and junkies can only mug or rob in private. I was not the same physically and more important mentally, similar but not the same, a changed person leading a more authentic life, realizing you don't automatically change and that you have to live and revaluate all that you've been taught by schoolmarms and your parents— now I live by how I want to not what I thought I wanted but the way

I want to not how I'm supposed to live, it isn't a straight forward leap but it is an experiment where I evaluate my thoughts but no longer in a dream, now I am awake, and miss the days I don't jog but I do walk to my liquor stores on days I don't jog, the only difficulty is feeling tired if I jog too much and now try and not break my personal best each day. At least I'm no longer a time server waiting for the weekend that would zoom by because I got up so late and before I knew it was evening. Now I awaken with the sun. Grandfather always awakened with the sun and he would be in the living room wrapped in his robe either reading the paper or some book. I still remember my past but it is no longer me I haven't completely discarded it but am no longer trapped in it even if I do fall back into old habits but once I realize that try and change it. But I still wonder is there truth? Does my experience of change lead to truth or is it only and illusion that I am on the right road? I don't know but Zoltan thought it worth the try to find out, and my birthday really put a scare into me was I a make-believe person who never finds out what he wants to be. Yet I have enjoyed growing older most of my former friends never said that but wanted to relive the days of yore. Now I no longer have to dress for success, even if I am good at it and learned how to select fine fabrics that didn't wrinkle unlike my father who only bought the cheapest, ill-fitting and uncomfortable clothes now mine last longer and so more expensive in the short run but cheaper in the long run and they look better. I only wore jeans at the railroad but now I am in public and when I first told her I was quitting she said she was willing to support me, that's when I realized she cared about me but I couldn't be supported by a woman. That was then now I'm liberated. What I love about her is that we can talk about everything and she said if you are unhappy quit and she had this second sense that could intuit what I felt, but she said no you are confusing me with your mother, all I know is what you say and how you act, at first I thought you enjoyed your job, she confused what I liked about the job that it was unionized and had a fantastic wage especially while going to school but now wanted to use my education not be a worker for the rest of my life. It took me a while to realize that as well. I knew I had been taught a man supports a woman, takes care of her, makes sure her needs are met, but it leads to a dull life and I was fortunate living in a peaceful world, no Hitler, no Uncle Joe Stalin on the horizon and a booming economy so I am able to make some choices and choices allow me a more truthful life—what's the sense of living if you live a lie, I don't need more things, rent don't even own a car and have no interest in going to the Hamptons—the new Coney Island, where there are few minorities, and I never liked the Catskills, the only place I enjoy is the city. What I like about my vacations is going to more plays. My boss suggested that I invest in a place in West Hampton near the train station, he claimed it was almost a ghost town, where few people live but plenty of houses and in the future throngs of Manhattanites will go to vacation there, and if you buy a place now it could be a gold mine in the future. But I have enough, yet respect him he always makes sound deliberate decisions and I thought myself lucky enough to sit at his feet but wasn't interested in a risky scheme.

She wore a black band around her soul, for her time stopped and she didn't even realize it, not even in the joys of remembrance but in her denial that she attempts to mask by continued inactivity, depression, naps in the afternoon, but it always pops to the surface, she wrote a letter to her son explaining her hatred only he didn't see it that way, where she explained to Joseph she only married his father for financial reasons but she should have never left her mother and that she could never forgive her father for abandoning his family to fight in a war that had nothing to do with him. Joseph showed us the letter and Esmeralda immediately felt sorry for her but I thought she must have been a horrible mother, but Joseph says no, and after all she did mail him the letter. Me I am afraid to become like her trapped with so few options in life and sometimes I can feel Joseph's passivity when he asks questions and expects me to know the answers, I don't know, I don't know is all I can tell him. Did Esmeralda only take me in as a duty after my mother was shot by the incompetent Mafia? He kills my mother but his intended target lives. Except even before that the best days of childhood were spent with grandma when she took me to the art museums, the Central Park Zoo and afterwards for ice cream at Café Nicholson, the museums and the zoo bored me but the treat of ice cream was a joy until I was old enough to only be with my friends and she was nice enough to understand, but even as a little child of four or five understood something was not right between my mother and her, I wasn't able to put it into words and my mother never said anything bad about her mother but my mother was oblivious to life and would never say things but she did run away from her at sixteen, and she led such a superficial life going out with a gangster because he would spend money on her and gave her baubles, probably stolen, she never asked. We sold them when I moved in with grandma, my college fund as she called it, my mother never even suggested to me of going to college, at eighteen she would have expected me to work at some low-paying job and get married and pregnant at 21, to a man who would take care of you. Grandma had given up on her daughter but she is good to me but she could never fool herself into thinking she had a happy life, a miserable daughter, two husbands both as she said seemed rational to marry at the time, to escape her parents' home and when a widow didn't want to be home alone at night rattling around an empty house and this was her chance to get to America, but no matter how hard she tried raising my mother, two husbands, lovers she was always lonely—she even told me she took to drink at times she was so depressed all attempts to quash her memory of Jacobo. How would that have been if it worked? There is a crack between her actual life and the memory of her life with Jacobo, she even admits she doesn't know what's true anymore, claims emotions are processed in the heart which influences the brain, and now I see myself afraid to love lest I get hurt like her, feelings are feminine reason masculine, is that necessarily so? Imagine she can never forget the war and all she lost and her life is torn between the past and future with no now and she can't have a normal relaxed life nor can it depend upon certain truths—at an early age she challenged all, normal for youth to challenge their elders but usually we settle down soon afterwards, but she has always refused easy answers, just like Joseph who likes theater that is difficult, she needs solid ground upon which to stand—she sees nothing wrong with me going with a man almost a decade younger than me and if he leaves me for a younger woman she will say well at least you had him for a while and you'll have that memory. She is a romantic; I became aware I was falling for Joseph when I looked forward to seeing him and no longer just as a friend and I began worrying about the future with him and I could no longer return to those halcyon days of friendship when I simply enjoyed his company. Sex complicates matters everything is changed, in friendship there is no erotic desire, we enjoyed the same things, friendship is more pleasant we don't have to always worry about the other and can enjoy each other's company doing the same thing, with desire each moment is not enough we want more always desiring more, and now the best part of going somewhere is coming home and lying in bed cuddling; everything is charged now there's no longer a fixed point that we revolve around, we now revolve around each other and I'm frightened, but I like being with him but to give him my heart and soul beyond my body and then he breaks it I don't know if I can live with that, yet being with him is the most enjoyable moment in my life, I try and get up for breakfast with the two of them when he brings back fresh bread and occasionally that delicious chocolate swirl, truly I feel my heart skip a beat, who could have thought breakfast could be so nice. Love is forgetting the old and replacing it with the new: before him my life was a trance but now acting has become more real to me especially when we discuss a character I am playing—he loves that I am preserving a heritage but I have to make sure I am not a slave to what went before and use my creative impulse not to repeat what others have done. He has this insight while I looked at it superficially but now I too research the character and not simply read the words in the script, now I'm ready for school: I think before I act—theater is not text it's visual. Thought doesn't change anything it's just another layer added onto the character's dimensions that modifies the character and makes her more real for me, and that doubles back on me in helping me find my identity that is different than before, grandma grasped that immediately said I was a much more profound person around Joseph but it has taken me awhile to realize that, but now that I do I am afraid and the fissure is I can't bring myself to accept this new situation and bringing my newfound love into my old ways of thinking, but love grandma says is passionate beyond lust it is the supreme gift that goes beyond mere feeling and invades your total self, and as you realize that your body undergoes a transformation but only a few select people are able to grasp that and understand it, most never get to that moment once in life, and don't truly exist but go through the motions of existence, so says grandma, never cognizant of their soul but only what happens on the outside: that is the alpha and omega of existence. I had to look that up, the beginning and the end of the Greek alphabet and I had to spend almost a full day at the New York Public Library, I thought they wouldn't let me in without a library card, what did I need that for, to find the right book that explained that to me, watching the call numbers appear on the screen in front of me, the guy sitting next to me just wanted to see his book lit up, it was fun. Who would have ever thought I could have fun in the public library, and so many people were writing away all day not once moving from their seat, I kept thinking maybe one of them is writing a play I could be in. For the first time I realized how little I know, how ignorant I truly am, that grandma was right I should have finished school but it's too late now. Joseph wants me to go back but I work in the daytime and act at night I have to sleep once in a while, besides the thought of listening to professors drone on is enough to give me a headache; however, I can no longer just act on feelings, thought has shaken me to the core and now I'm beginning to wonder about all that I believed. It's easy as a kid you have so many paths open to you but as an adult the paths shrink are fraught with consequences, yet am glad Joseph thinks I am smart enough to get an education while still insisting I act. He wants us to be free of encumbrances but he doesn't burn his bridges behind him at least not yet even when his boss told him he's quitting and moving to Israel, which Joseph has no desire to even visit he wants to go to Madrid or Budapest but he says it but will he actually do it is another story; he claims his biggest mistake in college was not going abroad but he was too cool to do that and figured he would do it on his own after he graduated, but so far hasn't done it. This rupture upon myself is forcing me to think in new ways and brave me is frightened, who would have thought it? I who laughed at my friends for being afraid to come into the city am now as scared as a newborn about what is, might come to be, and what can't be.

What I like about her acting is she gets to the essence of the matter, no bullshit, she lives the role, feels it, thinks about it yet when she comes home she is no longer that character. How can she be in the moment and then that's not her? I have to feel my way, think my way through any situation or act of perception yet she can do it so naturally—nothing comes to me automatically, first order, something has to be before me like a painter who can't paint from imagination but must have an image before him in order to begin; it's like the new word s/he but Esmeralda thinks it's silly adding a new word to our vocabulary that is empty, it doesn't have an intimate relationship with the language where we can see if it is a man or a woman or if we mean both or if we need to name a person use their name, everything is connected to the individual painting, it won't happen without the artist; and she blew my mind when she said even if we find intelligent lives on other planets what we would need to find is do they have art, plants grow by a chemical process but will they find art which is a human trait, or do lives bend on other planets by religion. How we got talking about art I can't remember but she immediately connected art to humane and the church to nature, their first difficulty in Spain was when Columbus found the new world, were the Indians human? The nocturnal council or the Grand Inquisitor had to debate that: only when it was shown that they had art did the church have to concede that Indians were human, only humans create art something totally different than nature. Cassandra woke me from my nap and said she came to a conclusion, she was sitting at the foot of the bed and had just come back from an afternoon rehearsal and Esmeralda was out for a walk, she loved to walk everyday weather permitting, that and exercise were now her passions in life, and she says she wants to marry me, and I'm thinking with me? she's not realizing the full extent of her words, but she says that the rehearsal finally convinced her that I am the constant presence in her life and even as she was performing with them realized she wanted to be with me, that they are nice people a powerful play that will be barely remembered in a small theater that nobody could ever find, and none of these characters have the inner strength that I have. Inner strength? How little she knows me but I am smart enough to keep silent and make a caring face wishing I actually had the resources she claims I have but it's my reserve they take for wisdom, I envy others and have a deep vanity but am afraid to look stupid and when I speak add nothing to the conversation but she claims actors only recite and have no depth of character, she speaks words with such intensity but she claims to have no idea what they mean, and she is always glad to come home to me, and when Esmeralda comes in from her walk we tell he we are engaged even if I thought we were a couple without the need for a wedding but she says the word makes us closer, one set of words leads to another and that leads to a closer relationship between us and if that is true then marriage should make us even closer, I say, or at least think because at that moment I wasn't sure what to say but I know I thought it but was afraid to say something and ruin the moment that I wanted to cherish, thinking about the moment made it once removed and as a good actor wanted to stay in the zone; no matter how much discomfort I feel while jogging there comes a moment when the endorphins kick in and you feel as if you can run a marathon and you begin to enjoy the run, but for me there is no feeling without thinking about where the feeling is coming from I can't just enjoy the moment as Cassandra can I have to see the moment, feel the moment and even if I feel the moment suddenly pretty soon my head kicks in and I begin to wonder—thinking is consciousness of my feelings so that thinking is my reality even if I have to feel it first in order to think it second and cannot think without feeling it because of my lack of imagination and always wonder if what I feel is my lack of feelings only thoughts which I say are feelings and may not be how I feel. Is my thinking initiated by thoughts or misinterpreted feelings? Yet I feel happy and groggy at this moment and as we tell Esmeralda the news she hugs us both and tells us that she is glad it came to this. Cassandra begins to do her salute to the sun exercises to calm her down that she wants to be over before she begins and I begin to make lunch, ever since I began to get up early use naps to keep refreshed during the day only when I am home, the days I work I need no naps, my mentor at work explained to me one way to slow down weekends is not to sleep in but get up early on weekends when I complained to him time goes by so quickly, only on weekends I can't get up early and not nap, and now don't like to jog on weekends so many people are out and about running all over the place you can't hear yourself think, but it's not a good excuse anymore because now many joggers are now running with earphones attached to a Walkman, so I came up with another excuse, Moishe's bakery is closed on the Sabbath. I may lack imagination but excuses I have. We drink coffee out of bowls but how can you drink coffee out of a bowl and sit on the toilet and read. I transfer my coffee into my J cup that has a handle and can relax in my morning shit. We were all thrilled that what we had was made official and she told us she hoped we would remain a couple and that she didn't want Conchita to go through life alone, she didn't see the age difference as anything to worry about if it didn't affect us and nobody could see what you could see inside of you they can only see your actions, which don't necessarily affect what you think but is only a series of perceptions of what you think but that the total process is a mystery and as long as you love one another and don't hurt one another you will be fine. Here I thought she was talking about Tomas her second husband but I was wrong it was Santiago her first who she shamed into fighting so that he could prove himself to her and he was so stupid, as she said, that he didn't even understand whose side she was on. He probably thought of her while dying, I thought, and she rarely thinks about him, I thought, and this is the first time I actually think I heard of her talking about him, who she said loved her beauty so but not her while my grandfather not only loved her body but loved her mind—possession of beauty is not true love. The three of us had some cheese on a baguette that Cassie had brought in from Veniero's that wasn't closed because it was Saturday and celebrated our newfound relationship that was the same as the old only now with a deeper meaning to me but Cassandra later told Esmeralda, who told me, that she felt no different.

When the priest came by to tell me I wondered what he wanted but seeing the serious look on his face I immediately knew what he was going to say, and when he said it you'd think I'd be inured to death but I shook, cried, all the while wondering why I was crying he was nothing to me but still he was my husband, he was killed defending the mother country against the Jewish-Bolshevik-Freemasons or some such gobbledygook the priest said who are trying to destroy our country, not that the British bribed Franco with a pot of gold to remain neutral so the British could sail through Gibraltar and keep their colonies in the Middle East; there was no sense in telling him we haven't had Jews in this country for five hundred years because to him all Bolsheviks are Jews and Freemasons are tools of the Jews, what nonsense, but his solemn face says it all, his hands are folded as he tells me Santiago is in the hands of God—hadn't he heard we killed God, but, of course, I could not say that to him, and instead listened or tried to listen as he told me he was killed by a sniper, and that his body is being brought back home but I thought really now I can wear black, what I should have done after we lost the war but wouldn't be allowed to, finally now to show my true colors but for the wrong reasons, and that's when I realized I can't live here and began thinking of ways to escape Madrid. I am sure of it even if I never actually thought that to myself. I really made no lucid decision to leave but it was a decision nonetheless made while listening to the priest talk about Santiago and his coming funeral and talking about God in such a way that I have to accept God's will but if you don't buy into his metaphysics he is just a silly old man who looks at you kind of funny almost as if he was afraid to be alone with a woman, afraid you will seduce him and turn him away from his beliefs, they can't be so strong if a little girl can tear him away, lust is stronger than his beliefs, but I know I didn't think that then only when I came here to the States did I ever see such predatory priests. In Spain they get their rocks off by torturing people, here where torture is not allowed they like to have sex however later I found out it's mostly with young boys not girls, but once when Tomas was silly enough to go to one priest and the priest met me not that I would go to confessional, not on my life, all of a sudden I started getting these anonymous phone calls and a man was breathing heavy on the other end and it became disturbing when it happened every day at the same time when I was alone in the house and I finally called the police and they traced the call to our local priest that Tomas had visited and I laughed the police were willing to prosecute him but I asked him not to do it anymore and the shame was enough to turn him away. Now I realize he probably wasn't even transferred to another parish where he could continue his obnoxious acts, but continued in our parish. Our daughter was becoming a teenager and I didn't want to hide sex from her but Tomas said she's too young and had insisted we take her to religious services in order to keep her teenage years calm. A lot of good that did. I can barely remember when the priest knocked on the door and wonder if the person who answered was me, of course it was me, but I'm not that person anymore, and I have no real memory only faded images of him it's so far removed from my new life, I can't even recall what Santiago looked like only that he was way older than me, true I have his photograph somewhere in my things, Julio could have taken that I wouldn't have minded but he left the personal stuff only wanted jewelry and electronics that he could hock, nobody would be interested in a picture of him. In the photograph my hair hadn't started to thin out, when I had hair in bushels so much so Gloria would wrap her hands around it until it hurt and when I couldn't take her twisting and pulling anymore cut it and she was so upset she screamed and cried but back then it grew back thick as ever. Now I wonder who I am when I see myself in the mirror is that me or am I trying to deceive myself. Thank goodness for cosmetics and I can put on my stage face, I may have only one soul but thank goodness many faces; if my life is to have meaning I should remember my past but all I can recall is Jacobo and what could have been not what has been not the constant changes the marriage to Santiago because I wanted out of my parents' house I can work I supported myself my entire life but I needed a man to wear a black veil and others left me alone thinking I was in deep mourning, of course some men got their kicks thinking a widow would need a man to take care of her, not only didn't I need a man to take care of me usually you had to take care of them I saw them as such little boys but all I can do is look back at that time of living in bad faith with myself my emotions could not have been invested in these men—Circe was correct men are pigs, all Spanish men want from a woman is they cook, clean and bear them children, how many abortions did I do, even after the pill, these women are so frightened by the priests they wouldn't even consider the pill, and they all had to be virgins at marriage, their mothers insisted. It was important for the future husband to be able to draw blood. Give me a break! I saw them as little kids trying to play adult but they saw themselves as so mature. I wonder did these kids ever grow-up? Conchita did, because I made sure she had the pill even when she objected that that means she's going to have sex but I insisted she not follow in the footsteps of her mother and have a baby before she was an adult, and she still fought me all the way, it's only now with Joseph or my newfound boyfriend as she likes to kid me, his red hair reminding me of Jacobo, and she says he looks something like him in the only photograph I have of us, we took it when we knew we had to part and even as it faded I had it retouched. Santiago is somewhere in a photo album and so is Tomas but I never look at them, once I kept Tomas photo on the dresser because he is Conchita's grandfather but that only lasted a brief time. When I left him I left him forever and now if he called he would see a different person than the one he took to the States, not that I am not grateful he took me, seeing the Statue of Liberty brought me the feeling of freedom, and the configuration of streets with its grid not square and church confirmed it—you can't get lost in this city with its grid except for the surreal streets in the Village that was not initially part of the initial grid and is thus able to stay aloof from the rest of the city, still I was quickly able to find my way around here and felt as if I had been here all my life. At first I thought I might be homesick but I was dying on Mejia Lequerica street here I felt the breath of spring and started to become this new person and when Tomas talked about Madrid I wondered what he was talking about he knew me as a woman with black hair who wore a veil I wore no veil in Manhattan. It was the old me he knew and had no idea I was the resurrected me and my only regret is not seeking out Jacobo. But I realized if he didn't search me out what good would it have done if I schlepped up to the Bronx, I didn't want to get him into trouble—my feelings are different at different moments of my life—he might still be in love with me but he too would have changed even if I don't want to admit that to myself and he might not be the Jacobo of old, so I told myself, even if I couldn't believe that, but why not we all change, and in my perplexity wouldn't be as resolved as I was if I didn't go chase after him. Joseph tells me he will take me up to his old neighborhood but he says it's not the same anymore and they now have Vista volunteers on the Grand Concourse, can you believe that the crème-de-la-crème neighborhood in the Bronx is now such a poor neighborhood that Vista volunteers are placed there. His dream in college was to go to Paris and say that The Champs-Élysées looks just like the Grand Concourse. He didn't go in college and now wants to make it a honeymoon destination. The dollar is very good now and I have told him to go to a three-star restaurant La Jamin where he could get the best meal of his life for under a hundred dollars and he has even bought a wine booklet letting him know which wines to get figuring they wouldn't have Jewish wines in an establishment like that. Paris is the only place I would even consider going to, I would never go back to the old country even if Franco is dead he's not truly dead his ideas live on.

Now that we know all about the slaughter the United States can't claim to be the beacon on the hill any longer, I remember that term from some history class, it's just another lying government that grandma told me about and now maybe the people will awaken from their slumber and call the government into account. We bombed the living shit out of the people of Vietnam automatically thinking a little more killing will bring victory and justify all the slaughter, all they did was lie about the body count in Vietnam, Joseph is particularly interested thinking that, it could have been him, even the Pentagon Papers didn't lay out in such detail the lies of the American government towards people of color. Now Grandma says we are the imperial Spain, Spain? I had no idea of its history as an imperial power but she says we were the first modern nation state until we were defeated by the English, we were the first nation to conquer large swaths of land in the new world and subjugate people to absolute rule, it all began when Ferdinand and Isabella expelled the Jews and Moors and consolidated their rule because of their belief in racial purity that the concept began in Spain and then the conquistadores went out to conquer or at least to get them out of the country, get rid of them, whoever expected them to win but most of Latin America becomes Spanish, and we hold onto the remnants of empire for 500 years until we lose Cuba and the Philippines at the beginning of the century. Who says I don't read? I need this stuff as research for the play I'm doing. If you ask me it's better not to be a world power. But can we get it into our heads we are no longer God's gift to humanity or will we rearm just to prove we can kill: to be a world power and the city on the hill are incompatible, the city is not even a real city but a metaphor look what the colonists did to the natives, even Ben Franklin commented that Indian women captured by whites always wanted to go back to their tribes but white women rarely did, yet the mythology is the reverse; our opinions are real we were taught in school about the desire to be ocean to ocean, manifest destiny, I don't know I never listened in class, I never understood any of this until I started doing my research on the Queen, the power behind the throne—why couldn't she rule in her own right why did she have to rule behind a man, all of a sudden I am becoming interested in this stuff—Joseph says it's about time I became educated, he sees me as self-educated with a lot of holes in my education, he's right I believed in what they taught us never even giving it a second thought I even believed the Chicago 8 were guilty wearing their long hair as a sign of protest, how stupid, I didn't want to understand that the war was a lie and thought the government was correct in not giving them permits to march in Chicago because the enemy would be encouraged, and I liked how they imprisoned Jerry Rubin and Abbie Hoffman and cut their hair, like Samson they took away their strength, and they showed photos in the newspapers of how they defeated them but now am beginning to realize it was a show trial, the court had no interest in justice only power and tradition and tradition is terrible; they were standing up against power and tradition and because they wore their hair long were thought of as effeminate but they were stronger than those men in crewcuts and white socks. Grandma and Joseph actually thought those young guys won, the old ideas were dead they just didn't realize it yet because pretty soon thereafter came legalized abortion, equal rights for women, easy divorces we aren't trapped with a man and the end of alimony, which is a good thing for women forcing us to work not be a stay-at-home mom. And then this wild thing where a man actually got custody of his children because he was a better father than she was a mother, not simply because the mother was a junkie or in prison but based on merit, no longer is it automatic that a woman gets custody of the children. I learn all this preparing for Queen Isabella, I get the part am excited do my diligent research, then the play collapses we get bad reviews and go down in an auto-da-fé; at first I instinctively supported the hippies we were both young but it's only now when I see how the powers that be destroy any idea of creativity that I am beginning to intellectually realize that I have been leading my life as a lie, now these ideas are going deeper into my consciousness, I'm halfway through my life now and all of a sudden I am beginning to realize I want to learn and think, pretty soon I'll be an old lady and then what, and even though I was never a feminist am now beginning to see things in a new light, I never went to consciousness-raising groups because I like men better than women, if you go to an all-girls high school you never want to see another woman. I never really thought about issues before but now am beginning to think about something and what I am thinking about is discovering who I am by thinking about what I never even gave two cents about, before I never thought about things only reacted to things now I want to know—at least now I can wear women's size jeans I like to think I helped bring that process about, even if I no longer wear blue jeans. Now we are talking about what we always assumed as the only way of acting, for instance I won't take Joseph's last name even if grandma thinks it's the law that you have to but she is mistaken it was always done so there was no law codified about that you must take your husband's last name only custom, there is a law that you don't have to give it up so the mother can have the same last name as the children. We were all simply trained to give up our last name, which in my case is my mother's last name because my father wanted nothing to do with us, otherwise it would simply be his last name not a woman's. Maybe I can persuade Joseph to take my last name, I asked him jokingly but he said he would feel uncomfortable doing that, why women have been doing that for eons, I now am beginning to have new ideas that occupy a different space in my mind and am acting upon them. The good thing is I no longer accept unequal pay and computers is a kind of new profession so the pay is not drastically unequal, still unfair but not by a large margin: equal pay for equal work nobody now can deny that and that has become our mantra also your mother doesn't work here clean up after yourselves, which we have to put up next to the coffee because boys are slobs. It all started when we found out about all the lies our supposedly democratic government told us and the massive cover-ups and the defense when found out that I was only following orders shocked the American people even if the government didn't have the balls to prosecute the ring leaders. Tradition is not what it once was and when the masses found out politicians, the military, the FBI all lied to protect their own asses this has sent a shock wave through the American psyche and it's now a new ball game as far as I'm concerned where the old rules are questioned and it's not the rules that are crucial but how we look at them. It's like when Joseph was bored in the hospital after his nose job in his sophomore year and he brought *Thus Spoke Zarathustra* to read he not only came out handsomer he said but intellectually wiser and for the first time in his life became a serious student and claims his grades actually dropped because he was now a serious student and now into his studies and reading more not simply what his teachers told him to read and couldn't even parrot back the answers on exams, not that he had more self-confidence because they eliminated his hook nose, that I have never saw pictures of. Now he wasn't just a pretty face, he said, but had some knowledge Nietzsche and Kaufman's *Existentialism from Dostoevsky to Sartre* were the two profound books he read while in the hospital even refusing a television because he was so enamored with those books. He credits those two works with the beginning of his education not school. Now it's my turn even if I am older than he was as a kid I wasn't interested in books, never went to the public library and we had no books in the house, not even an encyclopedia—put me in coach I'm ready to play the game, and Joseph and grandma do encourage me but I simply wasn't ready but it's never too late school might be over but education isn't it can be lifelong. He doesn't even feel threatened if I don't take his last name but only angry his mother isn't alive so that he can show that to her, at the hospital as she lay dying he asked if I would put a cross around my neck, or come on Ash Wednesday with ashes on my forehead—seriousness in play is what grandma said, as if I were Catholic and he could give her one last zest before she died. I don't know if he was serious but wouldn't. As grandma said you run into an atheistic Jew you're never the same again. Now that I am beginning to think what is and what is not I am beginning to understand the Jewish prophets there never is a true view only true points that the essence of Judaism is true that we raise ourselves up and

stand alone and not crawl on the ground like a snake. And each time now
that I listen to grandma or Joseph I learn a little more I may never grasp
the truth only approximate it but it's only when I begin to understand
what's been forced down me and what is what I recognize as false that I
begin or begin to begin. I actually wanted to light the Sabbath candles
but Joseph and grandma were shocked but agreed with me it's nice to
plan on one meal a week where we all insist upon eating together but
they didn't think it had to be ritualized. But we now all save Friday nights,
unless I am acting, as pizza night, I could say the prayer if I could read the
Hebrew but we have caught the essence of the family meal without the
words, and don't need the prayer, so I fooled them one night when we
lit the candles, not for religious reasons but because they were beautiful
and recited the prayer for *Shabbes* because an opera singer friend gave me
the transliteration.

I memorized every feature of her face I was married to the most
beautiful woman in the world, men looked enviously at me when we
walked down the street and when she told me go fight I didn't even
question her thought I would be the brave man she married, and I had
nothing against the Germans they helped us defeat the Judeo-Bolshevik-
Freemasonry menace that was threatening our country, and I didn't want
to lose her even if she never threatened divorce, divorce is impossible in
a Catholic country even if the only time I saw her in church was at our
wedding I just knew she believed in God everybody does, it was that
silence of hers that was hard to take, in the middle of a conversation she
would just go silent her mind elsewhere and I could never break into it
and she never told me what she was thinking about but I thought it was
because she lost the baby but I would give her another one: Marriage
should be all about togetherness and she was splitting off from me, but
as a war hero she would be mine completely. But she would never go to
church with me neither Christmas or Easter the most beautiful times of
the year not only because it was holy but because spring is finally coming,
why I loved the Easter service finally a breath of fresh air, not the white
sky of winter and long days stuck inside, now with the fresh air and color
in the trees we could have night life once more. Those Sundays after mass
stuck home with Esmeralda we didn't even say two words to one another,
I don't know what was wrong with her, the priest said give her time she
needs time to recuperate from the loss of the baby but it was more than

that but I could never find out what it was she wouldn't talk to me. To let time pass a little more quickly I would play with my stamp collection that I inherited from my father and never had thought much about until Esmeralda's silence and dream of faraway places, a weird dream for me who never went anywhere, who didn't like to travel, but she was far from me and I wanted to get far from her, she was never with me, I thought all this would change once we married and she began to appreciate me but she never felt for me, and the nicer I was to her the meaner she was to me and near the end I just couldn't take it anymore and thought if we had a child if she had a son to raise instead of a dead daughter someone to carry on the family name all this would change, but it is difficult to have a son when you don't sleep in the same bed, and go to bed at different times and never touch each other. Still I liked how men envied me when we walked down the street together and people knew us as important people especially those who claimed I wouldn't amount to much and here I am walking down the street with the most beautiful woman in Madrid, I didn't force her to marry me, she wasn't bewitched by my charm, have to marry me because I made her pregnant, just the reverse I made a legitimate woman of her, and for that she should be grateful to me—how many other men would willing take another man's child and raise it as his own. She is the personification of beauty and I went up in my friends' esteem of me because she was my wife. I wasn't the first in my group of friends to marry but I certainly married the most beautiful woman and it was worth the wait. When Franco was calling for volunteers to fight the Russians against the Germans I didn't even know they were enemies, I thought they were allies didn't truly realize what I was getting into, I had forbidden that subversive literature in my house, she wanted to go but imagine her mixed up with those dirty Jews, oh I knew she had met Jewish men before me and I wasn't her first lover but I forgave her seeing that she was a young girl easily corruptible or smitten by the devil, being captivated by desire with no parent to stop her makes her less responsible for her actions—I wouldn't have gone against my parents' wishes never I always pleased my mother who worried about me being single, who would take care of me after she was gone, and she didn't want me to be all alone—if she would have known my father would die so soon and that she would soon be all alone, I wonder if she would have approved the marriage even so she did it under protest because she thought she was a she-devil; Esmeralda refused to allow my mother to move in with us, never totally saying no but saying she would be happier with her sister, would be happier in the country, would be happier anywhere but here and she refused to even consider moving into my mother's place, she laughed that I would then be sleeping in the same bed that I slept as a child even if it done all the time she said the only condition she insisted upon is that we not live over the shop. She no longer wanted to follow the old ways and saw it as a tradition that made no sense, we are the new generation even if I had one foot in the old ways and one foot in the new I agreed because she would not even consider marriage unless I agreed to those conditions. So one night I just went off in the middle of the night and joined the Blue Shirts, thinking she would be proud of me but I immediately found myself among a bunch of devil worshippers, drunks, and no goods, I hadn't realized Jews were still in Spain, thinking they were expelled over five hundred years ago, nothing whatever prepared me for this and then we go out fighting, no training, no nothing a few days marching and all of a sudden I am in a war zone, I thought with my medical skills I wouldn't have to fight but we were all fighters, Santiago, Santiago march you have two left feet, run Santiago run, but this damn rifle was so heavy that I could barely walk, people thought I was strong but I was only fat and I hadn't run since I was a little kid playing street games and I wanted out only there is no way back it was explained if we deserted we would be shot, if we were captured we would be shot, if we disobeyed orders we would be shot or worse sent to a horrid prison camp and all I did was pray and pray wondering how I got into this, telling God I was a good man and got caught up in this by accident and if He would get me out of this I would dedicate my life to him, and if I was allowed to live would move in with my mother so that she would be next to someone she loved and that Esmeralda would have to accept I would not take no for an answer. In my letters home I told both my mother and Esmeralda everything is fine not to worry. In childhood I was a conquistador and never would have surrendered like my father did when the Yankees rode up San Juan Hill, but once the actual fighting began realized as I peed in my pants that I wasn't going to be on the front lines but hide in the rear, still I got shot on a guard post in the middle of winter when it was freezing cold and didn't even hear the bullet coming nor feel any pain only tasted some blood coming down the side of my face and tried to say mommy but was already dead. She couldn't have done any good, I don't think my comrades even realized I was dead I fell down so quietly I was never a troublemaker all my life why should I be one in death, I was stripped naked and not even given a burial no last rites but dumped unceremoniously into an unmarked ditch with others who had perished that night, and when the Russians captured the encampment buried their own in the same ditch, so I am close to the one who could have killed me. I am dead and haven't even lived and my last thought how I would live if I survived didn't matter because I didn't survive and never received a hero's welcome I was counting on nor the respect of Esmeralda that I would have gotten if I came home in one piece and she could no longer boss me around even if I was older than her and so proud to be her husband the tables would have been turned and I would have been the boss; my mother is the only one who truly mourned me, I should have insisted she move in with us okay we didn't have to move into her place I get the new but she could have come with us. But she wouldn't have moved in she couldn't stand it that Esmeralda smoked cigarettes and not only in the home but in public as well. And once I died she never thought about me again.

I have to believe I have a future, behave as if I have a future and not be morbid all the time, and I am excited when Joseph is around, must not let this culture get to me, as grandma says if it doesn't disturb you it won't matter what other people think, if only that were true, still the difference in age bothers me and when I am an old lady, as if I ever really thought about that before, even when I started smoking knew that wasn't good for me later in life, but I could never think of myself getting older, that happened to other people not me, and besides it was so far in the future that I couldn't imagine myself that far in the future, so now why do I worry about it so? It's only with him that I feel alive if he left now there's no telling what I would become and it does make grandma happy that we are planning a wedding it's as if she's marrying Jacobo—the mark of Jacobo is on his forehead: he does have that large forehead of academics even as he assures us he will never become a schoolmarm after the strike, but it's not her he's marrying but me and how will he feel in years to come; I am too old to bear him children will he come to resent me; he says we can adopt because he is a generous soul but in the end he will probably want his own, he also states his mother was over forty when she had him if she can have one anybody can, but I've had an abortion and that will have an effect. How do I know his mother didn't? Mother's never do, we can't believe our mothers were sexual creatures. He told me his parents married in December and by March he was born so she was no virgin bride, even if he never thought of it until I pointed it out to him, just thought he was born early, all that is hushed up in front of the children. He was born with a weak heart and the doctors couldn't do anything until he was six months old, and so his parents were extra pro-tective of him and claims at his first birthday party they had clowns and elephants. An unlikely story but he did survive the operation. Grandma asked if his father was active in politics but he didn't think so he had to earn a living from a young age and had no time for politics, he knew Jews were considered radical but he thought his father was the right of Genghis Kahn and never caught the bug of education, even as he insisted he get one, and when he wanted to quit and work on the railroad his father laughed and said be a worker after college first finish your school, that's why he had no qualms about supporting me when I went to college unlike some of my other friends, that I understand no family in my old neighborhood would support a girl going to college, what do you need an education for to be a mother? Unfortunately, he said it drove a wedge between us—educated people differ from uneducated ones, and my fa-ther knew that, he was no dummy just because he didn't have formal schooling; he was of the last generation of Jews with a limited education and no interest in the Talmud, at least those religious ones had the Bible to fall back on, but the uneducated ones were trapped between the old and the new, after the war everybody got a high school education, he didn't even get a chance to get that. Now something happened I say, I don't know what but kids can no longer read, drop out of school in record numbers, young girls still get pregnant but boys end up in jail, that's the big change I can see up in my old neighborhood these kids start way to young playing adult. Yes mama, Joseph says, but it's true no longer can you say a book changed my life as grandma said! Imagine that! it all started with the Teachers Strike of '68 when all of a sudden Hispanic became allied with blacks, all to decentralize the school system via community control but really to wrest control from the Jews who were doing well in the educational bureaucracy and the results are now a worse school system, when you think It couldn't get any worse it did, now students graduate who don't read and worse can't read, and those who dropout to find jobs find that there are no jobs for uneducated, and they quickly find out drugs pays more even if it messes up their lives. But I couldn't see into the future why should they. I only stopped smoking because it is a vile habit and couldn't stand the smoke. Joseph supported the strike still lives as if there's 4000 years of suffering in the world—grandma and I quickly realized the anti-Semitic overtones of the strike, but not Joseph and besides we didn't like to be lumped with blacks never believing that black and Hispanic would make a new coalition of the proletariat—most intellectuals supported the black and Hispanics against the teachers but why should Puerto Ricans have anything against the Jews, true most were schoolteachers but no longer landlords or even small shopkeepers that had long ago been filled by Asians, and the sons and daughters of the of the shopkeepers or landlords went to Harvard and broke down the doors of discrimination at the hiring practices of the corporations, Yale and some of the Ivy Leagues even rescinded its quota against Jews, what next admit girls? but I didn't like it that Puerto Ricans were called Hispanic, they're tenant farmers once generation from away from their parents going bare-foot. Grandma would always read Albert Shanker's column in the *New York Times* and said the union head's column was always more sophisti-cated, nuanced, understanding than the regular columnists who spouted cliché after cliché, Joseph claimed after the teachers strike he vowed never to become a schoolteacher and it would have been easy for him with his academic credentials instead he found this wine salesmen job after the railroad and wanted nothing more to do with education, called it a dis-ease which during the Great Depression was considered a great job with security, but the Depression was over and he didn't have a Depression mentality. He's not as pure as he makes out, he did take a few civil ser-vice tests and with his prodigious memory and test taking ability passed with flying colors and got called for the welfare system, the Rockefeller Drug program and Parole but refused to go, pissing his father off leading to a rift between them unsettled at his death, but even in a rift they always spoke to one another and he cried profusely at his funeral. Grandma said he was an intellectual but he laughed at that. He didn't want to be bored to death so instead worked as a wine merchant, which gave him time to walk between stores and not have to work 9 to 5. He actually makes a good salary but now has become restless and quit because he turned thirty and thought it was time for a change. Grandma thought he would go to graduate school, showing how little she understood him, he called that the Jewish solution, more education, instead he now is into real estate and can become a slum lord, only he says he will be a different type of landlord he wants people to buy their apartment, I never heard of such a thing why own when you can rent. He wants to marry in a synagogue thinks a religious marriage is more sacred than a civil one, it doesn't make a difference to me but if it makes him happy will let him go to a rabbi.

It served no direct purpose but indirectly served another when I couldn't believe what I was seeing glad in one way to see it in another wondering what am I doing here, but I couldn't just sit home and vegetate and decided at least on Fridays to go to museums and galleries, to do something with my life and it started when I went to the MET and went directly to Rembrandt's *Self-Portrait*, I loved looking into his haunting eyes and it forced me to think that I too can be a 'learned woman' one striving not giving up, then afterwards Conchita was in a Greek production of *Circe*, not on Broadway, they wouldn't have enough guts for this—this was a syncretic performance using Greek, Byzantine, Jewish sources, which allowed us to rediscover our past: for a thousand years we lived without Troy and its consequences until Byzantine scholars brought Greek playwrights back to the West and the Renaissance with its love of an individual ethos was drawn to this, and the more we learned more about Greek thought the worse it was for Christianity stuck in the Dark Ages—the Greeks demanded that characters use their minds, quite a blow to Christian fatalism and Conchita blew my mind and not in ways that she expected, she thought I might be embarrassed seeing her naked on stage her arm having a fake tattoo of two black snakes coiled around her left arm with red tongues hissing at each other and their eyes circled in red, proving she's a witch; I still can't get use to her naked on stage but have seen her nude before and it's her choice and I support that and she gets pleasure in titillating men's desires like Circe, the director knew where to place Circe so that the audience would know where to look when the voice and sounds came out, and Conchita has no self-consciousness even if she became aware of herself by the time she was four and no longer wanted to sit in my lap let alone be naked in front of me, she doesn't recall that but I do it was an important moment in her self-development when she could only look at the world through a glass darkly and no longer be free and natural, but now she is not afraid to show off her body, there is a tragic-pleasure in watching her perform, she has a good strong body, after all she is in the forefront of revolutionizing theater and actors have to stay in shape, and not catering to the prurient element in the audience but forcing them to look beyond nudity into the ideas she's talking about—all of a sudden you see something wonderful, beautiful and you can't even put it into words. At first men come just to see her nude but soon they grasp the ideas she's talking about and the theater is drawing them in as if there's no tomorrow, the dregs don't show up but educated people do both men and women not pandering to the audience and the greatness of the theater is that it destroys conventional way of thinking, to be a Puritan is not having to think. Joseph Peter Fuchs objects claims nudity destroys the drama, he still has a difficult time seeing her nude on stage and that she is destroying the spirit of the works when they use nudity and thus can never get at the meaning at all. That may be correct in the abstract but once you see a performance your eyes open up and of course in Spain those plays weren't permitted, the best argument for open theater, but in America there is a greatness and after some hesitation, debate, argument, the priests lost and now off-off-Broadway has become a mecca, a challenge to bourgeois theater, Broadway is theater without thought their knowledge no different than mindless feeling and at least this theater makes judgments between thought and schlock now that authority has been wrested away from do-gooders. Here the audience thinks it has a right to judge art is what they like serious thought mixed with gaiety not the general cultural decline of the lowbrows. She sits on the stage for almost two hours reciting her tale in front of a campfire, sometimes in the nude, sometimes wearing a robe, with a little musical accompaniment and singing in the background as she tells how Odysseus made his way to her and how she cured him of his love of killing, it was her voice he heard that says enough killing to end the Odyssey, change is the most difficult of all things. Any Tom, Dick or Harry can produce shows that are titillating but to make claims of beauty, goodness, truth requires one be serious but being serious does not mean you cannot be gay—have to be careful with that word it's now undergoing a metamorphous. When I look at art now it has to be beyond practical more esoteric that forces me to think, Joseph said that and he is correct, if you want to relax go to work. I don't want Muzak for the soul! Novelty attracts people but what forces us to think is the delay of informing us what's going on that excite us, difficulties in figuring out what's going on increase our desires and excite our imagination, mere suffering is not enough despair must lead to courageous action otherwise the bad guys just get their comeuppance, still art is only an image what is presented before us on stage only a performance and if I nap in it know it's no good, but what surprises me is that I am always the oldest in the theater, but at least Conchita's performance is mine; a moment of truth a part of my authentic self, and now I'm going back to art openings and galleries again like I once did but stopped for no particular reason and Joseph loves to come with me even if Conchita still can't get beyond her art: I love it when I can't figure something out but afterwards it comes to me when it becomes an image not simply a thought then it becomes alive for me while it was up on stage I was wondering but the image has to be mindful otherwise it's like hip-hop music words that I can't phantom even if the beat moves me—it has to be activated, erupt inside me for it to have meaning. Her nudity gets me started but theater is much more than applause and if a woman is to be nude on stage she must be saying something otherwise you are confusing the stage with a strip club, but if the audience only likes nudity there is no theater of the mind. Unfortunately now all that seems to matter is the applause of the audience knowledge and reflection count for little. Joseph surprised me once when he said they never saw Greek drama while in college, what kind of education is that? He's young yet and has potential but he still doesn't grasp all I say, and I like the way he challenges existing norms insists Conchita breastfeed, wants to be in the birthing room, insists that he be part of the childcare not let it all fall on her. Old fuddy-duddies can't be my friends and it is crucial action take place with thought behind it and then I brace myself realizing 99% of the population probably have never seen a live theater performance or even if they do they don't change their life because of it. Jane Fonda did *A Doll House* on television but how many women realized it was about modern feminism and as long as women stay barefoot in the kitchen change will not occur, you didn't have to leave your home it became another episode of television. Change is difficult, our hearts have to change not the economic system—Marx was wrong Freud correct, women now don't have to marry and get pregnant right away that makes us a little freer but when we can do things by ourselves like men can will we become truly free.

Conchita thinks that the heart attack did me some good got me out of myself and out into the world once again, but I think it could have been accomplished without the heart attack.

Why do I feel so uncomfortable around these people? No longer do I have anything to do with them, and even when I went back to the old neighborhood to walk around felt it was only in a dream inside a dream, I never would walk up there in person it's now called the South Bronx and is dangerous especially for a single woman alone—there's no honor among hooligans they'd rape, rob, kill an Hispanic woman as easily as a white one, in fact only minorities are left there as Joseph said Co-op City is really Jewish City even if Italian and Irish and other whites moved there, they were the first ones smart enough to take advantage of the opportunities blacks and Hispanics are too afraid to own an apartment, Joseph has this idea now of getting them to buy but we'll see. Even in the dream I didn't walk down my old block but the main street next to it, I could feel the warmth of the sun on my face and looked at the rundown apartment buildings, you could see through some of them they were abandoned, what nonsense to dream about this, I haven't been there in years and don't want to go back, then I bump into Hector and his new wife, but Hector was the wife, it just didn't make sense, he/she ignores me I get that he was surprised to see me in the old neighborhood, but his husband is surprised to see me and he can't hold his surprise in and I see the shocked look on Hector's face and I want to mosey on by not wanting to stop and chat but I can tell you he looked good, that's what you get when you ride the subway in the city you get to examine pretty boys faces and size men up quickly—you can't stare at them they quickly get the wrong idea but you can gaze quickly and see if they are beautiful or ugly or somewhere in between, safe or dangerous, Joseph thinks I am immediately drawn to beauty and the beauty he thinks I'm drawn to is the beauty of my father, as if I have any memory of him, that's just it, he says, you have an unconscious memory aided by some old black-and-white photographs that capture him at one particular moment in time that unfortunately was not his moment, and men who look like him are beautiful to you, the only difficulty with that theory is Joseph does not look anything like my father this intense young man who quickly realized he was starting out life at nineteen with a woman and child and abandoned us because he wanted nothing to do with us all he had wanted was sex from my mother not a family, pace grandma, I can only imagine what he was thinking, acting, doing but that was not what he actually was thinking, acting, doing, I have no knowledge of that only what I think he was thinking, acting, doing, and most likely that image is completely false but it gives me a way to think about him, even if what I think is wrong: I know that from acting where audiences have the most varied interpretations of my performance and abstract a few of the characteristics I am portraying which have nothing to do with the emotions I am feeling and audiences cut out what they don't want to see and only remember what they find interesting, which means they don't truly understand a nuanced performance. No it isn't my father I saw in these boys and it's not only safety especially if I pass 96th street on the West Side and all the white people get off the express train, of course I size him up that is my first order concern but it's deeper a fear a deep rooted fear that my future can quickly revert to my past that I've worked so diligently to erase and wish I could glance longer but I'm too afraid I will chose the one in a suit and clean shaven, quiet, the boring one, and it wouldn't be the image of my father because the men I like never look like my father who abandoned us—I remember as a little girl wanting to find him and he'd run up and hug me but even if realized I existed he had no idea what I looked like, only as I became older realized he probably has a new family and would want nothing to do with the old. My desires are rooted in bodies, acting is intuition before learning. The picture I have in mind of my father is not real, anyway, it is a pose and I have no idea how these men will look as they age, usually men get handsomer as they age and women get old, gray hair is attractive on a man not a woman, a woman's body sags more than a man, especially after children, I quickly look at a man's eyes top of his face his eyebrows his nose their I can see their uniqueness no one shape fits all. As a kid we were told each snowflake is different from every other snowflake and I couldn't believe it and I started examining snowflakes in the next snowstorm and it's true up close they are different no two are alike. Me too, I have to glance at the face as a whole before I look at the individual parts to see if it's an interesting face—why I worry about marriage I am not through looking yet, an interesting face means an interesting life, it's not only the outer face but how I think the outer face connects to the inner persona the fantasy of my rush, sure I have no idea if my fantasy is correct and most likely it's not, most men I know lead conventional lives, but I am a good actor and can quickly improvise and give them lives they could only wish for, or as Joseph says I have a good imagination and from looking at their faces can infer a life that is reasonably inaccurate or it has its scientific roots in phrenology—feeling of a person's skull to determine what kind of person he or she is, I know where that idea came from, Joseph read me some article in the Tuesday Science *Times* how they now realize autism is a physical disease not one of a refrigerator mother, and I immediately thought poor women blamed for their child's condition when all along they were not guilty—there is no innocence Joseph always reminds me only not guilty. He reads too much Kafka, grandma says, quoting his grandfather who somehow read Kafka before he became KAFKA and said we all die like a dog, shamefully, there is no more moral authority, and dog is God spelled backwards. But I do believe the lean and hungry look determines one's personality and body language is important for any actor—and now we can even tell a liberated man or woman so quickly because of the clothes they wear or the shape of the glasses—all liberated women now have the Gloria Steinem look with their aviation glasses. Why should I despise my old friends so much, that is the question, but I don't know if the dream was truly about them—why am I different from them? Pure chance I got out of the neighborhood, Joseph consciously made the decision to leave I don't know if I ever would except for my mother's death—collateral damage as it's now called, forced me into a brave new world now the only issue is freedom, can I be free and also a mother, and my new friends seem to be able to combine the two, of a women's night out, of men sharing in all the housework, of both men and women earning a living. When I look at the image of my old friends I see them saying to me why do you think you are better than us? Yes, it's because I believe in art, you stupid dummies, I want to say that art has opened a new sense of perception to me, I learned to look, look for beauty grasp at knowledge not say I'll see something when it comes on television so I don't have to think. They think they are ahead of me because some have husbands all have children as if life were a race to get husbands and children. Well pretty soon I will catch up in that department. Pregnant at my age, who would have believed it? It's early I can still get an abortion but all of a sudden don't want one, not because I am ecstatic but because Joseph and grandma are, I am nervous. When I try and explain this to Hector in my dreams he sees me as uppity and don't know my place in life even if he never would go so far and say that to my face. Pregnancy has been giving me these strange dreams but I won't become just like my mother I fought too hard to escape her clutches to fall back now, the difference between my former friends and me is they moved a little further north or out of the Bronx but nothing else changed they even begin to look like their mother and they never gave themselves a chance to find out who they could be—they refused to grow only repeat their parents, they are housewives, mothers, but not an independent person using the *kinder* as an excuse not to live, how many of them can I hear saying when my kids are grown I will have a life but I doubt if they can you can't just have a life: life is a preparation for living. I have to believe in this freedom and not succumb to easy temptations to revert to previous roles as I did in my dream and my old boyfriend changed into a she who only wants to marry her so as not to be able to learn what freedom is even if she still is responsible for her life.

What did I ever do to them? What does it have to do with me? I supported the Teachers Strike, thought the North was as segregated as the South because of housing convents and restrictions, I'm no dummy, besides Esmeralda explained how bad the public school system was to me intellectually, but I knew from firsthand experience it stunk. I'm not hurt only my pride is wounded, why me? what did I do to get treated this way? A bunch of rowdy kids wanna be tough guys come up to me with a knife, a knife no less, three, four of them, and I can't believe it and in the old neighborhood no less, no I'm not coming up here anymore and felt more at home here than anywhere could walk these blocks with a sense of freedom, knew every knock and cranny, obviously not every, didn't even walk to the other side of the street when I saw a bunch of kids hanging on the stoop, shouldn't have gotten off the main street, but I wanted to walk past my old building, now these young toughs are scared they believe the stuff the media is saying about them 'The Bronx is Burning' little thugs, I use to go around and hassle Dodger fans when they lost the World Series to the Yanks, but never pulled a knife on them, one held it to my throat I can still fear the scar but it's only imaginary I feel where he placed it there's no mark there, twelve, thirteen-year-old punks, I bled but I didn't even know I was bleeding until I put my hand on my neck and when I took it away so some blood and realized they cut me, never even saw these kids before one moment they're behind me as I pass them the next they're standing alongside of me—I remember when the riots took place and these kids were looting appliance stores, jewelry stores, electronic stores, or kids like this probably not them and I wanted go and loot a bookstore, break a window and take out some freebees cause nobody breaks into bookstores and I could get away with it, then was afraid cause nobody breaks into bookstores and I would get caught imagine the headlines in the newspapers, caught robbing a bookstore while the kids robbing the electronic stores would be left alone—they really did a number on the stereo stores but we have a good Bang and Olufsen stereo system so that didn't interest me, then finally said no I won't steal it's wrong. Now I know it's wrong after it happened to me, I almost laughed when they took my el-cheapo digital watch, and they had no interest in my credit cards or driver's license only the money in my wallet. You could have been killed Cassie yelled at me as Esmeralda washed my face and put alcohol on my wound—my red badge of courage or stupidity as she said, you think young thugs care you came from that neighborhood, you were an easy mark, I thought it would be a quick easy walk from one subway stop to the next just a small detour around my old block—my old neighborhood is not mine anymore, the old grocery store, delicatessen, Chinese restaurant, dry cleaners, shoe maker, and tuxedo rental shops all gone. Now I want to go back and confront them not to beat them up I'm a lover not a fighter, but challenge them what do they think they're doing wasting their lives hurting people and to get them to think about their actions, I lived here and I still live in the city they have no right . . . yea, yea, keep it a nice fantasy just don't go back there anymore was Cassie's admonition. There's no such thing as universal guilt, unless you're Catholic then there is original sin and a human being born guilty is just a milder version of original sin humans can make vows and break them and only humans can do that, but this is deeper they're blaming me for my white skin and I don't even have a black mask to hide behind, this is separate from my other actions and I am not responsible for what happened to blacks and Hispanics, even if Cassandra hates to be put in the same league as blacks, or Afro-Americans as the intelligentsia of the black community is now calling itself, I wonder if that term will catch on, as the Jewish intelligentsia is now calling the Holocaust the Shoah; am I responsible for unequal housing, the projects that lead to de-facto segregation in the city, slum clearance, the invisible wall that constantly moves where

Afro-Americans and Hispanics cannot go without looking for trouble, me all by myself: urban renewal separated the races and ghettoized the city and what housing practices separated externally schools separated internally and no amount of good will could put Humpty Dumpty back together again; am I responsible am I responsible for the city's constant debt, forget The Fall it's the bankruptcy of the city that's causing humans to live without a conscience—these kids should have been in school but there are no more truant officers eliminated in the budget cuts that allow kids to roam the street at all school hours. Back in my day you had to be careful of men in fedoras they could be detectives or truant officers everybody knew that. This can never be made right and no matter what I do I can't be free of this feeling that I had something to do with it no matter how ridiculous it seems—free will, conscience, reason all conspire against me—here I am thinking I have free will and am quickly reminded of my Jewish roots, not what I say or do but what I think, but these guys didn't hold a knife to my throat because I am Jewish but because I am white—the difference between me and the Third Reich is the State is not against me if I would call the cops they would investigate and all the power of the State would be against them a bunch of ruffians who one moment were robbing appliances the next people and it was only real to them when they made the television news, reporter after reporter commented upon the fact that in all these riots kids would rather watch it on television than turn and see it live, as some bank robber did when he was holding a group of people hostage and a reporter called and the hooligan answered the phone proving how ubiquitous it was. Cassandra is asking me, really yelling at me, why didn't you cross the street, but it's like I never move in a subway car when a black guy sits down next to me, I don't like showing I'm afraid or prejudiced, even if now I don't allow anyone in the building I don't know, especially a young black male, maybe now I will cross the street when I see a group of young black males. That's silly pride that will get you killed, keep your ego out of this, was her warning—that's it blame the victim I retort, I'm not afraid of a bunch of punks, I'm from the South Bronx, but of course mugged from punks from the South Bronx, the East Bronx was a neighborhood, the South Bronx a state of mind, as that term has caught on meaning slums not a neighborhood when I lived there. The bleeding seems to have stopped otherwise Esmeralda would have taken me to the emergency room immediately but at that moment I was only interested in my dissertation on free will and wondered if would ever go back there again. The war in Vietnam is technically over but now it has been brought home to the streets of New York and not only do apartment windows now have gates on them, and buzzers to get into the front of the building but storefronts now also have iron gates so hooligans can't throw rocks through the window and steal. I didn't report it because it was such a small act of violence it wouldn't count in the official statistics, which were never accurate to begin with because it put the city in a bad light and we were told crime is much lower than the newspapers report—there's no such thing as a crime wave the experts keep telling us. All we now could hope for is from out of the ruins a new city can be born again. Cassandra wanted to totally break from blacks, no more coalition, Esmeralda says as European Jews migrate out of the city Afro-Americans are losing their number one ally and with the demise of the Afro-Americans and Jewish coalition it will be harder for blacks than Jews.

At first I would record all my dreams into a tape recorder, colorful or not, but now that I am not sleeping alone I write them down in my 'Dream Notebook' changing colored pens each day but no longer remembering them as precisely as I did when I awoke and quickly stored them on my tape player, it's a little more difficult now when I can't recall them as clearly when I awoke in the middle of the night, at first it startled me to hear my own voice and I wondered who's speaking, but what surprised me most of all was they were so vivid and in technicolor—an acting teacher once said an actor uses everything and you have to access your subconscious don't let it stay hidden—an actor's moods and feelings are crucial to understanding the development of character and you have to use your subconscious and you have to make sure it works for you, repetition is your friend, what one doesn't know you can use, what you know you can't it's too artificial. I didn't record my dreams to help me understand my trauma but to make me a better actor, a role can't just be seen from in front of you it must be developed from all angles as a painting when in front of you can't just look at the drawing you have to see the whole painting, the whole gestalt, when Icarus falls to the sea for flying too close to the sun it's only a tiny fragment of the whole painting but it is the key to the painting, either it's seeing man with too much ambition and pride or he's so small in the corner of the painting that man's lot has no meaning and life goes on as grandma said when I accompanied her on one of her jaunts to the museum on Friday night, you have a better grasp of character because even as we speak we are thinking different thoughts and that's one thing I learned in acting class. Now that I'm going back to school again more to please Joseph and grandma but I think I can do it after having learned how to code that was a boring class but I learned how to do it, but none of these professors has a creative bone in their body, some of them are clever but you have to keep away from them. Did students have affairs with professors when I went to school? Must have happy hunting grounds, it's really a hot-house atmosphere even if I find these teachers a bit stifling, the good stuff isn't on the syllabus they rarely talk about ideas or plays, never read original sources, impose other people's ideas on you not allowing you the freedom to discover them for yourselves, confusing playwrights with their characters it's not as if they don't have some resemblance but it's still not the playwright, playwrights don't have lives their beauty is in their imagination not their actual life lived, it's in the theater where the play takes shape, even if Peter Brook's is now saying anywhere can be a stage, you still have to vanish behind the fourth wall. Joseph likes to read a play first but I like to see it performed where water is turned to wine, even if the scenery is only cardboard and wood with some paint covering the outer layers, but he sees the words not the illusion but when he sees me up there that is not me I am not that person I'm an actress playing a role—how many men have mistook a character for the person and the character knocking heads against each other, we create people who can't exist in the everyday world or if they did they wouldn't be able to create a character they'd be so ego-centric and obnoxious, good theater is metamorphosis a transformation, a spectacle not simply overcoming your pains with good cheer. I love going to the theater with Joseph when I am not engaged, that's the difficulty being in a show you can't see other performers, and seeing a good production just blows me away, it's not only the stage settings or actors playing roles but the whole production, the holistic approach and Joseph has a simple way of determining if he liked the play if he rereads it but I have to feel the magic immediately, you feel it in your bones, it's the closest thing I have to a spiritual awakening, a more real world than is accessible only to my body, glimpses of a life I could actually lead if I weren't an actress, it's that wild unconventional knowledge that I love: the one that came out of religious services as music from church services even if Joseph thinks it was the other way around men and women listening to stories reenacted by one person than another that somehow became sacred, in acting feeling is everything but only if it's based on intelligence or maybe it started by parents wanting to entertain children certainly it couldn't have come down from organized religion with its thou shalt not's if that happened it happened later when everywhere men were bent heavy by priests instead of being as they are. Still theater is a metaphor it's not real it comes from imitation our clowning around not taking ourselves too seriously and if I became Cassandra in real life grandma and Joseph would not be entranced and sometimes I wish I had the pleasure to stay in character and have the life I have on stage because when those stage lights go on and the house manager yells places magic happens and I am no longer this shy searching lost girl but become my character and when men go home have wet dreams about me, at least I hope I do infect their imaginations that men see me as the role not the person I am, acting is not genuinely true merely like the truth, why tyrants always want to ban it, it gives the audience the illusion of freedom or at least an opportunity to think about their lives. No wonder tyrants keep women under lock and key they are so afraid of them and their sexuality—too bad there are so few good roles for mature women. I have played queens to beggars but in the end it is usually a man's story, even modern women playwrights seem to be supportive of the man's position, I can't even go to the movies anymore because these women have half-lives and can't be without a man and I'm becoming more like grandma gravitating towards the classics where authors are aware women have sexually charged lives albeit sometimes unconscious, and in making myself Cassandra actually believe I am Cassandra and therefore have reasons to act as I do. I betcha I could pass a lie dictator test on stage. I never forget the stage is two connected parts, regardless of what Peter Brook says, the stage above and the audience below who have to believe what we put up above. We have to be before an audience to act and the audience can't be passive they have to engaged with us and we have to engage them if theater is to work, thank goodness for footlights otherwise if I'd see the audience staring blankly at us I would know we are letting them down, all I can do is hear their laughter, sorrow, sighs, no visual conformation what's going on, all we can do is mess with their minds, their mental states, let them have wet dreams of me, mental states are the images that stay with us they are what I record in my 'Dream Notebook' they are the world as the actor sees it not as a spectator in our lives but as a lived experience.

April isn't the cruelest month it's just a continuation of March's psycho weather, winter or summer or fall but no spring, and I wonder if we'll have spring, and in my head I know they'll never be a spring again since Jacobo and I parted, and that is the last spring that I can remember that had warm sunny days even as it rained the day he left, it's cold outside, not as cold as February but still I can't put away my winter jackets; the white sky refuses to turn blue and I haven't even seen a robin but only the dumb think a bird can be the harbinger of spring, there is no more spring, it only becomes a little warmer in May and then we go right into summer, at least now the threat of rain has turned into a drizzle and I don't have to carry my umbrella but I didn't listen to Joseph who explained probabilities to me and said it was cheaper to buy one good umbrella than a few cheaper ones, however I usually forget my good umbrella somewhere so I don't think I am saving any money with his calculations, better to just leave it home and carry my cheap one, who cares if loose that even as I see the sidewalks littered with el-cheapo umbrellas, and I never made the connection until Joseph pointed it out to me as his grandfather did to him, still I use my inexpensive ones unless the wind is out, and now I can at least see the sidewalk and don't mind getting damp as long as I don't get caught in a downpour, only how do you know it starts out nice but in a moment you can get soaked, yet I can't stay in the apartment all day, now that I can walk again without a stick, I have to walk every day to clear my head regardless of the weather, unlike men who retire and make a dent in the sofa they lie there all day long. That's Joseph complaining about his father in retirement who couldn't do anything and would lie on the couch all day, he tried to do things with his father but his father was too far gone by then to want to do anything, it's too easy to become trapped inside you have to force yourself to do things, I am now getting back into the habit of going to galleries and museums on Friday night as I did when I first retired and somehow stopped now at least I am using my mind again, it is important at my age to exercise my mind and not simply lie on the sofa, and of course I see Conchita whenever I can, and seeing her has allowed me to go to other performances as well, even if sometimes I am the oldest person in the audience, and interestingly enough one of the few females who go alone but here my age protects me men don't see me as an easy pickup. I much rather go with someone but now am getting use to my isolation once more, and I can be alone with myself, I have to be because most women my age aren't interested in going out at night but I just love wrapping my head around raw theater. Joseph explained to me how he loved walking the city with his grandfather much more than sitting up straight at his immovable desk with his hands folded in a classroom, and I can imagine myself beside Jacobo as we discuss what I've seen, I told him he should have been homeschooled but he never heard of that, imagine I could have been taught by my grandfather, he said, but that was denied him because his family didn't even know about it, but it's become more popular now for the wrong reasons: Christians don't like that religious values are not being taught and by religious values they only mean Christian apologetics not a search for truth, but a system of beliefs because if God is dead there is no truth they claim, which is secularism gone wild and religious nuts will have none of that and all of a sudden people are allowed to set up their own academies explicating the biggest lie of all, and refuse to teach scientific thinking, truth is self-knowledge, good is harmony and beauty is using your imagination, and they don't believe in understanding why things work as they do. Scientific rationalism is not just any old belief but a progression from belief to knowledge. He would have done terrible in one of those academies but I can see him walking around the city with his grandfather and learning, he probably learned more in a couple of hours with his grandfather than he did sitting all day in a classroom to a sequence of half-truths that teachers mumble, but life doesn't work out the way you want it to otherwise it wouldn't be life, life always throws stumbling blocks into your path and it's how you navigate around them that determines life. Do you give in or do you continue to search for truth? When you realize you can't affirm yourself everyday especially when life doesn't live up to your expectations then life begins and we are faced with a choice to continue mired in muck or try and break free and you have to face waiting for another fifty years or attempting to strive, it's so easy to give up when youthful idealism fails and you sink into a rut because your early dreams of success have faded, now you earn your stripes can you continue or do you give in to sloth, I recall those Sundays home when I didn't work and Tomas and Gloria were home, those days were brutal until it finally dawned upon me I can't stay home and take care of them and cook, clean and wipe up after them, no my life in the new world would not be a continuation of life in the old world, even if I couldn't just walk away besides walking away wouldn't help I would just go someplace else to lead the same life, it's only by thinking can we make small changes that can change all, all we have is a little freedom we don't decide the world we live in we are there, I wasn't thrown into a world it was there before I was born and had to adjust to a world forced by our circumstances, I now get it but I wish I had somebody to explain it me earlier it took me forever to figure this out on my own but it is better to have figured it out even if late than not figured it out at all. Oh this shitty rain will it ever let up or am I going to have to open my umbrella, at least I've learned how to dress for it with thermals and waterproof boots and it's not mud, you can't believe the mud we had in the war occasionally when a horse slipped in it he couldn't get up had to be shot so the Falange wouldn't get them. I don't let the little stuff bother me and can now walk the streets again, life throws curveballs at us, Joseph explained the baseball analogy to me I don't understand the game Tomas spent so much time listening to on the radio, the hardest part of learning another's language is the metaphors, bullfighting I understand real people can get hurt it's not like a sporting event where you play to win; theater is more believable nobody gets hurt or wins. True at first I felt uncomfortable going to the theater the language was difficult for me but I wouldn't be lazy and quickly grasped meanings, and true I felt embarrassed when Conchita was up on stage nude but I adjusted so it as part of the performance, she's not going to get killed and she's acting doing what she wants to do, not giving into the inertia that sets in when the bloom of youth fades and you have that pit in your stomach where everything is exhausting and empty; she becomes somebody else upon the stage and if she doesn't it's a poor performance but if the magic occurs and she's transformed into the other becoming Cassandra then Wow! I'm glad she has that. She never play-acted as a child and I'm glad she's getting the chance now, her career is starting to take off, directors and producers are noticing her still she won't give up her day job especially as we age our choices become less and less our options less and less and we can't immediately change our life it is a circuitous process, we can dream of changing but the actual act of changing takes hard work, usually we run away thinking that's all we have to do but pretty soon the old life comes back to haunt us. How many men divorce thinking they will find happiness at the end of the yellow brick road only to come back to the same ole, same ole and only when they die do they say with the last woman he finally found happiness not if he lived would have left her as well. Or these young kids of today who make irrevocable decisions so they don't have to think, have babies, become a drug dealer so they can spend years in prison saying I never expected to get caught, Yea right! Stupid jerk robbing someone in your grandma's building and leaving a trail right to her apartment, or women afraid to use birth control because they want someone to love, to hold, and they'll be different than their mother only to turn into her. It's a curse to be too pretty when young. Damn rain it's coming down again like when we were forced to watch as Jacobo boarded the boat and I threw my arms around him for the last time and Delores Ibárruri, *La Pasionaria* telling them we shall not forget you: 'Mother's women tell your children of the International Brigades and how the men reached our country to fight for freedom.'

Did she wear black? A veil? Imagine somebody loving like that but she did live in a different time where people thought you only love once in lifetime, one shot at love then it's over, not like us moderns where if it doesn't work you're outta here. I admit I was surprised when Esmeralda told me how she left her husband, and really didn't mourn the other one and saying if it doesn't work out why torture yourself yet would have been shocked if my mother left my father. I just couldn't imagine my parents separating, why, my grandparents did, but my mother and father were the rock of my foundation, to just up and call it quits, I couldn't imagine it. And yet kids have to go through this all the time now, I knew nobody who was divorced, a couple of widows yes but divorce I didn't even realize my grandparents were divorced only living apart until Robert, my friend, pointed it out to me, he was Dominican but wiser in the ways of the world than I was, but Esmeralda mentioned if he was Dominican living in New York in the fifties he must have been part of the Trujillo regime or connected to them, I don't know we didn't talk politics at age 8 but it certainly throws a new light on our friendship if his parents were part of the right-wing ruling class. It's wild how the future throws new light on the past and changes the past. Still he was my friend not his parents. At least now we are more honest not continuing with this farce that the family is the bedrock of society. Kids can adjust. Even women

FREDERICK MARK KRAMER

are having dalliances now I suppose they always did but now in greater numbers, a dalliance is weird but the new way of viewing marriage we are in a momentous moment of change and I truly can't grasp it because underneath this newfound feminism is a deeper level of insecurity and questions being raised, it's way beyond equal pay for equal work, maybe monogamy is a forced thing and people aren't made for it, some men have been arguing that but the family is sacred, now women are also but not seeing the family as profane and the societal implications are not easy to understand, we have to understand history in order to understand the significance of these changes—there is no more the eternal feminine, she is one of the boys. But as Phyllis Schlafly, a silly woman, whose misogyny helped defeat the Equal Rights Amendment by glorifying children, kitchen, church, but she was only a symbol of how men hate the new woman. The difficulty with these changes, which I support, unless it affects me, as Cassandra says, is I'm really good in abstract thought it's the day-to-day stuff I have difficulty with, hey I cook, clean and do the laundry, yes she says but you still think you are doing my job, these changes might have a strong influence upon society. When we talk about this they have no idea what I'm talking about they are so set in their ways and see nothing wrong with the changes which they have been in the forefront and think I'm complaining because I might lose my privileges but I am talking from something deeper. Yet when I first laid eyes on Esmeralda compared to the photographs she showed me she is more beautiful now than then, okay now she looks older is no longer young but there is a purity to her face and a delightful smile missing from the old black and whites and her eyes are etched in sensuality an enchanting woman, the first elder I met I thought I could have a conversation with, I'm around her more than Cassandra who's busy with work, acting and school, and she has forced me to open my eyes and see the world from a different point of view that looks so fine in theory but will it work in practice—such a profound difference in our thinking can't be explained by age; she has obviously thought about a lot of this while I go by my gut, I feel, she fights that instinct and tries to see things in a different way—one of the reasons I couldn't take this job anymore is I didn't want to become old before I became old, already I have to ration my pleasure, can't make love to Cassie and masturbate on the same day and have to make sure I can love at night only on the nights when Cassie comes home late do

I allow myself the solitary pleasure. Aging. I'm no longer the kid. And if I don't watch it pretty soon will become an old man. imagine I now get tired walking, I who could walk forever. Some friends think I am in fantastic shape because I can jog five miles but that isn't enough to slow my paunch and now I even have to watch what I eat. And exercise is not enough my mind seems to be going, this job steals time that I can be using to exercise my mind, and now I have to fight myself to go out on weekends, especially when Cassandra is not in a performance, it's so much easier to just stay home. At least we still don't have television that is a total waste of time. I'm learning despite myself at least a little each day to see underneath the surface not just look at things on the surface that there is more to it than meets the eye, first I look and see if it is pleasurable to me then I ask why before checking with Cassandra and Esmeralda and I am redefining my taste challenging my thoughts no longer thinking everything has to be in human proportion, no longer resisting uncomfortable thoughts forcing myself to reexamine my cherished beliefs, because that's all they are beliefs not knowledge: why should a couple stay together if not happy. I was really pissed when a theater critic let his opinions flow how this performance wanted children to follow their parents, listen to their elders and regard for our laws proving he didn't understand the play and uttered sheer nonsense it wasn't a profound opinion but it had dire consequences because reviewers of off-off-Broadway have more power than need be, now people listen to them and chose which shows to go to because of him, and he talks about feminism as bland self-overcoming not realizing how much discovery is involved in struggling to find out who we are and also in our wondering is there a rock bottom end to ourselves or is there no mind body self at all only desires and striving to overcome and no final resting place where our soul or consciousness are. He discussed the performance without discussing the writing, acting, sets, music, art, only what he liked or didn't and it wasn't open to question and he saw the performance without a historical perspective because now history is a dead letter. When I wrote him a nasty note did you see other performances of the same play or plays similar to see what authors are trying to say, he didn't even bother to respond. But it blew my mind how before we went to a concert Esmeralda and Conchita would listen to a record of the performance before they saw it. What's the purpose of that? They took art so seriously they wanted to see it in historical perspective not for liking or disliking alone. Esmeralda liked how the new theater with its over-the-top acting, music and stage settings were challenging the old order and Cassandra felt the new theater was showing the world new ways to live, but I wondered since I usually see art as pleasure for the moment but lately have been overcoming that belief and am now seeing art as serious with serious reflection, Esmeralda says there's more to art than pleasure, art has to force you to reexamine your life. If only theater was so serious.

When I first walked into my grandma's apartment I could smell the scent of ambrosia, the cloves, cinnamon lavender, she would keep these spices in her bronze cauldron on the stove at first I thought she was a witch, I had never noticed it before but that aroma was enough to make me feel scared, because whenever I came here visiting with my mother, rarely, but since she hardly wanted to go up to the Bronx we had to come down here, for a sixteen-year-old totally taken out of the old neighborhood and thrown into Village life it was quit scary, usually when we had visited she wanted me to sit quietly on the sofa, something I could never do and her apartment was so pretty I felt it was a museum piece never lived in, and felt uncomfortable sitting anywhere, in our apartment all my toys were strewn all over the place, back home in the Bronx we only had one bedroom that both my mother and I slept in, the double bed in the middle of the bedroom and my single bed nested against the wall, the other wall held our shared dresser and mirror, why my toys migrated to the living room as well and we never thought anything of it. Privacy was not a premium up in the Bronx, everyone I knew shared rooms with brothers, sisters, relatives, grandparents, only when I moved in with grandma did I finally get my own room, my mother's old room that she fixed up for me; back in the Bronx we shared the living room unless my mother was in the kitchen cooking and she didn't spend a lot of time preparing our meals, and in the living room we'd fight over with television programs to watch, but now we didn't have a television and I wondered what we would do at night. Did she expect me to read, or listen to classical music? Joseph had even said the reason I did so poorly in school was I didn't have my own space, but it was deeper when we got to geometry and the life of reason dreamed up by Plato my mother couldn't help me, only those kids whose father had a high school education here could help their offspring, most of my friends' parents hadn't finished eighth grade or English wasn't their first language so it was left to the child and we couldn't cope alone. I learned that in college. Once I moved in here my education began, she refused to get a television no matter how much I begged and cried, and she was educated not in the formal sense but she read all the time and knew where to place the decimal point, and my new school actually provided tutoring and all of a sudden I was told that I was smart, even if I didn't believe it, but acted as if I was and I was such a good actor that I transformed myself into a smart person, I acted smart, exchanged my coolness for melancholy, affected passions I didn't feel, turned my stupidity into wisdom, that eventually I couldn't take the mask off, I really liked getting out of myself not always thinking about myself, especially when up on stage loved playing female leads Medea, Celestina she wasn't simply Brigadoon and Esmeralda insisted drama open my eyes and even if I couldn't fully understand the roles I knew they were profound and I laughed because back at Walton, my old high school in the Bronx, the word bitch was used and there was a whole uproar whether the word was appropriate for a young girl to say and no concern how it fit into the play while at Calhoun we were encouraged to research our roles and understand the source of the character's motivation—this was the most fruitful year of education for me even if I had more drugs and alcohol than I ever had in the Bronx, I specifically remember walking into grandma's place and the woman in front of the kettle saying now this is your new home and even if I felt strange and the odors alarmed me she showed me my own room, and it wasn't painted pink, and I slept under a sheet for the first time in my life, at home it was directly under the blanket and this felt more comfortable than having a blanket directly on top of you, even if I had difficulty falling asleep I was so scared. She allowed me to take my records, some clothes and toys but wanted nothing of my mother's five-and-dime jewelry or furniture. She made me make my bed in the morning, why I'm just going to sleep in it again the next night. She had comfortable chairs and the living room wasn't designed around the television but there were reading lamps next to all the chairs, and books on the walls, I never saw so many books in one place, a whole library. In our house sometimes I couldn't even find a pencil to do my homework, no shortage of writing materials here. She even had a typewriter. And a fine stereo system not simply a record player with a good turntable but it didn't automatically bring down the next record, and when I complained, she said that isn't good for long-playing records, and my 45s were no good without an adapter and it was no fun changing records every three minutes or having to start over and replay the record, grandma listened to albums, so if I was to listen to my noise as she called it I had to listen in my room, because I brought my record player and clock radio down with me. She even listened to operas on 78s that I had only heard of but never saw. You'd think there'd be more music on them they were so big but they fooled you played very little music per side compared to LPs, that's why there were so many of them in a boxed set. Besides talking about noise who could listen to that screeching. When the music teacher said you can get extra credit if you go to an opera she immediately bought two tickets at the old Metropolitan House before it moved up to Lincoln Center, nosebleed seats but she said the sound travels upward and the higher the seat the better the sound, it may be good for sound but not to be seen and I loved seeing those men in tuxedos and women in gowns, and expensive jewelry but soon learned to enjoy the music even if I didn't understand the words plus the staging was mediocre so I didn't miss seeing a blur of staging and imagine we each had a glass of champagne in the intermission I was allowed to drink champagne and I felt so grownup and sophisticated. Joseph is envious that I actually had someone to take me to the old Metropolitan Opera House before it was torn down for progress and moved up to 64th street as part of poor people removal, destroying a neighborhood, it couldn't even support a bookstore until the homosexuals started reenergizing the Upper West Side, Joseph has told me enough times. But he thought the area was a slum until grandma told him it was an existing neighborhood but she thought the Bronx was a slum until Joseph told her it was an existing neighborhood, the publicity machine worked wonders destroying old neighborhoods for progress. He didn't even know there were such things as opera, concerts, performances, galleries outside of Broadway and the museums of art, until he went to college and they had discount tickets which he felt too cool to use. Niche opened his eyes, he always said. And you can't do that on your own you need someone to encourage you show you the ropes, and there I was fortunate grandma wasn't this little old lady set in her ways, she said If you don't go by yourself you'll never go and she was the only woman I knew who traipsed the city like a man, all of a sudden I am living in a palace not a hovel and before never realized the difference and it's difficult to go back to the old ways and one day stopped taking the train to the old neighborhood and my old friends, no one of my friends ever took the subway into Manhattan, they were afraid of the city, none of them had even gone to a special high school like Joseph, where the smart Jewish boys go, as we called it, but as he said at least I went away to college only one of my friends did, we were given no guidance city college if we were smart enough to get in and nothing else. Joseph complained boys lived at home with their mother until they married and then moved in with their wives. Only when they finally divorced their wives were they finally able to live alone, at least you had exposure to other worlds and to see there is a bigger world than bounded in your nutshell.

Who would believe this? who could have thought this? how can such a minor incident change the way we see the world? It's no Auschwitz which forever changed European history that when Joseph called it inhumane I reminded him that it was done by human beings. When Conchita moved in with me she confessed she never heard of the Holocaust. What they teach in American schools. But this! I always gave lip service to feminism, women's liberation, but thought they were too helpless why I preferred being around men to women at least they didn't stay indoors all the time like some Muslim, no more Moslem for them this black Muslim spelling is more phonetically correct even if Black Muslims still get no respect, covering their face from men's seductive glances; now if a woman isn't married by thirty and had children by thirty-five she thought her life as over even if she bought big curly towels to wrap around, a nice bathrobe, scents and gel for her bath, she was leading an inauthentic life because she was going to be home alone and there was nothing she could do about it since she didn't have a family—family comes first, and whatever relative called them they would go to their house for the holidays. Then this comes along and blows us all out of the water: some high school girls wanted to play baseball and the educational bureaucracy wouldn't let them, but those young girls found women lawyers who argued that the city ballfields belong to all the people not just boys and they had to open up their fields, somehow when Little League wouldn't let girls play that didn't catch public opinion, but this did, when the story leaked to the press everybody in the city was talking about it and saying it was wrong, I certainly did, even my barber did, this was no big abstract fight of are men and women equal, or even viva la difference, this was simply a case of feeling: can girls play ball or is that only meant for boys. Boys didn't mind girls playing only a few academic shysters did saying ball playing isn't ladylike, they could get hurt, but most thought if they want to play why shouldn't they, it was so clear cut that the fields belong to all students not just boys, even if Joseph remembers the ball fields in the Bronx occupied by men not boys especially on the weekend when these wanna-be youngsters would get together to play softball and the woman would sit alongside them and cheer and little boys could never get on the fields. His father even threatened to write a letter to their city councilmen asking the fields be reserved for young boys, but of course only threatened he never sat down and wrote a letter. This was like the South where colored couldn't drink at white water fountains and had to have their own and a judge said even if it is inconvenient that justice is inconvenient but we must have equality, could a judge have actually said that maybe I'm misremembering but he did say schools have no right to deprive girls of playing, running, jumping simply because some in the culture thought it unladylike. And the upshot is more people have learned about feminism because they saw how wrong it was to deprive girls of the opportunity to play ball. Now everybody sees what's messed up in this culture when a little event like this sparks such outrage and some judge ruled you can't discriminate on public fields and the Board of Education had to retract its rules and allow girls to play not just be cheerleaders, and the city didn't need a utopian project to see this as a right and the correct way to treat women. Of course Joseph said it didn't hurt their cause that some woman running in the Boston Marathon under her first initial and wearing a hoodie sweatshirt so nobody knew she was a woman was knocked out of the race by one of the judges but when her hood fell off and an official bounded down from the stands and body slammed her right in front of the television cameras for the whole world to see. But only because they wanted to see it, how many times has injustice been shown and nobody gave a shit, this time the stage was set, an idea whose time had come, unlike the Spanish Civil War where atrocities were shown to the world and the world said ho hum and was more interested in avoiding conflict than with the rights of Spanish workers and peasants. And even if the marathon was a private event and the organizers could ban whoever they wanted to ban it was held on public streets of Boston and the mayor and city council forced them to integrate—who would believe sports could play such an important role but Conchita complained sports that's all they give minorities and one in a million can make it into the pros and the rest languish, we'll have equality when women, Hispanics, minorities are allowed to be scientists, lawyers, engineers, not athletes and actors. But even she was impressed with the public's reaction to the banning of girls from public fields, and it caught the city by surprise—the jingoist press kept writing about it sarcastically but more but more people began to take it seriously that their tune soon changed and finally the city bureaucracy was forced to concede that if even one women wanted total equality she would be entitled to it, even if women's coaches were more practical and said women wouldn't be treated equally in sports until fathers or mothers said to their daughters lets go outside and have a catch. More people cared about this than the local school board elections that convulsed the city less than a decade ago where black and Hispanic were dragged into a coalition to bring community control to the schools and now the schools have gotten measurably worse, kids graduate now who can't even read, but now they can play sports, kids don't even read comics anymore only sit glued in front of their television sets all day watching mindless violence and advertisements to buy things, and can't even go outside anymore to play ball because the streets are so unsafe, of course that's not all students but reading is a good gauge of intellectual strengths but no magical thinking occurs in reading like in sports where they believe they will be able to get to college and parley college into a basketball career. Some black kid aptly named Moses jumped straight to the pros from high school and nobody talked about him losing out on his intellectual potential or that it was the worst thing that could ever happened to him, only said he could either get an education later as if it were that easy, or buy a college with all the money he received, the more cynical reporters talked of the sex, drugs and rock 'n' roll he could accumulate but what if he failed and ended up in a dead end job, only Carl Rowan a newspaper columnist said the most important thing that ever happened to him was to get a college education, education is too important to pass up. Joseph tells me of some of the star players during his high school days who couldn't get into a college and worked at Bickford's or Sanitation after graduating from high school and playing ball on weekends as they became old men in their twenties. Sports the opium of the poor. Why should that be any different for girls if they don't have an education, in fact it will be worse they will be stuck home alone with children. But this was a great consciousness raising stunt as Conchita calls it as sports has caught the public eye for a moment. Unfortunately it's not being against women having the right to use the school fields that is the main issue, the issue is how come there is only one special high school for girls and three for boys, really only half of one because up at Bronx High School of Science girls and boys go together while at Stuyvesant or Brooklyn Tech. It's all boys. I hope feminists take up that issue. No longer can you even utter under your breath why do girls need an education if all they are going to do is marry and have children, which in the past kept many a smart young woman from trying to fly, and the main issue is girls getting an education not playing ball, still it is fascinating to see how from this small level momentous changes might occur and who would have thought this little story would generate so much publicity and mushroom yet I still hope more will come of it than having a catch.

Girls now play sports, no more tomboys, girls who dressed as boys and played ball to the chagrin of their parents and who always hoped they would outgrow it, and most did, like girls lose interest in chess when adolescence comes around and they discover boys, but never discovered me. I like watching girls play basketball because they play the way I did, give and go, passing, jump shots not running up and down the court dunking or taking a jump shot and no team work. Thank goodness girls can't dunk! That's the only sport I can barely stomach. Esmeralda wants to go to soccer games, I have no understanding of soccer only Europeans played soccer and I knew no Europeans only refugees adults and their kids of course played baseball, football or basketball on the playgrounds of the city, only Zoltan kicked the ball to me and I distinctly remember it as funny an old man kicking a ball and he said if I kicked it back where he couldn't reach it I would have to go and fetch it, no problem for a ten-year-old, but for an old man out playing sport that was unheard of—my father never had a catch with me, I learned how to play on the streets. But now Pele and everybody is talking soccer and girls are playing even as I love listening to the clergy arguing against women playing sports quoting Deuteronomy that women should dress like women and men like men, but the cat's too far out of the bag for the clergy to influence all but a handful of girls, besides women have been wearing blue jeans since the

'60s, and women by calling attention to discriminatory policies, it's not simply that they wouldn't allow a woman to run but that a whole group of women are not able to compete, sweat, seems to have struck a chord in society, and they are no longer willing to be auxiliaries, cheerleaders, earth mother, the eternal feminine, they are now demanding the right to participate not to be man's helper drawing him back but now want to participate in the agony of defeat and the joy of victory and just as there was no law that women had to change their last name, they just did it automatically when married, now the masses are seeing girls should be able to play like boys, I wonder if it has any effect on Madeline, Matty, our neighbor's daughter younger than me so I barely knew her except for saying hello on the staircase but never played with her or stepped in her apartment, but I did give her my old baseball glove when I stopped playing, a Mickey Mantle model not Willie Mays that I slept with under my pillow and even if my mother said you don't give a baseball glove to a girl gave it to her because I had heard her fighting with her parents who refused to buy her one. Now people realize girls have the right to play right field. Interesting all she did was go to Catholic elementary school, high school and now I suppose graduated Fordham, a Catholic University or Thomas More the women's auxiliary but I hope for her sake she went to the Manhattan campus not the one in the Bronx then she could hang out with city kids and go to the theater not hang in the Ramskeller drinking cold beer or the Irish bars that dotted the uptown campus. I should call her and ask but am too shy, but she did thank me for giving her the glove on the staircase, even then I didn't invite her in to my apartment but asked her to wait a moment in the hall and I went and gave her my glove. You can't call girls tomboys anymore that would make them feel exceptional and here in the city there now are leagues where girls can play, I wonder if that is so up in the Bronx, they always take a few more years to catch on to current concepts, the only ones not playing are black Muslim girls not because it's banned in the Koran but because shorts are considered too sexy, immigrant Muslim girls are Americanized and play. Sports have done more for feminism then all the intellectual arguments—sport becomes the midpoint between ladylike behavior and unbridled sexuality, people think with their emotions not their brains and this idea of equal playing fields has struck a chord. Cassandra doesn't see much good in sports thinks it's going to be the same ole, same ole, that sports are going to set us free but only freedom can set us free and as usual Esmeralda worries women have much deeper problems than can they play ball, she is more concerned with illiteracy, poverty, second class schools yet even as I agree think sports is a nice first step, but both want girls to get a serious education. Cassandra is now really chafing under the schooling she received up in the Bronx and is disappointed at her night classes besides her work and acting takes too much out of her to put strenuous effort into her classes but she is determined to get a college diploma to prove that the Bronx school system couldn't crush her and to prove to herself that she has brains—once the professor handed out a reading list and she laughed it was so easy and not even required, the only thing required was the textbook. Gutenberg would turn over in his grave she thought wasting a printing press on a textbook. At U. of Pittsburgh all readings were required. And she is the only one talking to the professor the other students have no idea what she is talking about and worse at times no interest—these students are worse than when I went to school at Pittsburgh she keeps complaining they only wanted to party the women of today have no idea what's going on the world and no interest, and there are these are rank-and-file police officers getting a free education probably making more money than the professors with their LEEP grants, and so see this as a part-time job and all they complain about is how their wives don't want them to patrol with women police officers even if they have no objection to it their wives do. I suggested she wear an ersatz wedding ring to keep the men away but that only makes her safer for an affair, she said, instead she gives them a haunting look, she's a trained actress and her looks strike one to the bone, and if that doesn't work tells them to get their slimy hands off her. One even wanted to watch her sleeping, she tried not to crack up as he said that, said my husband would object to that. She's wearing the ring I gave her when my shoelace opened up and I bent down to tie it and she said yes, yes I will and it took me a moment to get it, but I gave her my mother's engagement ring that we had to have fitted, how come in the movies it always fits exactly? However the ring didn't stop the cops even if they respected it, I thought the silliness of the program would force her to drop out but she insisted and the price was good and the convenience even better so she continued determined as she was to succeed even as she stopped engaging with the professor because nobody understood where she was coming from and they would make cat calls when talking the difference between gender and sex how sex is lived by gender, or how race is understood as class, when she mentioned this the term 'heavy' kept popping up, catcalls. She wanted her education to be serious and she wasn't a prude she enjoyed a good laugh and didn't mind if the professor cracked a joke or two between thoughts but she was mainly interested in the thoughts but she wanted to learn how class, gender and race interacted and how these ways of looking at the world were interconnected not separate and finally couldn't take the cops anymore and heard about this program across town that was serious and you didn't always have to go to class and she could read these new Feminist studies and write papers on it and we bought our first word processor so typing could be easier, even if I did say it was only sociology but she disagreed it was creating a new field out of the old, and Esmeralda agreed it is important to see new types of thinking more than always being interested in parsing the old—to think is to forsake the old ways of thinking. Feminist Studies programs were looking at works as the products of cultural milieus not as eternally binding and inflexible. Why couldn't I have had realized that when I was in class, now I felt I was ready to learn, at least I am not like the former sports starts who didn't get into college and were now working as dishwashers in Bickford's one in Sanitation, or parkies, my time in school hadn't been given to learning and now women's' sports has put women's issues on the map replacing Vietnam and Civil Rights as the claim for social justice.

Spanish women think too much about their honor. I was wronged I didn't do anything wrong except love too strongly and I can't get rid of that thought, you can wash your face if dirty but honor can only be washed away with blood—garbage thought poured into us as children and that takes a lifetime to rub off, you can't just wash it away, you can't just remove it shake it off it's like the food you grew up with part of your psyche even if it's no good for you, you can't live without it and maybe it's not even bad for you, learning is questioning past voices deep within you guessing how they would act in our situation before trying to develop your own voice, if my parents had met a year later or even if they had sex at a different time I probably wouldn't have been born, it wouldn't have been me but some other poor schlemiel—would she be going through this now? Maybe not if she had a different childhood, maybe that child would have been totally different than me but they had me and if they

had me I have to have these longings not some other being. I only think
about him twice: once in the morning and once before I go to sleep at
night, not true sometimes he's with me when I have something to say
and I wonder what he would think, he who abandoned me despoiled
my honor, since he would never leave his family for me and suddenly
he left the country and my heart is rent in two like what the Jews do to
their coat to show mourning, only Joseph explained here in the modern
world they don't want to ruin a new suit so they now pin a black ribbon
on their lapel to signify mourning, no more ruining of suits. It doesn't
matter truth is formed from their ideas not whether you ruin a suit or
not. He wanted to wear his grandfather's suit at his funeral and tear the
lapel but his mother wouldn't let him saying you don't ruin a good suit
as if anyone would wear one of these wide-lapelled double-breasted suits
anymore, he thought, not realizing that they would come back in style
once again as well as wide ties, instead the suit hung in the closet until the
moths had a feast on it and they finally had to throw it out. He laughed
at the machinations of the rabbis like his former friend who now won't
shut the television off on the weekend, the rabbis say you can't turn it
on not that you can't turn it louder. Judaism to him is to get away from
tradition. He doesn't get it, Judaism for all its seriousness is also laced with
comedic elements, I learned that from Jacobo, for Jacobo fought tradition
with humor he hated the passiveness and resignation built on obedience
on ancient tradition as if that were the way as if there was one unique
way God gave Moses on Mount Sini and now all they have to do is wait
for redemption—ghetto mentality he called it, and he hoped to escape
from that in Spain only there he saw true ghetto mentality, the priests
are even worse than the rabbis wanting to ban all sorts of pleasure, even
hated theater, imagined that theater can give you negative ideas, acting is
based on deceit and what never happened can be more interesting than
day-to-day life, better not to enjoy yourself, even thinking about theater
debases the soul, oh if only theater were that strong. Joseph compares it
to criticizing academics of the '60s saying they ruined higher education
with their demand for relevance not the classics when in truth the schools
were at their best then not now with their watered-down curriculums.
Yesterday we went back to the Bronx the first time since I helped empty
my daughter's apartment if I don't count passing through the Bronx on
my way upstate but Joseph finally took me up to his old neighborhood,

'the Bronx is Burning' area that was shown on television, and I've always wanted to do it but never had the guts to ask Joseph but he said yes but we can't do it at night it's too dangerous but in the daytime is fine and we will walk on the main thoroughfares and keep off the side streets and we will be okay. He naively thought we'd be left alone because I am Spanish-looking not realizing thieves have no sense of honor and an old person is a good mark they can't see so good and can never identify them. And as Conchita said junkies never leave their neighborhood you don't see junkies robbing rich people on Park Avenue they rob where they are comfortable and that is their neighborhood and then disappear into the alleys or projects. It was a bright sunny day the first real warm sunny day of spring in May even if spring officially began weeks ago, and spring will never arrive for me since Jacobo left, but I thought a walk might be a beneficial way of relieving a memory and loosen its hold on you, unfortunately all it did was make it more powerful, the return of the repressed, but we took the D train to 167th street, his stop, and he even apologized for his New York habit of asking me to walk faster so we wouldn't miss the train and his letting go of my hand so he could bound down the steps faster and hold the door until I got there and I was out of breath the whole trip, he was frightened by my heavy breathing that I might be having another heart attack, but my heart is stronger now and by the time we reached his stop I had caught my breath; he had asked a couple of teenagers if they would let me sit because since women started working nobody offers their seat to women anymore and these two boys stood right up didn't even bat an eyelash decent kids who are just not taught anymore to stand for old people or pregnant women, and I slowly started to breathe normally, somehow I thought the trip would be over an hour, that's how long it seemed when I went to Gloria's house but this train moved and I don't know how he knew where to get off every station was covered with graffiti and you couldn't even see the station stop nor hear what the conductor is saying over the loudspeaker it's so mumbled and they speak so fast, I kept asking are you sure you know where to go? He laughed said you could disagree with me about anything except how to get around in the Bronx, I know the old neighborhood I can't get lost in the Bronx. Not that he knew every street he's not a taxi driver but he knows the layout of the Bronx like a homing pigeon and we kept on the Concourse and 167th street, and he showed me the candy store now a bodega, where his grandfather would take him for egg creams, where he bought the *Jewish Forward*, and the *Daily Worker* for his grandfather, the shoe maker which doubled as the local bookmaker, where his mother won enough for him to get a nice Bar Mitzvah, the five-and-dime store Woolworth's where they bought all their dishes and silverware, that was still there, these stores are where the women in the neighborhood worked if their husbands didn't make enough money but rarely did a married women work, you couldn't get rid of them they fed you breakfast, walked you to school, picked you up at lunchtime, made you lunch, brought you back to school in the afternoon then picked you back up at three o'clock when school ended, made a snack for you, watched you outside when you played ball, made sure you did your homework, cooked dinner gave you a bath and put you to bed, many times all before my father came home. Imagine how great he felt, he said, when he was finally allowed to walk to school by himself, only his mother must have allowed it but he didn't think of it that way. He also said if he had only played ball on the weekends like some of his friends he would have been a better student but he couldn't wait to be outside no matter what the weather. He couldn't show me his apartment building it had been gutted and now was an empty lot but the building beside it was still standing only you could look right through it on its way to rubble. All I could think was these were the streets Jacobo walked when he left me but Joseph said they weren't the streets his grandfather walked when he came home from Spain, they moved up here later when the laundromat business started taking off and they came into some money. This part of the Bronx was then considered the art deco capital of the world, lobbies were like living rooms, glass and geometrical designs dominated the buildings on the Concourse and grandma's building even had an elevator and a mural in the lobby of an ocean view surrounded by an island, he thought it was painted but his grandma said no it is made up of mosaic tiles imported from Italy. He lived off the Grand Concourse. As usual my thoughts were wrong. But even in its bombed-out shape you could see this once had been a beautiful area that now has Vista volunteers, junkies, homeless people, prostitutes—you would think the city would do more to keep it up, this was once a grand boulevard.

The Queen is the most powerful piece on the chessboard and that happened when Isabella of Castile became ruler with Ferdinand, grandma told me this story enough times but she never considered this the high point of Spanish rule because what's the sense of power if it doesn't make life better for the people, or even better for future inhabitants all it does is cause war and misery, imagine what the Muslims must have thought of the backward Catholics and their silliness, why men were allowed to marry only one woman not four as it should be according to the Koran. They had this high civilization and they must have seen the Christians the way the Romans looked at the Christians, an unfettered lot of ruffians, Joseph claims that not grandma. Yes they became the power but it was the power of exclusion not inclusion they couldn't live with others in their realm Muslims didn't mind who you worshipped Christians said you could only worship Christ and they set the policy which has made it impossible for Spain to modernize even as the civil war failed now we suffer the consequences of excluding the other, Muslims, Jews, people who run small businesses and we are continually forced into backwardness; our hero is Don Quixote who saw windmills as giants and forced us to always look backwards for our golden era, this was grandma. Boy was Joseph surprised when I told him how the queen became the most powerful piece on the chessboard, but probably was more surprised when I first beat him at chess, he never realized girls could play chess, the only girls he knew who played chess knew the moves but not the strategy and had never seen girls play chess after high school, in his whole college career not one girl was on the chess team only boys, never did a girl have a chess set in the south cafeteria and I would have never played the game except grandma gave me a beautiful chess set when I was five for my birthday and I just wanted to learn how to play and a neighbor taught me how to play and in junior high school took it as an elective instead of checkers or dominos and when Mr. Martinez heard I liked chess he let me take it with him and he taught me how to analyze positions not simply move pieces and if you controlled the four squares in the center of the board you would usually win, and don't take your queen out too early, and I understood strategic positioning and the value of pieces and you don't trade pieces unless you get more value or a better position. So when we played and he took his queen out early the game was mine all I had to do was wait. But grandma doesn't like to play anymore and these new computer programs are cumbersome, and not very good, but I think they will get better, at work all the men play Star Trek but that's just a random game in quiet time I like sitting over a chessboard, even if the two-dimensionality of the game is a pain, someday maybe someone will come up with a 3-D system. Joseph is no match for me and it's fun playing again but it takes so long for a computer to move on the higher levels that I get impatient, I should have sent Mr. Martinez a postcard letting him know how well he taught me. He would appreciate that because I do when someone comes up to me and recognizes me and says I explained a difficult coding problem for him, his smile brightens my day. I remember he was the only schoolteacher who came to my mother's funeral and was worried about me and was glad I was moving in with my grandmother, too bad he never knew I went to a serious school afterwards, he would have liked that, and he asked if I still played chess but there were no girls to play it with in my high school. He nodded said maybe I would get into it again after I finished my studies. I never thought of high school as studies. Now at least it gives me something to do sometimes backstage with cast members, again usually men, girls rarely still play chess after puberty. I can't play with Joseph he would get pissed if I let him win and he isn't on the same level as me. I never any good at hiding my intelligence and let the man win. I despise women like that who let boys win and who let men lead them to bed. We have to be independent, grandma insisted I not learn to type and I now pay the price for that now with my finger pecking what I would have given back in school to learn how to type with a typewriter with no letters on the keyboard it could save me a lot of time in coding, but grandma said you don't become a typist you become a thinker. I gave her the argument that I would always be able to get a job, good typists are needed my teacher said, grandma said good let her be a secretary you aim for more in life: if life crushes you then you learn how to type not before, instead I learned coding. They call me a natural but that's a hunk of shit I work my ass off at it. I can do minutiae and acting. I couldn't believe it in college these smart, educated women learning typing, home economics, curling their hair, makeup, skills that would help them catch a man, it cost me a fortune to get my essays and term papers typed up but I didn't care I wasn't going to be lashed to a desk. Now I sit at my computer station and don't move for eight hours, each time getting a little closer in coding before I could never stay so long in one place, now I even do foot exercises and hand exercises so I don't get stiff and even eat lunch at my terminal but I can sit and program all day long. Joseph envies me says he wishes he could concentrate like that. And luckily I didn't bother learning how to type, computers are putting typists out of business anybody can peck on an Apple. We were the first on the block to get one, for my courses, everybody says wait until next year they'll be better, so what, I need it now. I have to tell grandma and Joseph to back up always back up and keep hard copy otherwise all can be lost even if it is a pain in the neck to write a page, print a page and wait two minutes before a page gets printed, tear the perforated page off the printer, copy the page onto a floppy disc and then go back to writing on the screen, I am getting them trained on computers even if they don't like them they are the future and faster printers are on the way, and Grandma even goes to the senior center and is learning Basic and I am trying to get her interested in playing chess again. She says she learned it from Jacobo in Spain just like Joseph did from his grandfather as a little boy and they are a good match for each other but even as she says she wants to play again but she doesn't. She wonders which is the executive function in her life, her mind, reason, her body, sensual, or herself which is different than both of them. She thinks playing chess brings back too many memories looking at the pieces, holding them in your hand, planning your strategy and all that reminds her of playing in the middle of the night with Jacobo, and I guess, even if she would never say, before making love, and playing chess forces her to feel the civil war all over again and she is transported back in time and would wake up in a cold sweat having dreams of the war once again, and she said that back home when she lived with her parents after the defeat the hardest part was the dreams of the front where she saw so much pain and suffering that she doesn't want to go through that once again. Her happiness is mixed with fright and the game brings back too many intense memories, she once told me sometimes all she could do for the men is give them morphine and if not shot in the stomach some strong coffee as she took their names, rank and brigade and made up a medical card saying what they had done. I want her to fight her memories but Joseph thinks she should leave them alone. Whenever she talks about Jacobo it is tinged with hostility because the happy times are mixed in with the pain.

I never spoke of my past as being hostile I always thought I kept that hidden even when talking to myself, but Conchita tells me different, my darling granddaughter is talking and it takes me a moment to realize she's talking about Jacobo not Joseph, at least she's not ashamed to be seen with a younger man, even if I felt she was talking about Joseph because she was frightened of marrying him—marriage is serious business you gain and lose by it, and she has doubts, she claims she's not through looking yet but at the same time she's nearing forty and there are not going to be that many opportunities left and they've been together for such a long time and she is pregnant, even if she says she is willing to give up the baby I don't believe it that you can do when younger when you'll have or think you'll have more chances, choices, now this is it, I see all this in an imaginative perspective as opposed to a narrative perspective within time and space; she was born too young, not her, my daughter had a child before she could be a mother and I should have been able to prevent that but didn't couldn't she was out of my control by then and soon out of my house, she wanted her own place and she was going to be a better mother than I had been to her only she had no idea what mothering is all about and thought it was only being a friend to her child, she could ooh and aah but not think and love and she didn't want me around and I didn't want to be around and I didn't love her, there I can admit that now, and let her have her way—Joseph's parents loved him didn't let him have his way as a teenager when he wanted to quit school insisted he graduate, I gave in because I said I loved her and she had to find her own way, but I had the higher knowledge that a sixteen-year-old can't find their own way only get trapped in a way and find no way out of it. So she was bored in school that's no reason to drop out and have a baby; really a child born to a young mother has less life chances she has no maturity to guide her and doesn't even know it. But now she is of age and wonders if she will be a good wife and mother, that is a good sign, also, she wonders if she's the marrying kind, not such a good sign, how Joseph puts up with her sometimes is beyond me, he is a gentle soul who likes to be in her orbit and is always doing nice things for her, knowing she likes coffee in the morning makes sure he leaves some for her, bringing home flowers because it makes her feel appreciated even if he doesn't see her all day; if she had been born when Gloria was in her twenties then she would have had a little better chance, what chance did she have when all of Gloria's friends were dead set upon proving themselves as adults as little kids at too young of an age, smoking, drinking, dropping out of school having sex with the first man who comes along, playing at being an adult and this liberal country let them play at it not knowing what adulthood is all about, thought it was good for a woman to stay home with their baby made it into a social policy but didn't realize how corrupt it was allowing young girls to move out of their mother's house and set up their own at sixteen, they quickly caught onto the rules that welfare would set them up in an apartment and they could playact adults without suffering the consequences of adulthood and with no incentive to leave welfare, all she could do is work off the books to make a little and I mean a little extra money in a hair salon and employers were quick to exploit welfare mothers as cheap labor while her neighbor cared for Conchita cared for a few kids by allowing them to lie on the couch all day and watch television. The poor were the first to get the sets they knew it was a good babysitter. I was going through hell with Tomas until he left that I wasn't going to schlep up to the Bronx where I wasn't wanted. That was a mistake. Like the cry I made when I found out she was shot and I begged God to let me see her one more time before she passed, an insane cry for help and I knew what I was doing even if I don't believe in god prayed to God let me see her one more time before she dies, but it was a silent god, a hidden god, who refused to hear my prayer and she was dead before I even got to Montefiore hospital and it was this irrational wish of childhood drummed into me that burst out of me before I even realized what I was saying except I realized it as I was saying it but couldn't hold the thought back. Maybe I thought my life ended when Jacobo left but I knew it was over the night Gloria died. I couldn't believe I had done that but childhood does take its toll on you and all those years when I couldn't say no popped to the surface not my more rational belief that the gods were made by humans and have nothing to do with reality as Jacobo explained to me what I had intuitively thought, why else would I have run away like he did, but at least he gave me intellectual reasons for my disbelief, and it did surprise me how I screamed when I got the phone call about Gloria being shot how can you believe in a personal God who rewards and punishes in the next life for what we do in this life; Jacobo said God is dead, that was the first time I heard that and that the Bible was a fairy tale, it must have come as a shock but it seemed perfectly natural at the time so how could it have been a shock. I never truly felt for Gloria and my absence of love must have hurt her terribly and we both couldn't admit to each other we couldn't stand one another and she wanted a little one to hold onto like a doll, to be friends with, only little cutesy infants grow up and she couldn't be a mother to a toddler and she never had a chance to feel her oats the only reason I can understand why she went out with a hooligan—she was too old to be stupid but she never got a chance to be a teenager until Conchita was able to stay home alone at night and they would compete for boys, she was like an older sister to her own daughter not a mother because she never had a chance to climb out of the dark woods of teenage years—she still listened to rock 'n' roll music even into her thirties, never went to movies unless on a date and saw the crappiest films, never read a book, and probably never went to a play or concert, I could understand not going to Broadway that is expensive but there are other venues. But she did go to after hour social clubs, if she hadn't been killed before she would have been in the *Happy Land* when a disgruntled lover throws a container of gasoline into the building with no fire escape and one window and almost ninety people die trapped in the ensuing fire, which he didn't mean to do, the devil made me do it, all he wanted was to get even with his girlfriend who dumped him and of course she survives but they practically blame her for the attack and catch her as a welfare cheat working off the books and throw the book at her. Imagine seeing almost ninety bodies lying on the ground dead from smoke inhalation even the Mayor said it was the hardest thing he ever had to do and he was a marine in WWII. I once loved dancing now I rather sit and listen to music. Gloria was never able to reach that stage all she could be was erratic and drink booze to try and forget the curves life threw at her, she could never learn how to hit the curve ball as Joseph once said. His next door neighbor's son was so angry at his father for not letting him tryout after high school insisting he get a job that he enlisted right after Pearl Harbor and died on Guadalcanal, and he was a teammate of Hank Greenberg at James Monroe high school in the Bronx, one of the great ones, but thought he was better. I looked at him, Conchita looked at him, but he said the difference between an also ran and a major leaguer is the later can wait and hit the curve. Anybody can swing and maybe connect on a fastball but a curve requires thought and patience. When her idealistic demands of youth were defeated she couldn't get up off the mat and gave into despair. What I enjoy in watching Conchita with Joseph is the reminding me of my time with Jacobo and wondering if it would have progressed their way and also a moment of examining my life, something Gloria was incapable of doing—maybe I erred but I didn't do it on purpose but Gloria constantly went out of her way to sabotage herself and then complain about life's injustices, she had no idea how lucky she was, life changed after the second War, okay not in Spain but we were here she never had to realize how cruel men could be to their fellow man, and she lived in a welfare state that tried to take care of her only in taking care of her ruined her so that she expected to be taken care of and did nothing on her own, what was so terrible about having Conchita at such a young age is that she didn't allow Conchita to grow, didn't allow her to have a good start in life because she never considered Conchita's feelings and that had to be bad for any individual— even Tomas jumped at me that I was a mature woman when Gloria was born and I should have been around her more but I couldn't stand being a mother especially on weekends when I was trapped home with both of them and I let her go while we still lived together. Maybe I could have done more. But I couldn't it's easy to say I should have done this, especially when you put it so far in the past that it's impossible for you to do it, but then I wouldn't have become who I am now nor what made me this way: if you change one thing it doesn't mean everything else would stay the same, and I did my duty Conchita wanted to stay in her mother's apartment but I would not allow it and welfare wasn't going to pay for a girl to live alone, at least they did something right and she was forced to move in with me. I saw she could barely read, rarely did her homework, had no idea who the mayor was, but let her finish up there only next year insisted she get an education, there at least she discovered acting, which helped her get through those painful years, I knew I had to intervene to give her a chance and not become like her mother and to make up for the fact I had done nothing to raise her and if I had done something it would have been to make sure she hadn't been born and insisted upon an abortion even if it was illegal back then in those pre-McSorley days and I wouldn't have done it myself but would have found someone. Since I didn't stop her from being I had a responsibility towards her to give her some life opportunities and what I remember now is how it upset my life finally enjoying being alone and now to have this angry teenager moving in with me but I said to myself I have to give her a chance in life and finally Tomas had left, a decent if dull fellow, and I just didn't want to let him drag me down with him, I really wanted to feel the breathe in my lungs once more not be thought of as some man's wife but to finally find out what I wanted—a woman without a man is like a fish without a bicycle that was the tee shirt I wore around the house and laughed every time I saw myself in the mirror wearing it.

What the fuck do they want from me? I spent almost two years in prison only they had the nerve to call it rehabilitation. Shit, all we did was talk drugs. But I was no homo, stayed with my kind and we protected one another you have to stand together against the colored otherwise you will have no one to protect your back. Only as Petrie says we should have gotten rid of Hector all he did was cause fights he hated the colored so. The old timers told me I was lucky back in the day Hispanics were beaten on terribly because we didn't have enough of us to fight the whites or the colored. I finally get out, gave up on parole but still get it, and bingo get arrested again my first visit at the Parole office because I'm late, I get here a few hours late, who could find this place I don't know Queens and I have to wait hours in the waiting room. One of the guys even has the balls to tell me to read like I can read, I didn't go to classes liked clean-up duty better you knew what was expected of you, even if I liked the teacher and her nice red hair, fine ass, and I imagined she wanted to do it with me, a real man, not like those jerk-off social workers, real shits, only Hispanic correction officers were worse wanted to make sure nobody took them for junkies, at least white or colored officers were sympathetic, Hispanic would take no shit but they had to be careful they weren't real cops had no guns all they could do is put you solitary and that was crazy nobody to talk to for twenty-four hours, the scariest time I had upstate, in groups at least other people were around you and you could talk, even if I rarely spoke until Petrie said talk, talk they like that shit, make it up, you make parole quicker that way they think you trying to get rehabilitated, he was the smart one but they only wanted me to talk about my mother not anything else like if they'd give you a job when you get out of this place and all I wanted was a job in an office but no they kept saying we had a messed-up childhood and we have to get to the bottom of it and then some colored or whites would talk about you can't give in to temptation, religious fucks, you have to be strong when all around you are drugs. I never believed any of that just did my time and couldn't speak that bullshit and criticize my mother, what did my mother ever do to them she's an angel, those assholes, but the teacher the one with the flowing red hair and nice ass did try and help but I'm too old to learn to read, all I wanted was a job in an office, promised myself when I got out will get one even if I haven't the slightest idea how to get one and don't even own a suit and as Petrie said don't even know how to tie a tie. But you don't need a tie that much anymore you can go 'button down' he said, and I can learn that even if I have nobody to teach me. Grandma came up once but she's old and it's too far for her and expensive, mom never came but grandma did say I could live with them in the Heights when I'm released—Petrie read the letter to me but even if I behave myself one misdeed and I would be put on the street. My only letter and I couldn't even write back, Petrie said he would write it for me, he read letters for all of us and wrote some for cigarettes but he didn't play dominoes for shit said he liked chess instead and could only play that with one colored guard. They would sit all day making no moves always thinking and the guard was surprised a prisoner was so good as Petrie was, he would even occasionally win. The guard could have gotten in trouble playing with an inmate while on duty but he was bored and would bring out his chess set and play by himself until he started with Petrie. I finally get parole and they tell me I have to report to this place in Queens I have a drug counselor, Petrie said they didn't want to allow me to max out and have no supervision they thought it best for me to go home but have to report to a drug counselor once a week would be the way to keep me honest. But they closed the facility in the city and now I have to get to this place, I told the counselor that but he calls the correction officer, here they're not called guards, and he gives me a couple of tokens for carfare so I don't have to hop over the turnstile and says the next time I come back here they'll give me five dollars as spending money but first I have to take another drug test because they think I'm high because I was so late. Shit after I get off the subway didn't know which way to turn and nobody on the street knew where this place was. Better than when they let me go upstate at midnight and they give me a ticket for a Greyhound bus but no money to get home from the Port Authority. But at least I knew how to get to grandma's place but I take the wrong train and end up somewhere in the Bronx but the token booth attendant tells me how to go back downtown and get the A train and he lets me back in the subway for free, only you wait forever for these trains in the middle of the night but finally I get home to grandma's and climb the four flights of stairs and ring the bell. They weren't expecting me the facility didn't even write them that I was coming home just cut me loose and I couldn't even call they don't have a phone but grandma grabs me and hugs me and asks if I'm hungry and makes the bed and lets me sleep on the couch. My mother doesn't live there anymore and after I try and fall asleep grandma goes into the kitchen and starts cooking and talks to me as I try and fall asleep, and she asks me not to cause trouble in the building as she doesn't want to have to move again at her age it would be too difficult, but I want to say she didn't have to move because of me it was me not her that robbed but she would have thought that stupid she has to live with these people and she was ashamed of what I did, and she wanted to be spared their sympathetic look your grandson is a junkie. Who's stupid? I'm me not my grandmother. I did wrong and she moves out. Then she starts preaching once again that I have to grow up but soon I fall asleep having not been able to sleep on the bus and when I awake she makes me some food and tells me it's nice out go feel the breath of fresh air on your face, the breeze of spring, look at the fresh flowers Yea okay. Is she insane? But I go downstairs and walk the streets, don't know any of the kids on the block all Dominican now and walk up towards Broadway hoping to run into one of my old pals so I could get high. No more winos on the street it's all weed now which is okay by me. It feels so good I use the money grandma gave me even if it would be more nice to stick a needle in my arm especially today when I have to go see the man but think better of it, and now in Queens this guy is checking my arms for tracks but he can't see any I didn't dare but he says I'm high and luckily I belch and he can smell the alcohol on my breath and they don't send me upstate only upstairs and it's only for two weeks and this 'brother' tells me to be cool and I'll be out of here in no time and the drug counselor says I have to overcome my desire if I am to kick the habit. What habit I don't have a habit I can quit anytime I just like to get high.

In high school we would go on the weekends to the Bronx Botanical Gardens now called New York Botanical Gardens, when did they change the name? probably after the 'Bronx is Burning' for publicity sake never standing firm but trying to show their distance from the Bronx, a deceit but as the Gardens see it guile, they even have a train stop right next to the Gardens now so you barely have to set foot in the Bronx; it was an easy walk from my old neighborhood in order to pick up girls because girls like pretty things and would walk around smelling flowers, until one day by the river bed, which I had made a mental note so I could find it again having found it by accident, I ran into a girl I knew from elementary school and she waited for me to introduce her to my friends but I said nothing my tongue wouldn't speak couldn't say where do you live now? what school? let's go to the movies together? and we parted and here I am sitting under an oak tree near the Bronx River cursing myself for being so shy, why? I was never shy in my dreams but couldn't even get a word out, and I liked her so much in elementary school and wasn't shy about it back then she was one of the few girls I could talk to, but now couldn't say a word and there were three of them and three of us a perfect match but I couldn't say a word, big shot that I am. I saw the yellow witch hazels against the backdrop of the River and the light of the sun on reflecting off them, and thought Zoltan would be proud he always told me to notice my surroundings as I walked oblivious to all but what my inner radar could detect, saw the changing colors of the plants and flowers but dared not mention them to my friends, my erudition surprised me because I never noticed such things before and I was surprised she came up to me since we hadn't seen each other since public school. One of my bewilderments as a kid was reading in the *Post* how Bill Skowron of my hated Yankees came home one day and found another man in flagrante with his wife and I didn't wonder why that story was in the paper only why would a woman married to a baseball player cheat on him, back then I was bored with school so sports and using my fists were my main activities, now I smile I wasn't actually a bully didn't pick on kids smaller than me, never stole lunch money, but only fought those like me who couldn't control their emotions. I eventually outgrew it or more likely I thought then as I think now got my ass kicked by boys who grew faster than me then realized that was not true, it was when one of the boys asked me to touch his cock and I felt repulsed and he said if I didn't he would beat me up and my stare didn't scare him off, another lie stand up to a bully and they back down, my fists were ready if he made a move towards me, and then I remember him saying how are we going to fight can we kick blah blah and I went and hit him so hard it scared me I just pummeled him to the ground and his friends had to drag me off him and I never felt so scared in my life, I might have killed him. The next day he came to school with a black eye, a red eye and bruises all over his face, and that was the last fight I ever had in the schoolyard, it must have been spring nice weather and we were outside playing that's when most fights began. In high school I hadn't fought in years and wondered if I still knew how, girls appreciate tough guys, I told Cassandra, and she laughed saying no only a boy's version of us we like men who are attentive and charming. She never once set foot in the Gardens and didn't even know it existed. My first thought had been to squeeze his balls so hard he'd scream but it never came to that he started the tough guy routine and I just let into him. Why was I thinking about this? We had just come back from a ballet, my first ballet, and I recalled Isabel had danced for the school in the auditorium and I had said she's really good because I had seen her dance before and she would tell me all she wants to be is a dancer and even if I noticed when we met she had gone wide, put on a few pounds and was probably dancing no more, and instinctively felt that was a shame, but why couldn't I say something like do you want to go for a walk, to this day still don't understand it okay not to smell the fresh flowers or look at the yellow light and shadows of the sun upon the flowers or the buds as they started opening up, or even ask her for her phone number but these thoughts hadn't occurred to me, didn't even cross my mind, all I wanted to do was get away from her before I had to think of something to say. I thought that while sitting under the big oak tree, an unlabeled tree but all trees are oak trees to me, not Linden, Ash, or Pine and I said I should read the *Little Golden Book of Trees* I had from the time my friend and I would go to the American Museum of Natural History and Billy would steal books that I would read it when I got home. He only stole for the fun of it and let me have them. That's the first time I realized my mother had been throwing my stuff out after I no longer played with it. The book was nowhere to be found and when I confronted her she didn't even know what I was talking about a book was clutter and if I didn't read it no sense keeping it. I asked if my telescope was still around from when I had gone up on the roof and looked at the stars and grandfather bought me a little telescope which enabled me to see the planets and how I wanted to be an astronomer. That too was gone too. That was okay, I never realized to be an astronomer means you have to be good in math. And now I am taking Cassandra because my story interested her she now wants to go to the Botanical Gardens to see the cherry blossoms, who would have thought? Only she insisted we take Metro North the railroad to the Bronx. I refused. We can take the D train and walk the five or six blocks down the hill I said then go to Arthur Avenue afterwards for some Italian food. She still was a little frightened of the Bronx so we paid a fortune for railroad tickets when a token would have gotten us there as easily. That's what I get for explaining my 'love life' and needless to say that was the closest I ever came to picking up a girl. It's difficult she said, acting is easy it's all scripted but in life our thoughts, words, come out confused. The playwright had a chance to rewrite the actor to rehearse— rehearsals are safe spaces, some playwrights rewrite a scene twenty times and we actors do the same, it's not spontaneous combustion. Why can't I be cool? Show me the tree you sat under? Not only couldn't I find the tree couldn't even remember where the Bronx River was without asking directions, which I refused to do until Cassandra got tired of walking in circles and asked an attendant and we found the river but not the tree, I hadn't carved my name in the tree only in the gutter across from my building, so my mother wouldn't see it. I didn't even want to sit down and dirty my nice pants, no longer did I wear blue jeans that my mother would wash, so instead of walking alongside the river we went into some of the hothouses and being with Cassandra now was more exciting than my adventure with Isabel but not by so much I said to myself. I thought would have been so cool to walk into one of these places with a girl on my arm and now here I am doing it with a girl I love and its's a big deal not as exciting as I thought it would be. Then I thought everybody would look at me now people are actually envious of me she is so beautiful and I still don't have a grand feeling in my soul, now, of course, even wonder if I have a soul. Isabel was the one I would fantasize about being married to and how all my friends envied me being the first 'adult' of our pack, but now I see how that turned out for my buddies who married their high school sweethearts and even if I am surprised at how boring they've become it is a truism of my friends that only those who married their high school sweethearts are still married, everybody else I know seems to be divorced or divorcing or cheating. Only high school love remains pure and I wonder were these the only ones they made love to, they couldn't have had much of a love life. Esmeralda said I hadn't acted upon my youthful desires because you had a lifetime plan and you even realized these were youthful follies and deep down you wanted time and experience to grow alongside your desires and you didn't want to act to hastily and be trapped in a condition of perdition. I think I would have if I could have. Imagine going with the prettiest girl on your arm. We only have a moment to live, she had said, but yes what a moment to be the most popular boy in high school nothing can take that away from that. You can only love like that once she said, and I agreed but not too loud because Cassandra was nearby, and she said she had given her heart to my grandfather like that and was never able to give her heart completely after the first time and I felt embarrassed imaging my grandfather with another woman even if in my lifetime he never actually lived with my grandmother. I can hear my *avuelo* in my ear I knew what was better but did the worse, ah such a profound statement coming from a dead man and when I came across it in some book realized my grandfather's thought wasn't original only first love is.

If it's not done against a specific individual is it bad? I didn't do it against Joseph didn't even do it because men do it all the time, but I didn't do it in order to be like a man and have a scalp on my belt, even if I admit in the past I did it for that reason; men do it without thinking but for a woman it's different we have to have feelings connected otherwise we are those 'type' of women, and I never ever did it for money I did it for worse reasons, not even careerism I would have mentioned that but I had the talent and nobody ever propositioned me at work, they only do that to secretaries, you need connections, of course, but not as much as you think talent does win out the stakes are huge and people have to do a good job, unlike academia where they fight to the death because the stakes are so trivial, I had no family connections but I was able to walk through the open door, the front door—granted I started out as a temp. worker but keep on advancing, advancing more in my work place than in the theater world, where there are ten thousand young girls ready to sleep with the director or producer, but I didn't want a starring role so didn't have to start out sleeping with anybody only wanted a chance to show my stuff and to see if I really did have enough talent to continue and I have. I am not ashamed nor proud either that I didn't sleep my way to the top, your past comes after you but I did flirt with directors and producers but I would never sleep with them, what I did I did for no ulterior motive only to prove to myself I could do it. I did it because I could do it to confront my fears my fears were rational my actions not. Could have done it in the theater, not the workplace, you don't shit and work in the same place, the theater was of such short duration, no complications, but you have to work with these guys forever, and in the theater everyone realizes no complications and truthfully I never thought about the wife and the kiddies, or if I did think about them and how they'd feel I ignored the thought it never rose to a serious conscious level, didn't even think it would help me get a role, I didn't like to be thought of as a prude but still refused all advances, except how do I know they were advances if I never acted upon them, mind you never for a leading part there producers wouldn't take a chance on an unknown even if they slept with them, I saw that clearly, there like at the workplace talent is needed. Besides I didn't want love from these guys only a chance and even if I didn't sleep with them flirting with them helped me get started, all acting is dissembling, masking, deceit, like being at court grandma said, disguises for practical ends, only I had no idea what she was talking about. I thought of it as acting as the key to success, you think all my life I wanted to be a pipefitter, the joke in the theater world when actors take a day job and have to convince their boss that's all they ever wanted to do. Sometimes I wonder who the real me is. But it did help me get some parts climbing my way into the world I wanted and accidentally allowing me to rise at work, somehow my ability to code promoted me above the other girls who were afraid of the machine. Men might be promoted on promise but women are promoted on accomplishment. Then had to leave that job that had treated me so well, didn't want to but Joseph said I would always be considered a secretary/typist there who programmed on the side and if I got a job as a programmer would only be considered a programmer because that's what they pay me for. Besides then he said I would no longer have to dress as a secretary and could wear jeans, programmers were the odd bunch back in the day. Now the times are changing and we women are allowed to act like men but I never thought I would. It just happened. In class, not with one of the students, god forbid, they are so dumb but with a professor no less, or a former professor we met by accident in the lunchroom and started talking he was so nice to be around, an okay teacher but a witty conversationalist, had a fountain of knowledge too bad he never used that in class where he stammered and stuttered never looking up from his notes. Good notes, sharp, he said he rewrote them every semester, but he didn't like the class to talk he said he had something to say and by gosh he was going to say it, never liked being interrupted with questions which were usually deflections from knowledge as he called it, while I love short crisp dialogue on stage instead of long speeches. It came unexpectedly, I wasn't even on the pill anymore because I was only doing it with Joseph and he wanted a child, I was ambivalent but was beginning to see his point of view and I knew if I didn't do it soon the decision would be irreversible, and then he claimed we could adopt but if we were going to do it I wanted my own. He even thought my Spanish heritage could come in handy we could go down to Peru or Columbia and be able to adopt. I wanted none of that. I had to be the responsible one and went off the pill lest I find myself in a situation I didn't want to be in. At least I didn't have to save myself for marriage or have myself sewn up. Grandma quickly saw the benefits of the pill and it had no business being connected with religion even if the priests were against it, and I have been on it forever, but my doctor did say we don't know the long-term effects and now that you are with somebody it wouldn't be a bad idea to ease off it. How come then I meet this professor. All those other times it never went that far now all of a sudden it does. We met a couple of times by accident in the student cafeteria until he admits it wasn't an accident he was waiting for me and just 'accidentally' went through the line when he knew I would be there, men do that all the time, there's no such thing as an accident, I tried closing my ears but couldn't do that and enjoyed hearing him talk and developed a passion to enjoy listening to him, unlike his droning on in class when I thought he would never get to the end of his notes and I enjoyed listening to him and did look forward to his being there and was disappointed when he was out for a few days because he was under the weather, and I gave him my work number so we could chat anytime. He wasn't hesitant in calling and we made an appointment for dinner. You can't let a moment of desire ruin your life, I remember grandma warning me about this in college, and if you become pregnant you are going to have an abortion. Where was she now when I needed her. I thought I had it under control. We would eat, have a little wine and chat, end of story that's all I enjoyed his company, that's all, and I never expected any more, that's all, end of story, I knew what I was doing I wasn't carried away by passion I'm a grownup; first I said no this isn't happening then I said so what I'm a mature woman, then why not just to see what it's like, all the while believing I was in control of the situation. When passion leads it's hard not to follow but that's not the correct way to live, but I said that afterwards, during it's fun to be on the bottom for a change, we were sitting down in the Wales hotel room, a suite a bedroom and a living room, and talking in the living room on light gray chairs on the opposite side of the light gray couch, with one table lamp next to his seat and a cocktail table between us, I was finally coming to grips at what I was doing, not going with a professor but hurting Joseph and I vowed not to tell him, not to let it slip out not to hurt him because of my mistake, it was good but not as great as I thought it would be, and I had done it but so what if I hurt the man I truly loved with it, can I tell him I came to appreciate him more by hurting him. No, I vowed hearing my grandmother's voice inside me it's your fault don't go confessing thinking you'll be making it better by hurting Joseph; I had already told Joseph when we first started getting serious all the men I had been with so I didn't need to add another one. He had wanted to call all my previous lovers and tell them I am no longer available until I was saved by the bell, literally, the phone rang, he said don't answer it but how can you not answer a phone call, it could be my agent, and when I got off the phone a few minutes later I couldn't tell if he rethought or was relieved but he relented and we never discussed it again. Now I'm not pleased with myself not for sleeping with the professor but for not being able to tell Joseph my revelation that he is the one and for hurting him, even if I don't know if it will hurt him, it would hurt me but I am sneakier than him, he's an honest good-natured fellow who would probably forgive me. When we grabbed a taxi he wouldn't just get into any cab he wanted a checker so I would have plenty of room to squirm around in. But I won't mention it because it could put the relationship in jeopardy, and now that I am having his baby I'll do all I can to make sure the relationship works: there is a difference between character and morality and now that we are a team, even if I refuse to take his last name or wear a ring, it's like putting a hook through your nose, and he likes that because we are considered a liberated couple, but these are only superficial trappings, the reality is we are for each other. I've learned something that you simply can't give into your desires without thinking about it, just because it feels good in the moment doesn't mean it is good. I never slept my way up only down. Didn't even use it to get my foot in the door only out of the door. I know the difference yet I did it anyway. And now we are all three in a checker, Joseph holding my hand and grandma in the front, on our way to St. Vincent's, and all I can think about is this baby going to start off life living under a cloud, poor kid grandma said he's going to be what he wants, a doctor. They won't allow her in the delivery room but she insists upon being there and I doubt if any doctor or nurse is going to kick her out. She is the great-grandma. At least now I have a little more understanding of myself and am ready to do a Calderon play, I always felt uncomfortable doing him because he was the first playwright I read where women had reflective thought and I didn't get it. Now I do. I can proceed with caution from now on and Joseph insists I continue to act, to work, and to take classes, even if I'm not so sure about the later.

Question: How do you make a perfect Manhattan? Answer: Get rid of the Jews and blacks. My co-worker was telling me how he had overheard that in a bar in the city, one of those nondescript places where truth is spoken to power either under your breath or when you have booze in you. Why I tried to avoid such places but there's not much to do in the middle of the day if you don't want to sit in a movie theater, and how many movies can I see. Selling wine is so easy now I have my contacts and we're on a roll that I get bored quickly and have plenty of free time but nowhere to spend it. No longer can I read all day, and if the weather is poor don't want to walk around the city so I now spend too much time in bars, usually they're not crowded just old geezers and I keep telling myself not to go in and there I am sitting at the bar thinking that at first Cassandra didn't want children, I could live with that, but as I aged did want one and now that we are married thought it was about time, who expected her to get pregnant so easily, she was worried about her biological clock but I can go on forever and one day it was a fait accompli but I didn't believe it at first how can she get pregnant so fast, she's over forty what are the odds and then I wondered if she was ready to transform her whole life and she said yes, and was even ready to give up acting and she wanted to give up acting more than I opposed it but she still wanted to work she just felt she had to earn money not be dependent and she still insisted upon taking classes, she was determined to get her degree or at least get closer until the baby overturned everything. Here I sit drinking my beer wondering what I've got myself into. Somebody plays the jukebox which is a blessing I don't have to think, the only place I like jazz are in bars and I sit and listen to Nina Simone trying not to think, you hear all these stories of women getting pregnant at will it may have been at will but only when the body is seventeen not forty, at forty it's supposed to take time and also sex should be more pleasurable because we were doing it for a purpose but it was more nerve-racking not just for the fun of it, it was my duty to perform, sometimes I could, sometimes not, before I always could, yet I soldiered on and each time a gush of sperm released realized I could be fertilizing thousands of eggs but all I needed was one, Esmeralda suggested dissolving an aspirin in her uterus and that would work even if she had no idea why. My doctor laughed at this superstitious nonsense, said they have been doing wonders with fertilization treatments but we weren't ready for that and after all didn't need them. I don't know which act worked was it the one where I imagined this is going all the way up her vagina and I'm sure she'd be pregnant from this or was it from another one where my seed barely squirted out. She was determined to work until she couldn't work anymore and once came home crazy and I thought miscarriage and felt miserable, that's how I knew I wanted it, but it was from a hard day at work and standing in the subway, luckily she was healthy and in good shape (acting made sure her body was finely tuned) and she continued swimming at the gym instead of staying in bed and getting fat, strong like a bull is what Esmeralda said, who was surprised she was doing so much but you couldn't stop her even if I thought it might be harmful for the baby but women are now in control of their own bodies and she actually contacted a midwife not a doctor and would have the baby at home, which scared me especially because it was illegal. But what is legal is a debatable point and if it accidentally happens at home and you can't get to the hospital on time nobody says anything, midwives are now allowed to deliver but only in hospitals so we made plans that she had no intention of fulfilling of going to a hospital for the birth. What she didn't like was only one person was allowed in and Esmeralda wouldn't be permitted, I would be the one who helped her breathe and I did my part even if I was scared but more important she said to me afterwards was that I held her hand. We had a plan as if this was the most natural thing in the world even one of the five-year-olds on the block said did your wife give birth yet. It was a wondrous moment even if it was in the hospital because her water broke and the midwife couldn't make it quick enough and we panicked and took a taxi to the hospital, we could have stayed home we were there all day and night before the baby decided it was time to come out. And Esmeralda had only one job and she blew it, she was to take a photograph of the baby's head as it peered into the world for the first time but she was so caught up in the birth she forgot to take it, but she did take the first snapshot of the three of us together. The doctors were worried because Cassie was so old and panicked but there was no problem, she was doing fine and the baby was healthy and finally I was able to leave the hospital, I was starving, the nurses fed Cassie and even Esmeralda but not me. Here I am in a local pub drinking but also pouring some food in me. Thank goodness all bars in New York have to serve food. Now the real difficulties emerged, I wanted her breastfed, Esmeralda said bottled milk is as good—a clash of values, I wanted to wait and see what she looked like before naming her but Cassandra and Esmeralda already decided upon Jacoba but I didn't want her to follow in anyone else's shoes. A victory for me it became her middle name and nobody uses the middle name. I brought in a rubber sheath and insisted she get used to the nipple but she had a hard time adjusting to the nipple even when hunger became too much and pretty soon was on the bottle, I felt left out as Cassandra and Esmeralda took charge of the baby except my job was to feed the baby in the middle of the night now that we used bottles instead of a breast, otherwise I would only have had to carry her to Cassandra. Tomas came by once and we have a picture of him holding the baby and Esmeralda said that must have been the only time, she had purposely left when he came by so as not to relive old memories. The little runt upended all our lives a winter baby is difficult it's usually too cold to take her out and so we were all trapped inside with her. All of a sudden our apartment became too cramped, at the beginning her crib was in our room and we even put up a make-believe barrier to make believe she had a room of her own, but that couldn't last. We switched bedrooms with Esmeralda but that also wasn't much of a help even if her bedroom was a little wider. Life was no longer the same everything revolved around the baby as she had to be fed, clothed and napped over and over again. Esmeralda was getting old and I worried about her but at times the baby would cry and she would get to him before I did and there was a new vigor in her steps and she couldn't wait to take her out to the park. She was the first person she saw in the morning and many times the last she saw at night and I saw how my grandfather was with me because my mother told me the same story—the only time in your life when you get unconditional love, and it's not from your parents but your grandparents just for being you while parents always want you to do something. Esmeralda said as job classification go grandparenting is one of the best. I noticed I started getting gray hair, I could always see one or two but now it was obvious even if I denied it at first, it didn't make me look distinguished only old. Doubled down dyed it and refused to wear a hat lest I become bald, even if there was no scientific evidence that wearing a hat leads to baldness, I just knew it was true. At least we didn't have to go through the ordeal of circumcision, a tough decision for me, we had discussed it before knowing what sex it would be, and instinctively wanted to do it out of my Jewishness but also thought it was an old-fashioned myth that had no place in the modern world, but if we had to do it I would have insisted it be done by a mohel, a cutter, one trained in the covenant of circumcision and had more experience than doctors or midwives. I was ready to fight myself and not give in to the old ways and realized you really had to fight them they don't come off automatically when you become modern. You have to fight off the dark instinctual thought even if goes against everything you now believe in yet it does not diminish the unique worth of light.

I was astonished that this could happen to me, a regular everyday normal event that I didn't see as a regular everyday normal event to me, to me it was extraordinary: I who thought I would be alone my entire life, who would want to marry me, I who was prepared to live alone my entire life, I who thought I had nothing to offer anybody was now involved in family life, something I hated when a kid, which is probably why I waited so long to begin one myself, and when I took myself off the pill grandma was happy, but recalled how she thought it would be the death knell for her and would put her out of work, how when the pill first came along women could have sex without the fear of a baby nobody would come to her, but she quickly realized women weren't adjusting to it so quickly to the new ethic, it takes more than science to get people to adjust and preachers were helpful in reminding women of the sin of stopping procreation. Thank goodness they allowed her to continue making a living but she never told me that I only figured it out later, and now the only ones who get pregnant before their time are the poor usually Hispanic or black in the city. They still can't adopt the new way of looking at the world, they're the ones afraid of the pill certainly not educated women—and if Hispanic or black become educated they are no longer poor and see the world differently, Joseph has told me that enough times, education changes you, you only hang with people who have a similar education as you, religion, race, ethnicity are all things of the past only people who look at the world similar to you. Of course I don't believe that but it's true, our friends now are only educated. Grandma even volunteered to counsel, coach young Hispanic girls but had to give it up it was so mentally and physically exhausting, they saw her as this old lady not a Hispanic woman. The problem for educated women right now is we refuse big promotions because we want to start a family. Me. Couldn't accept it because I knew I was going to take maternity leave soon and I couldn't work in a high-pressured job, working sometimes until 11 at night and maybe one weekend day, I would have to be with the baby sometimes. I got pregnant on my own volition I knew what I was doing, it would make Joseph happy, we chose this it wasn't forced upon us, it wasn't an accident and yet I am still astonished that this happened to me, Joseph said when he first held Jacoba he felt closer to me than even the marriage, which hadn't changed a thing for me, but he said for the first time in his life he felt connected to the universe, imagine he wanted the name Jane but I thought that was too plain, her name has to have some oomph, and we settled on Celestina but nobody calls her that, she looks like a Jacoba: Celestina Jacoba Diaz-Fuchs. So much for his wanting her to have a simple universal name, and Joseph held her even before me then they took her away from me to weigh her and I wondered where are they taking my baby and he was right there and held her but I stuck my hands out and he immediately put her on my stomach, he told me afterwards he was so afraid of dropping her—it was like at the theater the father holding the daughter and putting her on my lap and I imagined in my head she fit snuggly unto my belly that it all seemed so clear to me this was my purpose in life, what I was put on this earth for and she was born because of what I did not some abstract idea of having a family—women marry and have children even if now the order is reversed or even the second part non-existent as Joseph says but I couldn't imagine having a child without a helper but no more is it shameful to be a single mother, the word has even changed from illegitimate child to single parent; there is something to having a family otherwise your life is empty. I've never thought that way before. Old age begins not like Joseph thinks with the onset of gray hair but when you start thinking differently. Oy. But he is still adamantly against religious superstitions and I'm glad we didn't have a boy to test those beliefs. And if we had I never would have agreed to doing it at home with the whole religious rigmarole, but now I'm beginning to wonder if you should throw out the baby with the bathwater maybe we should keep some traditions even if it only gives the baby something to rebel against and it does make one more intellectually honest yet he wants none of the stuff now being passed off as Judaism, musical creativity, ritual innovation, he wanted and didn't want a rabbi at the wedding said we must oppose all forms of superstition, only when I said we could get a woman rabbi did he agree, he likes messing with tradition. His stubborn streak overcame his rational streak, what I love about him is he's full of contradictions and he knows it, none of this macho bullshit for him even if Hispanic men are the most henpecked men of all only making believe they have all the answers. Now the answers are questions, we now must be a real family, Jacoba has to eat every day, has to be put on a schedule, our lives have to be centered around her when she cries and she is in the moment, she has to be held and there are enough of us. Do they ever get to sleep through the night? As Joseph says looks like her college roommate will have to rock her to sleep when she awakens. Thank goodness she adjusted to the bottle in the middle of the night breastfeeding is too exhausting but Joseph thinks the bonding is crucial. We are now connected to this world more than I ever thought you could be, no longer do we wonder what are we going to do, but so far at least we can go for walks together even if one of us is holding the baby or grandma babysitting. I give grandma things to do but she is content just watching her. Let her be happy she deserves some happiness in life, especially after I disrupted he life, imagine, and I can only see it now how hard it must have been for her to take me in, an angry teenager moving into her home, but she did it and didn't let me ruin my life that I certainly was capable of doing I was so mad at my mother for dating a hooligan and getting herself shot, as if she did it to spite me. If she hadn't gotten herself killed I would have been trapped in the neighborhood probably gotten myself 'knocked up' and never learned there's another life outside the neighborhood, they take the neighborhood with them wherever they go. Now I am a mother just like them, only similar Joseph says, not the same Joseph says older Joseph says, so you won't be a friend to your child but a mother to your child and you have lived a little so you know what is important in life and he shows me how correct he is because I see the next generation of my friends' children now grown up, the girls still drop out of high school and have babies even earlier than their mother and the boys go directly from dropping out into the prison industrial complex via drugs. Shameful that behavior I see these punks on the street having nothing inside them, they don't read, they don't study, don't work, all they do is hang out and have no idea of life outside of drugs and alcohol even those who actually kick the drug habit can't live without a beer in the morning, and more as the day goes on, they can't have pleasure without drinking, reformers should have spent more time on the abuses of alcohol than on their anti-theater prejudice—they shall make no graven images that's not only to worship idols but it was used as a way to show actors led despicable lives the unholy pleasure theater gave, and the intensity of the acting only promotes passions, ah if that were only true that theater is so intense. But the theater gave me more life chances, I am grateful for that, it got me out of myself even if I'm not the characters I sometimes portray on stage; it's always humorous to me when fans think that what they see upstage is me. I do not consider theatrical life normal but the exception even if Joseph thinks of it as progression to me it's still a little odd and there are no rewards in acting, least of all monetary I can see why some actors have to leave the profession once they have a family you can only do it for yourself and when you get a family you no longer have a self. *The Seventh Seal* might be the last film we see in years together, he likes unconventional films but conventional drama where the community wins out over the individual, but in movies he loves independent individuals: does life have any meaning or is there nothing there and you can only feel freedom in your final moments in the physical pleasure of your dying, Jacoba fell asleep and we decided to try it and agreed if she awakens we would leave but she slept through the whole movie. And he told me for the umpteenth time that his grandfather took him out of school so he could see this with him and I knew for sure at that moment we were a couple we repeated stories.

It's not clear was I content like an oyster in the ocean or only being tossed to and fro waiting for the end, hoping I could end it with some dignity and not be a burden upon the family, happy that Conchita found a man and even happier that she had given birth to a healthy baby; the baby has been a second life to me, really a first since I am deeply involved in her life more than I ever was with my own child, who I was happy when she finally moved out of the house even as I knew she was too young to be starting a family but glad she was out of the house, and after she left it was easier to ask Tomas to leave even if Conchita thinks that I'm glad she found someone from the family, i.e. Jacobo's grandson: no it is the baby she gave me that delights me and maybe I can make it all up to her what I didn't do with my daughter and granddaughter, I am grateful she found a decent person who treats her kindly not like the jerks she sometimes brought home—there's no such thing as 'the good', only individuals who are decent or indecent and Joseph is decent not in some grand idea but a specific individual who cares deeply about her, I saw that in him the moment we met even if I thought he was somebody else, he found her attractive and went for her even if he later admitted he was scared, it's only when we're scared that that person means something to us, and he did come calling because he wanted to see her again, he overcame his fear, a good sign, I like that in a man, a kind of arrogance not afraid to try new things, even if it fools you at least you've given it a chance not put off by them. If only we could know in advance but of course we can never know only think we know but we never know exactly how it's going to turn out that's why solitude has to turn into dialogue with each of us when we struggle to find our other half otherwise all you do is look like your elders but each individual has to try and figure out who s/he is and learn for ourselves, I'm glad Joseph is in our lives but more important is Jacoba I love looking at her, watching her fall asleep, holding her in my arms I can't get enough of her and feel my day doesn't start until I see her in the morning, poor baby they force her to sleep on his back we too had infant death syndrome but we raised babies with it, it's difficult getting a good night's sleep on your back, no wonder he's grouchy so much of the time, I like to rock her on my shoulder so she can get some good sleep while Joseph makes breakfast, and now he even put plugs in the electrical sockets so she won't be electrified, and she can't even turn over in his crib let alone crawl yet and of course I can imagine her putting a knife through the socket because everybody told her no, otherwise who would even think of such a thing. We never had any of these things and babies turned out fine. You put her down for a second and she starts crying she likes to be held and she has enough of us to hold her, more power to her she might as well get it all in now

I was afraid of spoiling her at first but Joseph said this is the only time she's going to be so spoiled let her have it, who else is going to spoil a baby as much as a grandparent. Not only is he decent but smart and when we first met I thought Conchita would discount him as being too smart, well-mannered, decent, for she still was on the lookout for the high school jerk, that she had been with and still thought in terms of the same ethnicity, religion, creed, or the children would be lost. Same old stuff the priests always told us only they mentioned the Jews as devils, as if there were any Jews left in Spain, it took a bit but at least her education started kicking in and she didn't believe that nonsense. The greatness of '68 was old myths were shattered and the old traditions were thrown out the window and now even mainstream culture no longer totally accepts the old ways. But even with her newfound education she still believed in the old saws but meeting a younger man forced her out of her old traditional ways, I recall her refusing to call boys in high school, good girls just didn't do that she was adamant as only a sixteen-year-old could be, now they do it all the time. It still was pretty much the same in college, her education never really touched her for all the bravado she had the education was still very conservative and she still wondered what others would think about her and not going too far on the wild side, she still dressed for classes and a new outfit each day lest someone think she spent the night somewhere, only later when she came back to the city did she get back into blue jeans once again. The bravest thing I ever saw her do was grow her hair long, even the Chicago 8 trial was about long hair, the powers that be couldn't stand long-haired boys, the result was when they were convicted the state couldn't wait to cut their hair, and made sure everybody knew about it by showing their mugs on the front page of the newspapers hair cropped, thinking these kids thought they were Samson but we took away their strength, but it was too late their defiance caught on, and the state didn't even have a clue, even their straight lawyers started wearing their hair long, and their ideas started transforming the culture, I felt so comfortable around them safe near them yet if I see large groups of Hispanic men hanging on street corners will walk to the other side. They haven't a clue the world has changed and now it's even worse young Hispanic men dropping out of school in record numbers because they are afraid of getting caught up in the drug culture so have practically no education at all, and now that here in the city they can go to college for free have no interest in doing so and are not prepared to do so, at least young girls are going to school so as not to be dependent upon a man, something feminism taught. Many of these kids can't even read or write, or as Conchita complains never saw a play in their life, almost think a play is a bad thing that could upset their moral equilibrium, not that they are afraid to leave their neighborhood, not that they would learn to think. Now that local movie theaters closed and kids have to take a subway or bus to movies they don't even do that, Conchita says, in public schools now they teach courses in Spanish in the afternoon what good is that the greatness of New York public schools was that kids would learn English there no matter what language they spoke at home. Now they don't even have that, now we have to worry about schooling even if we have time yet, and I insist and Joseph agrees with me that the early grades are more important than college, by then it's too late and we want to make sure she gets a good start in life and are already looking at pre-Ks. We want a day care connected to a university and Conchita immediately switches to Baruch so while she finishes up Jacoba has good care, and now she is going with renewed strength realizing Jacoba has a better chance of going to college if his mother graduates from college. No more fooling around I love taking her there the days Joseph is busy with his new job, and how she struggles to find her thumb with her mouth and now she's not even allowed to suck they say that's bad for her teeth and she'll need braces so we're supposed to take her thumb out if she finds it, which only forces her to do it again. They raise her by the book. Thank goodness I'm here so he can have some relief. Babies are not fragile they're tough, strong and cute for a reason how else are they going to survive; now at least I am getting my turn for the way I ignored Gloria and Conchita and truly can't believe I did that, but I know I did, never felt anything towards my own daughter and unfortunately it showed in how she led her life and now I can try and make up for it since it is too late to make up to Gloria all I can do is hug Jacoba. I know her mother loves her but she doesn't know what true love is, wait until she has a great-grandchild. I have to move the chair now, the sun will soon be in her eyes and she will awaken too early, I much rather sit with her than carry her all the time, Joseph said he would fix the shade, a man and his tools, but he's too busy so I better call the super's apprentice, his son, who dropped out of school and is now apprenticing but he told me the reason he quit was drugs were everywhere at Hughes and he knew he would become hooked and says he will take his GED at eighteen. I gave him some books to read but his father gave them back to me unopened.

When I saw Mademoiselle princess she captured my heart even as I was prepared not to be enamored with her, I don't want to relive the past nor get back into that life, I've struggled with myself too long and too hard to put it behind me not to think about Esmeralda, after all she did hurt me and I was good to her, brought her to America, she lied to me to get me to take her to America, said she loved me when all she wanted was to get out of Spain and she doesn't love the States the way I do. I am the son of a poor dirt farmer and the army allowed me to leave that life even bring my parents here to the city, not my sister she wanted to stay in Puerto Rico but her son moved here and I was able to help him get started, and by then had left the city so my nephew wasn't caught up in the gang, drug stuff. Gloria, my sweet daughter, did make efforts to stay in touch but not her daughter once Esmeralda got her fangs in her, only now that she has a child does she consider family important, and here I was getting used to be separated from them and she calls, my step-grandchildren are my grandchildren, I see them regularly also my nephew's family, so I'm connected with family again, I hated what Esmeralda did to me breaking up the family like that, all I lived for was the family and then I found myself all alone, I hated living alone with nobody to talk to, and when my new wife, not so new anymore we've been married almost ten years and she brought along her two children, answered the phone insisted we get together she knew how much missing her hurt me no matter how I told her it didn't, living with them was difficult at first I told the boys I wasn't replacing their father but in fact I was since their father abandoned them and that in itself is a world of difference, even Esmeralda told me that the first time we met, which I hoped would also be the last time we met, in one of her bohemian cafés in the Village, where hippies believe in abortion on demand and the death of God, Estrella was jealous but she need not be I may not have been an intellectual like Esmeralda but I knew the difference between a keeper and one who used me and realized Estrella was a much nicer human being even if sometimes I think of Esmeralda and what was but quickly come to my senses when I see the difference in how I lived then with how we live now, but to think about Esmeralda doesn't even make sense yet my mind does think about her I don't understand it, she wasn't nice to me and I get so depressed when I think back to those days. My recurring fantasy is to run away with her and when she leaves me again as I know she will, then will commit suicide. Does that make any sense especially since I now have a loving wife and two loving children, three grandchildren and am considered part of their family they don't see me as an interloper and the grandchildren love me more than their biological grandmother and they don't even realize that I am not related by blood, we are living nicely on my retirement pension, where else but America could you live so nicely on my military and work pension plus social security. Why think of Esmeralda who only caused pain in my life and I was so good to her, it just doesn't make any sense. Estrella is going to retire soon then we can travel and at night here we can look up at the nighttime sky and see starts just like in PR when I was a kid but then I didn't appreciate nature. You can almost get lost here in the trees, the locals call it a forest but it's just a clump of trees, they don't have forests in America, most of the wilderness was destroyed in colonization now they have ballfields where trees once were, and soon those will be destroyed as developers build housing tracts, farmers sell 500 acres but a house upon an acre is 500 houses, it's no longer the small community old timers remember, we even have a mall now making the downtown area kaput. I was surprised when Estrella said Conchita called she hadn't called in a while and I was happy and content not being involved with them and when the phone rang I wondered who it could be at this hour of the night, thought something might be wrong with the grandchildren but Estrella speaks to her son most days and we would have known by now but still thought it might be an emergency, who knows, give my imagination an inch and I can conjure up the most extreme horrors and when Estrella hands me the phone I hear *Abuelo* and I recognize something out of my past and immediately think Esmeralda is dead that's why she's calling and I'm sad and happy at the same time, and my heart is beating fast when she says I have something to tell you, and my heart is still beating fast as she mentions her new daughter and of course I am happy and excited for her then she tells me to come down and see it, she didn't even give me a chance to catch my breath and she wants me to visit and I speak before I even realize what I am saying, of course, of course, congratulations, I want to see the new addition to our family but all I thought about was having to see Esmeralda again, as if she ever cared about family, but somehow realized in seeing the baby I would be forced to see Esmeralda again; all well and good I will show her she wasn't the end of my life I was able to continue living my life and made sure I had photos of my new family in my wallet, yet I still think about Esmeralda even as I realized she probably hasn't given me a moment's thought since I left, she forced me out asked me to leave and I wasn't going to force myself on her and moved in with my folks, who couldn't understand the concept of divorce and thought that was white peoples' problem Catholics don't divorce—my mother had no idea of the changing world but my father said to me you need time for your soul to heal don't do anything stupid after I quit my job—I was surprised how in tuned my father this dirt farmer was I thought he just didn't fit in in this new world but he knew something and said you are my son and could stay here as long as you like but this will pass even if now you don't want to get up in the morning. I had to get up early my mother would be cooking dinner in the kitchen before the sun rose and making an incessant racket and after my father left for work would go in their bed and continue sleeping, how the two of them managed to sleep in a full-sized bed all these years was beyond me they slept together for almost fifty years until my mother died quickly after my father, she couldn't live without him, childhood sweethearts never knew the meaning of divorce. All of a sudden I was an orphan with no family in the past or the future. Esmeralda didn't even come to the funerals. My new wife says my mother was lucky to die of a broken heart, even if the doctor says nobody dies from a broken heart and named some technical cause, because it is hard for a woman to live alone after her man dies someone she has cared for all these years. Not that I expected Esmeralda to come but I thought Conchita would come but she said she was on the road and there was no use burdening her she hardly knew them. But she never respected family or she didn't even consider me family only the ex, even if we weren't actually divorced then we only divorced when it became easier in New York and I wanted to remarry. Even some of the guys from the Navy came to the funeral, guys I hadn't seen in years and a couple of friends from El Barrio drove up to be with me but not Esmeralda or Conchita. Now my wife hugged me when I told her the news, and our two sons, their wives and my grandchildren all hugged me as well when I told them we have a new grandchild, and the grandchildren wanted to know when she would come up and play with them.

Why can't I learn to enjoy myself? Is pleasure always connected with 'the good'? I simply couldn't be in the apartment when Tomas came by, I would have been polite to him but it would have upset me and luckily it was a Sunday and I didn't have to spend it indoors, and it was a nice Sunday so I was able to take the subway, I travelled from Madrid to Manhattan but rarely took the subway to Brooklyn, it wasn't so bad, a quick ride once the subway actually came, I thought it would take over an hour and I'm here in less than thirty minutes, only you can hardly read the subway stations with so much graffiti on the walls, Joseph explained I should count stops but I lost count, and the public address system mumbles, but the kindness of strangers told me how many stops even if they didn't know where I was to go, and you can see different people here in Brooklyn women still wear dresses and kerchiefs, dowdy types, not jeans and down jackets yet they were nice and I get off at the correct stop and was surprised the Garden was right there and I always wanted to see the cherry blossoms and thought today would be a good day to venture into Brooklyn and their Botanical Gardens, and I'm surprised even the red tulips have opened up, one of the gardeners told me today is the first day and I am amazed standing in front of the tulips watching them gulp the sun down, at least it's not raining out and this place actually has benches where you can sit and look at the tulips and cherry blossoms at the same time, this can't be an accident someone must have thought this out. Only problem is some old person is pontificating away as if he has something to say and people are gathered around him as if his thoughts are profound spoiling the quietness of the place, the Village is full of them, old geezers who think they know history better than those who live it always telling Trotsky how to run the world, park bench philosophers, you think wisdom comes with old age? Let them try instead of blabbing about it with their age old aphorisms when examined are only clichés of a previous generation, we get these gray beards all over the city. I have to move or people will think I am part of his crowd and worse have to listen and put my two cents in as if I have anything profound to say. I think now is the time to have a little pleasure in my life to look and smell the flowers and was surprised the red tulips opened up, and now I know I have a new favorite place to go to when living in the city becomes too hectic even if I never come here again but I must remember to come even bring Jacoba here it's nice and solitary and I loved seeing the cherry blossoms from a distance and now the tulips right in front of my eye, even if this man is never going to shut up more people are now crowding around him, what is this? why are people listening to him? He's interfering with my peaceful pleasure. Better to get up and walk around the gardens than have to continue to listen to this babble, as teachers who say they want to make a difference or this guy parroting Senator Moynihan that everyone is entitled to his own beliefs but not his own facts, and I can't help myself and say 'benign neglect' but nobody knows what I'm talking about how his policies almost led to the bankruptcy of the city, but I can't get into an argument I'm here to smell the flowers have a good visual experience and quickly make my way from my comfortable bench deeper into the park. It's safe here you can walk anywhere unlike the city now where you have to be afraid of the other guy and women can't go out at night now without an escort. Pleasure is determined by a human perspective we have to look for our own good and to look for some kind of good outside ourselves is silly even if most of the times I don't stop to smell the roses I do stop to admire sunsets, since the operation my sense of smell has diminished but my love of beauty only increased and no longer do I think to stare at flowers is not truth it may not be but it does make for a happier life—why I have to go to the gardens I need a stronger whiff than you get in the city, especially since I don't have to be home when Tomas appears. When younger I would have insisted upon staying to show myself I could take him now it's more pleasant to take an uncomfortable ride on the subway to somewhere that is pleasant and escape. I spend a good deal of time avoiding things I dislike now and I find pleasure in viewing the flowers even if it isn't necessarily good. Now if I can only learn instead of repeating the same mistakes but maybe I'm too old for that to happen, but make no mistake I say to myself as I find another bench away from the crowd, and I can see the cherry blossoms and red tulips below me but I cannot smell them, pleasure is important and pleasure is crucial for my happiness. Why didn't I come here earlier certainly I knew about it but who goes to Brooklyn? Joseph would have taken me up to the Bronx he knows the place well would go there to meet girls but it is difficult to get there, this is right off the subway line. Conchita laughed when he mentioned it she never ever went there or would even think of going there, never even went to the zoo was only stuck in her neighborhood until she went to high school and that only a few blocks away still in walking distance until I sent her to a real school. I walk toward Daffodil Hill and this man sits down next to me and takes out his sandwich and tries to start a conversation with me, why I like travelling on Joseph's arm—the last man who started a conversation was hitting on me, do I have my mace? Does he think me a teenager? Sorry to disturb you ma'am but I like to eat my sandwich on this bench it's the best view of the park and I like to feed the birds, actually he throws his crumbs at the birds, and like to look at the shadows the sun makes on the trees, he's wearing a suit, his shoes are shined, he's shaved, he doesn't look dangerous, but now I have to be afraid of strange men, says he's a teacher or was a former teacher of art at PS 20 on the Lower East Side Essex off Houston until the budget cuts eliminated art programs, mentally I say Jacoba can't go there, and he now has a good gig at the museum where he's an administrative assistant, what was once called a secretary and the pay is weekly so I always have money in my pocket and I don't have to go in a classroom again. When I turned forty teaching in the city became unbearable what they do to students and I just couldn't wait another fifteen years then I was laid off so didn't have to decide and this job opened up and I grabbed it and now I wonder if I'll ever teach again. This job gives me so much time to read and look at art and having lunch out in the gardens in the highlight of my day. He must be lonely he loves to talk. Could I have seen your work? Occasionally a painting of mine was exhibited but the art market has gone crazy now and dealers only want work that can sell for mega-millions not hundreds so I am not exhibited anymore. Sorry. I thought after my first exhibition you can only go up from there but there is no justice in art and I kept finding smaller galleries until non-existent galleries came my way, finitude is easier to grasp than infinity. Desires are different than pleasures he laughs, I wanted to be an artist, I moved into the city to be an artist but art is like a pyramid only those on top make a living from it and decided to become an art teacher to pay the bills and it was okay while doing it now that I don't I don't miss it nor regret leaving, especially as art budgets were cut and students would really act out in art class thinking art isn't serious not realizing it was the key to culture, all famous civilizations we know of are only because of its art. Now I rarely go to galleries and I've learned an enormous amount about art and love the classics they challenge me more than contemporary art only made for the market place, good art is a cry in the wilderness and it must grab you instantly the interplay between the eye and the mind you have to be able to finish with your mind's eye what your body's eye sees. You probably can give good guided tours? I'm not a trained docent who spoil the way people enjoy art besides there are too many paintings on a wall so people spend less time looking at one painting but try and see all in one swell swoop, I like looking at one painting and leaning as much as I can about it, I can tell if the painting is good if I go home and paint. An interesting chat and when he left said if you come by at this time most days of the year I will be here, you are the only person I ever met sitting on this bench and I hope you didn't mind my interrupting your solitude but this is where I sit. With his lunch time over I was all alone he was correct nobody else came and sat on this bench. I feel the sun upon my face what I wished most for when I was in the hospital with what I thought was indigestion but which turned into a heart attack and luckily some doctor realized that and treated me for it not allowing me to die in the waiting room, where I imagined I was climbing up a ladder and said I better get down Conchita still needs me, I always wanted to thank him but never found out who it was that gave me emergency artificial respiration and all of a sudden found myself being wheeled into the operating room.

Is this what I want? Is this it? I really thought I understood exactly what I wanted now that I've gotten what I want is this it? I wanted this? In college at a job interview was asked how do you see yourself in ten years I was too embarrassed to say, married two children job house white station wagon, all so ordinary, so banal, instead I said the truth as I lied I can't picture myself in ten years, only after the interview when obviously I didn't get the job did I wonder why I even went in the first place, I had no interest in working for corporate America, this was the sixties the times were a changing and I was caught up in the times, I heard my grandfather's voice, not the first time, his is the voice that usually comes to me when I wonder what I am doing, you didn't go to college to be a company man, no I went to be a lawyer but couldn't stand the law that had nothing to do with justice. Everyone, my mother, said I should be a lawyer because I talk a lot but I was learning to distinguish law from justice and they were antithetical. I felt bad not getting the job I didn't want and hopefully gained a little in the practice interview but I hadn't taken notes afterwards so would continue repeating the same mistakes in interviews until a friend mentioned I should take notes right afterwards of what I said I liked what I blew etc. so I could get better. I did but never got better, my charm, my humor just didn't come across well, which is why I was so happy when I found this job that I vowed never to leave it, but when I realized was on this job thirteen years and Esmeralda said I should get Bar Mitzvahed became depressed, thirteen years. The railroad job didn't count I was just a kid and my friend Harvey had worked there and gotten it for me. When I was on my own very few jobs came my way but did learn not to go where I don't want to go because I am so susceptible to outside influences and felt depressed not getting a job I had no use for. Even cut my hair, bought my first blue three-piece suit pinstripe suit, ate a good breakfast before the interview but now realize I have to keep my distance if I am to learn. So when this new job came along reacted with caution after all I have what I want now and am responsible for a family I can't just up and leave even if Cassandra said she would support us if need be, I just can't blow in the wind, but even now a decade later still have the same old weakness, I have no idea what I want, say A want B get C can't I ever get it together. From the outside it looks as if I'm moving along but deep divisions rent my inside. Others praise me for living my life but I don't need their praise I need to find out what I want, what is correct for me, then I can do it regardless if anybody praises me or not. What have I accomplished? Who says I have to accomplish something? President Jimmy Carter stagflation ruined my savings people are becoming deeper in debt and working longer for less, but he's not getting us into a war and has put Human Rights—that you do not hurt others—on the table of foreign policy concerns, still I no longer have time to pursue my leisure activities in the afternoon, can't be done anymore, my job doesn't go as far as it once did and I have to be out all day selling my wine. When Cassie and Esmeralda first met me they were impressed that I had a job not simply a loafer how can I live without working. It doesn't bother Cassie she thinks it cool a man cares for Jacoba and that I really earned my keep when she was born with jaundice and they kept her in an incubator and all he did was hold her all day long and to everyone's surprise she came home with Conchita, it didn't compute and doctors were amazed at how quickly she got better with affection, doctors understand bodies as machines but we understood love, the body is an organism and reacts to feelings. We have enough savings to last us a bit, and Esmeralda is not without income even if social security doesn't pay so much. The only reason we can make it is because we have this inexpensive housing, rents are skyrocketing in the city, some apartments are charging a thousand dollars a month rent— who can pay that much? Now you do need two people working to make rent a man can no longer be the solo wage earner nor the women who before worked for luxuries or vacations can no longer do so, the money is needed to survive. Cassie suggested I go back to school, law, MBA blah, blah but I'm not interested in school besides these professions are so hierarchical you can only go to the best if you are to succeed and the debt would be enormous that mostly I would be working to pay it off and then I ran into an old friend from the wine business, James Speir, and he suggested I come into partnership with him and now I'm struggling do I give up my comfortable niche and confront my demons or do I stay tied to this job. On paper the job looks easy but I know the difference between theory and practice and I would be earning less money quickly but my potential would be fantastic. He's in the real estate business and pioneer neighborhoods are now the boom. But we stay out of pioneer neighborhoods who knows if they will take off we wait a bit and go into hoods that are already past the tipping point. I quickly saw what was going on in the city because of my constant walking the city streets and how race and class are interconnected and that as people move into crumbling neighborhoods homeownership makes them conscious of the area around their home and force the city to provide some essential services, garbage, police, unfortunately not the schools ghettoization of the public schools is still continuing—the past weighs heavily on the present, you can usually tell when the neighborhood is changing when a Starbucks moves in or a bookstore opens up, I hadn't realized how few zip codes had bookstores until I started noticing, and the neighborhoods that are changing are those close to subway lines that get you into the city. I am becoming a denizen of South Brooklyn, the Upper West Side of the City and Jackson Heights, Queens, if a neighborhood is starting to go co-op we buy up a few apartments and make decent repairs, not cosmetic repairs so people will spend serious money not pay for a fixer up, we're dealing with New Yorkers who have a renters' mentality and can only call the super for repairs; in fact, that is our biggest difficulty New Yorkers can't seem to get into their head why own when you can rent but now with two people working their tax bill is quite high and the government seems to think home owners deserve more than renters and mortgages lower your taxes, and if we hold onto the apartment for a year or two can do okay, we're not big players but we are doing okay, and I'm such a good little Jewish boy who knows how to study the Real Estate Exam was a nothingness, even lawyers are now getting into real estate and I short-circuited the process. Still it's work and it now leaves me little time for leisure there's always something and you have to be ready, remember people think they are being evicted from their homes so they are fighting you hard, and I now carry a beeper so I can never be disconnected, Esmeralda calls it a leash. I'm always available even if it goes off at 2am. At first I felt important now I'm hooked into the system and can never shut my mind off even if I do enjoy always having something else to look forward to instead of the same ole same ole, there are always problems constant busyness nothing at rest and with constant motion the days go by quickly and I now like weekends where I can slow things down and don't do anything. But you can't completely shut your mind off even if I try and save weekends for Jacoba and the family, I now no longer jog just awake early sit in my recliner and stare into space drinking my coffee and reading the *Wall Street Journal*. Can you imagine me reading the paper? I never would have believed it but I can't start my day without it now. First I go to the business section. No longer do I wonder if I am capable of thinking rather than actually thinking and if I begin to think think ways of escaping running off with some pretty girl and becoming a famous playwright, even if I can't write a line but as long as I keep these ruminations inside me I can go on with my day, I am alive now because I no longer have a succession of thoughts that I will never activate yet am always surprised when I come across men or women who actually acted upon them— imagine that? the biggest difficulty I find in trying to sell apartments is the amount of divorces people actually up and leaving one another and moving to another part of the city, those apartments are impossible to flip. I knew I changed when I voted for Reagan we needed a strong leader to get us out of this morass.

Now it's color that fascinates me, previously it was the drawing that interested me rather than the color because color was only an added attraction, it was the figure that fascinated me but all of a sudden I see shades of colors and not so much the figure but the shades of color and facial textures, fascinating as I age I change or I force myself to change and not stay settled in my ways, no longer do I see time as cyclical but unilinear—bodily problems are now to be expected not a shock out of the blue, you can't get by old age without assistance everybody I know needs glasses either to read or drive some are even walking with three legs one even with a walker, I am one of the rare ones who doesn't need glasses at my age, but now will be willing to wear them as I did when I had to walk with a cane after the wheelchair; what I liked about Joseph was his going into a thrift shop and bringing me a silver-handled walking stick so I wouldn't be stuck with an old people's hospital cane, Conchita laughed but I liked it and we slipped a rubber tip over the metal point and I felt much better walking with the stick than I ever would with the cane, and I refuse to walk with the four-pronged tip that the doctor wanted me to put on, like I wouldn't wear old women's shoes even if Conchita says I'm old yet the difficult part of aging is how others treat you and don't take you seriously. I was always prepared not to become my mother, and whenever I caught myself thinking like her can fight it, but never expected to be thought of as old and I refuse to give in to conventional thought and only worry about my bodily needs I live in the messy reality of life of being human, and I no longer look at arts for only political purposes or of idealized bodies even if I still love to look at the *Death of Socrates* but now am politically conscious and don't like it that his wife is leaving him at a time like this so he can pontificate only to men, I'd rather she be there holding his hand while dying, but these are only ideal images each work of art grabs an abstract moment and codifies it but each moment has to be judged on its own not toward some non-existent next, I have no idea what comes next, I am with Joseph and walking through the museum not because he reminds me of my past but because of him himself and how he is one of the few men I know who likes to go to museums and look at art and I like to have his arm to lean on. The children will be our teachers. If he had been a relative would have been polite to him but nothing of himself would have come out but I enjoy how he treats me as an equal not as an old person, he laughs with me not with a nervous laugh to humor me—we can laugh at frivolous stuff or stuff that requires serious thought and he reminds me of home where only a few people did something everything else was within the framework of the Church rarely were there any freethinkers. I admired Picasso so even if he moved to Paris at least he lived the way he wanted to live how many people can say that and now we go downstairs to see *Les Demoiselles*, the Three Graces on the left the twisted ladies reminiscent of El Greco, whatever these women are they are not adjuncts to some man's imagination but people in their own right, only the painting is gone my one nice joy in this museum on loan to somewhere who knows if it will ever be back. He had to leave Madrid in order to paint like this, I explain to Joseph, and after the dictatorship would have killed if he painted like this. Joseph smiled laughed said wow these guys took art seriously. Imagine they'd kill you for what you painted here they would ignore you unless you got lucky to be a cause célèbre. Artists like the masses couldn't make waves there was only one acceptable way to paint, Joseph exclaims the communists are similar in Hungary Zoltan could only paint one way or he would have been arrested. Interesting how dictatorships and totalitarian communists see art as decorative to disguise reality, paint my way or else, glorify me or else, my way or else. Joseph has to change Jacoba but there are no changing tables in men's room I volunteer to do it but he refuses and does it on a bench in front of all and makes sure to throw the Pamper in the garbage where it can stink up the place so they will learn men have rights as well. He has become more serious since the birth and is forcing me to change as well as we go all over the city the three of us, only he is also working, looking for apartments and when he has to stop and speak to a super I am there to help with the baby. He's not allowing me to fade away but forcing me back into the world and I'm beginning to see deeper art is metaphor, everything is metaphor for the moment and the moment is activity not at rest and I am moving and thinking no longer is a work of art only if it advances some cause it has to have a certain beauty in itself otherwise like theater for children that has a moral purpose and the moral purpose is always the good guys win and the good guys are the ones in power who control art that is deemed acceptable. Now I am thinking again and don't have to be like a little old lady without a thought in my head but can decide on my own what to see and to do how to live and I'm no longer simply going through the motions, and when I feel like this feel blood stirring in my bones. After I recovered stopped exercising and now it's Joseph who insists I go on walks with him and Jacoba and it's when my doctor told me how surprised he was that I had healed so fast he didn't think I would ever walk without a stick, but I was too competitive and it came out in physical therapy and exercise when I pushed myself to the limits and soon was able to use the stick not the chair and now Joseph carries the stick when he dresses fancy. And now I won't go without thought. Imagine for so long I thought I no longer needed to think I was comfortable but without self-understanding thought turns to fallacy and I actually believed I was too old to change my ways yet I still have to fight myself not give in to inertia to lethargy and go places that feed my mind that's as important as my body and it's only in thinking that I feel myself alive, I can make mistakes, the only way you can live is to make mistakes it's not all given to you at once and life isn't mere appearance it's how we think that counts. No longer am I limiting my views because I am afraid to try and now that I look at both color and figure synthesize both and fuse them and immerse myself in life. Most people my age are already dead or have never lived in the first place so timeless eternity will be no different and it probably won't satisfy them now as it did when alive now I'm in unexplored territory, the first generation of the super old and there is no more next.

My life blossomed after my mother got herself killed in that barroom with a gangster, Yolanda even told me she heard my mother was actually involved in shooting not that she got caught up in collateral damage, she was in the wrong place at the wrong time but she never should have been there in the first place if she had decent values and now I can barely recall how upset I was, if I looked in my diary nothing would have been in it not because I didn't keep a diary but couldn't express myself, and didn't know my true feelings, nor in the letters I wrote to friends when I moved in with grandma, they were full of lies of how well I liked it here, really I was an angry S.O.B. but didn't have the ability to put that into words. I hated grandma and wanted to escape, didn't want to move away from my friends but welfare wouldn't allow me to stay home alone and one friend said her mother would take us in but her mother balked said I have enough trouble with you and am not going to care for somebody else's brat. Besides that's what families are for. My heart was frozen in grief, fear, anger and anguish, I was not alright even if grandma did give me space to breathe and at the same time glad my mother was dead she deserved that for the way she treated me but I could never say that then. Grandma said that, not exactly, but chastened her for going out with a hooligan, what do you think happens when you go with low life, you can't expect not to get caught up in it. A gangland feud just to be taken to a nightclub and bought some fancy babbles that to her was living the good life, me too but on my own not with some jerk, until I moved out of the Bronx into the city which opened my eyes to other ways of living, not everything is mere appearance or for sale, l learned that by being around different people than I was accustomed to, but it took time I learned the hard way, never book learning I had to feel it, when I recall remember being scared but refusing to admit it frantic but smug and now can't even imagine back when I was scared and frantic only think I was but not feel how I was, I didn't want to continue high school in the new school and grandma wisely let me finish the term up in the Bronx but she was just appalled at how little I knew; my study habits were nonexistent, my lack of math skills still hurt me to this day when I can't even figure out a tip in a restaurant, luckily I bought an expensive calculator makes all the difference, don't use it to find best buys in supermarkets but how to tip. Grandma taught me sometimes spending a little more is worth it in the long run you don't always have to buy the cheapest. Now all she has to do is convince Joseph who still buys the most uncomfortable suits because he doesn't like to spend real money. At night what was I to do she had no television and I realized it wasn't for lack of money she read. Who reads? None of my friends that I knew spent the night with a book, I didn't even have a library card but she took me to the Tompkins Square Library and made sure I got one when she saw me reading *Archie* thought it was time I began my education as she put it, and over the summer she convinced me to go to the private school and finish up not just get a job as a beautician or become a secretary, I had wanted to take a speedwriting course but she refused. Give yourself a chance first get an education. An old crow I thought she didn't know anything, if I could work in an office I'd meet exciting men. Oh boy! At school we drank and smoked but these private school kids smoked marihuana, when I saw my first rolled cigarette I thought it was heroin and my mother always said one puff and you're hooked for life, she didn't mind me smoking but said I couldn't take cigarettes from friends because they might trick you and give you a joint, not that cigarettes are worse and give you cancer, heart attacks, emphysema. All pot does is let you chill out. All us actors smoke it now. Those kids at Calhoun had such a feeling of entitlement and I realized they deserved it they were so smart, at first I wondered how I could keep up and I couldn't except for tutoring also I was ashamed at being left back having to repeat my senior year, that's when I stopped going up to the old neighborhood, all my girlfriends had graduated and here I was still a student but it was only for a year, and the following year the guidance counselor helped me get a scholarship, I had only spoken to a guidance counselor once up at Walton where she told me my grades weren't good enough for college become a beautician or a secretary and she had told me about the speedwriting course at Katherine Gibbs. Some of the Jewish girls went to City College and maybe one kid to LIU but college wasn't on the radar, and they all lived at home until married, in my culture I was the only one who went away to school, even Joseph stayed at home why he was so envious of me I got away. That's when I didn't feel so bad going back to the old neighborhood and hanging out on Fordham Road in front of Alexander's, all city neighborhoods have hangout places, usually a busy shopping street, and that was ours and we would usually meet there or Poe park, but that's all they were doing hanging out as if they were still in high school. They laughed at my fashion and thought I was acting white when I wore a nice shirt and slacks, you couldn't wear that in the old neighborhood because then they'd take you for a whore, nobody wore jeans in those days it took a little while before girls would be comfortable wearing them but by then I was long gone and I was beginning to realize that how I live is made by my decisions not that I have to follow the group and I did things for a reason even if I felt embarrassed explaining this to my friends for fear they would accuse me of acting white, I was acting but not white but making an effort to change myself and I saw this as a better way even if I didn't read as much as grandma who read everything. But in high school when I got the role of Pandora the first thing grandma did was take me to Pandora's Box a café no longer in existence as I found out when I wanted to take Joseph there and impress him with my intellectual haunts and it was here that I memorized my lines but it was gone. Grandma even took me to a bookstore and bought *Works and Days* actually bought me a hard-covered book, I didn't even realize bookstores existed, I only saw comics or paperbacks in candy stores, books were in libraries, I never saw a bookstore in the Bronx, oh some toy stores sold adventure books but usually those were for boys. Who ever heard of studying for a part, but I learned the myth, didn't want to at first thought it would get in the way of the words of my spontaneity but she insisted and to this day that has held me in good stead with directors when they realize how serious I am, since many actors don't read, and that was my first taste of feminism where I realized men assign all evils in the world to women. The Greeks Pandora, the Christians Eve even Calderon who totally transformed the story and I became a statue who becomes alive, the stage was darkened when Pandora is in the box and lit up as I leave the box, and everybody applauded and I loved the applause, but at first I was embarrassed to step out of the box I was so evil, but my teacher insisted I smile said that it's not you but Pandora on stage don't confuse the character with you, you are playing a character you are not that person, but I was afraid people would see me as her. Now of course I realize you have to inhabit the character you play, think how the character will think, act how the character will act during the performance, of course it was only a school play with parents, classmates and siblings in the audience but the applause was deafening and at the after party in a cast member's house—a whole townhouse in the West Village to ourselves where we smoked pot and drank champagne all with his parents' knowledge all they did was insist somebody come and pick us up because we were a little high and couldn't go home by ourselves and if nobody came we would sleep over until the next day, grandma came by at 3 or 4 in the morning and we walked across the Village, which was full of people out at that time of the night, I remember being surprised at that, the streets were rolled up in the Bronx after 8 or so and only kids were out at night or maybe a man coming home from work, and she was glad I was beginning to see what another life looked like but she didn't force me into this new life only this way of living is more serious and was hopeful that I would take advantage of my opportunities, and it was that second senior year that showed me there are different styles of living, and now that I had a taste, but a taste is only a taste, to live differently you have to develop more than a taste, you have to learn how to distinguish pleasure from a deeper understanding of living, that went over my head when we drank champagne, champagne is what Myrna Loy drank in the film we watched on late night television, she would drink three four of them and not be woozy even if my head was spinning as I walked home with grandma. Why am I thinking about this all of a sudden I don't like to reflect on my past?

It's crazy one moment worrying if we can hit our target the next the money comes rolling in, all of a sudden I am fully ensconced in middle age, a surprise, I've gained a few pounds, but no noticeable balding an occasional gray hair some aches and pains but normal for my age and I have to now watch what I eat not too much meat but otherwise am okay, I'm in good shape for a man of my age, when did I become a man of my age, no longer the kid on the block when all I wanted to do was make an impression as if now I don't, but now it's a more sophisticated impression even if I was never called the kid. I wanted this, I spent my whole life working for this other people would respect me see me as normal now our business is booming I have a family and we're about to make a big move. I always wondered how my father and grandfather could live like this now it's me, one baby and maybe another one in the oven so we have to move and be in a neighborhood with good schools, and we've been actually looking at places where the schools are good, Cassandra actually suggested Hoboken, New Jersey but none of us wants to leave the city, besides the difficulty with these new neighborhoods is the schools that are still behind the times. We walked there the four of us went into a bar for a bite and there was this drunk sitting, fly open, pants open and Cassie says you take me to the nicest places however it was the only place open on Sunday but it didn't seem to be a place where you could get a croissant or fresh bread or a decent espresso, but it does have easy access to the Village but we thought we might have to wait a little while before the neighborhood gentrified. Esmeralda felt sorry for these old geezers slowly being kicked out of their neighborhoods as yuppies, quichewazie as she called them, moved in. We all agree if we move here we will be unhappy and we keep looking because we do need more space. If we really wanted space we should move to the suburbs but none of us even thinks of doing that but our neighborhood is becoming so drug-infected that it's becoming dangerous for Cassandra to come home late at night, she now has to have the taxi wait until she's inside the building before driving away, and I have gotten to know my neighbors because we instituted a tenant's patrol and we all take turns sitting in the lobby barring strangers; now if somebody we don't know comes the tenant has to let us know he's coming and the landlord is in the process of installing a second door that can only be opened by a buzzer, and we have barbed wire on the roof so junkies can't climb in from another roof and Esmeralda only goes out with me on her arm. All the same a tenant came home discovered a burglar and he killed her before fleeing. It wasn't Julio he lives uptown, and when they caught him he claimed he didn't do it the police were picking on him because he was black even if they did find her purse, jewelry, radio, inside his apartment, the only thing he didn't take was her computer, he got caught trying to hock the stuff to a nick-knack store telling the proprietor that the costume jewelry was the real thing and the police check these places periodically and the jewelry led to him, he was a total stranger to me but some on the block actually knew him and had seen him drinking on the stoop because he couldn't get into the lobby, and the apartment house across the way started it when they became so annoyed at him drunk in the lobby constantly banging on his girlfriend's door trying to break the door down to let him in and the police never came to take him away. Cassie said they should put a uniform on him to scare burglars away when he got drunk and passed out. However, one tenant came after him with a baseball bat, he really lost it, and if it weren't for his neighbors would have killed him, and afterwards they decided on the tenant patrol. At least that woman is still alive. Norma is dead, hence the name of our tenant patrol. Still we don't want to leave the city, we're rooted, and I feel I gain strength from the city streets but we now have to worry about the other guy and I have to worry about the *kinder.* I just don't see the Hastings on the Hudson, nicknamed the sixth borough because so many Manhattanites moved there for the fresh air, schools, open spaces and gardens, I know it looks good on paper, fresh air, green grass, more space, but you have to drive everywhere, the schools are regimented and the boredom of that life scares me when all you talk about are railroad schedules, cars, and schools, I can't see living a serious life there only segmented but it's not only me Cassandra and Esmeralda think the same way but we worry about the school system in the city, what's going to happen to the children who go to school and can't read, we believe in democracy and all that and the schools play a role in our democracy but can we sacrifice them to some ideal. A new term has entered our vocabulary 'functional illiterate' students are graduating New York high schools not being able to read because of automatic promotion and that's only if they stay over fifty percent now drop out, of course the Board of Education denies it saying we don't keep track but the guys who did the report did keep track of students, and most aren't moving away going to another school they simply stop coming. This means that not only can't they think they don't even realize they can't think and are so unprepared for life. We are now convinced the city's education system cannot do the job, I somehow went to some of the best the city had to offer and it was shit imagine how it is now with no best, at least I learned to read and write. Without even a serious discussion it seems we won't move out of the city we do take advantage of the city it's not as if we're in the Bronx where only if you worked you went into the city, not use the public schools even if we met them at the entrance they would still be trapped within the school for eight hours, we can't home school we're all too busy for that, and we have to decide soon this apartment will become too small, so it looks like private schools will be our option and Esmeralda says The Calhoun School so it looks like the Upper West Side is where we have to look.

Grandma and I differ on so many things it's difficult to believe we are related, she agrees more with Joseph than with me and I'm beginning to understand why she loved his grandfather, even if I could never imagine mourning my whole life for a bygone love, she seems him reincarnated even if he was born before he died, certainly that had a lot to do with her upbringing where you only have one great love in your life, from what I gather while Joseph's mother napped in the afternoon, a sure sign of depression, Jewish women nap Hispanic drink, be careful of generalizations I can hear both of them saying, but it's true, yet Joseph says many Jewish women are closet drinkers and grandma that many Hispanic women nap, and both smoked at home but never in the street. We've come a long way baby both groups of women now smoke in public but not cigars, but his mother didn't even prepare dinner and she was home alone all day, it was his grandfather who cooked dinner and he spent time with him during the afternoon when he wasn't outside playing ball and it was his grandfather who took him to cafeterias, movies and walks, at least he had someone to show him the way, I had nobody until I moved in with grandma, never even been to the American Museum of Natural History whenever there was a class trip I was always 'conveniently sick' that day never liked leaving the neighborhood and never went on class trips. He at least knew how to ride the subway. He calls me a feminist but I am not a feminist except when I want equal pay for equal work, but he says everything is about the economy all the rest is peripheral. But I still believe in traditional values a man should take off his hat in front of a lady in a closed space, hold the door open for a lady, when I was on the subway pregnant needed a man to offer me a seat now I can stand on my own, but the trains never have air conditioning and I was trying to open the window to get a little breeze in and a man sitting right next to the window wouldn't even get up and help me open the window, we're all a little confused about the new values and don't know what is correct, heaven help us for living in difficult times, obviously I like it that now women can control their own bodies, and that girls can play sports, but why would they want to do that? At the same time if they want to why should men stop them. Because I act in classical drama silly men think I believe in the roles I play, I think a good actor could pass a lie dictator test all the time we dwell in the character, how come courts don't allow actors to see if it's real, we believe in the roles we play while playing them but that doesn't mean we are them. How many men have been disappointed in that I'm not the character—I can act the cool sophisticated woman but really am a bundle of nerves an insecure woman who doesn't have much of an education, why I am now insisting upon continuing even if it leaves so little time for the family, grandma always worried when I just blurted out stuff with no knowledge while her and Joseph have thought through their thoughts, opinions and know the difference between knowledge and belief: Truth is self-knowledge, Joseph says, good is using your imagination, grandma says, I think beauty is human proportion. But I have to submit to the arbitrary will of some producer or director but I never confuse their thoughts with reason, that's why Joseph says I have good intuitive sense but I'm not out to change the world people who try that become dictators, all I want is to act, it's Joseph who thinks he can make things better for Hispanics and blacks, not me, why can't he just make money why does he have to be a do-gooder? He feels guilty making so much money but he can't help let people make up their own minds they're responsible, but he wants to help and has this new idea. If people don't know what's good for them, you can't force them to act in a certain way: homeownership is not for everybody. He thinks Hispanics and blacks can't think and he knows what's good for them and what they want. Grandma says I've changed but I'm still not this homebody even if married still look only now keep it a fantasy I do have to take care of my husband and pump milk, lots of it especially now that I still going at night to school, and Jacoba doesn't like to drink from the bottle, but she will if hungry enough. I still am happy with our old furniture it's Joseph who shops for new paintings, he loves moving them around and like grandma likes the whole wall covered with art, not one painting to a wall that I like, antique dishes, hates to have one set, copper pots and pans, even brings home flowers that grandma appreciates, I sometimes forget to notice, I try, appreciate it but it just isn't me. He asks me but does it anyway, he has a good head for decorating even if he's not gay and no longer do I even buy cheap umbrellas because of him realize one good one lasts longer than three cheap ones and spending more at first really means spending less in the long run. Joseph says he had to learn that he wasn't born with that knowledge but I think he's rebelling against his mother who made him wear galoshes that you could never get on over your shoes and he now gets the finest he can afford so besides it looking good it feels comfortable and fits better as well. I never think in the long run, he's always thinking that way, says when he was up on 97th street bought a cheap fan at Tip Top but it only lasted a less than a summer when he moved in with us he and grandma insisted upon a good one at the Sharper Image on Madison Avenue that has a nice design and functions smoothly, I never learned this and after my mother died and I was shopping at Woolworth's a five-and-dime store I saw all the kitchenware my mother had in our home, and I would go to there to shoplift, that was the first store we girls go alone but even we eventually decided the cosmetics and fake jewelry weren't worth it. It was funny everybody would be looking at the colored girls when they walked in and we had the place to ourselves. Once I had a part-time job at Cartier's beautiful jewelry that I couldn't afford on my salary but when they had an employee's sale he insisted I had to strike and I borrowed money from him and grandma—paid it all back in installments, both refused interest, and bought myself a small pink-gold necklace something I knew I could never have afforded myself and wouldn't have spent so much money but he insisted and said you'll never get another shot do it, and just did it without thinking otherwise wouldn't have done it, still have it only am afraid to wear it now the streets are so dangerous but it is beautiful. He appreciates quality, and is preparing to leave our place is getting too small but I love this neighborhood and don't want to leave but he's right it's getting too dangerous for our little girl and the schools are just terrible, even

I can see that, at first I thought they were good enough for me they'll be good enough for her but watching the boys and girls in the schoolyard and how rough they are convinced me we have to find a good school.

It's difficult, or as Jacobo would say easier to believe than think, because all of a sudden all alone I've become frightened, real scared of the noise at night, I never was the way I once loved the night that's when life began, as a teenager couldn't wait until my parents went to bed and how disappointed I was when I realized the night was like the day, only when I left home to I begin to realize the possibilities of night and now I'm staying home again and I must get out. It's not so much the noises that frighten me as the new neighborhood, at least up here a woman out alone at night isn't taken as a prostitute, woman have freedom now only have to worry about junkies, but these street people up here are nice, considerate do help me bring groceries in for a tip, even warn others when sanitation is ticketing cars but they're not junkies with syringes up their arms but gamblers and street hustlers, and I usually walk on the main thoroughfares even if I love the little side streets and now force myself to take taxis at night when buses forget to come, feel uncomfortable taking a taxi never needed one before but now have finally agreed otherwise I might be stuck home all night—how did the city get so bad—'benign neglect' nobody saw it coming little by little some streets became unsafe to walk on, street lights stopped working and the city didn't repair them, garbage started being picked up weekly, abandoned buildings weren't being boarded up and junkies took them over, crack has replaced marihuana and heroin as the drug of choice, transportation in ruins, the schools a total mess, the police totally useless, no wonder 'white flight' but Joseph finds this place up here besides he said too many Hail Mary's to leave the Bronx so wanted no part of the suburb. He has two sets of friends some from the old neighborhood who have moved out of the city and his school friends who also left the city but when he comes back from the country, as he calls it, goes down to Katz's for a pastrami sandwich or Ratner's a kosher restaurant on the Lower East Side for pierogis and potato pancakes but really just to get the smell of the country off him. Art may have allowed him to see nature in a new way but he still can't stand it. The suburban fresh air is too good for him, he complains these areas have no bookstores, art galleries, concert halls, live theater, just a few malls and an occasional megaplex that shows crappy American blockbusters. His friends complain that if they rent videos at Grand Central they can only rent them for a day so if they bring a video home to watch for the week-end they have to pay overdraft fees. In the Village there are video stores but so far up here I haven't found one. But his friends don't miss the city but they never took advantage of it, those from the Bronx never went into the city and from school only to work not to museums, music or theater. In fact, he is surprised at how few of his friends actually went to live theater, most wait to see it as a movie, or maybe Broadway but never downtown to off, or off-off, and when he mentions plays to them they say distance. Why I'm learning or forcing myself to use taxis is I still want to take advantage of the city, so does he, Conchita is a denizen of taxis, she always makes deals with taxi drivers, everything is a deal and she has no difficulty running off the books, and the driver keeps it all. All this re-minds me how I listened to Mass, gospel, consecration and communion never understanding a word all in Latin and when they changed it to lo-cal languages actually said they shouldn't do that it takes all the mystery out of it but who was I saying it to I no longer went and had no right to tell them it wasn't mine, it never was mine all I liked in the Mass was the theater, how priests acted with their theatrical dress and change of clothes from white to black officiating at the altar, the solemn music the hushed silence where applause should be, and blabbing about the drama of Eden, the snake, Eve's sin in their sermons never how we are born into a world not of our choosing we are there, and are forced to be free in a world bounded by space-time, if separated in space you are separated in time, and chance and each choice we make is a leap into the unknown, now I wonder why Christianity hasn't come to an end after the Holo-caust, if we're created in God's image then God has some responsibility to us, how could God have allowed it to happen; that event was so horrible there can be no more redemption. At one point I must have believed most likely when my parents took me to Mass and I couldn't refuse but when I was older firmly refused even as my mother threatened me with eternal damnation, that I would burn in hell forever more, but by then it was too late I wanted nothing to do with them and started getting inter-ested in art and interested in Communism and from Marxism to freedom that is not bound by any tradition. It all started when I rejected the teach-ings of the Church and saw them for what they are and at first looked for utopian solutions until I realized this is impossible, we had a good enough cause in the war and still we lost, and decided to live in freedom instead, which was next to impossible for a single woman in a Catholic country and marriage became an option to get me out of my parents' clutches even if you move from one set of constraints to another and I found out to my shame that I had to behave now as a married woman even if that is not what you want but you don't know what you want, sometimes only luck can make your life better and you can make your own luck. I knew I didn't want, couldn't do what girls are doing so easily now be a single parent, and you can't easily throw off your family, your heritage, your culture it follows you no matter where you go, only in a careful examination of myself was I able to throw off false gods and begin to find my face if I wanted some freedom. Luckily I have a skill which gave me some financial independence even if I couldn't practice it here but then was able to develop another one so I wasn't dependent upon a man. I enjoyed my freedom didn't get involved in bars or clubs to dull my mind, I always had something to occupy my mind, didn't become a professional mother giving up her life for the kiddies, always gave Gloria hamburger while I ate the steak, now women can even go into a bar alone but I wonder if that is freedom, I feel like such a hypocrite if I deny them that right but at the same time they confuse debauchery with illusionary freedom. Travel alone yes, drink alone no. Unlike the pill, which is real freedom that Hispanic girls seem hell bent on avoiding—what the Church can do to you, and before they even realize it they are trapped as old mothers, their beauty faded with having babies on demand. How do we live? Are we born knowing right from wrong? How long does it take knowing how to live? Now I have conversations with my younger self but it's no use I never would have listened back then, you don't even ask the questions. Jacobo once said you don't live you exist like an amoeba exists only thought allows you to break through non-purpose purpose and break free of your entanglements and imaginary beliefs where we take the opinions of others as our own when we are frightened but if we can stop for a moment and pay attention we can begin to learn to think, that's why those moments with Jacobo are so satisfying not only the love-making but the intense conversations that allowed me to think in new ways his thought allowed me to spread my wings and gave me my first taste of freedom even as his were clipped when he left Spain. Something died inside me when he left but I was so happy carrying his child and when that child was born dead was depressed and wondered if I would ever walk again, I gave myself five years to escape and America became the holy ground where I was free not forced to be what I didn't want to be even if he had disappeared, I still recall the shock of how men would ogle women here, or catcalls and men actually thought we liked that, the nice thing about aging is those end.

It felt like I was shitting a watermelon and to my surprise didn't want it to come out, what did I want to carry an 8-lb girl inside me forever? no but I knew our lives would change drastically when she finally came out, induction did no good I couldn't push hard enough she just stayed there finally the doctors said I have good news and bad news, the good news is you're going to see your baby in a half hour the bad news is you're going to have a cesarean he was concerned that I was still retaining fluids, should have used the midwife and how can you argue with doctors when they say time's up and boom it moved so quickly. The recovery wasn't as difficult as I thought acting is a good profession for giving birth, I was in good shape and walking a lot helps all I wanted to do was walk home from the hospital but they insisted we take a taxi, wouldn't even let me walk around the hospital said no you have to stay in bed you could faint if you walk. You can't think of everything and this is much more exhausting than I ever imagined. Six months off from work, I'm allowed to work from home as if you can work in the house when a baby sleeps: one, they never sleep and two, if they do you're too exhausted to do anything but nap. Grandma and Joseph are helpful but still it fell to me to nurse her and that is exhausting walking around bloated until the baby decides to drink. How does the body even know to secrete milk after a C-section? Joseph even wrote a paper for me but was upset when he got a C and the professor saying he really didn't understand what Philoctetes is about when he made the joke that his moaning *oy* proved that the Greeks knew of Judaism and his cry *oy* proves he's Jewish? The professor had no sense of humor. We laughed but he never did another one for me. And after that I wrote all my own papers but that didn't change the nature of my beliefs, and even as grandma tells me all the time beliefs are not facts they still give me pleasure and a certain sense of certitude. Yea, like the belief I had that a nursing woman can't get pregnant again. Or the belief grandma had before she met Jacobo that Christ could not come down from the Cross until the Jews believed in him but Jews would never believe in him until he came down, that was pounded in her head by the priests and sisters but laughed at when she met Jacobo, or that I don't want another child, not now not ever not that it's too soon but whenever is too soon. There's' no one I can explain this too, Grandma and Joseph are so excited by this one they would welcome a second with open arms, only I don't want a second. I don't always want to have to think about the baby but that's all they do now grandma loves staring at her watching her sleep waiting for it to smile. When she held her she didn't want to let go. Joseph is too concerned with the day-to-day to enjoy her the way grandma does but he too at times can't stop staring. She never did that with me. If only I recorded their conversations I could write a family comedy even if few people care for family home movies anymore more interested in raw over-the-top productions, uptown may have wordy plays but certainly not downtown. We can't even go uptown anymore that theater is so boring movies masquerading as dramas and the only plays we see there are revivals of the Greeks, now I love this new theater that rips your guts out but now that Joseph is a father he is looking for more respectable plays something he can take Jacoba to and even schlepped her to the art museum and can't wait to take her to the opera. Just what she needs. Now we seem to be going through a boom of ancient Greek playwrights, for years you would never see the Greeks performed and they were only kept alive because students had to read them but now since students no longer read it's good theaters are performing them, only you can't get students to go to live performances they prefer movies where the characters are unreal than having to identify with characters who are so like themselves. We always thought word of mouth is the best advertising especially after the newspaper strike when there was no advertising but that doesn't seem to work anymore, sometimes only a star name from Hollywood or television will do. Maybe the newspaper strike helped the revival of Shakespeare and the Greeks because everybody heard of them, unfortunately however the strike really shut some small theaters. I didn't miss the news but what was going on around town evaporated, I don't recall the 1962 strike, Joseph does, he missed the sports section, I never was interested and now he can't even watch a baseball game it's slow. In high school he had a little action taking bets if you could pick three players who could get six hits and he made a fortune, until the strike and he couldn't get the box score, because students didn't understand the odds a typical ballplayer gets up four times in a game and would have to get two hits which is virtually impossible and finally he got caught someone bet a whole lot of money and won and he had to pay out. He gave up gambling after that. He wants Jacoba to start soccer as soon as she can. I think she should walk first. One of the things he likes about the West Side is they have children's soccer. He and grandma have all these plans for her and those plans keep them together and I feel like a stranger in my own home, I shouldn't say this even to myself but she does nothing to me, I can't seem to get close to her, I know she's part of me but she's out of me now, I feed her but it's grandma and Joseph who hold her all the time I've become a wolf to man how else to explain my feelings towards her. I'm not a religious person but do believe you can't live without love and to take care of a child you have to be able to do it on faith alone and if you believe that you will but if you don't no amount of intellectualizing can force you to change. They both don't want her to have a religion I was raised Catholic by my mother but my mother wasn't raised Catholic by her mother, my grandmother, they need religion in order to have something to break away from, and I'm more Jewish than Catholic even go to Reform Temple without Joseph who won't set foot in that place even for the food that he loves and I have to bring some home for him. He feels nothing Jewish, he said, left the temple after his Bar Mitzvah when the rabbi said God gave us this land and we have the deed right here, pointing to the Bible; but when I go there feel nice afterwards besides it gets me out of the house Saturday morning so I don't have to deal with making breakfast, it's a shame colleges don't have classes on Saturday and Sunday morning they would be filled with women escaping the home drudgery. Weekends are the worst even bad weather is better than having to be home alone all day with the baby. Imagine, I once thought I could never get pregnant, and then bingo as soon as one is out of the oven another one pops in. There won't be a second. We can't afford two even if we now have more space another would change me too much—once you have a child your entire life changes and what you once thought important flies out the window but now you start to wonder is this what you want, I was so happy being a Village girl now having to live on the Upper West Side is depressing, it's so far from everything, there's no theater up here only a couple of bookstores and movie theaters not even art galleries, but luckily a few nice cafés but you can't even find fresh croissants on the West Side we have to get Sarah Lee's frozen crescent rolls. The bakery across the street is German, has good German sweets and the aroma when you pass that place is enchanting, I walk down 86th street for the subway just for that smell. My life's on hold right now and I don't know how long I can stand it.

If it was only reason that propelled me not only desire I could have done more but it was mostly desire occasioned by thought I couldn't just stand and act but living fine and dandy but not the good life but had those terrible values hidden under the table and I knew I wanted out but didn't plan a way out just let it happen and even if there was a purpose to my desire it was too obscure for me to grasp, I didn't realize that there was something inside me that hated it all and I was treading water until I could learn to swim treating myself as an impersonal person as if I as a person didn't exist but only my inner self saw through this when I finally broke free of my parents only to be trapped by a husband who I had to be free of and then another then a daughter but I refused to let her get in the way of the newfound freedom I was discovering, all along I realized I had lost my soul-mate but I wasn't going to sacrifice it all for Gloria, she would have to live with me no longer was I going to live for others; that's when I made a vow to myself to begin living when Tomas finally moved out and hugged me the last time his hug surprised me otherwise I would have never let him hug me, he isn't a bad man, in fact quite decent, and never opposed me but I no longer wanted anything from him then my daughter gets shot what can a grandmother do, all my thoughts puff up in smoke I had to care for my granddaughter she was totally lost up there living all by herself and soon welfare was going to take away her subsidy. I told Tomas to get a divorce whenever he wanted I knew he wouldn't do it but I was wrong and when he finally met someone else divorce was doable in New York; no longer did he have to go to the Dominican Republic or have a lawyer do it for him, no longer was Nevada the divorce capitol of the States, those nice dude ranches where you stayed for six weeks while declaring residency a thing of the past as if we could ever have afforded giving up our lives for six weeks. Now I no longer have to feel obligated to him. If I had wanted to remarry I'm sure he would have gone to the DR but I had no intention of living with another man again only now I am with my granddaughter, her husband, and my baby, truly I get anxious if I don't see her and smile at her and

I love how she smiles back when she sees me and now I know why I
have loose skin so Jacoba can grab onto it. It would also almost be fun in
believing in an afterlife just to see the look on his face when I tell him I
am with his grandson. But instead I remember the failures of my life, my
failure to find happiness, truth, abandoned, taste degraded, living with
the herd, and the all that tempers my failure is that I take responsibility
for it, my attempts were failures but my failures were my attempts indeed
in failure maybe my granddaughter will succeed and some of it might
rub off on her the freedom part not the abandonment part but freedom
is too complicated for it to occur by osmosis—the feminist revolution is
giving her the intellectual strength to act what I could only do by gut she
now has thought, I still fight against self-deception but at least now it's
out in the open, now it's not a shame for a woman to have a job instead
of being with the family, no longer does she have to feel guilty not taking
total care of the baby having dinner on the table when the man comes
home keeping a perfect house, previously it didn't matter my beliefs only
affected a few not the culture now a few are affecting a few others and
that is affecting all and it's these women who are staying home minding
the hearth who have to defend themselves. The times are a changing. As
more people are becoming aware of these new ideas that women didn't
have to become pregnant from sex and that they could enjoy sex without
fear of children or now if a child is conceived you don't have to stay home
because of a child because there are childcare centers even if it didn't
mean too much individually culturally it is transforming the place when
whole bunches of people believe it, go for it, act on it, taken together
then society changes. Now that women have new thoughts no way will
they go back to the old ways and I am encouraged by young women
in the city insisting that girls get a good education and now they have
equal space in the top schools that were primarily for boys, of course
the Board was against it bureaucracies are slow to change but they had
to answer to the court and the court had to answer to society and voila
girls get a chance to go to good high schools, or as Joseph would say FM
(fucking magic) but he claims it doesn't matter the public schools aren't
any good but that's because he had such a bad experience and now top
colleges are even admitting women. Jacobo once said there is a special
place in hell designated just for school teachers but of course science has
shown us there can't be a special place in the universe for humans who

have no body we are our bodies, and brains are only connected to the body, old superstitions die hard and now that schools don't teach God some folks are creating their own special Christian schools to fight the ungodliness of secularism, I know from experience how easy it is to fall into the old ways and that you always have to be on guard fighting back the old comfortable ways of deception and even if I am connected to my younger self it really is a deceptive experience because I am only responsible when I became an adult—adult experiences determine who I am and it is that experience that has determined me and I'm always fighting my younger self who wants to imprison me in conformity—the I should have, the I should have, maybe I should have gone up to the Bronx for one last look at Jacobo but I didn't and have to live with it and I'm not sorry I didn't what good would it have served but only showing me I know how to torture myself, but I might have seen Joseph as a little boy but everyone says yeah until it happens but that's what makes me who I am you can't go picking and choosing what you should have done because how do you know what would have happened and the choice doesn't necessarily have to turn out your way. It's the failures that have made me who I am today trying to live with them and live with integrity, I have to give myself a C plus and forget the Benedictine Sisters and their monastic ways to get around all the strictures of confusion they put in front of us, my favorite being if you believe it was a sin in your gut it is a sin, your heart trying to tell you something that it is a sign of contrition as long as you constantly express regret: not to learn to think for yourself accepting that there are contradictory motives inside us and that you should develop strength to resist those internal desires that interfere with the rational desires. Otherwise all you are doing is the same thing over and over again only hoping for different results. Nothing absolves you or gives you absolution you have to refuse yourself in order to try out different forms of yourself. Did I stumble onto this before I met Jacobo or only by being with him?

Who I am is not who I thought I was and I realized that as I acted like father and that acting has now made me one when I was ready to give up my life for the baby; no longer do I want intellectual force from the theater I get it enough in real life my thoughts have nothing in common with the reality of things? My whole life has changed and all previously thought is gone, kaput no longer can I act as if I am the center of the universe even if thought I was doing it for the good of others, I was only truly looking after myself, I was doing it for me, me, me, and only for the benefit of myself hopefully I didn't make it worse for others it's only in the blackout where I had a little adventure that it started to become clear: we had no candles nor a flashlight but as long as I realized power would come on soon wasn't too concerned only inconvenienced and the following morning there was power and my adventure was over, but during the blackout was more afraid of fire with the whole city lighting candles but I had opened the gates kept the window open and moved the crib into my bed room for emergency egress if need be but there was no need, and was surprised when some of the street people knocked on my door and asked if we wanted candles and thanked them and when the lady discovered we had no flashlight came back with an earth-mother-sized one, a spotlight really, so you can make the way with the baby, when I climbed up on the roof to see the city it was eerie with few lights on and candles everywhere, and was only worried about Esmeralda she couldn't come up with us because she would never be able to climb down the fire escape so she had to stay in her basement all alone. She left her candle right by the door but I wasn't sure my actions were enough but it wasn't my actions that changed things but the way I thought, I would have helped Esmeralda if she held unto me but I wouldn't let her drag Jacoba down, maybe a fireman would have helped I was ready to act but luckily wasn't tested. Cassandra called and even if we were asked to keep off the phone in case it had to be used for emergencies we talked and talked for over an hour, and I knew better but still I wanted to hear her reassuring voice even as I felt I should free the line but it was too comforting to talk while Jacoba slept besides me and Esmeralda stayed in the basement even as I explained to Cassie I might have to end suddenly then I heard her say love but I said I doubt if we will and became anxious over the choice I had to make and realized I was not the strong silent type who accepts what comes but actually was afraid, I never imagined feeling that, and it was comforting to talk as long as possible who cares if it affects others I have an obligation to keep myself calm in order to help others but I wouldn't be able to help others if I was alone with myself I needed to feel connected with her even if she said we are all frightened and she couldn't talk as long as she wanted because other people needed to use the phone to call home, I calmed myself down by telling her we can escape

.lized afterwards how important she was to me, we

.ch other our true love but during the blackout our fear

we are to live. A peculiar feeling, she was in the theater

.ors and they had enough light to spend the night and in

, she said she would walk home. Afterwards we realized it

.te our heads there was no danger but while in the middle of

. so sure, here I was thrown into a dangerous situation and I

won. .ed what I would do: and how the world wasn't concerned with me but what I was going to do counted, I knew what had to be done but it is difficult to wonder if I could do it while the world no longer revolved around me, but did make this choice to bring the baby into the world and now another one on the way but did I do it to bind Cassie to me, my dream of her pregnant in the bed with me, it wasn't only my actions but my intentions, it's easy to see my actions I gotta do something, but my feelings were a mystery to myself as Freud said artists are sublimating what they can't get in real life into my imaginary life and I always liked that because I don't have an artistic bone in my body and can feel superior to artists who only imitate while my effort is to master the complexities of real-estate and housing law not a make-believe but a true expert. But is this living? Why should their way be any more correct than mine? I'm a big boy now is this what I want. Do my actions have to be considered as the kind of life I chose even if I constantly have doubts and what do I have going for me since I broke with the old crowd so I wouldn't be tempted to follow them and their ways—I no longer know one high school friend or buddy from the old neighborhood, believe in passion in the life you lead especially now where we have some individual choices and not forced to be a soldier, a Jew, a communist (I always felt you could only be a communist in the 1930s opposing the fascists) but that was then we are living after then and nobody says I have to be Jewish or a soldier. I slowly slipped away without my even realizing it and now there are fewer options opened to me, especially after the birth of my baby, now I have to earn my keep and can no longer even think of walking away from this life, but just because I am doing this doesn't mean I want to do this even if I don't know exactly what I want to do and nobody knows the uncertainty with which I lead my life. I am thinking this after having a normal conversation with Cassie and am ready to climb out the fire escape with a baby in my arm and wonder do my intentions really matter when its only with others that I begin to become myself. By m. power was turned back on and I could ignore what I thought during t.. night.

How come I lived after what I did? Everything ended for me that one morning at sunrise, one moment I looked up at the morning star wondering if it was Venus or Jupiter now I never wanted to see it again, I was just released from the infirmary when the order came they need ten men for special duty, fully dressed, and I was feeling better after days of dizziness and had met this beautiful woman who I had talked to all night long, but it was time to get back to my unit that I had recovered from what no one knew I had all I felt was dizziness, no fever, no nothing but I couldn't even stand up, one doctor said dehydration another the flu, affluenza, anything to give it a name but it was something that never happened to me before, healthy one moment then not but I didn't care I met this wonderful woman, alive, cheerful, beautiful, could think she reminded me of all the reasons I came here in the first place to get away from the gloom that was my life in the Bronx to live and change the world around me and I now have to catch up to my unit who were ordered to go to the parade ground and I dress and catch up with them pretty quickly as I walk looking at the morning star wondering how you can tell if it's Venus or Jupiter, what do I know about astronomy but only afterwards realize of course it had to be Mars, and said to myself will check it out when I get back in the world, but never did because after what I did it had to be Mars, who could have thought I would do what I did? I always fall short of what I said I would be but this was too much and there is no forgiveness for what I did. This failure is tragic I would never recover from it and all I wanted to do is forget it but no matter how hard I tried it snuck in by the back door and I was always depressed, I thought I had some nitty-gritty but had no idea what I was doing marching out to the parade ground in full dress uniform and somebody handed me a rifle while I'm wondering why we're marching at this time in the morning only I'm told I'm part of a firing squad: we are going to shoot one of our own as a traitor. We were all dressed in our uniforms as if this was a military exercise all that was missing was the drum and bugle—that he was a deserter I didn't even doubt but to go and shoot him this is murder not an execution, I may have killed men before when I fired my gun towards the enemy and a bullet of mine may have struck the enemy but

I'm not the greatest shot and if I killed someone it probably was from lack of medical care more than my gunshot: there he was all of a sudden right face and there he is his hands tied behind his back, his pants wet from peeing and so frightened; I have never killed in cold blood before, I can still see his broken body in front of me watching him die, hear our guns firing over and over, him screaming 'long live Stalin, long live Stalin' right before we shoot, not even realizing it was Stalin who ordered him shot. We were ordered to kill a traitor but before I always thought it was different killing a man in battle from one in cold blood, we're here in a righteous course how could something so right turn out so evil? It was wrong and I did it. We were standing so close to him, in movies it's always so dramatic music, drums, ready aim fire, all the sergeant did was say fire and I did it so I wouldn't be thought of as a coward for not obeying orders not that they would shoot me if I didn't do it I could use that as an excuse but it didn't enter my mind I never said to myself I'm not going to be a party to this affair, and I was marching with my comrades, I never should have done it no matter what they did to me, one of the reasons I came here was to escape the gloom and hypocrisy of my life and thought here I can start over but that didn't work I am the same person here as I am back in the city, a new place doesn't change me—I remember thinking if only I could start again then hey I start fresh here nobody knows me but it doesn't matter I'm still the same person doing things when I left that I didn't want to and here I am doing the same thing again but now it was worse I killed a man in cold blood before I only married and had a child. We watched him die the sergeant shot him in the head to put him out of his misery, we were all so close and couldn't kill him, we had walked up to him he was blindfolded so he couldn't see us but we would have had to look at him and were told to fire out guns, it all happened so quickly and I was a cold-blooded killer. No drum rolls the poor devil standing there in front of us, no priest, a fly buzzing around, did the fly have any idea what was going down, ready fire, just like that the sergeant bellows, he yells, 'long live Stalin, long live Stalin' and a volley of shots ring out, mine among them, we are so close we can't miss but of course we did we didn't kill him and the sergeant has to put a bullet in his head. Why couldn't he have done that in the first place? Because then it wouldn't have been a court-marshaled offense but outright murder like we did. Afterwards we were all silent but the world was no longer the same to me. I couldn't imagine doing something like that. It was within the Law we did what we were ordered to do, he was a convicted traitor and a deserter must be punished and it sets an example for other men not to betray the cause, but is any cause worth killing especially if it is not in battle—does conscience make cowards of us all, was Shakespeare a Crypto-Jew that thinking forces us to regret action, as Eric, my English friend said, why I always liked Hamlet he could only vacillate never did anything only killed Claudius by accident. here we were struggling to set people free and doing the same as the fascists. What resulted from this action is I never killed again after seeing a man die when I was in battle made sure my bullets went over the head of my enemies, the ancient tabernacle all of sudden acquired meaning for me: Thou Shall Not Kill. And to make amends gave up the woman I loved. No longer could I blindly follow the laws of the Republic, the captains, I couldn't up and disobey I was too much of a coward for that besides I would have been shot and they would have called me a traitor, so I kept silent but no longer did I believe in what I had believed in, not if you have to kill a man up-close and watch him die—a moment before alive, then in agony, and here I am killing a man whose name I don't even know but seeing him die in front of me and knowing I was the cause horrified me and I no longer was the same person I was a moment before, and when I finally left Spain defeated walked home from the ship my head low, not the kind of hero's welcome I imagined, good because I didn't meet anyone I knew because I was ashamed of what I had done, all I thought about was the pasty face and the man screaming in agony. I recall a barber, one of the International Brigades on the ship made some extra money shaving and cutting hair and cropped mine short, I can still feel the sun on my face and the witch hazel aftershave he rubbed on me, I didn't want to be what I once was and when I looked into the mirror didn't even recognize myself, good, I wanted to forget as much as possible—was I going home to my loving wife and daughter who awaited me with open arms, no, all I saw was the deserter's pastry face a man who I never knew and haunted by dreams of that face for the rest of my life and that my adventure to get me away from my life was a total failure and made me see what a terrible person I was killing a man in cold blood.

I am affected by what affects me other stuff gets lost in the humdrum, as I am sitting on the subway arguing with a man dead over five hundred years but his thoughts are alive to me, you can't have one without the other; he had answers to every question I have questions to his every answer, for him God was the unmoved mover because he was the first mover of the world, nature is God and because God was first he is supremely perfect and we are part of God and remain in God, even if we don't know his mind because he is the prime mover beyond our thoughts and there is an order beneath all this chaos. I take out my new Sheaffer fountain pen between stops, we're stuck as usual and an announcement comes over the loudspeaker saying, or what I think it's saying it's so mumbled, is that we will be moving shortly there's a train behind us, another case of the future influencing the present, and as usual I am too angry to concentrate when the train stalls so I make notes about what I read, as if notes will allow me not to forget, at least I have a seat and I make a quick perusal of the car see no pregnant woman or old person so try and get back to my studies, it's nice I don't have to offer my seat now at least young women work so they can stand and no longer do I have to play Sir Galahad, and realize up until the 20th century most people actually believed this stuff, I wonder how many do now or is it closet beliefs, since most people never talk God in public anymore except politicians dissembling the audience by making believe they're religious, or so I thought until I actually met some state legislators and realized how dumb they were and may have actually believed, now I'm beginning to rethink my thinking maybe God is not dead for the vast majority of people. My face gets contorted and the guy next to me asks if I am alright, and I tell him nothing personal I'm not frightened about the subway stopping only how the medieval mind gave way to the modern, he laughs and turns away goes back to his paper and says you ought to take my class. Now it's more brazen we're starting to understand how big the universe actually is and that a person, thing, whatever couldn't have lit the match to set the universe in motion or that the universe is too big maybe this isn't the best of all possible worlds maybe God had a chance to experiment on different worlds, or maybe man is truly alone. Have to be careful how I say that, and, of course, never to clients, but if you claim that Holocausts are created by small-minded men not crazy men they crucify you. At least now for some Jews, as the generation of suffers starts dying out, are beginning to open up the question, but see it perverse if there is no God anything is permitted as opposed to when God was alive and it was allowed. Can we ever look at this dispassionately? should we without the emotions, motives and desires, these historical studies forget people lived and suffered and now with eyewitness testimonies fading what will become of Holocaust studies, except there are unfortunately always new Holocausts popping up. Aren't I lucky, I think, to be born on this side of the Atlantic and not be touched by their madness, and can look at the sunrise or sunset while jogging around the reservoir in Central Park, I love going with Jacoba she loves the bouncing as I run. I get my pleasure being with her and I can especially feel it being stuck between subway stations watching trains go by us on either side of us. I start to make notes in my book when a woman comes up beside me, I'm afraid she's going to ask me for a seat, and I can count on one hand how many women have spoken to me on the subway, but she says I saw him walking the streets of Paris, who's he? and she looks at the book I'm reading that God brings inherent order to the world, how can that be he's been dead over five hundred years, but I like a woman who can start a conversation with a man on the subway now so many of them never look at anybody or are afraid to speak at least we get the wrong idea, I offer her my seat, the polite thing to do, but she's not interested in sitting just was surprised seeing somebody reading a hard-covered book so many men are reading newspapers and women romance novels, you can tell they usually have them covered in a plastic case, and nobody naps on subways anymore because of the danger. Obviously she had confused him with somebody else I quickly close the book so she won't realize her mistake and usually I am so proud to be reading a serious book on the subway and show it off, but even if riders know of the work they'll only think I'm a student. When Harvey saw my place with so many books wondered if I was still a student. I try and explain the basic assumption that life is not all or nothing but there has to be a combination of pleasure and thought which to me doesn't mean hedonism, and she replies like the old 'dedicated virgins' it wasn't that they didn't like sex but that they had a mind of their own and the only way they could use it was to escape the patriarchal family. A conversation with an educated woman, rare. I am thrilled at this young woman talking to me and see the envious looks of other faces, they think of me as Don Juan, wow! Some parts of ethics can be considered objective, she goes on, but we all live in situations that determine how we should act, there are no predetermined conditions each situation is unique and can be reasoned out even if the reason is faulty but you can only find out by doing. Is this a dream? I pinch myself. Is she real? She tells me how she's now reading this great book by a guy you probably never heard of Walter Benjamin, and I laugh but don't mention I read him in the Sixties and always wanted to go to Berlin because of him but dared not because then I would feel too Jewish, she talked about how he loved the vibrancy of the original in painting or music and I kept my mouth shut about how at least in copies or phonograph records we can see or hear works that would otherwise be lost to only the few cognoscenti, that democracy opens doors and now that I saw copies go to see concerts or see original works of art, except modern music that is difficult to listen to on recordings I like to see where Elliot Carter's music is coming from. Then I shut my mind up to let her talk not be afraid of the silence talking to a pretty girl like that allows me to change my view of myself, I'm not so old after all, can I ask her for a cup of coffee, a glass of wine? no that's too threatening besides I'm married, a father, but I want to continue the conversation and then maybe screw her but I would never cheat but instead would enjoy having a conversation with her. All the while she's speaking I'm wondering can I ask her out or is it going to be another should have, would have, could have, and do my usual nothing, she is talking about the good or bad, right or wrong and here I am ready to take the low road and appeal to feelings while she claims to be talking about the mind and moral reasoning and all I can think about is my penis. All of a sudden the train jerks and starts when I could have enjoyed twenty more minutes with her and most of us exit when the train finally pulls into a station not believing it can make it to another one as the motorman mumbles something into the loudspeaker, half the doors don't even open and so we crowd out, only those forced to go to Brooklyn have to stay on the train the rest of us will walk. The joys of the subway. She doesn't say let's keep in touch and I would have given her my office phone, I realized I wouldn't give her my home number; maybe we can meet again, nothing more I won't cheat and such a nice young girl chatted me up makes my day and I walk with a spring in my step even if I know I'll never see her again, and go to a meeting with my clients as I try and guide them through the labyrinth of forms needed to qualify for loans at banks, since I have this skill that can decode mortgages, open homeownership and I don't use my abilities to exploit people but make it possible for them to enjoy being a homeowner.

All of a sudden I'm this homebody, before dishes were dishes now they have to be washed, I like order but never could spare the time to clean up and now even feel self-conscious about having a cleaning woman, a domestic, how humiliating but I don't have the strength to clean after holding the baby most of the day and feel free when I can get away from all of them. My grandmother and husband seem quite adaptable to this new role, how did I get so entangled with life me who hated home economics classes in high school and now I feel I must act where before it was a treat now I need it to keep me sane. Where am I going to get the strength to do this, grandma thinks I can just stop acting everyone will understand a new mother but it doesn't work that way, if producers or directors don't see you they completely forget about you and if I take a hiatus I'm afraid I will never go back, never be able to act for the imaginative only the groundlings—it's happened to too many of my friends, a nice gig steady cash and they decide I'll only come back for the perfect part which never materializes. Maybe if I could start out on top, wouldn't that be nice. Acting is too important it defines who I am, I can work and take classes knowing that that's not me, acting is me, if I had to do them alone would sink into oblivion, I love the applause and not only do I want other people I have to see myself as an actor. I may be kidding myself but the key to me is acting, I can't give it up running lines it is too much a part of my life and too important to let it fall away, I know I'm superficial but acting is superficial always inhabiting other people but it's my way of dealing with the world—when on stage I feel so much better about myself and even if there's so much rejection in this profession the one acceptance makes up for all the failures, and the gratification allows me to put up with all the crap the constant nos and is the moment of my life. And I do have support I couldn't do all this by myself, grandma and my husband are supportive but still it is up to me to continue, I'm no longer an ingénue and the competition for mature women's roles are intense mainly because male playwrights don't know how to write for women, unfortunately, women playwrights now getting a start with feminism are so young they only see older women as shrews, parasites or a chorus of old biddies, not human beings having a life of our own, and there are so few parts for us, it would be wonderful if some playwright could write about our lives and fears; I'll be happy when these women playwrights address serious concerns not trivialize or ignore them. What the young don't understand is that we all age and while men still see us as wives, mothers or whores we are never portrayed in our own right. At least men playwrights pour out their fantasies on us women still are too afraid to do that. How can you write plays about solitude and spaces? I know the beauty of this when Joseph took the three of us to the Central Park Reservoir to see the sunset because there was so much smog in the air the sunset over the Manhattan was magnificent, colorful clouds, white clouds an orange and chartreuse sky, that's his way of liking nature in a park in Manhattan, he hates the real thing and usually won't take the time but he insisted and we walked to the park and of course Jacoba was crying and I thought he was spoiling her by carrying her all the time but he likes showing her the ducks and the refraction of light off the water, I couldn't squander my precious moments this way but he insisted and we spent a nice evening together but I can only take this nature for so long, and it wasn't even solitude there were multitudes of joggers passing us all the time, it seems as if everyone on the West Side has discovered Central Park, where only a few short years ago people were afraid to walk in this place. Still I won't go north of 96th street that is still dangerous but Joseph pooh-poohs it because he runs the whole park, says it's safe now the joggers have taken it back from the junkies. He still has the ability to take time off and enjoy artificial nature, he says he needs it or he'll go crazy and what can I say his new career is paying off, I was skeptical at first but this buying and selling seems to work. I never would have thought New Yorkers would want to own their own apartment it's so illogical to me we rent you buy a home not an apartment and we got lucky now that real estate tycoons have all these empty buildings they couldn't rent and they convinced the mayor they were on the side of progress and said you can use them for daycare facilities and charged the city exorbitant rents and since they donate large sums of money to their coffers politicians agreed and we now are beginning to have daycare centers in formerly abandoned buildings. The whole city could be out of bankruptcy if they eliminated graft for a year. President Ford told the city to drop dead, didn't even take the mayor's call, President Reagan told the Bronx go fuck yourself the government isn't going to wave a magic wand and fix this place, and both don't give a damn about corrupt city life, but Joseph thinks it forces the city to get up off its ass and not be dependent upon the federal government, but now the city is so strapped it doesn't even help theater, they never helped poor people's theater anyway but now no subsides for plays, short-sighted politicians want to cut the National Endowment for the Arts what do they think drives tourists to the city its beaches. You come to New York to see theater. Broadway shows are filled with them but we can't get them to come downtown, yet you take your life into your hands walking down 42nd street, the junkies, prostitutes, chicken-hawks, three-card-mMonte hustlers, runaways, now off-Broadway is trying to develop a response to unsafe midtown but AIDS is destroying Greenwich Village and they still haven't been able to get tourists to come see our shows, some people will go to the West Village to gawk but few will go to the theaters which are mostly in the unsafe East Village between Fourth Avenue and Alphabet City. He says if they ever buy a building they will make sure there's a theater in it and if there's a theater in it I will always have parts, but they're a long way from owning a building and are concentrating on staying small, his partner doesn't say grow or die, rather he wants to keep it a small business. A smart man I respect him. Joseph wants to invest in the Bronx, sees all those burnt-out buildings and says a perfect place the transportation is great into the city why not be the first, but Mr. Speir says wait, wait until the neighborhood begins to change who knows if the Bronx ever will, even if there are good subways into the city the Express bus has made it easy for people to travel into the city now but Joseph gets angry at that using city, state and federal subsidies for private transportation not for the subways, but it has allowed the people in the boroughs who wouldn't dare ride the subways at least come into Manhattan. He says okay we won't invest below Fordham Road but above it is still lovely, the fires haven't gotten there but Mr. Speir is skeptical and I was pissed when I heard Jahn's Ice Cream parlor closed where I would go with my girlfriends for a kitchen sink, a whole tub of ice cream, 30 scoops with as many toppings and flambéed. When my mother at first gave me ten cents for ice cream I complained said I needed a dollar for an ice cream you could never finish, Joseph replied with the same story his mother gave him ten cents for a pizza and he said we're getting a pie and his mother yelled who eats a pie. Cheapness knows no religion or ethnicity. Our mothers knew nothing of social activities. My friends from Calhoun didn't know of Jahn's mostly they were from the city and the boroughs were a phenomenon, and they wanted to go with me but I was afraid I'd see some of my old friends up there and was ashamed of them so I never took them, that's when I was carefree and could travel if I wanted to, now I have to plan around the family, Jacoba, grandma, my husband, a new type of activity, deliberation, no longer can I just act regardless of the consequences I have to think of the other, before it was only me, now the me is she and my life is on hold. Luckily I still am able to get roles downtown but my life is no longer so simple, now before I do anything have to make sure bottles are pumped, bresteria, even if I think formula is easier. Now my life is transformed from artistic purpose to maternal.

No matter how bad the pain is it could never be so bad as when I see her again, usually I'm fine until the brute fact stares me in the face, at first I wasn't even sure it was her people change over the years maybe she stopped dying her hair, cut it short, it isn't black but gray, she caught me off guard I didn't think it was her at first and usually when I see her I get a pit in my stomach even before I realize it's her that's why she caught me so off guard, when I get that feeling I quickly realize what's happening, this time I walked straight past her, she was sitting out in front of a café drinking a white wine—how can anyone sit out like that so the whole world can see you? I never liked that much rather do my drinking in a bar, she looked so French and she always liked the French that I wanted to saunter up to her and ask if I can join her and comfortably sit down beside her, yeah sure in my imagination, besides I can't stand wine it tastes like soda pop but I wouldn't have wanted to break the mood and besides I figured these little cafés only have wine not beer, and I would start chatting away saying you look good, lying through my teeth telling her how fine I am with my new family, then would give it all away by asking if we could meet discreetly just to discuss old times nothing more because I have a life now and wouldn't want to ruin it, and I wouldn't give her my phone number and we would have a nice conversation and all the while I would be scheming, I was in full body armor I had just gotten a haircut and shave at my favorite barber wearing a clean shirt not my work shirt, nothing of my work uniform when I travel in the city I leave my work clothes at home, no tie but nobody wears them anymore, my black leather pointed shoes, white socks, that I had thought looked so neat and I had bought on the spur of the moment at Florsheim and was feeling good after my haircut so was walking up Broadway and I saw her but she didn't see me and at first I wasn't sure her back was to me and as I walked wondered and crossed the street into the shade walked down a couple of blocks crossed again and walked up in the sun to make sure if it was her and I said if it was her I would go up to her and greet her if she was alone sitting outside drinking wine, a sure sign she wanted to be picked up, and I would glad-hand her, kiss her on the cheek twice, and offer to pay the check, and the closer I came the more I realized it was her, and she was just letting her hair resume its natural color, I haven't seen her in a few years, I'm not exactly sure in how many years and I don't remember her having a part on the right, usually no part but it's shorter now, and no longer curly and I noticed a little bald spot where the part is but her smooth profile skin, her smile were all the same and so when I wanted to say Esmeralda wouldn't have even said it as a question even if it was a question in my mind and I was ready if it was not her that I'm sorry I thought you were an old friend, but I was now sure it was her as I was recalling the Esmeralda of my youth, indeed as I moved towards her I was becoming more positive it was her and if she would have spotted me would have given her my cheek and acted surprised that I saw her and I felt my heart beating hard like the first time I saw her and this feeling always stayed with me even if it took a couple of sightings before I was able to get up enough courage to speak to her. How easy it is to speak to someone you don't care about. And even if she stopped loving me after twenty years of happiness I still have this crazy hope we can be friends but I'm not this young buck anymore, I no longer even run for the bus or subway not that I am afraid of a heart attack my heart is fine but my balance isn't as good and I'm now afraid of falling or slipping down the steps, I'm an old man even as I feel good inside me but now for the first time feel old in front of her sitting across from her, in my dreams, chatting away in my dreams, as the sun pours down upon my face and I pass her once more knowing I will not make another trip that would be too obvious and I can't even show her one of the aims I wanted to show her that I wasn't destroyed when she left me her sudden upheaval wasn't the end of the world, the world didn't come to an end when she asked me to leave, and I immediately think it was lucky it happened years ago because now I know couples who are divorced and still living in the same apartment because rents are so high neither can afford to move out. Two couples. But if I know two there must be more. And at our age we can't live with roommates. Still seeing half her smile was worth the pain I'm having now I just couldn't turn around because then she would have spotted me. I have been through enough and she seems happy, maybe she's waiting for someone then I couldn't intrude, maybe she realizes she lost a decent man and now mourns me even if I wasn't an intellectual and liked to relax when I came home and watch the game with a beer; a union organizer said television was bad because it would make men passive and they would never leave the home, another that it would cause sexual impotence a third ruins the eyes, I never stopped her from going out in fact encouraged it just didn't want to go with her to those silly plays she seemed to enjoy, I only got angry when she let Gloria move out she was too young to be on her own so she was pregnant and had Conchita we could have all lived together but that was the final straw for her she never loved her own daughter, I could never understand that. The only thing that angered me was not having dinner when I got home after I put my nine, ten hours in and was hungry. Rarely do we get what we expect from life but I would have liked to show her that not only have I survived but that I'm better off than before and enjoy every moment of my new life and I hope she had a good life after she left me. No I hope she had a sad life. No a good life. I can never make up my mind. I want her to have a decent life because I am a decent person and wouldn't want her to suffer but at the same time I wouldn't mind if she suffered for abandoning me. I was never as happy or unhappy as I imagined and I realize what I think about her makes no difference in her life. I could wish her evil but as long as I don't interfere in her life my wishes are nothing, I accepted my fate and could have been cool walking up to her and chatting her up but I just couldn't do it. Because spring has finally arrived and I feel good about myself in my new haircut and clothes, not in my work uniform, at least until I passed her by, all this takes place inside my head she didn't even recognize me as I passed by and even if I wasn't exactly sure the first time by the second was absolutely positive but it wasn't the same as coming upon her fresh and only now I am a little more hesitant in approaching her knowing the type of person she is while the first time I imagined her different than the way she was and now I no longer want to step into a hornets' nest of feelings even as part of me wanted to circle around her one more time and wait to see if she recognized me but I fought myself even if part of myself wanted to stop and chat I didn't want to: what would be the point to prove to myself

I could hurt myself, to show her she had no effect upon me, no hard feelings, nah I remember she wronged me by leaving me and because she did I will not forgive her and won't get involved with her again even if I stay depressed for an hour, day, week, month I will get over it.

The heart attack was a blessing in disguise got me out of this god-damned life, the doctor said I shouldn't move, don't lift anything heavy, don't smoke, don't drink my condition was such that I stopped going to the doctor, self-medicated, drank and smoked more took my grandchild to the museum I hate museums storehouse of culture for snobs thinking that art can be a bridge from working-class life onto high culture, but couldn't stand being with the family anymore, my daughter, her husband who was still affectionate to her after all these years but not a brain in his head, he gets caught stealing at work but they like him so much they don't fire him thank goodness then I would have had to hire him, family first, is what my daughter would have said, all I enjoyed being around was my grandson, he had great potential and he wanted to go to MoMA and I loved how he could become interested in art through my friend Zoltan, who he started calling Zorro and Zoltan didn't mind but now he's too old to call him that and is back to Zoltan, and how he always liked to go downtown with us when he bought art supplies or when we walked the streets, Zoltan loved walking especially in the middle of a painting, only problem was his mother wouldn't let him miss school as if he learned anything there—and how once he said to Zoltan you went to the art store without me? from then on Zoltan would only go on Saturday and insisted he learn a little Greek and less Latin, his real education, he said, was walking with him and his grandfather, I was proud of him learning dead languages, Zoltan not even realizing they don't teach writing anymore let alone dead languages, and you can't even find productions of Greek or Roman plays in the city, everything is song and dance but Zoltan felt freedom in America he could paint to his heart content here nobody cared if he was accepted, tolerated or subversive, as in Hungary after the '56 revolution, here he was ignored as most artists are unless they bring in big bucks. I felt the conformity would break his spirit but he felt alive walking the city streets like I did and we'd walk together and when Joey was capable and not want to be with his hooligan friends join us, he would continually say you can breathe in America. When he saw Paul Klee for the first time he literally said that that's what he was looking for fluid art not paint by the numbers art, which is so boring. He must have loved it being at my wife's place where all she had was paint by the numbers on the wall. I put him up when he first came here and needed a place he slept on the couch until Miriam couldn't put up with him he's taking over the living room I'm a stranger in my own house I can't use the living room and he moved into my daughter's apartment for a bit until we could find him a job as a furniture restorer then he could get a place of his own. I thought he might be depressed or something leaving his homeland but he liked walking the streets said it reminded him of the streets of Budapest, New York like Budapest I just couldn't imagine it, and after a few months found his own place on the other side of the Bronx found walking the Bronx exhilarating and loved walking the different neighborhoods, pleasurable, until he bumped into somebody who told him of a room to rent on the other side of the Bronx, and I never realized the Bronx had so many hills as when I schlepped up to his place in Riverdale. Only he said it wasn't Riverdale because it was on this side of the Henry Hudson Parkway and true Riverdale starts on the other side with its expensive private homes not apartment buildings regardless if the map says Riverdale is up on the hill, he moved in with little furniture had only a drawing book only later was he able to afford an easel and paints only we saw each other less and less as distance separated us. We still met in the city and Joey still always wanted to walk with me and we simply got in the habit of not telling my daughter especially when he played hooky and we went to the Devon theater an art deco movie palace on Tremont avenue in the Bronx. The only time he came over was the Passover meals that my daughter made and since I couldn't stand to be with my wife invited him so I would have someone to talk to, how did I ever marry her, how dumb of me I was taught only to go with Jewish girls that's all I knew were Jewish girls, did I ever think she was beautiful, maybe by default she is a constant complainer that life treated her rough, ha, she has it good indoor plumbing, a modern kitchen, living in one of the most desirable streets in New York off the grand boulevard what they called the Grand Concourse, where there are maple trees planted alongside the roadway to honor the war dead. I hope Joey doesn't marry Jewish. I didn't mind putting everything in her name what I minded was having to come back and live with her. How did I mess up my life so, I thought I was finally on the right track when I left for Spain never expecting to have to return like the prodigal son maybe I shouldn't have come back but I had nowhere to turn and was flat broke maybe if I held out a little longer something would have turned up, shoulda, coulda, didn't I couldn't live in the world I ran away from but neither could I live in the world I created, always at odds with the world and myself always trying to find happiness always doing something else, always running from myself; the doctor didn't scare me only encouraged me, he thought I would be scared and not continue as I had been not realizing I was running as I always did this time physically and I found out what I really think no more deliberations coming to the same conclusions fleeing until I could run no longer. Now I wouldn't have wanted Joey to be the one it was unexpected but not unwanted and his holding my hand made my demise pleasant at least I wasn't thinking of his screaming, bodies mangled, and no more fighting just my leaving quietly, my demise pleasurable. The Great Exterminator didn't want that. That's what Zoltan called the Angel of Death at our Passover Seder once he understood enough English but Joey said no at least he did it himself didn't send his minions to do the killing and my wife and daughter were shocked they would be talking this way, they had never heard criticism of Jews like this, and I said I couldn't imagine a God happy having killed so many people. We get what we deserve he claimed if we continue to believe in this barbarity and Miriam and my daughter called him a self-hating Jew because they had never heard such criticism. The cunning of reason escaped them. He had nothing to do with propaganda advocating nothing his painting gave him reason enough from the meaningless of life and luckily he wasn't called upon to be heroic the only time he was during the Hungarian uprising of '56 he fled, I lost my taste for heroism after seeing dead men up close their pasty faces staring blankly their body parts strewn all over the place up close—everything changes when life can no longer be lived and no amount of activity I did after I came back could erase those memories. No longer could I see paintings of human suffering never saw a Goya painting again, too unpleasant, there is no catharsis for those who actually saw suffering it only causes us to remember what we want to forget, I thought maybe away from Madrid I would be able to control my thoughts but they only became worse, even schnapps didn't help and you can't sit in the dark forever but it showed that I hadn't the slightest clue to who I was running away from Miriam then having to crawl back and she not even recognizing me my hair so short or as she said white not red, sticking my foot in the door which she finally opened taking me in even as she wanted to slam the door in my face, could have slept on the roof plenty of people did that back then especially when it was hot and you couldn't get a bit of breeze inside, instead I came home and stayed tried to be a good father and made believe I was doing the right thing until I couldn't take it anymore and moved in with my daughter. Could I have changed? I don't know. I couldn't forget that I know. Quitting guarantees you don't change maybe if I made efforts might have changed, life was a cruel taskmaster and the only way I could escape is this lying in my grave, drinking, whoring, working around did nothing for my life, she was pregnant when I came back but I raised him as if he was my own.

I never liked the man he wore too powerful cologne, jewelry and I think even mascara and Joey would say ridiculous things asking if I had an affair with him. Then I get this rare blood disease and my life is essentially over but I have seven more years to live. I never even learned its name all I did was get progressively worse and from healthy one day to feeling like crap the next, I fall down and couldn't get up and lie on the floor in pain, mostly, until my daughter arrives and calls the ambulance; it took the doctors forever to figure out what it was and then one day I'm in my home and the next an ambulance rushes me to the hospital and I never leave that place stuck in a wheelchair not even able to walk, but I can think my mind is fine so I know I'm trapped in this body then all I can wait for are visitors and the only visitors are my daughter, her husband, and my grandson only he can't be bothered and doesn't come every week he's too busy with his playmates or walking the streets with my husband and Zoltan, my daughter keeps assuring me I will get better and I want to stay alive and go to my grandson's Bar Mitzvah until I realize he's refused to have one the influence of my husband, no doubt, I married a vile evil man who has no respect for God. I should have never opened the door in the middle of the night no good came of it, I didn't recognize him I wasn't going to answer but he keeps pressing the bell and he would have awoken Molly—why did I listen to the rabbi he's not a preacher but he said my daughter needs a father and I was also pregnant but didn't know it yet with Jack, why we got along without him just fine as a bookkeeper I was making enough to pay the rent and when he left again I was able to support us all, true he did help and I had to take in Zoltan for a short while because we needed the money and he used him as an excuse to move out, his paintings were about nothing grotesque colors you couldn't see any men or women nor straight lines in his paintings and he never sold a painting, not one in his entire life unless it was to a friend who bought one out of charity finally I had to ask him to leave I thought he was such a bad influence on my younger one. Boys are so susceptible to bad influences and after my son moves away he becomes attached to Joey. Finally, Joey yells at me that I am derisively calling him a painter when he is truly an artiste according to my thirteen-year-old know-it-all grandson. What does a thirteen-year-old boy know anyway only not to have a Bar Mitzvah because of the influence of his grandfather and hanging out with the goyim smoking, sneaking on subways, he got caught we all know about it, and playing baseball in the streets—I had to buy a television set otherwise he would have never come over for a visit, otherwise he would go with my husband and Zoltan to the Central Arts supply store on 3rd Ave. and watch Zoltan buy paints, brushes, sketchbooks, he even brought him one, just what he needed. I kept seeing this gray snow on the set and when I actually went to watch a Little League game was surprised at how green the field was, it was always so gray on television, I never could understand the game no matter how many times he explained it to me. He even shut the sound off and announced the game so I would understand what was going on but he plays too much baseball and not enough studying, as soon as he gets home from school has milk and cookies and rushes downstairs to play ball with his friends, while the children of the communists, socialists, the red diaper babies are all so smart, even skipping a grade, he only wants to be a ballplayer claims his teachers know nothing teach only ideas already known, disobeys teachers, such nonsense from a baby but he gets that from his grandfather and Zoltan. He runs out as soon as he comes home from school. How can you be anything if you don't study? But Molly nor her husband can't get him to read except comic books, they destroy his mind, he buys them for a dime and sells them for nine cents, great businessman that he is, claims then he only needs a penny to buy a new one, not that he's dumb just bored, so far no teacher has realized that but I have tried taking him places only it was getting difficult to walk especially with him running so and he only wants to go to baseball games. He wouldn't even go to the Museum of Natural History with me says school takes him there enough. I wonder if he will come on children's day they hardly allow children under eighteen here not realizing that would be the best thing for me if I didn't see him daily I felt my day was wasted, I was the one who took him to school in the morning picked him up for lunch brought him back and picked him up at three o'clock in the afternoon, the highlight of my day until he didn't want to be seen with his grandma anymore. Ashamed I'm too old-fashioned. Said he wanted to walk home from school alone but he was too young to cross the streets by himself even if there were school guards at every crossing, he just doesn't pay attention he's in his own little world. Healthy one day confined here the next and now I can no longer be home alone and I can't move into my daughter's place I wouldn't be caught dead next to Jacobo, his smell even disgusts me. No choice where else can I go my son is out in California now and has no room for me. Besides I would be a stranger there. God gave me this body and I have to live in it; I cannot understand why God is doing this to me I have done what is right and respected and nobody can accuse me of being indiscreet even if I did have a child illegitimately nobody knows. God knows and is punishing me for my indiscretion. But I am not ready to go yet I do want to see my grandson Bar Mitzvahed and even if he doesn't take lessons because of his communist grandfather who once said to me my proportion of blood, phlegm, yellow and black bile makes me a depressive, the *meshuggner*, maybe someday he'll come to his senses and I want to see him say his prayers in front of the Torah, so far at least he doesn't want a Christmas tree likes his friends, but he does want Lionel electric trains as if we have any room to store them and he always goes to his friend's houses around Christmas time to play with them. But what he likes to do is burn the trees afterwards, I saw him playing with matches from outside my window in the park across the Concourse, and I was so angry told his mother what's a young boy like that crossing such a big street by himself, I had to get dressed and go downstairs to make sure he could cross safely and get home. He even plays ball in the street but not the Concourse the small street he lives on and I bring my beach chair out and watch out for him luckily not too many cars come by the side street. Once when he was five he darted across the street in the middle of the block and a car almost ran him over it scared me so I vowed to be outside and watch when he plays ball. Why was I ever born, God can take me out in a moment even if I'm not willing but I have been living an exemplary life and I won't mind being released from this body but first I would like to see him Bar Mitzvahed, ensconced in the Jewish faith not be a heathen like my husband who the rabbi said I should take back for the sake of my daughter. May he rot in hell, both of them for making my life so miserable. Now the doctor is going to stop by and tell me what I already know that it is hopeless but they always give you hope it's never it's over but we are treating it, and I can no longer live by myself and I can't live with my daughter as long as my husband is still alive. I told her I don't want him at my funeral, but he will come just to spite me. And my son-in-law just got fired from the Navy Yard, the war's been over a long time now and the government cut back his good-paying job where he would take the #7 train and see the Silvercup bread sign and now he has to find jobs in small factories which are also beginning to lay people off because they are moving down south where there are no unions, when he drove up the East River he would point to the Silvercup sign across the river and say that's where your daddy works before he was laid off. He has this job at Ketay but thinks it's soon going to be gone and they can't feed another mouth at least her husband stayed unlike mine even if my daughter cooks and cleans for three men who don't appreciate her. If God would be merciful he would let me finish my life helping my family and not rotting away in Lincoln Hospital.

Did it think it through? Did I deliberate and actually realize what I was doing or did I just up and go like I always do things, impulsively? Didn't care a whiff about the future just wanted to get out of the present, knowing only I couldn't stand this world and had to escape, don't pass Go, no need to pause and didn't even doubt that I was doing the right thing, if I thought too long over it would have done what I usually do, nothing, but this time I wanted to do something even if I had no idea what war actually meant and would have been better off not seeing those horrors that ruined the rest of my life—if only I could lead my life backwards, unfortunately we have to lead it forwards and I couldn't calculate the consequences but you can't calculate consequences all you can do is guess because if I could have thought about it wouldn't have done it but I quickly joined the Party so I wouldn't have to think about it got on the boat they called a ship the *Thersites* but when I returned wasn't the same person and had nowhere else to turn I was practically broke and didn't want to live in flop houses along the Bowery, that no longer seemed ro-

mantic like my adventure instead thought of Miriam's soft, warm eider-
down quilts but after one night with her realized my mistake, she didn't
even want to open the door and if I wasn't a little high after stopping
off in the tavern on the corner—drinking does change your character
and I started getting emotional, sentimental, and I hate sentiment, why
I shouldn't drink and I actually did miss those lugs and was almost to
tears upon seeing them again even if I hadn't thought about them once
while I was away, if only I had gone straight home instead of stopping at
Johnny's I wouldn't have been so soused and after she recognized me we
hugged and cried, but after my tears retreated into my usual silence and
sitting in the dark wondering what I was doing with my life right away
after we hugged and we never hugged before sober I couldn't stand to
be around her but you can't stay drunk forever eventually you come out
of your haze and wonder what you did even if it was delightful to see
my daughter the next morning as she jumped all over me daddy's home,
daddy's home, and hugged and kissed me. Her hugging me was the highlight of my life next to the birth of my grandson, that is, she married
a dull-witted decent man and all I thought of the marriage was that I
would have a grandchild even if they divorced but nobody divorces you
stay together or apart unhappy. It's apparent that I think by the amount
of booze I have in me, of course an Irish bar wouldn't have wine and
John the owner set me up he was glad to see me, I only learned to drink
wine in Spain, and since I can't stand the taste of beer was set up of shots
which gets me sloshed quicker. You'd think I'd be attracted to her but it
wasn't even close, no feeling whatsoever when I saw her again, I didn't
know how I felt but there was nothing remotely attractive about her in
her flannel dressing gown and face devoid of makeup, nothing changed
since I left eighteen months ago except me, you'd think she gave away my
clothes but they were still neatly hung in the closet but they no longer
fit as I lost so much weight, my toiletries in the back of the medicine
cabinet and boy did I have a hangover the next morning even told myself
I had to watch it I'm not so young anymore you can no longer burn the
candle at both ends and expect to be able to get up in the morning. And
the coldness of Miriam took all the heat out of me, one day in warm
Madrid the next in the cold Bronx. Me actually thinking I can start over
once in Spain and now back here again and that we can make a go of life
together, what was I thinking? I wasn't thinking like when I joined the

Communist Party because that was the only way to get to Spain. Then I was blackballed by the FBI and couldn't get any job I applied for before it finally dawned on me this government isn't going to let communists work and I couldn't forget my past even if I wanted nothing to do with my past I wasn't going to be able to let go of my past so quickly or easily. Banks wouldn't lend me any money but John did and he only charged a few points higher than the bank but at least I was able to open my first laundromat. When my grandson wanted to go to Aviation High School to learn a trade Zoltan said that Music and Art would be a better school you have to start early to learn art you can't play catchup and you can always learn a trade but you need a good education I insisted then he go to Music and Art and not be a tradesman, you can always be an apprentice but have to get your education while young before life gets in the way. Finally now that I'm dead I realize that simply getting along is not enough in life you need something deeper you actually have to live and living life is thinking life not simply following your desires: I escaped this life by being a soldier boy if I truly wanted to leave this life all I had to do was walk out the door not run away just say this isn't the life for me and I want to do more, it would have left them in a lurch but I didn't have to live with her to support her, I could have rented a place a few blocks away and still seen my daughter, nobody divorced back in the day except rich socialites who ran away to Reno, if I went to Spain could have gone to Reno I never cared for what others thought but yes I did otherwise I would have done it not wait until my daughter was old enough and move in with her. I couldn't have done that what I did had to be theatrical even if I hate the theater with its make-believe ways, pitter-patter and shallow optimism and distrust actors miming or changing reality, it's all easy to see now lying in the cold ground there is no punishment or reward your life is your judgment, I had no character didn't allow for real thought serious deliberation and that character is more important than action, if only I learned this before but I loved to act without thinking and even if I acted for all the right reasons, which I made up before and afterwards: I should have learned how to distinguish chaff from wheat go through the horn not the ivory but it's difficult to escape your past especially your gut feelings and get beyond the emotional to wisdom.

Why Oedipus complex I'm the one with the boobs, if you start from somewhere you have a fixed point to see how far you've come but if you have no fixed point how do you know how far you've come especially if you have nothing to hold on to—thinking has to start from somewhere, aimed at something, but all I have been doing is avoiding thought doing spur of the moment things that no one else does, I'm not strong like a lesbian, what's wrong with me already bored with good sex that I told myself would last a lifetime, that I convinced myself I would never cheat never get bored again, and I enjoy being with him; or as grandma says he's a wonderful person and I agree with her I am lucky he helps around the house, helps? he does it all, even brings the baby to me in the middle of the night so I could breastfeed, what's wrong with me can't I feel happy with what I have, after the baby was born we didn't have sex, of course, we were too tired but now we're having it again but how come I keep fantasying having with other men, not that I would do it, of course, but when I see a good-looking man on the subway my mind immediately flashes to us having sex and I think of him when I'm with Joseph, interestingly I thought it would be with the professor or a director but my mind never ever flashes unto them, once I went out with a professor who claimed he was a theater historian and lectured in London part time, sounded interesting, but he didn't know of Caryl Churchill or Howard Barker and did silly things academics did including lie about his travelling to London. I'm not a kid anymore okay in my twenties could hop from man to man and enjoy it but thought eventually I would outgrow it, settle down then I found Joseph and told myself this is it, it could work so I'm older than him he's a true gentleman, still stands when a lady enters the room, of course he now does it for show but nobody even gets that meaning anymore, grandma even had to tell me I never saw that before. What about intimacy, commitment, Joseph has it but do I need it also really all I want is my own immediate pleasure not even gratification but a nice feeling and each time get myself deeper in a hole wondering if I want to live this way instead of having a plan when these urges come all over me. I know I shouldn't that's what I believe but I'm hooked on the excitement and when I get it am horrified that I did it and can't wait to go home again—back in the day women had so few options at least now I have choices, sometimes I even laugh at all the choices I have, if I have choices why can't I choose; is what I am doing natural? What is natural? I always fall short of what I think I should be. However, there is a big difference when you love your husband and family and when you don't. Now because I do I am lonelier than I ever was. If you are stuck with a man you can't stand at least you know what your penance is, but if you are with a man you love how can you always want another. I'm not bad I don't want to be bad but still how can you stay with one man, are women built for monogamy? Granted we needed a man to take care of us, and father our children but we don't anymore can't we change? Grandma couldn't have Jacobo's child without a husband it just wasn't done but there are single parents all over the place now, one wag even suggested you could date the collapse of western civilization the moment middle-class women started having children without being married, no longer was it an illegitimate child but a single parent. Grandma had good instincts thought she wasn't going to force him to come back to her by telling him she was pregnant he had to come back to her of his own free will, and when he didn't her parents set her up to give her legitimacy. But all that is history. Now women have a chance to be free, and don't even have to wear his wedding ring, he does but not because he considers himself married but because he likes jewelry, I don't because it's none of my colleagues business to know if I am married or not besides married men love women who are married for their dalliances, safe, but I like the whole shebang the flirting, the daydreams, and if a man isn't what he says he is, I don't put up with it and leave, the sexually explicit dramas now mean more than ever and if it inhibits decent souls who don't want to get involved with a married woman somehow those are the ones I like, a little adventure. Of course we have to be careful now and I do carry condoms. I'm a free-thinking woman who has no use for tradition and like to carry my home on my back and as Joseph says I'm the only woman he ever knew who reads in the bathroom. It's not true of course but it shows how few women he actually knew. And grandma told me that Jacobo would actually carry *Hamlet* to the front in his knapsack but when he got home he must have felt all his dreams were absurd and just wanted to get back to the ways things were before and Joseph said he once told him before he died when he confused his age that he had learned nothing in life and each of us thinks we know it all when young and die realizing we learned nothing. He even called book learning stupid, silly, but he was always arguing with books I've seen some of his books all penciled up marginal notes, occasionally answering the author usually just saying grow up. Joseph said his grandfather couldn't read without a pencil and eraser and Joseph continues that tradition but he thinks about what he does I always skirt by on feelings never having a final goal in mind except maybe escaping from one situation into another, every time I finished with one man would find myself back in the same mess all over again with another, that they wanted to live with me but I didn't want to be with them when the sex became routine, I hate passive sex. I loved it when they ate my vagina did it up the ass, but then I wanted more and they always wanted the same, I was raised to think a woman couldn't be without a man and young I was attractive enough to have them hang around me like flies with unfailing grace and I would usually pick the wrong one before Joseph came into our life. What's wrong with me this is not natural. If this is not natural, why do I keep doing this? You have to play the hand you're dealt. I tried to be a good wife and mother heaven knows I tried but those first months home were a killer, I told them to leave me alone after 8 o'clock I'm dead, but if I could have seen where my acts led but I can't see ahead willy-nilly and when I looked at grandma knew I didn't want to end up like her, oh I love her but pinning for one man only one man I want no part of that, my so-called old girlfriends would show off their cherished babies as proud possessions not realizing they would leave them one day and then where would they be, Yolonda even wrote me a letter saying she was seriously ill and wanted to see me why? we broke over twenty-five years ago we have nothing in common and I've bumped into her a few times and we can laugh for a moment but it goes no further and now she wants to see me. If she wanted to see me she had twenty-five years, it may ease her conscience but I don't want to see her ill especially after twenty-five years. It has taken me forever to realize all the nonsense I was taught and finally said enough is enough just like grandma got her first husband to fight against fascism to get rid of him it took longer for her to ask Tomas to leave both were so accommodating didn't want to put up with her moods I am a little more sophisticated than grandma and want more from men than just protection all they saw was her beauty and weren't able to look behind it to see a mind at work but men never give women credit for hav-ing a mind only beautiful. Still I have trouble expressing myself getting a grip on my thoughts if I'm thoughtful I must be evil. Eve is seduced not in solidarity with the snake, Helen is punished for running away with a handsome man instead of staying with a quarrelsome old biddy, I remember Joseph explaining those things to me things he studied but that I grasped intuitively, and made sure to take classes that discussed what Joseph was talking about, at first I felt strange walking into a bookstore and then the clerk said we don't have romance novels here but mystery novels are over in the corner when I asked about philosophy he said we don't have those either, luckily in the Village we had 8th street and three bookstores where you had all the philosophy books you wanted then I found Fourth Avenue with all their used bookstores and you could find any book you ever dreamed of in one of these. Grandma says she learned English by reading the Greek tragedies then seeing them acted upon the stage, the stage was her English teacher. She loved going to plays that had little movement and talked straight so she could understand what was going on. Shakespeare was too difficult for her at first, language-wise not idea-wise. She loved America she said it was the future buildings torn down even before they were completed. After the second world was she laughed at the Germans and Polish who chose to rebuild their bombed-out cities as Disneyed versions of history—wouldn't people appreciate indoor plumbing, elevators, laundromats. Here now we have one of the greatest cities of the world and politicians let it go to ruin because women want freedom and it's safer to keep them home locked up or need a man's arm to walk the streets at night. Whenever women start wanting freedom men start getting uptight not allowing us to enjoy the novelty and excitement of sexual freedom. Now we have squatters living anywhere, drug addicts roaming the streets at all hours, once I was breastfeeding in the park and out pops some junkie and says can I have next? I never ran out of the park so fast. Good housing stock going to ruin, kids dropping out of high school and hanging on street corners to all hours who enjoy getting women pregnant but have no thought of the consequence of babies, all destroying life of the mind but at the same time off-off-Broadway is doing serious production and we get good theater within all this squalor as grandma says because when she first came to the Village nada, zilch there weren't even cafés where writers could connect only bars, thank goodness for cafés on the weekends otherwise I'd go crazy home with Jacoba.

How boring I've become, work, childcare, dinner, in bed by 9:30 and get up and do it again the next day. Did I plan it to happen this way? I was the 'kid'! The 'kid' strikes out, no longer am I playing at life, life has now become serious I have a child to support a family, I just can't get up and leave, can't even go for a walk when I want to, or eat when I feel like it, now when I walk it is somewhere, I almost feel like calling Harvey, my high school buddy, since I have become just like him, even if I never wanted to be like him—Rochelle an old high school fling called to invite me to an opening of hers but she couldn't even invite me she insisted I bring my wife along, why we weren't lovers, barely second base, Bronx ghetto mentality, but I do remember giving her a massage and wanting to enter her backwards but too afraid, the brain and penis evolved at different times; she has no talent except for self-promotion—be careful I hear an inner voice saying but she was too hot for me back then when we had this little adventure when a neighbor had the temerity to yell at us to shut-up while we were sitting on the stoop at 2 in the morning on a weekday and calls the cops on us, all we were doing was making noise and hanging out outside the building and he calls the cops, we get even by ordering pizza and Chinese food take out in his name for two weeks, but I'm not the same as back then and she could have changed as well but I doubt it she'll always be sixteen in my head—her talent was always for pleasure not thought, not even fragments of thought, art should be pretty she always claimed, having a different interpretation of painting than I did and to her pleasure was pleasing to the eye not struggling with a work of art as Zoltan did making it pleasing to the mind, Zoltan would compare paintings to spices each spice has a unique flavor but when combined a totally different flavor, I enjoy a pleasurable work of art but it also has to force me to reflect not just admire causing me to jump start my mind getting me to put thoughts next to images and that gives me pleasure, the combined effects of the eye and mind, be careful, be careful, I say to myself thinking about Rochelle is forcing me to think about myself can she be considered a 'shiksa goddess' I always think of them as Wasps but she was Irish—not substantial but a manifestation of something else, what? how did I get this way? did I choose? Well yes but I didn't think it through knocked on Cassandra's door and became attached and thought wow to be with a woman like that what would my friends say even if the truth is they don't think about me as I don't think about them—there's probably a symmetry of thought. I wanted her no questions asked but do I want all that comes with it, yes I did I imagined playing house with her but I had no idea what that actually meant, it was simply a wish that came true, heaven help you if you get what you want, I just went along it's easier to go along than stop and reflect but then that would have meant I wanted it I could have left but it shows it was deliberate in my choice even if it wasn't me who made that decision, but then who would it be. who made the choice? I who made the choice or the choice made me? The choice had to be because of what I did and willed even if I cannot remember actually making a choice it had to be what I wished for otherwise I could have walked away thinking must have made it so. She became pregnant by accident, she is too old all the doctors said pregnancy at your age is high risk until one of the doctors said pregnancy at any age is risky but you're in good health you should be fine and she chose him, and she probably thought it will never happen again and even if she wasn't old she was not that young decided to go through with it— she worked so hard for it, it wasn't an easy pregnancy but she continued working and acting, not afraid to show off her pregnant body on stage, not content to wear those big wide dresses she let her belly show, and now not ashamed of her body nurses in public with a little towel over her, all of a sudden I was a father but no amount of thinking about being a father can prepare you for the actual experience of being a father— they're so tiny I was afraid to hold it at first but once they snuggle in your arms you're hooked for life, I love watching her sleep, which of course she never does I never was so tired in my life and it isn't fair that after four weeks had to go right back to work, Cassandra claims she now works much harder than me, and I believe it when she puts her in my arms, Jacoba awakens each morning at 5:30 like a little CEO that I don't even need the alarm anymore. At least her day job gives her maternity leave even if she occasionally works from home. I should have stayed at the railroad they give women a year off with the birth of a child and of course the women never came back just took the leave. A good union perk. My father was disappointed I quit that job good pay and a good pension but I couldn't imagine giving up my life for a pension, maybe Jacoba will do the same to me: now I like to imagine myself a simple union worker with no difficulties, but recalled didn't want Cassandra to think of me as a worker not a thinker but now realize I was just using her image for what I wanted to do even if I didn't grasp it then, I didn't want to be a worker I wanted more from life than just a good income and pension, I wanted to learn to think. Biology is destiny I can no longer play with abandon—ah the magical images of childhood I never played with abandon only jumped on the bed with freedom until my grandfather came in the room. Her desire meant deliberation and I went along for the ride thought it would be cool to be a daddy not really understanding all it takes to be a father, the man responsible for a family. I should have known better my divorced male friends refuse to have another child with the next woman and lose them but they rather lose them than take on the responsibility that entails of raising another child. Brave new world. But they make a choice what choice did I make they have power over their decisions I was afraid to be left alone; if I could have held on a few more years ought can become an is, but I always imagined myself married from early college days on and my friends would envy me that I was starting out on life so early and we'd have a kid—all posturing is baloney, the difference between desiring and needing. Shall I leave? Wouldn't think of it love Jacoba and Cassandra and Esmeralda and wouldn't have it any other way except inside my head where I am never satisfied, I can't live alone no matter how much I dream of living alone, solitude is beautiful but only in small doses and want to ring up Rochelle even if it's only a cute fantasy but to actually do something would be an anathema to me, but she did say you were the man I let get away, but she had too much self-hatred to love, and I could barely stand her in high school why would I like her as an adult. Just because I'm married should that mean I can't play around inside my head. We married not because of financial reasons, or for the health insurance there was not ulterior motive we loved each other; is it cheating if I imagine playing the field. Don't ask why but now that I wear a wedding ring women flock to me. Where were they when I was sixteen. I wondered if living with her would make a difference with a piece of paper and it does I feel much closer now with the marriage certificate. She said to me it feels the same and we both liked the idea of living together and I didn't think it would make a difference but it has. Maybe I'm making too much of this I don't have to explain my action to anybody except I keep explaining it to myself and think it's endearing to be home with a wife and a child and live in a brownstone on the Upper West Side instead of an apartment in the East Village, the place is so huge Esmeralda suggested we get a house manager, and I'm not too worried about supporting them I am making so much money now in this new company it happened so quickly that buying the building at the insider's price seemed too good to pass up, and all these contractors gave us a good rate to renovate because they wanted future deals with us. Imagine to be out of checking plus and have some savings. My partner convinced me to do this before the baby was born and when I told him we were planning on marrying and he said let's do this before you have no time to change careers you can deal with people and understand complex rules of real estate law even if never took, or would even have thought of taking a business course, the technical requirements were easy as he said but it's having a soul that counts and I naively thought all I would have to do is drive people to the apartment so I would have to get a fancy car to show people I am successful but it didn't work out that way, New York is a rental city and the difficulty is getting people to think of apartment ownership the way people think of home ownership as something to pass on to the children or save on taxes but now with men and women working taxes seems the strong point. As usual I didn't think this through just thought it would be fun to do something different and who expected such an increase in revenue. I can't call Rochelle she never went through an artistic crisis she's still the same old high school girl.

It's a total change in my inner landscape no longer do I see my life as a toilet bowl but now it has a purpose, I have to be with her, see her, watch her smile, hold her close to me, if I miss it one day feel unanchored, no longer do I fall down and am afraid to stand up, I now enjoy just watching her lie in her crib, with Gloria I went crazy even Conchita was difficult at first an angry teenager ruining my calm but with Jacoba I finally feel as if I have a purpose in life, it may not be God-given but it is deep within me and justified now by all my actions. Motherhood is not my primary goal but now I stay home all the time to be with her and when the weather is nice we walk in Central Park, at least on the outer ridges of it I'm still afraid of the park by the reservoir but now there are more joggers out and the park is becoming safer, still I have to be careful there are glassine envelopes and needles in the playground part so I usually won't go in there even if Jacoba can't walk yet. And Joseph is much more serious now it's crazy how fatherhood changes a man no longer seeing himself as the kid but a responsible father who likes to come home at night and play with the baby, but Conchita seems to be the same as before only a little distant, I assume the postpartum depression that affects women after giving birth, thank goodness babies are cute or none of them would be alive they are so much work, feeding, pooping, crying, sleeping that's all they do. And now we're too tired from being with her all day to read, listen to music, and all we can do is get into our PJs early and watch television and they have a big one—standard size is now 27 inches not 13 back in the day. Conchita isn't around much at night doing a show but she pumps a lot and if she doesn't we have difficulty since the baby doesn't like the bottle and will only take it when famished and not without letting us know she doesn't want it. Conchita now needs her freedom, the acting, researching the part, the rehearsals, more than ever otherwise she's afraid she will become only a mother, as if that's the worst epithet that can occur to a person, but she's not alone in that regard, there are few stay-at-home mothers on the West Side all I see are grandparents, nannies and an occasional man out with the baby and some of us have started calling the parks department demanding they clean up the park in the morning getting rid of all the drug paraphernalia and it seems to be working. You now rarely see mother's not working and Joseph complains if he walks Jacoba to the park at night he has to stay a bit in the twilight because working women are afraid to be alone in the park but he makes up for it as he gets to see boobs, he likes to say as women are now more brazen and breastfeed in the street. One women even was arrested for breastfeeding indecent exposure what could men see that's so exciting in a woman feeding a baby, luckily the judge and it was a male judge threw it out of court, but you never know I'm sure the woman was frightened, some old biddy complained she was showing her breast in public. Made the papers, I think it happened in Brooklyn certainly wouldn't here on up on the Upper Red Side. Women now are anything but mothers, a friend of Conchita's had to come back from living in Rome where she considered herself a foreign correspondent occasionally writing for papers and magazines to take care of her father after her mother died and now is a full-time English teacher so depressed of being deprived of her identity, and once a week spends the night in the Chelsea Hotel and makes believe she's back in Rome, but she too is trapped in a role not of her choosing, women it seems never can have a life of their own. She has brothers why can't they help? Patriarchal rationalizations, women are caregivers. No matter how much this culture changes women are still responsible for the home fires, but now I'm glad to do it and I see how important it is for women to keep the home, Joseph tries but he still does the bare minimum, fortunately now he makes so much money we can have Sally to clean up all our shit. Conchita wants to hire a full-time nanny but I refuse to allow it I want to raise her for as long as I'm capable but I do take her to daycare a few hours a week just to get some rest—daycare is more expensive than college, and she does get more stimulation from them than at times she gets from me, all she gets from me is my undivided attention and love, which Joseph and Conchita insist is more important than stimulation so we do both. You have to see things by the spirit not just the eye. We have to raise our own children yet when I see me the poor who still stay home and raise them because they have no marketable skill all they do is sit in front of the television they are so overwhelmed by infants. I now work in a shift and am relieved when my shift is over and now take naps in the afternoon I never took naps in the afternoon now it's almost my nap time, but if I'm with Jacoba don't however if she's in daycare that day collapse into my bed. Still I would have it no other way, and when Joseph or Conchita thinks it's too much for me and want to treat me like an old lady I say don't you dare. My life doesn't always have to be self-centered I can enjoy the little changes of nothingness held together by who knows what maybe it is a continuous whole but it has separate compartments and I love it when people think I am the grandmother. Nobody up here knows any other part of me and nobody will if I have something to say about it, this life now has some purpose to it missing for such a long time. My favorite time now is pushing the carriage into the park, looking at the trees then down to Jacoba smiling as we walk along the edge and listen to the birds, and I have a nice conversation with her, no baby talk, and I can't wait to take her across the park to the museum, only I'm afraid I will get lost, walked across the park the first nice spring day and somehow ended up in a circle back where I started, but I laughed and realized one of these days I'll get the hang of the park, it's huge. It's also fun to sit and talk to other grandmas or the occasional men, the nannies are so ignorant I can't understand how parents would allow a caregiver who won't take the baby out of the stroller, won't smile, or won't even talk to the baby except to say you're small so what you say doesn't matter. At least the nannies from Jamaica passed the British A level finals and come here looking for work but even to them it must be humiliating. One of them even brought out a chess set and would play by herself since nobody else would play with her not that they were playing with the baby they just didn't know how. I surprised myself by enjoying it, as a young girl always wanted to be active and just couldn't sit and concentrate if the knight goes here the queen has to move here, and gave it up until I started playing with Jacobo once again and he was surprised saying you don't play like a girl, men somehow are always surprised if women play chess aggressively, know how to play combinations and have tactics. But like Conchita gave it up because I have to keep moving, motion is my set role, all other things are finite but movement is infinite, constant flux and after Jacobo hadn't played until I taught Conchita, I just felt so unwelcome in those dimly lit chess clubs that populated the Village even if I would occasionally play in Washington Square Park I much preferred watching to playing besides I could beat them in a minute even if I never liked those five-minute games it takes the beauty out of chess and was disappointed when the Sunday *Times* dropped its chess column I did enjoy solving their chess puzzles. I always love being by myself but can be with others as well, in fact I need others even if every time I'm with them I want to escape and be by myself and I oscillate between the two as Conchita who hates to be in a bad play but knows she can't quit even if the role is of no challenge and has to force herself to get something to flow, it's amazing she says how few roles there are for mature women, the men have the best speeches, lines, and define the issues, women play helpers and have to pat their hand and smile a lot, most of the staging is excellent, acting good, scenery fine but playwriting is getting weaker as more plays become television sitcoms. She thought with more women entering the field plays would have more substance make the women's parts bigger and more interesting, but it's still male-dominated, especially producers and she has vague thoughts of becoming a producer herself but she has enough on her plate right now and as a new mother can't do anymore, Joseph says he will support her but she refuses to see herself as supported by a man, no matter what she can't explain it any better than that like the first time she heard the word tiffin she thought she heard Teflon, Joseph thought *tefillin*, the phylacteries worn by the orthodox, but I thought everyone knew that word as a light midday meal when I never had heard of the term brunch. Now I love going with Conchita, Joseph and Jacoba and we can sit outside and drink mimosas or Bloody Marys—any excuse to get out and cafés are appearing up and down Columbus and Amsterdam Avenues, even if I feel weird living here me a Village girl never thought I would leave thought they would carry me out feet first from my apartment I'm getting to like the vibe here because of the park even if I never saw myself as a beatnik still I liked being around them and enjoyed walking the streets of the Village. Joseph had found a huge three-bedroom apartment in Riverdale on the other side of the highway the expensive section, and a great deal not Manhattan prices, nice neighborhood not ravaged by drugs good schools and close to the express bus or the railroad that could get us into the city within a half hour, but the streets roll up by 8 and Conchita put her foot down and said we're not going back to the Bronx where I was bored culturally and intellectually, and here I am liking the West Side with its banality and conformity, the side streets are still unsafe to walk at night and there are few cafés.

I don't really like it here it's too quiet, parks everywhere, not that I'm a stranger in a strange land I went to school here, but then I was only allowed to walk on the main streets the side streets were unsafe, Hispanics lived there—Broadway was truly divided the west side was for whites the east for Hispanics and blacks but Joseph found this lovely town house and this old woman sells the building because her husband died and she wants to move to Florida I thought he was crazy but he saw the future, and he's good at spotting trends and said this side of Broadway is on the rise, an O'Neal's has opened on 72nd and Columbus and it's not just the people from Central Park West going there, you can't get them to walk the side streets, but new groups of people are moving in, he meant fags now called gays, and they have a lot of money since they don't have kids—and he is correct the area is changing, the architecture lovely, the brownstones being changed into apartments with facades and cornices being restored, steps instead of stoops. I thought it was so cheap because it was dangerous and people were making lists as we moved in but he said nowhere as dangerous as the East Village and it has parks all around it. Yea but who's going to walk in Central Park. And this block is on a high school block with all the rowdy kids getting out at 3. But he said he did a sociological investigation and found that the kids ran off this block quicker than you can say Jack Robinson, they want to get as far away from their school as possible, and what made this brownstone so desirable is here is where Jamil Abdullah Al-Amin also known as H. Rap Brown was caught after robbing the Red Carpet Lounge claiming he was a Muslim cleaning up the area of drug dealers. An interesting career change, near here was also the Continental Baths which turned into Plato's Retreat, and we can go and be the only ones who really want to swim. The paperwork was enormous I don't know how he did it banks didn't want to invest in the neighborhood it was redlined but as he bluntly put it he was able to take advantage of the empty space where white banks, real estate agents, brokers wouldn't go and when banks put all sorts of obstacles in his way he just waited them out, paid the fees, all their missed appointments, demanding of in-person interviews and eventually by dint of hard work was able to get the mortgage and the idea of helping other minorities get mortgages by helping them fill out the paperwork and guiding them through the shit. Esmeralda was proud of him I didn't care so much for his do-goodism. He dealt with one problem after another the banks had put so many obstacles in his way but he negotiated until he found a bank or really a banker willing to give it a go when one banker said we don't invest in colored neighborhoods wrote to the president of the bank shocked, shocked I'm telling you what this banker said and finally was able to secure a mortgage, I don't know how he could put up with so much bullshit, bankers, lawyers, meeting after meeting and where he told me to sign I did I did he made sure I was an equal partner and I was worried I would be equally liable but he said the reverse if I die you'll have easy access to the place and not have to deal with the courts, always thinking ahead except he wouldn't die only his hair turned gray from the negotiations. One day I noticed it was all gray not brown. How did that happen? I wondered if it would turn white and he'd really look like an old man but it stayed gray and gave him a distinguished air, men age better than women and after months of negotiating we finally renovated, he even had grandma's bathroom renovated so she would be able to get in with a walker, if needed, which meant refurbishing the whole bathroom because you couldn't open the door when he widened the door frame because the toilet was too big so he had it replaced with a small oval toilet with a bidet, and we moved into the bottom two floors and rented out the top to help pay the mortgage and what he thought was so easy became a nightmare in reality because it was difficult to find quiet tenants, and we didn't realize how expensive it was to renovate what did I know about such things I'm Hispanic and avoided banks, my friends congratulated me in finding someone who knew how to do all these things, bringing someone in the family who knew how to make money and contractors veered over backwards to help because of future work and get on his good side for the new buildings he was restoring, parts of the city are now undergoing a metamorphoses as joggers were driving drug dealers out of Central Park, home buyers are changing the shape of neighborhoods making the poor, black, Hispanic uncomfortable in their own neighborhoods eventually forcing them to leave. Or as the co-op mongrels put it there is no hereditary right to apartments or as grandma said a hereditary disease affects us all. Not me Joseph said. I don't believe in original sin. Still other parts of the city did remain a cesspool of decay and he was right this neighborhood had more potential than our old even if an actor friend said he would never walk down that block and he was built like a brick shithouse but he lived in Rockland County and any Hispanic was a threat to him. The surprise for me was the street people who weren't drug dealers but people who just lived in too small apartments and would hang out on the steps they were a blessing in disguise warning us of drug dealers, and greeting me anytime of night that I came home always out so the street was full of people and you wouldn't get mugged with people on the street. We were in a pioneer neighborhood that was about to reach the take off stage from a traditional blighted area to one where new stores were opening up along the avenues and other apartments on the block were being renovated and from there it was a single step to maturity a full-blown neighborhood and soon the police were forced to actually ride down the block not simply stay on the main avenues that they were doing in the East Village but patrol the blocks as tenant associations formed and created block patrols and the streets were reaching ripeness. You knew the neighborhood was changing when Burger King tried to move in and the residents opposed it, and boy did love their crispy French fries. And Joseph said when Parnassus opened a used first edition bookshop that is the sign the neighborhood tipped only college graduates read. Grandma likes the place because it is close enough to the Calhoun School where she sent me but I like PS 9 but both think it as apartheid but it is a good school because parents from other neighborhoods are sending their children here even if it is outside their district. But we have time to worry about schooling and even if I believe in public education am frightened to gamble Jacoba's future with classes of 35 or 40. Joseph says he's not against public education only what they do to kids there. Esmeralda and Joseph like the greenery Central Park, Riverside Park, not just Tompkins Square Park, which is an outhouse compared to these huge areas—walking in either direction two three blocks and we are in sunny green spaces that are becoming safer as more joggers and dog walkers use them. The neighborhood is changing all around us, the bar where H. Rap Brown fled and was shot after aiming a gun at a cop closed and in its place is a copy shop. At least on the Upper West Side ghettoization was coming to an end.

I never could see myself as a caregiver, I smile as I say this and look over at Jacoba napping, even when married did as little as possible only wanted to escape my family, do as little as possible for them, not care for my parents, never had the ability to make life pleasant for anyone including myself—never had that pause, that artistic pause Jacobo always talked about, where you stop and wonder what you're doing is correct and artists who have it and survive it go on to make serious works otherwise go through life blithely now realize it was deeper there was nobody to make a home for if I did it could have been learned, I could have gotten better with experience but experience is nothing without thought but what did I learn from experience after each event I retreated back to exactly the way I was before it's only when I started realizing sensations are not all that I started to learn—it's like those superstars on television who always talk about practicing and practicing that's why they're so great, as if all boys don't do that, but they forget to mention that only one in a million becomes a professional; something is needed to make us dig deeper, something beyond mere skill, a desire, and to live a decent life you have to desire to do so it won't happen automatically, luck and a combination of other factors, and I've been lucky not letting the negative throw me off course, I made mistakes, the men in my life can attest to that, but didn't let that become the alpha omega of my existence—too often for women the man becomes determines their life and even if I always hoped to be with Jacobo again, one of my aims was getting to the States to spy him out: I never dared say that before there I said it but so what I didn't follow never went up to the Bronx to look for him, never sort him out in the phone book, true I went to the March on Washington but there it was for equal rights for Negroes, not true went with the Abraham Lincoln Brigade not that I knew any of them beforehand but hoped Jacobo would be present, even if he was dead, only I didn't know that then. My living was only in my head even if I wanted to follow him to the ends of the earth, now I need Jacoba. Joseph laughs finds it difficult to believe old people have lives thinks that's the province of the young yet when I finally made my way here with a husband in tow decided I couldn't, wouldn't, shouldn't do that, afraid of doing had never stopped me before and I never set foot in the Bronx until long after he was dead when Joseph took me up to the Bronx Botanical Gardens and by then I thought I was free of him—boy do I lie to myself everything I say about him is a lie, including this, and that has hindered me in my life it affected what how I should live but until I realized I might die never changed a thing even if I knew it was over in reason but not inside my mind where I kept believing what could have been only now that I found it difficult to walk up three flights of stairs and started getting dizzy and am even afraid of being alone in the dark, did I change my point of view. You can't change only one part of your past because who knows who knows where the change will lead but at least moving up here allows me the freedom to go out and about without having to think of climbing up three flights of stairs, forcing me out only once a day. Now I've begun to live not fantasize and how to make it happen here and am trying to make things well in my loving Jacoba, no longer will I be held captive to an imaginary goal but rather a real live physical baby, who won't be a baby much longer but will always be my baby even if I have to tell myself I am lucky as I had to teach myself I wanted two plush towels in the bathroom one to dry myself and one to wrap around me after a shower but I did it and afterwards said why did I wait so long for such a pleasure—don't postpone joy! I was never guided by what others thought and forced myself to wonder what I want and even if I thought poorly it was mine not something given to me from the outside. My thoughts are usually incomplete there is no sort of standard for judging maybe there is in learning a skill but not in life, it was easier to move in with them than not, yet even then knew I would not be a reflection of my husband, but had to become what I wanted to be even if I had little clue what that meant, that takes time, you have to be at least forty, forty-five before you can learn to think, but time alone is not enough you have to be able to come to a place you feel comfortable not hating being there—one skill I did have was the ability to make a living, when I didn't have the right pedigree here to be a nurse figured out there are other ways to nurse, and I could be alone and that cast a long shadow and I could travel to the States and begin to feel pleasure walking the streets here in the city, and all the pleasure I had here being by myself was better than the thing itself, the home but that thing is now changing now I am finally being able to stay home now I'm thinking about my long-playing records was actually better in itself than in the thought about it. Also Joseph bought me a new-fangled CD player and I have to admit the music sounds better on one of these if it doesn't just crap out as it sometimes does, I am finally learning how to be myself, growing up learned that from Jacobo even if he couldn't do it himself, I did say I would let him go after twenty-five years, another lie said to myself but at least I don't think of him with the same intensity, even if I do test and compare everything to how I think Jacobo would react, I now can care for other people and see what makes them happy and help them except most people lead such desperate lives I wanted more than that, a man would make me happy, a child would make me happy, a grandchild would make me happy, a job would make me happy, more money would make me happy, until they realize nothing can make them happy unless we make evaluations and find the balance. Certainly not being yourself and only living for others can't be the purpose of a woman. Tomas's family was still in Puerto Rico when we needed help and by the time we moved them here Gloria was five and I no longer needed them but at least we raised her decently until she got the wrong ideas into her head and had a mind of her own that she was so caught up in she couldn't see straight and thought who gets the most things in life wins, a nice hedonistic calculation but she didn't figure having a baby as a substitute for life puts you out of the running—she refused to develop a sense of self and wouldn't think only feel and never could have long-range plans she would not worry about the consequences thinking that by doing she was leading the good life, you don't start out knowing you start out doing and experience that is only physical never gets us beyond our animal nature: anybody can drink anybody can do drugs but it takes a moment of thought to say wait if I do this now I won't be able to get up tomorrow morning and think. Or what do I want out of life to be with these jerks all the time. There are no perfect choices you have to condition yourself to search for that not simply go with the flow, now I'm making a much more strenuous effort with Jacoba than I ever did with Gloria or Conchita, with Gloria I thought it would happen naturally but she only became a stick in the mud at least I insisted Conchita get an education so she could have the ability to change, revise preconceived notions of what living is all about—we don't know only have preconceived fantasies and only when confronted with a crisis do we begin to conceive how we want to live and break away from experience and develop a spirit observe our life and love becoming not being; we're not angels we don't have total knowledge only partial knowledge and we have to learn to use that or we never learn new ways of thinking. Stop crying Jacoba I'm here.

Does anybody know the real me all they have are images of me all I have are pictures inside my head and both have very little to do with who I was—all the people who know me only knew a small portion of me the shadow of me and I cast a big shadow but there was nothing behind it. How do you know a person? What we know is mostly what we see and I was this idealistic person who wanted to make this world better even as my wife thought I was running away from family responsibility by making a fool of myself running off fighting in a war I had no reason to fight in. The draft occurred later but then our government didn't want me being a communist and the government had no interest in my combat experience even blackballed from the army because the government didn't want veterans of the Abraham Lincoln Brigade, good I was drinking too much then to probably be of any use, what people thought of me had some resemblance to truth I was a bum who barely survived but that still wasn't me all the time I was drinking would tell myself to stop yet there was a kind of pleasure in just being and not having to think and accepting my fucked-up life without torturing myself in trying to understand why I followed orders or worrying about one moment to the next. The older I became the less I knew myself, my memories were reminders of what I had done but I could never grab on to them they grabbed me and let me go grabbed me again one moment smelling the aroma of the dead another gaping holes in their body due to the shelling, and when the fighting was over the dreams began. I wanted to be friends with my employees but had them call me mister—I am not who I am; would cry myself to sleep many a night wondering if I could change this and to my surprise my tears were warm, I knew I would have to stop but I had to get it out of my system nights were the worst and it was easier to go bed blotted than kill at daybreak, and not have to dream and see his face over and over again the man I killed at daybreak who yelled 'long live Stalin, long live Stalin' not even realizing it was Stalin who ordered him shot, I drank and caroused and even if went with prostitutes on Prospect Avenue, blow job or meaningless sex, it didn't mean anything, I was still a good family man, supported my wife and daughter, raised my son as if he was my own, but it was only when Joey came around that all of a sudden I became interested in the family, by then I was living with my daughter and her good-for-nothing husband but at least I had a grandchild who would stop crying in my arms, who would smile when I looked at him, I loved rocking him back and forth in my rocker I bought from the five-and-dime store so we could have a nice place to sit when he woke up in the middle of the night and all of a sudden my intentions changed and I stopped heavy drinking and when I held him the terrors of my night subsided, they never went away but at least I could get a handle on them, I couldn't do it over that was impossible but I did say I would never do it again, and did try and lead a more purposeful life holding onto Joey, feeding him the bottle, only the poor breastfed back then the rest of us used formula, while trying to figure out why I ran away in the first place until I began to believe I never ran away and if I no longer said I didn't I hadn't and more important said I will no longer live the fool I will start taking care of myself and I couldn't do that but slowed down my drinking so much that Molly kidded me we got a telegram today from Johnnie asking if you were alright we haven't see you in a few weeks. And Molly had no sense of humor. Started drinking beer and wine instead of hard stuff Molly thought maybe then I would get closer to the Jewish God but that God was dead to me and I had to see a living God and started a debate within myself trying to find reasons for his existence and remembered the intense friendships I had in those eighteen months in Spain but could never find reasons for a belief. The Holocaust clinched it for me what kind of god would allow such a thing to happen, but I stopped going with floozies even if that was the only sex I had but that only made it worse for me but I did give my wife pleasure when she threw me out but by then there was nothing left between us even our carnal gropings were few and far between and by the end were totally rejected by her. Hopefully she still stayed in touch with the father of her child. She never told me who he was refused to talk about it. When I couldn't stand her anymore moved in with my daughter and her good-for-nothing husband, who really was a decent man just such a dull boring fellow all he could do was come home and listen to the radio he never left the confides of home, because they needed help paying the rent, nor did I forget my wife and still paid the rent on the Concourse apartment. The laundry business practically ran itself. It was common back then for parents to live with their children and I needed to make sure Joey didn't grow up thinking this was the only world and would take him into the city every chance I could get him away from them, when he was a baby for the first year of his life my daughter never took him out of the neighborhood afraid to travel with him, I would take him to the local park, didn't need the carriage could carry him up the three flights of stairs to the subway nor need the carriage stored in the basement. I always had to help her carry the carriage up the three steps she was so helpless that it was easier for me to take him alone. He would sit on my lap when we went downtown or on the bus to the zoo and once he started walking we could go every-where. On weekends he went with his family in the car. Cars were being made again after the war and a comrade Jose Robles who also couldn't get a job after the war, the FBI still blackballing us opened a garage and he checked a car out and said this is a good used car, it couldn't have been Jose Robles I didn't know a Robles oh my god Robles I didn't have a clue until this moment thought I was so clever didn't even know his name he was the guy I shot. Imagine I thought he owned a garage in the Bronx, I am a stranger to myself, he was such a klutz couldn't even figure out how to put a condemn on, said it keeps breaking and we told him to grab it from behind and put it on, I talked him through it Wayne Simmons that was the guy who owned the garage, he must have had penis envy to ask me such a question—nobody knows about him today but he immortal-ized Jose Robles he didn't even look Spanish he was a colored man who worked for me and enlisted then when he too couldn't find a job used his skills to open up a small tire repair shop in an alley way and when he raised enough cash, I helped, opened up a storefront garage. He called it the Jose Robles Garage, that's why I was confused he must have been on the detail with me. As soon as I died my daughter sold the garage before her husband could get his hands on it and run it into the ground and saving the money for Joey's college fund but when he got accepted to City College she refused to spend the money on a private college where he could roam freely. Only it was the laundromat she sold the garage went belly up when Wayne wouldn't pay protection when the hooligans came around, I did, and was left alone. Did I live without knowledge of myself?

My big break came when I auditioned for a role in a Peter Weiss play, I had no understanding what it was all about all I knew was that I wanted it, street theater, guerrilla theater the stuff the old timers couldn't understand reminded them too much of agitprop when all the old left cared about was the class struggle, I remember in one of our meetings an old geezer said you want to know what a good newspaper is it's *Pravda* the real paper of the record. Pravda? That surprised me I never thought of the Soviet Union as a bastion where we were leading out lives I saw them as this repressed culture, they even barred Allen Ginsberg because he was homosexual how could anyone believe in the Soviet Union especially after they invaded Czechoslovakia: the most wonderful poster I saw was Russia out of Prague U.S. out of Vietnam some young man held up at a protest rally, but the old left was against the young and everything we stood for, sex, drugs and rock and roll and now this old leftie is moving upstairs, how is she going to manage walking up two flights of stairs plus the twelve steps leading up to the front door, at least she has no cats that the stereotypical old lady has. She was kicked out of her apartment and needs a place, not exactly kicked out as Joseph explains but a benefactor of capitalism, her landlord gave her fifty thousand dollars to vacate her place she really didn't want to do it but the money was too good to pass up and she figures she could live here until they carry her out, her only concern is moving so far downtown, she loved being by 100th Street and Broadway close to the center of the earth, near busses and the express subway stop that took her anywhere in the city, cafés, movie theaters, Lincoln Center, good shopping and grandma and her seem to hit it off so it might be a good match to have someone to commiserate with both exiles as they put it even if grandma admits she's no longer an exile because she speaks English now it's when you lose your language that you truly become an exile and she never insisted my mother speak Spanish which of course meant I never learned it; I hate these old lefties, Joseph doesn't take her seriously so he doesn't mind but they evoke all I hated about the old left standing in the way of progress. Marx, Marx, Marx, no thought of progress, of Camus, Sartre, Simone De Beauvoir, even now Joseph refuses to let me take his last name, says I have a career and so what if Jacoba has mine; he wants to show the world we're a liberated couple, if we are so liberated we shouldn't have married I'm not cut out for marriage or like gay couples living together it doesn't automatically mean monogamy. The sad joke going around now is how do Jewish men convince their mothers they're Haitians. And now that we own property it's much easier to share married than single and taxes are lower this way—the government is against you and a whole set of procedures get in the way of being single and female and we couldn't have put Joseph's last name on the birth certificate if not married, or you could but it was such a rigmarole it was easier just to marry, and now he now feels closer to me I feel more distant now being classified as a married woman and mother instead of as an actress. I feel as if my freedom has been slowly eviscerated, funny how these terms can affect you so. Now this old CPer is really something her father actually went underground in the '50s with the passage of the McCarran Act making the Communist Party illegal, Joseph laughed he was from a workers' family and they hated the communists more than anybody, especially after his grandfather died, who could have ever believed these people were a threat. Even grandma realizes the changes now are more dramatic than tectonic, from a vision of a radical classless society that is easy it's out there nobody is affected to one where the inner consciousness is transformed and we can live different lives than our parents, society has made a sea change—and even now I wonder why it took me so long to accept the pill, to become free and not define myself via marriage, children—how many childhood dreams did I have of a princess rescued by a prince and having a gorgeous wedding where I was the center of attention in a brand new wedding gown. I actually wore slacks and a blouse never would have a priest only consented to a rabbi because Joseph wanted one, he wanted a woman rabbi because they are not accepted in Judaism he liked that, I wanted nothing to do with religious fundamentalism always thought religious leaders the biggest hypocrites and both grandma and I love this new secularization that hopefully one day will destroy all religious identity but as all mainstream religious are going kaput nobody with any sense believes in them evangelical religions including Hasidism are booming—Joseph read somewhere that religious marriages have a better chance of lasting than secular so I agreed to make him happy and Danielle also thinks religion the opium of the masses so at least grandma has someone to talk to when they walk to the park. They disagree about mostly everything except capitalism even if they both are living so well off capitalism—one step forward two steps back, and we all laugh at that because the past weighs like a ton of bricks upon the living and the living is now a majority of all the people who ever lived, I like growing older life has been good to me and as long as my health holds I'm learning something about myself to be more of an individual, the individual is not identical with the group, similar but not identical, and that I don't have to have a group mind, at first I believed all things were of God and believed in the celestial hierarchy but now see more of the flux of time, feelings, thought without connection to any celestial harmony and am an individual of these times educated with the language to express what I intuitively feel and can add thought to those feelings now have more respect for Clytemnestra she's a mother whose daughter has been killed—motherhood is a powerful emotion, why I'm a good actress is that I can inhabit a character's insides even if don't always articulate it and that's where grandma and Joseph are correct there is a gap in my thoughts my ignorance comes from my lack of education and it surprises them at times and it's not just schooling it's that I'm not interested in the stuff they are. Joseph only likes the truth which for him is business while for me truth doesn't have to be the beauty of those classical poses of ballerinas, modern dance suffices for me, and his theater has to be about something but theater doesn't always have to be about something if it isn't about something doesn't mean it's crap because by definition then it forces the audience to think and art doesn't just have to entertain and even if the audience is passive and inarticulate doesn't mean they can't be aroused and preconceived notions challenged, you have to begin where your audience is. When I had extra-marital sex didn't think much of it, it made perfect sense to me not to become trapped I didn't think it would lead to other things.

What did I ever do that was correct? Did I ever learn? Now young people interrogate me. look to me for answers when all I have are questions I feel like a stranger in my own home, I don't even know where to shop here there are nice parks here that I can walk to but who cares I get my energy from the streets not parks, I like to breathe the air of the Village smiles of the neighborhood people who see you not these large box stores, I was on line at Louis Lickmann's, the German baker that has such a good aroma coming from it, not realizing it was the last day getting a black and white and all these old shop-girls were crying because it was the last day, the usual reason high rent for a nickel and dime business, and I order the last black and white and the man behind me says he wanted that, too bad, then he goes into a rant about how his wife is a Stasi agent spying on him and that he's an East German writer and drinks it's not even noon, and he's going to include me in his book because he's writing about the New York in '68 and Germany in '33, I ask him the name of the book and he mumbles *Anniversaries* but I never see it in print. Maybe I would do it differently now. Up here that was the only conversation I got all day, nobody talks to one another here Conchita and Joseph even brought in a tenant older than me but who they thought I could have a conversation with have something in common with but do they think I'm a kid who goes out and plays and makes friends with the first person I see, as if I could just jump into friendship with an individual without hard work; she seems pleasant but I don't want to interfere if she's a loner and much rather be the queen inside her own head than risk discussion where her ideas can be torn apart. However, she did say she would like to go walking with me, but she can't walk very far. It's fun being with ex-commies but she doesn't seem to flirt with men and takes women libbers so seriously, the frown on her face is permanent and I don't think she can laugh, she must have had a miserable life hidden by her commie bullshit, but the only way I could know this is if I engaged in dialogue with her but she hates small talk, but what other kind of talk is there, she seems to think the world we live in is a mirage and only when capitalism is destroyed will be able to have a true existence, commie claptrap, a worker in the morning, a scholar in the afternoon, and an artiste after supper, another utopian dreamer by people who hate facing the reality of living, I believed it but outgrew it, modified it, kitsch, boredom and cowardice are all words for the same struggle meanwhile life goes on behind our backs in the struggle to get up in the morning and live decently. Everything I once believed in is falling away as I'm forced to live uptown, nobody forced me but I didn't have enough strength to say no, besides I want to be near Jacoba, it's hopeless I can't live by myself anymore and I know that even if moving up here is against my better judgment I had to move with them no matter what discomforts I feel, just looking at Jacoba takes some of the pain away only my mind refuses to accept that I no longer live at home. My brain seems to be racing along two tracks the quick pace of this newness and my slow thinking of the way I want to live my remaining years, it's difficult I can't even take the subway downtown the stairs are out of the question and even the stations that have elevators are slow and smell of stench, urine, if they work but are usually broken, and since there's one elevator repairman in the city I have to wait until he comes around again to this elevator before I can use the subway, I wouldn't mind taking the bus but I can't even climb the big step up and the drivers rarely stop by the curb so I have less of a climb. Soon the curb on the street will become too high so I now have to avoid public transportation and become like Conchita taking cabs everywhere only I can't take a taxi to the Lower East Side it would cost a fortune, Joseph occasionally goes with me but I can't keep him from his business he now earns so much to allow us to live like this. Even Conchita is impressed at how quickly his business took off and he's actually doing some good allowing Hispanics and blacks to buy apartments not forcing them out of the city like most landlords are. Manhattan should be a city for millionaires a real estate tycoon said, so it's not for the old because we are no longer safe because we are easy marks and Hispanics have no qualms mugging Spanish old ladies. Equality. When I see them hanging on street corners I want to talk to them how silly once a Puerto Rican ran past me grabbed my purse and knocked me down and didn't even turn around to see if I was okay, if he'd did that now I'd have many broken bones, my balance isn't as good, my eyes probably couldn't even identify him and it all happened so fast and afterwards at the station house the police found my pocketbook in a trashcan of course all the money was gone but at least I got my identification back, but still Joseph insisted I call the credit card companies and the policeman said I was lucky I wasn't pistol-whipped, that had happened to a neighbor. The city is full of animals now children of children young mothers unable to control their offspring not the cute little baby they hoped to raise differently than their mother raised them are now unruly teenagers. Joseph says this is a safer neighborhood than where we were from but still felt comfortable there here still feel uncomfortable. What was that movie we recently saw on television where the kids walk up the wrong staircases and the grizzly old women teacher tells the younger one as they walk down the street we're their best hope and only chance they have—public schools can't even do that anymore the kids are dropping out like flies, fifty percent of high school students now never finish. The image of the old woman trying to reach those hooligans has stuck with me—what was the name of that movie? It looked like it was filmed in the East Village but Joseph who knows the city said East Harlem, and not everything takes place in the East Village, could have fooled me, why live anywhere else. But Joseph thinks when I get accustomed to the West Side will never want to leave. I doubt that. What's her name just knocked and asks if I want to go for a walk in the park. I like small parks for sitting not big monstrosities where you can't walk too deeply or the junkies will get you. What's her name says joggers are more plentiful now and junkies have moved up north past 96th street and Central Park is safe once again and junkies around here stay in the projects, and Joseph made sure not to move too close to a housing project that is still dangerous, projects only mean trouble. To try and fix up the projects the city tried to get people to buy their apartments, ownership means responsibility and even if it was subsidized the tenants wouldn't think of owning, why Joseph rarely targets people who live in projects to buy co-ops, only those who have a spark in their head will he be on the lookout for, he even thinks the side streets are safe now especially with the new sodium lights that brighten the streets almost making it feel like daylight. The two good things the mayor has done is putting in sodium lights and making sure dog owners clean up their dog shit so I no longer get it stuck in my corrugated soles. If only he got rid of the pigeons like they said they would their crap gets into buildings and corrodes the underpinnings dropping debris on the streets not to mention shitting on people, instead they freed all the crazy people from Bellevue but never built the small shelters to house them and who now wander the streets without supervision or medication.

Now not only do I see my first grey hairs and my belly getting rounder I have to diet and sleep more and this job is slowly destroying my creativity, no longer can I read a book on the subway, read and reread, I either stare blankly out the window or read the newspaper and if I finish have no idea what I read and have to go back to the first or second paragraph to find out what this was about and even if I finish the article have no idea what the implications are my mind wanders so; no longer can I concentrate so that I miss my stop, journalists write as if we live in a vacuum, I must try and get back to serious reading, maybe begin memorizing poetry once again, what's glasnost, perestroika? who's Gorbachev? All I'm doing is going from one real estate deal to another now my tombstone can read: He was a dealmaker, how useless, depressing, I want to breathe come up from drowning in paperwork look inward but if I do I see have a child to support, bills to pay a wife who seems to be becoming more distant—I can't recall the last time we had sex, desire kaput, you can only have desire if you want something and all I want is a good night's sleep and even if she's next to me think she is somewhere else probably with someone she met at a play, unlike me who choses women I see from the subway—the subway is good pretty women get on get off and I can enter another's life for weeks until I forget what they look like, at least I can laugh at my follies Cassie is having a difficult time sometimes sullen other times a spitfire but if I look at her gently and put my arm around her sometimes I can calm her down but around her I'm always afraid something will set her off as I slowly empty myself of all my held beliefs that I would never become like my parents worse yet as I age I can see how I'm starting to look like my father and if I don't watch it will become him not grandfather who at least had a life before he settled down with my grandmother even if would never have the guts to do what he did, besides now who would I fight for the Nicaraguan Sandinistas a third-rate communist regime, they don't seem like a cause worth dying for, worse yet I'm sounding like my mother it's wrong what he did abandoning the family to fight for somebody else. What happened to my drive, desire, what did I ever want to be I know I didn't want to be a lawyer or go into business, all my friends were going to law school I knew I had enough school no teacher put me on the edge of my seat all they did was talk about what other people said never lived themselves, and I couldn't wait to be done with it now all I do is live in the world without a thought in my head that isn't concerned with business or the family is this the place I want to be? God I'm lucky I know that even know where I am the graffiti is everywhere and if you don't know your station you would never find it, how can tourists find their way and even when I would get off at the wrong station enjoyed walking the only time now I feel alive and I can always find my way—I'm so Manhattan-centric though I still get lost in Brooklyn, and Queens, but never the Bronx, however, I never go back to the old neighborhood, did meet Harvey a friend from there walking down lower Broadway we passed each other then turned around and both smiled but didn't even time to go in for coffee, just said hello, shook hands, I feel uncomfortable in this new thing of hugging men, he told me how much he liked the old neighborhood and how he loved to play ball on the weekend, and I laughed and got off a good line, you played on the weekend I played all the time why you went to Science then Columbia before he enlisted in the Army, me Music and Art then City College, he's a big shot now me a small time real estate broker. What I like about the old neighborhood friends is we can laugh together. We'll get together sometime soon we exchanged business cards. Sure. What I love now is letting the sun hit me in the face, the warmth of the sun on my cheeks as I walk almost as much as coming out of the dark movie theater into the sunlight and being blinded, I remember seeing *Julius Caesar* with my grandfather at the old Devon theater on Tremont Ave. in the Bronx and surprised he only wanted to see it once, I loved sitting through two or three performances, I was in no rush to get home, and afterwards wrote a play for Miss Shitface but she said it had little redeeming social value, didn't reflect well upon the school, and upset the class, but *avuelo* liked it. Movies aren't the same without him, him being with me is different than my imagining him with me because I would be ashamed of what he would see how I turned out—I'm not the person he thought I would become, he had hope for me and all I carry is his memory not his spirit with me, yet I don't want to do what he did—am I too afraid to see how low I can go. That must have been part of his motivation women now are onto it when they divorce their husbands, sell their houses, kids, jobs, and hate their old lives and make sure they see nobody from that life. I seem to be seeing a whole lot of them the quiet types who you had no idea have such vivid imaginations and it all keeps tumbling out as they join the foreign legion even if the French Foreign Legion is no more somehow women have picked up on this idea and these women somehow becoming renters in the city or an occasional one with enough money to buy her own small place. Interesting how they want zipless fucks but I never mix business and pleasure, lawyers do that to get pretty divorcees down on their self-image, or as Cassie says how else are these sleazebags going to attract a pretty woman unless she had lost all confidence in herself. At least Danielle occasionally went to the theater and claims to have seen Cassie as Circe except she didn't like the slowness and repetitiousness and it weighed on her that the men didn't rise up in rebellion of their fate, proving she didn't understand the play, but she actually went to the theater after she abandoned her husband and child became a therapist actually grandfathered in as a licensed therapist with no training by being hooked up with a Sullivanian group who sent her patients and who she lived communally with believing you couldn't have normal monogamous relationships in a capitalist society and the family is the cause of all our troubles until they decided to move to Florida. They were always so social never liked them in restaurants they would all sing and celebrate together making a big show of hugging and prancing around of being a family not caring about the other customers who liked quiet. She too doesn't have a television so she and Esmeralda can read together. The sun is non-existent the clouds so depressing, luckily I know how to dress warm, wool socks and a hat, I had to get out the crowds were too depressing and I was afraid the subway would stall again between stations, at least the heat was working—how many times did I want to pull the emergency brake just to air my frustrations maybe the powers that be would pay attention and fix it, be the leader of a rebellion, I'm not the only one getting out and walking, since the subway strike more women are walking also wearing sneakers and switching to heels at work, we walk together, apart, not smiling, women never smile on the subway, where was I? what was I thinking about? oh my unhappy life and how the subway is a metaphor for my life, wouldn't it be grand if I could just start a conversation on the subway only I wouldn't even know what to say and I'd be afraid she'd think I was trying to pick her up, which I would be, but wouldn't want her to know it, and only would want a little banter to help me get through the morning and dream about what I could have said so I could let her image roll all over me at night—boy am I good at taking an inch of a look and transforming it into an adventure and which has no chance of being real since it is nothing at all, I wonder how *avuelo* felt when he realized war is war not an adventure and he has a real chance of dying or not coming through whole or imagine having to take the life of a real person not some abstract idea of a man—did he shoot over their heads or did he frack like Americans in 'Nam did, no wonder the army doesn't want another draft. He came home after that experience and according to my mother never once talked about it and now I assume it's because he met the true love of his life and let her get away not that he actually killed another human being, a person, and that upset him so.

Looking back, I wonder what I never wanted to happen, happened, and now when I'm awaken in the middle of the night and find my way to the bathroom in the dark wonder why I lived my life for myself and not for others or did I live it for others and not myself, no longer am I sure, sure about anything all I like are the cold tiles on my feet as I sit over a toilet bowl reminding me of the cold of the war when all I wanted was to be old and say with satisfaction that I lived my life, now I'm not sure anymore, the hardest part of getting old isn't the physical ailments, my body changing, I expected that and I can get by with medication, it's how weak you become and I have to stay strong and fight to stay left. Is life continuous or discontinuous like those early Greek playwrights and sophists who believed in a meaningless universe that scared the philosophers silly. When looking at the world as continuous is it a supple fiction where I grew up in an environment that I didn't like and simply split, ran away, took a few men down with me but they were collateral damage for getting involved with me then I ran away again this time into nobody's arms first moved back with my parents until Tomas took me to America and here actually had my first taste of freedom had a child but when I couldn't stand him anymore asked him to leave, and my daughter figured it out that I couldn't stand her either, all by herself and left me the first chance she could, then I finally found some peace living all by myself, but surely the seeds of my destruction was my first act of rebellion leaving home and finding Jacobo, I hadn't led a one-dimensional existence but if I look at it from the outside it seems continuous but there are definite motives for each event depending upon how I felt at that precise moment, that no amount of thinking can recapture, and it wasn't as clear as I make it out to be in retrospect but I do remember the heartbreak. Joseph says what blew his mind in college weren't the courses they were all insipid and boring but the gestalt the new way of thinking that was developing inside him learning of the superior pleasures of the mind, poetry, music, theater over idleness and sex and drugs. He recalled how his friend Harvey told him he must see Sartre's *The Flies* and was blown away and had to go to back to the Greeks, of course he had heard of these plays what college student hasn't they were kept alive by reading but he never saw them acted and claims he felt just like those Renaissance thinkers who came across the Greek playwrights for the first time, gods don't exist or at least don't care about our lives nor influence our lives and wondered how would the ancient Hebrews have thought about this after they were exposed to Greek literature via Alexander's conquest, a well-ordered soul blown away by flux, a world that doesn't get its values from a God. Did they see nothingness and meaningless of the universe as opposed to the theologians? Did they forget about the Bible and following its strict rules and become secular and leftist? That's what his grandfather said, also the only man besides Joseph I ever saw read in a bathroom, he loved to slowly read the Greek plays let them wash over him but then we would talk then he would go back to them trying to truly grasp their meanings, and that he did teach me even if I am not a bathroom reader, it takes time and a small well-lit place to read and think and let your imagination run wild. Unfortunately growing up, before Jacobo the Bible was the book, that's all we knew but only with him did my education start. I had to feel my way towards education and the transition between belief and thought took a long time filled with a lot of setbacks and traps along the way, at first thinking that the men I grabbed onto would set me free but each new beginning soon morphed into the same ole, same ole, and when I look back from a distance wonder how I was ever able to become free, it wasn't a smooth ride I kept falling and failing bumps and bruises; how unfortunate I didn't keep a journal to see the crests and troughs maybe then I would recall better except now I know there is no Archimedean point of inflection from which you could see it all but each moment is coordinated with another and then you end up sitting upon a toilet bowl in the middle of the night your feet on a cold tiles wondering upon the meaning of life. How can you measure pleasure I can't stand people who lead perfect lives not only are they lying there not even having conversations with themselves? Danielle is a bore has answers for everything I go to the park with her and she can't shut-up listen to the birds, watch the clouds move across the sky, always yapping about the workers' movement as if there is a simple worker whose true needs are being denied because they desire the wrong thing by false consciousness and are alienated from their true nature. At least she didn't say *Pravda* is the paper of record only claimed the *New York Times* was good when it reported the truth about Moscow, not that their crack reporter, their man in Moscow Walter Duranty, was a fellow traveler. I'm still pissed at the *Times* when they knew of Mayor Lindsay's plan to raise subway fares but didn't report it lest he lose the election. He would have been creamed if voters knew of his plans. I'm fighting myself at different ages, all visions of a perfect society are bullshit they collide with the truth and now that I am slowly making my way in the dark back to my bed want to believe I know nothing maybe I have five years left, ten at the most but my legs still work even if they look like jelly, and I have to continue to hone my body for the ride why I go walking sometimes with Danielle others by myself to discover my new neighborhood, that and tai chi, which I passed on to Conchita who now does exercise even if she doesn't like to walk but realized after the birth she has to take better care of herself, my youth, middle age and old age exist side by side and went by so fast in retrospect but living them were slow I can't eliminate any of them because they are part of me, maybe I could have stayed longer with Tomas, a good fellow but I would have been dead by now, a boring fellow and what I liked about him is he got me to America and I stayed long enough with him to pay him back but I can only imagine him as an old man unlike Jacobo who I could visualize only as young—he even accused me of sleeping with other men, silly stuff that I wouldn't do while married even if now it is socially acceptable not that I believed in the sacredness of marriage or that I would be considered a slut but saw it as something that would have hurt him and I didn't want to deceive him, I didn't succeed but tried, he never would divorce me until he met someone I'm happy for him, I didn't need a divorce I wasn't going to marry. I have to shut my mind off if I'm going to get any sleep can't keep having these fights between my young self and old self, can't keep arguing, having this question and answer drivel, these blankets are too heavy and I roll off them, Joseph thinks I think so much, my brain's too tight that I must have Mariano blood in me, what I like about him is we can laugh together, he's also not afraid to have a conversation with an old woman.

I'm always on the subway going from one place to another but now I can no longer even read the newspaper on these trains I get so angry at the delays, the lack of heat, the doors not opening, that I stand and stare out the window until I can get to walking distance of where I want to go and bingo am out on the street no matter what the weather, actually rented a car thought it would be cool driving clients from one place to another but then spent so much time looking for parking that I finally decided to park illegally and pay the ticket, it would be cheaper in the long run, but soon thought that silly, besides driving in city traffic was a headache, my hand was always on the horn, and our planned Sunday drives upstate, to the country rarely materialized so gave up the car when I realized I could walk faster than I can drive across town but now I tire so easily, who could imagine that I who would walk from the old neighborhood in the Bronx to City College now can't even walk a few miles. So now I wait the thirty minutes for a downtown local that inevitability stalls no longer do I even play Sir Galahad and offer a seat to a woman, unless of course she's pregnant or elderly, and I mean elderly, cane, at death's door otherwise I say why should they be riding the trains during rush hour— forget young girls who glide through life without a care in the world, I'm too lazy to try and get them to smile say hey I'm not sixteen anymore, as if I ever met them when I was sixteen, sometimes I even think they're too old for me, and hey where have I been to think that, all I do now is work and come home to the blessed family. Oh yes received a letter yesterday from an old acquaintance from the school for fools and her news startled me, at first I hadn't the slightest clue what she was talking about then at the bottom of the letter she mentions our friend Claudia passed, she was always too hot for me her energy was contagious, her beauty made me nervous, always talking taking hold of my arm, I kept thinking she was being polite not that she wanted me and when she offers me her phone number gave her mine instead and never heard from her again. I knew she was sick for quite a while always said I should call but never did, I recalled seeing her few times after graduation and she had this cheerful look and always was glad to see me and I thought I'm so lonely and she's so cheery fuck her. She was a film critic and loved the films of Al Pacino and actually bumped into him at Bloomingdale's and had the nerve to ask him for an interview but he said he didn't do interviews, she didn't pan him afterwards, still loved him and was making it as a part-time film critic and was happy writing film articles and at least she was doing something intellectual not marrying and raising little kiddies. She was smart. I called and asked where the funeral was, it was private but her classmates are going to organize a memorial service and I will be invited to that. I wondered if her mother was still alive that must be the ultimate horror to bury your child, I knew her father had died when she was eighteen and remember thinking that her father must have thought he had done his duty getting her to graduate high school now she can live on her own but he was wrong eighteen is too young to be without family and she drifted through school using alcohol, drugs and sex as panaceas. It seemed obvious to me now I have to live long enough to allow Jacoba to graduate college, I said to myself after reading the letter, which means I have to exercise more and immediately leave the subway and start my new regime and say I have to do this all the time—no longer will I carry an attaché case but will walk with a light knapsack and maybe start jogging again. Can I even run the reservoir? I know I can walk it taking Jacoba around and around while she sits in the stroller crying no interest in the sunset or the ducks. She's a diva in training. Is her mother still alive? Once I ran into her in the street carrying a dress I bought for Cassie and couldn't wait to show it off to her a Valentino dress, and she laughed saying for my birthday my boyfriend gave me money and said go by a purse just like my father said to my mother. The apple doesn't fall far from the tree, of course, I have exquisite taste and only get gifts people would never buy for themselves. Was she married? In college she said she would never marry but we say a lot of things in college that don't turn out to be true. Did her cheerfulness relent as the illness progressed and all of a sudden become afraid, or did she face death with equanimity as the big C. receded from one part of her body only to reappear in another. It would be nice if her mother is not the last one in the family. Upsetting. Imagine I never get letters only junk mail then to get this and I couldn't even say goodbye because the funeral is private and I doubt if I'll go and see my ex-classmates again, I never participate in reunions. I vow not to die in front of Jacoba it was too painful to watch grandfather much better to ride off in the sunset, yet when I explained to Esmeralda how grandfather died she said at least he didn't die alone. I don't even know who to write a note to. There's nothing to say anyway except I would always fantasize about fucking her but she was too hot for me, too popular for me yet we sat across from each other in a couple of classes together and she talked to me and once I gave her my notes not realizing that I had been doodling in the margins and drawing her bangs and flip luckily my artistic talents were so bad the face didn't look like her. She was so pretty, better to leave that out and write some bullshit never the nitty-gritty—sexual thoughts are transgressions saying that would be bad form, more and more writing is becoming journalese not dramatic or novelistic, no longer is anything left unsaid, wondering, now all has to be laid out there, except I don't know what I truly feel, as if I even know half the time, or if say a word of truth the whole edifice will collapse and even if I tell Cassandra what I really thing about what she's done it will hurt her so I think it is better for me to be silent—I haven't enough guts to get up and fight people. How do you sum up a person's life, do you merely count how much time was spent on pleasure versus pain? You can't you can only live. We are all sad most of the time and only happy in dying well. Did Cassie have a smile on her face as she did it or did she even think about what I would say, this is too much I have to clear my mind if I am to get ready to make a sale, if I am to make a living, to go on with my life I have to smile a lot.

I was feeling better and thought maybe I need an aspirin and I'd be okay, then somebody turned the switch off and I was gone, crazy how I still go on remembering as if nothing happened grasping for truth throwing off old memories as I threw out old clothes, books, papers, discarding as if in discarding could start over again never wanting to recapture old articles bring them back from decay, museum pieces, much preferred starting over I no longer want to remember but the past keeps on sneaking back in, what do the living know about dying? Death is not like living, no way, and it's difficult for me to describe the discombobulated thing you become because you are no longer something with a body and you don't get to choose what memories spring to the surface, it warms you up when you think but at the same time creates chaos, it isn't pleasant, there's no time here even when you examine it from the outside because you are not participating in anything worse if you don't participate you're not even believing even if you like to believe you are, a bell goes off each time someone thinks of me as if I'm still around but the bell dims quickly and for some people never even rang except at the moment of death. Zoltan for instance came to my funeral mourning went up to Joey put his arms around him, hugged him said I was a decent man who helped him but never lived don't be like your grandfather find out what you want to do and do it. I didn't help him for praise, did it because he needed help after the failed revolution in Hungary and the memory of his brother who was a friend from the Spanish Civil War. Molly always hoped there would be a hell where I would burn, her mother was more forgiving at the end only because she was afraid to utter such thoughts, the only time I ever heard her swear was when she cursed my Spanish Civil War exploits but this is worse than at least in a hell you exist, you feel something, there is no name for what you feel here, there is no existence in this type of place stuck inside your memories and each new image is too weak to come up with terms even if some Jewish thinkers and their Christian followers or Christians and Jewish fellow travelers who live among them but are not part of them, Jewish homes are unlike Christian Jews live in time, Christians in space, we put a Mezuzah on the front door, the only time I ever kissed it is when I made it home from Spain, Christians put icons upon the wall, now only Joey is so Americanized he doesn't realize the paintings upon his wall are only recurrences of former icons and reputes the Mezuzah and doesn't even realize he's abandoned the old ways. When I first held Joey he smiled as if he recognized me then spit up over my new shirt. He will find them soon enough fall back to traditional ways, you don't even repeat here you don't even gather information here, all you do is get a disposition towards the past in remembering it, I finally am beginning to grasp that if you don't follow those old traditions they will die out like Ladino, that is just barely surviving before it passes from the earth, it has to be lived you have to engage with it if it is to survive, you don't even have to believe just use, participate and that he will not do until the crisis hits him, then he can get rid of all the excess but the core will remain even if it can't be defined because there is no essence without participation, is it absurd to say I am Jewish if I don't follow the tradition and even if he actually said the *Kaddish*, mourners' prayer, for eleven months, daily, not weekly but daily before he went to school, actually wore one of my wide ties that he would take off and put in his pocket once finished with temple lest he be made fun of in school, and this from a boy who refused a Bar Mitzvah and I had to talk him into it his mother wanted it so, then he was Jewish since then nada, nothing, zilch, he claims to have a Jewish head but only in willing, doing, acting, does one become Jewish, without thought even put on thought it is not Judaism only play-acting only in thinking do you start to know, to begin to know, and in acting the rituals become part of you they don't exist in the ether because there is no longer this, Judaism exists only in inhaling it, then it becomes real. How do I begin to feel this? Certainly not living when God was dead and if dead religion must be dead as well because both have the same attributes even as in a modern painting there is a balance narrative and illusion, it is in the likeness there is a connection. The idea that a Jewish God exists independently than the people who believe in him—nobody believes in Zeus anymore but does that mean Zeus' justice doesn't exist: now we just call it the Jewish God. The Greeks first asked how shall we live, the Jews said thou shall not, even if the Greek playwrights and sophists believed in a meaningless universe both thought that if abandoned by a God we can make our own rules, and if we deal with justice we have similar views, teachers need students, but do students need teachers? And a true teacher is always learning even if he can't put it into pleasing words there is no reason to believe it is not true even if doesn't come from up high. This is what you get when you think for all eternity, life is a metaphor for life unlike Zoltan who thought life was over if he stopped painting and put a sign on his easel to remind himself, gone fishing, but in his case it was somewhat true he would take the subway everyday to Rockaway pier and stand all day in the sun watching the water casting his fishing rod into the sea and throwing his catches back in repeating the same motions over and over and I can imagine him smiling as he throws the fish back in the water thinking he's saved the life of the fish only the act of catching the fish so weakens the fish that he becomes easy pray for other fish, this lasted all of a week or two then he was back at his easel. Since I can begin to grasp this I can grasp the disposition between the hidden God, mystery, human tidings things have to exist even if they are described metaphorically and error is not heresy but the continual struggle to find our way between knowledge and truth—never having seen justice only law I know justice is timeless not historical, and my continual struggle to find a way between thought and truth not simply grabbing food from a shelf as in a supermarket. What I miss when I force myself to think like this is being able to pleasure myself, I knew I was getting old when I could no longer do it to myself, of course my wife was of no help we already parted and she despised me and one day I couldn't even stand her anymore couldn't get out of bed and moved in with Molly and her new husband, parents moved in with their grown children back then, but even when I discarded most my things and was ready to begin anew all I did was collect new things. Got rid of all my suits, shirts, ties, books, papers, only to buy new suits, ties, shirts, when I died there must have been at least ten unopened shirts inside my dresser, occasionally I would like to buy a new shirt but if you wore it it wasn't new anymore. When my wife went into the hospital for good they trashed her place discarded everything leaving it in the front of the apartment for the super to discard, when I died the same all my belongings stored in the trash except for my ties they gave to Joey who only laughed at the wide ties, who wears these anymore.

Joseph no longer finds me exotic, the other, when he first met me he couldn't wait to show me off to his parents now it's as if he wears a black silver cord around his waist like pious Jews once did only he does it to separate his past from my future no longer am I pure to him, not different from other women; he has given up looking at me, and even now if I don't see myself in the mirror wonder if I exist or not and even when I see myself wonder who I am looking at, am I still this stylish woman who dresses well wear scarves that gives me a French look and boys still flirt with me?—I consider all men boys who need a manual to help them learn, distinguishing only younger from older none of them having a brain in their head all they want to do is run away with me or sleep with me all based upon my looks and haven't the slightest clue who I am—where were they when I was sixteen then I was ready for their craziness now I'm too set in my ways, even if I haven't stopped looking yet, but if they saw behind the image, I'm not the characters I play, and they see a reflection of what is not, and they don't see me shaking like a leaf fearing the look of the other and they will find out how much of a phony I am unsure, scared going to the bathroom a million times before a performance and still can't get over performance anxiety smoke one then two and sometimes three cigarettes at the same time before I go on one in each hand then two in one hand, and if by chance I glance at myself in the mirror think this is uncanny that this is me and sometimes do a double take and wonder who that person is staring back at me and it takes a moment for me to realize it is me. A mature woman who is responsible for her looks is a delight to men's eyes and women are no longer jealousy of me because they realize how hard I have to work at keeping my body in shape after one baby and one abortion, a body changes after a baby and your mind does after an abortion. I just couldn't have another child and now Joseph hates me. Who would have believed I could get pregnant so soon after giving birth, I was still breastfeeding and barely got my period when all of a sudden I was pregnant; I had to have an abortion of the second child and hadn't realized you could get pregnant while breastfeeding I didn't want it but Joseph did and has hated me ever since, grandma knew, said it could happen but I didn't know and couldn't subject my body to another pregnancy and have two children in diapers less than eighteen months apart, our bodies change after pregnancy and I'm no longer the slim young woman nor can I be anymore after giving birth. It's charming how many young boys want to pinch me even if I'm old enough to be their mother, and of course, I won't let them take advantage of me that way but I can see how they confuse me with my stage name I should only be able to be that person I play on stage night after night, I feel so good playing different roles much better than my coding job that does help pay the rent even if he says I no longer have to do that he makes enough for all of us to live on, but I still won't give up my freedom and independence, even if I say I am doing it for tuition and I do feel good paying my way not simply using the money for vacations but schooling is important and when I mentioned that I did okay in public school Esmeralda laughed and said the more you learn the more you earn and gifted and talented programs are now separate but equal programs separating the middle from the lower class. When we chose a daycare that had Hispanic children in it Jacoba only played with the two white Jewish girls wanting nothing to do with Hispanic or black children who played too rough for her. I thought we could take her and pick her up so she wouldn't be infected but those boys and girls couldn't play well without others and there were so many kids in the class with only one real teacher the others are volunteers who want to help but have no idea what education is about. Joseph won, grandma won, we couldn't let Jacoba stay there it would have been a disaster. Grandma said you can believe in public education but you can't let them do what they do to your child. What they do is a crime and this in one of the better schools not a public dumb-shit school up in the Bronx. It's now a tale of two cities one public with lower quality education, low employment, and serious health problems the other private with good schools, high-paying jobs and you live longer. She lasted all of two months before she cried one morning and just refused to go, what was I doing sending her to prison, and since we are Hispanic Joseph was wise enough to give her my last name as her last name private schools bent over backwards to get a Hispanic child who could pay the full boat and show the world how they increased their minority representation, Joseph insisted I come to the interview in my business blue, he had made sure Jacoba had a nap and some cookies beforehand so she was in a good mood and played well with others. The little narcissistic one, Madame princess, still thinks the world revolves around her and with her grandmother it does. He learned this in the playground when occasionally a parent but not a nanny was with the child and children played together but nannies sat with nannies, mothers with mothers and men apart but once in a while a mother would have a conversation with him, more often grandparents he said and that's how he learned which school had a lower enrollment than usual and was able to get Jacoba in the middle of the term. I was worried she wouldn't make friends but it turned out easier in the middle than it would have been in the beginning of the term. We separated soon after and I moved back to the old place I just couldn't stay uptown anymore, go to the park with her on weekends, drop off at school if grandma couldn't get up on time, and be in the same room with Joseph and his silences. Nothing's wrong, nothing's wrong he would say whenever I asked but I knew he was angry and hated me for what I had done but was too ashamed to say it, he thought he could live with it but he just couldn't. Life is visual I know that from acting and I couldn't stand being treated with such contempt, I first started going out with actors, with actors no less, actors aren't serious we just needed to wind down after a show but then it came on me the old bugaboo that I wanted it liked playing the lead, flirting, doing it rather than going home to a silent bed, didn't tell him why hurt him but kept coming home later and later, at first wouldn't do it said it was wrong why ruin a marriage, and then one night without thinking, but of course I knew what I was doing, came home not at all and he knew, grandma knew but I wanted it no longer wanted not being wanted wanted being wanted and enjoyed it and remembered how much I enjoy it, because I am an imaginary creature know how to take on different roles even could play with a French accent or English, never had to use a Hispanic or German because they seem too rough for American ears, and after I did it once found it easy to do because being a housewife was a harder role to play since I had no idea who I was even when I gazed at myself in the mirror. I do look marvelous, not even forty, even if I am approaching fifty, only if I could feel that way but we are who we are on the outside only it took me awhile to realize that, Joseph is a real nebbish but kind and true and loves me even if he is so boring and living together is so difficult and monogamy so boring. But I'm now supposed to be a responsible woman who gave up living no longer a fly-by-night Holly Golightly, I just saw her on late night television and what I most remember about the flick was the opening scene where Fifth Avenue is a two-way street when I was in a cab and he made a left and we went directly into traffic and nearly got killed, the cabbie didn't realize Fifth Avenue became one way, but cars moved out of the way and on the next block was able swing right and I got out and walked to the audition and couldn't believe that happened to me that I could have been killed in a car crash, here lies Conchita, I wasn't Cassandra then, and now here lies Cassandra a shameless hussy, and everybody would be looking down at me mourning me until I realized that there is no place to look down from only now I am looking up wondering what's going on at home without me. No longer am I the starlet who doesn't get the part but an old woman even if I don't look it when I gaze into the mirror.

When I first went to this East European nouvelle cuisine restaurant somebody told me Trotsky ate here all the time and later the golden boy Max Eastman would also eat here, I laughed nobody even knows about these people anymore, like Solzhenitsyn who was able to stay human under extreme conditions and now nobody reads him anymore yet at one time he was the most famous author in the world, but this restaurant gained significance for me when I knew its history even if I didn't believe it, still I tried to enjoy my food, once I loved going here but now the food is tasteless—Joseph had a different feeling when eating out since his mother's home cooking was fried, boiled or baked until all the flavor was eradicated he loved eating out with his grandfather, but his grandfather never took him this far downtown, a shame, we might have bumped into each other, the big difference now in the city with women working all the time families eat out more or order in—when I first came here it was only single men or an occasional woman now when I walk into a restaurant it isn't strange to see a woman eating by herself, too bad the food isn't as good as it once was. Imagine if I could have walked into the Odessa restaurant and there was Trotsky sitting at one table or a little later the golden boy or even Floyd Dell, but Americans aren't historically conscious with their short-term memory are only interested in celebrities. I wonder if Dell ate here, now there's a name from the past that I haven't thought about in a hundred years why think about him now? I guess I always loved when he said the Village is getting too touristy and expensive after the Great War, imagine what he would think now as kids from the tunnels or Jersey come in every weekend, now even I'm a tourist. Even saw, but it was pointed out to me Isaac Bashevis Singer in a restaurant on the West Side because he lives in the Belnord, and actually went to Parnassus book shop and banged on the window and the proprietor a cute bald-headed man opened the door and liked me immediately and showed me his books, and tried reading him but he talked of such simple silly characters unlike all the Jews I knew that it was too stupid for me, his Jews were so ignorant and superstitious and were shocked if they saw a woman smoking in public she was the devil incarnate not simply a human being enjoying a moment, and his god was silent and unknown so that anything could be believed. But I want to wrestle with a book read it slowly and wonder. What I enjoy however is women who wear wigs so as not to be stared at by men and now Hassidim wear sexy wigs because they are not allowed to show their own hair and are more attractive in wigs; I tried to find this charming but couldn't, ignorant people hold no special place for me, I like those who struggle with a man's gaze but not define themselves by it and take responsibility for their actions, why I'm having such a difficult time now waiting for Conchita who freely chose to leave, which I approve of, but at the same time she is missing out on the joys of Jacoba, she doesn't know what she's missing in not raising her child, I never knew you could love someone so much. But she's young yet and wants to live her life her way, have an adventure, but you have different feelings the older you get, no longer is an action a unique singular event it has consequences it is a duration connecting each moment with another moment in space-time, like a symphony contains all the notes before it but now sounds different when you hear it in totality and each moment is part of modifying the past, it's not a straight linear process towards an ending but the acceptance of new ideas as they now become available— yet what I struggled with is easily accepted by the next generation only they have their own difficulties, so Conchita can leave her husband but we realize abandoning the family is not so good for us, or now women can smoke but it gave me an early heart attack, the doctor was quite blunt give up cigarillos or you'll be dead in five years. And no longer did I say otherwise I'll get fat or some such nonsense the fear of an early death was enough, that and three hours a day of physical therapy. It's still difficult for me to believe I will be an inanimate body I'd much rather believe in an afterlife where I could see Jacobo again but now not only is God dead and the universe so big that man is so puny but science teaches us he doesn't even exist. Why it was difficult reading the stories of Singer people who believed and didn't know how to disguise it as the world moved from a mechanical society to a modern one. Even now people go to church believing in free will and we have a choice to do good or evil with or without grace it's no longer simply a matter of dogma. At least faith is being questioned, discussed, not simply accepted but still marriage and death are marked by religion not divorce. What I expected never happened, religion did not die with the killing of God, when I first landed here was surprised how irreligious most Americans were but that was on the surface, scratch them and you find deeply religious people with strong superstitions. Joseph at first would eat sweet-and-sour pork as an act of rebellion but now won't touch pork, nor make it for Passover. He says his tastes have changed but its old-fashioned religion rearing its ugly head, taboo. It was only Zoltan, who at first welcomed the communists with open arms until his brother disappeared into the Gulag, that allowed him to start with Conchita who I just saw walking in front of the window and will be here momentarily, what do I say to her? she's missing so much not seeing her daughter grow up but she has the right to be free not tied down against her will, but what goes through her head is it the impulse of family or it her education, which taught her to be free, but whatever I say it will only be the tip of the iceberg she has to decide for herself.

I can't believe how this anxiety gobbles me up alive, with men at least you can have a conversation with, we women are stricter and are terrible to work for but now at least we don't have to clean up after men, men are such slobs and actually expected women to clean up after them, they are good at going to strip clubs to relieve tension but can't seem to keep an office clean until some woman manager wrote a sign clean up after yourself your mother doesn't work here but still I try and avoid women bosses as much as possible, and I've been told that as well, men at least get their pleasure in domination but ever so nicely because all their pleasure comes from work, or so I have been led to believe but now what for me is only a day job for these new managers is the alpha and omega of existence and they attempt to take away whatever little freedom you could find on the job—all they want to do is prove themselves, prove how tough they are and it's there way or the highway, all lies that women are supportive, Joseph thinks they have balls but I don't think they want to take you down I would have said guts but they really are pains to work for, which is why companies now have had to create Human Relations Departments the back fighting is amazing, the narcissism of small things as each of us demands we do things her way and that leads to conflict, men at least can take it outside we women can't and back bite, shameful how we behave especially with a woman boss, usually I do what she says not wanting to fight tooth and nail over some insignificant thing it's too stupid unfortunately nothing is given to those who don't fight and I feel petty doing it but if I don't fight for my rights I won't be recognized as a human being and my colleagues will walk all over me but if I stand up to her and let her know she is worth no more than me maybe, just maybe, she will leave me alone—only she wants to clear this place of old blood but if I let her know I am not someone she can mess with—you can't play masochist to a sadist and its cruel for them to know this about me, to think this about me, bosses can't stand independent types and am I still clever enough to recognize that and make believe I still depend upon their input no matter how stupid because they are so invested in this project, how many damn backups do you need? As long as she thinks she's imposing her will on me as project manager and I recognize that we can get along—now all I do is complain—I hate these fallow periods with no acting work and my life becoming a shambles and not even an audition to go to and I go home now every night to an empty apartment I can't stay forever in the office and now don't want to leave this job even if more and more offices are going high tech and I am in demand because they need a woman to train other women in the technology and I'm not afraid of machinery as a lot of woman are this is so much better than those miserable Home Economics courses I was forced to take in high school, even thinking about them lets a cold chill run down my spine, where I learned how to set a perfect table, cook for a man, and when I went to a real high school felt ashamed to tell my newfound friends of the courses I took, luckily I jumped on the new technology, as soon as computers came out I was enthralled even did Joseph's spreadsheet he was so comfortable using a pen and pencil until I showed him by altering one figure in the column all the others can get altered as well and he became a believer as long as I did it for him. Joseph hates the computer and I still have to do it for him but I love exploring on it, how I learned was to explore nobody taught me, early on most employers didn't even realize machines had functions besides faxes, I'm still amazed how people laughed at faxes in the '70s why do we need so much speed can't we just photocopy and mail, wasting so much money on technology can't you spend the money on improving the city, as if the powers that be would ever spend money on that, when they kicked the mentally ill out of hospitals for being warehoused did they ever build the small group homes they needed, as my social justice warrior says, or as grandma says, the reason why there is no integration in the public schools is because the powers that be don't want it, it's easier to keep the poor uneducated, the city shuts down libraries in poor neighborhoods, doesn't pick up the garbage, force the poor to live in segregated housing so segregation in the schools didn't happen according to the law, makes sure poor people don't know how to read, lets them graduate high school as functional illiterates, movie theaters are closed in poor neighborhoods so they have no place from which to exercise their imagination and travel makes them feel unwanted in other parts of the city but allows them to develop doo-wop, hip-hop which have no saving grace, if only they would give schools computers kids could have a chance, the only difficulty is figuring out which technology to buy and the scandal of computer magazines when computer companies gave free hardware to journalists of these magazines in return for favorable reviews. Most executives still don't know the difference between hard- and software and when a journalist writes a favorable review because he is personally affected the company makes millions and the reporter then gets some more kickbacks, it's like the '50s quiz shows that were fixed. I pretty much have now figured out how to tell lies from truth, salesmen say yes to everything but I now speak to the software engineers and see what they can or cannot do. My poor boss so rushed and ordering equipment that is already obsolete but she refuses to transfer power to me because she wants to make sure I don't have any—when she was throwing out all this paper I had to say slow down this is the operating system, she didn't even know what I was talking about and now if the system crashes we have no paper trail and we have to go in from the front not where the problem originated. Now no one can keep up with the technology it's changing so fast as the old men are quickly finding out and retiring early since all they can do is manage the old way because they don't have the knowledge required for the new technology. You can only boss if people recognize that you have some ability and you can only do that if you know the difference between software and hardware and all of a sudden they have to be dependent upon subordinates and when buyouts come around they are the first to go, of course they are too good to pass up but these guys have no other abilities and the next twenty years are going to be hell for them. Poetic justice! But who cares about these old fogies it's the new generation of women bosses that are making my life hell and they are never going to be satisfied always wanting more no matter what I do for them, no matter how I make the manual easy for them to read but you can't learn programming from a manual and now if only I could leave this job and find a gig that's not a hostile environment but I don't want to jump into an unsettling situation especially now that I am mentally beat up. At my age I ought to be able to live my life as I want to live my life not have to be an older woman looking for a new job. This is too disheartening.

All these connections who would ever thought they matter, who could have realized how successful I would become, a kid from the Bronx who only played ball and had no interest in learning, my parents kind-hearted with not an ounce of business sense in them and no connection to the outside world, I had thought I left their world behind after my Bar Mitzvah, I still don't know why I did it. I didn't want to have anything to do with them thought I was adopted, we had nothing in common, couldn't stand Hebrew school and wanted nothing to do with the world of superstition, my mother actually asked that I say *Kaddish,* the mourners' prayer, for her for eleven months after she died, but I could not imagine her dead or the world I lived in ever changing and no way was I going to go to *shul* for eleven months, yet of course, did it for my grandfather before school every morning would go to the synagogue and say the prayer before riding the subway to school, luckily it was in Hebrew and so I hadn't the slightest idea of what I was mumbling as a prayer because once I saw the transliteration knew I wanted nothing to do with these old saws that glorified God's name and supposedly helped the souls of the dead find peace in the afterlife, which I didn't believe in at sixteen. I never liked this idea of a supernatural God beyond time and space imposing laws on us, a sudden flash just illuminated this to me, it wasn't a thought out position but all of a sudden realized all this is bullshit. Sin isn't punished by hell and virtue heaven instead they are their own rewards even as my grandfather said even if you don't consider yourself Jewish others will and cites some anti-Jewish slogan that a Jew is like tree planted with worms in the roots, the worms are the Jews. I didn't know what he was talking about then. Of course I knew about the Holocaust but that was so long ago over there not here. I even wanted to see those anti-Semitic films, *City Without Jews, Jew Süss, The Eternal Jew* to laugh at them as we laughed at *Reefer Madness* but those films weren't available. I would imagine only Jews would go the goyim weren't interested and my first big business deal was going to bring those films to America, a pleasant thought to while away the hours in class, when I told friends about it they thought I was crazy only sick minds would want to see that anti-Semitic diatribe, Ezra Pound was a great poet but a virulent fascist and traitor, this is totally inappropriate. I never liked being defined by the other, one of the reasons I moved out of the Bronx and into the Village was here you were who you were not who your parents, class, race was yet now am so successful only because of my connections, the jobs I got were because I was Jewish, albeit a Jewish atheist and the friend I made there who opened up this door for me into co-ops and people buy from me because people think I'm smart even if I have no outward manifestation of Judaism, don't practice it even go out of my way to ignore it, it plays so little a part in my daily life, but it is this nepotism in the broader sense, my creed, that has allowed me these unlimited possibilities not to mention Cassie's good fashion sense that allows me to dress well, she even bought me colored underwear even when I mentioned I wasn't gay she said men feel better wearing nice underwear and even threw out my torn, ripped underwear that I would wear until disintegration, I never understood what was wrong with torn, ripped wife beaters and briefs, I do feel cool wearing them, she learned that in acting, how you feel affects your performance and you dress the character even if what you're wearing is not seen in the performance it helps make you a better actor. Is this the secret not Judaism? I still can't believe how much money we have and we always want more, what seemed like a phenomenal amount before I had it now we can barely live off, especially with private school tuition and two households to support, even separated we still share the same bank accounts, keep all our money in the same pot, we still do things together, yesterday we went for a picnic up at the Cloisters and we still sometimes eat dinner together as a family. The only things we can't do is vacation in the Hamptons or go to the South of France, something we always said we would do. Now I don't even hesitate to take taxis, I don't walk, where before I would always walk or ride the subway now say home, the Upper West Side without batting an eye. How will I survive without her? It was fun when we had less money and lived in a rent-controlled apartment in the East Village and occasionally would walk over to Battery Park and sit in the sand, our own private beach until the city finally developed Battery Park City from the sand they used from the construction of the World Trade Center and I would see the orange sheath they covered it with and was disappointed when the buildings weren't orange. Suddenly like abracadabra I went from making a living to a great deal of money and now am always short, simply by realizing which neighborhoods are at the jumping-off point and ready to switch from rental to co-op and the young quichewazie now realize the advantage of ownership even if the poor really can't understand the concept and still think of owning is a home not an apartment and easily take the cash buyout and move further away from the center. We aren't tearing down buildings but upgrading them unlike the Bronx where the housing stock was disseminated by landlords burning down buildings for insurance, here we are giving tenants a good sum if they move out or help them get mortgages so they can stay and we even helped some tenants flip so they could get a bang for their buck. Unfortunately for most of them they don't have the business acumen to take advantage of this, and of course the black tenants don't trust me being white, fortunately the Spanish do with my broken Spanish, which I am getting better at. Still it's people's homes we are talking about and they get frightened some even hiring lawyers—a waste of money, property rights win and we have the law on our side, it only adds a little more time to negotiations which could be better spent than on their shenanigans. Do tenants think courts deal in justice? Judges don't know the meaning of that word, only law not morality or ethics precedent not a continuous updating based on human beings changing circumstances. I love those lawyers who say property is theft, do they think we're in the Soviet Union, it usually takes only a day for the court to throw their case out even if almost a year to go to trial and by then negotiations are deadlocked and some of the poor have already moved out losing out on a chance to make a few bucks, tenants have no right to live in apartments in perpetuity just because they were born there—apartments by definition are transient even if Esmeralda has hers for over forty years, and now her granddaughter is living in it, thanks to me who when we moved refused to give up a rent-controlled apartment and sublet it but even she knows it's not inheritable like ownership of a piece of property but if a relative now lives in the place for two years has the right to her name on the lease, which Cassandra will do in time. It's amazing for me to see how many Koreans, Chinese, Russian Jews can band together to form co-op associations that lend money to each other and help people start business or move into a co-op but black and Hispanic won't, can't. They live in such lovely brownstones, wonderful architecture but don't seem to be able to get together to buy only rent and landlords have so little incentive to repair that brownstones are falling apart, they call the city hotline numbers and really expect the city to do something when all the city does is say no, no and maybe slap them on the wrist then they go back to the usual no heat, hot-water building falling down around them, strips of concrete actually falling from the building, probably due to pigeon shit getting into the masonry besides shitting on people. When the city said they were going to get rid of them people applauded until we realized they were going to kill them not capture them and let them roam free upstate. What do you expect from a city government that allows neighborhoods to deteriorate? I attempted to take a taxi to Morningside Park recently, no cab would go all the way so I took a gyps cab, we're not yellow is their slogan and was blown away by the beauty of the park and the lovely brownstones on the side streets, the nice housing stock facing the park but all the buildings are in total disrepair and nobody was fixing anything, in fact I was the only white face around there, but it was the middle of the afternoon so I wasn't frightened, and probably was thought of as a parole officer or welfare worker and wanted to check out the neighborhood it was so close yet so far, right down the hill from St. John the Divine and Columbia University but both did nothing for the place and I couldn't get any tenants even to think about co-oping their buildings why should they put money into this piece of shit that's the landlord's job or the cities and weren't interested in investment opportunities, and all the city wanted to do was destroy the park as a way of solving social problems. Way back in the '60s Columbia wanted to build a gym on it but students stopped them and this is a park also designed by Frederick Law Olmsted who designed Central Park and the city wants to make a parking lot out of it. Central Park is now becoming safe once again as joggers are using the park forcing junkies out; the same could happen here, there's no police presence besides they don't go down the side streets and are viewed as an occupying army, the station house is built like an underground nuclear bomb shelter above ground, not one window in it but if the local tenants could form block patrols and force the city to pick up the garbage this can be a good pioneer neighborhood but now it's too dangerous, two hooligans even stopped me, big brave me, who peed in his pants, luckily some elderly ladies walked by and the hooligans respected them and I was able to flee. One of the women asked if they were bothering me because I was white, I thought old. Also I notice the public schools here don't even have the illusion of decency or gifted and talented programs in fact discourage white people from enrolling so they can continue to get federal funding for poor and disadvantaged students. I learned that in the playground. Columbia University faculty never send their children to the local schools, even married graduate students don't. These schools are unfit for human habitation according to one professor.

No? Yes? No? I don't know? Esmeralda looks grandmotherly but she's had this charmed life not only does it look good on the outside but in her living it. Here I am sitting in my big room drinking my bottle of wine all alone and as the years have gone by the more I drink of it, and she is downstairs with her family, I need a little buzz to get some sleep but she sleeps soundly, or so she says, being with her family—when I asked her if she was afraid of death after her heart attack she said no because she wanted to live, but maybe she's on too much medication now to drink, it certainty hasn't stopped me, and her daughter liked a beer when she came home, sometimes we would drink together when she needed to unwind after a performance and I was the only one up in the house. I'm sorry, my fault, when I asked her to put it in writing my lease and she took it wrong thinking I was trying to screw her when all I wanted to do was protect my rights but this single life warps all my thoughts and sometimes I am too direct with other people because I am afraid other people won't recognize me as a person only an old lady, she carries a flow chart in her head and I wanted her to be sure she saw me as an individual and not kick me out on a whim. Instead she left. Her working has really done a number on her and she has difficulty distinguishing friends from acquaintances—I can hear her, I have a good listening technique I pay attention to the way the unconscious works, good training from my years of doing psychotherapy, and I saw how unhappy she actually is before she w she too realizes how difficult reality really is and with truth the burden is a little easier to bear even your loneliness, I found out more about Cassandra ith Esmeralda in the park, when Esmeralda exploded, in, she was so disappointed in her moving out and not her own daughter's infancy and hoped Cassandra wouldn't hat didn't interest me as much as her living with two men, married with and one she carried around in her heart, how many women do that can't be satisfied with what we have and make up fantasies about the other. Now her granddaughter is actually acting upon it she can't stay married she feels the itch down below. Women cruising scares most people. I still believe the family is the destruction of us all, but now that I am alone without family wonder what's going to happen to me in old age. After all my mother at least had children to care for her I have nobody since I left my husband and daughter. He's remarried and wants nothing more to do with me, but maybe if I saw my daughter now we could get along. When I was married I was living with two men really living with two men the one I was married with and the one I was living with in the Village, telling the one I was married that I spend the nights in Connecticut after my classes rather than coming home late at night, then taking the train down to the Village and spending the night with him and I used different variations of my name Danielle, downtown Ella uptown Danielle so would know who was my friend from where at any given moment and not have to rely on my memory in the different worlds I occupied. Uptown I was a therapist downtown a professor until one day someone called from uptown wanting to speak to me and my husband gave him my downtown phone number and I realized he knew. I asked her how she found me and she said Jim gave me your number and then I realized he knew even if I knew it the moment she called me Danielle. I thought the shit would hit the fan but he said he didn't mind didn't like it that I attempted to deceive him but that it's okay, only it wasn't okay and later on I found out he wasn't so pure because he too was involved. Only to him it was amusement for me I couldn't live without both and the danger: when I had a fight with Marvin and he wouldn't let me in the apartment and pushed me out he accused me of trying to break in and got an order of protection against me then I got one for abuse against him for pushing me out the door and Jim had to be the one to negotiate between

us—we would both tell him what we wanted from the other ɛ
room and he would repeat it and the three of us lived like that for a w
until Marvin got sick and I was the one who nursed him, cared for him,
made sure he took his meds, for five years before he died and his children
didn't even invite me to his memorial service and I only found out about
it because friends called and wondered where I was and was shocked I
wasn't invited. I didn't break up his home they were separated before I
met him, okay only two weeks later but it wasn't me who broke up his
marriage, the home wrecker, he even said he wasn't ready for another
relationship and I didn't force it until he came around in the meantime
I was lying to Jim, dear Jim, who I loved but who couldn't satisfy me
and didn't do anything to stop me from leading my double life knowing
about it all the time and he couldn't even go to the political events I
loved because he found them pretentious—a true academic, fixated, rigid,
talking about stuff nobody is interested in and living in the clouds except
when having affairs with students, but he was a man when he found out
about it and very much tried to make it work. My double life was too
important for me, he said, and as I explained to Esmeralda and for therapy
and teaching you need stimulation otherwise you wither away and it
becomes the same ole, same ole, but if you engage your life your work
is engaged as well, and I would go to demonstrations, marches, political
debates, psychotherapy mixed with radical politics. We broke with the
old ways of living and I had absolutely no contact with my family, not
go by yesteryear's truth but discovering new truths, the group was now
my family. When Marvin died I struggled with his family to get back
some of my belongings and all I wanted were my writings, which they
trashed in a fire in Riverside Park his daughter said to me, and my IBM
electric typewriter an expensive purchase when my Underwood broke
and I went to get it repaired at Osner's Business Machine Shop on West
78th and Columbus when Stanley the owner with his wife Mary said get
yourself a good machine you're a writer and these typewriters are made
for college students not professionals who do one, two term papers on it
not use it daily, you need a professional machine and I proved to myself I
was a writer by splurging on this top of the line IBM electric typewriter.
Word processors may be better but I had to feel, see, touch, erase, go slow
with my work not rush through it—the difficulty I had making a living
near the end is now everybody wanted to rush through therapy not take

the time it needs, therapy is slow going but insurance would only pay for psychotropic drugs not therapy. Finally, I bought a new computer but it stayed in the box I always waited until next year because everybody said next year's model would be better and when I finally got one Marvin was no more so I had nobody to show me how it works. One day he comes home tired and goes to lie down in the bedroom and dies instantly and he was only sixty-two and I decided to flee New York moved to Hollywood, Florida but the heat and humidity were terrible, the driving crazy—you have to drive everywhere and I could drive a bit but those left turns from the middle lane were hair-raising, I could read a book in how long it took a red light to turn green, but worse was the boredom and within a year was back looking for a place in the city, put most of my stuff in storage and was living on friends' couches until I found this place and since I can still climb stairs grabbed it and vowed never to leave the city again. I told Cassandra my story when she would come up for a beer and unwinding, she must have told Esmeralda because at first she wasn't interested in going for a walk with me then relented. And when we started walking together really looked at her and saw she wasn't the stereotypical grandmother I made her out to be, even if she had yelled at some little boy get away from my great-granddaughter you bum when he was playing wild in the park, but an attractive older woman whose body is reasonably firm and her mind sharp.

Sound is the boundary of the sea and land the civil war is the boundary of my life before and after I was never the same even if I had to go back in time to the before I was not the person I was when I left home and I only moved back in with my parents because it was the only way to survive in a defeated country, I had to emigrate internally but that didn't mean my life was the same I was already planning my escape, my mind always thinking even as I played the dumb girl but I knew I couldn't do it by myself that I would need help, I had no such guts, a fearful little kid who couldn't live on her own—what would have happened if I moved out, it just wasn't done you couldn't do it, why didn't I board the boat would he have turned me away?—right then I knew somehow I would make it to America and as much as my granddaughter and Joseph think it's a trap it has lived up to my expectations, they don't know what fascism is—it's not the marching and rigidity they are only outward symbols of a deeper trend, what it does to your mind, how it forces you to conform how you can't even use your own language to think, to clear your mind of rubbish, how it censors your thought and the only way I could get a little freedom was to marry. There was no other way to escape and in marriage you get a little freedom so I rather be married than a dutiful daughter only I didn't want to be a dutiful mother to Santiago's child, for my love child yes but not Santiago's child, he would have loved me to be barefoot and pregnant stuck in the kitchen but then I wouldn't have been free, being in love offers you possibilities and gives us new insights into your condition having children would have forced me back to reality and no longer could I be the creator of my own soul, sex then becomes a tool of enslavement. If I had a child by Santiago, my life would have been a toilet bowl using my child as an excuse for not living and Santiago would have wanted more babies and I might have surrendered to him like our defeated nation. Tomas came along at just the right moment he didn't truly come along I created him a small man who got power by being seen with me and I used it to my advantage I may look pretty like my mother but I have a brain where she didn't and rather than go along with the way things were used it to plot my escape, especially after Jacobo. After I found out what love truly is and it got me to wonder about myself, who I wanted to be, and the world that didn't fall apart when I had sex that was pleasurable instead my old ways of thinking began to crumble and shake to its foundation and no longer could I go along and be passive and started taking an active part: thinking is beautiful and love is love of thinking and all of a sudden my whole life was different and I started making mental notes to myself to divest myself of all that I had previously been taught and fill my head with these new ideas and by doing so transformed myself and started believing in what before I only felt and I started becoming who I wanted to be while fighting to become less of who I was and no longer would be this purely passive individual who waits: women wait, I was not going to wait and even if I had to go home in defeat even while the guns were still firing and I could still see the blood flowing inside my head I began to start answering questions I started having with Jacobo and realized if I wanted to live I had to live—the world I tried to change wasn't changing only coming back with a vengeance but it on the ship was no longer the world I wanted any part of and the civil war ended for me the moment I was on the *Ajax* for the States, when I first mentioned this to Conchita she thought I meant the cleanser. I had a deeper desire a desire deep within me that may have existed before as a young girl who went to war, but now it came to the surface and now no longer did I crave adventure as much as to escape this trap. My mother cried when I left but I wouldn't let her tears stop me, all thought begins from love, desire, and that helped me grapple with the woman I wanted to become after I had to crawl back to my parents or when I first landed in this colossal city and saw how big the buildings were. My parents were ashamed when I came back pregnant and quickly arranged a marriage for me before I was showing and Santiago was glad to have me and promised to raise the child as his own, that was the beauty I had and the status my family had and he thought it would be fun to play house with me and I saw the respect he saw in people's eyes when he walked down the Puerta del Sol with me; all of a sudden he shone he was no longer a small-time pharmacist but had climbed the social ladder and hadn't married a woman from next door but one from the upper class and I used that to my advantage and took no shit from him, but I suppose he was waiting for the baby to exercise control over me. Did I realize it at the time or do I only realize it now? Now maybe I can articulate it better but I knew it at the time no way was I going to be his wife as I had been a daughter, even if my mother was so happy that I was finally married and wouldn't shame the family. When I returned from the civil war I was already a woman and that made all the difference, the church be damned, Franco be damned but he was never damned lived forever even in death nobody believed he really had died. Generalissimo Francisco Franco is still dead, Chevy Chase on *Saturday Night Live* kept repeating over and over and nobody in the States could grasp that people in Spain still couldn't believe he finally died, especially after receiving so many health bulletins that he was recovering nicely and resting comfortably. He probably was dead already. I was through with hypocrisy and knew if I didn't act would be trapped forever and wouldn't let the church be part of me it was a fight to the death and I wouldn't give in married in church because that was the only type of marriage allowed—imagine the shock when my love child was born dead, stillborn, nature sometimes messes up and now Santiago was happy thinking now I would then have a child of his, and he must have felt relieved not to raise another man's son but he never mentioned it. And I had to be very careful not to carry his child, I would love Jacobo's child Santiago's would have been a stranger. And when I finally did get pregnant again felt nothing for Gloria only that she helped me get to America with Tomas, to get away from all those dull Spaniards who I regarded with horror. Immigration officials were so nice to me a Mother and a bride. Santiago fought with the Fascists to prove to himself he could be a man but that's not true he left for war in order to prove he could be brave to me because I detested him and would no longer be content with home at home above his pharmacy and his mother never forgave me—the death of her only son and she accused me of not loving him but by then I wanted nothing to do with her and didn't even answer her letter when she accused me of not loving her beloved: you did not stand by my son and you let him go off to war just to be rid of him, you signed his death warrant and smugly looked on. You have no love for anyone except yourself, how could you raised by parents who never loved you. You begrudge me the happiness of being with my son just to have an easier life you are not a human being. I told my story to Danielle on our sit on a park bench, she loved to sit not walk, she asked why I didn't go home now that Francisco Franco is dead, I said this is home I am living where I want to be living, use the language I want, and it wasn't possible to go back the people will never change.

Maybe I became who I am because my mother pounded me over the head with religion because I can't shake it as easily as I wish. At sixteen I could I knew what God was and there was no god, how could you believe after the Holocaust, grandma explained that to me but still I act as if there is an eye in the sky, as if all my actions are being watched, as if anybody would care about me—what if there is a minute chance that reason alone isn't the answer would I want to change my ways? We now know the stars are not pinpricks where you can get a glimpse of heaven because there is no up or down in the universe yet I still can't get those images out of my mind, not that I go to Church, churches are empty they even have to sell off some of their real estate in order to continue, and if this continues within a decade they all will be out of business, will they have a fire sale? It would be a good thing if they continue to keep their schools open and fight the monopoly on public education, if it wasn't for grandma, then Joseph, I wouldn't have been born again, I wanted Jacoba to go to Catholic school but they are adamantly against it had a fit even if it was so much more affordable, Joseph claimed we make enough to be able to afford a good school. What's the sense of us making so much money to save for college elementary school is much more important, the habits formed there are the ones that stay with us throughout our life, and he is correct I think kids who play well with others have a better chance in life than those aggressive ones, and I thought of my religious beliefs and my hatred of going for religious instruction even when they bribed us with milk and cookies, that got a laugh out of Joseph who would have loved to be dismissed from public school for religious instruction and envied us Catholics who got dismissed early on Wednesday, an hour early, for an hour early he would have believed only he didn't realize how lucky he was not having to listen to those nuns drone on about a virtuous life, you think those pious rabbis were any better, he countered, if only Judaism wasn't powerful enough to get Jewish boys out of school and when they were strong enough they got the public schools closed on the High Holidays, but what good is that the only fun of being Jewish was getting off school while my friends were stuck in school, he always said. My mother had sent me to Catholic school for two years but the discipline was too much, even if they talked about how the cosmos is full of love I am a free spirit and couldn't stand it until one day I simply refused to go and now I'm thinking about sending Jacoba? I remember how free I felt when my mother finally consented and let me to go to public school because she couldn't stay home every day with me at home—free at last, free at last, and the public school was so much easier I did no work, I could read already and had to wait until most classmates could catch up. And here I am wanting my child to suffer, I don't understand myself, it's bad enough I still pray to a non-existent God, cross myself when I pass a church, because of all that pounding when I was little, that's probably why I'm so confused as an adult, I'm still afraid just like a little girl, but then I wanted a prince charming to rescue me now I know there is no prince charming but that you have to rescue yourself, Joseph is a decent soul but no prince charming. I thought I was free when I left school early and moved back in with grandma, even actually told her that I finally lost my virginity but she immediately had me fitted for a diaphragm, afraid that I wouldn't take the pill all the time and let myself be carried away into pregnancy. I actually see women on the street nowadays asking young girls directions instead of men thinking of solidarity with women but these girls are idiots and don't know how to traverse the city only their neighborhood, mature men however do. Now I'm the one who has to be responsible, how did that happen? I have a child! She has a stranglehold on me now the only time I can talk to Joseph is when he calls me at work because when she is awake there is absolutely no conversation in the house—she is not cute and quiet but rambunctious, I told Mademoiselle princess that the world doesn't revolve around her but if she had half a brain would have told me to shove it I'm going to *Mimi*. Grandma laughs, says hippies are the strictest parents. Nobody loves children the way grandparents do and it's true the world now does revolve around her and thanks to grandma I can leave, now I have peace not living with them we tell her she's not the cause of the breakup but she doesn't believe it but doesn't realize we had her to save the marriage, which can't be saved, but now all of a sudden living alone after living with so many people is not as exciting as I thought it would be, I actually turn the television on when I get home to have some sound. And all of a sudden enjoy drinking tea with a madeleine as Joseph suggested, I didn't even know what he was talking about, he said Proust, I still didn't know imagine an educated woman not knowing Proust but now I enjoy reading him drinking tea and dunking my madeleine in my tea cup. And I was going to buy it in hardback but decided to spend the money on a charming Sevres porcelain tea set instead and read him in soft cover, ouch. The cozy however really doesn't keep the tea warm in the pot and I should get a samovar, but that would ruin the effect. A refined aroma tea is not the tea from tea bags, but fresh tea in a ball with a little milk and I now put a sugar cube in my mouth, like grandma does from what she learned from Jacobo and I thought that cool, a pleasant way to relax but I miss the garden in back of our house. Danielle that stranger who moved in loved pontificating there so it soon lost all interest for me I couldn't stand her she seems so pretentious, Joseph and grandma seem to like her so I couldn't say anything but I would have never let her move in, I like men better than women, I like boys so much better than girls but boys always seem to want a threesome. Some fantasy of threes and it's always two women. I have to remember I had a secret life that my mother knew nothing about and I'm sure Mademoiselle princess will too but is it better to have it with rich kids rather than poor ones, I learned more about drugs and sex at Calhoun than I ever learned up in the Bronx, where I only learned to smoke and curse. Yet I turned out alright so it couldn't have been all bad, is this a sign of old age I'm starting to agree with my mother. Next I'll take her to church, what about a confirmation?

That would appall grandma, Joseph wouldn't mind he would see religion as a way of controlling children with guilt. He was even angry when I told her that we lived together before marriage. Parenting makes cowardice of us all.

Do you know how much I have to fight my conscience just to get up in the morning? It isn't easy getting out of bed, I know I'm not throwing people out of their home, people haven't lived in these places for generations, besides renters have no God-given right even if they were born in them, and I am not kicking them out and throwing their furniture on the street, forcing them to seek shelter in a homeless facility, we are paying them decent money if they will leave and if they accept can live in the Bronx or Brooklyn, further out, with some savings. New York is a rental town and many do not understand the benefits of ownership and no matter how hard I listen can't get them to grasp the fact that they will be saving money by owning instead of throwing it away on rent, why should I own an apartment it's not a house? I can persuade younger couples especially if they are both working and they have no children, or gay couples the benefits of ownership but minorities who I thought I could help want little to do with me. They see me as a landlord. The government think owners are better people than renters and you can get nice rebates on the interest so that yearly you're paying less than you would be in rent and you get equity if you sell making big bucks and all I hear is it's taxed, so what at least you have the money to be taxed on and the government only taxes on 80% of the profit, money you wouldn't have had if you hadn't listened to reason. And banks can't or won't change their ways; minorities mainly black and Hispanics have difficult times getting mortgages even when I help fill out the paperwork or they feel uncomfortable going to banks, banks don't like to look at off the books income, steady, legal but since not taxed banks say it doesn't count and people who have no debts or credit cards can't get mortgages, and redlining is severe. Some can't come up with a ten percent down payment otherwise the money would flow and can't ask family and relatives for help yet some of these brownstones have the key ingredient location, location, location, in the city near a major subway stop, a park, good shopping, the only apartments that are bad are those near projects, those projects not going away and the kids who live in them are only going to get worse, many of these projects are Amazons all women and children no men, children with different fathers because so many men are in jail and no men around unless off the books, you don't expect the women to wait around do you? Cassie says, and these kids create havoc outside the projects, these women really do need a father around to discipline the kid even if Esmeralda thinks fathers don't bring discipline it's that these are kids raising kids they're too young to be raising children little more than kids themselves, best not to live near them unless the Supreme Court decides that the Housing Authority can do its duty and kick out tenants whose children are convicted of drug offenses. I know bleeding-heart liberals say it's unfair especially if the mother or grandmother is law-abiding but how else are you going to clear the projects of drugs, junkies shouldn't be allowed to ruin projects as they ruin the city, drugs are a plague on the city, it's bad enough the housing stock is aging and Department of Housing is losing many qualified workers to retirement and replacing them with MBAs kids who have no idea what it takes to run a successful project only know strategies that never seem to work but they swear by them. What's so difficult about keeping elevators working so the elderly living on the higher floors can go out once in a while and not have to climb up thirteen floors, they should never have built these modern projects over six stories, then at least they were safe and people knew one another, now they're too high and nobody knows their neighbor, at least projects usually have heat in the winter, something you can't say for all the tenements. Those that we buy and fix up the number one cost is a new boiler. But little surcharges usually can cover that. And we don't scrape we do a good job. It's fascinating how we don't necessarily have to paint and plaster as much as undo paint, plaster, years of neglect, underneath is beautiful old woodwork that we now restore, bring back to the surface. I see what has happened to the city with my own eyes, eyes are a good tool for seeing to see what is going on around eyes don't deceive especially when added to experience and thought, when neighborhoods fail they don't get better by themselves you have to make a conscientious effort to right the wrong and when ownership happens people begin caring for the neighborhood you just don't stop at the door to your apartment but you sweep the sidewalk, call sanitation when garbage is not picked up or abandoned cars are left on the block, do home repairs, call the police when crack houses are used in run-down abandoned buildings, the only difficulty I find with brownstones is their skylights, lovely for the sun to pour in or see the nighttime sky and the white splotches of light on the black surface only you don't see stars in the city so all it is is dark and worse no matter what you do junkies will break in and that costs a fortune to close up. We did it in Danielle's apartment, of course, she complains, but I didn't want junkies sneaking in and terrorizing us, she thinks I'm a worry wart. And now that everyone realizes rehabilitation doesn't work the solution is to lock them up instead of dealing with the underlying problem and what happens when these kids get out built like brick shithouses, all you do in jail is lift weights, where are they going to go but back to mommy. Jail is no threat anymore no bugbear most, many in the neighborhood are in jail and it's a rite of passage: the good thing is that our consciousness is changing and people are beginning to wake up and see how drugs are bad for the community not some black or Hispanic kids telling the police we are the acting proletariat fighting to change the system and groups are now willing to do the hard work for neighborhoods and try and make them whole once again. And homeownership helps I keep telling myself—all conscience is habit customs conditions what parents, teachers, say, oh my god am I getting old believing in my parents and teachers, the savior of us all? Imagine if I was the kid caught with drugs and my parents were forced to move and I was responsible they would have had to take me with them where else could I have gone. Lucky I didn't cut school but now Hispanic kids tell me they can't be in school drugs are everywhere and they're afraid they'll will get caught up in it so drop out to the dismay of their parents, who can't understand why the schools can't be drug-free zones. Khalil Sumpter a kid at Thomas Jefferson high school in Brooklyn pulled a preemptive attack on Ian Moore and Tyrone Sinkler who he thought were going to bully him and fired first killing them in the school hallway and it wouldn't have made an inch in the dailies except the mayor was going out there to give an inspirational talk and where the mayor goes the press goes so it made the front pages of all the papers and the Mayor was shamed into agreeing to finance metal detectors at the front door in some dangerous high schools. Right now developers are not building housing for the middle class let alone the poor but we are trying to restore the housing stock and even then the city government is fighting us tooth and nail forcing us to have to prove everything instead of being on our side when we try and improve the community, making

sure we follow the letter of the law, environmental regulations, fire regulations, building codes, but almost allowing the west side of Manhattan
to be destroyed by putting a six-lane highway through it, not supporting
mass transit, Westway, from Battery Park City to the George Washington
Bridge, oh they don't say to the bridge only to 43nd St. as if all cars will
just get off on 42nd St. and not want to proceed further north, plus all
sorts of access roads and exits that would destroy existing neighborhoods
but Marcy Benstock stood in their way and the courts agreed with her
the environmental impact statement was ignored and even then the government appealed but eventually they lost. The government is the enemy
of the people wanting to spent money on traffic not transit. They should
make a statue of her across from Jane Jacobs, not, we only make statues or
name streets after military leaders or esteemed politicians. On our small
scale we do not break the laws and have lawyers check out our agreements and insist our clients also get lawyers not use ours, as it is some
clients still want to bluster their way through pay off inspectors: the fire
department has a good policy fire inspectors are there only temporarily
and if the building isn't up to code and there's a fire a year or two down
the road the inspector may be the firefighter caught in the fire because
he has to go back to firefighting after his year or two inspecting is up.
Wonderful strategy in theory, except it doesn't work in reality, doesn't
stop the inspectors from taking bribes and we are forced to pay off otherwise our construction work will never get done even if we are up to
code. Our renovations move slowly but they move and one reason we
are successful is that we have a decent reputation even if I always feel bad
when we take away peoples' homes even as I realize that's not true just
superstition, confusion, guilt talking to me and yet I know it's not me for
all our calculating, planning, research, organizing and thinking no matter
how well we chose pioneer neighborhoods it's just damn luck that has
come my way.

I rarely think about my mother nor my father if there's a hell my
mother must have joined him there by now but inside me she lives on
more than I care to consider; now women can live more fruitful and
imaginative lives but I have her values inside me and no matter how hard
I try and shake them they don't seem to want to leave, I thought by
coming here to America would finally be free of them but they are still
inside me, now women can slam the door and not come back, I couldn't

do that on my own needed a man to live until finally I couldn't live with any man ever again and now here I am living with Joseph and Jacoba, Conchita has moved back into our old place. Of course she has invited me back but to live without Jacoba doesn't seem worth it. I have no idea how my parents met, they must have told me but I never was interested, living with them was totally uninteresting all they were concerned with is do people like you, am I religious enough, and they had no concern for me as a person, living with my parents is totally different than how I live now, and looking at old sepia photographs of them, my mother looked quite beautiful even if it hid a hideous soul. My mother always thought she would die young, always a drag, while my father thought he would live to be a hundred—if it were only so. When I received the telegram I knew I should go back for the funeral but was afraid Franco wouldn't let me leave because I had criticized his regime, and even little criticisms go a long way with scared, frightful people who make a big show of toughness but are little bullies instead I walked the streets of New York in the middle of winter, just left the house with no coat on just a blouse and wandered in the Village for hours until the cold finally numbed me and fortunately Tomas was home because I left without my purse, keys, wallet, identification, and when he asked where I was didn't even know just walking and Gloria was bigger by then and had her own key, we didn't even have a phone so I couldn't have called if I had wanted to but I didn't want to just wanted to walk and walk be alone with my thoughts and one of our neighbors gave her milk and cookies when she came home from school, it was that kind of building where neighbors looked after one another, I must have come home after dark because all I remember is Gloria yelling at me where were you don't you know it's dark outside, why didn't you tell anybody where you were, as if she was the mother. She always loved play-acting at the supermarket she loved making believe we were sisters and mommy is going to be angry at us and we shouldn't tell her where we were. This time she went too far and I yelled that I received a telegram that my father had died, which stopped her dead in her tracks. Why didn't you tell me? I had read it and thought I left it on the kitchen table but I had crumbled it and thrown it away then took it out of the waste basket and read it again to make sure I read it correctly then lit the gas and finally watched it burn over the stove. I could still see some of the ashes on the stove, afterwards my mother closed herself off like a nun. That's how she always was but now she had a legitimate reason to be this recluse and my father was no longer around to mask it. Without him there was no one and she was no longer this beautiful young woman who had men to play with her only my sister was left and she never forgave me for abandoning her to my mother. I could have become my mother but I fought all my life not to be like her, if only she had the ability to be a little affectionate I wonder what effect that would have had on me. Would I have run away so early, met Jacobo, changed my life? I know you can't change one aspect of your life because who knows how it would have influenced other aspects but I still have this ability to think this and despite all her yelling and ministrations to the contrary to return to the fold I knew that I was only bidding my time and that I would leave Spain and not return until after Franco passed, but who knew, could believe he could ever die, then I was young knew we all die eventually knew it then also but wouldn't believe it then: and when he finally died on November 20th, 1975 proving once and for all there was no God for if there was a God he would have died long ago, in the colonial war in Morocco, if God can see everything that will occur, he should have known what type of man he would become and not allowed him to be. I have no desire to see their grave, the last time I went to a cemetery was when Gloria died and then I only went so Conchita wouldn't be alone and said this is too depressing, I didn't even go for Joseph's parents, and I didn't really want him to be alone but couldn't go, but I did have food ready for him when they returned, he claimed that was a Jewish tradition but it was a human one. You always take time out to eat. It's fascinating to see how close Catholic and Jewish traditions are before religious leaders take deep breaths and try and separate them. Just sitting out here in the twilight, Joseph made sure I have a rocking chair in the garden the garden belongs to all of us but since mine is the only door that leads to the garden I like to think of it as my own private spot, and whenever I sit here and rock my mind likes to think backwards and I wonder if I could have led a different life, if I had been allowed to study or would I still be the same person I am, something I will never know, but when the sun sets and I sit and ruminate I think of a past that I never had, I never cared too much for the life I lived especially after we lost our country, I still stayed there but it wasn't mine anymore but a fascist regime, inward emigration describes how I felt until I was able to leave and that's all I cared about. Santiago would never have left and when he finally left his mother lost all respect for him, as if I ever had any, and didn't even want to even walk down the street with him, when he was serious would laugh and when he was funny be stone-faced—it's sad to think feminism came too late for me—God will come but too late for us. Now young girls go on grand tours by themselves women didn't do that in my day, oh maybe the English because they wanted to get away from their dreary climate—English women and their sketch books were everywhere but not French, German or Italian, it certainly wasn't Spanish we would go nowhere without our husbands. Now it's so simple even colleges offer a year abroad back in the day it just wasn't done. As it is I never became housewifely, I give myself credit for that but still my only ambition was what I didn't want to do I had no idea what I wanted except escape. The stifling ambience of provincial Spain, the church, the military became home—life that is afraid of living only liking order and routine, what was in my power was only the ability to marry and I tried to use that to escape, knowledge and marriage are two opposite forces and I didn't get a chance to achieve much at least Jacobo allowed me out of my shell at least that's why he's so central to my imagination, he allowed me to think for the first time and to feel the power of knowledge, it's like when I watched football such a boring game but when Jacoba plays all of a sudden it's exciting and I hope she kicks the ball, even Conchita has gotten caught up and tries to come to the games, Joseph thinks she's too young to play ball but loves that they sing songs afterwards, and he even has started jogging once again but doesn't bring back fresh bread as he did when we lived on the Lower East Side—since Louis Lichmann's closed nobody on the Upper West Side makes fresh bread anymore, progress.

There is a huge discrepancy between what I try to do and what I do, how I think and what I've become, how did this come about, all I set out to do was become a working actress and now I am a successful data processor, sometimes actress, unsuccessful mom, and divorced woman who when I go up to my Jacoba's school don't even know which class she's in, luckily there were only two so I quickly found it, and after she saw me at the assembly knew I could leave and not have to sit and be bored. She wants me to go with her on school trips but I'm too busy and my company doesn't give time off for school trips like Joseph's; since Joseph is the company he has made it a company policy that parents can take off for school trips. I'm glad and sad I can't take time off and I am as far removed from childcare as you can be without being totally out of the picture, it is easy to become uninvolved and seeing her alternate weekends is not conducive to keeping informed. Grandma went down to the boat basin but she couldn't keep up with the kids walking and the teacher was in such a rush to catch the *Clearwater* that they didn't wait for her and she had to take a taxi home. She missed the fun of going out on the Hudson river with two dozen screaming school kids, and I will never forgive the teacher for walking so fast, what's the rush, even if grandma says it's okay, she was looking forward to the trip she didn't want the students to miss it because she couldn't keep up, afterwards Joseph bought her this beautiful bamboo cane with a red silicone handle that her hand fits comfortable around even put on a rubber tip so she could have a good grip on the sidewalk from the Cooper Hewitt Museum, and it didn't look like one of those old people metal canes. But I doubt even with the walking stick she could have kept up. Don't get old is all she says, but what is the alternative? Just a couple of years ago I hated walking with Jacoba she walked so slow and I would get exhausted but now she must have gotten some muscles in her legs and my little Mademoiselle princess actually walks ten blocks to be with her friends instead of taking a taxi. All this I now hear from grandma or Joseph because I never take her or pick her up from school I'm usually too busy at my job or acting late into the night and it's too early for me to get up there. Joseph can set his own hours besides nobody buys an apartment early in the morning even banks won't see him before eleven, managers are always in meetings, so it is his job to take her to school and they now both walk, with grandma they taxied, she loved getting up early, waking her making breakfast for her dressing her and taking her to school, only now she can do most on her own except cross the street by herself so Joseph is the one who takes her and he refuses taxis. He's still loves to walk and insists she do it with him. I thought it was all over in one of the company reorganizations and maybe I would get a good letter of recommendation but a woman over fifty has no chance in this job market, it's even worse than acting, nothing personal but we are going in a different direction, we don't need two people doing the same job and of course the woman would have to go but to my surprise I stayed, promoted and a huge raise because of Joseph's negotiating skills, I would have said alright, I'm cool, whatever but he insisted upon me asking for more and boy did I get a once in a lifetime raise and it wasn't a bonus but my annual salary, he said be careful maybe they're making sexual advances towards you, but he reads too many newspapers, these are professionals and our job is efficiency even if we are the most inefficient company I have ever seen, belief in managerial knowledge is like a former belief in God taking for granted but never proven—besides men only like twenty-year-olds not mature women but I do have to be careful sometimes men's fantasies get away with them and they think of Hispanic women as ho's with an enormous sexual appetite; he was always disappointed when I wasn't sexually abused so he could sue them. He says you're a mature woman can handle improper advances and we can have a college trust fund for Jacoba. When I told him I work with women he says he's not prejudiced he'll take money from women. Now I'm working with men again, men on their 2nd, 3rd wife, younger, of course, kids from all of them what do these men see in these younger women who don't have a brain in their head. I was surprised when I met a few of them I can see why they want to stay home and be a mother they can barely hold a conversation, I never had a meaningful conversation with anyone of them, they don't read, go to plays, go to concerts or art galleries, they simply yap only about their children or how tough they have it because their husband has to pay so much out in child support and alimony. They don't even seem to mind being stuck home all day with an infant, especially as the man has to work later and later promising he will leave at five but usually leaving by seven. The men are nice, sometimes when they are working late or when I am between gigs or have a late show we go for a drink and I enjoy being around them, warm a pleasant sense of humor and safe. Their idea of marriage is you don't cheat but men never considered it cheating yet the correct interpretation is inequality because it was okay for them but not their spouses and even in the era of feminism it is still the double standard. Yet when I did it it made perfect sense. I pinch myself, but how do I know the pinch isn't part of the dream, whoever thought I would be hobnobbing with upper management and they are so much like us, and what is special about them being so educated and all is that they do come to my performances, insist upon it, appreciate it, and since I no longer play nude parts I have no problem with seeing them outside work. I thought they would come up with excuses, the times not right, we couldn't get a sitter, blah, blah, but they even drive into the city by themselves and don't even want comps. Real *menshes*, character, brains, interest in the world around them, the only adults who come to my performances are bourgeois. They realize how important acting is and I would disappear as a person if I didn't act and some of them wish they had continued along artistic paths they dreamed about when younger but gave up when they weren't instant successes and became pencil pushers instead. Even producers no longer proposition me on the casting couch but wonder if I can get a donation from the company. Now sometimes I wonder if I got the gig because of who I am or the money I can bring in, why I like voiceovers or commercials better, there I know it's mine not what money I can bring to the table, and really that's where the money is better than in acting. Crazy world. We both make enough now that either one of us could stay home but both of us need to work and have our own space. I would go crazy being home all day with Jacoba, still I am the one who feels guilty for leaving them even if Joseph stays he's gone most of the time now that she's in school. At first she wanted us to stay outside the school and always be there for her and I thought let's tell her we are she will never know, but Joseph refused said his mother lied too much to him, that he still gets angry over her lies thirty years later and that he vowed to tell the truth: we cannot wait outside the schoolyard for you but will always be there to pick you up. After a little crying she accepted it. And when she went to the doctor for shots he always told her it would hurt but not too much and that it was okay to cry unlike his mother who said it doesn't hurt. He is so much more patient with her, listens to her asks her opinion. His mother was only doing what the temper of the times said but he doesn't forgive her that easily she messed him up because she was messed up before him but that's no excuse for Joseph. You would think as a parent he would be more understanding he vows to do the exact opposite of his. I have so much, my life so successful and I want less but what to cut out. Of course I can have another affair be just like a man when bored strike out but it's only temporary satisfaction and doesn't get to the underlying elements, now it's starting to become boring switching from one man to another, and I refuse valium, I wouldn't even have to get a prescription all my friends use it but I want to feel the pain and benefit from it, after all I am an actress, and an actress first, I keep reminding myself. One of my colleagues actually took it during his dissertation defense, what's the good of not feeling it. It made him a stranger to himself. But he didn't care he passed and wanted nothing more to do with them. How can you live and not be in the world of the other? Grandma feels lost if she doesn't see Jacoba at least once a day, she still makes her breakfast, and is there for her with milk and cookies, and a good hug before she goes to bed—let her get that love now even if I doubt she will even remember it, but Joseph has taken many photos so she can know what grandma looked like after she's gone and realize how important those bonding moments were even if grandma is not doing it for the future but in her unconditional love of the moment, however she probably won't even look at them if she's like me, but Joseph has said enough times he will keep talking about Mimi so it will become entwined in her, part of her gestalt, her language, her thought. We now live in this crazy moment where the old rules are being tossed out and new ones are being created. What was once considered damned is now accepted—women no longer have to stay home with the kiddies, we can keep our own last name that really is only our father's last name not our mother's, abortions are legal, drugs becoming so, and I have no moral qualms about living my life, only is this freedom or a sign of decay not a strengthening our values, having to live with choice?

Does an act first start in the head or in the hand? Is it physical or mental? When I visualize it never is how I envisioned it. Cassie once told me when she would hang out with her friends in high school they would smoke, shop, playhouse and imagine themselves as young mothers and their daughters couldn't pull anything on them because they knew it all but when she went to a private school they'd go into Riverside Park discussing ideas, poetry, colleges where they would be free, and she quickly saw she was out of her element and had no imagination beyond the everyday and wondered why they would be discussing school work, ideas and getting laid before they went to college, the books they were reading in class and they never had any doubt that next year they would be in college. It was expected of them and they expected it, while up in the Bronx few friends from school would go onto college, rarely did one of her classmates even have the average to get into City College and nobody even dreamed of leaving home and going away to school, while here that's all the girls talked about. Last night I had this dream where grandfather and Esmeralda were going by bus to Spain together along with Cassie and me only the bus breaks down and she goes off in search of food and I wonder if she will make it back, but she comes back in a motorized wheel chair and I quickly get the association still in the dream, we had just seen a play, a musical, Cassie and I still do things together, and one of the musical numbers 'wheelers and dealers' about a bunch of old people in wheelchairs playing solitude and dancing. I found it utterly obnoxious but why in the dream were grandfather and Esmeralda holding hands rubbing their faces and both so young-looking, then I decide to go for a walk since the bus isn't repaired and pass a movie theater where the owner steps out wearing a sweater over his sports coat, I don't get that and make a mental note to recall that and figure it out when I awaken, because I don't think that was part of the play and he comes up to me says hello offers his hand but I haven't the slightest idea who he is and continue walking only to come upon a young couple of a boy and girl, that is important not a gay couple I think, and they are talking about how the boy is a landlord up in the Bronx, I immediately grasp that I keep thinking of investing up there but something always holds me back, I want to go up to them and say The Bronx? but am too shy—even in my dreams I can't be a hero, besides I never liked young girls who giggle and still can't figure out how my partner left his wife of over twenty-five years for a woman half her age who hasn't an idea in her head, he got caught having an affair and didn't make much of an effort to keep it secret and left his wife for her and is now sleeping on his boyhood friends' couches, as well as other friends he knows from high school. I continue walking before it dawns on me the bus might leave without me and I'll never be able to catch up, it can move faster than I can walk, and I turn and say no problem all I have to do walk on the side of the road the bus will drive on and I will run into the bus but all of a sudden a big porcelain wall looms in front of me that couldn't have been there when I started otherwise I would have noticed it I'm not that blind to my surroundings, I walk straight but there is no tunnel thought it— how can that be? To the left and right are two slits but I know I walked straight and now don't know which way to go because I'm sure to get lost—the porcelain wall I even get Esmeralda is rethinking we should redo our old-fashioned bathroom put molding in, a good shower, and a toilet bowl more ovular in shape not the vintage stuff we have, what I don't understand is why I'm stymied which way to go and I don't want to make a commitment either way and am standing there waiting for the wall to open up and as I wait the bus could be getting further away. Finally, I awaken in my usual cold sweat and roll over to my side of the bed, I now usually go to sleep on Cassie's side and when I awaken in the middle of the night switch to my side, and usually by the time I reach the other have figured out my dream of missing Cassie, usually a not very complicated latent meaning and I can continue my sleep but now feel stymied. Kafka at least has a door only meant for him even if he isn't allowed in it, I don't even have a door only a porcelain wall with no tunnel through it staring me in the face and with no way to get through it. My life is blocked, I stay awake for the next couple of hours telling myself ignore it it's only a dream but I want to finish it so I can get back to bed, my dream usually finds its purest form when I am totally awake and begin to realize what it's all about then it loses its force over me—if you can't wrestle with a book, interrogate it, question it, what good is it? Only after that can you read for pleasure. Now I realize the impossibility of my vision and only in actually does it come to fruition nowhere how I imagined it. I can never visualize how a project will turn out not because I can't see the final form until it is completed and the setbacks along the way always alter the final result, I wonder why am I thinking about my grandfather and Esmeralda together again, that's not my life and theirs is over at least my grandfather's is, Esmeralda is waiting, and she's been with a few men since him didn't wear black and my grandfather is buried next to grandma—is that bus going to Spain? Why a wall? All fragments. Is my life a series of fragments from my past? and I'm not going to be able to understand my life unless I realize that. But is there a deeper meaning or do I always see surface reality as the meaning. If life has a deeper meaning it is eluding me. Usually I can decode my dreams but this one is so powerful that when I awoke was glad it was only a dream. Why do dreams have to have meanings? Is this because of Freud that dreams have to be about something. Maybe if we don't listen to the Bible, God talking to us in dreams, or Freud our id talking to us and deprive them of special meanings maybe when the original set of assumptions about them are forgotten their meanings become problematic and there will be no way to grasp what the new is promulgated in the old. Why do dreams have to have meanings it's only because I read when I read Melanie Klein they have different meanings than Jung, I should do an empirical test and take the same dream to a Jungian, Kleinian, Freudian and see what they say, never to a Sullivanian because at least Klein and Freud didn't know what they would find Sullivan and his groupies always know. Danielle was a couples counselor who didn't even believe in a housekeeper, common sense, if you have a housekeeper half your problems are already solved. But these interpretations are only reasons after the fact not a realization of an unimaginable imaginable form to me. My dream originates in the dream itself not in the parts which I grab from everyday life—that had to be the worst possible moment when I saw how bad my life is stuck behind a wall and have to be more careful in living because I now go out so infrequently and the best part of the dream was that I wanted to leave at intermission but there was no intermission probably the director was afraid nobody would come back if there was one because Cassie only reads for pleasure not wrestling with a work while I struggle and don't only want to be entertained want to wonder, but Cassie will never leave a work in the middle if they have enough guts to go on stage she will see what they have, she will also tear a book apart and read sections of it I would never do that. She probably learned that from Esmeralda who says she can't schlep heavy books anymore and has no qualms of carrying sections. Besides my lunch and business papers I carry in my attaché case the Portuguese writer Saramago and am grateful to him for introducing me to his compatriot António Lobo Antunes and his movement in space-time that is more real than my world; I can read on the subway, but not Lobo Antunes for him I need quiet time to engage, read, reread, a room of my own, my comfortable reading chair, a light and my fountain pen to argue with.

The war is over, the Second World War is finally over, do you comprehend that, understand that the end is finally over Europe is once again free, there is no longer a wall between us. Conchita thought grandma must be losing it the war has been over almost a half a century, I've been calling her every night because I am so excited. It's useless to talk to Danielle she wonders why anyone would want to leave a communist utopia. I sit and watch on CNN, I insisted we get cable television so I could watch the collapse of communism live and talk to her incessantly about it, never thinking it would happen in my lifetime like her I thought this was here to stay. No the actual fighting has been over but not the peace, England went to war to protect Poland, not Spain, that was the second country to fall victim to fascist occupation, Spain was the first and after the war an Iron Curtain enveloped Eastern Europe and now that has fallen and Europe is whole once again. Again? Joseph asked. Eastern Europe has a European sensibility not a Russian one but nobody of this generation knows that because it was behind the Iron Curtain and they erased its historical parts, even many Eastern Europeans have no idea of their own history, the Poles have a little more freedom in the arts but still don't know their own history, the Romanians are clueless of their past, Hungarians don't even realize they were an equal part of the Austro-Hungarian Empire, the second greatest power in all of Europe until it all came tumbling down, Czech's don't even know who Kafka is because he wrote in German but was Czech through and through, and Albanians don't even realize the war is over they still have trenches in case the enemy invades, these countries will actually have peace in their lifetimes and now maybe the Soviet Union can go the way of the Dodo bird. But they are too strong. Immediately after Russian troops were removed from Eastern Europe the whole edifice collapsed. You have a more benign view of the Soviet Union, I know them for what they are, we had a good cause in Spain and they helped to make sure we were defeated, everything they did was against democracy I was present at creation when they destroyed most of Central Europe and started calling it Eastern a real threat to the peace of the world, you knew the Soviet Union from the '60s when a bunch of old farts ran the country and the Party was a laughing stock but not after the war when they were a real threat. I even woke up Jacoba and brought her downstairs so she could see the collapse and I was a fellow traveler until I realized how antidemocratic they actually were—we had to support them at first they were the only ones fighting the fascists but they were even worse fascists with a larger vocabulary, they believed in freedom for the working man only they were more authoritarian, bureau-cratic not people-orientated nor did they believe in individual freedom, a bourgeois concept rather for the good of the state, which meant the good of the politicians, they talked the good talk the brotherhood of mankind but that's because they couldn't deliver the goods so talked about false desires versus needs as if they could deliver either—socialism is an inef-ficient economic system and everything they did was to cover that up. I never thought I would live long enough to see this day, only yester-day this day was not possible I tell Joseph who still can't believe I am so antisocialist. I like to imagine the look on my fellow travelers faces as if they could believe this is happening. I feel like hopping on a plane and celebrating with them but it's only a fantasy I can't travel much anymore. The question now is will the Baltic states become free, Joseph and Conchita with their poor schooling don't even know Lithuania, Latvia and Estonia are occupied countries. Joseph says he thought they were always part of the Soviet Union, which he actually calls Russia, not an indestructible union of free republics established by Russia as it says in its national anthem, and Conchita said she thought I was talking about the Balkans. Joseph thinks that when McCarthy got rid of all the China experts in the State Department, the '50s purge of all competent knowledgeable people who understood that part of the world the US foreign policy went kaput and small-minded souls who had no notion of history, nationalism or even spoke the local languages set our foreign policy and education adrift, back decades. Why we ended up on the wrong side of history in Vietnam, he said, and were hell bent on killing me or even worse letting me come back as a cripple so they could prove the world we're tough. Silly understanding of history, the US didn't help us in our good fight they too wanted to keep the peace at all costs and the cost was the Second World War. Communism was a real danger after the war but by the '60s was a dead man walking nobody thought it was serious only powerful unless you were a dyed-in-the-wool Party member and the Party was mostly FBI-supported so they had a bogyman to fight. I love watching them chip away at the wall, throw down huge chunks of it, love watching the masses fleeing through Hungary our Secretary of State saying we have contingency plans for everything but not a mass exit, try and imagine Havel meeting with Husák in the grand ballroom of the Municipal House, imagine how it must have felt for Havel yesterday a dissident now meeting with the premier in this gorgeous oak-lined room, elected president of the *Magic Lantern Theater Company* only to have to decline because he's elected head of the Civic Forum and soon its first democratically elected President since the war. Shameful a good playwright having to turn politician, politicians are a dime a dozen good playwrights come along once in a thousand years, the Greeks, Shakespeare, Calderon playwrights who question the existing order, but this is a happy moment, too bad Jacobo isn't here to share it with me, I'm sure he would have changed as well. Of course Conchita and Joseph have no idea what I am blabbing about but they should be able to see the smiles on peoples' faces as they taste freedom many for the first time in their lives most haven't been born with it. I had that for a moment in the Spanish Republic and somewhat when I landed here and set foot in America, I loved seeing the Statue of Liberty it meant something to me then too bad so many immigrants now fly here and don't get to see it, but we all went to one side of the boat to catch a glimpse of it that I thought the ship would tip over—too bad they don't put up a photo of it at the airports, that is America's greatest symbol when fleeing terror. With the collapse of communism, a new era of peace can be envisioned there's already talk of a 'peace dividend' of taking the money from military and putting into civilian projects. The difficulty is that I know the East Europeans only through their literature and I have to be careful it's as if you only know us Spanish through Cervantes. The few dissidents I've met are really peasants in their head and we now live in enlightened times I wonder how these citizens can adjust to the modern era. Enlightenment takes time. Now I can snuggle with Jacoba she can't stay up so late to watch the screen and fell asleep as the whole history of the world is being played out, maybe she will learn about it someday not let it be swept under the rug as so much of American history is. At least I know what to read her, when Conchita came to live with me she was functionally an illiterate and they let her graduate. She could read *Archie* comics Joseph read *Superman* but at least it didn't stop him from reading Nietzsche. Only on his own he says they never mentioned him in class except to say he coined the term God is dead but never anything of substance of what he said. Yet we believe so firmly in education and I smile as I see the graffiti on the wall in West Berlin and the gray stone ugliness of the communist side of the wall. This is all ancient history to them.

As a new mother I spent all my time worrying never time for myself, did I pump enough milk, is Joseph going to be okay home alone with her, can grandma be so involved at her age, will she suffocate while sleeping, will the handles of the carriage fall off and she'll roll into the street, and I also have carpal tunnel syndrome not from sitting at the computer but from pushing the heavy carriage and can't flex my hand, I never had a moment of peace: trapped inside all day, didn't even go for walks, it took forever to get Jacoba ready that besides going to Dr. Lang, the pediatrician it just wasn't worth it. And it was impossible to go on the subway the space between the turnstiles was so small a carriage didn't fit and you could never attract the attention of the subway clerk, Joseph never had difficulties he could lift the carriage but I couldn't. He said he was a knight without armor to mothers when he lifted their baby over the turnstile otherwise they would still be trying to catch the clerk's eye so he could open the gate. Where could I have gone anyway the streets up there were so unsafe, Central Park was unsafe, at least in the East Village I know where to walk and I'm much more comfortable around here. In the park I refused to walk north of 96th street, didn't even walk north of 96th street on Broadway even if Joseph says you can walk all the way up to Columbia, as if I would want to walk there. I finally got to see the fabled West End Bar but it was full of drug dealers. That place doesn't have long to survive. The first time I ever came up this far north was when I got on the wrong train as a kid and all of a sudden saw I was on 125th street but it was above ground not underground and knew I made a mistake and quickly got off the train. Luckily I went into a candy store on the corner of 125th and Broadway and told the owner's wife my story and she put me back on the downtown side and told me to transfer to the uptown #2 train at 96th street, that was the first time I used my feminine wiles I had the fifteen cents for the fare, fifteen cents can you believe it, grandma remembers everybody complaining when the fare went to a dime, but I didn't want to spend the money, so played the lost little girl and it worked and I got home without having to spend my precious fifteen cents and that was the first time I saw precious Columbia University that didn't interest me in the least, I knew 'my kind' never went there, nobody told me that I just knew it like a lot of my early thought just known without any reason why. It was only when I began to think, engage, learn to act, that I began to develop an appreciation of thought, when I started paying attention to my surroundings and wondering changing the way I thought that it became a transforming moment abandoning myself and stop listening to the silliness of my vague thoughts, as if I knew all the answers, and open myself up to others. It requires effort to get these silly ideas out of your system, my mother never made the effort, and I did begin to get an education at Pitt. But now the times are a changing, a victory of the working class over the bourgeoisie, as grandma said, we needed more educated people to compete with the Soviets who had launched Sputnik and our kind can finally go to Columbia, and it's this lack of thinking that hinders us and now some people have better life chances by replacing old values and vague thoughts with new exact ones, and I was finally able to tell Joseph and grandma that one night, which quickly became two or three, I needed to be off duty and that I needed my own time, it was hard enough in that the only time we got to talk was over the phone Madame princess never stopped crying and at least Joseph gets to go to work I did not have such luck stuck indoors with her all the time, it was difficult at first but she cried and cried according to Joseph but when she was hungry enough took the bottle not the boob it was the same milk only in a different container. At home I would be exhausted when Joseph came home and could barely stay up past nine, I couldn't remember when I had gone to bed that early. Grandma and Joseph would read to her I would summarize but what surprised me was how Jacoba wasn't interested in the story but the numbers on the bottom of the pages, she was always looking at the numbers, good Joseph said she can go to Columbia, a woman interested in math is worth her weight in gold. After she finally fell asleep I had to clean up all over the place, pick up everything, do the dishes, clean, laundry grandma was too old and Joseph thought housework meant me. He did cook dinner however but it was unnatural how we quickly assumed societal roles as soon as Jacoba was born. He became the provider I was the stay-at-home mom, until I couldn't take it anymore. Thank god I only had six weeks leave and that was considered generous. Some co-workers were even surprised I came back they didn't expect that. The problem became what was I going to do with my time off, I wouldn't go into a bar by myself, even if women could do that by now, even if Joseph thought I was running around with old friends, I wasn't seeing anyone and I still even feel uncomfortable going into movies by myself so instead went and saw plays, dozens of them, I could go downtown to plays and cab it home, I loved going to ones where friends were in the cast and then afterwards going for a drink even if I was wasted the next day with Madame princess. I didn't even ask for comps, just surprised them and they were delighted to see me in the audience and we enjoyed each other's company, they loved celebrating after a performance in a bar. The theater with all its faults is what stimulates me the most—art is never real life that's what's so good about it, it expresses the concrete physical forms in a little adventure not the everyday, and going back to my regular life seemed dull after a theater experience. The gulf between theater and life is greater that the news and philosophy even if they both have features in common, art is complete nothing else is, someone always has an answer in a play not so raising children there all you do is what's easiest and only those who don't have children have answers, they think children nap, sleep, and you can read not collapse on the sofa exhausted. Children humble you you think you know it all and quickly realize how little you know. She will never watch TV as I plop her down in front of the screen to shut her up. I can see my mother smiling, she always said I hope you have nasty children just like you—me? I never thought anyone would want to marry me least of all have children by me. Now you don't even need to be married to have children wedlock is a thing of the past but how can one person care for a child? They're not dolls but bundles of desire with wants and needs that don't fit into your life. It's only because of the help I could survive and I couldn't do that too long. I didn't even want to breastfeed it takes so much out of you but grandma and Joseph insisted and I fell for it realizing my mother gave me formula and I vowed to do the opposite of my mother, besides nothing is better than nature, except it takes everything out of you and once she tasted the good stuff wouldn't touch formula barely took the pumped bottle. My little gourmand. If only you know this in advance but if you did nobody would have children. Imagine women feel this as the fulfillment of their lives, not to raise them only to have them. The clock watching, I was over the hill weak, nervous, didn't know what it was went to the doctor for a checkup and came out pregnant, more women are probably driven to suicide by being mothers then unrequited love. Motherhood was a figment of my imagination until it happened even if they can't sit still long enough to sit on your lap—there is no such thing as a natural mother only few mothers who can stand their children, I couldn't wait to go back to work and dreaded weekends until finally I couldn't even come home.

You can only have what you can lose, let's assume I didn't go off on an adventure then I never would have met Jacobo and wouldn't have come into contact with his ideas and they wouldn't have been cemented in me and allow me to flourish, his ideas inside me took time to grow and it helped me change a little at a time otherwise I could have gone the way of my childhood friends who never thought a day in their lives besides thinking about their bodily needs and what others have impressed upon them, the sheer pleasure of my life has been being allowed to grow having more doors open to me than I ever dreamt possible, except chance could have also influenced my life in ways I don't know about because I think I would have been different anyway, before Jacobo, I didn't believe a word my parents said, or the culture around me but it might not have gone anywhere without this 'forbidden fruit' something so different than anything I encountered that it gave me intellectual credence to my doubts, without thought it becomes mere revolution, which always leads to the same ole, same ole, only with thought does it become rebellion, a different way of life, and every time I think of the way I could have been shudder—the arc of my development comes from my body, my imagination strayed and I actually saw him not as he was but how I saw him not as a human being a creature of flesh and blood—he has had a good run inside my mind and has haunted me from beyond; I was never a college student, we women weren't deemed suitable to learn only to bear babies, but as Conchita realized most of her girlfriends drank and smoked and only searched for a husband when she went to school—how many young girls married upon graduation. She tells me she still knows women married since then but others are on their second or third husband, I hope that's not true now but they probably can only disguise it better, she learned so little in class why I wasn't so disappointed she didn't finish but now that she has graduated and even if she didn't want to go to the ceremony nothing was going to stop me. Joseph always complains nobody was interested in ideas all they were concerned with was good grades and teachers would always mark up his papers in red but never want to sit down and discuss ideas with him. He once explained how Claudia, the girl that was too hot for him, kept talking to him, flirting with him, holding his arm, touching him, but he kept seeing her as being polite not that she really wanted to be with him and couldn't believe it and when she offers him her phone number offers his instead. Once, so he said, she was impressed with his answer in class and allowed him into her group afterwards even if all he wanted from her was a piece of ass. A black mass, a piece of what was denied him because she was so attractive he dared not approach her, he wanted to ask her to see *Last Year at Marienbad* at the Paris theater but was too shy to ask her beauty made him nervous, her energy contagious. Back home I was trapped the only way out was marriage something I thought I would never do and I did try to be faithful at first, but I didn't want to be considered a harlot and

Santiago was so dull and boring that I knew I wouldn't have any trouble with him and if I wanted to go anywhere had to drag him he always wanted to be home, he didn't even want to see newsreels of the *Degenerate Art* before the Nazis destroyed it all, thought they actually were part of the Jewish, Freemasonry, Bolshevik plot to destroy society leading to the corruption of society. He actually despised avant-garde art and thought people who even looked at it were morally corrupt. Even today I can't stand beer it reminds me so of Santiago, and I don't even feel guilty he went off to fight just to impress me even if I badgered him he did it on his own because he thought women love war heroes, he still had childhood fantasies in a grown man's body but not in his mind, because he never was with a woman he still classified us as either whores or mothers, which reflected how the church saw us, not as human beings with the same desires, fears as men but as evil vines twisting and turning up a tree wrapping its tentacles, vines, around the tree not as a lost human beings with our own thoughts and dreams but always busy doing something for our husband and children, breathing their air almost as if we were the child as opposed to having an adult life, an unconditional love of abandonment not a realistic love of equals. Now all I want is my solitude but back then was afraid to be alone for all my talking about it, but growing up means being alone, and it's not the end of the world if a woman is an old maid. It was in meeting Jacobo that I was able to begin to understand this and that I can eat in silence not always have to push the conversation along even if I required to do this with both husbands, but I wouldn't sit at their feet and ask them what's troubling them, at least with Tomas I was able to get to America, and as soon as I walked on the sidewalks felt free, no one cared about where I came from, who my ancestors were, what my religion was, it was me, just me that people knew; it was an unexplainable feeling at first where you were no longer attached to your old way of life and I could breathe for the first time in my life, and the Village had clean air back then not as polluted as now, clean streets except for dog shit and cigarette butts,—women even brazenly smoked on the streets I remember being shocked by that: the rapture I first felt when I walked those streets was not hindered by guilt or conscience, that only came about when I imagined what if take the El up to the Bronx but even as I imagined it knew I would never do it, I loved him too much to ruin his life. Not that I believed in fidelity but he did and in times of true self-doubt actually blamed him but quickly realized what could have happened to me if I hadn't met him and so no matter how much I suffered in the new world, I knew that it was better to be here than back in Madrid, but the initial loneliness was painful it takes time accustom yourself to a new way of life, now I have ersatz solitude then it was real still I realize how much better off I am here than there, my intellectual ark led me to the streets of New York, and if there is a Platonic heaven where only minds exist I can meet Jacobo there and Joseph can say to him your time of boredom is over and we can continue our intense conversations—how will it be meeting him without a body? It was his body that first attracted me later his mind, or as he said first the belly. We all have our follies but at least mine got me away from the church and fascists, a poor man's freedom to be sure but we had enough not to be common riff-raff even if back home we were considered wealthy and I had to learn to live poor. I wasn't a hoarder but I did have enough clothes, stilettos, swollen feet, slit skirts, that showed my ass, and my eyes and lips ringed with mascara and lipstick but quickly was able to adopt to the American way of casual dress and only later able to wear slacks and a bandeau instead of a bra, I felt too old, late, for the braless look. When Conchita started wearing overalls she wore it with a tee shirt she felt too old to go without the tee and wouldn't go braless either and wore a bandeau under her tee. However, she loved wearing a mini-skirt on campus and all the boys staring at her and making cat-calls. Women weren't allowed to wear jeans on campus. She would get delight in fueling their imaginations. Now at least there are comfortable shoes for women back in the day there were only high heels and old lady shoes, which no self-respecting woman would wear until their tendons gave out and I take credit for being one of the first women to start wearing sneakers, even If I had to try on men's sizes, back in the late '40s. Still I felt uncomfortable wearing pants until the young started that in the '60s. Before my heart attack said I won't deprive myself of so much pleasure in smoking, afterwards quickly changed my tune, I started my life as an adult by doubting the Christian version of truth because of a chance meeting with a Jewish anarchist.

I cannot leave the house without my 'war-paint' involuntarily I look in the mirror I'm always on the prowl especially now there I am no longer on the Upper West Side but back in my old haunts and can now walk as freely as I once did—hard to believe but I know every nook and cranny of Loisaida now morphed into the East Village as hipsters move in and feel at home only on my street. I knew all the street thugs the girls moved away but I still see the boys hanging but they won't be hanging around much longer they still don't realize the neighborhood is changing, besides grandma new all their mother's and now that their mothers have passed these men think they have a right to the apartment in perpetuity but as Joseph says when landlords couldn't fill them up they did but now that they are in demand landlords will evict them. But it was more of a neighborhood back then now we seem to be drawn into atomistic pieces, nobody knows one another or cares for one another—I always thought they should have made a statue to Leona standing guard watching the children play in the street, she was the glue that held the neighborhood together, and I still like to walk on streets that you see little kids playing you know they're safe and instead of Leona you see mothers and an occasional father not so many grandmothers anymore. I like to see fathers pushing baby carriages that never occurred back in the day. My body is myself and that is the unique part of me and so far my body feels okay, melancholy has been lifted from my shoulders since I came back here, I went to the doctor feeling low and depressed, he said young mothers often feel that way and gave me some Paxil which only made me more lethargic and I had to crap all the time and there are no places in the city where you can just go to a bathroom, how many bars, restaurants, did I have to go in and just order a quick drink in order to use their bathroom, especially since they did away with pay toilets because gays were using them as rendezvous points and the city wanted to control AIDS. Once when I couldn't hold it in and did it all over my underwear and skirt I snuck back into the house and washed them out before putting them into the laundry I was so ashamed. That's when I decided to get off the antidepressants. Grandma's heart attack was important for me I realized then that I have to keep my body in shape or that could happen to me, I shouldn't go that far because my being an actor does mean I have to keep my body alert and somewhat in shape but I did stop my nicotine addiction and quit before everyone else did even if I thought I would gain weight but tai-chi helped keep that under control and when I got back into it after the birth my neurasthenia, hypochondria, hysteria, boredom started to fade but only really left when I moved—all I want is to live the rest of my life in freedom not be tied down. I mean I wouldn't mind living with another man again, having breakfast with him, holding, touching, that is nice but I don't think I'm cut out for that type of life. I didn't want that as a kid but then I did and even laughed when all my ideas were reduced to this simplicity, married with children, and now all I have for that is guilt, guilt that I have abandoned my daughter but if I stayed with her I would have ruined her life, better she be around caring people than one who was going crazy. Or as Joseph says I love how you use your reason to calculate your passions, what he means is I am 'mind fucking' him, and when I finally couldn't get out of bed in the morning, didn't know if I was going to awaken sad or happy I started smoking again then I knew I had to make a change, besides now we know secondhand smoke is not good for children it gives them asthma and I when my daughter didn't want me to kiss her anymore because I smelled so bad realized I had to stop again and that's when I went for pills. My body recognized what my mind refused to see, I thought I could handle it being a stay-at-home mom but I couldn't and now that I'm here feel trepidation when I have to go back uptown, so much for my tenacity and will power but a little sniffles showed me the way, I just didn't want to get out of bed. If this were the Dark Ages you could have said God pointed the way but we are at the end of the twentieth century and God is dead and the old ways of looking at the world no longer work, like when the Athenian playwrights challenged to old heroic culture of Homer and started questioning their ideas, the same thing happened to me, the old ways are no longer the ways to live or one way but not the only way and maybe the Greek playwrights understood it, it's that life is tragic not our tragic flaw. I never thought of myself as a feminist just an independent person but now am beginning to rethink all. My body showed me not the medical advice of how to live with myself but the feeling that I had to escape that prison and all I wanted was fresh air. Strange to say fresh air in New York City but I wanted not to have to rush home, be with the baby all the time, pump milk all the time or my breasts felt engorged. Physical exercise helped and as soon as Jacoba turned six months off the boob, now I miss the orgasms. Who knew? Those were the best I ever had. When I walked back into this apartment, the first thing I did was pay for it to be painted each wall a different color and the ceiling white, I wanted it clean and clear, also picked up the linoleum and had the floors sanded, neighbors thought a yuppie was moving in, very few people recognized me from the old days and I recognized very few. Now my exercises and my walking have gotten me back into feeling life, a good acting gig also helps, imagine me playing the mother I am still the child inside my head and I had played Iphigenia once, the promotion I take in stride the money it gave me allowed me to remodel besides it's not as much as it thought after taxes are taken out. Still as grandma says it's enough and I can still help out uptown. I really can't define what a good education is but I know it when I see it. People now say we're giving our daughter an elite education but it's elite in a good way, at Walton when I graduated some girl received enormous applause because she was waitlisted to Barnard, but the boys and girls at Calhoun all went to good colleges and we were well-prepared, I wonder what the results were did she get in? Would she be able to do the work? I feel much better acting again and can even walk home after the performance because this part of the city is becoming safe once again, thank goodness for Bratton and clearing junkies off street corners, let them stay inside they're no danger to the streets then and he makes sure police cars are where junkies like to hang out. Modern statistics are taking the streets back from hooligans and it means that not only white people but us as well can feel safe. Hooligans are not class conscious I won't rob a brother, they picked on their own more often than whites but only killing of whites make the press, especially if it is a blonde woman. Then they had a field day. I now have the freedom I once had but lost on the Upper West Side here I know people not a stranger in a strange land and I can even walk in Tompkins Square Park at night and still not get a swing at two in the morning, but now I don't want to swing anymore. The only thing I do miss is Central Park we have a few small playgrounds, one park but nothing compares to Central Park, it takes my breath away, and when I first walked it couldn't believe it wasn't natural that they could shut the water off anytime it was all man-made, that this was something the city fathers actually planned Olmsted and Vaux designed every bit of it, from the lakes and ponds to the woods, hills and valleys, unlike now where all the city designs are highways so you can't walk, the park is a place to stroll. My difficulty is that I can't get up there more than twice a month and whenever I do I make sure to walk in the park either uptown or downtown and then at its end take the subway back. Luckily all trains go to the Village so it doesn't matter on which end or which side I end up on I can get something to take me downtown. I look forward to that walk more than seeing everybody. I shouldn't say that. But it's true. Unlike grandma I can walk the steps in the subway she can only take subways now that have an elevator that are usually broken, of course, and since there is only one elevator repairman working for the transit authority she has to wait a month before the elevator is fixed. Teenagers like elevator surfing like we used to like hitching a ride on the back of a bus but we never broke the bus these kids seem to break the elevators. Boy were the police surprised once when they stopped us and I was a girl doing it, even then I was somewhat of a tomboy. Joseph laughed when I told him that story he said he was afraid to do that but it was easy hop on the fender and hold onto the window when the bus stopped or was going slow. He never even snuck under turnstiles a moment before the subway came in so we could hop right on it. Then the city got new busses with no back fender, fixed us, but by then I was too old to ride busses anymore I was interested in boys and looking glamorous like those blonde bombshells in movie magazines, using makeup, eye shadow, mascara, lipstick, pimple removers, perfumes all stolen from Alexander's on Fordham Road. Grandma can't even ride the bus the last step from the bus to the curb is too high and she could fall. The city says the new buses will have an extra step, we'll see. Maybe then she can come down here. She'll be amazed at how the neighborhood has changed, nannies, men walking babies, street people gone, nobody sits on stoops anymore, nobody gambles or play dominoes and now that all apartments have air conditioning nobody sits on the street just to get a breath of fresh air, gates are starting to disappear from the windows, barbed wire has been removed from rooftops. Grandma's beach chair has gone the way of the dodo bird: bourgeoisie culture is atomistic, the breakup of the community into solitariness.

No matter how I lie to myself I'm not prepared to say it's over and no matter how many times I say it it still doesn't ring true, or when she says I'm back for the baby or grandma I like to think I'm included in the equation, I have to mean something to her even if she can't explicate it in words and I keep imagining she's running her hands through my hair like the first time even if I am now practically bald—or will be soon enough. I'm always busy now because I'm afraid to be alone with myself, to forget myself. I saw an old man on the subway balding on the top very long on the sides and said that will soon be my look, and the first time she didn't come home at night she did call and I didn't say you could be dead in a ditch somewhere only she said I was at Beckett's *Not I* and she met up with the actress afterwards, but it's only a one-act how could she be gone that long; she explained later he friend took hours to wind down from playing a mouth and they spent the night drinking. That was the first time she went without me. And it's true sometimes I find her actor friends pretentious, having fake emotion, believing all life is art not worrying about making a living, I waited up as long as I could finally fell asleep on the couch knowing I would hear her come in but she came in and didn't wake me only held me tight and saying I love you while I pretended to be asleep. One night what's the big deal she needs her freedom I am a nobody and I can't keep her chained to the bed. Nice image, nice thought, even said she has the right to freedom creativity not complacency but I didn't believe a word of it; I wasn't stopping her from acting as if I should get 'wife points' for that, I made sure she went back to work I knew she was going crazy at home all day alone with Jacoba and grandma, and she wanted to contribute to the family income and taking care of Esmeralda who had an income, albeit a small one only social security, there was no pension in her line of work, illegal abortions and sewing young girls up to seem a virgin. Besides whatever savings she had was eaten up by inflation. The next night she brought home daffodils and to my surprise they lasted more than a week, I put some plant food in and lukewarm water, not cold, somehow I knew that but I don't know how, and watched them blossom and die—their beauty was in watching the whole gamut from blossoming until death, and now when I feel depressed coming home to an empty apartment stop off at Surroundings, until they closed and then reopened, my favorite flower shop, and buy some orchids because it makes me feel nice and am trying to learn how to enjoy myself. She started dressing alluringly, no more business suits, her shoulders showing, a dress split along the middle where her boobs were and sometimes a small necklace downward, dressing provocatively but within established limits. She wasn't going braless that was too un-corporate and out of fashion, but she was pushing the limits of the dress code. She complains I no longer buy her Sacher Torte, Marzipan or Black Bark but Louie Lichmann's has closed and Universal Chocolates has now gone out of business, as the owner said you can't have a nickel-and-dime business with thousand dollar rents. I laugh because before her I only knew of chocolate with cream stuffing didn't know of imports. I remember wondering if she's too sophisticated for me and would I be able to keep up, she was my dream come true, a beautiful woman with a mind who expected she would use her mind against me. Because of her a little nobody like me became the center of attention whereas on my own would have crawled back to the Bronx. I loved walking down the street with her, holding hands, letting her define me, catching the glances of envious people—with her I lost all reason and thought only want to be with her, who when she said oh baby my heart almost dropped and I realized all I wanted was to be with her, that my only goal was to be around her, we didn't have much money, only later did the money start rolling in and I realized I became normal commonplace, no longer the maverick but a married man with a daughter. She says I tried to control her, not true, I felt closer after the marriage even if she said she didn't. I know I can wait until she comes to her senses I have the tenacity of waiting and all I am doing now is waiting for her to come home, no matter what she does I won't leave her I said but it was she who left me. Waiting for what? patience for what? is this what I want to live my life waiting? Can't I live differently? When she moved back into Esmeralda's old apartment with the subtenant moved out I still was patient but the voice started getting louder inside me. We still do things together share the same bank accounts, and occasionally eat off each other's plates but no longer order the same food. My fingers have grown chubby, I'm balding, have a little pot belly but now I have to watch myself lest I become like those old men I despise the mediocre, smart men who know something but are oh so dull, I never invited them home or forced Cassie to meet them I knew she would despise them why should she have to suffer with them let their wives do that, boring but polite men who basically I thought I could do without so never advanced as far as I could by avoiding their parties and social gatherings. You do it enough times and they learn not to invite you. Now I get tired in the afternoons, never before did I need a nap but now usually can take a quick snooze because I feel down but I want more, my member still gets hard seeing a pretty woman on the subway fantasying about her, and when I have anxiety want sex even more. I love looking at their naked beauty but would never/ever start a conversation with them they are so serious-looking and I am so frivolous. I can't even talk to my colleagues anymore they're only interested in the job or sports, women are now interested in sports, and I no longer have the patience to watch a game. She was the one who included me in serious conversation knowledge for living not simply book learning but that *Je ne sais quoi* in knowing how to enjoy life, how to live, and now feel more intensely alone all I can do is make money. It was only being with Cassie that I could feel the blood rushing through my veins, my heart pumping, and I could go beyond myself. What am I going to do? I'm not too self-destructive I have a child to look after and I did promise myself I would do my best, even if I know my best isn't good enough and I don't deny her access but that's because I want to see her, I've seen too many men who when they divorce quickly get out of the loop. I can't have that. She may be creative but I have the knowledge to stay with the family even if I'm so dull and boring. When I look at Jacoba sitting in the high chair or sleeping think like God looking upon his creation and saying it was good. Cassandra can't do that. Why did I not awaken that first night and see how she looked why did I pretend to be asleep, was she disheveled, her lipstick smeared or am I just imaging all this?

I never saw so many hills in my life, the whole West Side is uphill and in both directions everywhere I want to walk is a hill and it's getting difficult to walk around but if I don't get out at least once a day go stir crazy inside—we went to the Grand Canyon Joseph thought it would be nice to be in nature. Hell no! It was jammed packed with tourists and we went out of season drove into the North Side of the park, the unpopular side, stayed at the hotel and got up early to see the sunrise but what was more impressive was seeing stars at night—a whole sky full of stars, I haven't seen that since Spain and I still could find the Big Dipper pointing towards the North Star and the Little Dipper but not Sagittarius where the Milky Way flows, we didn't see that but we did see meteors and an artificial satellite, at least we thought they weren't airplanes, too bad they didn't have an evening tour of the nighttime sky they had tours for everything else, as it was I could only walk on the rim my balance isn't that good anymore and was afraid to walk the six miles down to the bottom, Joseph did got up early walked about a mile down but became afraid he wouldn't be able to make it up because of the altitude, we get out of breathe so quickly at higher elevations that he walked a little while kept hydrated took some photos and decided to call it a day met all these climbers on the path with headphones on just like in Central Park nobody listens to nature anymore, even saw a man carrying a boom box, so the solitude climbing up was ruined by those climbing down—he doesn't like to listen to music while walking or jogging even if he thinks nature is silent. He is obsessively compulsive about his solitude and silence and refuses to listen to music in his runs or walks while Conchita loves walking with her headphones on it drowns out thought. I wish I could have walked more but after breakfast would walk around the rim and in some forests they were paved and it was difficult to find unpaved trails except going down the canyon, which I couldn't do, I started went a few steps my stick helped but was too afraid is this the start of old age, afraid to do what I once could do not when I went out of the house with two different shoes on? I grabbed one it looked like the other and they fit the same but outside realized my mistake but didn't want to admit my mistake and continued walking hoping no one would notice, even if back in school wore two different-colored socks, but that was deliberate we were all doing that to set a trend, and I only stayed in the Park for about an hour feeling the sun on my face, the breeze in my hair and then couldn't take it anymore and scuttled home. When I went to Jacobo's gravesite I wore two different-colored socks and swore I could hear his wife saying wakeup Jacobo your mistress is here. I visited him dead but not alive that would have been stalking and placed a small stone upon his headstone to show I visited the Jewish tradition. The socks were two extremely different colors and would have been noticeable except nobody looks at old women. Now I make a mental check before I leave the apartment but I'm sure it will happen again and again. I thought I could flee to nature but this is nosier than Central Park and all the trails are full of people, you have to be friendly and smile—where solitude ends worship begins so there is no existential loneliness in a National Park, I am more alone in the city than anywhere else. It's only by being with yourself that you can learn to think. And women have had difficulty we never had a room of our own unless it was a sewing room like my mother who had a little shack in the back where she would go and sew otherwise we were never allowed to be alone, we couldn't walk alone, I always had to walk with friends, schoolmates, cousins never by myself until I came to America—that is the freedom of America being able to walk by yourself not going into bars, movies or theater alone, but being able to walk and yet how few women take advantage of it, even if I now see more women driving alone but they are driving going somewhere nobody can drive for the pleasure anymore like Tomas would do after the war when the roads were much less packed. And still if a man's in a car with a woman it's the man driving, except Joseph and Conchita, Joseph can drive but he knows Conchita really loves to drive and he gives her the pleasure. And I know she can't think too deeply while driving, she always has the radio on and does have to pay attention to the road. Walking allows your mind to wander only when you cross the street do you have to stop and concentrate and one of the great games in the city is walking avoiding the lights crossing only when you have the light, just meandering. Okay I cross the street when I see a bunch of blacks or Hispanics on a street corner they only see an easy mark no respect for age and since all want to be cool in front of their friends it can quickly turn ugly. To them it's the sound of two hands clapping not one hand clapping and I didn't mind the cat-calls but the cursing and the violence are abhorrent. I would love to go up and lecture them but they would only laugh. Too bad Jacoba is too young to remember this trip but it is not for memory only the moment that we take her, Conchita offered to babysit but she works all day and night so would have had to hire someone and we both didn't want to go without her and we have taken a whole lot of photos even when I look at old photographs it only brings back a superficial feeling I can never actually remember the moment and I have thrown out a whole bunch of old photographs to Joseph's dismay, never throw out the past. Now the only time I feel young is when I can give some happiness to others, Conchita, Joseph and especially Jacoba and it is good that Joseph can spend time with his daughter, how many men or women can actually do that in this modern hustle world, he makes sure she gets to the playground every day. And if you're not with children when they are young you miss all the joy of them, they don't mellow with age. This is what great grandmothers are for so when they become teenagers listening with their headphones and don't remember us hopefully it will lead to a good sense of self inside them to counter their base desires.

I can only read at home now, no more can I read Marx standing up on the subway going to school, Freud in candy stores drinking an egg cream, Spinoza when I went to temple with Conchita because she wanted the Jewish experience, Nietzsche in recovery from my nose operation, Schopy in the bathroom. Now I have to be sitting in a reading chair with a pen in hand and no longer even read in the bathroom, and if I find a seat on the subway just stare at the window like a zombie, even if a pretty girl comes on I rarely let her intrude in my fantasies. If I try and read I wonder what I'm reading, I still carry a book, wouldn't go anywhere without one, but rarely open it, no longer do I have an external conversation going on with an internal one—a character saying what I think he should say as opposed to what he means to say and I could do this almost simultaneously, but now accept the right that she has the right to be free, I can't force her to live with us, be patient who knows what will happen, but I also want her to refuse the charms of others, her polyamorous, and never want her to see other men again, haha, she said she was going to leave four times but didn't each time and we'd get into fights in public places when we tried to have some alone time, and I'd say do you want to get into this here? Interestingly she's still living her selfish life while I now only live for others, oh I have selfish moments like the time I walked into The Bohemian Bookworm asking for *Piers Plowman* and the bookstore lady said Pierce Brosnan, and the sex was marvelous, so much for making love with an educated woman. And she has altruistic ones like asking us how many rocks did you see when you went to the Grand Canyon, but usually we are in conflict, perpetual conflict, it was funny when it happened to my other friends but now it's not so funny, she no longer wants to be a dutiful wife but I never wanted her to be dutiful, self-mortifying I had enough of that from my mother, but that doesn't mean she has to abandon us, why can't we live with both. I have to force myself to get off a few stops before and walk to my next assignment, I now like walking in bad neighborhoods that I avoided for so long because the city is safer again and I can see some of the neighborhoods that I refused to walk in, I was in Brooklyn the other day came across this huge park in the middle of nowhere called Sunset Park and was shocked that their actually is a park in the area called Sunset Park, it's on a hill with a nice view of the water, the Statue of Liberty, the World Trade Center and lower Manhattan, and I never associated the neighborhood with a park but small housing of Italians, Irish and Hispanic. If the schools weren't so bad here and if the subway ran at more regular intervals, the local R train is terrible in Brooklyn, this might have been a good pioneer neighborhood, when I was first told about this place I was so Manhattan-centric didn't realize he was talking about Brooklyn and it took two, three phone tags on the answering machine before we met up. And now

I have that 'crazy' look on my face if there are still muggers around they would see you don't mess with me look, however I still have to be careful because some junkies are so clueless they would see any white guy as an easy mark. It reminds me of 7th 8th grade where bullies would ask you to touch their cock or squeeze their balls, I always said no I wasn't going to be called fag, and they left me alone and I must have gotten that look back. I'm not an easy mark. Still I only walk on side streets where I see kids playing otherwise walk on main thoroughfares. Business continues to boom, we pick up apartments quietly, pay decent money, do a decent job on renovations, not half-assed cheap like some of our competitors, we keep records of good contractors and guys who pull a fast one and we give this information to clients and we have developed a decent reputation for fairness. Big deal Cassandra left even if she still has the keys, she did give them back but I gave them back her daughter still lives here, not to mention her grandmother. She said she would invite us over to her place after she fixed it up but so far no invite has come. It's also a third-floor walkup so I don't know how many times Esmeralda can go. And she still does come and visit Jacoba and her grandmother when I am not at home. I never even thought of asking her to leave, why not? With me now she's stiff and formal and whenever the phone rings hope it's her and dread if it is her, now I stay home nightly to project normalcy for Jacoba and she still crawls into my bed in the middle of the night, I love having someone to sleep with even as I realize I shouldn't and promise tomorrow I will break her of the habit, Dr. Spock and all that. I actually thought of going to live with the Hasidim in Williamsburg, Brooklyn to start over, the simple life, their love of dance, the Jewish experience, a moral tradition, ties with the past, except they expelled me from the group they were dancing to God I was just showing off, besides they are so uneducated and dumb they didn't even know which end was which in a telescope, but I did see in Williamsburg a good pioneer neighborhood that was on the uptake, there was a used book store and a Starbucks, sure signs the neighborhood was going through an upgrade, and that thought actually gets me off the subway and stop into a three or four brothers for a hearty breakfast, they offer me the newspaper but I refuse at least I don't read them—I can't fall back on God only push forward, Israel is the most anti-religious country, women I know who immigrated from Israel have no knowledge of the Bible and claim it's a retarded country, besides

Judaism isn't my home when I met this woman who says I could only live in a city, I am my own woman she screamed reminding me that the Jews created God out of their own loneliness. I thought we'd break up after that but she did call again saying I called good evil and evil good and she understands that Americans have no understanding of the world and I actually had to defend America who she accused of being public enemy number one for not standing up to evil and being so goodie, goodie, I thought she was messing with me but she seemed to like me and when I told her I was from the Bronx she said I always heard the New York public schools had this good educational system so many good writers came out of the Bronx who always said they learned so much in public school. What? true if you were a top student they coddled you otherwise forget it. No school system yet created by man ever destroyed the spirit of a child, she said. Obviously she had never been to a public school in the Bronx. We could laugh together. So I am in sheer hell thinking about Cassandra and have pleasant images of my newfound girlfriend, only she's not a girlfriend yet but we do enjoy doing things together, I live on borrowed time hoping to live twelve, thirteen more years until Jacoba graduates high school, that seems to now be the only reason I'm put on this earth and I have to be careful lest I succumb to despair. The good breakfast stretches my stomach usually I'm afraid to eat a lot in the morning so I can get through the whole day without a nap but today felt hot and needed an air-conditioned restaurant to cool down and tell myself I won't bother with lunch until after I check out the apartment, it's important that I stay on top of everything be the project manager I want them to know I'm around and checking up and if they need help make sure they get it. We have small contractors who are grateful for the work not the big firms who have dozens of jobs this way I can be sure they will get the project finished on time: no bullshit but a decent job. Once I would sell apartments without appliances letting the clients chose their own and could actually sell it cheaper and the new owners could get the appliances they wanted but this is New York and former renters were not expecting not to have kitchens and bathrooms that didn't have full appliances and didn't know how to shop for appliances now we make sure the apartments have European kitchens and nice oval toilet bowls and clients seem to know that and appreciate it. Kitchens and bathrooms are crucial in a sale, wood floors also help even if they are a pain to care for—all this takes extra time and money but I have plenty of time and we have extra money to do a good job. Only life depresses me my life is drifting downward and it's difficult to examine my life all I see around me is an inferior product and all I do is go through the motions.

How do they know? What give them the right? I didn't want to come here I wanted prison where I could do straight time, you do your time for the crime and you're done but a lawyer told me Rockefeller program is better you do less time all I had to do was cop to the Rockefeller program but I'm no junkie I'm Julio, I wasn't like these guys I can quit anytime, and now my mother keeps telling me I'm angry all the time—what do I have to be angry about, all that bullshit they call group therapy, who needs that I just wanted to mind my own business and do my time, I didn't need their shit to sit in a circle and show your weaknesses in this big room and this elderly white dude talking who knew what he was talking about this old geezer with his long hair and jeans and he blabbed and blabbed said I never did an intelligent thing in my life, I wouldn't go with any black dude but there were only black and white dudes there very few Hispanics and I couldn't stand those. I saw no purpose in this. The therapist is talking about sexuality and saying fags are okay, fuck him, I don't do tricks for anybody never sold my body on 42nd street, don't suck cocks, and he said we are the people we want to be, all bullshit, smartass guy wearing glasses, why did I have to listen to him, I wasn't like the others, I had to stay in a place like that because I would be released quicker but it was upsetting all the stuff they were telling me that I hated my mother, that I was queer, I much rather have worked in the kitchen than have to put up with their bullshit, some bullshit that I strike out at myself because I hate my mother, I love my mother with my heart and soul, and I'm only using junk so I can get some happiness trying to recreate the first time. I can stop whenever. But they never asked me that. My life doesn't revolve around junk and if they had said it simply and not add all the complexes it's just you know or don't but the old white dude kept hammering away at me in sentences not simple words that was difficult for me to understand. He said dreams matter. I don't dream. He told me I should learn to read, why do I have to read I just need a job in some office 9-5 and I'll be okay, he says go to plays, who the hell goes to the theater, my mother has never been to the theater neither had my grandma, nobody I know goes to that shit, the white dude says we all have imaginary identities that we can see in plays, shit man, I know who I am and I have no imaginary identities and didn't feel bad except for being in this place, and I don't want to punish myself, what bullshit, who wouldn't want to get out of this place where you have to spend 24 hours a day locked up in a hole, and if you misbehave they send you to solitary. You go crazy there, no brothers. I've learned so much more about drugs upstate than I ever knew on the street and this self-punishment is what I brought on myself for copping to this program, I did it to myself. The call me colored but I'm Hispanic have nothing to do with those niggers they have no respect. I was trying to teach myself to read like the pretty woman teacher says I should but I was going crazy looking at her with her blonde hair, pearl white teeth and cutesy smile, but I still couldn't figure out the meaning of words but she was better than the old white dude who kept talking about my mother, what does my mother got to do with this? I bet he could read but everything I did was screwed up in this white man's world—why did I have to go through all that crap couldn't they just tell us what to do, what they wanted not talk about it. And then they'd ask about your mother, always your mother stuff you shouldn't tell anybody he wanted to know in front of a whole group of colored and whites with a few Hispanics and then others would jump upon you saying you're bullshitting, lying, you wanted to do it, and go on and on and all I wanted was out, never said a word in those forty-five minute sessions that always went on for hours. If I had a girl to love me and I had a job, I wouldn't need this crap I can imagine myself coming home to a wife and little children, but these guys said I wasn't ready for love. How do they know? Said I was too selfish? Selfish my ass I just didn't want to talk in front of strangers unless it helped me get out quicker. And what they talked about. At least back in the cell we talked drugs here about our past but the past is over they said the past is the future, bullshit, the past is complete. I never thought about it. Don't I want to be happy, they said. I was happy on the street I wanted to say but was scared to say aloud because then they would all jump on me that I was lying. How do they know, they're not me? I'm Julio. I don't care what happened when I was a baby I cared about now and I don't hate my mother. I loved my mother she said I could go back and live with her once I completed my sentence but the old white dude thinks I'm going to end up back here if I don't change my ways cause all I'm going to want is another fix, and that I should start thinking where I want to be in ten years. I know outta here. I'm young and all I know is I hate this old white dude who's he to be giving advice that nobody is listening to. How come he gets to say things? Did he ever live on the streets? Always talking about truth, the real, but not understanding what it is to live on the streets had life too easy—white boys always preach, it's okay with a priest that's what they're supposed to do and I don't listen to their crap about God always watching you and you don't have to go to church but you're forced to go here for early parole, it looks good if you finish this shit that I participated in group therapy sessions even if I never speak because it has nothing to do with the real world. And I have to do better the first time at the parole hearing when they asked me do I love my mother I started cursing at the SOB's but now I learned to take deep breaths and not lose your cool, don't let them see how you tighten your fists, yes I do I will say, I don't want to do anything that will hurt her, I will say, I'll be ready for them the next time, let's see if they can trap me we talked a lot about this in the cells I was ready for their games. All they like to do is refuse you parole nobody gets it the first time, I thought I would now I know better and won't blurt out something stupid, the second time I knew what to say, say it nicely, don't let them see you get angry show them I am not a prisoner of my emotions but a prisoner of society and that I'm trying to get my GED, that looks good even if I have to sit through Shakespeare that looks good on my parole application and if I get my GED they will give me one, they got plenty to give says the pretty teacher. She gives me books to read but who wastes their time reading if it's not on the test. She says we should see Shakespeare, all life is in Shakespeare, who's Shakespeare? In group therapy we tear each other to pieces and she thinks Shakespeare can help me get through that, how we don't love anybody but ourselves and that we purposely go and hurt ourselves and what we need to do is show remorse but when somebody attacks me I become violent, even if the white pretty teacher with the pearly white teeth and curly blond hair said she couldn't imagine me carrying a gun, but you needed one on the streets otherwise junkies would take advantage of you knowing you couldn't go to the cops, never got parole, maxed out, got arrested again and again. Glad I'm out of that fuckin place now I only drink beer soon as I get up, no more junk makes my money selling my methadone.

I did what I wanted and if it occurs again I'm ready only it never occurs again in the same way, or maybe if I had gotten Jacobo it would have
ended differently, because I think it doesn't mean I can do it—Conchita
didn't like the way it turned out and left, I'm impressed with her ability to
do that, but she left a mess in her wake, Joseph with his aristocratic pride
in being chosen can't admit that she has left him, granted we have enough
money for caregivers but he says imagine if I had to hire a stranger to take
care of my child I wouldn't even know where to begin, do I ask them to
fill out an employment questionnaire? But I can pick her up after school
and even if walks miles ahead of me at least she still doesn't cross the street
by herself and waits at the corner. She needs her mother; I know now I
regret how I treated Gloria but only in retrospect while living it couldn't
do any different, changes in the body change morality and I always felt
justified in what I did, she was a lost child. I still have images of her
in my head being totally dumbfounded having no idea what's going on,
stubborn, fussy, ungrateful, I abandoned my daughter so cannot criticize
Conchita; when the world refuses to turn out the way you imagined it
the only way you can survive is to reboot, I will raise Jacoba until I am
no longer able. Jacobo helped me remove my blinders and once I went
back to Madrid saw how difficult it truly is in being free, at least here
in the city you can start over. I planned my escape well, too well, who
knew I would live with Tomas so long, and I wonder did I consciously
know what I was doing or am I now putting a story on it to try and
make sense of my life: falling in love with men who could liberate me
from my parents and luckily he didn't own property otherwise his family
never would have let him near me: chastity guarantees paternity, property
passed to legitimate heirs; and when they failed realized I had to do it on
my own—life is lived not thought and then the pain of loneliness begins,
did I transfer to living alone that I had when living for others. What I
loved about the Village was as soon as I set foot in this country realized
women could go anywhere by themselves, take walks when depressed, I
just avoided Tompkins Square Park late at night too many boys bunched
together but I could walk up and down Broadway, Houston, the Bowery,
7th, made a perfect square and usually there were people on those streets
at all hours, avoided the deserted streets, parks, bars, could walk and you
didn't need a man on your arm in the evening, my daughter thought she
could do nothing by herself if you didn't have a man you were living in

sin. She never grew up. Played by her own rules, thought Mafioso men were the highlight of living, she never did get to look at a Rembrandt *Self Portrait* of him sixty-five, broke, his art sold at auction, no studio from which to hang his hat so he goes and wears it tilts it on his head and you can see in his eyes what next? And he paints one of the most powerful portraits ever painted. I took Jacoba to the Met last week and made sure she saw that painting, only artists can go on everyone else would be defeated. This was also the first painting I saw when I walked all the way up Fifth to the Met and rode back down in a double-decker bus, sitting on top in the breeze. I knew exactly where the painting was, I was tired from the walk and the museum usually has too many paintings and halls for me soon you don't realize what you're looking at, but if you go to one painting and stand in front of it for minutes you can appreciate it, it's difficult to do with Rembrandt so many people pass in front of you to say they've seen Rembrandt but I was able to stand for almost a half hour before crowds came and then took the open-decker bus back downtown. The bus driver recognized me from when I would take Gloria on the bus in the middle of the night to stop her crying and let me on not at the bus stop. Unbelievable. That kindness made my day. He asked me out and I told him I would if I could but that I was married and he respected that. I should wear my wedding ring more often, it's easier that way. I wanted to take Gloria to see it when she didn't feel like going to class in the 5th grade, I said stay home with me spend the day with me we'll go to the museum. She did but only liked the lunch room and gift shop, and she felt too embarrassed in front of the nudes. Conchita wasn't embarrassed and now that the museum is so close a little walk across the park I take Jacoba all the time. Let her become an aesthete. But I only take her to one or two paintings so she doesn't become overwhelmed but she likes the suits of armor and also the Guggenheim where she can run up and down the circular dimensions and up the slant to touch the paintings to the guards' dismay. We've been kicked out a few times and barred from the suits of armor for climbing on the horses. Museums are not interactive enough. Joseph laughs in elementary school they always took him to the American Museum of Natural History, never art museums. Conchita never went she hated class trips and was always conveniently sick on those days. Now she has art all over her body that she's performing again. Her artistic will is as strong as Rembrandt's and I notice how many more women are leaving 'the good life' i.e. married, house, children, and seeing that life as a trap and moving down into the city again. Conchita had it all a husband who cared for her, supported her in her efforts but she gave it up. These women do the same. But Conchita feels awkward having Hispanic women clean for her but otherwise she would have to scrub the toilet and do the laundry and wants none of that. I still talk to her on the phone so I know what's going on with her and she knows about Jacoba. How much can Rembrandt's *Self Portrait* save us from the hell on earth, I prefer real life to imaginary tales but I need both. No longer am I trapped in my body but I still use the little one as a substitute but soon she will be on her own and too big to sit in my lap. What then? I am a creature of the moment shattered all over the place trying to make up a story so my life makes some sense but still living in the moment and can't stand religious zealots or Marxist fanatics who still live on the foundations of a glorious future. These folks are in agony until the day they die then expect to live in wonderful bliss, a mind cannot be made whole except by art: art gives reason to live, even if I feel bad because Conchita does have a moral responsibility to her child she also has one to herself and her baby is not abandoned she has a loving home and she does keep in touch with her and I have commissioned a painting of her in her room so she knows who I'm talking about and even if a painting is not an actual original individual person at least Jacoba has an image of her in her mind's eye. It sounded good but now I'm starting to wonder it leaves her in confusion and must try and find a better way to keep her acquainted with her mother. It is the lighting of Zeus not the wailings of a Wandering Jew that will allow her to live, even after Jacobo left me and since then my life has been a shadow at least I had a chance to live: what doesn't kill you makes you stronger.

I tried, really tried, made an effort, each time I climbed the twelve steps up from the street to our brownstone, I made the effort said to myself each time I climbed those steps make an effort, I am going to enjoy this night, be with my baby and my husband, they can write that on my tombstone, I failed. You have failed Conchita. There are defeats and there are failures and I have failed miserably but have not been defeated. For over a decade now I tried to be a good wife and a mother married or not no matter what you call it we were a couple then a threesome it has the same connotations no matter what you call it otherwise there has to be a separate term for each, but it's no longer cool when freedom is blocked that violates my purpose, I thought I would be able to do more in marriage, more in motherhood, I was wrong as a single woman I have freedom and no matter how much loneliness—my body turned to ice and each time I started walking up those twelve steps I became more rigid the higher I climbed and couldn't shut my mind off and started automatically walking up to the entrance and another night in purgatory. Luckily I am a trained actress and knew how to play my role but what about me, unfortunately I wasn't honest with myself I was not facing myself and would shout and scream so as not to have to listen to myself and didn't want to admit to myself how lonely I was. I don't know if I knew I must have known you can't keep that a secret from yourself and I couldn't wait for the weekend to be over even if before I always prided myself that I wouldn't end up like my mother and here I was my mother incarnate. If there is a hell she would be laughing. Hell is something that if you don't believe eliminates the whole God thing—how can there not be a place where the just can look and see the unjust suffer so and think they led virtuous lives by being saintly, it should be fun looking down at those in agony. Do I have the right to be this far away from my daughter? This was all that I worked for and now realize as I walked up those twelve steps to the front door wondering if I wanted to play the victim then realized I didn't want to be the victim and that one day I turned around and walked down those twelve steps turning sickness into strength I knew I wasn't coming back, I am a creature of my time I am not becoming I am and with the pain and the heartache knew I could use those conditions creatively, somebody said that to me once but then they were only words now the words had life breathed into them: the only way I can live is to be free. I remember thinking that as I climbed down the twelve steps immediately forgetting that I had put my key into the lock but the seed germinated in my mind and once germinated wouldn't leave instead blossomed as I walked up the twelve steps once again even as I told myself count don't think I had thought of a new way and there was no way to stop thinking about it, and luckily I walked up again because I had left my key in the lock and the thought kept breaking into my dreams and even I no longer thought it when counting the twelve steps was thinking it all the time—there can't be anything beyond this space and nothing behind time that's why there can't be a heaven or hell and

I am going because I have to leave. Whatever I try ends in failure, the only way out is to get up and leave otherwise I will be here for eternity and only I can end this since I did this to myself. I didn't know what I was getting into I thought marriage would free me not trap me, then my body has a child and after one popped out another was about to come— that's what happens when you have sex while ovulating grandma said, but this time I refused and he's hated me ever since, even if he hasn't said a word about it. And if I was to be not become I had to be free of them. But I still love all of them no matter if I can't live with them, but they are also loved by others and it is better for them to be loved by others. Joseph is too much of a homebody not to have a home. At least I haven't killed Jacoba I am no Medea killing her children to get even with her husband for abandoning her. Me thinks that was too drastic, I had no choice I had to get an abortion for my sanity I had to free myself. Virtue belongs to me at all times in my thoughts and I couldn't make this second accident my entire life. I despised Yolanda and my old girlfriends who let themselves get pregnant in order to trap themselves now they have reason to scream at the trap they laid for themselves as they say girls 14 to 21 think they know it all. Freedom depends upon myself if I gave in it would have been impossible to continue, as it was it almost was, and what would have happened to me if I stayed in this glass palace prison, I would have lived because that is what I do but it would have been sheer torture. I never would have been able to act again, to continue in art and finally only in getting what I thought I wanted realized how unhappy I was. This was only given to me by my upbringing, my culture, my religion but that was not all there was something more, that I learned from grandma and even if I couldn't explain it I could start learning things, and that allowed me to move in a more articulate way of wanting to live, living is not only beliefs but can have some knowledge and this provides a nice basis from which to start even if you can't see it being taught. It was there all along I just couldn't see it. The only way to find out what I want is to have it. The next time I didn't run away walked up the twelve steps then walk down again, I simply didn't walk up the twelve steps but let them know so they wouldn't worry, wrote Joseph and grandma a long letter, typed, because my handwriting has become atrocious because of word processors at work, explaining that I was not abandoning them but finding myself, I have to live my own life not be a robot, and even if I feel terrible in doing it I left did not abandon them and Jacoba is not alone in the world and she has a family to love her and even I live in pain and am embarrassed in what I am doing but I still love them. If I was to be human again I had to leave, it wasn't even at the first step that I thought this I thought it over a million times before I actually did it and refused to climb those steps one more time, I turned around, imagine that, without even thinking and if I was thinking would have thought I should turn right back but didn't and kept on walking to my friend's couch—I was no longer going to live with lies concealment, boredom.

I now walk everywhere, walk again, avoid the trains as much as possible now that they are safe, go figure, but walking calms me down, I can't even watch television, tried taking an afternoon off and sitting in a movie theater, a waste of money I have no idea what was shown on the screen only it looked just like a television movie not cinema and I always liked films or cinema, at least foreign films that came from art or theater, painting, set design, costumes, not television but these young filmmakers seem to recycle old television shows, and now have found that the best way to be alone with myself is to walk in a crowd and so when I go to art museums or galleries look sharp in my beret even expect people to come up to me and ask artistic questions, and that did happen when Lilliana bumped into me at a gallery opening, we were both there for the same thing: free wine and cheese. I know the difference between mannerism, baroque and rococo, linearity and perspective, I didn't sleep through Mrs. Pollard's art history lectures and film strips, of course I did, everyone did, the professor had no feeling for art but knew everything but felt nothing, no passion only talked formulas, academics are so mediocre, she didn't paint only criticized those that did, I was thinking about her when someone bumped into me, apologized said I looked interesting in my beret, black turtleneck sweater and tweed sports jacket, and really was involved in the paintings because I was talking to myself, no I said remembering my boring art history class and I really don't like these objects on the wall they are of nothing. She laughed you want easel painting to support the government, totalitarian art. No I like social realism not socialist realism. We laugh, she says I'm the only person she's met in America with a nice smile who knows something about socialist realism. She had enough of that. Where? Czechoslovakia, left after '68. Prague, I said. Yes, she replied. My favorite city. Have you been there? No I said. Go to the East Village, it's like Prague. I've been there. She heard Kafka could never finish his novels, wondered if Joseph K. would ever get to the Castle, and never heard of Meyrink's *The Golem*. What is to become of me I wonder every time I am with a new woman it's like a tabula rasa while talking to this attractive woman and I see men's gazes all around me, envious, no longer can I fool myself that I am doing what I want or what is right. What is right is that I am out of the house looking at Albert Oehlen's 'how to go on' at the *Dia* center, with art that has been declared dead many times and a pretty woman bumps into me and I have nothing to say but instead of mumbling actually ask her to go out for a drink with me and to my surprise she says yes. We talk about Gulag grotesque as a description of Soviet architecture, totalitarian art how Hitler and Stalin had the same ideas that art should glorify the state and particularly the Leader or the Führer, I thought I understood life is a good job but a job is a job, she is an artiste, a set designer, involved she doesn't go to work her life is her work. I understand every word she says and all I'm thinking is will I be able to meet her again or is this going to be it. I have left most of my childhood friends who only like to remind me of my past that I wish to forget, and rarely have dinners with acquaintances from work the only person that I still have conversations with is Esmeralda. I want to introduce her to Esmeralda. I thought she would take me to a noisy painters' bar, and nobody would suspect that I know how to make money and am only good at that, they wouldn't know I am a caregiver and can cook, my beret would help them think of me as a painter, instead she took me to a coffeehouse, Caffe Dell' Artista on Greenwich where we sat and talked the whole night over a café au lait. I have skills but in living am a flat zero. I have to learn how to live but I doubt if anyone would want to go with an old man such as myself, I don't even know how to date. Esmeralda laughed when I told her that while I was out on a date, even if I didn't consider drinking in a café with a set designer a date. I wondered if I could hold up my end of the conversation. Esmeralda warned me about setting myself up to lose, and I was ready but still I had little to say. But I started recalling moments in Ms. Pollard's art history class and I knew about art, history, life, had gone to plays, which I found out to my surprise most painters didn't, Lilliana at least had an excuse at first, the language barrier, but she speaks it well enough now that I got up my courage and asked if she would like to go to a play with me. She said she didn't really like plays, too bullshitty can we go to a movie instead. So the next night we went to a double bill, not really a double bill because movie theaters stopped doing that at the end of the '60s, but we saw *Russian Ark* by Sokurov at Lincoln Plaza, a 96-minute film taken in one shot of the Hermitage museum in Petersburg, and then she took me downtown to the Quad to see *Band of Outsiders* an old 1964 Godard film where they race through the Louvre in nine minutes and forty-three seconds. After that we were a couple. When I finally took her to my place she complimented me for a non-gay man you make a comfortable home. And it is me I am the one with taste, learned, but we eat off linen tablecloths with fine china and silverware, we do have oil paintings covering all the walls, rugs not carpet on the floor, and comfortable furniture, quilted pattern sofas and reading chairs, some of course getting destroyed by hurricane Jacoba. When you come home you should have something nice to look at. Antiques but lived antiques not museum pieces that you could not touch. This certainly didn't come automatically or learned from my parents, we never had paintings on the wall, not even paint by numbers, nor books, except romance magazines, nor carpet only linoleum, but I learned from grandfather, then Zoltan, then Esmeralda and Cassandra, until it became me, even if many times I was so down that I couldn't look up at the beauty, that's why I loved going to see artists at work and seeing their struggles, seriousness for the sake of seriousness with no hope of future reward but done with a sense of humor. I can feel it when they try and then words become trite and the truth is difficult to explain. Even if I didn't have Jacoba, nor Esmeralda to take care of I know I couldn't be an artiste. Lilliana really does it. She lives in a pigsty in Westbeth a small bed, hotplate, no gas, she shut it off to save money, and the floors dripping with paint, clay, clay models all over the place, and paper drawings all over the walls. Why it was easier for her to stay at my place then for us to gather at hers. She actually did have a convertible couch that opened into a double bed just in case, but she usually slept on top. I wouldn't force a guilt trip on her and was prepared not to sleep with her on the first date, but women now have no such qualms. No man is a hero to his wife and I wondered if all my sufferings was to bring this about and I couldn't wait for Cassandra to find out, but, of course, I wouldn't be the one to tell her. She saw all my insecurities and still wanted to be with me. When she found out I came from the Bronx she wanted to know if

I was beaten up like the stories she heard, so much so that she has never been up to the Bronx, afraid it's too dangerous. I tell her worse, I was the one who would beat up people at least up until the fifth grade when for some reason I stopped fighting, I still don't know why I don't think I was beaten up too bad, I would get hit but I gave it back. One guy once asked me are we going to fight fair or are we going to kick and I laid into him before he knew what hit him and was pounding him on the ground. Maybe I stopped after that afraid of what I could do. She inspired me I loved her legs wrapped around me, especially when I dreamed about that since the moment I saw her long slim athletic legs—I may have a dead mind but my body surprised me and we could do it over and over again, never could I do that with Cassandra. Now I don't want to live without her but do I have the right to ask for more. My parents vegetated can't I just exist for the next twenty years—do I have to have a goal? You can ask a question like this when you are flat on your back and wonder if you'll ever get up again, not when a woman is on top of you squeezing the life out of you and you're having an orgasm. The rules are changing and I no longer have to follow the old edicts, still I vow not to leave Jacoba or Esmeralda she will have to live with us or I spend some time there but my main duty is still to the family. Even if the old ways don't work anymore and women have an independent income and the idea of freedom is in the air but it all depends upon education—imagine if she had graduated U. of Pitt. but that really doesn't matter because education is deeper than schooling—she is creative and artistic people have something to live for not just play-acting at life—going on vacations when you don't want to go on vacations, I can't stand driving out to the Hamptons or the Berkshires, why would I be doing this I much rather be at home seeing theater, movies, artistic shows, concerts and occasional poetry reading, than be sitting under an umbrella under the hot sun on a beach or walking in the mountains with ticks. And when you go out to eat dinner at night the whole town is in the new hot restaurant, so hot that nobody goes there anymore, a Yogism, I thought it fun challenging the old values until it happened to me, now it's not so hot. I like the idea of coming home to a family. This new breed of woman is making my life more complicated, I always talked about wanting to be free even if I hadn't the slightest idea what that meant—yes I did, I never wanted zipless fucks, always thought lovemaking should mean something, never wanted to be a playboy with a waterbed, never wanted a mustang or vacations on beaches, I know what I don't want but what do I want? I try and see my breakup as a misfortune not a tragedy, you can recover from misfortune tragedy takes you down— why I still go to art shows, and artists don't have an easy life but can do it, so why can't I. Now at least I have somebody to do things with and maybe I can parley that into something. I haven't told Esmeralda we are a couple but I think she knows, we go to art galleries, movies, I still can't get her to go to off-off plays every weekend and we both have similar tastes in only looking at a couple of paintings otherwise the exhibit becomes too overwhelming and not afraid to talk in a museum art should be discussed not bowed down to. Simultaneously we both decided to leave after listening to Kurtág's string quartet at the Brooklyn Barge rather than let it slip out of our minds. However, once I step outside into the bright sunlight am lost but Esmeralda has said she will stay with Jacoba she must be loved and she does spoil her but what is a great-grandmother for than to spoil a child with love.

How did it turn out like this, why couldn't he have said sure I'm cool with it as long as you don't upset the family? I never cared what other people thought and it could have worked if he had been agreeable. We were connected at times I couldn't get enough couldn't wait to tear myself into his body until I met someone else then someone else again, I would have been okay if he had met someone too as long as he kept it away from the family, and if he would have asked me to stop seeing someone I probably would have. He didn't see my heartbreak, I was going crazy being home all day with Jacoba, I really didn't like being a mother, boy is this hard to say. He just didn't see it. Said I have to stop seeing him how could I do that? It was only a blow job. He could also have gone out with women I would have understood. Maybe if he would have said I could stay one night away from home we could have worked it out but he said he couldn't handle it, was too jealous said that if I left now maybe in five years he would get over me but if I stayed he would always be in pain, I had no idea I was going to do it, I was walking up our block, walking up the twelve steps to his not my place and I said no, left my key in the door and had to go back for it, thought about it halfway up and then before I even realized it turned around and walked down the steps to the subway and back to the old neighborhood, not the Bronx I would never go there, besides my old building has been torn down after a fire when the hood was overrun with junkies, back to where I lived with grandma, I know some actor friends who moved into the East Village and even if they are paying a fortune in rent compared to what grandma paid because the East Village is now chic and which thanks to Joseph we haven't given up so it is still under rent control, you don't give up a rent-controlled apartment he said we'll sublease it and if the landlord finds out then we'll fight in landlord tenant court. And the landlord never found out because he no longer collects rent in person but has a company do it, and grandma pays the rent under her name and the subtenant pays her, and we don't make a profit, a good legal strategy in case we're accused of illegal subletting. It was only a thousand square feet and we've outgrown it years ago but you don't give up a rent-controlled apartment. I spent a few nights at on my friend Sophia's couch wondering when I would come to my senses and go back uptown. But I was a burden their bookcases overflowing, their closets were filled to the brim, paintings all over the wall and worse only one bathroom. That was fine when I lived with grandma and Joseph but now that I had gotten used to more than one this was impossible, I couldn't be alone in this place and I needed time for myself, I shuddered when I walked in these people were so nice and considerate, so overbearing only concerned about me, I was thinking about how to move out what place to get after all I earn a decent salary I could find a place when grandma called and said our subtenants were moving out. Once again I led a charmed life. All of a sudden I had an empty living room and I had the floors sanded and put a Navajo rug in the center. That was the only item grandma could buy when she was at the Grand Canyon gift shop that was made in America everything else was made in China. I covered the cracks in the wall with paintings, Lisa constantly moved hers around so she wouldn't get bored looking at them we had never thought of that and I vowed to do that. Lisa had invited me in no questions asked she must be use to people running away before me there was a high school girl who couldn't stand being with her parents. Location, location, location the East Village is hot now, a name coined by landlords when trying to sell apartments on the Lower East Side thinking its proximity to Greenwich Village would help them sell them, is becoming safer and she can make a little extra money between gigs by letting people stay with them, but she still takes taxis home if she comes home late at night. Her boyfriend can accept the fact that she's out late at night why couldn't mine. She said when I'm ready to talk I will and she saw no reason to force me but it makes no sense for me to talk to her and was glad to finally have a place of my own. Everyone expected me to be happy, married, child, jobs, a wonderful home, a built-in babysitter, and the place was finally renovated, totally, the walls decorated, the floors finished, the bathrooms brand new, one with only a toilet, sink and shower without even a curtain, only teenagers need curtains for showers, an eat-in kitchen, but I couldn't stand the place felt trapped even if this place is made for people to be happy in. One more step up and I could have been trapped for life without even a chance of becoming and so without thinking I cannot recall one thought about leaving even if I had my doubts it wasn't even a fantasy I turned around and walked down into the abyss to Lisa an old friend from the theater, who I actually bonded with when we were both nude on stage together, nothing like a little nudity, titillation, to bring out the best in men. I'm wondering what's so wrong with this life, she says nothing, offers me a stiff drink she has no *café con leche* and I have to laugh she has not even a quart in the house while we buy two, three gallons of milk a week. She's from Madison and drinks her coffee black and instant. With her I began to realize there is something to being successful and happy and I liked the life she was leading. Lisa liked that. Happiness is a better judge of success than work, it's how you live that counts, grandma always said that and if my life can actually change I want to do what is pleasing to me and I won't live the way I lived before. The only theater metaphor that comes to mind is playing the dying scene, I still think theatrically not business-wise, but I am modifying that scene to play the living well scene, living well is the best revenge, no longer will I be on my deathbed wondering if I lived the life I wanted to but will lead the life I want to—a weak analogy I know because we now die unconscious in hospitals not surrounded by loved ones but it's the only scene I can visualize, wondering did I live the life I wanted. Will I call out mother. I hope not. Joseph says I use to many theater images but he always does what is expected, why he is a reliable man and easy to be around, I can't do that anymore I want more mostly I don't want to play the victim, not become my mother. Maybe I should look my father up, never cared before to do that. Wouldn't even know where to begin, just a boy my mother dated who knocked her up and took no responsibility. Now I no longer want to be about family, children, my husband, baby, they will no longer be all my thoughts, always part of me but not my central part, always thinking about other people but now I'm better off than before. This is not acting this is me: I'm not a character in a play, strangers are always surprised when they meet me off stage that I'm taller, shorter, smarter, dumber, more secure, insecure not realizing I'm acting. It doesn't make sense I still wonder if what I'm doing is right abandoning my family but my conscience was strangely silent when I sat across from Lisa never wanting to go home again. I knew I couldn't stay there forever and had no idea what the future held and wished I could take a long hot bath and put a big soft beach towel around me, but can't the place doesn't have a tub only a shower, and when I first moved back here went to Mays up on 14th street as they were going bankrupt and bought two large soft beach towels that I like wrapping around myself— uptown I never bothered with baths nor the good weave these towels have. Now finally realize I have to take care of me nobody else will and pursue what I like not what I think I want.

This Danielle is quite a character, whoever would have thought, I can't believe half the stuff she says my difficulty is I don't take old people seriously and smile and laugh about what they say but don't think their memories are accurate or they simply make it up. How could she have lived with two men, who's going to put up with that except she really believes it as she says it and is sad now that it has come to an end. It's ended because both are dead. I couldn't even conceive of doing it and she did it. You can either do it so know it works or grasping it thinking about it but in thinking about it you don't realize if you can do it or not you have to do it to realize if you can do it, do. Do I have to do it to find out I can't do it? She must have given those men something for them to live like that and when I see her smile and her vivaciousness realize something was going on. I would have been banging my head against the wall, she claims to be a child of the '60s even if she's too old to be that she certainly grabbed onto what liberation meant, self-liberation no matter how it hurt children, and now her child is getting back at her writing poetry that breaks in the line and refills it with hate, astonishing, complicated but not cutesy poetry of a daughter writing on the distinction between feeling and thinking and how can you feel without thought: she always gave me chopped meat and kept the steak for herself. But there are no words that can express her anger at her mother. I can't imagine the pain she is going through.

I was appalled, stunned, shocked by her daughter's decision to take her away without even having a chance to respond they even threatened to take her by force against her will to take her out of our home even as she lived here over six months already and was quite capable of managing on her own and put her in a home for senior citizens up in Riverdale at the border of the Bronx where it goes into Yonkers. We have tried to contact her but so far she hasn't called back. Her daughter has guardianship, we didn't even know she applied for it, we might have appeared in court and testified even if the law is firm family comes first, even if we insisted she could stay with us our house would be considered a temporary solution not a permanent one and wouldn't have held much water with the judge. Legality is all and family has first dibs unless you can prove contrary, and we couldn't use my psychological arguments even after what the mother did to her and she is still angry at her mother and has never forgiven her mother and now only wants to do what's best for her mother put her in a nursing home to wither away. Of course she might deny it just as the mother denied she was hurting her child by living with Marvin: unconscious motivation is speculation even if true—why I like drama it's all speculation therefore all true. Who can read non-fiction anymore they take motivation, speculation out deal only in what people say as if they speak truth, I know I lie to myself all the time about Cassandra. I really have to stop and think in silence to get an aspect of the truth of what I think and then I usually am shocked at what I think, and then I have to cover it up and give a pleasant answer to myself and it's even a recurring pattern and think I should ignore it—are there parallels between children and parents or are there too many complex gradations between one and the other for me to say I am positive this is the truth. Can we ever know the whole? Does she want her mother's money? There has to be plenty if she sold her apartment moved to Florida then sold there and then came back. We're not talking chump change and Frank, her husband had a pension and that and social security should pay for the nursing facility. She's playing the concerned daughter so much I think she's acting the concerned daughter only doing it for her mother's benefit, her mother was living on her own, she was forgetful but it wasn't that bad that she has to be institutionalized, at least the State now regulates the homes not like the Nursing Home scandals of the '70s where they were rat-infested, unclean, and subject to elder abuse, now at least the places are clean and well-lit, a sign of decency. If she had moved her closer in the city Esmeralda could visit as it is it's difficult if not impossible to get up there unless you go by express bus and that means somebody will have to go with her and that somebody means me. It's shameful what has happened in our culture the elderly have so little freedom and I say it so brazenly as if this isn't going to happen to me because I simply can't imagine myself old but remember the old wives tale *avuelo* told me where the father cuts off the head of his father because he is old and infirm and then his son takes the scythe and his father asks why, for when it's my turn for you. Is this how we all end up and our belongings left outside our door to be thrown away as trash. I bet Danielle wasn't thinking she'd end up this way sad and not even knowing the reasons she's sad probably thought she'd get old gracefully and be the same person she always was. We all have blinders on. Esmeralda has made me swear I won't put her in a nursing facility. Cassandra said Hispanics don't do that. If it were only true. Besides Cassandra is only Hispanic when it suits her. When my mother could no longer live alone I couldn't move in with her, to live with her would have been the death of me, and I couldn't even move back to the Bronx it depressed me so much to be there, and she couldn't move to my walk-up in the city. To move back to the Bronx would have been admitting total defeat, it was bad enough when she would look out the window waiting for me to come by or when in school waiting up all night until I came in making impossible demands upon my freedom, as it was I was ashamed to tell friends I still lived at home until Cassandra gave me the ultimatum live alone for a year before you move in with me, which lasted seven months. One classmate, what was her name? anyway couldn't live at home and her mother threatened to have her committed and she finally moved in with her social studies teacher and they lived that way for years until they finally broke up and she swears he saved her life that without him her mother would have prevailed. I wonder if she will institutionalize her mother when the time comes? Pauline Phyllis that's what her name was or Phyllis Pauline. I remember being envious that she moved out of the house and was living with a teacher and thought he was taking advantage of her but she claims he saved her life she couldn't live at home anymore and her mother actually did try and have her committed but she was able to fight her off until she was eighteen and then according to the law she was an adult and when the affair ended she lived a normal life unlike boys who when love ends go off to war. But I loved going over to her house and making believe I was an adult but always had trouble calling the teacher by his first name as he insisted but I could only call him mister.

This old gray mare ain't what she used to be just grayer, no longer can I walk with Danielle and surprisingly I miss her not that she walked much mostly we sat and observed old men flirting with young women, she called them 'dirty old men' but I thought they were just keeping themselves alive, if a young girl ever went with one of them I'd be surprised especially the ones who combed their last piece of hair around and around on the top of their head. I imagine she is unhappy in the nursing home, it's too sad and too difficult to visit and it's depressing I keep thinking soon that could be me. Conchita promised she would never let that happen to me but Conchita doesn't live with us anymore and now I'm more dependent upon my old lover's grandson and if I become too difficult he will have no choice but to put me out of sight. What good is all this living if it doesn't prepare you for dying? I have no belief that the gods will come to my aid, besides there being no such thing if they did exist what makes you think they would care about me and my immortal soul. My soul isn't going anywhere there is no soul without a body. We now know the universe is much bigger than we thought and some commentator has already said maybe He can't take it in all at once, why always a He? and when She looks away I'll be sent to a nursing home. It's terrible feeling so helpless—what's the good of living if you end like this. Without a decent body you can't live and each day is more difficult than the last—medicine helps but the side effects are painful, if only I could give up my will to live, no longer can I think through a thought or even have pleasant sensations, just try and be a little without pain. Some silly social worker, giggling, told Danielle that many women start new lives here, a young woman who has no idea what it is to be old and D. avoids her when she can. She can no longer hold her wine glass, wears diapers, can't hold in her urine, and on weekends there are too few aides around to change it and as her memory evaporated her depression lessened, they are connected. When I asked Joseph to complain to management they were responsive, the place is clean, the beds made every day but she lives in a dormitory setting without privacy she's in a nightmare from which she can't awaken. The problem is once our bodies begin to desert us our minds falter and all this suffering doesn't make you a better person or enhance your self-esteem only forces you to admit you're living too long. Will I have the courage to end it when I become too much of a burden? How do you know? You can never know for sure and I was ready after my heart attack and look what happened living became better, I started taking better care of myself I got stronger I can walk a few miles and I can truly say right now I'm in the best shape of my life walking and doing yoga daily—back in the day you weren't considered a woman if you did sports. Now I see both men and women jogging all the time and if you jog you can't smoke or have to give it up to run better and less and less people smoke or is it fewer and fewer I still get confused with American idioms and these are not interchangeable, less and less refers to quantity, I think, and fewer people are waiting for their first heart attack to give it up. Before my attack I would laugh when someone told me to stop smoking but now am glad I did but if it only allows me to live like a vegetable— are bodies without souls rotten smells and soiled thoughts unable live a full life? The charm of walking down to the Museum park is gone, we would sit and watch people feed the pigeons, New York never got rid of them as they said they would because their crap gets inside buildings and ruins the infrastructure and we would watch old men flirt realizing all the power we once had and didn't even know it. Old men never spoke to us. I'm not afraid of death, only dying, never have been always loved the way the Greek poets, dramatists, tales they told about the gods their seduction, theft, way worse than human beings then Plato comes along and the gods must be beyond reproach, perfect, so bans poetry from his perfect city, as if man can ever be perfect. Ancient Jews then Christians must have loved him, some philosopher didn't even ask if the gods exist only they had to and be perfect. If they are so perfect what is Danielle doing in a nursing home? Fundamentalists still believe we have no free will and that God sees all, knows all, if this is true why doesn't He make changes, at least modern man has some notions of independent thought that God is not universal surveillance but a moral fiction. I certainly would have left my parents earlier when I started to learn to think if I only could, of course, all I thought about was Jacobo, but soon learned you have to think more than just about a man, if it wasn't for my damn thoughts that I thought life could have some meaning and that I had to think about what I was doing in order for life to have some meaning it had to be more than a pleasant outing. Why? All my thoughts didn't help me I went back to my old life when thoughts became too scary. Joseph disagrees says I had no other choice. Not true we have choices we just don't take them. He would have run away lived on the street turned tricks in Times Square anything not to be them. No he says he was a goody goody all his thought of being a free thinker was play-acting until he actually did it—you can think about it but you have to actually do it for it to become real and you feel it. Knowledge doesn't have to come from thought but from experience and that experience can lead to thinking. Surprise, surprise but what if the experience doesn't lead to knowledge what then. You have to be able to think it through to grasp the idea. But what good is all this thinking when we end up like Danielle your thoughts do you no good when your children have legal authority, who can be like Sophocles and recite portions of *Oedipus at Colonus* to convince a judge he was of sound mind when his children wanted to declare him incompetent. I better start memorizing parts of *Don Quixote,* he isn't the jester everyone thinks he is he wants to uproot evil and loves a pure woman, Dulcinea, who cannot exist—what is it with men and their fantasy women? At least he fights oppression and believes in self-sacrifice, for Quixote everything exists for something else now each individual lives in his own universe, and when the universe crashes down there is nobody to pick up the pieces: you can't make an omelet without breaking eggs. There are no more idealistic people.

Why couldn't she just do something silly like killing herself to let the world know she still loves me. Is that asking too much? I would look good in mourning. Even as I think this realize nothing I say will affect her and that I don't truly want her to kill herself, but it's fun imagining instead of saying get on with your life. I spend more time at work, I don't have to think there I know the job, walking more, checking apartments more, getting better at finding new neighborhoods near the tipping point then lock up some apartments by offering decent prices, which let other tenants know I'm around and they become comfortable with me and if the time comes don't switch to other real estate companies, and only occasionally am I called a slum lord and at first was surprised at the anti-Semitism of some of my clients, since Jews are usually not landlords anymore, the garment district is no longer predominantly Jewish and school teachers are no longer mostly Jewish—those days are over the kids of these parents moved on to be doctors, lawyers, stock brokers, risk arbitragers, so it's not an economic prejudice but a stereotype and like Conchita who long ago changed her name to Cassandra, we changed or added Clayton and Company, sounds more goyisha. And if a building decides to go co-op we already own a few apartments and don't need to buy more. The difficulty is New York is still a rental city and tenants are fighting for their homes and still don't see the advantage in owning but now it's slowly changing the young couples with both working see the tax advantage, especially when it is two gay men who both make good incomes and are taxed to the nines, and can't even take the marriage deduction. Most clients can't grasp the tax code but when we tell them of the specific advantages some get it, while local pols rant and rave about keeping developers out of the neighborhood but never talk true conditions that middle-class educated people are making the city more responsive to their needs, garbage is picked up regularly, police now actually patrol streets and eliminate pockets of crime, block associations keep crime down and co-oping actually gets residents to know their neighbors and we've become accustomed to increases, too bad they now actually have to charge tuition to City University, but why shouldn't they have to pay some education becomes more valuable this way, besides it's now open to all high school graduates not just the elite. If only I could have a body without a mind, all this looks good on paper and I no longer have to pad my resume I still have to live and that is the difficult part, being with Lilliana helps, but I've come up to a dead end, this is the limit to my life, I can't have fun anymore even if I wondered yesterday if all of my family history all their struggles were all there to produce me the apex and now see all this as nonsense and I can go no further am too depressed. Just as I was deep into self-pity I received a call from Esmeralda that Danielle was kidnapped from our place and put in a nursing home in Riverdale near where her daughter lives, and claims she doesn't have all her wits about her and Danielle called and feels isolated and without friends, her health has declined from eating, talking walking to lying in bed all day, but since we have no legal standing and besides that's her problem I have enough of my own but I handle Esmeralda with kid gloves even if she's up front with me but still supports her granddaughter. I may not have a soul but I do have a body but I have more than a body I have a self and while this is difficult for my body it's worse for my sense of self that is demoralized and I see my-self that is different from my body even if my-self and body are one; if I can keep my body from getting heavier, walking, and now all of a sudden being careful what I eat and when I am about to fall asleep after a night of watching television instead of directly going to bed make sure I brush my teeth, saying I will get over this and I don't then want to go through the pain of a dentist because in the midst of my depression didn't take care of my-self. That hit me when I went to the dentist and all of a sudden I had four cavities and in the dentist's chair realized I should care, and while the noise of the drill frightened me, luckily she had gas and I was able to see words float out of her mouth as she told me I had to take better care of my teeth and I thought the self is important as I grabbed onto the chair and held tight with my hands even if I didn't feel the drill but the noise of the drill scared me. It was enough of a scare that I now brush my teeth three times a day and wouldn't allow my body to deteriorate and I would care for my-self. The life I am leading doesn't impress me too much it's not that my soul is out of joint otherwise I could simply stay on my late night schnapps and all could be honky-dory, but my-self is an entity to itself it doesn't admit progress and can only be what it is, can't be weak and ugly or handsome and unhappy: my-self is not one of these but all of these in different degrees, I don't have an ounce of goodness in me but am a good provider and a lousy lover, still tremor when I have to perform and a cold shiver runs through my body and I get cold when I am naked in bed, at times I want to hit her for making me perform get out of myself, and then I want to plunge a knife into Cassie for putting me in this situation but not because it's wrong and I would go to jail but because I have no right to force her to be where she doesn't want to be but when I hit her my prick gets hard. I can't reason with her but it would be nice to guilt trip her and she gets me so angry, yet nobody is forcing me to care for her grandmother, or our daughter and she actually ends up cursing me in my dreams for being so good— since when is good better than truth or beauty, she actually says to me or what I can remember, I don't know if I can continue but am afraid to do something else: my-self is something even if my soul is not as I dream of taking her from the back. Those were the words flowing over my head as oxygen flowed through my nose and I was done for the day. I walked home and napped. It was worse than drinking a bottle of wine at lunch and knowing when I got home all I would do was sleep. This was deeper and all I dreamed about was Cassie. My life is so low that I couldn't wait to go back to the dentist and have more cavities filled. While under the gas said do something nice for yourself and bought a nice first edition at Pomander which, surprise, surprise my dental insurance wouldn't cover even after I explained it was part of my dental recovery. It was too nice of a book I was afraid to carry it outside, afraid to underline it, afraid to read it, it is so expensive, so I have an unopened first edition of Antonio Los Atunes sitting on my bookshelf in Spanish no less they only had Los Atunes in Spanish not Portuguese, and try and teach myself Spanish. If he had written in French, he would be an international bestseller. When I awaken in the middle of the night look in on Jacoba who went to bed by herself fully dressed so I helped her into pajamas and sat in the dark in the living room, more and more I like doing that especially when people are home, alone by myself I usually put music or the television on and plenty of lights, as I said to myself that I have more passion for her in her absence, I don't think I loved her as much as I do now. My-self is a jumble a confused mess but at least my body is having sex.

I love my mother so much that I would never do anything to hurt her. Rest assured right now Danielle has a place right near me and that she can use the phone to call anyone she wants. As she was at Joseph and Esmeralda's place until last week I now have to get her new pairs of shoes, the ones she's been wearing are falling apart. Danielle is not in prison she can come and go with someone as she wants all she has to do is say where and approximately when she's coming back. The home only wants her to be safe and also provides medical care 24/7. Esmeralda and her family can come and visit anytime provided they tell the nursing home in advance and they can even go for a walk if they desire. Despite Esmeralda's version I have no desire for her not seeing her friend and she knew from the start that hers was only a transitional space. My only wish is to be absolutely sure Danielle is getting the care and attention she needs and where I can know what's going on, which was not the case at Esmeralda's. After my father's death she wanted to stay in the apartment more than anything and nothing I could do would convince her to move somewhere else. I did everything I could so she could stay in that apartment a few more years, helping, networking, despite Danielle's firm insistence not to have anything to do with old ladies from protective services but these remarkable people used all their talents in finding a place in Danielle's life, not only did these old ladies volunteer they succeeded in gaining

Danielle's confidence and she started participating in their activities and made many friends, without there care and devotion she would have been forced into a home for some time. Then she couldn't stand the cold and somehow got it in her head that she had to move to Florida. The weather is nicer there but she was trapped all alone and couldn't drive. She came back but not to the old place. I found her an apartment on the West Side but the inevitable happened and she fell one night and was trapped on the floor until a friend called the next day, before that she had resisted the idea to live with other people and was always getting angry at me for suggesting it, me being the only obstacle for her living alone. Nor was she then aware and had no idea of her illness and how it affects her so. How can it be otherwise? There was a consensus around the necessary of a transition and since her new building was going co-op and Joseph was so supportive and said we are looking for a tenant we all readily accepted this idea especially as she wouldn't be alone. But Danielle completely lost the notion of time and didn't even know how long she has been living with Esmeralda and her family and was surprised when I told her it was over a year, for her conversation is without memory of what was just said and she has no sense of my presence. However, there was not a moment when she asked during this period do you want me to stay with them? She didn't have a clue where she was and she was not too happy living there, it was understood right from the start that the stay with Joseph was temporary in want of a long-term solution of us finding a spot for her in a nursing home. That was the solution thought out by me with the help of the professionals specializing in her illness, her stay with Esmeralda and her family depended upon the evaluation of the professionals and their understanding of her need and by me her only daughter. My wish is to be absolutely sure that Danielle is getting the care and attention she needs and where I can know what's going on, which was not the case at Esmeralda's. Danielle's social worker phoned a month or so ago and informed me that there is a room available at the nursing home, which also happens to be one of the best residences and I have visited many of them, this gives her a fair chance and I am positive she will be happy there. Danielle has Alzheimer's, her health is deteriorating. Esmeralda and her family have done a wonderful, kind job helping Danielle not be alone, take walks, have someone to talk to, and not keeping Danielle away from her friends this past year and for this I am grateful. But it was difficult for me to go and visit her there and they openly rejected me from their sphere of friendship and barred me from speaking to my own mother or spending large amounts of time with her, and also I have been made aware from stories by Danielle herself how unaware she is of her own safety needs and Joseph and his family seem not to fully understand the level of care she needs given her condition. A psychologist and a social worker helped to determine the feasibility of Danielle staying at Esmeralda's and Joseph's place and both understood that a person with Alzheimer's needs in terms of care are and what Joseph and Esmeralda were prepared to accept. These people were specialists and when my doctor called and emphasized it's not easy to get room in this place and if you want it you should accept it, if I had waited for some crisis she could have ended up anywhere, I couldn't live with that. I cannot deny this is a difficult decision for me and extremely difficult for Danielle, she is at a point in her illness where any change is disconcerting and destabilizing. But this has to stop, any change is going to be a source of stress for her, and now that she is in the nursing home she can live and evolve in a living condition that will offer her the best compromise between being continually alone or accompanying by health professionals in a cheery and kind environment with care and compassion for those who love her and only want her happiness.

He talks about Judaism all the time yet he eats pork, ham, bacon, and grandma says he's one of those God-infected atheists but if you say God it already exists better not to mention it at all, he sees Jewishness as a mixture of Spinoza and Kant but lately it's been Rothschild and Boesky. I have no such illusions ever since I gave up crossing myself passing a church, left to right and when grandma laughed at my superstition and said cross yourself right to left and you're a Protestant and left to right a Catholic. How silly. That didn't immediately set me free from the belief, you can't change beliefs so easily, but it was a start, I stopped doing it in front of her so she wouldn't think me pious and eventually forgot and stopped doing it altogether. That was a start. This is more difficult, I never realized living alone could be more difficult, I have to keep reminding myself I chose this that I no longer wanted to live a married life, that in movies Hollywood wraps things up so neatly, sentimentally, that once you have a man your life is complete. It isn't true. That was not my life. I am beginning to realize that I have made the moral jump and that I want things to be difficult. Cute when Joseph once said he wanted art to be difficult and now he says did I say that? and all he wants is to be entertained. He says I'm still a kid questioning, wondering, being, and maybe he's correct because I fell into a trap not all at once but inch by inch and the only way to escape is to leave, I could have stayed that way forever unless you force yourself, I keep telling myself, and once I started there was no turning back even if I know I'm hurting others, I can't deny that but Mademoiselle princess doesn't cry inconsolably she has grandma and her father, I can't go back to that way of life I have to accept that, and Jacoba has a loving home and she is not being abandoned and if I don't do this will not have a life worth considering. Otherwise how can I live with myself, this desire of mine is to be who I want to be without preconditions because I have no religious reasons for doing it even if I can hear a priest say stay in a marriage a woman's place is beside her husband, at least no longer under, but to take care of yourself you have to be selfish, to live for others altruistic and give up your ambitions. I am not blind or deaf I know I am affecting others and not only intellectually but emotionally as well. My leaving is upsetting grandma, Joseph and Mademoiselle princess but Mademoiselle is the least cuddly baby she can never sit still long enough. Last night for the first time that I can remember actually went to a movie by myself, me who always had a date—a woman going to a movie by herself just wasn't done, and saw *Alice Doesn't Live Her Anymore* what claptrap she had a man waiting for her at the end of her ordeal and I was bored silly not because I had separated but because I was angry at myself thinking this would help me pass a night away. I should have gone with Joseph and his grandfather to see *The Seventh Seal* at least there a moral crisis is presented when the knight comes home to Sweden after the Crusades and mass death and people are forced to wonder about all their old beliefs and begin to wonder if life has any meaning. All I did was sit and finally when I couldn't stand it anymore, when a man came into the picture, walked out and instead of going home to my empty apartment and doing the dishes, walked down to Princess Pamela across from Katz's deli and had fried chicken, collard greens and black-eyed peas, I usually don't go since I'm not a doyenne of soul food but didn't want to be alone, and she hugged me like a long lost child because grandma had helped her start when she had only an 8-seat restaurant in her walk-up apartment in Alphabet City and grandma lent her some money to open, now she has this small place on East Houston, she still wears her red wig but doesn't sing much anymore but the food was good and the apple cobbler stuck to my stomach. Now I will hire a housekeeper to clean the floors, do laundry, wash the bathroom and kitchen, and have to get myself into another play otherwise I don't know what to do with myself. It's only in acting that I find happiness, it's like a drug and I realized that when I realized how satisfying it is. This is what you get from being half-assed educated certainly growing up Bronx didn't allow to see things differently; it was an old-fashioned neighborhood where everyone knew your mother and thought they had the right to discipline you. Grandma opened my eyes to a different world, still if I was educated earlier might believe art is only a phantom a lie. Catholics believe that, they believe anything except truth only want to follow ritual doesn't matter if you believe as long as you follow you're okay with the big *gantse macher* in the sky, as grandma says sometimes only a Yiddishism will do, as long as it looks fine, nobody cares how you feel—what are people saying about you, looking good. But that doesn't make it anymore. I still use religious similes, metaphors to put meaning in the right frame of mind even if I use them for different things, there is no regret anymore it doesn't help me live—wouldn't it be nice if I could live, I hope to live again but at least now know what I'm after, and am not waiting for my life to begin or to get my just rewards in the next life, it is life I worry about. How I live will determine how I live and how happy I am and my half-assed reasoning, thinking, intuitiveness all now go into myself and is part of me not simply following rules that I must do even if I didn't create them: it's me, a combination, or me and the change in my life. But it's so disheartening to come home to an empty apartment that I leave all the lights on and I have made it a habit to leave something nice to look at on the dining room table when I first come in, even buy fresh flowers because it makes me happy; it's a new type of thinking, it feels strange but correct putting order into my life as opposed to going with the flow. Who knows if this will work? But I gave Joseph the keys back I don't want him to have the illusion that I will be back someday and share his bed. Knowing a man's brain, he'll think I made a copy. But no longer will I live the way I lived; who knows if this is right but it is the right way for me and now I am thinking not purely acting but Joseph doesn't think this type of thinking is the right way, he claims he never stood in the way of my acting, working, living, all true but you have to do what you have to do that's what grandma said and I think she's proud that I am not into laziness and turning against myself by living a lie. You have to live an active life, a creative life, use it or lose it she says. She surprised me as she always does I thought she would be against my leaving but she can always see beyond the moment and she would ask what's the purpose. I may not have an answer but at least I am trying and I'm not the first and even if I fail I am not the first woman to leave her family in search of a different life. It would be nice to crawl into a bed with a man once again without Jacoba between us, or have breakfast with croissants and freshly brewed coffee then maybe somebody could tell me how the French drink coffee out of a bowl and read at the same time. But right now this is not my life and I am back in this old apartment where I started out my intellectual life.

I somehow imagined that if you did things the correct way they would work out, I sowed my wild oats or if not sowed I wasn't so wild but I ran with the boys before I settled down to a life of responsibility and to my surprise have done what everyone else had done—you don't go against nature and at first just did my thing but began to realize that doing what nature intended means never getting out of my own skin, and that if I am to do something had to do it get out of myself and be with others and caring about others, and then I thought I was doing right not because everyone was doing it but because I wanted to do it and now only know families, rarely to go with single people anymore except Lilliana and of course Esmeralda but she's too old to go looking for a lover. Now when I go into one of my old friend's bachelor apartment I shudder could I live like this, dirt everywhere, books all over the place, windows dark and moldy, tables covered with junk that you can barely walk in their place—at least gay men have a nice apartment, clean well-lit places, they enjoy being couples, bachelors don't even use the kitchen, pure chaos inside their apartments dissoluteness with nothing to distinguish the place from a pigsty—I thought I avoided that in marriage, that I escaped dormitory living also by my own efforts by moving up the chain of being having a well-maintained apartment. There is a leap from being single and living in a pigsty to responsibility and a nice apartment. I hate it when I become so sentimental it's like watching a movie unfold before my eyes, luckily I wasn't an action type guy and my thoughts of going over to her place and knocking some sense into her never materialized, I'd feel too ashamed. I couldn't discuss her extracurriculars maybe if I could we would have communicated better, but what was I going to say let me watch it will be fun, listen to her adventures afterwards, have seconds after him, I couldn't do that it would have destroyed me, wouldn't have allowed me to live with myself would have given me too much pain, I just can't live for thrills or that she is bored and wants a little excitement, it was fun playing house for as long as it lasted, shopping for furniture, antiques, oil paintings and drawings to put on the walls, the oak kitchen table with different-colored chairs that were bought in different stores but which fit together, almost like a jigsaw puzzle to be enjoyed by putting the pieces together. That was living, my happiest moments cooking for all of them while they were chatting away in the living room, all gone, lost, being with Lilliana is nice but not the same as living with Cassie, Esmeralda and Jacoba. I went with the flow, it was all easy never questioned no real thinking and not doing anything different only ersatz living free, thinking I was living in moderation between extremes never able to go wholeheartedly into anything and look what it has gotten me, lying to myself, kidding myself, that I was living correctly: no real thoughts to my actions just a defense of my actions. Now I have to face unpleasant truths moderation is a piece of shit what I want is to be free not be outside myself and be like nature, nature has no goals is indifferent to worldly matters oh of course I had goals or at least some that looked like goals but I accomplished those without thinking, I must stop that type of thinking and try and get back to authenticity to decide how I should live, feel, be active once again not put limitations upon what I can do but also function as a free human being. What's the use, I can't be except who I am, I can't be different now I even feel uncomfortable in jeans, I can't even figure out what I want except what others don't want and I don't even know what others want. I want more of an intellectual life, why I enjoy being with Lilliana yet those artistic types bore me so, not a brain in their head, oh competent, very competent in their craft but can't think beyond it and hold such conventional views except in their art. And they are my fun time. I like hooking up with Lilliana it's not meaningless sex instead of hookers, that I couldn't do it was too meaningless, now I even like being on top something I thought I would never do again. But with her it's only one night stands as she can't stand being around Jacoba, actually took Jacoba to a play and Jacoba behaved, she rented a baby, spent the night with her but afterwards said all you do is think about them they are demanding and this has convinced me I don't want children, and here she was having a five-year-old girl imagine if she had to deal with an infant. I think I would rather live alone than have a succession of one night stands, and I keep wondering if I have something to offer, yea a five-year-old and a grandmother who's not even mine but the lover of my *avuelo*. It's only the money that gets me out of bed in the morning and trying to remember I had goals once even if I can't exactly recall what they were and I do look forward to actually having an actual lived experience again between my self-destructive deeds claimed as moral actions especially when I could bind them in my soliloquies—I used to like that in the theater but now that the theater has gotten rid of the fourth wall I can't hear their thoughts only see their actions, just like TV and movies. I find this cheating but wonder if I would find it different if I could think. All I have been doing is lying to myself so much so that I think it's the truth and it isn't unless I think it all the way through, how can you want to live with a person who doesn't want you? But how can you measure truth? is it by your own conscience or is to some outward standard? I want to start again but does that mean I have to be young again, yet I am so stuck in my ways or can I create my life in my own image otherwise all I am doing is what everyone else is doing. I have to develop confidence that I can do new things—can I learn to live anew? How can I just start anew but I never wanted to be my parents, only *avuelo*, especially when we went on our walks, but now I hate going back to the Bronx, get so depressed back in the old neighborhood and wonder if the subway will run, but that's okay because I can walk downtown like I did with him. I am happy walking, in walking I can let myself go but if I am to live life want to be doing something no matter how afraid I am to try—it's only by applying the most rigorous standards because it doesn't come automatically to me that I can change. Can I change? How many times have I said this but that doesn't mean I can do it? I keep going without direction. Making money is no direction just something I lucked into and am good at but if I'm going to live I'm going to have to start figuring out what I want. Now all I am good at is figuring out what I don't want. No longer will I simply follow my gut because my gut is fear and I remember my mother saying she never took me anywhere my first year so all I did was stay in the neighborhood. Funny I think of her now, I rarely think of her but I did make sure Jacoba travelled the first year I wouldn't keep her only at home or the neighborhood, I only know it because she told me enough times I have no memory before language; my first memory is when *avuelo* took me to the playground and swung me real high and ran under the swing to the other side and swung me back and me laughing. Is that true or is that another false memory because he told me that a million times as well. What starts out as ordinary might be able with effort to become non-ordinary.

Like a record scratching and repeating itself, or if I were a man instead of a woman, as Jacobo once said when I wanted to ask him not to leave and he answered my unasked question that I had to think about life not our parting but how we are to live afterwards and we can't be afraid of this absence because we will meet again even if we never met again, now I miss walking or sitting with Danielle in the park under the blue sky watching clouds go by, listening to birds, observing young lovers walking hand in hand. I just can't go up to her in Riverdale like I couldn't go to the Bronx and confront him. In a minute I would have left either husband for him but he was too scared to leave his wife and he believed in the responsibility he had as a father—he did part from them but regretted it and according to Joseph stayed until his daughter was grown before splitting and only moved in with his daughter when he couldn't get out of bed. I didn't know that. If a woman could be a man nothing would have changed he would have waited for death I couldn't have saved him, it's a delusion of women that we can save man, I have enough trouble saving myself from my own fables. If I look backwards can see the whole broken up in fragments never a whole life that made any sense only from a long distance can I see how one project led to another but it wasn't continuous, logical, there were large breaks in between and while I still live it's all only fragments, maybe after I'm gone somebody could see it as whole, I certainly can't, there is no whole life leading up to this and only when I make efforts to live do I feel the intensity, and I don't know if I have it within me to do it one more time and then one more time after that until time is no more, I can't keep going over my past or blaming Jacobo he is not responsible for my life even if he made living more difficult later, at least he pointed me in the right direction I remember first meeting him and what attracted me was his sense of smell, even sick he smelled different than other men, he smelled healthy and different from other men; I can't shut my mind off from wondering how life would have been with him, not only did I lose a lover I lost my best friend the one I could talk to about my problems but how long could I have continued under his tutelage, one must up and leave their teacher and when we parted realized I was left to my own resources and couldn't live the way I had lived before, I was now forced to live free because I had seen a new way of life and for that I am grateful and don't want to forget that as opposed to living the boring dull insipid life of my countrymen, my parents, now I was able to break free of the shadows on the wall only I couldn't go back inside and help others, he taught me how to live and it is my memory of him that keeps me alive even if I couldn't go home again, but you can't forget the past when I began to live and if I am to continue must stay positive and use that energy not to change the past but to refocus on the future. I couldn't have lived my life regrets and all, pleasure and all, pain and all, if I hadn't had a moment with him. I hear myself being silent, no longer giving advice, of course taking care of Jacoba is taxing and I hope Conchita comes to her senses and finds out what she's missing, but now that Danielle is not around I have no one to talk to. Would it have been so bad if she stayed here? Of course we can't care for her as nursing women can however she would have been in life not confined to a room, here she would have been alive, true she probably will live longer up there, they will make sure she takes her medicine, makes sure she eats, attend to her sick needs, but so what we need more than clean sheets to be alive. So what if she would die a few years earlier down here up there she exists not lives—why I made Joseph swear he wouldn't put me in one of those places. Joseph has a difficult time when I talk about dying he doesn't want to see it but talking about it doesn't make it come any quicker and I'm ready I have my affairs in order and I try not to keep any secrets from him, he knows where all my papers are. So does Conchita. But still I worry did he just say that to appease me but if I became too difficult would he institutionalize me or will he put up with me, or will I have enough guts to end it all if I know it's the right time. *Adios.* But how do you know? I'll never know. Is it time to visit his grave once more? No enough he's not there. And the last time I went all I kept thinking about was will the bus return am I going to be able to get back into the city, so my time wasn't spent with him but only worrying about the bus, I found the grave easily enough, cleared out some weeds easily enough, but kept saying I can't miss the bus it runs every hour and there's no place to sit and you have to stand in the hot sun, I can only think about the moments in my life don't have the ability to see it whole—is there such a thing as a whole life not pieces sewn together, fragments, there is no one traditional goal except maybe when young to have a life, when old to say you had a life but in between are the difficult moments and if you know what you don't want and you know that first then finding out what you do want takes more effort. We all want to be happy but what makes us happy, living how we want to live but you have to struggle to find that out otherwise I could have slid back into what I didn't want, of course my ideas changed as I grew at first I wanted adventure then some man who would watch over me and even thought it dandy if some boys fought over me but when I had an adventure and saw men with shrapnel wounds slows tearing their body to pieces realized I didn't want adventure anymore and settled quickly on being bored with my first husband and who thought I would think him brave if he enlisted not that I despised everything he did including him telling me to think of me kindly if he didn't come back. Such claptrap, sentimental folly of boys raised on war movies. He was a mamma's boy in an adult's body but a child's mind and once he left quickly realized if he came back I couldn't live with him because I realized marriage imposed more restrictions upon me than my parents, imagine he expected me to cook and clean house for him like his mother did. That's when I realized before I simply knew it now after Santiago realized I couldn't live the way nature intended but had to find my own way and realized nature provides no values, big eat little, a sunset is beautiful but an earthquake not, nature is wrong if I am only put on earth to bear children, cook and clean and sacrifice my life for my husband, I now have so much respect for single women with the resources to have children than I ever had when I was sewing them up or giving them abortions. In my times you just couldn't be a single parent unless widowed. I thought a husband would give me a happier life, wrong, in my time religion was for children, it was a venial sin to kiss a boy a mortal one to have premarital sex with him, but I wasn't a total failure I did learn from it: there is no fear of death because death is the end but what I do fear is the loss of being with Jacoba and Joseph and now that I am enjoying life will hate to leave it; there is no certainty in my life it's all bits and pieces and no matter where I look I can't find a whole but only specific instances where I lived and didn't even realize it until afterwards other times existed not living.

My life is getting a little better, doing more with Lilliana now and feel more like Don Quixote chasing windmills than Kafka trying to find out what the Law means and can I gain access. My life is a series of masks and now I have put on a new one of a contented bourgeoisie, no longer do I get into arguments with carpenters, painters, subcontractors, contractors, electricians, once even asked one electrician if he wanted to step outside, luckily he didn't he probably would have killed me, and don't blow every mistake out of proportion just step back and try and charm them and it seems to work people are nicer when you are nicer to them, I've become easy-going—a little sex goes a long way, I was anxious didn't even know if I should put my arm around her but knew I had to have sex with her or lose her, don't put women on a pedestal Esmeralda said to me we have the same needs and desires as men, she insisted and it's fun not playing the grieving husband all the time, and I say to myself that I won't keep silent all the time if something bothers me say something don't let it fester let gentleness sweep over me and when a waitress spilled coffee over my morning paper said so what newspapers are filled with crisis after crisis does it matter if I miss one; reporters talk in such clichés and only go to press conferences anyway don't actually investigate, too expensive and besides English majors now only can write short sentences. I was walking down on the Lower East Side and bumped into murals by Samo, same old, same old, only now Basquiat is famous and his graffiti are now murals, art is starting to give me pleasure once more, even went with Lilliana to a 'dramatic monologue' usually I don't like one-character plays, usually we get language that disguises thought, exposition but no denouement but this time the final outcome wasn't ignored—a play where one character came on stage dressed in red, bows, and recites a poem that catches everyone off guard, then leaves the stage and comes back with a cat, and in the background is a white screen which starts showing slides of the city and violin music is heard, as the lady speaks only to her cat, and then her glasses fall off her head and she goes down the floor and laughs, and she changes from a matronly lady to a murderer and kills her cat then she gets up and sings and dances while holding the dead cat in her arms saying how much she loved her cat and we have to respect animals all the while music is playing and her dress is slowly becoming undone, and it was a work of surprising charm something I had never seen before, and afterwards Lilliana and I had to go to a café just to talk about it, even if she was a little confused because of her language skills and she usually preferred simpler plays. I couldn't recall having such a good time at the theater in a long time but Lilliana wanted more of Aristotle's three unities and the next day went to the library in Red Hook and wondered if Red Hook could ever be gentrified they don't have a bookstore, café, Starbucks, art gallery and not even a local movie theater, that had closed down when movie theaters closed in the '70s but it did have bar after bar with cash registers not the new computers and the busses here are awful and I had to walk from the Brooklyn Bridge subway stop and that could have been the highlight of my day but I wanted to go the library and work, to find a copy of Aristotle but none was to be found nobody read the ancients anymore the librarian said after I spelled Aristotle for her, it was good to see the old neighborhood being recreated in Brooklyn even if developers were telling me this is the next hot neighborhood, I didn't see it. I couldn't find anything there the library's bathroom wasn't even working. I went by the water and thought it would be nice if there was a ferry service to the city I could get back in no time. I sat on the pier wondering now what. Am I becoming a sentimentalist but I hate sentimentality wasn't it Hitler or Stalin who would cry when he left the theater but never could hear the cries of the people he killed. I couldn't wait to get back to Lilliana and tell her I was far away from the city and wondered if I would get back as an actual real live bus approached and I took it not knowing exactly where it was going but asked the bus driver to let me off on a subway line—all subways lead to the city. Haha, the G didn't the only subway line in New York that doesn't go into Manhattan but it led to a stop that did and I felt good being back in civilization. Is it a Manhattanite's duty to bring civilization to the boroughs? Then I don't know how I got there but the Lower East Side beckoned and I walked its streets once more and saw the old graffiti and of course thought about Cassie and wondered if I would see her and what would I say and would we catch up. She usually spends 'quality time' as she calls it with Jacoba now one day a weekend sometimes two but usually only one and they do nice things together and I don't deny her this because she does stimulate her as opposed to me always struggling to get her washed, fed, dressed, off to school, making sure she does her homework and then have to do it again the next day that I have no strength to stimulate. At least now she brings her to her place and I can spend the night with Lilliana only now Esmeralda is starting to be afraid to be home alone and so come back more often. Other families share parenting so this is not new for only her and we think it doesn't disrupt their lives too much but I wonder, sharing children is awkward and unattractive but at least the child knows he or she's loved by both and they don't get confused where to go, just because it hasn't been done before doesn't mean it can't be done. It's being done all over the Village and the West Side showing that fathers can raise children but of course it's done without the court's consent they still can't wrap their heads around it and think the child needs the mother, one home and the father can see the child during the summer. The courts think it not natural for a mother not to raise their offspring unless mentally or physically unable otherwise they think they are hippies even if they follow conventional paths in all but childrearing. Cassie is still the only one I know who can pick up newspapers with her toes and roll those same toes across my penis. If only we could talk but the phone is the instrument of the devil and instead of our talking on the phone we now use it to communicate instructions not conversation. Mea culpa I sometimes get so angry at her we can't have a decent conversation imagine how I will feel when she takes a lover or shows me a lover, I can't stand the men she seems to be with in the theater I could never have a decent conversation with them, all they knew was acting and were very conventional in everything else and one even asked are you a Marxist? Yes, aren't you. They could smoke pot but couldn't think, I thought they might read while waiting for auditions but most didn't read or if they read it was mostly best-sellers, or books that received a good review in the *Times*. Imagine that. She always brought home to dinner the same type of man and I always wondered what she saw in them. All she did was show me she had no taste bring men and women who couldn't earn a living but did have good manners and dressed unconventionally. Male actors were the first men I saw wearing an earring in their lobe and women were the first to start having tattoos all of wild beasts—punk is everywhere, spiked hair, safety pins in their nose, like the fashions of the '60s they caught on but not the underlining thought, when I sat down among the Goths they were nice people dressed weirdly and with black nail polish but without a brain in their heads. Kids have a right to rebel but it's only when they do it against me that I get pissed. Twenty-four hours, a complete action all in one place that's what Aristotle meant, I didn't have to walk up the steps of the Tompkins Square library on East 10th street walking does my brain good and it came to me even if surprised me by not coming at two in the morning and waking me up and I walk past the old apartment instead of going to the library.

I saw on television the *Bronx is Burning* and all evidence that people lived there was wiped out and decay had turned living neighborhoods into piles of bricks and you could almost hear wolves howling at night some of the streets were so deserted, houses that I played in, apartments that I passed were all gone, some of them were the most beautiful in the Bronx all destroyed ripped to their core, pipes stolen, and streets deserted. Those streets at one time were pulsating with kids we girls jumping rope, double Dutch, playing potsy, hopscotch or just rapping on the stoop, boys ringalevio, Johnny on the Pony or stickball now there are new buildings replacing the ones torn down with a little different address—prefabricated houses replacing stone and mortar and if kids ever get to play on these streets again maybe they can come alive, meanwhile the Bronx has no soul only bricks no community. Three story apartments replace larger old apartment buildings with well-decorated lobbies, there's no money for that, everything functional small projects cement like fortresses with all the windows facing frontward, but no charm, now instead of Hispanic, Jewish, black are Caribbeans, Mexicans and an occasional Hispanic who hasn't moved. The Bronx is back. He calls, sometimes I haven't received a call in days other times ten phone calls a day but I think nobody's called because he hasn't called, when he calls I speak to Jacoba even if she still is uncomfortable speaking on the phone, and I get to hear his voice and we can now have almost a civil conversation. He still hasn't forgiven me; I can hear it in the tone of his voice. The surprise is Jacoba can actually call boys, they've been doing that since the '70s, I knew that but I recall never having enough guts to do that they had to call you: an unwritten rule, women were sluts if they chased after boys. I think this is great Joseph has mixed feelings but when he tells me she's sick I become concerned I don't like it he gives her an aspirin to mask the fever and then let the school worry about it. And I do worry if they supervise enough one boy fell off the slide and no amount of hugging could stop him from crying the headmaster finally called his mother who also couldn't stop his crying he was in so much pain that she finally took him to a doctor who had to set his arm and put him in a cast and he finally shut up. He had a broken arm. He's the one my daughter calls. She feels guilty because she pushed him. At least now we talk and she visits and we can spend 'quality time' together if she doesn't have an activity on the weekend. Playdates are in, sports are in and they're all so much more programmed kids just don't go out on the street anymore and play it has to watched by a parent or nanny. I usually make arrangements with Joseph after I speak to Mademoiselle princess but I always get the feeling he's standing right over her ready to grab the phone away if I say something inappropriate. I know I did the right thing I couldn't have stayed another minute in that house but loneliness sometimes is so bad I go into the bathroom to vomit for no reason at all; I became so frightened actually went to the doctor who said there was nothing wrong with me, no brain tumor, cancer, multiple sclerosis all that I had been preparing myself for—what the imagination can do to you, but it's still as if I'm falling and can't grab onto anything and feel the heat on my body as I go down but can't catch myself yet I don't fall. It's fascinating how social control works trying to be an individual I see myself branded as a bad mother, luckily my actor's training I have good balance, I toss and turn don't sleep well, I who always could sleep through the night, could sleep through anything now any sudden noise from the street wakes me, forget it near the 4th those firecrackers drive me crazy, but this year couldn't take it anymore and left on the 2nd and stayed up in a hotel in Woodstock because the noise of the patriots was so deafening. Grabbed a Greyhound bus and left the city for a week. These patriots think they've discovered noise. I did this I am responsible for this I wanted to move out I always remind myself and no matter how bad it is now it is better than being trapped up there. Marriage, motherhood the kitchen isn't timeless it's fostered by social control. Grandma wants me to come back and enjoy my child but I can't, maybe I'll be alone for the rest of my life, I was prepared for that before Joseph came into my life, I never thought anybody would ever want me and even when I dreamed was never the perky good-looking girl and even then I was never interested in neighborhood boys only boys who could think, that was the best part of college life meeting boys who could think not only say 'Kookie, Kookie, lend me your comb' as if I would fall for the chatter of the neighborhood chumps who were always combing their hair back and into a duck's ass. We had to be careful growing up boys would use condoms with holes in it to impregnate us so then play house with us. This was even before the AIDS crisis, grandma prepared me for that when she actually gave me condemns but I was so embarrassed I put them in the drawer where my mother found them and gave me hell and wouldn't believe my explanation. When I moved in with grandma I carried my own condoms grandma's orders, she was never embarrassed to go into a pharmacy and buy them. I also knew she was a backup before abortion was legal. These kids now all they want to do is get laid before college only with AIDS they are now into oral sex, boy am I an old biddy. I remember being surprised then disliking it at first when Joseph would feel me up in public places thinking what that would do to my reputation, but he was always discrete and it replaced romantic displays, our little game. I felt a hand in my ass on an up escalator in Sax's at first I couldn't believe it didn't know what it was but when he squeezed turned around and saw the grin on his face and then I started rubbing up against him in a crowded subway, our secret private enjoyment. Sometimes he'd come up to me like a stranger and try and pick me up on the bus, or feel my breasts, discreetly of course while I rubbed his private parts, those events fueled my juices and the sex later that night was wonderful. I love orgasms but not with any Tom, Dick or Harry it has to be with someone I like and if I never have it again masturbation will have to do. Grandma must have done it most of her life she couldn't have gone out with men back in the day, I would have known about it and her husbands weren't lovers, but women weren't as educated back then to look out for their own pleasures only in pleasing men and their family. No longer will I plan for the future it only gives god a good laugh and I'll let come what may, now I don't even mind doing the wash and folding the laundry it gives me something to do before we had a housekeeper I still have one but I do the laundry, I've now become like the old women that I always disliked because they would tell your mother if you did anything wrong and your mother would slap you across the head never listen to your side, going to the basement with a basket of laundry and use every machine because I go once every two-three weeks, Joseph couldn't stand women like that hogging all the machines but I take pleasure in doing it. Yet I feel guilty social control isn't only totalitarian, at least then you know who to fight, but worse by our own individual feelings that are more powerful when we try and break free of the cultural norms.

Theater in America are Christmas pageants, you would never know there is a crisis in the country as these pretty plays are put on as the country is falling apart, religiosity is running amok, ninety percent of the people believe in angels, twenty-five percent are part of the Prison Industrial Complex, the court system a farce, poverty is increasing, education non-existent kids graduate functionally illiterate, except for the well-to-do (why I don't feel guilty using the private school system) and I'm having this wonderful life. I now enjoy plays once again even if they have talk backs, I don't speak am too shy but enjoy listening to speakers after performances unless they are academics who giggle or say nothing profound but I'm impressed with those who can talk historically, philosophically not those who indoctrinate students and have no interests, hardly any student has ever been to an off-off-Broadway play, let alone a foreign movie or a poetry workshop—is it going to be on the test, while I do love listening to playwrights, poets, even actors who sometimes have something important to say—why this overblown respect for academics, what good has come out of the university? All they want are comps because they are professors. What knowledge do these almost tenured have? Tenured have none they have given up intellectual pursuits once ensconced for life, most live without challenges to their life, without joy, complain how underpaid they are—no joy in intellectual activities overcoming their fears seeing something different, the fear that constantly nags at me to start studying again, that insists I go with Lilliana to plays once more, to poetry readings, to concerts, to art galleries, i.e. to live in the mind once again not always concerned about business or the family. Of course I still do my parenting Jacoba doesn't like to hear the word no so I try not to use it, take her to her activities, spend time with her, bring her with me when I can, but let her live her own life, no longer do I have to dress her only feed her. But deeper I feel myself regaining my courage to live, fight inertia do things and stop being afraid to fuck up. What does this mean? I still have duties, responsibilities I won't off half-cocked but it's sure fun to imagine I could—might I be living a lie all that bullshit drummed into me as a child that I can't shake off no matter how much I say I don't want to end up like my parents, maybe important truths are just done and not thought about because there are too many practical reasons or are all practical reasons fear of the unknown instead of joy. Joy is living in thought not an imitation of thought that my business dealings are and I can have a million reasons for not getting up from the couch, but it's only in doing that I begin to live again, my rebuilding: my daughter knows God exists and maybe for her she does, but for me living isn't for another world but in this, not above or beyond but here and now. I have to recall that bring it back into my conscious memory living is not an imitation of thought it is thought. No longer am I so positive that God is dead, maybe I have the wrong notion of God the Judge maybe it's a way of life. When I stop feeling depressed, disjointed or that times out of joint but am engaged then I can tacitly assume the existence of a higher power, and that I'm not too old and set in my ways to begin anew: it's certainly fun doing things again instead of sitting home and lying on the couch with my wine. Now I go to coffeehouses and art openings and listen to intellectual discussions, something I always wanted when in school. I'm not too deep in a hole that I can't climb out with the help of my friends, friends I still have a few, not business associates, I rarely socialize with them, nice of them ask about my life but since they have no lives it's usually a short conversation but the few people I know mostly I know through Lilliana. The hardest part of the breakup was not only Cassie my lover she is also my best friend and I miss that more than the lover. I am careful now not wanting to have my best friend be my lover and have acquainted myself with a few others. Now is the moment I can begin to take charge of my existence so if a God actually exists He/She/It must be a trickster to put me through all this just too able to learn a little truth. I love it when the young preach to the old without a bit of responsibility and say go for it man, as if I can automatically change my thinking when it didn't turn out how I thought it should. If only the theater, which I have such great faith, would deal with these issues instead of their fictions, at least now some classic plays are being reproduced and I enjoy them more than contemporary ones because they deal with issues of contemporary value and have the audacity not to solve problems but ask them, you see in them something beyond the moment; no one can describe the inner conditions of man as a playwright, we can't escape this umbra and the inner is where all serious issues are as compared to the daily crisis of the press, films or contemporary novels. The Soviet Union has collapsed, first Eastern Europe when the Berlin Wall fell, that was the greatest theater of them all, imagine a playwright became president of Czechoslovakia, we celebrated together and Lilliana told me that her mother and father celebrated the fall of Berlin in '45 and he was still wearing his concentration camp shirt, the shirt he came home in; now the Soviet Union itself showing saying false needs are not true needs we have true needs not capitalistic imposed manipulation, inner qualities count, intentions count, people with a decent inner disposition are not going to commit crimes or injustices. Even though the Soviet Union has collapsed they are not willing to talk let alone confront their past. Maybe it will be like the Germans the grandchildren have to confront their fathers and grandfathers. We of the '60s tried and failed to change the world, but it did change me, it showed me you could live a different way not have to conform to the old rules, I loved the graffiti, the powerful questioning, not the drugs or the clothing styles, the theater but not the novels, and now realize art may not be able to save me but at least it allows me to get through the day it doesn't have to edify me to see the imperfections of the world. Maybe I can produce some of the plays I want to see produced even if nobody would come except I was taught by my mentor always use other people's money but if I use my own who knows what will happen next. It would be better than walking across the Brooklyn Bridge stopping and thinking how nice it would be to hit the water it looks so inviting, even if they now have put up a fence around the edge I could climb it I was raised by monkeys, as a kid I could climb up fire escapes in back alleys and scamper over rooftops with the best of them. Would my last thought be of Cassandra wearing a black veil at my funeral? Neither weird foreigner seized leisured heights; fantastic my last thought wouldn't even be about Cassie but a ditty we learned in high school to know what words go e before i and the teacher forgot veil. I couldn't even die with her on my lips. And since there is no afterlife couldn't even catch a glimpse of her wearing black—would she even come? But I have Jacoba, Esmeralda and now Lilliana and no longer do I even like to tempt myself by walking across the Brooklyn Bridge, my doctor prescribed Valium which gets me out of bed in the morning but it doesn't feel like me only me going through the motions and I wanted to feel me, and I wasn't so down that I couldn't get out of bed in the morning and to make sure I didn't OD flushed them down the toilet. I'm weak when it comes to temptation. I won't let Cassie define the rest of my life. At least I can say let no one envy my life.

If only I could say that to those discussions, why should the theater make life easier, there are small theaters that can show raw performances and have philosophical discussions afterwards instead of shows that bore you to tears. Maybe I am giving too much credence to art to save you, but being creative for a non-creative person looks so enticing instead of pencil pushing. Should I go back and study art, maybe I should have done more in high school but it was only when I saw *The Flies* that I truly fell in love with the theater and wanted to go to travel to Paris, imagine being in Paris of the '50s and you could see Sartre, Camus, Beckett, Ionesco on stage, of course I never did. I can't take it anymore, I hate walking out on a performance but this is monstrous I can't even follow what they are saying it's so conventional—show don't tell, give me a break, I remember when critics criticized Sartre his speeches were too long but I loved his thoughts, imagine he thinks hell is other people wouldn't it be nice if you had to justify yourself to others instead of to yourself. When Vaclav Havel was first done off-off-Broadway I immediately bought tickets thinking the whole NYU community, Columbia students, maybe even some City University students would come but all that were there Lilliana and me and Czechs were family and friends of the actors. Lilliana said he never had a chance to truly develop as a playwright because he became involved in politics. He was magnanimous he helped others and got dirty hands but at a cost of his true self. Can you quantify which is better? And then afterwards the pedagogue squealing we have to write everyday if we feel like it or not. I dislike these academics who make a living from art not doing art. What does he think art comes full grown out of the head of Zeus, this isn't a classroom you're talking to lovers of theater adjust your thoughts accordingly; living means being morally connected to others but politics is temporary and how can morality be connected to the transitory. Only in the theater do we have the ability to stand outside real time and think differently but now the purpose to the theater has shifted to get to the next level, from off-off, to off and from off to Broadway? What about truth?

If only you could know in advance you could make plans know how it turns out, the logic is, of course, it's going to catch most of us, but when and those going through it have no need for logic, how many times have I wanted to ring his bell and crawl into bed with him and imagine when Jacoba wakes up and she finds me there while Joseph makes pancakes and waffles in the waffle maker I bought him for one Father's Day. He mentioned that he was at his happiest making breakfast for all of us, he loved to get up before all and set the table before everyone awakens and have fresh coffee made when Grandma and I awoke and he loves hearing us talk as he works in the kitchen. We could all be sitting around the dining room table as if nothing had happened, but I can't. It's too painful. You can't. I won't. Not that I wouldn't mind admitting I am wrong but I'm not and I keep telling myself or lying to myself that I did the right thing and am glad to be free from them that that cannot be my life that is not the way I want to live. I am not cut out to be a family woman and if there is a correct way to live the family is not for me no matter how much I miss this. The family is only a label nothing corresponds to it maybe it looks like there is but there is not. Yet it was done by me I wasn't forced into a marriage I wasn't contracted to the family, my husband isn't a brute, in fact he's a nice man who is happy now that he has found another woman but I wonder how I will feel if I ever meet her. Some stranger will then become the mother of my child. Will I be able to live with that? I will have to because a woman who is there day to day will be the mother of the child and they will probably have the other child that he wanted. When he marries I will be free of him, haha, I will become angrier and at the same time glad he has found some happiness. And it will put finality on it that there would be no chance that I will get back with him even if I will not be happy with his remarriage. And yet this is the only way out of the situation I have to accept his remarrying. Is this natural? What is natural? I can't be with one man why shouldn't he be allowed to be with one woman. I am close to fifty I want to be able to live, imagine a half century soon I will be fifty I always thought that old but I don't feel old—two half centuries make a century what I once thought of as ancient that is until it happens to me. If I now don't begin to live when am I going to, I'll be an old lady before I even know it and won't have a chance to do anything, this literally is my last chance and I should take advantage of it not wait until Jacoba is grown; there are no rules we live in the modern world and now I have the potential to try and I no longer must do what others have done, we have choices now, no longer are the old ways the only ways: women don't have to live in a family anymore. The choice was mine to walk into the house or not, I decided to turn around. When did I get so smart, certainly not in school where I never cared much for book learning—acting is intuitive but now I see woman is a woman is a woman with no prearranged destiny, I can't find salvation through the Church or faith in Jesus, a woman has a right to be herself and duties and responsibilities come with those rights not duties and responsibilities imposed upon us so that we have no choice, I am my grandma's grandchild I listened to her too much and I left to look after myself and once I began thinking like that it was no longer what others expected of me how they expected me to live but finding out what I want to do, and no longer did my happiness lay in being a mother and wife rather the bitch came out because I was not happy, no longer could I live not being happy I rather live with this anguish than the contentment of being unhappy. Freedom liberates even if it means I'm lonely and I wonder how I will get through my days when not working. At least on the job I don't have to think except when my thoughts breakthrough in the middle of the day for no reason at all. I am not thinking about my life and all of a sudden it rushes up and catches me off guard, all these mistakes are mine but only in making them can I find out who I am. It has been difficult to get back into acting harder than I thought producers love ingénues and all these youngsters now have degrees and know so much and there are few roles for older women, even women playwrights have a difficult time writing for older women, they are either mothers or grandmothers but fulfilling a function not having a life, I turned down the part of the grandma who sits home all day and grunts oblivious to the world, I shouldn't be so critical yet there are roles for older men and they aren't as stereotyped. Playwrights can't seem to get beyond false images because of their limited perspective and teachers still scream the same thing show don't tell as if that is the most profound thought in the theater; there are no perspectives of grown-up women as women she has to be attached to a family in order to be alive not simply lost souls struggling to live, no God telling us how to live. Maybe I should be more forgiving to my mother but all she wanted was one bling after another, one thing after another and had no thought of her own only wanted to impress others with her little trinkets: to live is to think and create, life doesn't get better in time only harder. Time doesn't exist only the past emerges and the future has not yet arrived. This idea that I am the creature of my times is crucial because it's not fundamental but deeper about me and it's how I have to live, how I want to live, and this is the most important point, this is more than book learning it's a wondering and it's the most profound kind of wondering I can think of; this insight was a feeling that I grasped at first and only later acted upon when I walked up those twelve steps and realized all that I had previously believed was not true and now was in for pain and loneliness but if acted upon this could I truly say I began to live. Somebody at work called it a midlife crisis, pure bullshit I could no longer live with myself nor could I lie to myself anymore, couldn't exist on that level any longer but can I live now as a human being or am I just going to fuck it up all over again.

It is getting difficult to climb the steps usually I don't have to but to take care of Jacoba and walk up for dinner. In the middle of walking the phone rang and rang I was finally able to retrieve it and it was Danielle calling and talked and only asked me to repeat a few times what I already said, she sounded so sad, then said you know I'm not coming back you do understand that don't you, and that made it impossible for me not to cry, I asked how she called and she said an aide dialed the number and when we said goodbye I am not even sure she realized it. Her leaving and my granddaughter moving out are depressing me, I respect her decision I know marriage isn't for women but for men and know Joseph promised not to put me in a nursing home but what if he has no choice. Meanwhile Jacoba has to be loved. She walks faster than me when we come home from school but she stops at the corner and won't cross the street without holding my hand. Marriage was for eternity but eternity back in the day was only twenty, thirty years now we live so long we can't be held to a promise we made while young, we are not the same people we were when young even as I like to imagine my timeless first love without the difficulty of aging. I hate walking up the outside steps but it seems so much easier than going inside my basement apartment then climbing the steps from the inside, but I hate this urban architecture where they have these crazy side spikes so children won't slide down the steps, it also means old people have no place to rest, I catch my breath, I'm on the third step already, Danielle's phone call almost out of my mind, but I'm lucky now I could never have carried Jacoba up in the carriage, even had to insist they get a lighter one that I could push instead of a Cadillac of carriages that was too heavy for me to move around. Fascinating how I never believed I would get old, that it wouldn't happen to me, or that my idiosyncratic way of thinking has now become commonplace no longer just a dream but from a perspective from which we now live. Fifth step. That men and women are not bound forever is now considered natural and when thinking like this keep the pain in my legs from hurting too much, everyone believes this now; I wonder does this mean the old ways will come rushing back. Only the poor are still caught in a time warp and the women are still children, kitchen, church, it's difficult to be around Hispanic girls they have no idea the world has changed but the cat's out of the bag as Conchita says and when I volunteered to tutor some girls at Brandeis High School they had no interest in learning to think, and to my surprise some couldn't even read, in high school and illiterate. How did they allow them to pass? Not even romance magazines they could only look at the pictures. Seventh step. We must start again from the individual not from the social class teach one child to read and you've saved the world no longer do I believe in generalizations, yet it upset me so how dumb they were that Joseph suggested I give it up because it was so upsetting and at first I didn't want to so it as my mission but soon realized Onomatopoeia was laughing at me. She knew it all at fourteen and wouldn't even carry condemns and sure enough got pregnant. Says her boyfriend is different is going to drop out of high school and get a job. Where have I heard that before. I spoke to her mother her mother refused to let her get an abortion said she would love her grandchild and that she Poeia was wild and this would calm her down and the three of them would live together with or without the boy. I tried to insist that she finish her education but the mother said she can get her high school equivalency at sixteen now she's smart. Ninth step. It's easy to be against poverty but changing the inner disposition is difficult as if education is the only answer. Of course that keeps the poor entrapped in a system but that is just a statement of fact not an evaluative judgment. It's that they are not given a chance to grow. It is difficult to make people become free than we thought all our actions did was make them more dependent upon government than capitalism. At least capitalism allows room for non-conformity—try and imagine avant-garde theater in the former Soviet Union, no such thing art had to ennoble the masses. According to Lilliana art in Czechoslovakia was populated by security police and plants and would complain anytime an artistic work deviated from socialist realism, the workers were always the heroes and the bourgeoisie always the bad guys and samizdat literature was always seized by the state. I betcha

Americans would love to have an audience of the police rather than the nobodies that comes to serious productions. Conchita complains all the time nobody takes difficult stuff seriously all they want to be is entertained and her bar is lowering all the time now since there are no serious productions she is now going for fluff, crisp and short, just to be working again and I hope she finds something. The eleventh step is a doozy, crash, I have to be careful and not fall down, Joseph says he will get it fixed when the weather warms up, here I have to hold onto the spiked handrail my balance isn't as good as it once was. Can she do it? Did I do it? Can you jump off a cliff and live by yourself? I know I have a million regrets and when I look backward wonder if I could have lived differently but the one regret I don't have is that I lived the way I wanted to even if it only makes sense afterwards, while living I could make no sense of my life. Maybe happiness isn't automatic it only comes by learning and training, you have to be able to stand away from the hurly-burly and extricate yourself from it—failed but tried, not a bad tombstone. But who succeeds it's a constant practice of reinventing yourself: I was reading about this new study that our frontal lobes where we make decisions don't stop expanding until we are in our late twenties, no wonder that little twerp thought it cool to rob his grandmother's best friend, and now he's dead of AIDS probably didn't even realize he had it thought it was some rare form of cancer, no wonder Poeia thinks it cool to have a baby before she's grown, no wonder the courts won't allow this as evidence it would mean all those hooligans don't truly know what they're doing, it's simpler to treat them as fully grown adults and lock them up for twenty years it's called being tough on crime. Bingo, made it, still can do it. Now all I have to do is find my key under the mat, nope Jacoba did that, I'm in. Don't get old. Who would believe walking up twelve steps could take so long and take so much out of me that I can't even hold my purse and walk at the same time I need both hands for balance, luckily I still do yoga which helps my balance but it's still a struggle and I'm almost out of breath, I can't even take the subway anymore elevators are usually out of order and climbing those steps are too difficult. Now at least buses have gizmos that allow the step to be lowered so I can get on and off, even if enough of them are usually broken and I have to wait for a bus that works. Worse are those people in wheelchairs who can only get on through the back and half of them don't work, taking the M11 but has shown me it passes two hospitals and they run them without the mechanism working, couldn't they run them across routes that don't have hospitals on them instead of making them stay out in the cold waiting for a bus that works. Do I ever do what I like? It's only when I keep challenging myself but now I can only go out once or twice a day it is too difficult to navigate these steps especially in winter with ice everywhere, but Joseph always brushes the steps right after a snowstorm still there is black ice. And luckily for me there are street people, gamblers, domino players, who help me and it's going to be a shame when they get kicked out like back on the Lower East Side as gentrification takes place, they are always the first to go. The neighborhood is turning there's no stopping progress, the local bodega even now has a cappuccino machine.

You can't understand what's going on in America if you don't understand emancipated women and their uncertainty. The rejection of the Equal Rights Amendment is not as bad as it seems because most of the rights are already custom even if not law but it leads to a deeper level of understanding how conservative this place is. From western New Jersey to Eastern California are the Badlands, except for maybe a university town here or there, and these places refuse to recognize the anger women live with without basic equality, which not only affects women and also the poor and uneducated but them it will not affect even if they know as well as the middle class how the country hates women by holding them to a different standard. The immediate is a particular moment when we women want basic equality but not only wage equality for example when young girls, really their parents, sued the Board of Education and said they were entitled to equal access to good high schools—of course the board resisted but public opinion forced them to do it and not with all deliberate speed, which authorities then met by concentrating on deliberate in ensuring racial equality would not result. Women insist on being free now, and no Women's Right Amendment is going to stand in the way. The Equal Rights Amendment is a perfect description of what goes on, most women still marry, raise a family but more now are choosing to go to work as well and it's this aspiration that defines us even if state legislatures won't support us it doesn't mean it won't come into play and now we are fighting even sexist language that Joseph laughs at now having to write he/she but it is a beginning where people are finally waking up to what's going on. New ideas are sweeping the country and because women believe in it it will fly even if many say I am not a feminist. I never thought I would consider myself liberated, a feminist, but now along with many women I have come a long way baby even when I am home alone every night with nothing but what I call freedom. This idea is difficult for me and even for Joseph who supports women's rights until it affected him personally and is now not so sure. That pause between beliefs and nature. And now white women are attempting to get equality for Afro-American women but are not putting it on the back burner as the early suffragists did when they claimed slavery was the more important issue. Now it's equality for all and even gays are demanding rights no longer to be arrested just for being homosexual, only difficulty is Afro-Americans while politically liberal are socially conservative or as grandma says are the most virulent ant-gays there are. It's easier to see the struggle of gays because they are dying by the barrelful but if they don't get institutional legality the next generation will have to start all over again, only recently have I begun to think in generational terms, the byproduct of turning fifty, once you are fifty everything changes and you want to institution-alize equality so it can't be forfeited so easily, why conservatives aren't giving up on abortion but now trying to nibble it away at the corners; the right of women to have an abortion is the law even without her hus-bands' consent so now they are saying you shouldn't be able to have a late term abortion after the second trimester because then the fetus looks human, head, body, arms, legs more like Charlie Brown but if it were a human being what would it matter what it looked like it is alive at conception or it is not, not how it looks. But if they can keep women pregnant they can keep them home in the kitchen and dependent upon a man, especially where they have no daycare so women have to stay home and care for the baby, you get to think about these things when your home alone and have time to think, I even joined a woman's book club, not a woman's book club but only women come, men have no time to read, I'm free from the hustle and bustle of family life now I come home and read, talk to friends, I purposely got rid of the set so I wouldn't sit in front of it all night long and start to believe what's on the set, news, entertainment is real. I could have been an A student if I studied this hard when I was in school. School is wasted on the young. The world is seen differently now when I have time to think and read and I am also volunteering with No More Nice Girls, a feminist theater group like the old Bread and Puppet Theater performing on the street to raise political consciousness, here they use placards and chants instead of puppets and minor performances, even if we believe equal rights are inevitable why not push them to come quicker. Inevitable can mean a long time look how long it's taken for Civil Rights for Afro-Americans. What's the world so afraid of giving people equal chances. Thank goodness for pot it makes thinking much easier. In college some girls thought since I was Hispanic I had easy access to drugs, I didn't, scared stiff of them, only later some women in my book club have gotten me into it. The Equal Rights Amendment didn't come in isolation but along with Civil Rights, gay rights, anti-war movement—why the sixties mattered and you can't understand feminism until you grasp the whole picture and you can only grasp it looking backward inside it all we can see are multiple forms of control, men are boys scared of erotic women. Maybe I shouldn't bother I wonder if I am speeding things up with my activism I rather get back to acting I had to give up a part because rehearsals interfered with my schedule, the director wanted total commitment but I could only give that at night not during the day. I'm not ready to give up my day job. Parts for older women are few and far between and this one comes along and only in the theater can I shut my mind off and not have to make real acts only gestures that I cannot do in actual life; in the theater I could have quit been a hero but there is a pause between reality and the imitation: rent. The world may have no meaning but life certainly does, but as grandma says my rent is low enough, now it is but what about in the future, I have to save up for old age when I am alone with no family to support me. Fifty changes everything. Some hecklers even were against old people moving in together unmarried because neither wanted to lose social security benefits, it embarrassed the children and Congress actually changed to law that a woman no longer has to be supported by a man but is entitled to keep the social security she has. Only companies want to get out of the undue burden pensions cause them and claim when a woman marries she should lose her first husband's pension because she is now supported by another man and private companies can get out under the burden of pensions. Can you believe it? At least the courts still won't allow that. Who knows for how long. The only way you can see this unfolding is after it unfolds, at least I am on the right side of history even if I still can't believe this is happening to me and it's been so long since

I thought this way. Do intentions count or is it only actions? It's good using my mind to fight bodily inertia.

The first time I looked up in the sky through a telescope and saw the rings of Saturn it looked just like the pictures I had seen of Saturn, what did I expect something different but still seeing the actual rings was greater than a picture of them, and when I looked away knew there was no heaven only infinite space that science has now confirmed. How can some religions deny scientific thought is beyond me, but the hatred of science is virulent, which is probably the best way to go since you can't have a rational debate with religious freaks, their religious midrash is that God is outside time and space but practically it must mean there has to be plenty of planets out there surrounding other stars and we are just one planet among many and we must live life like other peoples, but only when we use our reason and art do we rise above our instinct. I love Joseph very much he's truthful, good but not courageous, he is doing a wonderful job both of us but he is becoming smaller in his dreams, all he wants now is contentment, peace and quiet, he doesn't even go on short business trips anymore and he no longer finds challenges on the job he's been doing it so long. He's not doing what he wants to do, and probably no longer even knows what he wants to do, he goes so deeply into playing the role of dedicated father going to all Jacoba's events, PTA meetings, play dates when he can, this new word because children cannot simply go out and play because of fear of crime and junkies even if New York has started rising and hooligans are now in retreat, the police are getting illegal handguns off the street targeting minorities and confiscating their guns but parents still fear and children must be supervised at all times, can't even go to a movie alone but have to have an adult with them at all times. Jacoba is so scheduled she has her own calendar and Joseph doesn't always tell her what's up next least she become overwhelmed. To children all this is natural but even Joseph knows she's too regimented and this is artificial, that you need time away from grown-ups free from parental influence, to be allowed to play by yourself. He always complains that he hated being home all the time and couldn't wait to run into the street after school and play. He's a bad actor, he doesn't want to live like this but can see no way out of it, he wants to make up for Conchita not being around and sees his obligation, obligation is not the correct word, because then it is a response to the other, this is deeper his primary love, he hardly goes out with Lilliana anymore, she calls they talk but he's not interested in being with her weekends which he saves for his Jacoba and now has accustomed himself to this lifestyle and thinks he will have time once Jacoba is grown. That is probably the only abstract thought he has but how many people have I heard say this and what they give up is their freedom and can never recover it: freedom is inner time which we have to force ourselves to take or we become so caught up in the daily we forget how to live, and he now doesn't even like to listen to others talking about their humdrum existence, it bores him silly, so he doesn't dine out unless it's with one of Jacoba's friends who invite him to a Shabbat dinner but can't stand it when they try and set him up. And since women don't have time to cook anymore Shabbat dinner usually means Chinese takeout or pizza. When it was his turn he surprised the parents out when they made fresh pizza using a coke bottle to knead the dough, and the kids loved it. He is impressed with families and doesn't think anymore and is always surprised when couples announce they are getting a divorce, he thought them so happy; he doesn't even take Lilliana to plays prefers instead to walk with her and even then he says he has difficulty talking anymore outside of his business. Poor Joseph. He's now big on computers, we had the first computer on the block as soon as he saw the Apple he bought one and can spend hours in front of it after Jacoba has fallen asleep and Jacoba insisted she be able to play with it and she now has computer time. The first generation of computer programmers are now Luddites as computers program computers, computer skills change so quickly they're now talking of the Internet whatever that is. They tried to teach me but I couldn't learn, Jacoba wasn't even allowed on the computer until I set it up for her that lasted no more than two days and she quickly surpassed me, I have no idea what she's doing. They even learn on computers in school instead of reading, I think it takes up too much time that could be spent reading and thinking. Now Joseph is resigned to his fate but I try and tell him he has to live he can't spend all his life caring for his daughter she will come to hate him for it. He now takes his happiness in small doses and says he likes to be alone, but I don't believe him he was such a gregarious guy when we first met. He spends more time in the office but he says he has to the company is expanding more than ever and he has to show the new hires the ropes. Lilliana doesn't want a child by him what more does he need, other women he dated were silly all they wanted was marriage and children one even thought he wanted her to spit on him and she did and he left so quickly what could make her think that? He didn't want to go through with dating after that, the main reason he doesn't want a divorce is he doesn't want to admit it's over, they can't even use health insurance as a reason to stay together, he uses hers but he could get his own, or an apartment, how many divorced couples now live as roommates because the rents are so high. He still carries the torch for her, they still share the same bank account, and all money is in the same pot, even if they live separate lives and in fairness Conchita has told him she's not coming back. He's sleepwalking through life, no charm, only living for others but you have to have a self not conform all the time. He thinks, and we've discussed this, solitude is not all it's cracked up to be that there's no real world you'll find beneath the surface, what he seems to like now is our dinners together, he claims that and raising Jacoba are now his purposes in life but grave subjects he doesn't want to talk about—forget Jacobo let's talk Jacoba, he said, when I once mentioned his grandfather, and I've kept my mouth shut to him about that ever since. He's content when we have dinner with some wine, he loves drinking red wine after letting it breathe for an hour, says it gives it a better taste, and he's the expert but I haven't noticed that. He has no hidden life or if he does I am unaware of it; it's difficult enough to keep track of Jacoba's day and needs I can't also be attuned to his. He claims not to have a personal life because it is difficult enough to keep track of the changes in real estate and tax law that he can't trouble himself with self-examination. A likely excuse for not taking responsibility for your life; he keeps business separate from pleasure and never sleeps with his clients, that's what they have divorce lawyers for, he jokes. We still can laugh together so I am not like his mother because he never truly talked to his mother and he sometimes thinks but dares not say I am his true marriage to his grandfather albeit an ascetic one. What men think! How did it take women over five thousand years to realize men have no knowledge of the world only physical strength which they used in farming and somehow that became the distinction, men outside the home did the physical work and women cooked and took care of the children leading great men thinkers to believe that women were natural homebodies, the coming of farming worked, it fed more people than hunter-gatherers but it put women out of the occupational force, now we have bureaucrats, workers, an occasional artist but women became regulated to the home. Thinking must be learned what we are taught in school is not the only way there are other ways of living which somehow has gotten blotted out of herstory. At least he hasn't said I want a wife who will stay home and cook, he never said that, he has some intuitive sense that women are meant for more than just that, he doesn't look for fake answers but he still needs to develop a self so that he cannot simply accept what he is even if he looks good in a suit. He has to develop the strength to answer himself and find out what he wants not let the culture dictate it to him. When young you follow or you rebel it's easier only as we age do we have to make decisions of real consequence, he's coming in the door I can hear him bounding up the steps as if he's happy to be home even if Jacoba no longer greets him at the door, for that he will need a dog, but I can get up off the couch and quiet the record player and greet him at the door smile at him at the door, for a man that's important like milk and cookies for Jacoba when she comes home from school. Humans might not count in the greater scheme of things but when you walk through the door it's important to have someone to greet you smile at you so you can continue your evening.

How many masks do I have to take off to uncover who I am, the real me? am I the jolly businessman only interested in solving problems, the dedicated father, the bill payer supporting a family so we can have a nice home, the lover of a woman I like to do things with, or the lonely soul who I pretend to be when falling asleep at night: a conundrum. I became the guy who dreams of escaping it all and living in Montreal in the summer and Boulder in the winter but now that Prague is becoming exciting, the Paris of the fifties, maybe there; I have this nice fantasy before I fall asleep where I actually own a car and migrate between these Montreal and Boulder before I decided on Prague and have an exciting life only sometimes come down to reality when I realize before Lilliana how many dates I actually was on that were so superficial that by the time I came home couldn't even remember them, except for one who lived with her mother, I thought she was too old to live at home and when I tried to say goodnight she clung to me so that we spent the night in some hotel. Poor girl her father died and her mother is afraid to be home alone. Note to myself: don't be a burden to Jacoba go off to the elephant burial grounds to die. I bought a cemetery plot the moment she was born and have serious long-term health care insurance even if it too expensive. I say that now but I'm still young, okay not so young, what will happen as I age I've never felt so heavy, not physically heavy, jogging has helped me keep the weight off, and walking does me good, and at least I don't have to smell the urine mixed with pot on the subways and the homeless not being able to bathe, they actually no longer have a place to even wash, the bathhouses of the Depression were closed to fight AIDS in the mistaken belief AIDS could be transmitted through the air like other viruses, because viruses are transmitted through the air the analogy was AIDS could be, even if empirical evidence showed it came from unprotected sex, the toilets at the bus and train stations closed in remodeling to keep the homeless out and sitting on the subway we have to smell their odor against our will, but at least smokers now have to smoke outdoors so we don't inhale second hand smoke. Some hooligan up in the Bronx even went to bed with as many women as he could with the AIDS virus in order to infect them didn't use a condom conveniently forgetting to mention he had AIDS. Who knows how many he infected. When caught the public was outraged but he violated no law even if women wanted him to get the death penalty, but the law didn't flinch arrested him for parole violation and the state legislature made it illegal not to tell if you have AIDS. For a bit I had to struggle with a condemn, but now Lilliana and I have an exclusive relationship, besides sophisticated women now carry condemns in their purse, even if it's like going to sleep with your socks on. The best thing about being with Lilliana is walking across the city together especially after we spend the night together, the city is so quiet and safe at dawn. Do I have to know who I truly am each time I pull off one mask another appears? Is there a me beneath the exterior or do I just exist in this crazy life of mine—what I truly enjoy in these early morning walks is the solitude walking home by myself. Maybe it's good I have such a poor memory so I can't always recall the bad moments, I now take notes everywhere even got excused from jury duty when I told the judge I couldn't do it without notes, surprisingly she understood and excused me. I am different in different situations, as a father I accept whatever Jacoba does, even as I wish she would be more intellectual and at least take dance courses, I've told her she can stop going to school if she would do ballet. She has no interest. I should have said no ballet under no conditions are you allowed to dance. I pushed it too much. She now won't even play the viola, which I suggested guaranteeing she would play in an orchestra there are millions of violin and cello players but much less viola players. She played in one concert left the stage, left her viola and the sheet music that Esmeralda brought home, dear guess what you forgot. At work I won't put up with such shoddy workmanship and even will push contractors past the breakpoint if they do a sloppy job. With women I only seem to see them as sex objects, especially if I haven't had sex in a bit, with Cassandra I always wondered if I could do it. I still can't get her out of my mind, I tried getting up as soon as I started thinking about her trying the behavioral modification approach that my body would stop thinking about her because it wanted more sleep and I would be free of her. Haha. Now I still think and simply don't fall back asleep in the mornings. Except when I was with this dynamo who wouldn't let go and said she knew a hotel on 41st. between Park and Lexington that she occasionally goes to when she's had enough of her mother and lives alone for a night, and she had no compulsions about taking a man up to her room, the fear of being labeled a prostitute no longer scares women and I realized she had needs just like me otherwise we would go insane, as if living with your mother after a certain age wouldn't make you go crazy. She left early in the morning but I couldn't get up, couldn't even get it up, and just laid in bed staring out the window onto the building across the way, I had offered to walk her down but she saw no need. She said I also live with an older woman. But Esmeralda isn't my mother, I could never live with her. God almighty have I now also forgotten her name. Such profundity. The more I reflect upon myself the less I see that there is nothing there and how I look to others is the way I am becoming to myself. I have no true self just a bundle of nerves and shifting thoughts fortunately know a little history, and it's not ancient, and I am not forced to become what the other thinks I am and not overly concerned that they will see me as the Jew, or the cosmopolitan, because realize even with all my faults that I am responsible for the other, at least my family, and maybe I never encountered God and can do nothing about that, but I have encountered others and try and treat them decently, it's inborn or at least inherited from my *avuelo*. Poor homosexuals one generation of free love and bingo it's all over AIDS everywhere but I have never overtly discriminated against homosexuals, in fact supported them because I knew they were the ones that first transformed a poor neighborhood to a bourgeoisie one with their dual incomes and refined tastes, I am different to different people as the occasion demands and my clothes indicate that, with friends, sweater or sports coat, at work suit and tie, don't buy this dress-down Friday and even shine my shoes weekly. If I am lucky can remember the role I'm supposed to be playing and act accordingly but each time I learn something something gets in the way. I can't be a boss to my daughter nor a friend to my employees. But I am friendly to my workers and bossy to my daughter. He who sees me last usually gets his way, I am both exciting and dull, feel good and bad and sometimes don't even know until I get up for the day, look handsome with my graying and ugly or I begin to bald, it all depends upon my moods and there is this struggle going on inside me and sometimes I win and sometimes lose, only I don't know who's who. It would be nice if I wasn't a bottle of contradictions but I know I have a responsibility to Jacoba and Esmeralda so can't ride off into the sunset, Montreal in the summer, Boulder in the winter, Prague anytime. I hate Cassandra for forcing this on me but I also respect her for doing her own thing and refuse to call and lay a guilt trip on her. I realized this leaving the hotel and a black cat almost crossed my path, not that I am superstitious didn't see it as a sign, but said if she comes back or not it has to be on her own volition, and instead of the black cat crossing my path I crossed his as he was under a car, and was looking for a ladder to walk under wondered what the sheep entrails would say if I could sacrifice one. I can't shut my mind off and give meaning to a mere event, superstition dies hard with me.

How did I become who I am? Can I point to one specific event that if I did over my life would have taken a different turn? Is it my dissatisfaction with causes that wouldn't allow me to be like everyone else, couldn't stay in a marriage I tried but each time I knew it couldn't be forever yet each time I rethink my past it's something else that I am dissatisfied with and each time the past is different even if I try and view it objectively me always gets in the way? My way is right for me but does that make it right for others? Is Conchita doing right not seeing her baby grow, missing out on this time? Should Jacoba live like I lived? But yes let them have an independent life not be the victim of any false ideology, the great behemoth, the state, of believing the whole world is corrupt and you can't be neutral. I did believe that once, even as I can't believe I ever believed that—no choice is harmless, we all must choose sides capitalism destroys workers' lives as the army kills workers, even believed in collective guilt and the only way to fight was to fight collectively; now I almost wish for a separate kitchen that's how much I believe collectively. If I didn't have my own ground floor apartment never would have moved here and Joseph understands if there was ever a man who understood a woman's need for a room of her own it is him, that I couldn't be with the family all the time probably because he never had a room of his own until Jacobo died, before that he lived in the same bedroom as his parents and when he got too old for the crib moved in with his grandfather. He made sure Conchita had a room and also Jacoba in his architectural remodeling's, Conchita laughed calling it her sewing room but he wanted her to be able to have some privacy. Now that she's split we don't know what to do with the room, now it's difficult to make new renovations while people are living in the home. When I began I thought I had all the answers now I only have questions, at first I thought only about the proletariat and thought they were the only group that could promote change, because I wasn't a proletariat as Joseph said, he grew up in a proletariat household he realized the proletariat weren't change agents. How far to the right of Genghis Kahn are they? Boy are they conservative the most you get is an occasional liberal when young. Joseph even votes Republican, Jacobo would turn over in his grave, he thinks we need strong leaders besides in New York a Republican vote doesn't matter much but it's because he's a successful businessman and wants less government control and lower taxes, but they're the most venal white men I've ever seen stealing the country blind, obstructing justice, misuse of public funds, theft, and now Reagan will get his comeuppance for the CIA selling crack to support his anti-communist crusade; Joseph claims no party speaks for the workers and there's not a dime's worth of difference between the two it's not as if the only choices were communist or fascist now we have peace and even if times are complicated they are not deadly. We fight over this but good-naturedly, he claims nothing makes sense anymore in the post-modern world, left and right converge, he acts as if he understands the modern world and its desire to be unique and he is not ignorant of the avant-garde during the Great War, the Weimar Republic, the Spanish Civil War and how the wars destroyed the history of the working class even East Europeans have no knowledge of their history, totalitarianism ruled for so long, they haven't a clue they were part of the Enlightenment, thinking they were poor serfs until the Russians liberated them: Russia was for the people so why did they have to kill so many of them and institute a tyranny of bureaucracy; you only see Soviet culture as their history the great beast devouring its own. Now that the Russians skedaddled maybe they can find out their own history but we Spaniards haven't and Franco's been dead over fifteen years already. Now no longer will I make compromises won't align myself with feminists who only want better working conditions not transformation of the society feminist politics is becoming like working-class politics not transformation but our piece of the pie, and now that the Soviet Union collapsed shows a revolution cannot be made in somebody's name because all they did was suppress freedom in the name of the workers not of workers. Economic well-being is important but you have to have the whole enchilada. Kids now don't even know their own history, some not even that there were two world wars, that there was a Cold War and when the Berlin Wall came down World War II finally ended. Maybe now there won't be a separation from East and West. That there is a difference between a painting by Picasso and one by Basquiat, difference between Messiaen's *Quartet for the End of Time* and the Stones, even if heaven help me I'm getting to like the Stones as my concentration wains. Nobody reads American writers anymore, Joseph heard of Sinclair Lewis, Theodore Dreiser, Clifford Odets but never read any of them they weren't considered relevant in the '60s, I accidentally found *Arrowsmith* in a laundry room the first paperback I ever read, I picked it up and couldn't put it down even if before I disdained paperbacks it seemed to trivialize reading: a scientist with only one purpose in life scientific research who challenges the existing state of medicine and his life loses all meaning because his vision is so narrow but he challenges the existing state of medical culture, nowadays people think the world exists in a vacuum not part of the struggle for human freedom and the fight against force, the great beast that devours us and we become dependent upon it instead of learning to think for ourselves and we start actually believing what the tyrannical state says is right, no alternative thinking develops, now each generation thinks of itself as unique not part of the great chain of being and kids today think this is the way it is. Yes, mama, I can hear Conchita saying when I insisted she read and get educated. No I want to start my acting career, I let her because I couldn't stop her and also I was proud that she was going to do it and the only way to do it is to do it not just think about doing it, like so many mothers now who tell me they are going to have a life as soon as their children are grown. I wonder. Yet I even told Jacoba when she was bored in school one day the more you learn the more you earn she seemed to appreciate that. We can't seem to have a total personality anymore everything is bifurcated, job, home life, thought, entertainment all we have are artificial constructs imposed upon us by the great beast and serious thought is no longer seen as natural, we need quick answers to everything not reflection, the shadow becomes the image not a ladder upon which to climb to see the true. But will I believe this tomorrow when I wake up and I wonder who is listening to me because I don't believe in yesterday and who knows if I will believe in tomorrow, I seem to only live on inner time of my soliloquies.

If this is living let me wake up dead. My son died such a miserable lonely death and there was nothing we could do the doctors and the nurses wouldn't even let me touch him lest I get infected and I was told to burn all his clothes. At first we thought it was cancer but now I know it was this new disease AIDS, God's punishment to homosexuals, only Julio wasn't homosexual I know because he told me, and we aren't Haitians, he might have been with some but he usually only stayed with Dominicans we hate Haitians, they're black, but the doctor assured me it isn't a Haitian disease, but I didn't believe him because they always tried to sneak into our country but we kept them out. Now I understand it is this homosexual disease but he wasn't homosexual he was raised Christian baptized in holy water and had Your precious blood to wash away his sins. O Lord even if he never went to mass I still pray for him, wouldn't let him be buried out in Potters field insisted he have a Christian burial in a Christian cemetery out in Brooklyn, Greenwood. When he came home from jail he tried to be good, promised never to touch drugs again and went looking for jobs but nobody wanted to hire an ex-junkie with a prison record who couldn't even read or write. Even if he promised to be good he couldn't. Promises can only take you so far then it's up to the Man upstairs. We all went together to buy him a suit and a tie, he didn't even know how to tie one and my daughter and I couldn't help him, but the salesman showed him and told him how to loosen it so he could reuse it, and we polished his new shoes a good shoe shine helps but it wasn't enough. He was too intimidated by personnel department that he would only ask other laborers if they had a job and then left when they told him to go to the office or come back tomorrow, which he never did, and then would tell us the job was filled. I even called Esmeralda even if I was ashamed I wanted to help my son and she was glad to hear from me and gave me Joseph's number and he said he called but at the funeral she told me he never called. Joseph might have had a position for him, Esmeralda said, but he knew how to avoid anything serious, she said, but she hugged me and told me to keep in touch but I am still so ashamed. Then he went back to the bums on the street, the no-good types who only hang on street corners making wide eyes and catcalls at pretty girls but not even able to sing doo-wop like the boys in the Village did, all they do is hustle and drugs. And all of them have been in and out of jail and now they are encouraging younger boys to follow in their footsteps and carry drugs for them because they're too young for prison and of course the little boys know no better and these men are like gods to them having been in prison. Then he said he wasn't feeling well, felt like shit, bleeding from his ass, difficulty breathing but he wouldn't go to the doctor until one morning he couldn't get out of bed but we thought he was feeling like he did when little and didn't want to go to school, we tried calling doctors but doctors no longer make house calls and finally we had to call the ambulance who took him to Medical Center and after weeks of tests said cancer and he had to have chemotherapy but it didn't do any good he died by inches. If only we had known, but how do you know so we kept him as comfortable as possible until finally he had to go back into the hospital even if he didn't want to it was too much for us, he needed round-the-clock care and we couldn't do it anymore, after all I am an old lady and we thought he would die quickly but it wasn't quick he kept hanging on, my daughter thought they were forcing him to live for the insurance, we weren't paying, couldn't afford to, it was Medicare and Medicaid that pays hospitals and they wanted the money and wouldn't let him go. This is a God-given disease the priest said and I just couldn't believe that, sure he wasn't a great person but he was a human being suffering needlessly and there is no justification for anyone to suffer like that Esmeralda said, this isn't the wish of the devil but a medical condition he caught in prison. She is good to talk to. She came to the funeral I know it must have been expensive gypsy cabs aren't cheap but they always run and are not yellow, we recognized each other right away. I thought she wouldn't recognize me I've grieved, changed, so much but she said my gestures were the same, and she is as beautiful as ever, we hugged promised to keep in touch and she insisted that we make a date so as not to leave it up in the air. She was always a good friend and didn't let what my grandson did to her affect how she treated me. And I then knew my dream was silly that she would desert me so I left her first. Also I kind of hoped that Julio would go with Conchita but smart women don't bother with druggies. Especially when she had an educated man, and she up and left to go get a college education. Previously women might have put up with that like they put up with men who beat them, no more. As Esmeralda said when I said my man is old-fashioned, she quickly understood and said beating isn't a sign of love only power. Esmeralda explained that to me way back and why she's paying a fortune to make sure her granddaughter gets a good education. She was always smart. She knew how to stand up to anybody and not take crap from them, remarkable woman back from a heart attack as beautiful as ever, she refuses to give in. Now what have I got to live for. She told me I have to walk every day, get out of the house every day do something with my life otherwise lethargy will destroy me. I am too thin, barely can walk pains in my heart and chest, and she thinks I have to become more active. As if there's any reason to live. I loved my grandson when little had to see him every day and still see in my mind his smiling face as he learned to recognize me that sweet cherub faces with not a care in the world and I could watch my daughter sleeping and even in her sleep she was always worried about Julio. I loved being around him smelling his clean body kissing his smooth face, knowing full well with boys you have to get your kisses in early before they start to run around and dislike affection in public or private. My daughter got pregnant too young quit school just like Esmeralda's why we became such close friends, and the girls were both alike never liking school. Esmeralda was too smart for her own good, always thinking never deciding without reflecting only book knowledge, my man said, not street knowledge thinking she was better than us by going to concerts and plays by herself without her husband, movies aren't good enough for her. But he was wrong. He never trusted women who did things by themselves. She had a good husband not like the jerk I had and yet she asked him to leave, I never understood that he was a good provider. But she thought she deserved more from life and even if I never could understand her I liked her we could talk and laugh together and she never thought women are only good for producing babies. She even helped with funeral preparations I thought the church wouldn't allow him to be buried because of his homosexual disease but she spoke to a downtown priest who never mentioned AIDS only cancer and said he was now in a better place. How can any place be better than with me?

What I don't have and can't build upon are memories of Jacoba and me, I keep in contact with them but it is superficial I am not their everyday, I rarely see her and have no idea what goes on in her daily life, at first Joseph would write and let me know, then call at night and tell me, and grandma would do the same but as Mademoiselle princess became more demanding they didn't even have the strength to do that, and now even Joseph admits he couldn't wait until she could dress herself and start to take care of herself, at first he couldn't wait for her to talk so she could use words instead of crying all the time, and even if he is exhausted from her realizes she gives his life meaning. I can't work like that always on, call me selfish but I have to have a life of my own, yea right go on auditions where you know the producer is dumping your resume in the circular file but at least I am alive with projects and have this good-paying job so I don't have to supplement my living doing commercials or reading for the blind or as the audience increases we're seeing that people now like to listen to books in the car or at home, and this has meant more jobs for actors, imagine that people don't like to read only listen to books, yet actors say it's good pay even if you have to stand all the time and schlepp up to the studio in Stamford but my friend likes it being able to chill out along the railroad line. She told me about it but the books she records are frightful, silly romance or detective novels, and I've tried reading them but they are so boring, repetitive it can all be condensed to a pamphlet, middle America ugh: is it really reading if you're listening and don't underline, tear out pages or memorize? How can people read this stuff? I know it helps put them to sleep but art should be more than fluff at least when actors read it has a certain panache, especially with all the different voices, people often confuse nature with art, see a beautiful sunset and say isn't that fantastic yes but if you think about it it's natural like a rainbow only when we make a conscious decision is it art if no conscious decision forms it is nature not art. If I can only continue to go on auditions and not get discouraged parts will come they always have, but maybe in the past because I was this pretty ingénue and now there is a dearth of roles for mature women, a shame because I know so much more now, but I can't concentrate on the past that's ancient history but try and have a future. I still enjoy acting can see myself acting until my last breath, if I get the chance, a terrible profession in that others have to choose you, playwrights can compose regardless of the circumstances but actors need an audience, the sentimental weary roles they have for old women are pathetic, life is more fun than playwrights imagine, the past may be part of us but it's our living that has gotten better, this doesn't play well to writers, producers, directors who only think of women as wives or mothers, not having adventures of their own. How is my daughter going to remember me? Now I am thought of in the imperfect tense: she often said she would do this but never did, or will she remember her mother as this flawed parent fleeing the ones she loved for her act-ing. Motherhood can't just be what have you done for me, but that's all children feel until they become of age and learn to think for themselves—why adulthood is so much more important you are your own boss not a prisoner of childhood but responsible for your decisions. This duality is difficult for me unlike Joseph who is there for her but I love her as well a mother's love is real even if it can't be shown every moment I have too much on my plate and now I can at least look out my dirty window at the streets below, I have to ask Clyde to come up and clean, I wonder if he's even still in the neighborhood, the neighborhood has changed so much, come to think of it I haven't seen him around. When I was liv-ing uptown I felt like I was always staring into the abyss until she started Russian daycare, a woman who took children into her home had it fit-ted for children and had extended family members help out so we knew they would always be there instead of regular daycare that has such high turnover, then I caught every childhood illness, now at least I have plenty of time to myself, too much, it would be nice to have a gig at least Jacoba isn't on my mind all the time, enough of the time but not all the time, when we were living together when Joseph came home all he wanted to do was play with Jacoba which meant she never fell asleep, his way is not my way even if I can't help myself noticing little girls on the subway or on the street but only on weekends with their father. I couldn't go on otherwise I would have needed pills or liquor and there would have been a sudden accident, how could she leave her daughter like that. Who's this? it wasn't me. Besides I wasn't through looking yet just because I was a mother doesn't mean I've become a nun, this was not what I signed up for. Yet I was no youngster and the craziness of youth should have been squeezed out of me but it's all bottled up inside me, I wasn't ready to give it up and it exploded and now realize I won't let that happen again, I have to come to grips with my feelings let them out not keep them bottled up but try and keep them under control not keep telling myself it didn't matter, it does, and I did hurt Joseph bad enough when I aborted his child but to go out with other men must have killed him. At least tonight I'm going with Leo, he's going to meet me and we're going to go for a drink so I don't have to stay home alone—the East Village now is filled with nice local bars and McSorley's opened its doors to women in the '70s, I took part in the street demonstrations so much that I refuse to go into a place that discriminated against women, besides now it's for the younger set, I much rather go to Milano's besides it has a jukebox. Luckily we can walk the Houston Street bus comes once every hundred years, Joseph and I actually saw it once and hopped on even if we didn't need it to say we rode it, didn't even play our game of making believe we were picking each other up. Can't I have one goal in life and everything be subordinate to that, which is the only way I can confront my demons and continue acting. Here comes Leo I barely recognize him out of a suit, he looks so funny trying to look cool, a consultant, I would never dare date a colleague but a consultant won't be with us long and he's made starry eyes at me long enough I shouldn't let them go unanswered a power move not a loving gaze even though I don't make it a habit of dating and working in the same place. I can always move back in with Joseph, Jacoba and grandma if this gets too hot but tonight I just don't feel like being alone the void is too great not great enough for me to climb back up those twelve steps but deep enough that I want some company. I am now better than before and if I go back all this will be in vain I must keep going even if I lie to myself all the time somehow I know this is a better lie than living the one I once did and if I go back all my movement would have been for nothing just as if I had stopped acting because no one offered me a role. Acting is too central to my existence for me to stop it even if acting is full of uncertainty I can only live with that uncertainty—the times without acting are dread why I constantly do showcases, even if I still have to go to the bathroom and throw up before opening night but as the show continued my insecurities lessened. This is all real, leaving my family, living alone, looking for acting gigs, meeting Leo for a drink then coming home to an empty apartment that I now leave all the lights on not just one, then getting up in the morning and starting again. At least I'm not wondering what I'm doing trying to feed Jacoba satisfy a husband and trying to enjoy a well-lived life in a house. Acting is transitory thus my life is transitory—what you previously did in acting doesn't guarantee another project—not bad thinking, at least I'm using my noggin again school wasn't a total waste on me. Only should have done it when we had Jacoba could have had free daycare. Joseph wanted to help and write my papers but if I went back wanted to do it seriously to show myself I could do it and refused his help.

What does she mean by freedom? I don't understand her words her words are opaque does she mean no responsibility how can that be free-dom. Abandoning me okay but Jacoba, at least she is now seeing her on weekends, letting her visit taking her to museums granted I'm afraid she'll bad-mouth me in front of her but she doesn't and wouldn't, only my irrational fear. Can't I stop judging myself Cassie isn't like that; my parents much have put the fear of God in me because I can' stand my-self when I do that. No bad dreams, if only I could shut my mind off to them. I refuse to criticize Cassandra in front of Jacoba, too many children are torn between them that way, at least we're civil and maybe she can visit one night a week and take her to school the next morning, it's not regularly every Saturday or Sunday but at least it's something only once didn't she want to go when she had to study of a test; it hasn't affected her school work she's a good student her homework done nightly and her school is smart enough not to confuse rigor with enormous amounts of work, which still allows her to have a social life with her friends. Cutely they kept saying soon you will be old enough for homework and they couldn't wait to get it and now she relishes it. We do things together at night and during weekends she plays with friends, too bad she just can't go outside and play but there are no kids on the block and even as the streets are becoming safer according to the papers nobody actually be-lieves it, parents still take their children to movies until they're teenagers, Cassandra always asks about her daughter never our daughter and how she hopes they won't grow up with fear and she can lead an authentic life: one who can leave her husband and child? What is an authentic life to have no social responsibilities as a daughter, wife, grandmother? Isn't freedom responsibility? Or does it mean a truth that only she can understand in the recesses of her imagination. We live in a culture we are part and parcel of that society, rooted, we can't live without roots our sense of meaning comes from our past and her not having it is interrupting her soul, how can you be authentic if you are not an individual part of a larger culture. She thinks only acting is truth. It's a job, a difficulty job but a job nevertheless it can lead to something higher only if you abstract it to a sense of truth but if all you see is the shadow you aren't getting anywhere—art can't free us from doubt only increase our anxiety we have to look beyond sight and sound, I hate the curse of a happy ending where artists can't let the image stand for something else and have to throw in a last act in heaven or at least in our minds, she seems to think acting is honesty while the rest of us lie but is there anything wrong with making some money to provide for your family, she still wants adventure, the unknown, I like to be in bed by ten, she likes to fill up her empty space with activity the type of life I usually can't stand; why did I ever fall in love with her? the sins of youth? If I would come home to a woman who was sitting in darkness or screaming or vamping in sarcasm; I've calmed down but still can't pull the trigger and divorce now am even dating a decent woman but I'm truly afraid to codify it by putting an engagement ring in a candy dish. That's what *avuelo* did to Esmeralda when he gave her his ring. Am I that truly afraid to get involved again, I know this if I do get involved I'm never going to love as completely as I did with Cassie the pain of separation is just too great, just hold back a little. Yet Jacoba thinks of Lilliana as a step-mother with all the insecurities that brings about the evil step mother who does what a real mother would never do. Wonderful fairy tales being promulgated when over half the kids in her school have parents divorced, divorcing or living together. One couple even got married even if they had said beforehand we don't know how because their son kept saying why are you living in sin when he was a pre-teenager and they wanted him to try and calm him down, and they are his biological parents. She has a world that I don't want to enter into, it's her truth but not mine, mine is to take her to school every morning, make sure Esmeralda gives her milk and cookies, make dinner, and make sure she does her homework before tucking her in at night, and she's not allowed to go to sleep crying. And Esmeralda and I both agree she must have down time her whole day can't be scripted, she must play with herself, develop her own imagination not always have an activity provided by us. I never miss a game even if she barely kicks the ball. Esmeralda loves it because she was never allowed to play sports that was for boys and even if takes her forever to understand the game she loves to see girls running, jumping, kicking and working up a sweat. I bring a beach chair so she can sit and watch, but I have to remind myself it's her game and not boo or hiss opposing players only cheer and be positive, good try when you stink. I bring snacks when it's our turn and the mothers realize a man doesn't know what to bring so they give me lists of oranges, fruit slices, grapes, even if would bring cookies and cupcakes, and they bring apple cider spiked with rum so we sit and watch calmly. The thought that a man can do what a mother can do is an anathema, to them, the world is divided between competent mothers and the rest of the world, and it's true I always like to deal with mothers who have an understanding of psychology, when I would have mid-winter breaks and classmates would come over because the school year is so short and vacations so long, mothers made sure we had enough goodies for the kids, they have a smooth easy way about them knowing what is expected, not the uncertainty of Cassandra, no confusion they even bring trash bags and now while women are challenging the existing order it's good to see the old ways still exist. Without sounding like an old foggy the old ways have a certain charm even if I never could stand my own mother always being in the house never leaving me alone, these women keep the world comfortable and safe even if nobody wants that anymore. Once the old ways are challenged however it's difficult to see how we can go back, all, not most, all these women have jobs not one is staying home caring for the little ones, or if they do it's only before they can go to daycare or get help. Thank goodness for Esmeralda we at least didn't have to hire anyone even if new research is showing daycare is better for children then staying home with mother, grandmother—the sanctity of family life, those who go to daycare do better in school, economically and seem to have happier lives, at least that's what the preliminary data shows, it's too early for long-term studies. Hard to believe? Goes against the sanctity of motherhood. I always have difficulty when it's my turn to prepare soccer snacks but I'm getting better at it, now even bringing Gatorade along with water and fruit slices but I still bring chips these little Indians have to have some treats. The coach jumped up and down the first time the girls did a play he designed, instead of them all running to the ball. Weekends are difficult after working all week I want a little break and this soccer depress me that I almost feel like envying Cassandra her freedom even if I want none of it. To change would mean to destroy this life Jacoba would suffer and I want none of that, that's why I refuse to think about Cassandra in the middle of a soccer game, when her thought inexplicably surfaces I push it down but at night I still dream of her coming back to me or me running away to Prague and start over, warm fantasies that allow me to fall asleep, and usually I am living with Lilliana. It is shameful that these actual women don't behave the way my fantasies think they should nor do they even want to be considered sex objects anymore. Besides what difference would it make wouldn't I end up the same person anyway, how many men, and now women do I know who say I'm going to move somewhere and start over only to end up the same way. You have to confront your daemons in my case responsibilities running away is no savior. Sometimes I wish I were old and could give advice but Esmeralda says don't rush it you'll be old soon enough besides nobody listens to the old, it's never over just new problems and new challenges. Someone scored a goal. Someone yelled at me did you see that your daughter scored a goal.

She said I wasn't courageous only truthful and good okay I agree with but to say I don't have courage is to believe in militarism keep up that myth that those men who kill are courageous it is more important to take care of a child than to go fire a gun, saying I'm going in, doing it for my country, my friends, who knows what other reason not to take responsibility for your life and then take someone else's life. Taking care of children is not glamorous you don't win medals they're not going to celebrate your life but still it is courageous, so I didn't want to kill in 'Nam really only didn't want to come back crippled, physically or mentally, and I've seen too many ex-soldiers, Harvey, who have had difficulties adjusting to being normal, whatever that means, alcoholic, suicidal, drug-infested, abusive but Hollywood rarely ever shows what happens afterwards, as they rarely show what happens after the lovey-dovey stuff wears off, we seem to have this need for a happy ending, a lot of ideas have changed because of the '60s and mine was one of them, dropping acid and marihuana were the minor part, the intellectual part was that it opened my mind showed me a different way to live that I didn't have to follow the prescribed path and could use the intellectual learning and consider a different way of living, who would have ever thought I would become a successful businessman, family man, property owner, even if I despised my education I have to give them credit they showed me a different way, granted back in the day we wanted to change the world ideas were in the air you could almost touch them, breathe them, mostly of course we were breathing pot even trying harder stuff anything not to become the hated bourgeoisie, a rich man who bought playthings, imagine car window that went down automatically you couldn't wind them down, bling, granted I still am not that crazy, I live well and deserve it but don't go whole hog don't have to dress just to let people know I am successful rather I believe I am helping people have home ownership and realize how good that is and how good I felt when we achieved it and I think these families do as well. I've done some good it is decent for people to own their own homes and I help make it happen, besides the tax breaks you get some investment that you can leave to your children and it also means you become part of the hated bourgeoisie, as long as you don't confuse being the owner of a small home with the ruling class, that's two entirely different species and we discussed that ad nauseam but back then I didn't grasp the difference between a small home owner and one of the big shits, it has a different meaning for us than it once did when I discussed this in the abstract—it worked well in theory but not in practice, why can't people make up their own minds instead of calling it false needs as opposed to their true needs, as if anyone knows what true needs are beyond housing, well fed, clothing, a job and a decent level of culture. That's what I can't stand and it puts my ideas to the tests but how can I have conversations with people who don't read, how many houses have I gone in where they had no books, pens or pencils or art on their walls, never go out unless it's to a bar or visiting relatives, never theater or poetry readings, but I have to tell myself that's their life it's not for me to judge, those idiots. This has nothing to do with a home, except many are now house poor, but it's a style of life it's an attitude, a feeling about what you think is important and culture is usually the first to go, as art is not in the public schools because they want to concentrate on science and math as if that is supposed to indicate intellectual rigor, even if an era is defined by the art, novels, music it produces, seeing one Rembrandt can change your life try doing that with one equation. It all starts within the home, a place to raise a family and when you own your own apartment you know that you belong to the community and that affects how you treat your family and that has nothing to do with the apartment itself but how you feel about it and if we view the home as a trap or a museum as opposed to the physical place where you live. I understood that quite early my secret to success is selling to gays who had disposable income, then to couples where the woman worked as well, then everything became worse, housing coasts went skyward in neighborhoods with good schools, daycare became more expensive, and taxes were killing dual income earners, we were selling people what they could afford even as I was selling a style of life and I didn't let segregation get in the way, my *avuelo's* teaching and when some banks redlined and refused to lend to Afro-Americans or Hispanic civil service workers I found others that would and helped them file the forms so they could get home loans some laughed and said didn't I realize banks don't do business with them, but I steered away from big banks and found them decent mortgages in neighborhoods that were changing, started having safe playgrounds, no glycine envelops and broken beer bottles strewn all over the place, it's amazing how the streets are cleaned and theirs shade on the streets or there are more playgrounds in decent neighborhoods than poor ones. Still urban renewal highways kept the poor hemmed them in and we couldn't change that. The difficulty are the schools, but schools in middle-class neighborhoods are better than the poor because parents are involved and keep the principal honest and raise money for art classes the board cuts, some public schools even hire real live artists not academic types to teach drawing, painting, acting part-time, a smart way to use the money getting professionals who can always use the money. Artists help bring an imaginative ambience to the public schools where you can smell the tears in the walls. Housing segregation is de jure in cities which leads to the public schools as well and I wasn't afraid of breaking the code, of course real estate agents know it and support it, so do banks, city and state officials who deliberately keep separate but unequal schools, the only reason we don't have equality in the public schools is because public officials don't want it and to move out they build housing projects that are now all minority and I was able to find tenants who wanted out, had no prison record, a good conduct discharge from the armed forces and so I helped people move out of the projects and give lie to the tale that when minorities move in property values go down. Occasionally someone would sell prematurely in panic and if I was cool could buy them up but I'm not that type of guy, and there is simply a shortage of good apartments in the city and our biggest obstacle was getting co-op boards to sell to minorities and once we showed them good assets they were forced to agree lest they be considered racist. There was never a quota on minorities, Afro-Americans or Hispanic and property values never decreased only word of mouth prejudice which we didn't listen to. Not easy but at least I was doing some good. However what I never expected in some neighborhoods was the refusal of the public schools to change to the new situation even if all there remedial specialists were no longer needed they kept them up didn't update their curriculum to for the more educated students who came in knowing how to read, and didn't even prepare for the influx of new people and the elementary schools became overburdened and overcrowded and this created an dislike of middle-class parents, even with the rise of apartheid, gifted and talented programs and some parents if they could afford to started using the private schools by middle school, and the new middle class jumped on the charter schools while the board and union complained they should be in public schools and stay ignorant. Some schools tried all sorts of tricks to attract children of the middle class, Latin, chess, STEM, recess is now drill for first grade, but mostly public education became a pipeline to prison: everyone says they support public education only when you see what it does to your child do you usually take them out by middle school. My hatreds were such, I went to New York City public schools in the golden age, '50s to early '60s that I knew true hatred. Some high schoolers had to drop out of school to their parents' dismay otherwise they were afraid they would become addicted, fortunately the Board of Education actually responded and lowered the age to take the high school equivalency from 18 to 16 and these kids passed with flying colors. Where were they when I needed them, I had wanted to do that but you had to be 18 and by then I was a graduate and never went back. Now I have to rethink our business plan because buyers who own a co-op usually can't afford private school, thank goodness my colleagues are still discriminating in the suburbs and steering minorities to poor housing with weak school districts regardless of the Fair Housing Act of 1968 that prohibits discrimination based on race, or religion, keeping me supplied with a steady stream of customers. Unfortunately, the next generation of students are now having difficulties finding jobs, just because they graduate high school as functional illiterates and the job market is changing and union jobs are getting more difficult to find. Co-ops were not exempt from discrimination but New York lawyers came up with creative solution condominiums where you don't own shares but own your own apartment and can sell to whoever you want without board approval and that opened more doors. It wasn't designed to help working people but it helped and now parents of students stuck in terrible schools are even trying home schooling and regardless of what I thought, I couldn't wait until Jacoba was free from me always having to be there, it seems to be catching on, the religious right loves it to teach Christianity and so students don't have to suffer the slings and arrows of secularism and New Yorkers love it because it's one of the few places where students can get a good education, and of course the Board of Education is against it saying it doesn't socialize them well even if they do better on all exams and get admitted to good colleges. Now I never talk about the masses anymore only individual men and women who have some control over their lives and the lives of their children even if they have no idea the '60s ever existed because the school systems have tried nothing new except a fad or two. Now it is the real estate business that is forcing changes in public education, can you believe it.

He's using duty to hide responsibility, freedom, all under the guise that he doesn't have to confront himself, it doesn't mean what I was taught it to mean through my grandmother who said we are responsible for our own lives and somehow I still associate living with her not my mother who said I would never be happy if I didn't live the way everybody else lived, said I should live like my neighbors, but I never could accept this as a way there is no right life for me all part of the television dream factory which she bought into watching her soap operas, they never showed unhappy couples or what happens as the wife's eye begins to wander, all women were there for was to make life happy for their husband and that made them happy not a life of their own. From movies to the theater is an unsettling development movies like television continues the old life but when you start going to theater you start to question what's going on as you learn new ideas and see different perspectives but if it's too upsetting you retreat into comedies or musicals, but if you continue you go onto drama and learn to think in different ways and that lets art affect our lives. I stopped watching television early and began striking out on my own after high school, college was no help, how come they never encouraged time abroad, Spain was out of the question, Franco, even I knew about him but what about Mexico City or Buenos Aires to study, could have studying acting or thought there but college was so Euro-centered back then it never occurred to them to send students anywhere but the capitols of Europe and they didn't encourage it. Now they do, I gather some schools even require junior year abroad, students must hate that, those dumb schmucks, what I wouldn't have given for that opportunity. But as grandma says sometimes we put our missed opportunities so far in the past that there's no way we can make up for them, now it's too late for a woman to travel alone, even if I sometimes hear of it usually its students or of almost student age not mature women. We still have a long way to go. My first encounter with travelling abroad was when we were first dating and we both wanted to go to Paris, every Bronxite wants to go to Paris not London or Berlin, now maybe Prague everyone says it's cheap, I was surprised I thought he might want to go to Budapest especially after we came back from Zoltan's funeral his friend who escaped Hungary in '56, Zoltán Tóth, the Hungarian artist who always talked fondly of Budapest and was instrumental in getting him to go to Music and Art high school, and would take him to jazz clubs in the Bronx Club 845 on Prospect Avenue where he heard Dizzy Gillespie or Thelonious Monk, after-hours clubs sure—but live music in the South Bronx it was much safer then and you could walk the streets especially since Zoltan didn't like to go downtown to go uptown and they'd walk the streets of the Bronx; we went up to his house after the funeral and he shared one bedroom with another man and I pointed out to Joseph he's gay and he looked at me in shock, it never entered his mind that his roommate was his 'special friend,' but two men living in a one bedroom and he used his living room as a studio, what do you think? He also found out he disliked American culture and didn't take its art seriously but did he have it nicer in Auschwitz or the Gulag. Here nobody bothered him and he was allowed to paint freely and his lover worked so he wasn't exhausted by his day job. He didn't even have to ride the subway and come home too exhausted to do anything but plop in front of the set. Without even knowing him I knew he was real, an authentic being who practiced his art even if he never sold one painting in America and he had helped Joseph grow up and even if they didn't call it a *shivah*, the funeral meal the last meal between life and death, only a final farewell, the neighbors helping to prepare food after the graveside service where his roommate mentioned that art opposes science and looks to the soul not the body and if we are to be judged it will be by our beliefs not our deeds then morphed along theological lines wondering if Satan was created by God or is his equal and that Zoltan was dismayed that communism might exist for centuries but art is an act of faith that communism will one day fail; it was a Jewish mourning and even grandma came to a man who was so instrumental in Joseph's young life because it brought her closer to Jacobo, even if she had never met him. I remarked that art is a demanding profession like acting but acting is worse in that you need an audience at least a painter can paint under any conditions, he created he did not sit still but worked at his art, his whole life he was a painter without any compensation, yet he would always talk smack about America, his 'special friend' said and never got involved even laughed at feminism as he lived off his lover's earnings. He was all but married to another man only gays don't call it that. But luckily he had a spouse so he wasn't out cruising even if he might have been too old for that, but grandma said you're never too old for that, and his husband saw it as his duty to support an artist, isn't that the definition of a wife. And the meaning of this will never change it's always the wife who has to support the artist, too bad I don't have a wife, I had one grandma reminded me but let him go, she said, one who cooked, cleaned, you have to like a man like that. But it only looks good in theory not in practice. Husbands will always be life and the idea that they can change is ludicrous, men can step outside the family but women are forced to toe the line. Tradition, but now that women can earn a living and not be forced to look after the kiddies a new world has opened up to us and the meaning of words can now change without too much difficulty. Be careful I tell myself even in the gay community the same roles appeared, change isn't as easy as changing definitions, the old ways can take on a life of their own, at a disco some jerk was dancing on the floor his face in my crotch and it surprised me for a moment and I had to ask him to stop—young blood, but I wasn't going to be meat for his sexual fantasies, even in my office it's obvious women can be seen this way, but it doesn't mean I have to be that way, flattering as it is at my age to be considered sexy. My date with Leo turned into a disaster a little sex and then he thought he owned me wanted always to do things with me couldn't grasp that I was horny that night, lonely that night but only wanted a one-night stand and to have to be around him and say no all the time was too much. He thought he could win me over by always being at my beck and call I learned never again at work, no longer am I the cutesy type but didn't like it when he called me bitch. It showed me how little has changed even as I tried explaining to him I'm not the settling down type finally I had to tell him I was separated, I hated bringing my personal life into work, but he said he wasn't the possessive type, I had to laugh at that, he certainly is all men are if you have sex with them they see you as theirs. He wanted to go to church with me but I told him I never saw Him as part of my life and I couldn't understand how an educated intelligent man could still go to church if the old man with a white beard never existed as I realized with him words change meanings he saw faith as inborn not connected with devotional readings of the Bible but went anyway. The meaning of words are not the only ones I give to it; grandma would be proud of me at least I don't follow the crowd. It's taken a life time, long enough time to fight my insecurities they have formed too much of my life and now that I am fifty am trying to fight them to find out who I am myself and challenge these infantile insecurities and not get caught up in this culture of narcissism which is difficult to remove. I'm sorry I never met Zoltan he seemed to be able to go his own way, but he was an exile and had another country from which to draw upon. Look how long it has taken me to remove the cloak of childhood even if I never believed still felt it was the correct way to live until Leo told me his nonsense. Grow up is what I actually said to him. At Zoltan's service when we put poppies over his casket I saw how fragile this culture is when afterwards Joseph and I made a pilgrimage back to our old neighborhoods in one of my nostalgia runs and saw weeds growing between the cement, abandoned streets where family and friends once lived and almost like a Little House on the Prairie the streets were that deserted. Here I learned much that I now realize was false but it's deeper I have a connection to this place I never thought I had I thought I had thrown the old ways off but you can't pour new wine into old skins and now realize I still have a long way to go—why I like being with the young going to discos they are not so set in their ways but then you have to put up with their silliness like the kid dancing in my crotch, even if my nipples felt hard with him dancing I can even feel them getting hard now just thinking about it. By now you'd think I'd be able to understand these things and I can actually begin to feel and see that I am closer to the end than the beginning and I still like to stretch my mind and body to get the kinks out but now wonder that I have questions where before I had answers now I'm no longer even sure of the questions. Life is tricky, grandma said, and now I am beginning to see the absolute non-clarity of many words and the problems of life appear stronger than ever. The quagmire is will I keep it up or will I settle and fall back into the old ways but now am beginning to see that I have to continue even if I don't know where the path will lead but can I develop a life attuned to my new way of thinking. At least I no longer have to worry about making babies, only caring for one. Has my life moved from fate to choice? Here I am I can be no other. I never understood Macbeth in school how could he be killed by a man not born out of a woman until Jacoba was cut out of me, I am a slow thinker never ever could understand how Cordelia could be so in love with her father what did he ever do for her.

Not one to bend his knee for art Alphonse Laurencic spiritually tried to decorate his prison cell in Franco's Spain while being held in prison incommunicado in order to get him discombobulated, depressed and suicidal he used color and form—a mental use of colors to bypass his depression with colorful images but there's no evidence it transformed his behavior but it transformed his life by what he saw. Art saves decent men, the mean cheap bastards the dime-a-dozen type it doesn't even affect; it doesn't even matter if they renounce torture for each soldier that does there's always another to take his place and afterwards is anything explained by torture except the ability to deny it, if only Franco and his goonies were unhappy with all their wealth and power that would be so nice but that doesn't seem to have that effect on indecent people. The American president had to wear a bulletproof vest after his assassination attempt but that didn't discourage him, evil is too trivial to be affected by exchanging one bad guy for another; why can't these guys suffer like Agamemnon or Lear, theater no longer discusses this, now the theater is really dead, truly dead, and they should put nails in its coffin and have a mock funeral, Conchita was finally in a serious play, at first she was enthusiastic a young director who had all the right ideas at the read-through but then panicked during rehearsals, and said we couldn't get done in time and quit saying I'm sorry as if that covered everything, he wanted to go home to Mommy over Labor Day even if it was right in the middle of rehearsals and they bring in this new director who could only play it safe, he realized the challenge of what he was under and was afraid of the implications has the characters whispering on stage, literally whispering so those in the front row might here it but nobody else, lest radical ideas be heard. He mistook the performance for truth not theater advancing the way of truth. She couldn't get out of it, even offered to direct it herself luckily nobody took her up on it, and the producer a real Mister Fixit brought in this new director, who only liked chocolate chip cookies, which Conchita brought him instead of baking herself, he likes store-bought over homemade as a reward but the play now lost its edge and became an ordinary melodrama—maybe it's only a chance encounter with history that gives plays meanings now we are in a peaceful time and only when the enemy thinks new things up can drama foreshorten that event. But does theater change anyone's mind? Conchita, Joseph and I loved the drama of the '60s, early '70s when it challenged existing ways and was hopeful but this new director quickly succumbed to ennui only seeing novelty not meaning, narration following the same old patterns, the past is the future, the future the past and could never figure out how the two merged—that requires an intellectual effort of making strange the everyday. Joseph went with me so I didn't have to travel downtown alone almost as if it were a dark stormy night and we went to the West Village and we were able to get a sitter and Lilliana joined us there, the first time she would meet Conchita afterwards, we took a taxi, I was appalled he would splurge so much on me but he said it's easier this way and he settled in a taxi as he always uses them, but I feel so uncomfortable in one and we saw all this bottled-up talent on stage wanting to explode break the fourth wall, a polyphonic stagecraft, theater, music, and set design about a woman confronting herself as a younger, middle-aged, and older woman finally a play about a woman Conchita said only the director has such a difficult time with older women thinking of sex, loves, men and he saw her as his grandmother not a woman in her own right, a stream of consciousness play with two different women playing the same woman not at specific different times but at specific different moments repeating lines one said and giving them different meanings, a fascinating theatrical experience bogged down by directorial indifference, a committed director could have done something but he didn't like old women having a life of their own, only saw them in relation to the young as caregivers and interfering with the freedom of men. Provocative music not deliberately bland, and he even had the younger woman play a muse which Conchita rejected automatically, everyone knew this play had potential dramatic oscillations, a serious dialogue taking moments from out of her life and out of conventional notation making it stand alone for what it was not somebody's lover, mother, grandmother a woman of seduction, faithless but not with a mind, declaring life is important remains aware of its own demise and even if we have to die and all our activities are futile when compared to that it is crucial that our voice be heard, a voice struggling with truth and not false optimism only her place wasn't a world where people gave up or settle for the same old crap. The playwright raised the issue are women biologically driven or are we products by our culture: economic equality versus gender difference, updating the old nature versus nurture; motherhood is a trap and yet one of the finest moments in our life, even had a fine riff on which shoes she would wear sneakers, flats, or high heels and they had implications for her day—hard to imagine a serious discussion in the theater but what other art form can do that where you can get into serious debate with yourself, novels are getting shorter and shorter and no attempt at discussion of issues, movies are over the top asking 'let the force be with you' and repeat happy endings of television; music is no longer held as a direct expression of the world. I no longer go to poetry readings but many of them are about finding happiness in sorrow, and painting has gone further off the grid now trying only to be sold for billions. It was a good performance considering the circumstances and afterwards we met for some schnapps and Joseph introduced Conchita to Lilliana and they both smiled and sat next to each other but didn't talk much even if they would have a lot to say to one another. Theater is much better when you discuss it afterwards and see where it was pointing to and where it failed, of course, we never said Conchita failed her acting as one of the women was fantastic, but we discussed the directing and how it could have been better, and I didn't even have to worry about catching the subway home since I knew we would cab it again—it does take a lot off your mind not having to worry if the subway is going to be working. Finally, she was able to get her feet wet again and she wants to take it further with another director, she even sees it up for some awards unfortunately it's not only up to the actors who knows if producers would be interested. The writer was willing and he had also wanted a more avant-garde set of color, lines, not simply a severe bedroom but a visual surrounding affective stage design that Lilliana said she could provide one that rotated depending upon the mood of the character and since the director wasn't there we could talk as freely as they wanted even if we understood that he was called in at the last moment and panicked and when you panic you go back to the same ole, same ole, the writing was rich and scenes were needed to explore the verbal acrobatics that goes on inside a woman's head They needed at least a few more meetings to discuss how to perform this once more before they settle on a director and then see if they could find a theater in which to perform, theater goes on way past midnight even if the audience is out by ten, nine thirty in this case because even if the city is getting safer nobody believes it and people's lives have changed and many people are now get up earlier to commute, jog or exercise and like to be in bed early not late anymore.

Me, myself and yours truly are all supposed to be the same yet are all different there seems not to be a central place where I exist it's everywhere but I don't know how to equate it to my different personalities, especially when I think about Cassandra, there I am in ecstasy and it's so pleasurable thinking about it that I can't stop thinking about it even if I know it's all a lie she isn't coming back and we can't continue as we have been, even me, myself and yours truly understands that but I can't accept that it is impossible or should be impossible since I have moved on with my life; adulting means I should not let it happen, her image is okay but I must not confuse her image with reality and letting her continue to treat me this way means she's enjoying hurting me and I shouldn't be with someone like that no matter how much I say I want to. Am I a stranger to myself? Who's talking to whom the self I am or the self I want to become, I now have this lovely woman who I enjoy being with, doing things with, having sex with, being silent with, walking with, going to the theater with, yet when she's absent hardly think about her, she's not the grand passion of my life only a nice moment and we've been together a few years now and haven't broken up even survived a fight or two and from what I can see she hasn't gone around and slept with other men just to get at me, and I certainly won't hurt her the way I was hurt—is this happiness, which isn't even bliss but a moment of relief—it's happiness for itself that matters not what I get out of it. I'm not concerned about happiness in the next life, or a deep happiness but small joys that allow me to get through the day and now that I have found someone want to go for it don't worry about how it will affect Cassandra or Esmeralda, even if I do worry about Esmeralda and she will live with us as long as she wants even if I can't tear myself away from my despair and loneliness, anger, revenge, and each time I think about Cassandra it messes me up and I can't fall asleep at night or if do wake up in the middle of the night and make the mistake of looking at the clock wondering if I'm going to be able and fall back asleep and get enough rest for the day as I get into an argument with me, myself, and yours truly and find it difficult to calm down, anger gets the better of me and no amount of reason can get me to accept the fact that Cassandra abandoned me, she has the right to leave to lead her own life and I can't force her to move back by guilt tripping her with Jacoba, and I have attempted to keep Jacoba free from our dissension and still have contact with her mother, and I keep telling myself not to be angry or envy her life of freedom remembering I have a new life even if this new life I want to run away to Prague and start over or even if before I had the life I wanted, we were taking a bath together and I blurted out will you marry me and she answered even before I finished my thought one day and from that moment on we were engaged. Is the start of middle age when I can finally let go of my anger that my life didn't go as planned— that should make a God laugh. Job gets it all back double-fold in reality I didn't suffer as much, her splitting is the link to my new life, still I can't shut her out of my mind and what she did to me is frightening and I'm afraid on my deathbed will call out Cassandra hurting Lilliana but really was glad when she saw me with my new woman—let her know what she missed and I like me, myself and yours truly better when I surprised Lilliana with a dozen pink roses for our anniversary of the day we met, I never did that with Cassandra. Lilliana knows Cassie hurt me but she says keep on going it's not the end of the world as she keeps silent about her previous loves. When you are silent it's more than one or two. Of course she had lovers we live in the modern world but not an irrational passion. It's not as if I don't know I'm doing something shameful but knowing and stopping is two different things. Now I long to go for long walks to clear my head, don't care to see blue skies, trees, nature, only walk on sidewalks reading street signs and tee shirts on pretty girls, trying not to be stymied by traffic lights but each time I am somebody else and many somebodies quickly fade away—is there something inside me that I can call I: is there an innermost central processing unit even if my experiences can't identify it as I keep changing? My attitude keeps changing sometimes when she leaves I accept at other times don't, it was too long, too intense, she couldn't stand being adored and now I have a calmer more mature love where we see each other as adults, or am I afraid of getting hurt once more. Cassandra loves falling in love I enjoy being in love. My thoughts have changed but does that mean I have changed? I still feel like the kid who was infatuated with her and followed her like a puppy dog, but it's only in separating that I am finding out who I am and I am a mystery to myself there is nothing inside me that is the overseer of who I am. Very important. At work I have no difficulties I am who I am and lately some people have even been commenting how courageous I am in still dealing with gays but I don't even give that much thought, I'm easy prepared to take their money, it's more difficult with lesbians who don't have as much money but as long as they don't have children usually we can find a place for them to own. I'm up on the latest AIDS stuff and how men can put their pricks in each other's ass I still find difficult to comprehend, but as Cassandra complained I am like white bread and never went up her ass yet I only have to think of her sweet smile, her laughter and a cold sweat overcomes me. Women hugging, kissing, touching that I enjoy thinking about I love the gentleness of it. It's simply an accident I exist I can't seem to have been born for any purpose no one asked if I want to exist but I am happy not exuberant at the thought of my upcoming marriage even if we have agreed to continue our separate existences. She doesn't want to share expenses wants no one to tell her how to spend her money. It's this type of thinking that confuses me always wanting to do something else or be somewhere I'm not, is my performance like wearing a mask so there is a fundamental cleavage from what I do and what I believe— good actors become whom they play I am convinced a good actor can pass a lie detector they are not just mouthing words they are the character, Cassandra always believed that but maybe I think too highly of actors after all they are only playing roles not the character themselves. Yet I refuse to believe in the utter uselessness of my beliefs all beliefs are not equal there is a hierarchy of beliefs and I continue to struggle to understand mine and articulate them recalling when my *avuelo* told me the story of Babylon I wanted to sneak across the border and hang out in Babylon and how the shadow of God still exists in me even if human history means something. What does it mean to be free of God if I still struggle with it only now using more sophisticated concepts and ideas as that girl on the subway who came up to me because she liked the look of my face and asked if she could pray for me? I wondered who she meant.

We women are not built for monogamous relationships this romantic cliché is the biggest lie of all, I bought into it I admit it but how can you expect to have what you had for all time, okay if all time is twenty years but it withers before it dies and we now live longer and have more opportunities—romantic love to a single partner was possible when we are young but we are not the same people as we age and I'm no longer the individual who fell in love with him; if I can fall in love why can't I fall out of love still when I met Lilliana a pang of jealousy pored through me, depressed me, surprised me, a well-dressed woman wouldn't have hurt me as much but she was a younger version of me, it caught me off guard. A well-dressed woman would be a floozy but a woman in blue jeans, braless and comfortable within herself was a surprise and she held onto him the way I once did, who would have thought I could be jealous of my previous self, I could see why Joseph wanted to be seen with her and wouldn't let me define him, they were affectionate together without being bombastic, she is attractive, smart, intelligent and knew how to hold her tongue and when to speak she may appear shy but I could see that she speaks her mind. I shouldn't have come but grandma was there and he wanted me to meet her but I shouldn't have lied to myself saying this is only postpartum depression and I was feeling so high after the performance I just couldn't go home. In the midst of my blues I knew I wanted to stay and feel this I always knew this was bound to happen that it would happen some day and said I would be ready for it but can you ever be ready? but I am a true actor and something deep within propelled me to be a charming person and what I had done in coming was correct this is who I am even if I can't remember feeling that as I sat alongside them I know I must have felt that because I know how to get into the role of an actor and even if I am starting to doubt my feelings my memory tells me I didn't want to be in that relationship it would have been the death of me, but I was unprepared for my feelings seeing him with another woman I wasn't ready for that I was in my reverie from the performance crossing Bleecker not thinking where I was going maybe I should have gone into some Irish bar, even if I can't stand those places and a café seemed like a nice place to meet. They saved me a chair. I hesitated for a moment when I saw them and finally realized what I was doing meeting my ex for the first time as an ex and his new fiancée, maybe I should have turned around and walked out made up some excuse later but he saw me and stood up so I forced myself to go over and he introduced me and she was charming, polite, deferential and it was awkward but we are all adults so could pull it off. Immediately she complimented me on my acting just what an actor wants to hear and said she hadn't seen such a moving performance in years, probably true most plays are television comedies now. As if I was in a dream I just couldn't grab onto anything felt I was falling all night long thought of Mademoiselle princess and how she would take to having two mommies and can't recall much of the conversation after that only that she smelled healthy as if I went into a movie that a critic said I must see even if I had no idea what it was about. I just didn't want to talk about the past and I don't think we did I can only recall bits and pieces of our conversation almost like my life except I know and am fully aware that life is a total story not moments strung together even I can only remember pieces of it, my thoughts and feelings are more important than my words, words only have meanings when you believe them, but I really do have to concentrate more and be in the moment even if the only time I actually do that is when I'm acting on stage and can put my character's words into my mind and they become mine, and I won't play that character off stage, stage is special and I save it for that moment in the footlights, especially when the lights are so bright that I can't make out the audience only hear them and when I left the Le Figaro darkness hit me, a moonless night with streetlights not working I was surprised how dark it was walking home when I thought of some of the things I wanted to say, I knew he wanted me to see her and that my independence is important to me but by the time I realized this I was on my block I could see all the lights on in my apartment, it's so much easier when a playwright puts words into my mouth, as I now understood that I have never lived alone before all I wanted growing up was to be free of my mother I thought she was such a powerful woman only now do I realize how silly that is she had a monopoly of my infancy but was only a limited person and all I attempt was to free myself from her—are all kids like this their whole life attempting to break free from their powerless mothers? Once I thought we would always be together now he went home with another woman and by the time I figured this out I was walking up the steps to my empty apartment where I had more than a tea waiting for me, the sky now was totally dark not a star not unusual from our living room but tonight I noticed it that the sky had turned as dark as my soul without even going through different shades, I think some streetlamps must have been lit along the way I couldn't have walked all the way home in pitch black darkness but if they were I didn't notice them, I sat down drinking my scotch looking out the window trying to get hold of my thoughts, the window is clean and I can see the street and also my reflection or as I said my soul itself, I knew there was no sense in trying to sleep and tomorrow wasn't a work day so I could sleep in, grandma still gets up early but I no longer do unless it's for my day job and even there I can come in by ten and leave by six, unlike some colleagues who get in so early because of such a long commute and then rush home for the children. I wish I could be with grandma now we had such wonderful conversations not the same when I am with Joseph and his new woman. But now she's too old to walk that much and I can only talk over the phone or in my head, her voice is always there, I can still see her rolling her eyes at me when I become too animated, but I hardly imagine Joseph and in conversation I rarely think of him as a conversant—what I liked about him is his body but it is to grandma that I am continually explaining myself or trying to understand myself. As I sit looking out the window watching a couple holding hands on the stoop across the street instead of dealers selling junk wondering who that person was that I am who was I dealing with in the café and am I this gentle soul I think I am or am I plotting dangerous revenge, I am becoming aware that I am confronting a part of myself I don't like and have to be careful and not become the shrew I am capable of being, this I know without even giving it much thought. Joseph and his new woman can actually replace me even if nobody says anything she will be there day to day, no longer do I even know what's going on in his life only what grandma says or what Jacoba tells me and I am very careful with her not to show anger—give Joseph credit he does try and keep me informed but that's because he still thinks I will walk back up those twelve steps but that will not happen. How will his new girlfriend feel? It's silly getting sentimental, I'm not the type unfortunately women have been stereotyped that way and we have to fight it not to be it, luckily now times are changing and being married no longer defines a woman only divorce or lesbianism does in the Village and Greenwich Village is still one of the few places women can be alone and not need another on our arm. My difficulty is not that I fell out of love but that I hurt him and I had to lie to him and he couldn't deal with his feelings and tried to overcome them instead of kicking me out thought we could actually live beyond them, he would have never been able to, the first time I got caught up in passion but what about the second and third, it infuriated him but what did I prove only that I could hurt. What it proved is that I'm not this well-mannered kind girl I thought I was and was not what I appeared to be or what he took me and it took me awhile to realize that: I didn't mean to hurt him only prove to myself that I am free, even if there are limitations to my freedom there's also a hunger that couldn't be satiated by the way I was supposed to be, now that women too can make choices who knows if they are correct.

Who knows if I'm doing the right thing by my daughter bringing a stranger into the house? Not really bringing her into the house we've agreed to live our separate lives but together, I can't believe this I never thought it would happen to me again you can step into the same river twice, it's not the same water it's always flowing, this time I'm not messing with superstition that religious marriages last longer, we're getting married at city hall then walking across the Brooklyn Bridge to and having a nice lunch on the waterfront, Esmeralda and Jacoba will meet us there, I'm nervous can't wait for it to be over and rules except want to be married again but I know she couldn't live full time with us there are no universal rules except maybe what my mother told me to do, but memory tells me that I didn't always listen to her I've made this choice and I want to live with it even if I can hear doubts creeping into my skull doubts implanted by my mother, but I have to be careful she also loved me maybe the wrong kind of love but loved me nevertheless and it's because of that love that I am able to stand on my own two feet today; she was always afraid and never took me out of the neighborhood the first year, now it's called postpartum I called it mommy and made sure to take Jacoba all over the city so she not be like me, we travelled bus, subway, car, even if I was depressed and exhausted I thought it was important for her future mental health she be able to travel, I balanced working and taking care of her, lucky I was the boss so had more free time than most, and most of the time I was the only man in the playground, my life was put on hold as I cared for her now I'm slowly coming out of my shell getting married, the divorce finally came through no difficulty we just had to file papers and wait a year we agreed in advance to divide everything, no lawyers why let them get rich, I can see why lawyers fought tooth and nail not to allow no-fault divorce also they now have ethics, can you believe it? they're not allowed to sleep with their clients, Cassie wants to know how will they get sex nobody in their right mind would want to touch them only when you are vulnerable are you attracted to them, but she had told me all along she doesn't mix business and pleasure and if she used a lawyer would never sleep with him, I can't be around them for too long their illogic that masquerades as logic depresses me bad enough I have to be around them at closings. I am trying to be a good father and I can only be a good father if I am a good friend to myself and this feels right. Esmeralda even said it wasn't good that I should be so alone and somehow Jacoba knows she has to be gentle with me as she knows to be kinder and gentler to Esmeralda than she is with me, Esmeralda loves her unconditionally I put demands upon her. I know I have to do more if I stay like this will go crazy tonight when Jacoba was acting up couldn't take it and walked out, of course but I just had to clear my head of her babblings I wanted to go to a bar but I hate bars so went into the local movie theater and saw James Bond, what rubbish, I was too tired to schlep downtown to see a play, besides they're hard to find at the last moment but this movie was so bad I didn't even stay until it was over, the audience was hooting and hollering they didn't know you're should keep quiet during a movie and finally just stood up and walked out didn't even take my buttered popcorn, couldn't take my soda because I spilled it who can carry two things at once, that popcorn was huge and I asked for a small it starts gigantic, and the soda to wash down the popcorn lid opened and out spilled the coke, one of these days maybe they'll have cup holders. It was a weekday night I expected nobody to be at the movies, it was packed doesn't anybody have to get up early the next day, finally couldn't take the noise, the crowds, the hooting and yelling and went across the street to see Almodovar's *High Heels*. I'm a sucker for a happy ending the mother realizes her mistake in abandoning the family for her acting career dies. Too bad she didn't commit suicide with a rope or die like a man on her sword after what she did to her daughter. My most treasured moments are just beyond myself even as I watched still felt sad about walking out on Jacoba to be by myself and I promised myself not to do this again or more accurately I won't leave for such a long time, as usual when I get home she will have forgotten what we argued about and gave me a warm hug, the family has changed me and it's no longer anything I can reason out and it touches me to the core. It is fascinating how I changed once she came into my life and there is no other word that can describe it even as she pushes all my wrong buttons, I won't do anything anymore without thinking how it will affect Jacoba, and I think she gets along with Lilliana well enough that we can make it permanent and she isn't going to replace her mother and she doesn't want children she's made that perfectly clear even if I wouldn't mind one or two more, even if I wouldn't mind one or two more am I out of my mind even thinking that I can't do that to myself. Cassandra has a difficult time being with one and lately has hardly been seeing her especially as she now asks her when she's moving back yet she still is good to her as I explain to her her mother has a right to live the way she wants. But now that she is beginning to realize this is not natural I thought by now she would be accustomed to this enough of her friends have divorced or remarried parents, but she isn't and it's affecting her schoolwork from being an A student she now barely passes, and from being a goody-goody she's now a troublemaker in class, Esmeralda loves that she never liked cutesy girls and neither do I except when it's my child. I couldn't stop thinking about Jacoba and Cassandra while watching the movie or even do two things at once anymore I even make lists of what I'm to do otherwise completely forget. To break up the monotony of my thought I asked Lilliana to marry me and to my surprise she agrees at least now I have an excuse to start living again and by the time we marry maybe we can do more things together instead of my only pleasure being watching Jacoba asleep and sometimes awakening her in the middle of the night telling her I need a hug and we hug each other then she falls back asleep and has no memory of me waking her the next morning, partly it's my fault she's doing poorly in school when Cassie first left I couldn't be alone bought a television and we watched too much together instead of her free time and now she watches all the time getting me pissed. She even wants me to buy her one for her room if I get that along with a microwave I'll never see her. All this thought about my marriage but nothing about my being arrested for child neglect, not really arrested given a summons god forbid you leave your child unattended under the age of ten, she was eight and has been home alone before, I hadn't realized Esmeralda wasn't home but when I came back the police, social workers, god knows who were at the house do you know how dangerous you are to your child. What was my crime? Leaving a child unattended who was not yet ten. Some old biddy called the police and at the door was a uniform police officer along with a social worker ready to kidnap my child for neglect, luckily Esmeralda came home and they saw she was not black and they backed off, still I was given a summons that I intend to appeal to the Supreme Court, until my lawyer told me to take the class because if I fight it they will put Jacoba in foster care until my case is heard and that could take six months, no decent parent can let that happen to board your child with strangers while you fight an order, and they wouldn't even let her stay with Cassandra because she's not living here and so I pled guilty and now take parenting class where I find out everything I am doing is wrong, and after six months of good behavior my permanent record is wiped clean, and my lawyer says imagine if you were a single mother they might have taken the child away for neglect but as a man the courts have respect for you.

The sounds of sweet silence I always love coming by the river and listening to the nothingness, the ice melting, the waves lapping against the shore, the birds, a symphony of sounds that I never really listened to before Jacobo pointed them out to me and away from human chatter besides the church hated nature and we never learned to appreciate it, like Shakespeare the church banned nature, only they couldn't truly ban nature but saw it only as God's lower orders man is the naming creature and all creatures are there to serve man why the big debate of the early 1600 hundreds in Spain are Indians human if not they could be considered natural slaves like blacks, but sitting here quietly listening to sounds that I hadn't known existed heard every day but never listened to was as powerful as listening to Shakespeare in New York especially since my English wasn't that good and I wasn't able to follow the dialogue but the acting made words superfluous. The first Shakespearean play I ever saw was *Troilus and Cressida* at the Provincetown playhouse, a surprise since hardly anybody did Shakespeare back then O'Neil and Shaw were all the rage but Shakespeare sees Greek soldiers for what they were not heroes, good men, virtuous men, but vulgar charlatans who utter sweet nothings and even when he was being deadly serious couldn't do without Pandarus's irony, and comedy, why I loved it, and when I finally was able to find a copy and sat with my dictionary because I was hell bent on perfecting my English it was then I knew I was never going home again, like a Dantean in hell who would always be wondering about his homeland but would never set foot in there again I would make every effort to fit in, and even if Tomas wasn't interested I had neighbors who were educated women not afraid to be seen without a man on the street and we made our way across town and felt so comfortable in the Village that even to this day I can go to the theater without a man to define me—the simplicity of the stage, that evoked the mood of the characters, the atmosphere of war, kept me thinking of *Guernica,* the pain in the horse's head, the indiscriminate bombings, which would have been an appropriate design for this play, Shakespeare understood that war destroys all scruples it doesn't bring us to a higher morality but lowers it when they sack a city, kill the men, rape the women, nights of terror the inhabitants don't live in their homes anymore but as mere objects and those that survive will live in fear of the new rulers, and I always felt entitled from birth to my superior position only in the civil war did I learn the truth of the matter—I went in a childhood fantasy with a rifle over my shoulder to the front, fortunately for me women were not allowed to fight and I had to help clean up the mess afterwards and as I began to see the horrors of war couldn't believe what I actually believed and couldn't believe what I had done even if I felt it was the right thing to do felt so uprooted knew I had to leave this land and cut off from all I had previously thought and seeing this play in a strange country, barely grasping the language but getting at the emotions did I begin to feel at ease, at home, not deracinated, and walked home promising myself that I would read the play the next day, and back then you could walk the streets at night and not be afraid, that was true freedom for me. I would take Gloria out every day I didn't want to be stuck at home all day long, I'd go crazy staying home with her all the time, and I would get the carriage from the basement storehouse, luckily the super was always around to help me carry it up the three steps, those carriage were so big and bulky luckily we had a storage room in the cellar where we could keep them also bicycles if I remember correctly and we started walking towards Fourth street where in used bookstores I would find Shakespeare in the back. Walking was the only freedom I had when Gloria was a baby now it's also my only freedom only I go much slower with my stick, and refuse to use a walker the stick is sufficient and even if my balance is no longer as good as it once was and I walk precarious close to falling I walk otherwise I will give up the ghost and if I hurt myself I hurt me whoever me is rather than resign myself to being stuck at home all the time, leaving my homeland made me realize I had to change my ways because I wasn't wedded to a brutal country that was a mere accident of birth and living here allowed me to develop real thoughts not simply body sensations and only because I left was I able to begin to open my mind getting away from the closed atmosphere of fear and helplessness, it felt good leaving even if I realized I was fooling Tomas I did give him a daughter and tried to stay with him and felt scared coming here at first not really knowing the language but Tomas was a good supporter and I learned English pretty quickly being with young mothers in the playground every day and didn't need Gloria to translate for me, it is here in the States that I learned what it is to be me. Reason is humanity and I lived in a community of like-minded souls rather than Spanish-speaking neighbors coming up from the island. Still it wasn't easy being uprooted and in my darkest days would tell myself at least I'm not under the rule of *El Generalissimo* and would go for long walks at night when Tomas came home and cared for Gloria and became American by free will rather than by birth; for those who don't have it freedom is the greatest gift and those born here take it for granted. It's like thinking drinking illegal booze is the same as drinking in a nice bar. Once a young girl from Appalachia stayed with us as an au pair and wasn't comfortable with all this freedom, she had never been in a bar before that served alcohol she came from a dry county where they smuggled in alcohol and at first she thought it was the same thing until she learned the value of excess and would come home drunk every night and she was afraid of her potential and we finally had to dismiss her because I couldn't allow her to be drunk around the baby. At least I wasn't forced but left on my own free will that made a difference, I looked at horror on those European refugees who were forced to flee their homelands because of the

Nazis or the Soviets and surprise surprise most refused to go back after the war ended or communism disappeared, I always thought I would go back after Franco passed because of my love of Spain for my responsibility to Spain to help them learn about freedom, as Plato said we have to go back in the cave and help them learn what they are seeing are shadows but I just couldn't, it was impossible for them to change they were so corrupt and I thought maybe in a generation or two—the Israelites wandered in the desert for forty years really to get the slave mentality out of them, let the old generation die off, and I used the excuse I was too old to go home and now I am too old but it dawned upon me after he died I couldn't go back my home is here, even if at times I feel I don't fit in here and don't fit in anywhere but I fit in here more than anywhere. I was also afraid didn't think confronting my fear would make me a better person even as I wondered would I now come to the States with a man I barely knew, I did it then but wouldn't do that now and now my only desires are personal and maybe to die with some dignity. Those old terms patriotism, nationalism, algebra are all too abstract for me. The nicest birthday gift I ever received was the night Conchita told me she was marrying Joseph she didn't mention Jacoba until she was sure and that surprised me I never thought she would want a baby and I said to myself I have to make up what I did to my daughter who became pregnant and moved up to the Bronx to escape me at least I tried to make it up to Conchita and now hug my great granddaughter every day and make sure to kiss her, interestingly how values change as you age and remembering is different than perceiving, but maybe my memory is getting better because I have this pain in my side and my upper left leg that doesn't seem to be getting much better and makes it difficult for me to get up after listening to the water flow down the Hudson. Happy days.

I laughed when he first suggested it I wasn't laughing at him but the idea, I could always tell the difference between the moment and the historical, communist education does that to you prepares you for the long haul with their always talking about false needs of the capitalists as opposed to the true needs of the revolution, and I thought he must have been crazy, me, who would want to be with me, me, he must be out of his mind, here in this country were they don't allow girls any freedom he wants me to give up what is most precious to me: what feminism hasn't really begun to engage in the hard work of forming a party and advocating for real social change instead of piecemeal, in a culture that still glorifies marriage and motherhood rather than the individual self, where once a woman becomes a mother that's all she becomes, her being is kaput, even in marriage she loses freedom, and yet I thought of him as one of the most courageous men I ever saw when he was in the playground with his daughter, he usually is the only man there, not a hundred percent true anymore now that I have begun to notice here in the Village or even the West Side at least on weekends you do see some fathers, even some pushing baby strollers, no longer do the police stop him and ask what is he doing inside a playground, he pointed to his daughter, he laughed as he told me that but a week later found out in the same playground a baby girl was kidnapped and maybe the gendarmes were worried a kidnapping sex slave operation was taking place because a detective was the one talking to him otherwise you never see them telling him he couldn't be in a playground without a child that's the law and he pointing to Jacoba and Jacoba comes running up to him saying daddy, daddy because she fell and was bleeding from the nose and he calmly takes out a dipe-and-wipe and starts drying her and holding her, even police in dictatorships don't take father's away from their children in front of the children, what do you think they were dealing with Jack the Ripper. Yet they still shackle women to the playground, they sit on enough benches they could be judges. It's still mothers who are the caregivers or now nannies in bourgeois homes and mothering is only talked about in getting paid maternity leave, more childcare at work, time off from work for class trips, as if motherhood is eternal, why can't men nurture, if Joseph can do it other men can as well, if men become caregivers then workers' rights might accrue. Still I got scared, really frightened for the first time in my life when I didn't get better, and the pain kept coming and what at first thought would be a day or two convalescence turned into a few days then a couple of weeks and finally I had to go to the emergency room without health insurance, but my friend lent me her insurance card, fooled them but was so worried they would catch me and throw me out or worse arrest me for fraud, that I'm not sure it's worth it, Joseph visited me every day and made sure I had fresh soup along with his other duties, I knew he cared for me but not this much and I slowly got better it was a severe case of the flu nothing serious but it knocked me for a loop and because I'm a freelancer didn't qualify for health insurance, which I never needed because I am healthy do my exercises regularly and never was sick a day in my life, that is until now and I was shaken when I came out of St. Vincent's, they must have known I was using an alias but they were good about it and made sure I was taken care of regardless, and I came home to a well-stacked refrigerator so I didn't have to leave for a couple of days of rest and boredom that Joseph said is the road to recovery being bored at home but stay let your body heal. How did he get so smart? Afterwards we discussed it I was against it but there seemed no other way this was obviously going to happen again, you don't get stronger as you age only weaker and I realized how lucky I was when I saw what they billed the insurance company, I would have been wiped out and it wasn't AIDS that everyone at first feared—I've only been with Joseph and of course I quickly wondered has he been with prostitutes that disgusted me but he assured me he hadn't he just likes looking at them at bus stops and you can easily tell the prostitutes they're the ones still at the bus stops after the bus pulls out. At least I asked him for a day or two to think about it didn't acquiesce immediately even if I knew I would, what else could I do? Health insurance is important. They really force a family on you in this country or you have to become a secretary and take drudgery work in order to have health insurance, that I would not, could not, do, a friend suggested adjuncting but adjuncts don't have health insurance besides I rather have my teeth pulled than be a teacher, finally, I called a lawyer who did say marriage would be the best way to cover myself unless I was prepared to pay for it out of pocket but that would have denied me the right to exist, COBRA was so expensive on my limited income and it's easier to marry and be covered by your spouse—this shouldn't be allowed to happen imagine in this day and age a woman forced into marriage only here it's not called bride capture only the prudent decision by a free person. How free am I? I told him I would never wear his ring that was too much a sign of ownership but I feel guilty it sets a terrible agenda for other people that women are not allowed to be independent selves but can only be free in marriage. We agreed right away not to move in together but continue our similar ways only now I do feel closer to him against my better judgment. The more women succumb to this type of thinking the worse off we become, oh I'm not against marriage if a couple wants to but forced to, even if nobody put a gun to my head I was forced into this I could see no way out, why can't we have universal health care like they have in ex-communist countries, and as I say it realize how stupid it is, we had full coverage only terrible medical service here we have good medical service only terrible health coverage, the hospital took care of me made sure I got well and did all they could for me. He knew this was important to me and had planned getting a divorce anyhow but deeper he likes saying he's married, besides Cassandra really wanted her freedom and he would never stand in her way. I was worried about being a mother but he said we will continue as we have she can still call you auntie, which is okay by me I never wanted to change diapers. He laughed said the hard part isn't the physical it's the mental always worrying, a parent has a woeful imagination and can think horror anywhere. That's what binds girls to being afraid they have to be given the same freedom as boys. A boy can't be raped? Rarely is a girl just used to frighten young girls. He didn't even feel ashamed being the only man in the park and I considered him courageous for that, men think of courage as the ability to kill enough of that crap taking care of a child is more courageous than going off to war, and he loves watching his daughter sleep only wishes she would do more of it. He says I remind him of his friend Zoltan who he did things with and I can fulfill the same function with Jacoba even if she doesn't like going places with me. He thinks she will get used to me. I doubt it. Joseph actually had no experience parenting his father was never home but his grandfather was and he was loved, you need love nothing else matters I grew up under a dictatorship but had love so much so my father had a heart attack coming home from the train station after I left, but my mother wouldn't tell me for a year because she knew I would feel guilty and would want to come back but that would have been against all his wishes and she cared for him until he died without my ever seeing him again. I would write and my mother would write back, apparently the KGB were even at his funeral thinking they would catch me only my mother was too clever and didn't let me know until after he was buried, I didn't even know he was in the hospital only he could never come to the phone when I called, he was sleeping, or working or out, never home. And my father they arrest for teaching Sartre, the examiner says who's this Sartre we'll bring him down for questioning as well, for being a subversive one of the most honest forthright men ever to exist and he claims he was lucky only a couple of years in prison then he gets to come home a broken man. He says when he first came home I was sleeping in the crib and he was afraid to go in and wake me but mother insists and I hear him and he was afraid I would be frightened a bogyman in the dark but I stood up in my crib and hugged him and we were close from then on. Him they arrest and the courts realized that he did nothing but there is no innocent when the police arrest and he was sentenced to five years' hard labor and only served two and left with damaged health he who fought the Nazis and supported the communists was eaten up alive by them and spent the rest of his working life as a window washer never allowed to teach again. Americans don't understand this idea of freedom because they are little followers not creative individuals and I have a deep distrust of the family, courts, or social institutions they are not the places to solve your problems all they do is follow precedent which is the rule of the past not the future, look how long it took Brown vs. the Board of Education to become law and then nobody did anything about it. This puritan heritage of theirs is bad they won't even consider allowing the morning-after pill in this country while it is in use all over Europe, the only birth control for women is they be stuck in the kitchen and making babies, even federal funding for abortion was stopped quickly so now only the well-off have access to abortion. The courts will only change when society forces them and here I am giving in to one of my most feared nightmares marriage. The old way of life must go kaput and a new one emerge, be careful, I hear myself saying, we tried that and the old way reasserted itself with a vengeance, women had equal right to work in communist countries and be miserable in communist countries and do all of childcare and housework in communist countries, there was no freedom there only the same ole with a vengeance. It's only those who say things for our own good, really only means their own good and not what's good for the individual; no women without thought could fail to grasp this marriage is a trap for us and we have to grab men by the balls and squeeze if we are to get at the forefront of thought, our thoughts reflect how the world should be not is.

I can't recall how I felt first coming into this place thank goodness I have such a bad memory and can only recall abstract concepts not actual moments, I know I didn't like it here but not the emotions connected to that being in such a big house away from my beloved Village yet it looked so nice from the outside but I do recall thinking I can't walk up these twelve steps to the front door, but Joseph showed me how I get through the basement right into my apartment and I could slowly walk up the steps inside, more steps but not as steep, and Conchita thinking this big house is a prison that she didn't want to have to manage, not only that but I'm not interested in remembering it's over and done with what good does rehashing do no longer do I actually think about the past—of course I do but in a vague unfamiliar way where it no longer is me; I am actually happy in this house even if I know it can't continue and I like my genteel poverty enough money to live sufficiently and time to walk to the river and the parks, this I learned from an old friend who gave up a nice gig, is that I am now more engaged in living than I ever was when I was working and I do all I want to do now besides going into work. He goes to concerts, auditions, art openings and walks everywhere, well I go nowhere but walk everywhere feeling stronger now that I have three legs to carry me and the heat of summer is finally over and I can walk a little more and not have to carry a water bottle everywhere and don't miss the subways at all, if I can't walk to it I won't go, even if I did go out to Coney Island but that was too far on the subway and to my surprise not a single person offered a woman with a stick a seat so I couldn't board that train and had to wait twenty minutes for the next one to leave the station. But I had a pleasant swim the waves weren't too high and hadn't forgotten, walked the boardwalk to Brighton had a Russian lunch and walked back easily and am now finally learning how to use my leisure time, look how long it has taken me to develop the use of free time and now I realize what I do in my free time determines how I will live the rest of my life, and I don't want to spend it going to doctors. No longer will I compare my past to my present or even wonder if was the same person young as I am old, my thinking is different than now and my body isn't the same anymore, my relationship to time isn't the same anymore, how can I be the same person, I am different then than I am now, even my memories have changed and I look back at the exciting life I created and was able to live, and that makes me who I am: I know I was a lover, wife, mother, grandmother now great grandmother we are all one in the same but I am not the same in each incarnation, I'm happy now walking home and it's still hard to believe I call this home but I am actually comfortable here and have no idea why I was anxious moving up here, they have beautiful parks the area is close to the water, and I love looking at the architecture of the brownstones, a strange situation feeling what I don't want to feel. My relationships have only gotten better and I'm still human not dependent upon anyone and if I can help it will remain that way, humanity is more than instincts we can also separate from it and I see that clearer than I ever have before and this free time is my serious time not secondary or a moment grabbed here or there and it's not only sensual pleasure when I get to be by myself it is essential to my identity and when I am robbed of it decreases my emotional and moral awareness. Moving up here has taken me away from my memories of the Village and made me into a more interesting person, shamefully I am one of the few old people I see reading on park benches, instead of just staring straight ahead flat-faced waiting to be called. I notice I enjoy walking more, swimming more, if my mind was engaged while going somewhere, too bad pocket books are no longer so small to easily fit into a purse. If I have been wrestling with some ideas, I can then force myself to enjoy the moment otherwise I am marking time. And as the eye doctor said I have one good eye for short vision one for long so they balance each other out and I am one of the few people my age who don't need to wear glasses. Now I realize I forgot my keys and it looks like I'm going have to walk up the twelve steps and ring the bell, and as I wait for somebody to come to the door my thoughts keep slipping away from me but at least I didn't have to think about climbing those steps, they'll be the death of me, not from a heart attack my heart is good now, but from losing my balance but I was able to do it, slowly, and am I surprised when Conchita opens the door, she came by to help and wanted to be outta here but also wanted to see me before she left and so she waited being bored with her own daughter who as she told me later couldn't make conversation with her and I knew something should have been up when I heard the strings of Wagner blasting on the new CD, the Tristan chord is unmistakable, dissonance opens the piece and is the key to the piece, and while listening to it feel I am watching myself thinking, not the all-seeing eye in the sky but me watching myself, and we hug and holding her feels right that I don't want to let go. We have a grand kiss at the front door we're happy to see each other and she tells me she feels anxious being here but had to wait to be with me. If only I could think a thought through instead of jumping from one to another it doesn't get fully formed and I notice how she's changed gotten a little heavier probably from a poor diet and not enough exercise but keep my mouth shut, she comments on how she likes the new paintings we put up, really Joseph and his continual movement of works of art so as not to get bored or take for granted any one piece he likes to constantly change them, he says he learned that from me but I only did it occasionally he does it all the time. We all refuse to see art as interior design and constantly looking for works we like to be hung up on our walls and when we tire of them sell them and get different works. We don't do that with furniture however there we buy comfortable pieces that Jacoba has ruined and so now we look for strong fabric but our living room is lived in not a place when company comes, unlike Zoltan's friend Ferdinand now part of our extended family, who went back to Riga after communism finally collapsed to visit his sister and was surprised their apartment looked exactly the same as when he left it, except for the television, same furniture, dishes, paintings on the wall, the country was so poor they could never afford new stuff. Conchita is excited to see me, I can see she dressed for me but she says she doesn't wear jeans anymore especially since the kids are wearing them with tears and patches and she thinks she looks funny dressing as a kid. We sit and shut the CD off so we can talk, Jacoba comes out of her room for a moment hugs and kisses me I ask about her day she says good, I know enough to ask pointed questions she tells me what she did, then goes back into her room and I am alone with my granddaughter. She's glad we still have no television in the living room, she has become addicted she says, but here we watch in the den, her old sewing room, together this place is a lived home and she says are you going to offer me sherry but we have our usual tea, some things never change as Conchita says.

Something is wrong with me but I have to wait forever up here at the Veterans Hospital like I had to wait for social security and social security supplement finally I could no longer pay the mortgage and the bank wasn't sympathetic and we had to move back into the city, somehow was able to get into the projects unsafest place I ever lived in, and was able to shield, or as my neighbor said, really hid my little savings from the housing authority so I have enough for them to bury me. Neighbors all without kids but their grandchildren living with them, wild, raucous will kill you for a drug, a big difference from where I lived with Esmeralda there we looked after everybody here nobody knows anybody and now little gives me pleasure but I'm not dying as the doctor said just wasting away nothing terminal just declining, I live here now with my wife but it's so unfair to her she never lived in the city before and this isn't the city only a terrible neighborhood, occasionally my granddaughter comes up and visits I can't go down to her it's too far, she's not truly my granddaughter but I did raise her mother but what's the use I have no idea what's going on all I think about is the past and wonder if my life has any meaning. Sure I did the right things served my country, helped my parents get out of Puerto Rico married a woman who carried not my child raised her as if she were my own but she was never really my own her and her mother would fight so much that she couldn't wait to get out and got pregnant the first chance she got, divorced Esmeralda when she wanted me to, remarried started a new life up in the country but was all the same, except when younger I could play softball, that I enjoyed, even had a new knee put in the winter so I could be ready to play again in the summer, lived happily for twenty years until I retired and couldn't pay the mortgage and had to come back here. Who would have thought, luckily I am a veteran got high up on the list to live here, took it the first place they offered noisy as all hell kids playing in the park to all hours blasting their radio, taking drugs, all I do all day is sit in front of the television, mindless crap even can fall asleep in front of it, except Johnny Carson is off the air and nothing good has replaced him. I have to get up off the couch and do exercise only it hurts too much and if I go for a walk I'm an easy mark for these savages better to stay home at night besides sometimes I can be waiting over a half hour for a subway train into the city and I'll be damned if I'm going to cab it, even gypsy cabs that aren't yellow and go everywhere don't like coming to the Bronx. I don't like looking backwards but I know I did at one time and I liked going to movies but the local theaters around here are closed everything is in the city now and most movies are boring to me because as Esmeralda would say I'm boring but I like cowboy movies, the Cisco Kid and his sidekick Pancho, I was raised listening to them on the radio, standing on a stool and listening to the plastic radio over the ice box and miss them—now at least I've found the ponies, and it gives me something to do, but because they announce the winners too quickly Conchita brought me cassette recorder and I record the results then go over them slowly, I'm getting good at the track, make thirty or forty dollars by playing favorites and it gets me out of the house in the morning when I go to OTB, I don't make much nor don't I lose much, just like in life where I was afraid to take chances and now it gives me something to do with my day so my mind doesn't fall apart. It's only sitting up here at Kingsbridge Veterans Hospital that depresses me, I tried walking here but my knees hurt too much I take the bus and of course get here an hour early thinking maybe they'll take me early, ha, all I do is sit for an hour until my hour or two regular wait begins and all they say to me is I'm getting old can't go into a hospital because nothing terminal no dementia only cardiomyopathy and diverticulitis, each doctor telling me something different but one aide said you don't want to come in here and he's right, I don't want to be in a hospital or force fed. I have no friends here like my softball friends only other lonely old men I meet at OTB the Catholic church forbid OTB from being on the block of their school as if it would corrupt the young, more likely what do they have to fear from old people. The extra blocks walking hurts my knees even as I get more exercise but now at least I get out of the house daily, my newfound passion, I'm sure Esmeralda would disapprove she and her highfalutin ways why don't you read go to the theater listen to music, but I'm a simple guy, she was the only person I know who went to the opera imagine she wanted to take me but luckily I wasn't going to buy no tux, I didn't need to impress besides I would look funny in a monkey suit. Only walking to Off Track Betting allows me to shut my mind off and not think about myself but concentrate on the money I'm going to collect and on the way back look at the list my wife gave me and go shopping in Grand Union, she wants me to go to more than one store but I like the supermarket because I get it all there, but how these ladies can put up with that place is beyond me. Besides OTB and shopping I occasionally do the laundry and can go into the pizza place right next door and put a dollar in the juke box and listen to old songs while waiting for the laundry to finish, I have a slice while it's washing and sit there silently listening while it is in the dryer otherwise I never go out, except up here to the hospital. It's only when I'm home that I continue to think about the past and what might have been and the more I think about it the less I understand and the more I see the meaningless life I led and can't see myself moving forward only dying and how I'm going to be able to handle that—once I thought myself so lucky to have such a beautiful intelligent wife and a daughter who loved me never realizing it wouldn't last my daughter would move away and my wife would ask me to move out. I never had heard of such things. A family is sacred as my mother said to me only it's not true. My mother warned me but it wouldn't have mattered I wouldn't have believed her, she said your wife is too pretty, too intelligent I thought she was jealous Spanish women are so much more sophisticated than island folks not even off the farm, she even smoked in public which shocked my mother. My mother couldn't read and this woman was going to museums, operas, art galleries. And she was right pretty soon Esmeralda wouldn't even come with me to visit my parents and I took Gloria so I wouldn't have to be alone with her on weekends when she was doing her artsy things. And then out of the clear blue she asks me to leave and brings shame on the family, of course I didn't do it at first but when she didn't even bother to come to my mother's funeral that was the last straw, who could believe a wife would do that. Our daughter never forgave her she would have been honored to know her the priest gave such a nice service such nice words about her being in heaven with God now and he knew her so he knew how good of a person she was, you could have thought she was Mother Mary herself as a wife, mother, grandmother and she didn't want to hear nothing of it only said to me grow-up. I didn't know if I should laugh or cry I never heard such blasphemy she was my mother and had no life outside of her family and I wondered now that I was an orphan who would take care of me; if only I could say to her one more time I loved her enjoy the taste in my mouth of being around my mother one more time, you love a mother more than a father a mother is always with you, what did I do wrong, finally a doctor calls me soon I will be out of here and can wait for a bus to take me home but she wouldn't come to the funeral of my mother said she had nothing in common with her she was my wife she had a duty.

The hardest part of aging is getting out of bed, my bones ache, my left hip my right shoulder but I still do my exercises, a group of ladies do yoga in the park early in the morning but I have to get up so early to get there and I'm needed at home to help Jacoba prepare for school and then it's too late to get to them—great-grandparenting is a full time job, but when she finally leaves I can get started on my day, walk to the park sometimes having to go in a bush, I have no fear of bodily excretions especially in a city that closes public bathrooms, bushes have helped many an old woman, Joseph tells me men are built better and will do it between parked cars and he's not even old yet, you'd think the parks department could fix toilets where children play or toilets placed strategically all over the city but all you see are restrooms are for customers only, but I know places to go and where they are so I don't have to ask. I love to walk, examine vanishing points, appreciate the trees, sky, nature or city streets even playgrounds, aging means I no longer look at virile young men's bodies now I much prefer watching young boys and girls run around in the playground, a sure sign of aging, watching the youthful zaniness of young girls who are more focused now on what they want to be and now have a sense of humor and how young boys follow them around their pants low down but rise up when they come into contact with one. I love how girls can talk to boys, I could never do that unchaperoned they were always these strange creatures to me and it wasn't allowed to meet a boy all alone so we never truly knew them. But now I know a few little truths that I could tell the girls but still remember how we thought of old people and they must think the same way so it is better to just observe and have private conversation on thoughts, and it is impossible to understand them we come from such different worlds but I love their red cheeks and expectations of life that it makes me happy just observing them: this does more for me than my exercise, but the walking stick helps me get around since my balance is becoming precarious the doctor said I should use a walker but so far have refused that would hinder my movement too much, she suggested that I also get a wheelchair and I told her she's crazy. It's bad enough the bus step is too much now but there is access-a-ride only you have to wait forever for them to come—there are more things in heaven and earth Horatio than are in your philosophy, and one of them is old age. Don't get old. Of course Hamlet was only concerned with his mother's quick remarriage than getting old. Wow! How did that come about? I haven't seen a Shakespeare play in quite a while and as a materialist why would I believe that, I never believed that before—Conchita always said she would love to play Hamlet but they rarely do cross-gender Shakespeare even if boys played women's roles back in the day, she always thought men never get the essence of his character they play him like a confused man but he's really a woman who wasn't weak only had no power, Claudius only dies by accident not by Hamlet's hand. How did that thought hit me out of the blue? Oh wasn't Shakespeare playing in the park at the Delacorte theater and just saw

Hamletmachine with Ferdinand—the mind does work in mysterious ways. Shakespeare knew that Jacobo told me that and I can't forget him even if I can't remember what I had for breakfast this morning, him telling me that I can remember. Nobody talks anymore about what I know, there's no more talk of the Spanish Civil War, the fights of freedom, communism being the last great hope of humankind instead it was terrible because all life their lacked freedom, and look what happened when the wall fell then pretty soon the commies fell. Ferdinand is fun to be with besides his tenuous connection to Jacobo, a connection only true in my mind the lover of his brother's friend, close enough for me, and he too knows the same history as I do, even has it at a personal level, claims his mother and father were bombed by the Germans, Russians, English and Americans as they were in hiding during the war and his mother was pregnant with him. Joseph brought him a piece of the Berlin Wall so he could put it next to Zoltan's grave as a reminder that he got what he hoped for, wished for, but never got to see, the collapse of communism not in centuries but a few years after his death. Joseph said his grandfather finally stopped believing in communism not with Khrushchev's speech about the cult of personality that was only to reform the errors of the past not eliminate communism but when they marched into Hungary in '56 and he saw all hope for reform was impossible. All that seems a million years ago but with Ferdinand at least we share the same history and he escaped communism like I escaped fascism and the past was personal history not something out of a textbook. Now I'm speaking with some unknown tongue I never even met Zoltan only went with Joseph so he wouldn't be alone and come away with a new friend. Only he lives too far in the Bronx for us to see each other often, but he does come down once in a while and that person is still alive wants to move into the city but says he first has to empty out his apartment, which should take him forever. And I don't like going up to the Bronx because of the associations with Jacobo even if he lived on the other side of the Bronx. The mind is a mysterious creature: if a person exists he's alive and dead no longer exists, so why do I resist. How lucky he is not to have a body to drag around with him. What silly thoughts you old biddy you, how can I believe such nonsense. Ah Horatio, but I have to keep trying to find my voice—being is physical even if I don't know what it all means, but when I'm bored all different voices come to me especially as I now have to go behind a bush and pee. I know where my unseen bushes are, joggers use it all the time only on the East Side do they have porta-johns but they're so disgusting it's better to do it behind a bush. The joy of New York are the parks thank goodness they are safe once again, if only we could fix up the waterfronts as well. New York is the only city that doesn't use its waterfronts for people. Luckily I know enough to carry a small roll of toilet paper in my purse. Even marching I realized men were built better when we had our first break I wondered what for and the Sargent says you'll see but then I could hold it in forever, then I could stand the cold or the heat, and as my body changed what becomes painful or joyful changes as well. I live in the now but it has a past that disturbs the present and makes me wonder about the future. I still exist and Jacobo exists within me but beyond the moment, go figure, and it's no longer a lived moment even if I feel more alive thinking about him even if then I was somebody different than I am now—at least when I'm squatting he comes to me with all clarity even as I must concentrate and not drip and once finished that thought comes upon me like a tidal wave—it's more me than me living something that is me even if it's only inside me—ah Horatio there's more to living than goes on in your philosophy.

This play is fantastic, finally a play well-written about women's lives grasping the meanings of myths and rituals women are not only animal-istic creatures and how we have to fight them, and I'm fortunate to grab this part, my career has been on hold for years and now maybe I can take it to the next level with a good part, and we're doing it off-off-Broadway where there is energy; you won't get that in a big 199-seat house even if it's filled, which it rarely is off-Broadway is now becoming as bland as Broadway, and I feel better about myself having a purpose again, it's terrible that actors need an audience yet I feel better only when working as an actor, and now we're bringing on board a lighting guy, a sound designer, and a publicist so maybe others can find out how good this play really is. My only past that I can recall and feel with some degree of accuracy was when I was in performances and the parts I played all other memories are remembered not felt they could have happened to anyone only those parts happened to me. Now I no longer remember the lines but do remember how I felt in each scene I was there while at my job I wonder how much am I there I mean I physically I'm there, do what was required of me, but I was never truly present and when I try and recall the projects my memory keeps slipping away, it's now obvious I really wasn't there if I have to spend so much energy trying to recall it, and even when I see it in my notes have no idea what it meant, and can't recall with the intensity that I can recall my roles which I was not me but the characters were me they inhabited my skin, they were more real than me, and now I'm back in the life not concerned with my job, and again enjoy living in with them. Never could I understand those souls who believed everything has to do with the serpent, but this is a miracle I'm thrust into this life once more and that's what I like—religious zealots have it wrong my soul is part of my body and my body forms part of my soul; this set evokes timelessness, not a specific moment, it's not a Greek play even if it could have been written by Euripides it has ceremony and ritual but it has more, it doesn't try and make sense of life the playwright combined elements of Greek plays and even wants a masked chorus but we may use sound instead to depict the moods going on inside a woman's head instead of a nude chorus of men and women, we are discussing this now, still I like the idea of male nudes the female body is everywhere but they never show the male one, and the new director wants to insert this, perfectly non-perfect bodies no more of the stylized thin men and women of fantasy, use actors not models and all of us can sing and play multiple roles and we all take turns being the characters and the chorus, a real ensemble piece, when clothed we wear the same clothes we don't spoon-feed the audience as many plays do we force them to think, when I switch from clothed to unclothed when I am carrying a puppet I really don't have time to get rid of the puppet but it works beautifully when I dance with the puppet. The director argues we make choices and are responsible for our own lives and we can use spontaneity up on stage and we can feel each other's choices, dilemmas, difficulties, and this play seems to have caught the eye of the cognoscenti and might even be reviewed, especially now that we have a public relations man on board. Granted never by the major newspapers they are afraid to come downtown. Except now the Village is gentrifying so who knows how many real Village people will be interested, but people still come here to see avant-garde plays even as all the art galleries have moved up to Chelsea because of the usual reason, high rents, and have been replaced by high-end boutiques and clothing stores. It's weird walking around here now, when Tower Records moved on Broadway it revived the whole block instead of empty storefronts we now have clothing stores and shoe stores and people actually walking down Broadway it use to be so scary walking them at night but the small shops that operated alongside with the increase in foot trade are now all gone and big box stores have moved in. As grandma says nothing is as permanent as change. So far the boom hasn't affected the side streets so small avant-garde theaters are still operating and these playhouses allow for actors' sophistication and spontaneous thoughts, and our director likes that, what's not to like actors are not sheep, and we can depart from the script within the framework of the play, and the writer is fine with it sees theater as a collaborative process and doesn't insist his words be the final say. Who ever thought my marriage would come in so handy? Tears are universal and it's the heart break we go through and the mistakes we make in our minor struggles as we talk ultimate meanings to try and get to moments of life, happiness, now my ideas are on the stage and acting can help me think in different ways by examining painful memories and having the ability to have whole new sets of interpretations and experiences and the emotions attached to it, if you experience it differently the second time around it is not as painful as opposed to the insanity of going over and over it again and again and expecting it to change, there's a tragic pleasure in having sympathy with someone else's life even if you wouldn't want to go through the real life experience itself, terror, anxiety, sorrow is mitigated when you can see these things outside and not have to actually live them, you feel them but they are not yours and you can free your imagination and wonder how you'd react. I always like the term tragic pleasure, written by someone who knows what she's talking about, most stuff written on theater is nonsense, Aristotle demanded three unities he must not have seen plays performed the only unity you need is action, it must have an actor grappling with life and adulthood not worrying about the next life, acting isn't a dress rehearsal but an attempt to become self-sufficient—okay nobody can die for us and we all die unprepared but it's how we live that counts. And when this play is over I must thank Allah for allowing me the opportunity, I'm a mystery to myself where did that come from? Wouldn't it be great if I could have lived the straight and narrow without widening turns, no, tried that, bored out of my skull saw the sinful effects of living and when I think about it gives me the shudders, never have I felt so happy in acting, other roles were alright and when looking back sometimes my anger would dissipate because I wasn't allowed to explore the character to the limit, but this one we all went out together and bonded so we could feel each other as the same characters. Now I need to get my bed rest it's such a demanding performance this is too serious to take it lightly who knows if another chance will occur, I learned that in college when a visiting fireman (guest lecturer) said don't go for moderation, that's mediocrity, forget it, and now I believe it, even in college started reading the Greeks, Shakespeare, Calderon and became a well-prepared actress. If I had studied like that in high school it would have been easy wouldn't have failed music, failed music not because I didn't know music just never went to class. Grandma was proud of me hitting the books after I left even if she complained it would have been helpful earlier. I'm glad we have this new director who understands what the play is about and has these interesting visual thoughts that he translates into emotions and feelings.

Just as when heat comes in contact with cold it loses some of its warmth my life has been declining since Cassandra left but now is getting warmer with Lilliana by my side. The nights are no longer horrid, I get through them sleep through most of them feel better on a good night's sleep and there's always a new neighborhood to check out, or to help someone get a mortgage, or racism to fight, all that gets my gander up and I no longer come home to an empty apartment, of course I do, Lilliana doesn't live with us but I feel as if she does, she comes over many nights, we have dinner together and occasionally she stays the night especially on weekends and I try not to think about Cassandra, I knew we would be together since we had spent so much time together and at our age when you have so much invested in each other it's difficult to break. Imagine me married again who would have believed it? She wants to find her Jewish roots and take my last name and we don't even have children together but I'm against it, let me have something of my radical '60s left in me. If she has my name how am I different than anybody else, I'm still trying to become the adult I wanted to become and don't want to give in so easily. She has one quality that overrides everything else she is nice and I don't need anything else. Why do I keep fighting this my mother is dead what does it matter if I bring home a Jewish girl or not? It was fun bringing home a *shiksa* but now aren't I too old for those sort of games. Besides I don't have to explain anything to her I'm a grownup allowed to live my own life, only Esmeralda grasps my humor and she approves. At first I thought she might hold out hope I would get back with Cassie but she's been in more marriages than me and said you did the right thing. I'm learning once more realizing success in business is not enough I have to have a life for myself and can't be satisfied being in business and parenting alone. Now at home I have a quiet side no longer pacing up and down maybe I can be easier to live with. It's difficult confronting myself and having to pick and choose who knows if I chose the right moment and the more I wonder the more I confuse myself. When doubt creeps into a decision, I see this all the time, buyer's remorse, where doubt creeps into a decision but usually I can help them overcome it but not all the time as they move further and further away from their decision because of their fears and since our memories are fallible we don't recall what we thought when and are harder on ourselves than on anybody else, it's more productive to accept our initial decision than drift think of everything that can go wrong—you hear that self, I was amazed to get married and I didn't talk myself out of it, even if I still wait for Cassandra to come to me at night. The walk over the Brooklyn Bridge was okay but walking back was nicer because we saw the city skyline at dusk, meeting Esmeralda and Jacoba for brunch made it lovely too bad Ferdinand couldn't make it but his access-a-ride couldn't find the River Café. This walk has to be my favorite in the city excluding Staten Island and Queens where I look for new neighborhoods to gentrify and wonder who would want to live out here in the boondocks. But people do. I usually invest when the neighborhood reaches the second stage, not the take off stage not caring to be the first because then you might get caught and the neighborhood will never take off, there are no rules only feelings otherwise the Bronx should have risen long ago good transportation into the city, large apartments off the Concourse, some nice parks and shade, but sections of Brooklyn and Queens with small brownstones, no parks, and lousy transportation into the city are booming while the Bronx still stagnates, but at least there's no drug dealing or if is it's indoors not on the street. No more crack houses, the police broke those up and the abandoned buildings are being renovated and you can walk safely on city streets, god how I missed that I didn't realize that until we started getting it back, slowly imperceptibly slowly we gave up our freedom of the streets staying indoors or on main thoroughfares and not going into unknown neighborhoods until all of a sudden I realized I was trapped now they streets are usable again, the parks clean again, the city is breathing life. Granted I'm still afraid to walk in certain sections of the Bronx, nor do I walk in housing projects late at night it's a shame our ownership plan failed in the projects it might have done some good in making them safer as it is the Housing Authority has lost too many competent employees due to retirement and the technocrats that replaced them can't seem to do anything to maintain them and they have to be maintained otherwise they fall apart. We're still a rental city and the poor didn't have a feel for home ownership, it was all unreal and too technical for them even if the down payment was doable. But it's how one feels that determines if you rent or buy. Now there's not as much difficulty in getting people to consider buying they see the tax advantages, equity, only when they start to have children do they think of moving especially in neighborhoods where there is no gifted and talented school program. And if there is they stay and if they make enough money by middle school families will spend it on their child and chose private school. It's only those that look for really good elementary schools that leave the city early. When I check out the neighborhood I look for one good elementary school and boom does that neighborhood take off, better than Starbucks or even a bookstore. But enough of them now it's me going in the take off stage even if my daughter doesn't want Lilliana to replace her mother, which surprised me since that's not strange anymore what's strange is homosexuals living out in the open, and gay and lesbian parents having children when I was growing up you never saw gay parents out front I never knew even Zoltan was gay, as if there's something wrong with being gay and all I wondered is can lesbian women have an orgasm like heterosexuals, men are built better all you have to do is rub us and we come, but women can only have clitoral orgasms without penetration but Esmeralda explained that was all bullshit, Esmeralda and Lilliana immediately understood you weren't confusing children by telling them the truth but to me it's still awkward. But why should it be kept secret secrecy is probably the worst thing and they seem as harried as other parents only now and then can get on their high horse when someone expresses an anti-gay sentiment or won't let their kids play with there's. And now that I am getting accustomed to it am beginning to change but I admit when I first heard it wondered why be gay and have children. I have to stop going over my life and somehow it coming out differently and start concentrating on the future and enjoy the moments I now have and accept who I am.

So he married. He is the marrying type likes to be settled down. But it surprised me I thought I would be okay with it and I am but it still hurts, who could believe that, a mere Jewish girl no less, but a Jewish girl who had no knowledge of her own history living in Prague a pretentious woman but gentle and nice I have to admit that he did well for himself, living apart but married and he didn't marry in a Temple as he insisted when we did, I can take some credit for that, I'm proud of his growing up no more of that religious nonsense now he won't make a pork roast on a Jewish holiday it shows you care, obviously confused thought pork roast or smoked ham now he makes brisket and with panache. He started lighting the Friday night candles after Jacoba was born and said we should all have a meal together on Friday night no matter what we did during the week one night a week should be special for the family. He learned how to cook because his mother was so bad and his *joie de vivre* includes how the food should be presented and we started eating off a well-set table, fine china, flowers, and of course fine wines that he had learned when he was a wine salesman. At least he put his skills to good use, when we were first together he was leaving the person he was for the one he wanted to become and now Lilliana is getting the one he became not who he was. Once we went to Henry IV a sophisticated French restaurant and he confessed to me afterwards that he always wanted to go to one of those type places, he was easily influenced by Hollywood movies that showed suave sophisticated men dining in places like that, and he wondered if he would ever have another date to be able to go to one of those places, and now he can do it all the time, in fact while living together he liked to go to fine restaurants to learn what good food tastes like, the process of shedding his old skin and acquiring new tastes and I'm glad I was part of that, it was the end of his old self but not the end of me, I have to keep telling myself that he didn't support me but he encouraged me I have to give him credit for that, he was making enough money for all of us to live comfortably but he allowed me to work, as one of his colleagues put it, and insisted I continue to act yet I didn't want to live as a bond serf; an independent woman means a self-supporting woman otherwise it's all vocation, and I was a pretty woman used to getting what I wanted and I could terrorize him if I desired or become adjusted to laziness and as grandma said I should do neither, beauty is not a guarantee of happiness. I had to listen to my inner strivings otherwise I would have gone along, gone along; this is what's behind all my thoughts unseen but the underlying principal of all my appearances I had the good life of deceiving myself until I couldn't anymore, the *pneuma*, the breath of life was blown into my nostrils, the divine spark and I could no longer live the life I was living. It hurt to leave my family, Jacoba, grandma and Joseph but I knew they would survive he is a good father, provider, and Lilliana assures me she will not replace me, but what if she wants children by him, what will happen to Jacoba? I can always take her back, ha. Grandma assures me she wants no children being around Jacoba is exhausting enough no one ever told me how hard it is all you see are images of happy women taking care of children not the constant worry and exhaustion, somedays I didn't even get out of my nightgown until 4 in the afternoon wondering why I had her. Why do women have to see life in having children? Without children your life is never finished with them the end of an artistic career, I've seen it so many times. Without children you are always in the midst of some project that only death interrupts with children life no longer is but becomes about others one for other people unless you have a wife to care for them. Men always say what women have to do then criticize us for not doing what men are doing but we don't have a wife to care for us, and grandma did it so can I. At first I only wanted to act for the glamor but now see the profundity in it, but I did want to do it and took steps to make it so not sit on my ass and wait for something to happen, early on I realized the effects of drama combining the dead with the living and forcing us to confront our fears instead of burying them. Acting isn't about rationalizations but about the dead who live inside us. I left my old girlfriends who only could think of nothing but getting pregnant, marriage, and the movie version of the good life without thinking and would be always waiting around for something to happen but never had thoughts of their own, some of them couldn't even leave the neighborhood until the hood burned down around them, and no one of my friends would come downtown to visit I always had to go up to them until I didn't anymore. Leaving home for college was a good excuse. Nobody from the neighborhood did that. Acting is the unifying thread of my life not simply doing but loving and while I did and do it it transforms me. When acting the day has meaning when out of a gig and only working at the bank I have to confront myself and try and give the day meaning, living is more difficult on those days even if all I do is sit in an office and play with my computer it's not the exhilarating tiredness I get from performing, still I throw up before each opening night then I'm okay and when I first started I had to overcome this now the reverse to overcome the inertia of pure working work out on nights that I don't perform to keep my body in shape for those moments and to give myself something to do. Now I have my usual anxieties and go to the bathroom every ten, twenty minutes but at least don't throw up. There was a moment even if I don't know exactly when that I started seeing acting as sacred and if I knew when would bottle it, when all of a sudden everything made sense I was living no longer going through the motions of living waiting for my life to start, instead now I was actually living and was living seriously, when I became liberated from my old friends and the old neighborhood, grandma says I should be happy with this not many people get to experience that especially women in this culture, for them the peak is the marriage or maybe birth of the first child and they are the center of attention for a moment, and go to their grave no smarter than a teenager and are dull, boring until death finally catches up to them and ends their useless babblings but for you it's the everyday you found a profession you can grow in. They erect statues to mothers but who cares that's not for me. It's like when I gave up smoking and started breathing in fresh air, I wondered how could I have tolerated that polluted air so long, a filthy habit. When grandma had her heart attack the doctor lectured her and said he wouldn't treat her if she continued smoking and no longer did I see it as cool. Being an adult wasn't what I thought it would be but now have to admit that the pleasures of childhood don't compare to the freedom of adulthood, the stakes are higher now.

I still have my projects, I want to see Jacoba grown, I still love walking and feeling the sun on my face, still love meeting new people and having discussions with them, listening to music and enjoying Joseph's happiness even as I wish Conchita would have some more, but I understand her and even if it difficult for me to accept her actions I realize she is strug-gling with her freedom, is she deceived by what she's doing or is she the deceiver in leaving her home and family? Joseph insists I continue seeing her but it is difficult public transportation is so difficult and I still feel awkward taking a taxi. We now basically meet for dinner up on the West

Side when the theater is dark. Her life is getting back on course but I still think she is missing something even if she says I can't miss what doesn't exist. You may feel sad for me but that's not me. At least now she does see her daughter but it's difficult to imagine her truism good for all of us, yet when I look at my life from the inside not superficially I did similar things and I didn't miss anything because it was not me I was somewhere else until I learned to lead my life and I have an interesting life, my way, what more could I ask for in that I created my own life not allowed my life to stagnate, maybe I should have worn black the rest of my life and I have powerful memories of him and did wear black metaphorically and still believe in him even if he is dead, he is only physically dead inside my imagination he still lives even if Joseph knows him differently than I know him, yet sometimes wonder, in my despair, would he have recognized me if I had actually gone up to the Bronx and met him. My sufferings are not his he knows nothing about it and I like to keep it that way. You can't experience what you don't have all you can do is feel sad about not having those experiences not having the means of having them and who knows if I would have had them what would have happened because I didn't have them doesn't mean I didn't want them but in not having them lived a different way. Now I want to watch my baby grow up. I didn't see Gloria grow up nor Conchita, Gloria was a nightmare to me and Conchita was a burden when I had already decamped upon my new life but felt obligated to help knowing she couldn't cope on her own. I feel sad I never got back with Gloria but what could I do her values were so senseless that it pained me being around her. She refused to think only looked at the surface of things was only concerned with what others thought of her and was man crazy. She had no inner self. Maybe I should have made the trek to the Bronx but I didn't know he left his wife. How many times did I imagine knocking on his door and wondering what his reaction would be? Would it be discontentment, shock, awe, his bafflement especially as I imagine it when the lights are dim in the hall and he can't recognize who I am, how would I react to that disappointment? Adulthood begins in disappointment when we realize the world is not as we thought it would be. To have seen him one last time except each time I saw him would believe the same thing the last time but each would be only the first in series of last times that never happened and it's in these moments not taken that I regretted yet had to face with strength, courage, not the future anymore but my past, wow, I don't have much of a future anymore and the past is over and done with so all I have is the now but the now is never now always a second or two behind my thoughts, I exist in the moment and have to elevate that feeling it doesn't come naturally, usually I've been unlucky but did get lucky with Jacoba who has opened up my eyes to a wider world. I fought for truth but it was Jacobo who showed me how life participates in its own growth and we have to continue to grow or die it's not a moment but over a long period of moments, continual, constant, that can lead to an estrangement from the past and a struggle to make our way into the unknown picking myself up each time I fell down: a repetition with a variation. Not bad. It ended with Jacobo only he came rushing back into my mind. I didn't want to live without him but you don't die because you don't want to live with somebody unless you do something to help that along, and believe me I thought of it couldn't imagine going on and wanted to eliminate the pain and was bored, indifferent, why I accepted my first husband as a suitor didn't care anymore, he wanted to fuck me let him fuck away I wasn't interested, couldn't care anymore saw no meaning in living only sleepwalking going through the motions thinking maybe it could get me out of my parents' house nothing more not thinking about the future couldn't imagine having one, with the second my marriage the ring was always off. Girl was I scared back then and couldn't think it through, too depressed and imagined Jacobo coming back to Madrid for my funeral, wedding anything, then later coming to America seeing him once more, all nice irrational powerful thoughts that I had in my imaginary conversations with Jacobo prior to my going up to meet him in the hallway of his Bronx apartment but it was never the last until it will be my last. The future was bleak because the present was unbearable when the present became bearable the future became doable when I realized I had to do something with myself, and changing locations was not enough because I carried crazy around with me and more was needed, I wanted a life even if I had no idea then what I wanted and felt homeless in my own home but this was home and here in America felt loneliness but not homelessness, especially now that I can see real homelessness on the streets of New York that remind me of Spain after the civil war, or others of the Great Depression, this time stayed married longer than I should for the *kinder*, Gloria, until she left and I couldn't stand marriage any longer. But I had found my home in the Village and am glad Conchita still has the place, Joseph wouldn't let me give up a rent-controlled apartment said they are too rare we will sublet and now Joseph has put her name on the lease as the granddaughter. Joseph quickly understood the new changes in the law and even if he cut his own throat let us know about how a relative has the right to be on a lease and the landlord can't do anything about it if she lives there two years prior. He insisted that he won't force her home she has the right to her own life, I wish I was as smart as him and he only speaks to Conchita about Jacoba by phone otherwise he has no conversation with her it upsets him too much. He said to me he wants to make this new marriage succeed and knows what his lonely nights were all about and wouldn't wish that on his worst enemy. My talking with Joseph is like my conversing with Jacobo, Conchita exclaimed when we first met Joseph and I mistook him for his grandfather, at least I no longer have solitary conversations with Jacobo as long as Joseph is around. When I first came to this city besides the tall buildings and that Americans drank cold milk instead of warm like in Spain, I was so lonely all I could think about was searching for Jacobo and finding him in the Bronx.

Life is easier when you have someone to love you. Can I quote you? All my bravado going out the window of not wanting to face the truth of loneliness my subtle shifts of thought to evade this. This is the stuff dreams are made of who could have imagined this could happen to me, I certainly couldn't when your down you wonder if you can get up again, I found a woman who loves me, theater, art galleries, concerts has a subscription to the opera, after having stayed home alone so long we go out nights and the beauty is I don't have to go looking, it was only luck that we bumped into each other, I never talk to strangers especially pretty women lest they think the truth I'm trying to chat them up, but she walking by and fell and I helped her up, you fallen for me? and she laughed, but her leg was bruised with gravel and I had my little first aid kit in the stroller and helped clean her up telling her this is going to sting and she laughed iodine no longer stings and she had a strong threshold of pain and she assumed I was safe because I was with a baby, and afterwards said she wanted to keep in touch with me, and I hand her my business card, what else do I need it for except for picking up women. Finally I was a knight in shining armor even if was only in escorting her to the train station, others who had gathered around wanted to call an ambulance but she refused she was only shaken not stirred and more embarrassed for causing so much trouble and my Boy Scout knowledge was enough to put a band aid over it. I could lend her Esmeralda's walking stick she could walk as a gran-dame but I was sure she would refuse. And I didn't even mention my ex. I talk about her too much hi, I's separated, so I definitely didn't bring her up, by the time she left we agreed to meet again, a real live date. Who would have believed it? At first I thought a one shot deal and maybe I can get a little sex out of it, but after our first date knew we would see more of each other and I almost forgot about sex, until Esmeralda told me she would leave if we didn't do it. We had such a nice time at P.S. 1 looking at one painting, we both liked the idea of examining one piece of art only she took notes afterwards instead of seeing wall after wall because then you see nothing, and we both chose a gallery that had fewer people none were empty and I learned the difference between the Apollonian surface and the darker realms of Dionysius and how art can give meaning to life and the obscurity of existence, how painting developed out of these simplistic tropes into a much more complicated affair alogical and nonlinearity instead of only color and perception, where man is caught in the middle having choices not everything is predetermined and our struggle is to become free, that an individual is made up of heredity, his environment, parental upbringing he is not thrown into the world the world is just there, and the fairy tale of heaven and hell, and that it makes sense to scare people with hell so they will behave only if there really was a heaven people there wouldn't be able to stand the sight of people in hell and this must be the same for all art, and she was impressed with my knowledge, only she said communists didn't believe in heaven or hell only in this life and it was miserable enough; a dinner afterwards, nothing more and the next weekend we went to a concert and she loved the idea of continuing our talk how helpless we feel in the modern world that we should do something but feel downtrodden even here in America where one is free and won't be put in jail for your beliefs it's better to keep quiet rather than try and stop homelessness, nuclear proliferation there's no more enemy and they keep building bombs. But I was lucky I say to have been born here not there during the war. Imagine most people in Czechoslovakia have never known freedom because the last time they were a free country was between the crazy wars and most of them have died out, she said, and communists, who wouldn't let you be responsible for your own life and reduced freedom to nil and you are lucky to have been born when things are plentiful even now women can get an abortion or an education, in communism we could get an education but we had to do a double shift work and home and so freedom wasn't work only drudgery; it's not free will but luck of the draw, chance, I said, if you get decent parents, good nutrition, a decent education, you have a chance, yes if you don't live in the Soviet Union or its environs you have a chance. What good is saying that the blows of fortune won't affect the real you when ill health, poverty, or lack of opportunity obviously do. Still I see the effects of economic poverty all around, drugs, homelessness, teenage pregnancy and I am a committed capitalist since it helped me get out of the Bronx even as I realize bureaucratic structures get in the way of fair housing. Insidious governmental policy burnt the Bronx down, landlords made more money collecting insurance than rent in apartment buildings and that is if you could fill them, now we need a vacancy tax otherwise landlords keep empty storefronts off the market waiting for box stores to replace little shops and they can deduct the lost revenue off their taxes, why now around Lincoln Center is practically a mall where all the stores are similar and small shops can't afford the rent. Are you a Republican, she asks? Absolutely the Reagan doctrine brought communism to its knees by opposing them not trying to coexist. A nice talk over a bottle of red wine, that she knew how to order asking the waiter not a maître d' which is the second best wine for the price not simply getting the most expensive. Too bad I wasn't wearing my beret but it was good to be out of my dark suit, colored shirt and bow tie and on a date only I was scared about making the first move but at least I was moved by conversation. Only afterwards did Esmeralda explain that I better have sex with her, women like sex, and I would lose her unless I did something. We stayed together I put my arm around her, she didn't object, and we even stayed together after our first argument where I was ready to bolt only Lilliana said we can disagree but that doesn't mean we can't be together, as long as we attempt to understand one another. It sounded sensible even if I was afraid of another fight and maybe she would withhold love, did your mother do that to you, I don't know, I said, but even if I could remember it I could remember it incorrectly and would need independent corroboration but even if it is false that doesn't make it untrue to my feelings. From that night forward we started doing life together, sometimes on weekdays if I wasn't dead tired, calling every night, and we became a couple, or friends started seeing us as a couple and then you begin to see yourself as a couple—tradition, ritualistic gatherings made us into a couple but we can't count our origins as the only reason we stayed together it was our life together that defined us not our lucky encounter. One day then we decided to make it permanent and went down to City Hall and then walked across the Brooklyn Bridge to celebrate.

Movement is the key to acting, my acting is better not only is it not it also works when it becomes part of me and I become part of something larger and it has to be informed motion not spastic movements but determined, practiced in advance, rehearsed, otherwise it is nothing at all—all acting is locomotion otherwise nothing, dialogue has to be spoken as part of a plan and showing the characters logical developments but words are not all there is in acting, it's the way they are conveyed, the unique ways of speaking that get to the contents of the play their relevance to the whole and what guides the inner life of characters—I never come to the stage to act my part then lead a different life afterwards, before, during and afterwards I am that character, inhabiting her bones so to speak even when I have no more scenes there has to be a full understanding of her roll: She is living the moment, when I was playing Cassandra or Clytemnestra there was the curse but more important was how Clytemnestra was feeling that her daughter was murdered by her husband I kept that right in front of me at all times, the erotic action of the play, her desire for justice and hatred of her husband the gap between heroic virtues and human ambiguity; when an actor grasps the facts her stage appearance alters dramatically and we can only learn about a character from portraying her if we can open ourselves up to her particular dilemma not by being the closed beings we normally are, we play different parts, small, large, but all our characters are directed at the totality of the play. Friends have marveled of how different I am on stage than in life, some have not even recognized me at first, one of my little victories in life. I find it difficult to talk to people who say they never go to the theater. What do they do with their lives? But if the theater doesn't show us our understandings of others, if we can't use dramatic theater to portray life experiences then I agree it's better not to go; there's no reason to go if we don't catch the ambiguities of life not clear concepts, we learn in ways that are good and bad, and the beauty of the theater is crossroads where we can deeply feel moral issues and theater or at least good theater should aim for reflection not only entertainment. Too bad I am not famous enough to be able to turn down roles that make no sense, so I have to make sure every character I play has a moral responsibility for their desires either retaliation or in love, depending upon the situation and I have to get into the mindset so they are not black ciphers or messengers, even if the playwright thinks of them in that way. There is always something going on in my mind but am careful not to let it carry over into the character whose mindset I am trying to inhabit and my character was doing something before she came on stage and is going somewhere else afterwards, the gestalt of the character. Now finally a role that I can bite my teeth into a woman questioning, questioning, questioning but not giving up on life and not only someone confined to the kitchen and children. I always thought you couldn't change the past but now realize if I think about it differently it changes inside my head and when I conceptualize it differently and the past actually does change as I come to the difficult conclusion by seeing facts differently, no longer could I stay married to grandma's lover's grandson. I was happy if she was happy not concerned with my happiness seeing myself through her eyes I lost something of myself something of who I am and I didn't see myself as a person who wanted to continue looking, living, and became this inauthentic individual but acting is about authenticity and had to carry my professional training into my private life, and acting prepared me for anything and that is a good reason why one should undergo acting training to prepare you to think. The stage is a gamble, the gamble that I can convince someone of my point of view but that in itself is no guarantee they will accept it, but I can at least show them a different point of view. The only way I learn is to feel first and if others can feel it maybe they can imagine something different even when they don't agree with the character, I am all my characters and that's when new feelings begin that sometimes makes their ways into our consciousness, we can only grasp a character by her actions and how she acts is how she really is. Why I had to leave, walk out, the written word is unknowable until life is blown into it and it's clarified into a living breathing human being. The old biological theory of vitalism that God blows life into your nostrils may be dead, but in acting the soul runs through your life, life isn't the sum of the parts but the kernel out of which we make ourselves. Now I could have reached this point by accident but then it wouldn't be mine I need to use it, determine it, and growing up has allowed me more freedom to enjoy living not simply sensual pleasure, no late nights, theater after midnight anymore, my body won't allow it now I have to train for a role, exercise, eat right, the stress and anxiety alters the way I sleep so no more smoking and drinking parties, making sure I don't have too much sugar, no more sodas, only milk late at night, I lose too much weight during a performance to let myself go and no longer does my body automatically recover. Maybe that's what growing up is all about to begin to understand your life before it's too late. The first thing I did when I moved back home was to redo the bathroom and shower so I could wipe away all the pollution and with my new electric tea kettle made hot tea and sat down at the kitchen table and said now what. Now that I have left my old life how am I going to start my new and even if spent too much mental energy living that one, the more you spend the more you have, I knew I would have some for the next. I thought, incorrectly that I would immediately get over the old but there is too much back sliding my body couldn't wash it off so quickly I kept telling myself I made a mistake and I should crawl back until I got over this self-indulgence and wanted to go forward not backward, backwards was too painful, everywhere I saw confusion couldn't see what I should do, got a bump in pay on the job said what about a better title, then laughed more money is better, my limitations are great after all I can't work all the time especially when I am in a show, and eventually saw the truth I must be who I am not simply exist as who I pretend to be. My thoughts have expanded from the tension between what I thought I was supposed to do to what I want to do. How wonderful it is to be in a serious play once again and be doing what I want to do, that has been the success of my acting not if some director or producer casts me but that I am in a profound role once again, it's the inner character that counts not what they are saying. Unfortunately too many writers, producers, directors are afraid to look at older women characters with their flawed physical bodies with lust and there are less demand for nude roles, those only go to ingénues. Director say I don't look fifty as if they know what a fifty-year-old woman actually looks like. The beauty of a play is its totality put in another order and you would destroy it.

Why do I get here so early? There not even open yet and I have to wait outside rules are rules as the woman said. I have been spending long periods of time in waiting rooms, my cancer therapy has to be changed there's some growth in my leg has been observed, an infected tooth needed extraction to rid the body of dangerous bacteria an ER visit was made due to a near fatal blood clot in my lungs, other than that I'm in excellent shape. When our brains are out men would die, Macbeth knew it, Shakespeare knew it, I know it, it's no big deal but my body doesn't want to admit it. I have a reason to live and want to see my great-granddaughter grow up the finishing of my project and it is a worthwhile goal even if I will end before my project will and she will be sad about my demise but it will be the natural order, if the reverse occurred I would be devastated, as it is I'm worried about random acts of violence. However if she went to sleep at night and didn't wake up in the morning she wouldn't even know she died only we would and that would be horrible. A couple in one of Joseph's buildings recently poisoned their children then themselves because their debts were too great, they couldn't make the mortgage and couldn't pay tuition at Bank Street and everyone is talking that they shouldn't have killed their children, but to be raised without your parents would have been heartbreaking the parents knew what they were doing and thought it was the correct thing to do. The sadness is the children didn't have a life but what kind of life would they have had being raised by strangers, and they didn't even realize they were going to die, poison was slipped into their food and they went to bed as if were just an ordinary night and they didn't suffer and now won't suffer being dead. There is no moral ought there is simply to be, we are accidents in creation, there is no god above judging or a higher reality and even if you buy into the eye in the sky you still have to look at it from the end point of view, and there is no end point of view except we die, sure I wish those kids would have lived but who would take care of them, love them and not just look after their physical needs, foster care? Nobody adopts foster care boys over two and the boys were eight and ten nobody would have taken them in. Perfect means thou shall not, no excuses, but this is too old of an idea in the modern world—oh we would have all given lip service to the rights of children but they would have had none, we would use our sophisticated vocabulary to come up with some excuse why nobody would take them in and they would become wards of the state, there is no perfect only imperfect individuals. The palliative care nurse told me how many children want to end their parents' suffering with a pillow over their head but can't do it, conscience doth make cowards of us, and the parent continues suffering for no reason, and all the child can say is why did I let them suffer so what good did they derive from suffering so and doctors are afraid of the Law and the law has this slippery slope connection you let one person be euthanized and all of them will be, never that decisions should be made on an individual basis. You have to be prepared, at least now you can have a living will which doctors and emergency rooms don't take seriously but you are a little happier knowing you have made some effort to control your life and if you have a little consciousness left don't have to open your mouth for them to put a tube in. Now at least they opened the doors and I can think my sobering thoughts in an insipid waiting room you have to resist the law and the doctors and the hospital, medicine is becoming more religious not wanting to let people alone even if we don't want anything to do with them and somehow what goes on in our heads are not taken into account. Will I have enough guts to end it when I can no longer lead a life of dignity and become a burden upon those I love, of course, I claim I will, but will I? But then it might be too late and men make decisions and men are good at making decision for others but never for themselves and always want us to hold on as if there's going to be a miracle cure on the horizon, you can't regret your decisions our future is not guaranteed and when it's gone it's over; I wouldn't give up my unhappy days for nothing, I wouldn't change a thing I am responsible for my life even if life is no longer a series of future projects because I might not want to be what I turn out to be all I have is this moment to decide my future now and the future collide as I am not going to do it, and thank the woman but walk out of the doctor's office: no longer will I have treatment to be doing something but do nothing and see what happens; the now has collided with the future in one moment, I can imagine my future, recall my past but I can only act in the now but who knows how I will feel tomorrow—time is spherical not linear depending upon my mood; I can write different autobiographies depending upon how I feel at certain moments, I want my past to change but I can't just change part of me because who knows what would happen if that part changed, would my whole future change as well, and my now is always based on

am doesn't only depend upon my past and even
, obliterate the past I can make adjustments. Yet I still
_y mother's voice inside me I can never completely turn her
, when she died I thought I was free of her but quickly realized her death affected me profoundly, I valued her, understood where she was coming from even if she continually called me an idiot with her superior smirk and her values were so bad that she could never untangle them and each time I think about her I relive my whole life. Heredity not my moving to New York uprooted me. I must not think to hard I start shouting at her and I spent too much energy escaping her influence not to be like her at least with Jacobo I had moments of freedom—one moment of freedom in a previous lifetime of drudgery allowed me to continue, but at least I had that how many people can even say that. How many only think of physical pleasures as being free not being with someone you love. Even if Conchita thought this was my second marriage I know the difference. There is a momentary pleasure in getting up not waiting for the radiologist and deciding upon freedom but will it last. No longer will I have to wait for doctor's who are never ready for you and no longer can I even read in these waiting rooms but I do like these MP3 players it makes waiting easier. And if I were real cool now would die my hair blue, that sounds better than getting my body radiated or even tattoos all over my body. Tattoos look disgusting but I admire the women who do it who can mark themselves not let themselves be marked by a man, no matter how exhausted I am I will walk downtown in the park, the sun feels good, a warm winter's day, and at least I am liberated from doctors, will not go to them anymore.

How come I only have one talent in life making money? Can't I do more? Granted I'm good at that but so what, can't I do more. But what? It's crazy I understand all those legal regulations on housing how they intersect upon color, and the covert meanings, which of course are not too difficult to grasp, keep the poor, read Latino and Afro-Americans in their assigned place and not let them leave the ghetto: like the law you can't have a criminal record to get a loan, and the police patrol ghettos so they're sure to catch some kid, a law that sounds good but is designed to lock out the poor from the good society, so they can't own and can't find a job, the new Jim Crow. Stop-and-frisk policing can now stop anyone— read a young poor person on a hunch for what looks like a crime in their professional opinion, that is only a guess, not that they've seen something which is now called racial profiling no matter how they disguise it, and it becomes a crime on their professional rap sheet. Sometimes we can steer around it if banks don't redline and are willing to give people a second chance, and I have to admit broken windows did get crack dealers off the street and back into apartments, so the streets are safer. My basic technique is to put the mortgage in a woman's name, only now more of them are getting stopped, equal opportunity; and sometimes men don't like to think they are dependent upon a woman, for them we tell the banks upfront, they are going to find out anyway, and I bring him them to the interview, I let them see him as a human being and banks and co-op boards are usually willing to give people a second chance. Unfortunately too many poor families are usually run by matrilineal elderly women and these grandmothers are crucial in the raising of children while the daughter works and that presents difficulties, but I'm good at getting around these regulations, here I can see myself as whole not a fragmented self. But I want more? What? Do I just want to help individuals suffering from discrimination like sitting in a tragic play sympathizing with the hero without condemning the society that creates it? they're so concerned with status, power, wealth why be worried about them except the playwright tricks you into manipulating your compassion. Last night I was chatting with Lilliana and Cassie came out of my mouth, where did that come from, I wasn't thinking about her, not that I don't, and Lilliana asked if I think about her a lot and I lied and said no, sometimes, but I didn't know where that came from, didn't bother to tell her that I write letters to her in my head, she is my witness, tell her about my day, a nice activity I have as I'm about to fall asleep, or if I awake in the middle of the night, but at that precise moment hadn't been thinking about her and had no thought of her, and was embarrassed by my revelation, at least it wasn't my last words which would hurt Lilliana or while I was making love to her and I've told Esmeralda to put a pillow over my head in the hospital if I am about to say her granddaughter's name. She has that ability she could catch Jacoba scrunching her brow, pursing her lips, and knew exactly when she was going to crap before she did. All I can think is that a few days before I ran into Conchita's acting friends who I had once told about the school that Jacoba goes and she was waving to me on the street and said what's the matter didn't you see me waving, yes but beautiful actresses don't usually wave at me, and she thanked me profusely really loves the school, but this time she totally ignores me, and I wondered why. Can this be the reason I thought of Cassandra? Why must I always be hearing these different voices not only different but struggling to escape when I have someone to love me. She said she would support me only she can barely support herself. And no matter what I am not going to cheat on her I know how much that hurts and won't do that to another person and meaningless encounters are it's only a blow job Cassandra said, it made perfect sense to her but it hurt. If I don't continue to work, I will do something else but will not harm another. So far it's been lovely coming home and having a home cooked meal, glass of wine and nice conversation, Esmeralda even gave us a candelabra as a wedding gift and we light candles and even have fresh cut flowers. I can ask for nothing more yet am still dissatisfied. I never mentally write Cassandra while facing Lilliana it's only when I'm on my side of the bed, or if I'm sleeping alone that night, that I compose my masterpiece, it relaxes me and I gently fall asleep. From now on when she crosses my mind late at night I will go into my lists of '50s Giants baseball players, basketball players, all New York City baseball teams, all black New York City teams, boy do I have lists up the kazoo and maybe they'll help me fall asleep, at least I still sleep through the night it's rare that I awaken and usually because I am cold, that's the only fight we have she loves to sleep with open windows but now I have a down quilt and two thick blankets for weight and am usually okay but if I do awaken start writing on colored paper, different colors for different nights, my favorite is when I wrote in colored pencils—all that I imagine I must have had in childhood except there is no one left I can ask. Now that I want to ask crucial questions where is everybody. I do remember my grandfather having a cheapo fountain pen and refilling it and I did recognize that five-and-dime pen in one of my dreams, but I wasn't sure if I was fully asleep or trying to get to sleep and then totally forgot about it in the morning only to continue the dream the next night. I wonder what ever happened to the pen? Is it my subconscious talking to me, if so, why in riddles I'm a big boy say it straight out not in my fragmented selves. I don't even have to drop acid if only I could understand what's going on. When I actually do try and get my thoughts on paper they come out so banal, so full of clichés, narrative storytelling that I can barely reread before throwing them in the circular file. Yet I think my thinking thoughts so profound but I can never put them down on paper if I could I could become a playwright writing insipid dramas but at least not being shot at by war mongers. These guys are crazy another war this time with Iraq, albeit a short one maybe it will solve problems and not be a cause for rage, but now we have troops in the Middle East and that can only lead to more wars. Cassandra can star in one of my plays? That would be a kicker: Have her cry and moan how she lost the love of her life in war, I like it better than saying I want to be free. I better not become a playwright writing humdrum tragedies based on Cassandra leaving me, the whimpering individual not the tragic hero, typical human loneliness attempting to be on a dramatic plane.

Do I know anything for sure? What have I learned in my long life? I know I exist and each time I think of myself I am having a conscious experience know that most of the time I am not even aware of my existence I just am and am not even aware of the experience. It's like when I meet people on the street and haven't the slightest idea who they are, or when walking with Jacoba and I tell her look at that glorious sunset even if she looks and hasn't a clue what I'm talking about but I tell her wait until you've grown you will begin to appreciate walking just before sunrise, I remember doing that and liking watching the sun come up and bring to life all that was around before even the light of day was light then you didn't have to look out for the other guy, but now can't get up that early in the morning anymore no matter how hard I try, and again crime is down so it's safe for a woman to walk the city streets again at all hours. Rarely did Conchita and now Jacoba notice their physical surroundings, I had to point it out to them they are so engrossed in their own thought and what I like seeing is the beauty of the sky, the rustle of the trees, the shadows formed by the sun, the loud noises of the police cars, fire trucks, or ambulances that interrupt my revels and now the backup beep of trucks that interfere with nature. Joseph refuses to allow Jacoba to put her hands over her ears as a train pulls into a station tells her that's not what New Yorkers do only out-of-towners, New Yorkers are accustomed to loud noise of garbage trucks grinding away, buses idling and sirens never stopping and we pay it no mind, not a hundred percent true it all plays into our imagination as we walk the city streets and all I know is that sensation of thought comes from the outer stimulus, I tell Jacoba pay attention walk don't think, she can forget to look when crossing the street and luckily she has quick enough reflexes, I no longer can count on them and while walking in the sun, moon or nighttime sky, which is important in my life, I have to be aware and can't become too engrossed in nature and now see nature only secondarily as my mind is always looking around me even if what's going on in my head is what counts the environment is important but now I am becoming more like Conchita who always walked in a different time and never truly saw what nature had to offer, she was always an alienated soul like New Yorkers who don't go to the theater but say I'll see it when it comes out on television as if they're making a profound statement instead of leading the wasted lives they lead that never confronts itself. The most they'll do is go to movies and consider it cultural event but you can go to movies in Buffalo, Detroit, Oshkosh, the only place you can see serious theater is the city see works that you have to wrestle with not that dumbs you down or you go on date night, in the past you would 'dress' for the theater not wear a new pair of blue jeans, but something special, new blue jeans are nothing special, it was dressing up not an ordinary experience, not like going to the movies or staying home and watching television. Danielle was that way, never wanted to dress up, and I liked her but I could never get her out of her ways, I should give her a ring but it's so difficult talking to her she acts as if she knows who I am but she doesn't remember me or Joseph. Joseph when he goes into clients' homes likes to see if they have books and how they're shelved if all the same size he says book club, if no books wonders if he can deal with them, how can you have conversations with those who mouth clichés he asks because they've given up on learning only interested in relaxation as if the mind isn't a muscle that you should use. How absurd some people are think themselves happy or unhappy when all they really are is content—but why should I let that be my definition of happiness. Now I have to worry about this not so new urban architecture where there are no places to sit, covered in metal so kids won't hang out but that means I have no place to rest, thank goodness Joseph bought me a stool cane, light, but at first I didn't want to use it I liked my walking stick but now have to if I am going far and I have to plan my walks more carefully can't just walk and avoid red lights because if I don't have my stool can't stop and rest my legs. On the benches now I am a familiar face and I love feeling the sun on my cheeks even as tell myself there is more to life than mere sensation, pleasant as it may be and except for my physical deterioration I'm okay. Except for that! I have enjoyed aging never had the desire to be young again not that I truly could get my emotions under control but they didn't dominate my life, sure I liked looking and random encounters but at least didn't have to deal with AIDS, as Conchita says the fear of AIDS has made her a puritan. No more crazy sex that usually makes me feel young especially after we realized AIDS is passed only through semen it has really done a number on the acting community at least I'm not afraid of touching them and hugging them especially as they needed the warmth, even as Joseph pulled away from me after I touched them. Ah here comes a security officer who's going to tell me I can't sit here even if I speak Spanish to him but I did get some relief and still have upper body strength so I'm not stuck in a chair, and it's only a block to the park and I can make it to where there are benches and can rest my weary bones. As my bones become weary I start thinking about myth not because I believe in the eternal sky but sometimes the only explanation for a fact over time is myth, it works they can describe life experiences better than words ever can. Some lives are cursed, can that be, so much confusion in my thought even as I try and make myself clear that life is meaningless in itself we have to give it some purpose, but I like to begin with experience before going on to purpose—Jacoba is doing well in school again which should give her a good foundation if she can go on and realize what she learns has to be applied to her life and draw on her consciousness and not let it fade away, but if I go on from that thought become perplexed how the thought we experienced are acquired as if that's the only answer and we can change the thought once acquired like acquired traits, first I felt then learned to think tried to distinguish truth from belief but always wanting more, never satisfied; now I know only two things: I won't be a burden and would like to leave something to Conchita and Jacoba, my girls. When Gloria left I didn't feel a sense of failure as I do now growing old and walking in the silence of winter, luckily not a bitter cold day but a typical New York winter's day gray and overcast with only occasional snatches of sunlight on my face, which gives me warmth. Tomas didn't understand how relieved I felt with her out of the house and he couldn't forgive me for not going to visit her and to have heard from his new wife that he died has hurt me more than I realized I thought I was over him— loving was more important than living and I wonder if he died realizing that and when you can no longer love it's time to split and I wanted out and did it then it became my turn to figure out how I wanted to live my life instead of just going through the motions we women are able to do this easier than men because we have access to our emotions and they're not blocked by false images of progress, science and technology: I'm glad now men are beginning to see the way not covering up their ways but admitting their insecurities. Why I like good theater one becomes aware of something else not only the tragedy they represent but how one should live.

The planes came and went leaving destruction in its wake nobody knew how to deal with martyrs, I wasn't hurt only scared because I listened to grandma inside my head, how did this gray matter turn into a brain, I don't even know if she actually said it or not but I thought she would have said it or something like that, listened and got the hell out of the building even as loudspeakers were saying stay everything is under control, I knew that line, come on baby show me you love me and I didn't fall for it, or as Joseph says I have a brain and it allows me to think so I can be both miserable and happy at the same time, walked down the stairs in the dark, pure chance I took a staircase that was working and got out of the Trade Center before it collapsed, saw the smoke and fumes rising and walked and walked, couldn't use my cell, trains and busses weren't working wasn't sure what to do not a far walk to my home, stopped into a store and bought a pair of sneakers, forgot to take mine from the desk and just walked and walked trying to avoid the smoke, I wasn't alone thousands rushed away but those poor souls trapped and then I heard about the thumping nobody knew what it was at first and later bodies jumping off the roof because they were trapped, some colleagues, I had to go to funerals, but I walked up to Joseph's place, Liliana greeted me, she too had walked up we huddled around the television as Jacoba could walk home by herself, she's off to college next year so now we are looking at colleges and I've told her I'll break her neck if she drops out, grandma came upstairs and started cooking and we all ate together that night, lit a candle in the window that night for no particular reason, but no one wanted to be alone that night. I know I was happier being with them and could prove it but when I went home to an empty apartment felt depressed, needed to be with others, nonsense I said only I felt this emptiness inside and even if he has remarried we are still one, and I thought better to be with them then be by myself and when the phone worked called his office he was clever enough to leave a message on his machine saying he was going home and I decided to join him, also the smoke and fumes were making their way uptown. As I walked wondered how he could do this to me? selfish me, him getting married not even thinking about me. Fascinating how I could hold onto two thoughts simultaneously, I do and don't, and I was serious: I do want him to be happy and am depressed because he is happy, I want to be happy but living with a man will not make me happy, I want to have someone to come home to but that won't help me, maybe I'm not meant for happiness even as my art is flourishing, how can I be happy if I'm getting what I want and still am unhappy? I couldn't get much deeper in my thoughts the streets were so crowded everybody walking uptown because subways and busses were not working and I was surprised about how many young people had no idea how to get out of the city because all they knew were subways and busses and I had to give directions to the bridges to the Bronx, Brooklyn or Queens, forget it to Jersey or the burbs nothing was leaving the city and luckily I was in good shape so could walk but that night needed a good stiff drink. This wasn't the time for ordinary thinking, and we all needed something to lift our spirits, Jacoba explained that the teachers asked if our parents worked in the World Trade Center and she said I did, and the teacher called her into a special room and told them a plane had hit the building but that people were alright by then Joseph had called the school and told them to tell her I was okay but they never relayed the message and she was worried stiff until I came. It was difficult for him to get there as well and grandma could no longer walk that far but she could walk home and is alright now with all of us still nobody can believe what happened and they keep showing the buildings falling down over and over until we shut the set off in disgust. Lilliana insists I stay the night and truly now I want to be by myself but can't fathom going downtown on a night like this, and agree but stay awake in bed that night thinking I have to continue to fight my complacency and fight myself and not give in, and let this be a wake-up call that all is not given and it can be taken away at a moment's notice. No one act can define a life if I am who I actually say I am I have to fight for it I can't burn all my bridges so I don't fall back but it's so easy to slide back into the old ways and the next morning receive a phone call from my boss and we are now on an old-fashioned phone tree to find out who is alive and who isn't and we are told nobody will lose pay because of the incident. Incident it was an act of revenge. I became nauseous once more, and now it wasn't even for a play, who knew the shape of the theater, and if the play would continue; now is no time for doing art. But art is needed now more than ever, no repetition each performance brand new even as I mouth the same words nightly my thoughts connected to the words are different and I can really feel alive on stage—sacredness takes over. I want to get back on stage and to stop feeling sorry for myself, some families have it a lot worse right now loved ones perished: go to work one morning and don't come home that night. Going back home the next day I tried to get it under control, get thee behind me Satan. I am a real coward and have to fight for every little thing but I won't say any Hail Mary's or ask her to intercede no White Beard can save anybody, this event has to be the death knell of god. How could a god let this happen? Can it be undone? We have to stand on our own two feet not be saved by an unknown power. Nothing to be done and I walked home, the streets are eerily silent, yesterday walking up here we saw some airplanes up above and everybody looked thinking we were under attack only to find out later they were our planes protecting us, except nobody told us and we were all scared. It would take a couple of days for the streets to get back to quasi-normal but I said to myself now I should try and have a life, one drink didn't let me think that but it started me in a new way of thinking that I was glad he was happy and wasn't going to interfere, I thought I had to work the next day without thinking where was I to work and I checked in with our theater people but as of yet nobody knew anything and tiredness of my daily life today didn't tire me as I wondered what would happen next. Now at least I can make out clearly what I want, no more of the 9 to 5 only acting is what counts, except I got just what I didn't want acting got postponed because nobody was in the mood for theater and many off-off-Broadway theaters were too close to the rubble, and work resumed pretty quickly and everybody had time off for funerals of those that didn't make it. I would have survived anyway it was only the people on the higher floors that perished most on the lower were able to get down and leave the buildings in time. What I couldn't make out clearly is what do I want after this. You'd think it would be easy, I had made up my mind to leave work and now here I am back at the job not wanting to be alone and waiting for the theater to start up again, as usual half-assed do I make my way thought life and don't know where I belong, disliking this new pay grade where I never get a chance to finish my own projects and always getting new ones, usually then a bottle of red helps. That Y2K was quite a mess luckily we were able to fix it for twenty years and by then I'll be outta here safely retired. Okay I won't be too hard on myself I survived and I don't have to do this but you are so you want to do this and if I'm wrong at least I'm living so have another chance not simply am no more, there are no shortcuts the only way to do that is to do this and I shouldn't be ashamed how I live my life because when it works it's beautiful, my idea is to keep up those moments that can't be kept up forever, if I don't attempt all I will have are regrets—why do I always picture a death scene conversation and me saying at the last moment I led my life the way I wanted to, when all those people died without a final farewell or even a moment's consciousness did they know they were dying. I guess those jumping off the roof did. What were they thinking? There'll be no last act only everyday scenes besides who's going to hear my final wishes. Probably Joseph will be burdened with that or Jacoba if I live long enough. If only I could be the same person I was when I walked home after 9/11 then I was sure but now I know as usual the best isn't yet to come and have no reason to believe that, and I'm not the same person tomorrow as I am today when I knew I'd have a doozy of a hangover if I didn't stop drinking and flushed my last drink down the kitchen sink—only liquor stores were quickly opened the next day, I knew I had reached my limit if I wanted to act that night and still hadn't realized there would be no theater for a while. It's only in thinking that I can get a grip upon myself not the stories I lie to myself about and now is see myself the I who embodies who I am and as I can think can continue. I will not go on as before. The clouds are low I can't even see the moon because the dust is everywhere I know the moon is out there because I saw it the night before the incident but now can't see a thing, I feel just like when I moved in and tried looking out the window and couldn't see a thing angry at my mother for abandoning me so but trying to convince myself that I can't be angry at her she didn't choose to be shot, but she did choose to go out with hooligans. Finally I convinced grandma to hire someone to wash the windows so she wouldn't have to climb outside and sit on the windowsill and do them. Only in solitude can I talk like this and smash my thoughts especially to myself, I hate when that happens and it happens too much and it scares me when my mind is full of false ideas and I can't have one honest thought, which can get me on my way to others, but that only happens when I recognize it and not let it elude me, and again I can begin to recognize who I am who's always running away from herself and can laugh at myself trying to live authentically especially when I talk falsely to myself. I have to stand my ground because dishonesty always tries to sneak back in.

Maybe I should have kept a journal all these years but I wouldn't want the girls to see the kind life I led but why not the truth couldn't hurt but probably they'd have a different perception of me and not only see me as a grand- and great-grandmother but as an individual a human being with wishes and desires of her own, what would I say? Only one thing that I was loved and glad to love and he changed my life so in just meeting me and I had someone to be with me all my life. Or would I simply not say what is most important fill my journal with my daily nothings. There hasn't been a day gone that I haven't thought of him even after I promised myself not too, not only was he my lover but my best friend and all my conversations were with him, or when I couldn't fall asleep he would come to me and put his arms around me, of course, it's easy to love him he was never there never that real, I was most always in love with him, I had the most joy with him, there were others and I lived with them but he was the phantom figure, a shadow inside my creative imagination, that kept me from them, not he who was a flesh-and-blood individual because I did have difficulties with real flesh and blood after having been with him so long, for all of eighteen months but what an eighteen months it was my lifetime education rolled into a love affair. He had to leave go back we were defeated but he could have stayed only his wife called and I knew he would just didn't want to believe it but simultaneously enjoyed the last moments and made that moment last as long as it did until he boarded the *Polyphemus* at the twenty-minute warning and then I let it sink in he would be gone forever and my life is over in twenty minutes even if live another fifty years, and I was correct even if I lived another seventy years I was wrong lived longer than I imagined, and became a woman after the moment he boarded the *Polyphemus*—that was the moment of transition from young girl to widow it even dawned on me to wear black, which I have around my soul but it allowed me to see my life in perspective and I overcame my family, my country, my prejudices and to wallow in freedom even if I first had to go back home, I knew that was temporary and also knew I was going to leave Spain, it was the Second War that made me come here not Paris—that's what I initially dreamed to be free in Paris but not occupied Paris, and send for Jacobo imagining the joy on his face when we had a nest in Paris, I would have it all set up an apartment where he would join me as if we never parted and if I remember correct I had no doubts that he wouldn't come. When that dream failed I refused to flee from my life and knew I would come here somehow and America did bring freedom into my eyes, there's no better place to start over than America to break with the old ways, I remember seeing the Statue of Liberty in the harbor one of my key memories, too bad nowadays immigrants come in by plane and are greeted by a cold reception room, maybe they should put up a replica of the Statue at least as a photograph, framed, spacing like a surrealist montage that would give them a sign of hope, I felt as if I finally made it and my studying English paid off—knowing the language allowed me to adapt quit quickly and I didn't have to start from scratch, and I didn't live among the Spanish, later the neighborhood changed around me, but first it was the Eastern Europeans and we all improved our English together, the Spanish refugees only talked of going home I had a home but had no intention of going back to it, besides the Generalissimo never was going to die and they wasted their lives waiting for him to die. I did not want that to be me I wanted to continue living imaging I could now have a life and in that loneliness became who I am now and even with all my failures and back sliding wouldn't trade places with anyone I managed to stay alive and recreated myself even if it wasn't with Jacobo in paradise and even as I always wondered if I would bump into him and he would return. Sometimes I wondered if a creature of the Book would have enough guts to live by his instincts could he have violated the blood purity, or would have left again. Those moments were fleeting I rather go back to the moments of pleasure they are more tinged with meaning not the defeats I would have suffered, the defeats were only temporary setbacks; if you live long enough you can see beyond the moment and not everything is total despair the way I felt when I gave up upon myself even as now I realize they won't let me go and wonder how to end it even if I don't have the guts to climb up on to a chair and end it, I still walk even if I have difficulty, ah what our bodies do to us, but

.onger can I walk uptown/downtown, but I
.aily even up little slopes and refuse to allow Joseph
.er I can walk up steps and the doctor said that's good for
.ut what I miss in life is good conversation, after Jacobo none
good enough for me to have truly intelligent conversations with,
.ven if Conchita and Joseph and now Lilliana try they are too young
and always saw me as an old lady not an equal for friendship and in
friendship you need equals and Jacobo was greater than all the equals.
Silly goose. How many times have I told myself enough, enough no more
talking about him or thinking about him but then what would I think
about, who knows but my thoughts always meander back it's comforting
like Conchita's teddy bear that Gloria washed because it was filthy and
destroyed it and she was heartbroken for days. She doesn't remember it
and Gloria never took her feelings seriously but now whenever I get
Jacoba a gift I buy two of them just in case. Conchita says it's a waste of
money but I waste money in other ways why not make sure she's happy. I
still see the future, I'm planning Jacoba's graduation I have been privileged
to see her grow up, and I feel depressed if I don't see her at least once a
day and being with her does cheer me up even if she now likes to leave
before breakfast and gets home so late I insist she have breakfast with
me, I doubt if I'll have any more lovers, how long have I been celibate?
I must be all dried up unless the Dybbuk comes to me at night. If he
does, I hope he looks like Jacobo. I'm more Jewish than him he hated
such nonsense called it myth, superstitions from the past, and so did I,
but now that I'm older start to see religion as attempts at truth, sick of
the myth of the isolated individual we are not isolated but interrelated,
we are all Dionysians now, go figure, age plays physical tricks upon my
mind just like noon when the shadows are small.

I'm almost of age now, even if my family still treats me like a baby
and I can't wait to get away, not to be beholden to them, not to be
like them, to be free of them, I've applied to early admission so I know
that I will be out of here, used my mother's address, zip code, since no
picture is permitted they will think of me as Hispanic, I know where
I'm going, and want to know what it's like to be free of them, I want
to get married and stay married, I've already lost it, all the girls have,
we don't want to go to college as virgins but we know the difference
between sex and having a litany of men around and half brothers and

sisters. What appalls me is not knowing who you are going home with at night, to come home every night to a strange lover—wouldn't you blurt out the wrong name? It is safer to be on the straight and narrow then to go off on tangents like my parents did, all three of them. When Esmeralda came to school of grandparents' day she surprised them all by refusing the elevator and walking up the stairs and I was huffing and puffing walking up those five flights and she lit into me that I have to start exercising before I got too fat, she was always the one who insisted I do sports, she said too many women sacrificed a lot so young girls could be more than cheerleaders blah, blah, I told her I rather do schoolwork and get into a good college and I get no pleasure in running after a ball that I kicked, I'm smart school is easy and I can take advantage of my middle name, schools want minority kids now, and I plan on taking advantage of it, the better you do the more opportunities will open up for you later. *Mimi* dominated the room with her discussion of the Spanish Civil War, which the history teacher never heard of, saying it was the first battle against Fascism, and the Western Powers refused to help and Franco won paving the way for the dictators Hitler and Stalin. Personal stories are always the most moving they make history come alive, the teacher said and *Mimi* told a good story about how the people rose up but were defeated by men with better equipment and supplies not ideas but once the idea of freedom was understood it couldn't be squandered and it went underground until Franco died. She says women have more freedom than ever and men have more freedom then ever but you have to use your freedom. She spoke in perfect English with no trace of her Hispanic accent and really did hypnotize the class, one girl even came up to me afterwards and said I wish I had a grandparent like yours but she had no grandparents. Mom doesn't buy that but Lilliana does she wanted me to go to Stuyvesant rather than LaGuardia not because Stuy is better Music and Art is more creative but it's more important to get a good education, education and good habits are important, besides dad didn't like the new building says it has no soul compared to his school the one near City College, that was fine by me I got into all the special schools but went to Stuy because of the better education even if there acting is piss poor compared to LaGuardia I saw what those guys produce and what we produce but my mom wanted me to go to Music and Art, she still calls it by its old name, you can't begin too early to have an artistic education and those who begin late are always behind but I wanted a good foundation my *Mimi* impressed me no doubt about that, she said I should learn how to write critically, think, be flexible the difference between most people is not innate skill but education, I couldn't understand how they could have a big fight over girls getting an education as if girls aren't as smart as boys, then I will then drop out the second half of my senior year to show them I don't need college. She always liked that name because that is what she called her grandmother and wanted to respect her. She expects me to leave and go away to college and so does my father who never went away and says that was the worst mistake of his college career, says it's a good experience, I don't want the experience I want to be out of here. My mom is afraid all I'll do is party, but I'm not like her, she thinks I'm too young for this, I'll show her. I still remember the first play she insisted I go to she was in the cast 8th grade my mother was practically nude on stage and she's raped as a thirteen-year-old and bites the penis of her rapist but is afraid to tell anyone what happened. I still shudder when I think of that nudity and simulated rape scene, but she says as a play this is fantastic but unfortunately in real life it is horrible, and she tells me she knows the playwright that's why it's so difficult to act it but she wanted me to see some real good theater before I went to high school. Afterwards we went out to eat and I almost thought for a second my mother and father would get back together they were so nice to each other, and I had a hot chocolate with whipped cream and cookies, I still don't like coffee even though I promised myself that this year I would learn to like it for college and my trips abroad where I will sit in cafés, and there you have to drink coffee. Even now when I go out with my girlfriends or even boys I'm in charge of cafés because I know the places my parents took me, and one of the girls has even taken drivers ed. and has access to a car so maybe I'll be free of that, why do you need to drive in the city? At sixteen she got a car from her parents but it's almost impossible to drive into the city parking is difficult even going the opposite way of traffic but there is no opposite way of traffic cars are everywhere. My father doesn't even own a car says it's impossible in the city and says we'll rent only we never do. He says he will drive me down to my college we'll take a road trip down south. College will be fun to be on my own and not have to tell people where I'm going or when I'll be back, when to eat dinner, what to eat, the freedom from them is the best thing about college and it's far enough away I can't come home on weekends. My step mom loves Saratoga says it has a great theater program but it's too close and I told her I want to go far far away, she laughs but she supported me and helped me find Hendrix College, a strong liberal arts college near New Orleans, says I have to be near a city otherwise I'll go crazy in a small town, and it's an easy forty-five-minute bus ride in, I usually don't trust elder's advice that they never followed all I know is I don't want to be like them. And believe me I'm not. I have my own ideas and own dreams and I'm not going to follow theirs. My best friend, Kate, a year older, says college is nothing compared to Stuy. She says because I can read and write college will be a snap. They worked us much harder in Stuy they didn't even let up the last semester and they do fail seniors. Laura another friend couldn't breathe after high school and took her freshman year off to travel, my father was against it but Lilliana thought it was okay sometimes kids need a break, but my father is always worried then they won't go back, travel after you graduate, he says. He wants me to do junior year abroad so he can come visit. Dad wishes he had done that but nobody encouraged him but everybody is encouraging me. I want to go to Spain and am working on improving my Spanish, still angry at *Mimi* for not speaking to me in Spanish I could have been bilingual and had an easier time in Spanish classes but nobody else in the family spoke it but so what. She knows nobody there anymore but I want to see her culture and where she came from, she has broken completely with her culture and her roots but I think they're important to reconnect to. This is the new part of what I like being a senior is getting off a couple of stops before and walking all by myself along the Hudson to the school, no adults are out now and hardly a soul except for a few joggers and it allows my thoughts to come alive dreaming about next year before going to school, I learned that from *Mimi* who always walks and thinks and my mother likes to do that as well before a performance. My friends have never been to the theater, some to a Broadway show, others to Lincoln Center but none has ever gone downtown to an off-off and my mother wants to know how you can even talk to people who've never been to live theater, don't read books only know television or the media that reeks of mediocrity, go to art galleries or concerts, and if you don't go you will never have a taste for real thought, it's only theater that allows you to know what's going on otherwise it's one crisis after another, we are condemned to life, grandma says, not to live outside life but to live in it, she says, even if it's dreadful we are forced to be free.

It's all been done with mirrors, how did I do it? I didn't. She grew up by herself and now she's off to college. Will she sit at some professor's feet can she even sit still? So many kids are now so over-specialized that I haven't the slightest idea what they're rambling about and they're in such debt they don't have time to mess around they have to become serious so quickly—four more years then I can stop, my wife says you can only talk to artists, stop it, she's not my wife, only my first wife a polyamorous child murderer, with me on the losing end, of course I love you, you piece of shit, but the fragmentation of knowledge is serious now and I hope Jacoba doesn't become too technical and not have the ability to adapt to changing times, there's so much knowledge now nobody can grasp it all and you still have to live and college doesn't teach that, life isn't all about the job. Tell that to my daughter who at eighteen thinks she knows it all, hopefully she can unlearn in college or am I putting too much emphasis on school. It takes time. But at these prices I want instantaneous results. Yet we all insist she should go thinking that if we don't we haven't done our duty as parents, and even Lilliana insists upon helping saying even if I am not her mother, she has told me so a million times, still it would be wrong if she didn't get an education, and anything she gets there will be helpful but it's more important she get away from us and learn at her own pace. We still always talk about her even if she's gone and now she has our total attention more so than when she lived here. We wander ever upwards until the sun clips our wings and we come crashing down, our little white legs sticking up, and we can only hope we did a good enough job as parents that they don't fall flat on their face and can't get up again but land with a thud and pick themselves up and go forward no matter what curves life throws at them. Cassie told her this is your chance in life to shine make the most of it, but Jacoba doesn't feel this is her last chance, one thing good about education is it gives you a 2nd, 3rd and 4th chance, and America is full of last chances especially after you have some wine in you not like Europe or the former Soviet Union where they can hurt you so badly you can't even rise and only mute silence, violence, wins, a remembrance leading to a pain so powerful it is still difficult to talk about and it's better left unsaid and let amnesia set in. Being around those who suffered so much has at least taught me that, soldiers can relive their fears, horrors, friendship, victims cannot. I can even meet my old high school buddies for a moment at least before we go our separate ways but those who truly suffered cannot even talk about it, it only comes out in drips and drabs how many Holocaust survivors did I meet who would never say a word about their experiences and Lilliana's friends who suffered in the Russian prison camps still can't talk about it at least death will be the end of their suffering, a day laborer in the underworld is much better than survivor's guilt, and each time I meet them realize how lucky I was to be born on this side of the Atlantic, *avuelo* never could talk about his experiences, maybe I was too young, but Zoltan never did either nor could the neighbor who lived in our old apartment house who had a number on her arm, she even wore long sleeve blouses even on the hottest days and when I saw it once and asked she said when you're older you'll understand, I never understood how people could be so cruel, and she was our next door neighbor who lent us her apartment to make a party at my Bar Mitzvah when we couldn't afford to rent a hall, which I didn't even understand what they were talking about a hall, couldn't they just use the lobby, and what was supposed to be a happy time I found her crying she was thinking of her son lost in the war. I gave into the family pressure *avuelo* asked me, if it wasn't for *avuelo* never would have had it, wouldn't have said all right I'll do it, certainly not for the gifts, there were no gifts back in the day only money which my parents always had their hand out because they knew I would lose it and put it in a bank account for me, big deal I wanted gifts, and when a cousin a few years later had a Bar Mitzvah was going to buy him a baseball glove, something I dearly wanted for mine, the family talked me out of it saying you only give money, however a few years after that when he married I had graduated college and didn't give in to family pressure and instead of giving him money bought him an original work of art. Not bad for a twenty-something, I thought then finally standing up to the family. He promptly gave it to his parents I saw it hanging in their place he had no use for art. But when friends married continued that tradition and they loved it because that was the only art work they had in their first apartment. But Fanny, our neighbor, was the only one I knew who took in borders, I had heard about that during the Great Depression, but she needed company more than the money, but during my Bar Mitzvah we moved all her living room furniture into his room and shut the doors and opened up the doors between her bedroom and the living room and had this huge space for our small family. Even my grandfather showed up he usually would be no where my grandmother was only to be buried next to her for eternity. And all the money I received my mother held out her hand for my college education. Afterwards my grandmother bought me a baseball glove, my prize possession until my mother threw out all my prize possessions. Zoltan gave me a painting not of the Torah portion that I read for my Bar Mitzvah but from the *Book of Job,* the eternal wandering Jew who is not Jewish nor eternal, that is the first painting I ever owned and still keep it hung up, my mother displayed it in the living room so company would think we were so cultured. The only books we had were in my *avuelo's* room my mother didn't like books cluttering up the living room. I didn't take the painting when I moved out but when I cleaned out the apartment got rid of all the furniture and old photographs unnamed and undated, but kept the painting and hung it in the living room and also kept my grandfather's ebony and white chess set that he taught me chess on, his inscribed copy of *Hamlet* from his friend Eric Clayton that he had read in the trenches, even his Telefunken radio was discarded. However my comics, basketball, toys, and other paraphernalia were all gone when I emptied my childhood home. How dare she. Otherwise I wanted nothing from the past. I can't look back at my childhood without anguish I hope my daughter will not be the same way. She is out of the house now still doesn't realize it's not temporary because she comes back on holidays but if education is to be a success she will want to find her way not live at home again, and if she wants to go to graduate school will work a few more years otherwise I'm history.

Life is difficult and my life is not for everybody but I wouldn't change a thing, even if I miss not raising Jacoba and it's depressing now that she's gone, she tried to pick the place that is the furthest from here but also made sure to choose a place she knew she would be accepted, and at least she wasn't hoodwinked into thinking only Harvard would do— the horror of schools only talking selective college not good colleges for you, and after she leaves sometimes it takes me all day to get out of bed I'm so depressed then I remember the howl that came deep within me the first time I left them, but it also meant I would wake at 2am helpless—at least Jacoba says she understands my leaving and doesn't call it abandonment anymore, Lilliana has been good to her and she is the one who insisted upon a reconciliation and took her down to me when she was too young to ride the subway alone. Now they are safe again but Jacoba doesn't like the Village so rarely comes—go figure. Her father fell in love with the Village and never wanted to leave he only moved up to the West Side for space and the school. Since he like me hated the public school system we insisted she get a progressive education and now she's off to a small liberal arts college in Arkansas. At first she wanted to go to Claremont in California, her father wanted McGill in Montreal, but she realized she might not get in early at Claremont so decided on one far enough away that she can't come home on weekends, Montreal she never even considered, and here she thinks she will get a good well-rounded education. Let's not overdramatize I did okay at Pitt and Joseph here in the city, I think she is no longer a virgin, girls are not as intimidated as I was and they do that now also oral sex because of the fear of AIDS. Grandma made sure she had a sex education and even bought her condoms, yet when she began ovulating the doctor told her she could now have a baby she screamed in fright but then she was only twelve. Joseph and I can only have functional talks even if I wouldn't mind having conversation with him we have lost that ability I hurt him so but I didn't mean to hurt him just free myself from an unhealthy situation but intentions don't count only actions do: your life can only be defined by what you do. I've learned that from the theater, you can say anything but what you do is what counts. And some people are not meant to be with one person their entire adult life, it's just not natural, I couldn't give up my ambitions but didn't indulge in shameful conduct in order to hide that but live my life after all I fell under the umbra of my grandmother who repaired my childhood, really took a broken child and glued her back together stronger and more beautiful than before—Kintsukuroi, the Japanese art of repairing broken crockery with gold paste and making it prettier and stronger. Only I was stronger than grandma she never let go of a lover who abandoned her I left him behind me: a student does a teacher wrong if she doesn't surpass the teacher and always remains a student. I and me are two different persons, I wish they could be united but they can't I am always somewhere else. I gave up what I loved for freedom which was more important to me than security and when I could no longer live that life and saw so many bored people who had given up on life and only wanted to live through their children who would only end up just like them, mediocre dull people with a nice standard of living and vacations, all we ever talked about were children and their summer places, or their jobs that allowed them to live that life. We never could have conversations they were afraid to let their masks down and see what they became and I had to escape before it became too late only grandma understood and she hoped I would stay in touch with Jacoba, which I did even if is extremely painful when she leaves. I thought it would become easier after Joseph remarried but it only became more difficult, who expected jealousy but Lilliana is so nice she overcame me with gentleness and now even invites me to family affairs. Grandma, Joseph and her went to all my performances even taking Jacoba when she became old enough even Joseph came but he refused to have anything to do with me but went for Jacoba, he still didn't hinder me being with Jacoba or acting. Lilliana doesn't have an evil bone in her body, how disgusting, but Joseph couldn't overcome his anger which of course made me angry at him for seducing me which is nonsense because I seduced him, I'm older, but what does reality have to do with thought. Intellectually I'm grateful he's found a decent woman, he's happy in a family while I yearn, yearning to be free that I still don't know what it is but you can't die from yearning only inaction, and it's not as if I planned it or thought it out in fact wasn't even thinking about it just one day like any other day, the sky was gray, a cold tremor lit up the air, and I couldn't walk up those twelve steps, my key was already in my hand, back then you always had it outside your purse and almost halfway up simply turned around and went back downtown to a friend, I'm sure he and grandma thought I would come to my senses but my friend took me in no questions asked and I slept on the couch, but she insisted I must call home and let them know so they wouldn't worry, a spur of the moment set me free, the action not the intention counted, not a moderation which is only short for mediocrity; I refused to live a lie. Joseph saw it as stubbornness that I abandoned the family but it was my stubbornness in not leaving earlier that made it so much harder and made me full of self-pity, which was easy, I admit, I was comfortable in it, I hate to admit it, freedom is loneliness and suffering especially when you don't have a family, but I became tired of playing the role of mother, housewife, competent person, content Frau—all rationalizations after the fact, but needed to live once more. Only grandma never condemned me but said I should keep in contact but only when she became a little older could I see her otherwise she would have torn at my heart. Mothering is not my thing, many women can't be mothers only society doesn't us a choice and we become servants of sacrifice all weakness in afraid to live our own lives, putting responsibility off on the children as a crutch; my high school friends having babies from the first asshole that comes along so as not to have to live a life. Grandma always called that cowardice and I agreed with her, I guess I always was a rebel, until it happened to me and I realized it's true and what doesn't kill you makes you stronger and decided without even deciding that I have to be the real me whoever that me is.

Zoltan saw with color, when he was teaching me how to draw I would be amazed at how much color he saw, I see things in black and white, he saw shades of black and white, and I still love black and white movies but now at least I can see the main hues red, yellow, green and blue but it is Lilliana that points out the shades of them to me, great art student that I was, Lilliana sees more than the four primary colors and I always loved how artists could see more all I have is the ability to make money, somewhere, somehow I grasped the utilitarian function of real estate and am able to translate that into sales and even when the economy tanked was able to land on my feet because I didn't panic and bought some apartments and buildings at lower prices than they were worth, banks somehow got it into their head to lend money to open up new business rather than shore up existing ones and I was able to leverage bank loans and wait until the economy rebounded—real estate never goes out of fashion and once a neighborhood flips it usually doesn't fall back to the old ways especially now that crime has gone down and a new generation started making money and hated being taxed and saw the benefits of home ownership—this city is still a renter city but more neighborhood pockets are changing and now women even have their own decent income, some of my best customers are now lesbians since both women have good salaries, and once gay men came out of the closet I made a windfall because they had substantial jobs that now is almost the same for women. And my saving grace is I loved the color green. The only difficulty is if something goes wrong, and it always does, I can get accused of homophobia, me who consciously went after gay men in the '80s, shook their hand in public going to show I didn't fear AIDS, now being accused, of course I feared it in the '80s but knew it was transmitted sexually not by touch, thank you Esmeralda who kept up on these things, now being accused of influencing boards not to rent to lesbians not capitalistic moral injustice. I who know the difference between justice and kindness, kindness doesn't have law behind it you do it of your own heart and I tried to help gays and minorities secure decent housing and many of my customers started cohabitating no longer having one-night stands and they became an economic force in the city and some of my best customers: two men with disposable income and now two women with the same, what more could I want and boy could they decorate and throw lavish parties, women not as much, I love going to their parties and sometimes Lilliana is the only woman there but she never felt uncomfortable they were adults who treated her with courtesy devolving the stereotype that one gay played the man-woman and the other the womanly-man, they were as complicated as we were. The money is good when you open up the market to new people and not let prejudice get in the way. And everybody loved Esmeralda she could have a conversation with anybody and never believed reality was fixed but in constant flux and she loved talking to different generations of men and she taught me how to see things generationally as more and more married men were coming out of the closet and that time doesn't stop with each new generation. And I am good keeping up technologically loving each new iteration of the computer, internet, cell phone, and was always able to change with the times, to be accused of homophobia by two young women? I who am in the forefront of change, who loved eliminating tape switching to disc and now headphones it makes subway riding so much more pleasant, now nobody reads on the subway anymore, my old skill of knowing how to fold the *New York Times* and be able to read it on the subway is gone the way of the dodo bird and now I am always in contact with the world not having to continually check my answering machine, the sound on these new devices is terrific imagine if we had this in the '80s when we were stuck on the subways all the time it could have made it almost bearable, best of all is good riddance to the spreadsheet now I can show clients with simple clicks of a button how much their monthly mortgage, maintenance, will be, to be accused of prejudice is unthinkable. At first gays then lesbians were afraid that boards wouldn't let them in and co-op boards are crazy and the courts don't like to interfere and it is true in some cases, especially those who were actors and boards didn't not like

actors just the parties they threw, but as boards began to see that homo-
sexuality is a life choice not a disease and that gays were not always actors
and they liked the people I brought to the meetings, I always made sure
that the board saw individuals not deciding in a vacuum, they began to
see them as human who could pay the fees and since they were educated
people began to realize all they had been taught was false unlike those
who thought being gay leads directly to damnation. There my difficulty
was more with black co-op boards. And there you couldn't have a conversation their mind set was already made up, they had no idea they were
living in the modern world but rather still lived in the dark ages of superstitious nonsense, the Dybbuk, that Lilliana reminded me and I recalled
seeing that old television show where a dead soul inhabits a living body,
who could believe such nonsense exists in modern times am I accused of
poisoning the soul of the old lady? and a rabbinical court is going to judge
me, on the Upper West Side, no less, this isn't a shtetl, I only go to the
Reform Marrano Temple because religion provides answers for scared
minds like myself who are not sure. When these women contacted me I
knew they would be trouble because from the moment they awoke until
they fall asleep they never shut up, how can anybody put up with them.
Mostly I'm worried how anybody could take this charge seriously but I
did receive a registered letter ordering me to appear before the rabbinical
court. The Temple has a rabbinical court? I don't know if I should laugh
or cry Lilliana cries but Esmeralda laughs who knows what Cassie would
say. I didn't want to go thought it all to nonsense but was curious and
the court was serious didn't trivialize the issue, men dressed in suits not
black robes but I didn't like it was only men as Lilliana said men see their
mother, wives, sisters being taken advantage of, they're pussycats, better
get some women in the pool, and so some old women were called but
Upper West Side women not old biddies who would sit on their beach-
chairs in front of their apartment and judge everybody and they all took
the charges serious it wasn't simply a get together they took their roles
seriously as I sat there in disbelief.

When they call places that which is not becomes that which is and
I'm always surprised at the transformation that takes places inside us as
we prepare to go on stage and even after all these years still wonder at the
crossroads as I transform from this shy little girl into a magical woman,
there are many ways to accomplish this but usually I zig and zag, fall

down, pick myself up, go on, there are not only two roads to finding your way but many byways and when I'm acting I find the real me and sometimes I even surprise myself when I look at myself in the mirror and say who's that my face has changed so, my game face comes on, and all of a sudden I am this character, the true Cassandra has nothing on me and I have no other purpose in life then being on stage I don't exist other than here, could I be someone else, I doubt it, or I would have to discover who I truly am or as Joseph once said I am the most severe judge of me but I did have to develop this hard exterior to steel myself against the onslaught of my thoughts and fear of failure, learning how to say no in the process to anything that interfered with my goals. It isn't easy especially when grandma said grow up but I have grown up in a sense that I now realize I don't want what everyone else wants and am willing to go for what I want and to do something else would have been a horror for me, my only wish is that I could have understood this earlier I could have constructed a more perfect life and practiced my skills with more speed, but I can't change the past and I needed my life with Joseph to force me to change the future otherwise the future would have been the same as the past even if the past wasn't an abomination to me it was comforting but I like the unknown more, getting new parts breaking them down into chunks, memorizing them, working with ensembles becoming part of a team, fending off producers. Each time I think we will never be ready on time, we don't have enough time, not enough rehearsals, we don't know the characters well enough to interact yet by the end of the show we've never had such a good time together and can read each other's minds and I'm not the same person I was before we started and no longer have to use the bathroom incessantly. The life of the theater. Where else could a Hispanic girl from the Bronx get to play such magnificent roles be so many different people and meet so many interesting people, even be interviewed but asked such dumb questions about me not the play, but you have to do it in order to help sell tickets, usually it's a feel good story not a hard-hitting piece as if the demands of acting demands only a dumb response. You have to put up with a lot in order to be successful in this business, you have to be as hard as nails to accept all that rejection, how many young actors do I know who quit after a year or two if they are not successful, as if you can be an overnight success in this business or if not it's not for you, I much rather hang with artists who haven't given up than those who settle for mediocrity and then blame others for their failures not their own laziness and love of contentment, boy is that living in bad faith. It has taken me almost a lifetime to learn this, there is no way only ways, luckily I never had a mentor and so am able to try different paths and even when I entered into a marriage I should have known better but how can you know better you have to try it, feel it, see it, experience it, it wasn't doomed from the start only I couldn't give it my all, I hadn't stopped looking yet, I just didn't want to do it, constantly made mistakes and hurt people that I love and imagine they hurt me more than they actually did—my family is able to get on without me and I am hard to their calls, I don't want to be pitied nor only be with them or feel sorry for them because how hard it was living without a mother, it's what you accomplish do what you want with your life that counts if anything counts, I say that now about to go on stage but what about all those nights of loneliness can I balance that against the few nights of exhilaration. Is there a calculus that can handle that? Uncertainty leaping out over acceptance. I couldn't live behind a man's trousers, at least we women don't have to wear skirts anymore and can stand on our own two feet, of course, I got lucky off-off-Broadway stages bloomed up while I was coming of age and I didn't have to make my way to Hollywood because downtown became this haven for meaty roles and searing drama and I also have a nice gig at the bank to tide me over fallow times— never much but always enough, modest poverty that has allowed me to live, and grandma's rent-controlled apartment was a godsend, of course I remodeled the place wasn't going to sleep in the same bed I slept in as a child: replaced the walls, remodeled the kitchen and bathroom, had the floors sanded everything in the apartment changed but it's still the same apartment grandma still resides there in my head; learned how to live, shake the tiredness off me to feel light, good eating habits and exercise helped but it was deeper I was doing what I wanted to do how much higher can you feel than that, no longer did I attempt to please rather lived feeling life flowing in my marrow—love that makes living easier that makes a character come alive especially if you have director who says do it one way and if you say can I do it this way and they see your point of view, allow it, good directors are like that open to different interpretations, not my way or the highway. I no longer wait if I have something to say but jump right in, I'm not that kind of Negro. Unfortunately nobody understood that reference directors don't read. You would think they would they have plenty of time and there's Kindle now so you can even adjust the print if your eyesight is too bad. I can't do anything anymore without my glasses. But some directors are talking about using computer graphics what next? If they use the computer creatively it can be a valuable tool in setting the mood, but you have to be careful in grade school we all saw filmstrips that would make us learn and in college we all had language labs that would make us learn and I never learned Spanish and was happy when filmstrips came on so we could talk amongst ourselves. All shortcuts to learning fail, learning takes a long time and practice maybe you don't begin to grow up until you reach fifty. Lights up.

How did this happen? I thought I would have more time? I'm ready, of course, but not ready, of course, glad that I saw Jacoba off to college— what a treat to see her grow up and only be with her for enjoyment— thank goodness for little girls, only she's not so little anymore well on her way to becoming a woman and having a life of her own, and luckily I saw Conchita one more time in a performance, she's up for best supporting actor but acting is its own reward she doesn't need awards to tell her that, she knows it, too bad this play needed some reality her feminist rant without respecting the reality of others made this not one of her best roles, but it did get the play noticed, even reviewed, but the defenders of tradition, custom criticized her in great numbers, one of the most popular plays she has ever done. We all went as a family and that brings a smile to my face, who would have thought I believed in that even Jacoba came on her last night before leaving in the morning instead of hanging out with her friends, of course she did so afterwards, but at least she spent her last evening with us I never would have done that I never believed my parents did what was best for me. Soon no more me. I'm tired want to fall asleep but am afraid what if I don't wake up. How will I know? I always thought I would go gently but am surprised how hard I fight to stay alive, stopped smoking, exercised, ate well, still the body loses in the end and destroys you. Couldn't tell anybody then they would have treated me as a sick person, didn't want that, only when the pain became too great did I have to check it out and by then it was too late but I knew it would be too late that's why I waited like I did even as I tell myself that I shouldn't be afraid and take deep breaths—nobody can die for you we all have to die alone and the youngsters have no clue what I went through to keep it from them, and even if they are to sympathize with me they wouldn't have the fear I do and can't understand my whole life has been a lie, one big lie; lying about Jacobo, the fire has gone out a long time ago but it was easy to keep it blazing inside me than have to deal with it, our souls won't reunite because we don't have souls without bodies, will I go into a dreamless sleep or will I go somewhere else? When the body perishes the body doesn't even know what it's doing only the me, the me inside the body does and soon there won't be a me anymore; have to think quickly before the drugs take effect which will lessen the pain but won't allow me to think, why me? tomorrow I won't see my girls anymore, won't walk in the park, feel the sun upon my face, have breakfast with Joseph, maybe in my dreams—dreams at my age but I still dream my body hasn't taken that away from me, always onto something else before I finished what I was doing now at least I saw Jacoba graduate and my plan for her is not hers, she wants to transition to a boy, hormone shots, cut off her breasts artificial penis, sorry I'm going to miss that. Jacobo taught me freedom is to choose too bad he couldn't but for that I am grateful what would have become of my life if I hadn't met him, would I have been someone else but I did learn from him and think still I would have become me. The pain is lessening and I am becoming groggy, the nurse is standing over me asking if she should call my family it would be nice to hold their hand one more time, feel their warmth one more time, but I don't want them to see me without my war paint, they'll remember me this way not the way I was. They won't remember me after a bit. How long can you be remembered anyway? Does it matter if you're remembered? It's not the bottle that stores the wine it's the wine in the bottle that's important. At least I can laugh or try to. It's not too great even if I can no longer dance. What do they want from me? what do I want? I didn't think I would be so scared thought I would be ready, all my paperwork is done, not that I have much but they won't have to fight over it that has destroyed too many families, proportioned my estate fairly, and if they fight it's them not me. A shame Conchita and Joseph couldn't hold it together they were made for each other, but they're each a decent person and I'm glad they found happiness in their own ways, the fire's gone out and I still want the ashes, how silly, I could have danced with him all night even if he couldn't dance, I took pleasure in dancing he had two left feet and no ear for music, so different from any other man I ever met, gentle, kind, listened to what I had to say took my dreams seriously, he's the one who gave me the fire that allowed me to continue in a world not of my choosing, blew life into my soul, allowed me to see the world in a different way, didn't have to settle even if he settled he helped the one who came after him. Maybe the Dybbuk isn't so wrong just has to be modernized, imagine thinking of that at a time like this, I surprise myself as I drift off can't shut my mind off. At least I have been fortunate and my mind has stayed clear until I no longer have a body. Maybe I can look out the window but I can barely see that far and what does it matter if it's midnight or midday and yet want to know: at midday you begin at midnight you end. How much time left? Is that the morning star or a light from the lamppost? Have to try and get my thoughts under control in order to experience this not simply to fall asleep but tell myself what's going even if I can't report it to the world, the gates of the garden are opening the birds are tweeting, a bright light is dawning it's the beginning of the day can't be I always knew I would cease to be at night, must be an illusion, I'm not having enough food and hallucinating, try want to realize what's going on, is that Jacobo waiting for me on the bench will he be the last name I utter, soon there will be no more, shameful I haven't completed all I wanted to complete, a wasted life, always going from one place to another, one project to the next, now there is no more next, keep your eyes open girl, but I'm so tired and the sun is at its peak will I be going off to a nothingness or is my soul moving to another world? The body/soul problem there is no . . . you silly goose.

She died alone didn't even tell anyone the severity of her illness kept saying she couldn't walk but was getting better we thought she was going to the hospital to see a specialist about her leg, she refused to be treated like a sick person—all she wanted was to be known as a nurse in the Spanish Civil War and was lucky in love, nobody will know that because we surreptitiously buried her ashes in an urn next to Jacobo, even if Joseph felt awkward about her going up in smoke, we are finally doing something together after all these years, Jacoba was starting college and we were afraid the courses would overwhelm her so we decided not to mention it until it was over, I forget grandma had a life before me, us. I can only think of her as my grandma who raised me after my mother died and made sure I received an education, said you don't have an equal chance in life without one, but she had a whole life before she took me in shy of my

18th birthday when Tomas told me he was not my biological grandfather even if I had only known him as my grandfather but that she was pregnant when he married her so he wasn't my biological grandfather but of course he was my grandfather, decent man who only treated me nicely, but they never explained the truth to me until Tomas did when I turned eighteen and felt I should know. Grandma said she was always going to tell me but never found the right time, their big secret was nothing I was glad he was my grandfather, more like a father to me since I never knew my father, I guess I could find out now with all that DNA stuff but what's the purpose. Grandma I wronged you but we couldn't live together I couldn't care for all of us and take care of myself I had to shake the dust off my feet and live alone, you always said a granddaughter repays a grandmother poorly if she always stays a granddaughter and I know you wanted me to, insisted on, that I live my own life otherwise the clock would stand still and you didn't want that, still why didn't you trust me I wanted to be there with you, hold your hand with you, be with you, and we buried your ashes I was not going to allow a church service, and we recited some Spanish poems I know you wanted to be cremated, some of you lives in me and I couldn't put you in the burial plot with Tomas, let that be for his current wife, it would be funny if some stranger came by and thought you two were lovers with a long happy marriage but we wanted a plot that was best for you and besides I wanted a place where Jacoba can come and remember you and do right by you to let her know where she came from and feel alone when she is all alone in the world, only we couldn't put what you wanted on your tombstone that you were a fighter for freedom and were lucky in love because you have no tombstone, even if Joseph called his old friend Harvey, a funeral director, only to find out from his wife Katherine that he died nine years ago and he didn't know what or how he felt, sad because his old buddy that he laughed with died but he died so long ago that it felt bad to be sad, and had wanted him to carve an asterisk and put your last words next to Jacobo and Miriam or even carve another headstone, but that would have been sacrilegious you knew who your lover was and you don't need the world to know about it. The night we came home from the hospital Lilliana hired college musicians to play Schubert's *String Quintet in C major*, Janáček's *String Quartet no. 2* and Kurtág's *Quartet Op. 1* your favorites, music that thinks and evolves as it goes on, and we sat around having a candlelight last meal with a place set for you, we washed your body, brought dry ice so it wouldn't decompose and lit candles to slow down time and we could spend as much time with you as we could. Joseph's phone call came out of the blue we hardly speak but immediately I knew something was wrong, I haven't lost my artistic intuition that when I lose will know it's time to hang it up, he was so stern told me to get up to the hospital immediately you're dying and he only found out about it because the nurse called him, she wanted to die alone but the nurse wouldn't let her, he said the nurse said she is dying and you better hurry up and I immediately left work I thought you were only going in for leg not the seriousness of the illness, I was sure you would tell me that, I had a right to know, but you didn't want anyone making decisions for you. I should have known you never told me or my mother that Tomas wasn't ours and now I think about being lied to all those years even as Joseph says let it go, let it go, that's the way they did things back then you can't judge by today's values. But you should have known better, you lived by truth not what people thought yet all she thought about was a man she had a crush on as a teenager who she hasn't forgotten and stayed perfect in her imagination, it's only when you live with somebody you see all their human peccadilloes not fantasy; when you hear their loud bellyaching in the middle of the day that cuts off all reflection and numbs your body to the core, I wanted this? and you ask yourself how you got into this and wonder if he feels the same way you do. The midnight gong has sounded the quartet has left, Lilliana is cleaning up and Joseph and I are sitting here in silence, I know I should get up and leave but tonight to go to your apartment alone scares me, I always thought I was living there temporarily even if I totally remodeled the place, fascinating her generation covered up the features when I removed the linoleum found these wooden floors and had them fixed up, fascinating how her generation covered up beauty I even redid the bathroom and kitchen, removed walls added closets, even if the landlord said they would become permanent fixtures I live there now let me enjoy the place and now the landlord wants to co-op the place so I guess I can pass it on to Jacoba. Joseph has told Jacoba to let Lilliana live here after he passes then she can sell it. He's always the practical one. If a God is everywhere and circumference nowhere then grandma will be happy with this memory of her. We finally called Jacoba so she wouldn't say how dare you and she came up to mourn; her friends are all gone, her lovers all gone, only the family is left and I insisted she be cremated, her last wish but not so quickly, we needed to remember. Lilliana prepared quite a spread and I can still hear the cello inside my head and grandma spoke to me through the pulse of the melodic line, by the time I made it to the hospital she was cold and all I could kiss was a dead body, she was no longer there, brushed her hair back so she looked okay, she was never vain about her gray hairs I am always surprised when I see her photographs as a young woman looking just like me and it would be an honor if I ended up looking like her, she led a full life never a shrinking violet she started over many times never satisfied always trying something new adapted always trying to find for herself her place in life, constantly becoming as she put it even when I had no idea what she was talking about and only learned as I grew up, when I turned fifty it became clearer. She lived a life of her own making developed her mind that had no actual purpose until she developed it, she had enough money throughout her life not to be a slave to it, and basically enjoyed her life. What more could you ask for?

What was I to say? She didn't have dreams of despair yet she despaired, but she slept easy and sound knowing she lived the correct way, or if she didn't she never told me, but then again the gap between our ages might have made that difficult. At first I was too young and she condescended to me and I thought she was too old to take seriously but we learned to treat each other as equals, did we ever have a moment together as true friends. every funeral that you attend forces you to think about your own, but at least Cassandra and I agreed no religious hypocrisy we waited until Jacoba arrived and both of us knew she should be buried next to *avuelo*, she had told us enough times she wanted to be cremated, how am I going to live without her? not hearing her feet walking down below, talking to her, listening to her talking to me, just me, I'm only thinking of me, I'm ashamed, but it's true. We loved each other and I'm sorry she couldn't get it together with my grandfather maybe he would have been happier. He certainly wasn't happy with grandma didn't even attend her funeral, my mother begged him even to say see I lived longer than you, but he just couldn't he lived differently than my mother understood, I inherited his beliefs and my weaknesses are my strengths not sufficient to make me someone else but making my life a little easier. I couldn't just live for myself, having Jacoba taught me that, and finding Cassandra and her at such an early age made my twenties so much easier to get through, now I can no longer reach for the stars and have to live within my own self, which is this constant wanting to run away but always drawn back to responsibility—I wanted to travel but never did, now when Esmeralda is gone it might be too late to visit the capitols of Europe as in my imaginary trips, but Lilliana says she wants to travel, so I might yet get to see Madrid and Prague. What surprised me is when the hospital gave us her ring, I had heard about it never saw it apparently the ersatz wedding ring my grandfather gave her before he left that she kept it all these years and must have known she was dying because she wore it and we put it in the urn when we buried her next to my grandfather, I wanted to put up a cube, a revolving square like the one Astor Place but Katherine said that was impossible and she had moved heaven and hell to allow us to take Esmeralda home with us, the hospital didn't want to release the body to us only to a certified funeral home so she called and made all the arrangements and she delivered the body to our house, carried it up the twelve steps, laid it out in the back room, told us about the dry ice and when it was time to remove the body did it for us and returned the ashes. Esmeralda has died how will I go on, maybe she lived a little too long to have to suffer like that but how do you know when to go, her last few years were painful, of course when the pain became too excessive she stayed in bed and then I knew she was ill, but usually she was up and about and I had no idea of the seriousness of her condition. She wanted it that way. I respect that but dread her loss, she was the silent partner in my conversations not Cassandra even if it was Cassandra's body I was imagining it was Esmeralda I was talking to especially in the photographs where Cassandra looks exactly like Esmeralda when she was her age. I kissed her, hugged her, shagged her, but it was my inner conversations with Esmeralda and maybe she saw me the same way as my grandfather. I never had a better education than being with her and am able to feel more alive because of her, that's what education does that to you all I keep thinking about is me, not how she felt, just me. The '60s opened the door to more intellectual opportunities even if nobody thinks anymore and their eyes are wide shut, too bad my grandfather didn't have this opportunity I lived in more prosperous times than him had more education than him, had a good foundation, what I have what was denied him; didn't see the body as evil learned to appreciate the sensual and escaped my surroundings, those who only follow tradition where if you broach any criticism of their way of life is looked upon askew, I just can't imagine living with your own kind I so badly wanted to escape them and to meet the other, and all I met were educated people and I now realize that today I have very few friends who aren't college-educated, not that I'm picky or obnoxious only I wanted to escape their provincialism. It must be similar to Esmeralda who first came here to break off with the old ways and learn a whole new way of thinking, acting, doing, making, or as she said you have to try and live act as if you want to live, it must have blown her mind when she first came here afterwards we engage in interpretations I wanted to learn how to live and somehow ended up in real estate, but it didn't destroy me it's only my day job it isn't etched in stone I have a life beyond working, it's not boredom I still have time for reflection and conversation, I still read Lobo Antunes, Jelinek, and the Hungarian László Krasznahorkai, go to concerts, listen to Mozart, Schubert, Kurtág see the Greek classics, Shakespeare and whatever she's in, do things, now I will do less legal contracts even if I am one of the few people in the world who can actually grasp the meaning of those things but want to get back to a deeper understanding. As Lilliana said you can't lose them all when the Temple threw out all the charges against me, I had this great speech prepared my indignation rose to a high pitch, I was going to ridicule them in my speech, when the board simply refused to hear their bullshit said we are a religion based the 'moral law' of Spinoza and Unamuno, we're not prisoners of human bondage, of fear, of self-deception or ignorance, even if we have to die, and have no time for such foolishness. She opened the world to me and I won't close it upon myself and I want to get back to the old ways before it's too late I have set up a trust fund for Jacoba to go along with the 401K so she should be able to finish school without debt, but college isn't as important as elementary school, few realize that anymore their thinking sees childhood then adulthood not the interplay between childhood and adulthood and that no adult thought doesn't have a childhood wish or fantasy behind it, even if it's difficult to see the cause and effect—Cassandra had a discussion with Lilliana about emptying out her downstairs apartment and I insist she take the photos of her family but leave me some of Esmeralda but I now feel the solitariness of the house without her, I can't even go downstairs into her place to gather her things, let the women do it. How do I shut my mind off? Lucky in love she actually said that to me but maybe she meant all of us her life was never easy but she never lost her way, full of zigs and zags but always her not someone else, came here with nothing but knew it was better to live free than in a shithole, a comfortable shithole but a shithole is a shithole, to be free an individual needs time and solitude time to reflect and think, not be trapped in the day-to-day or fear your government so much you give up caring what's going on around you; you played well with family and friends, caught the moments between seconds, your life wasn't meaningless and you lived how you wanted to live. What more can you ask? What more can you say?

Drawing by Nicholas Vagenas